# MONTANA WESTWARD BRIDES

BOOKS 1 -4

AMELIA ROSE

# CONTENTS

## THE RECKLESS DOCTOR'S BRIDE BOOK 1



## THE RANCHER'S UNEXPECTED PREGNANT BRIDE BOOK 2

## THE LONESOME COWBOY'S ABDUCTED BRIDE: BOOK 3

## THE SHERIFF'S STUBBORN SECRETIVE BRIDE: BOOK 4

*This book is dedicated to all of my faithful readers, without whom I would be nothing. I thank you for the support, reviews, love, and friendship you have shown me as we have gone through this journey together. I am truly blessed to have such a wonderful readership.*

# THE RECKLESS DOCTOR'S BRIDE BOOK 1

# CHAPTER 1

Lucy couldn't tear her gaze from the staring, dark eyes of the dead man. His lifeless body lay face up on the ground, dried blood staining his dingy white shirt at the neck and across his abdomen. His long, curly, deep brown hair had bits of grass stuck in it and his tan, wide-brimmed hat lay close by, no doubt knocked off when he'd fallen to the ground after his assailant's attack.

"Lucy, go back to the buggy, and—."

The emotion-strained voice of her future husband startled her even though he stood right next to her. "What? N-no. I'm all right. I've seen dead bodies, just not with so much blood on them. I'm not squeamish, Sam." Bile rose in her throat, despite her claim, as she watched a fly crawl across Ernie's face.

Lucy looked up when Sam's hand settled on her shoulder. "I wasn't implying that you were. I just meant that we need to go back to town to fetch Sheriff Ryder. He needs to see this before Ernie's moved. I want to get back before scavengers disturb anything, or anyone comes along and moves him, or tries to steal his belongings."

Her eyes widened in disbelief. "Would someone really do that? Take his things?"

Sam's jaw tensed. "Yes. As you've seen, this land is still untamed. There are those who wouldn't think twice about stealing from a dead man."

Stifling the anger his response stirred, Lucy said, "Well, if anyone does, I hope they have nothin' but bad luck." She looked down at Ernie with a pang of sadness and regret before returning her gaze to Sam. "I'm so sorry for your loss, Sam, and I'm sorry I didn't get the chance to meet him."

Sam blinked his blue eyes and swallowed hard. "Thank you, Lucy." His voice was a trifle thick. "I know you would've liked each other."

Lucy gave him a tiny smile. "I'm certain we would've."

She followed Sam over to the buggy and waved away his assistance. Settling herself on the seat while he took up the reins, Lucy wondered who had killed Ernie and why. "Why would someone want to harm him?"

Sam's hands tightened around the reins for a few moments and a muscle in his cheek twitched. "I don't know, but I'm not going to rest until Ernie's murderer is brought to justice."

With a slap of the reins on the horse's rump, Sam put the buggy in motion. Lucy hung on to the seat as the buggy lurched forward, her heart thudding in her chest as she realized how dangerous this unfamiliar land could be.

It felt like she'd moved to the other side of the world instead of halfway across the country. The suddenness with which her life had changed in the short space of time since she'd come to Spruce Valley, Montana, alarmed her, and she wondered whether coming here had been a good idea after all.

~

*Two days earlier…*

*Why does misfortune seem to follow me around, like a dark cloud hovering over my head?* It wasn't the first time Lucy Magee had asked herself that question, and she suspected that it wouldn't be the last.

Trudging along the muddy road, lugging one of her suitcases and her reticule, Lucy prayed that someone would come along to help her. She paused to catch her breath and a rivulet of sweat slid down her spine as she sat her suitcase down. The early June day had dawned, muggy after the heavy overnight rain, and the lack of a breeze made it even hotter.

Consulting her pendent watch, Lucy groaned in frustration. According to the timepiece, she'd have just been arriving in Spruce Valley, Montana to meet her prospective husband. However, her stagecoach driver had passed away while driving the conveyance about an hour ago.

As she'd been looking at the passing scenery, Lucy had noticed that the coach had started veering off to the right toward the edge of the road. She'd leaned her head out the open window and saw that they were approaching a bend in the road. Instead of the horses turning to the left, they'd trotted straight ahead.

Leaning further out of the window, Lucy had shouted to the driver but received no response. The horses had started to turn, but not before the right-side wheels of the stagecoach had slid into the ditch and gotten mired in the muck.

Although she'd been bounced around in the coach, Lucy hadn't been hurt.

Once she'd gotten her bearings, she'd alighted from the vehicle and approached the driver's box. The elderly man had been slumped over and leaning to the right. As she'd gotten closer, he'd pitched forward and fallen off the coach into the ditch.

Horrified, Lucy had picked up the skirts of her powder blue traveling dress and rushed around the coach to his aid. However, as she knelt next to the man's prone form, his open, rheumy blue eyes told her that he was gone. Tears of sympathy and fear had slid down her cheeks as she'd closed his eyes with trembling fingers.

After saying a prayer for Mr. Trasker's soul, she'd taken stock of her situation. She wasn't a skilled driver, so she couldn't guide the horses in getting the coach unstuck. Thinking perhaps that she could ride one of them, she'd attempted to unhitch one. However, the scared horses wanted nothing to do with her and she'd left them alone after one had nipped at her.

Her only other option was to go for help. The thought of traveling alone along an unfamiliar road had filled her with trepidation, but she'd had no other choice. So, she'd chosen to take the suitcase with her most important possessions, and strike out for Spruce Valley on foot.

Now, taking out her handkerchief from a dress pocket, she wiped sweat from her face and then took a drink from the canteen she'd found in the driver's box. Her empty stomach announced that it was time for the midday meal, and she opened her reticule. She'd purchased a couple of Johnnycakes that morning before they'd gotten underway, and she unwrapped one.

She'd almost finished it when thunder rumbled overhead. With dismay, Lucy turned her gaze to the darkening sky and wanted to cry. Her luck just kept getting worse and worse. Gathering her things, she started hurrying along the road, determined to get as far as possible before she got soaked.

~

ALMOST SIX MILES AWAY, Dr. Sam Slater stood on the porch of Frost's Mercantile, which doubled as the stagecoach depot in Spruce Valley. He checked his watch and his brow furrowed with deep concern. Jed Trasker was the most reliable stagecoach driver in the southeastern area of the Montana Territory.

Sam knew something must've gone very wrong with Jed's run, because he could count on one hand the number of times the old man had been late. Not only was he worried about Jed, but also for the woman who was traveling all the way from Buffalo, New York to marry him.

He almost used the sleeve of his white dress shirt to wipe sweat from his brow until he remembered that it was the best shirt he owned. It had cost too much for him to ruin it with a sweat stain. The ones under his arms were mostly hidden by his dark brown suit vest, which he couldn't wait to shed.

Once upon a time, dressing in anything except a full suit had been unthinkable when in polite society. Of course, that had been before he'd moved to Spruce Valley from Trenton, New Jersey three years prior in November of 1865. Montana Territory had only been signed into law one year before that, in May of 1864 by President Abraham Lincoln.

Most of the Territory was still wide open wild plains, which had appealed to Sam after all the carnage of the Civil War. As an army doctor, he'd seen more than his share of death and had struck out for the frontier, craving peace and desiring to help fill a shortage of physicians in the new territory.

He fished a handkerchief from his trouser pocket, mopped his sweaty brow, and consulted his watch again. Eleven forty-four, it read. His disquiet deepened, and he sighed. A loud, rumbling growl of thunder reached him and he hoped the storm would go around Spruce Valley. They didn't need any more rain after last night.

After another ten minutes had passed and still no stagecoach, Sam left the store. He crossed the dirt street, his booted feet sinking into the quagmire as he walked. Upon reaching the wooden boardwalk on the other side, he made his way past the small, squat clapboard building that served as his office and headed down the street to the newly built sheriff's office.

Entering the red brick building, Sam spied Sheriff Josh Ryder—who'd been elected to office one month ago—sitting at his wooden oak desk. Josh looked up from the journal in which he was writing and smiled. "Did you bring your bride-to-be to meet me?"

Sam barely kept from running a hand through his sandy blond hair as his frustration mounted. "I'm afraid not. The stage hasn't arrived yet."

Josh's coffee-brown eyes filled with surprise as he looked at the clock on the wall opposite his desk. "Jed's never been this late."

"I know. I hope they didn't have trouble with robbers or Indians," Sam commented.

Josh closed his journal and got up. "Guess we best go find out."

Two other stagecoach drivers had recently had run-ins with robbers who'd stolen their cash boxes. Josh was working on catching them, but the thieves were smart and fast, making it hard for a law enforcement staff of only one to nab them.

Spruce Valley was located squarely in Crow Indian territory and every so often, they got riled up and caused some mischief. Of course, that was usually when they were warring with their hated enemies, the Lakota. When he'd moved to the area, Sam had been surprised to find that most of the Crow Nation was friendly toward whites.

So, although it couldn't be ruled out, Sam doubted that Jed had met up with troublemaking Crow warriors. In fact, many of the Crow in the area knew and liked the elderly man. No, something else was holding Jed up.

Sam said, "I'll go saddle Atlas and meet you back here."

"Fine by me," Josh agreed.

As soon as he stepped outside the sheriff's office, strong wind and fat drops of rain buffeted Sam, turning his mood even darker. He jogged back to his office and turned down the narrow alley between it and the wayside inn next door. The Honeywell Inn was a small establishment, boasting only four rooms for rent, but the owner, Bill Eckert, served good food and drink. He also employed a local widow, Greta Royal, who kept the place spic-and-span.

Reaching the livery stable behind the Inn where Sam boarded his horse when he was in town, Sam refused the stable boy's offer to saddle Atlas and did it himself. Swinging up on the big gray gelding's back, Sam trotted him outside and headed for the sheriff's office.

Josh was waiting for him, already mounted on a sorrel stallion. "Nice day for a ride," he commented with a wry gesture toward the sky.

Sam smiled and shook his head as the heavens opened, releasing a torrent. They turned their horses and headed east out of town. The bad weather on top of the missing stagecoach seemed like a bad omen to Sam. His anxiety intensified, and he urged Atlas into a faster pace. With a toss of his head, the powerful draft horse mix surged forward.

~

SODDEN AND MISERABLE from the deluge, Lucy sat on her suitcase. Her chin propped on a palm, she sat hunched forward, her elbow resting on her knee. She watched raindrops slide down a limp lock of her black hair that had fallen in front of her face.

Her right boot was stuck in the mud a short distance away and she'd placed her bare foot on top of her left boot, which thankfully hadn't been dislodged by the sucking mud. The thunder and lightning had died away, but the downpour continued.

Having looked around, Lucy had discovered that the area through which they'd been traveling was quite remote. There'd been no roads meeting the one upon which she'd been walking. No lanes, trails, or houses in sight either. Once the evil mud had stolen her right boot, Lucy had given up, plunking her suitcase down and sitting on it to wait out the storm.

A new sound caught Lucy's attention. Looking up, she saw two men on horseback approaching her. She almost stood up but remembered her bare foot at the last moment. Thrilled to see them, Lucy waved at them as though they were old friends she hadn't seen in months.

"Yoo-hoo! Hello!" she called to them.

Relief washed over her when the men stopped their horses close to her. It grew even stronger when she saw that one of them sported a worn badge on his rumpled black vest. Running into a lawman made her think that perhaps her luck was turning around.

Both men dismounted and the other one approached her

with long strides. Looking over his tall, rangy form, her gaze encountered intense blue eyes set in a rather rugged face. One wouldn't call him classically handsome, but she thought his strong jaw, slightly crooked nose, and high forehead were much more interesting than the more refined features of some men.

His brows drew together, and she was touched by his concerned expression.

"Hello, miss. Are you all right? Are you hurt?"

Offering him a wan smile, Lucy replied, "Other than feeling like a drowned rat, being stuck in the mud, and stranded due to a nasty twist of fate, I'm just fine."

The smile that curved his mouth captivated Lucy. "I'm glad you're not injured and judging by that lilting Irish accent, I'd wager that you're likely my bride-to-be. I'm Dr. Sam Slater. Am I right? Are you Miss Magee?"

Lucy's heartbeat rapped against her ribs as excitement took hold of her. "I am! 'Tis surely Providence that brought ye along just when I needed ya most."

Sam held out a hand to her. "Well, Miss Magee, the conditions may be less than desirable, but I'm still very pleased to meet you."

Lucy slipped her hand into his. "And I am indeed thrilled to make yer acquaintance."

"Glad to hear it," Sam said. "Let's get you back to town out of this terrible weather, and you can tell me how you became stranded."

Sadness replaced Lucy's relief over being rescued and her smile slipped. "I'm sorry to tell ya that Mr. Trasker has gone to his great reward."

"Jed's dead?"

The man with Sam had asked the question and Lucy turned her attention to him. "Aye. I believe that his heart gave out. The stage went off the road and got stuck. When I went to investigate what had gone wrong, I found him slumped in the driver's box. Then he fell off into the ditch. I went to assist him, but there was nary I could do. He was already gone, God bless his soul."

"I'm sorely grieved to hear this," the man said. "Jed was a good friend of mine."

"My condolences on yer loss, sir," Lucy responded.

His expression equally sad, Sam said, "Miss Magee, allow me to introduce you to Sheriff Josh Ryder."

Josh held out a hand to her. "Pleased to meet you, ma'am."

Lucy shook hands with him, thinking that he was also handsome in his own way. He had rather sharp features and wasn't as tall as Sam, but his brown eyes held warmth and intelligence. "Likewise, Sheriff."

Sam said, "Let's get going so we can get you settled, Miss Magee."

"Please call me Lucy," she said. "After all, we'll be married soon enough, and I don't see any need for formalities."

Sam nodded. "In that case, you must call me Sam."

"And call me Josh," the sheriff said.

Lucy smiled up at them. "Well then, Sam and Josh, I'm more than happy to get out of this swamp."

She held out a hand to Sam, who easily pulled her to her feet—or her booted foot, anyway. Josh retrieved her other boot and Sam steadied her while she put it on and tied it.

"There. That's better," she said.

"I'll take your suitcase and satchel, Lucy," Josh said. "I'm sure you'll want to ride with Sam."

Lucy's gaze left Josh to find Sam's eyes and she blushed at the twinkle in them. "Right."

"Sam, you mount up, and I'll help Lucy get up on that big galoot you call a horse," Josh said.

Sam cast him a dark look. "Don't make fun of Atlas." He swung into the saddle. "He's stronger than three other horses put together and twice as smart."

Josh chuckled as he assisted Lucy onto Atlas' back. She tried to hide her embarrassment at having to hike up her dress a little to achieve the task of mounting. It exposed a good portion of her calves and she adjusted her skirt to cover them more as soon as she was settled.

Looking down at Josh, she saw him glance away quickly, his face a little pink. She pursed her lips but said nothing. She supposed she couldn't fault the man for a little peek, but that didn't mean she had to like it. When she glanced at Sam, he turned around fast, but she knew he'd also been looking at her legs.

"I'll thank the both of ye not to ogle me so," she snapped.

"We didn't mean to, ma'am," Josh said. "It's just that I'm at eye-level with your leg and I sorta couldn't help it."

She glared at Sam. "And what's yer excuse?"

Lucy's challenging tone both amused and shamed Sam. She had the right to be upset about strange men staring at her shapely calves, but he hadn't been able to help himself. It had been a long time since he'd had the company of a woman and Lucy was very desirable.

Even with her inky hair plastered to her head, her dirty dress, and a smear of mud on her right cheek, her beauty was undeniable. Her marvelous gray eyes were stormy with anger right now, and her delicate chin thrust forward in defiance and Sam thought she was the most beautiful woman he'd ever laid eyes on.

"I was just making sure you were comfortable and

couldn't help seeing your legs since they're right there," he said. "I honestly didn't mean to offend you, Lucy."

She was quiet for a few moments and then nodded. "Very well, then. I believe ya."

Sam smiled and turned back around. He tapped Atlas's side with his heels and the horse broke into a trot. Lucy's arms came around his waist and his pulse jumped at the contact. He was glad she was putting safety above shyness and concentrated on the road ahead, shoving the way she felt against his back out of his mind as best he could.

# CHAPTER 2

An hour later, Lucy reclined in a tub of hot water, washing the mud and grime from her skin with the jasmine soap that Mrs. Royal had brought for her. Although her room in the Honeywell Inn was a little stuffy, the bath still felt good. Since her hair was already wet, she decided to wash it.

Once she was done, Lucy finished up and dressed in her best dress from the suitcase she'd taken from the stagecoach. Luckily, it had proved watertight and her belongings had remained dry. She donned petticoats over her shift, along with a simple white corset and a white blouse. She finished the ensemble with a pink paisley cotton skirt. Her thick hair would take a long time to dry if she put it up or braided it, so she left it loose around her shoulders.

Collecting her beaded drawstring purse, she left her room and walked down the hallway to the stairs. The aromas of savory meat and ale made her stomach rumble almost as loud as the thunder had earlier. At the bottom of the stairs, she turned left into a large dining room in which five square tables stood.

Sam was standing by one of the windows with his back to her, gazing out of it. Lucy took in the breadth of his shoulders and the way his wavy blond hair curled over his collar. He turned around and she realized that he must've seen her reflection in the glass. Not wanting him to catch her staring at him, especially when she'd just chastised him for that offense, she pretended to look around.

"Hello, Lucy. Feeling refreshed?" he asked, walking toward her.

"Aye, thank you." She gestured at the room. "This seems like a lovely little place."

Sam smiled and motioned to the table she stood next to. "It is. Please, sit. Mrs. Royal is getting us something to eat."

Lucy let him seat her and sat her purse on an empty chair.

"Other than the very last part, how was the rest of your trip?" Sam asked as he joined her.

"Exciting, nerve-wracking, and very, very long," Lucy replied. "And not a journey I care to make again anytime soon, if ever."

Sam chuckled. "I remember making the trip and I felt the same way once I got here. Maybe in a few years, once traveling gets easier, you'll want to go back for a visit."

"Perhaps, but right now, I'm very eager to start a new life."

"Ah, yes. Ready to be free of all those siblings," Sam remarked wryly.

Lucy frowned. "I love them, well, most of them, but even if I had wanted to stay, Ma and Da were pushin' me to marry."

Sam leaned his elbows on the table. "Yes, you said as much, and I still find it hard to believe that there wasn't a single eligible man in the whole of Buffalo, New York who would marry you."

Lucy arched an eyebrow and lifted her chin. "Ye have that backward, Dr. Slater. There wasn't a single man I'd met in Buffalo *I* wanted to marry, so before my father picked for me, I took matters into my own hands."

Sam gave an understanding nod. "I think you did the right thing. I'd say that even if you hadn't come here to marry me. I'm more forward-thinking than some men and believe that women have the right to decide their own destiny."

"I gathered that from your letters, and it was one of the reasons I chose ya," Lucy said. "I didn't want to be trapped in a marriage with an overbearin' man."

"I have my stubborn moments, but I'd never hurt your feelings on purpose, Lucy. It's important that you know that about me," Sam informed her.

"Thank ya. I appreciate that."

Greta arrived with a large tray of food. The tall, thin woman gave them a warm smile that made her green eyes shine with good humor. "Here we are. Some nice roast beef, mashed potatoes, and green beans." She placed steaming-hot plates in front of them, along with glasses of lemonade. "And when you're ready for dessert, we have some nice custard pie and coffee."

Lucy's mouth watered as she looked at the food. "It all looks wonderful. Thank ya, Mrs. Royal."

"You must call me Greta." The middle-aged woman patted Lucy's shoulder. "Now, you just let me know if there's anything you need." She gave Sam a stern look. "And you'd better be good to this young lady."

Sam chuckled. "You have nothing to worry about, Greta. I intend to spoil her."

Lucy blushed and laughed when he winked at her.

"Glad to hear it," Greta responded. "I'll be back to check on you."

Lucy bowed her head and said a silent grace before tucking into her food.

~

SAM HID his amusement as he watched Lucy attack her food with gusto. He could imagine how famished she was after all she'd been through. After a few moments, he turned his attention to his own food, happily filling his own empty belly. As usual, the food Bill had prepared was scrumptious and it didn't take long for each of them to clear their plate.

After sopping up the last of the gravy from his plate with a piece of fresh bread, Sam sat back. A couple of minutes later, Lucy did the same thing and let out a sigh of contentment.

"The cook here is excellent," she commented.

"Yes, Bill is quite talented," Sam agreed. "I know you'll want to rest tonight, but tomorrow I'd like to show you my ranch."

Lucy was eager to see the place she'd soon call home. From Sam's description in his letters, it was a beautiful piece of land. "Aye. I'd like that very much. When will we wed?"

"Is Sunday too soon?"

Lucy fidgeted a little and she seemed to mull that over. Finally, she said, "Sunday will be just fine. I brought my dress, so there won't be any need to shop for one or have one made."

Sam guessed at the source of her anxiety and put his hand over hers. "Lucy, we don't know each other very well yet. I don't expect relations on our wedding night. Before we take that step, I'd like to become better acquainted. My house has two bedrooms, so you'll have your own until you're ready to move into mine."

Her shoulders sagged and a relieved expression settled on her face as she squeezed his hand back. "I hope yer not offended, but I'm happy to hear that. I wasn't sure what yer feelings were on the subject."

Sam gave her hand a last squeeze and released her. "Well, now you know."

Greta arrived with their coffee and custard pie. They ate their dessert in companionable silence, enjoying the treat. By the time they'd finished, Sam noticed that Lucy looked fatigued.

"Lucy, why don't you go rest and I'll pick you up around eight tomorrow morning," he suggested.

She sent him a tired smile. "Aye, I'm quite tired and now that my belly is full of such good food, I feel like I could sleep for a week."

Sam rose, and she followed suit. "Then I won't keep you." Moving closer to her, he took her hand, and brushed his lips over the smooth back of it. "Goodnight, Lucy. Pleasant dreams."

Looking into her slightly dazed eyes, Sam was certain a spark of attraction sparked between them, which pleased him. He walked her to the stairs where Lucy turned to him.

"Thank ya for everything," she said. "Goodnight, Sam."

He gave her a smile and a nod, and then took his leave.

~

WONDERMENT FILLED Lucy as she and Sam turned down the lane to his ranch the next morning. After growing up in a city, the vast expanse of farmland that spread out before them was a surprise to her. She'd gotten glimpses of fields and forests on the trip to Spruce Valley, but she hadn't yet seen a ranch.

A small one-story, white clapboard ranch house stood a little way down the lane on the right. A large red barn had been erected farther down the lane with wooden fencing running out from the back of it. Several horses grazed in the pasture and a couple of dogs came running toward the buggy.

A sea of prairie grass stretched out as far as Lucy could see, meeting the dazzling blue sky above the horizon. Maple and birch trees dotted the ranch and there was a white bunkhouse on the left of the driveway.

Sam's voice interrupted her thoughts. "I know it's a little plain, but I left it that way purposely. Same with the house. I thought it would be nice to decorate it together, to make it ours."

His consideration touched Lucy. "'Tis a lovely piece of land, and I'm sure the house is, too." She gave him a teasing smile. "And I certainly don't mind giving the place a woman's touch."

His grin made her pulse skip. "It needs it."

He halted Atlas in front of the house and got out of the buggy. "You go on ahead and I'll start bringing in your luggage."

Lucy said, "Aye," as he helped her out of the vehicle. "I confess that I'm anxious to see it."

He gestured dramatically toward the house. "Then by all means."

As Lucy walked along the path to the porch that ran the length of the house, she envisioned the walkway lined with colorful flowers. She could also plant low shrubs in front of the porch. Stepping up onto it, she noted that the wide plank boards had been freshly painted a gray that matched the shutters and contrasted nicely with the white house.

The screen door was painted the same color, but the inner wooden door was white. Lucy liked the ornate brass doorknob and doorknocker. Opening the door, she stepped into a small foyer, which opened onto a hallway. The hardwood oak floors gleamed, and the walls had been painted a rich cream.

There were several doorways on each side of the hallway. The first one on the left revealed a large parlor with three tall windows. The weather had cleared overnight, and sunshine streamed through the glass, filling the room with warm light. A green-and-white floral sofa, love seat, and two wingback chairs were situated around the room facing the fireplace that stood between two of the windows.

Lucy envisioned her and Sam sitting in front of a roaring fire on winter nights. She would perhaps work on mending and he would read a book. A giggle bubbled from her over her daydreaming. She turned when she heard footsteps in the hallway.

Sam, lugging one of her trunks, halted in the doorway. "What do you think?"

"Well, I only got this far, but if the rest of the house is as nice as the parlor, I'm going to love it," Lucy replied.

His grin lit up his amazing eyes. "I'm glad to hear it. Well, I'll get this to your room."

Lucy followed him. "I'll come with you."

"All right."

As she walked behind Sam, Lucy couldn't help admiring his fine form. His broad shoulders tapered down to a trim waist and his trousers hinted at a nice backside. Her cheeks heated, and Lucy tugged her thoughts away from that subject.

The next room on the left was the dining room which led into the kitchen. Since Sam hadn't told her much about the house yet, Lucy was surprised to see that the sink had a pump in it. It would be much more convenient than having to constantly haul water from a well, especially on wash day.

Sam joined her in the kitchen just as she came out of the pantry and she commented on the pump. He said, "I'm glad you like it, but don't get used to it."

Lucy's brow puckered in confusion. "Why not? You're not after takin' it out, are ya?"

His lips twitched, and she knew that her Irish phrase had tickled his funny bone. "Well, I am, but only because a friend of mine who's a master plumber is coming from New York City next month to install indoor plumbing."

Lucy's mouth dropped open. "Indoor plumbin'! We didn't even have that back in Buffalo. Of course, we're rather poor, but still. Only the wealthiest had a water closet." She narrowed her eyes at him. "How can ye afford that?"

He leaned a hip against the counter and crossed his arms over his chest in a pose that pulled his shirtsleeves tight around his biceps. Those biceps, his slightly ruddy complexion, and strong hands showed that he was used to hard, physical work. He might be a doctor, but it appeared that he didn't spend all his days in an office.

"Mike Prentiss and I grew up together in New Jersey, but he left to be an apprentice with an engineer when our formal schooling was through. I helped him start his business and now he owes me a few favors," Sam replied. "He was out here last year and said the water table on my property was high enough to support indoor plumbing. So, you'll be the envy of Spruce Valley since no one else except Bill has it."

Lucy couldn't help being thrilled at the prospect of having such a modern home. She'd never expected to live in a place with running water. Not only that, but the cookstove was a newer, eight-plate model with a double oven, which meant she could cook more things at the same time. The pantry was large and very cool, despite the heat. Food would stay fresh longer in it.

Smiling at Sam, she thought she'd have married him for just the kitchen alone. "I thought ya were just teasin' about spoilin' me."

Sam straightened and stepped closer. "No, I was serious. After all, what's the point of having a beautiful woman if not to spoil her?"

The sudden heat in Sam's eyes sent Lucy's pulse galloping. His compliment made her blush, but she was determined not to be bashful. She was a grown woman of twenty-four—practically a spinster—not a young schoolgirl with a crush. And Sam was a very handsome man who seemed to find her attractive. It wasn't as though she'd never been kissed, and it seemed as though Sam had kissing on his mind.

Wouldn't it be good to know if they had any chemistry before they kissed at the wedding? Call her wicked, but Lucy didn't want their first kiss to take place in the presence of other people. As he closed the distance between them, Lucy's breathing grew shallow.

He raised a hand and cupped her cheek.

Suddenly, a female voice cut the quiet of the house. "Hellooo! Yoohoo!"

Sam frowned as he dropped his hand and took several steps away from Lucy.

"Dr. Slater?"

"In the kitchen, Mrs. Stavros," Sam called out.

Lucy gathered her wits as a plump, seventy-ish woman entered the kitchen. Her dark eyes glittered with curiosity and a welcoming smile curved her generous mouth.

"Hello, Mrs. Stavros." Sam motioned toward Lucy. "Allow me to introduce you to my bride-to-be, Miss Lucy Magee. Lucy, this is Mrs. Delphina Stavros, my neighbor, good friend, and our mayor."

Lucy's eyes rounded as she gave Mrs. Stavros a small curtsey. "Pleased to meet you, ma'am. I've never heard of a woman mayor before."

"How do you do?" Mrs. Stavros greeted her in heavily accented English. "It's good to meet you, as well. My husband Anton was the mayor, but he passed away last year. No one else ran for mayor, so I took his place." She chuckled. "There are only around two hundred people in Spruce Valley, so usually, there is not much to the job."

Lucy said, "It's still impressive to meet a lady mayor. It gives hope that perhaps the rest of the people here are a little forward-thinkin'."

Mrs. Stavros sobered. "Some more than others. There are those who are not happy with a woman holding the reins, but I do not let them bother me."

"Whoever doesn't like it can go hang," Sam chimed in. "You're doing a great job and I hope you stay at it for a while."

A pleased smile lit up Mrs. Stavros' eyes again. "You're much too kind, Sam, but I appreciate your support."

Sam noticed that the older lady carried a large wicker basket and nodded toward it. "What do you have there?"

Looking at Lucy, Mrs. Stavros replied, "I must confess that I became very curious when I heard that you'd arrived and just had to come meet you when I saw Sam's buggy pass my house." Sadness pinched her handsome features. "I can't believe that Jed is gone." She sniffed and pulled a handkerchief from her skirt pocket. "He was such a good man and a good friend. I'm going to miss him."

Sam put a comforting arm around her. "Me, too, but at least he didn't suffer. He's in a better place now."

Mrs. Stavros nodded and dabbed at her teary eyes. "Yes, you're right. Anyway, I knew you most likely hadn't thought about preparing lunch, so I put one together for you." She handed the basket to Lucy. "I thought Sam might take you to meet Ernie, so there is enough food in there for you all."

Surprised by the heaviness of the basket, Lucy thought that Mrs. Stavros must've packed enough for a small army. "How thoughtful of ye. Many thanks."

"That's what makes her such a great mayor," Sam said. "She's always thinking ahead."

Mrs. Stavros waved away his compliment. "I must get back home to help Elena with the children. My daughter has four little ones and they keep everyone stepping. Lucy, I look forward to becoming friends. You must come for a visit soon."

Lucy beamed, thrilled to make a friend. "I would enjoy that very much. Thank ya again for the food."

"You're quite welcome, dear," Mrs. Stavros said.

"I'll walk you out," Sam announced. "I'll be right back, Lucy."

"I'll be here," she quipped and watched them walk from the room.

~

SAM GLANCED at Lucy as he drove his buggy past the barn and headed for his sheep herder's camp. Her black hair, which she'd put up in a low bun that day, was hidden by a white cotton sunbonnet. It was saved from being plain by the pretty, swirling green and gold leaves that had been stitched around the brim.

He looked away from Lucy, facing ahead again. Try as he might, it was almost impossible to keep his eyes off her. Irritated by his immature behavior, Sam forced himself to be a good host instead of acting like an infatuated schoolboy.

"How long will it take to reach Mr. Red Dog's camp?" Lucy asked.

"The better part of an hour," Sam replied. "I'm glad it cleared off so we can make the trip. I wanted you to meet him and tell him about the wedding."

"Will he come to it, then?"

Sam smiled. "Ernie's not much for Christianity, but he'll attend just because I asked him to."

"Because he's an Indian?"

"Well, he doesn't have much Indian blood, just an Indian last name. His great grandfather was a member of a Crow tribe from this area," Sam said. "Ernie doesn't consider himself white, or Indian, or colored—just a man. And he doesn't have time for any religion or believe in *any* god."

"But he's still your friend?"

Some men might not like Lucy's straightforward, inquisitive nature, but Sam was enjoying it. Although she might not have had much formal education, through their correspondence, he'd learned that her Uncle Liam was an educated man who'd insisted on teaching his nieces and nephews as much as possible.

An avid student, Lucy had soaked up her uncle's lessons. As a result, she knew a great deal of mathematics, writing and reading, and history. Sam had been impressed by her intelligence and knowledge as much as he had been by her beautiful picture.

"Ernie is a good, honest man," Sam said. "He taught me everything I know about raising livestock and conducting cattle drives. When I first arrived here, I was surprised to find that there were so few people in town, which means fewer patients, so less income. I had to do something to make money. I became friendly with Ernie and he pointed me to my land.

"He grew up herding sheep, so when he offered his services as such, I took him up on it right away. He helped me put together a good herd and I made him my business partner. I take care of things around the ranch and he takes care of the sheep."

Lucy's smile drew his attention to her mouth, and he felt the urge to kiss her again.

"I'm glad that ya have such good friends," Lucy said.

Sam reached over and took her hand. "They'll be your friends, too. You'll see."

He enjoyed the feeling of her smaller hand in his and was glad when she didn't pull away. The back of her hand was smooth, but the light callouses on her palm proved that she was used to hard work. This was a relief to him because life in their remote, frontier area could be harsh and hard work was crucial to survival.

He lifted her hand and pressed a kiss to it. The blush that blossomed in her cheeks and the way her eyes darkened made him want to kiss more than her hand. Giving it a last squeeze, he let it go.

They chatted almost the whole ride, and Sam couldn't remember the last time he'd enjoyed a conversation so much. He was almost sad when they arrived at the sheep herder's camp because he didn't want it to end. With an internal chuckle, he reminded himself that he was going to have a whole lifetime to converse with the special woman riding beside him.

Nearing Ernie's camp, Sam grew concerned when he saw only a few sheep around the area. Normally, they were milling about, grazing or sleeping. Ernie's dogs, Chip and Millie, were nowhere in sight.

Swinging his gaze to the right, his disquiet deepened when he saw that no fire burned in the pit outside Ernie's shepherd's shed. No smoke rose from the small pipe sticking out of its roof, either.

Stopping the buggy next to the shed, Sam called out, "Ernie! Are you here?"

Upon receiving no response, a chill of dread crept up Sam's spine. He got out of the buggy and Lucy did the same. Sam walked toward the shepherd's shed with long, urgent strides, calling out to his friend. However, still no answer met his loud calls.

As he was about to open the shed's door, Sam noticed something out of the corner of his eye. To his right, peeking out from around the corner of the shed was a man's boot. But not just any boot. The sight of the worn, dingy, tan hide of a moccasin boot caused Sam's heart to leap in his chest because he knew it well.

Rushing around the corner of the shed, Sam found the body of one of his best friends. Sam fell to his knees beside Ernie and began assessing him, even though he knew that Ernie was dead…

# CHAPTER 3

*The Present...*

"ARE you sure you won't bury him in the cemetery?"

Sam offered Reverend Paul Gibbons a tight smile. "I'm certain. I've finished my post-mortem examination and I'll take him to his sons. He once told me that's what he wanted if I outlived him."

Paul sighed and leaned back in his wingback chair. "Very well."

Sam stared into his sherry—the strongest drink served in the Gibbons' home—and then looked around the comfortable if sparsely furnished parlor. It wasn't mostly devoid of decoration or bric-a-brac due to religion, but because Mrs. Gibbons found that it made her housekeeping easier. The time she saved on such mundane chores as dusting and sweeping, she used in pursuing her true passion—music.

Sam's sadness thawed slightly when Mary's spectacular soprano voice swept up and down a scale, the sound carrying easily to them from upstairs. "Annette sounds in fine form."

Paul chuckled. "Yes, she does. The voice of an angel. What a pity that none of our children inherited even half of her gifts." He straightened again. "Are you certain that I can't even pray over Ernie or—"

"Paul, I know you mean well, but I won't go against Ernie's wishes and have him haunt me. I'll take his body out to the woods in the morning, as promised, and give him to his sons," Sam insisted, growing irritated.

Paul lifted a placating hand. "All right. It just feels so wrong to not do something for him."

Sam's anger abated at Paul's contrite expression. "You *are* doing something for him—what he wanted—and I'm sure he thanks you."

Paul nodded curtly. "Does Josh have any idea who might've done this?"

"Not yet but give him time. Josh is as dogged as any bloodhound and twice as fearsome as a bear," Sam replied. "Although, if I find out who did it—"

"You'll turn him in." Steel laced Paul's voice and filled his dark eyes. "Don't utter one more word of sinful intentions, Sam."

Sam's fingers tightened on the arm of his chair and he knew it was time to leave before his anger sharpened his tongue. He forced himself to relax and finished his drink. "My apologies, Paul. I'm just out of sorts."

"I understand how troubled you are," Paul said. "But don't let Ernie's death pull you into darkness again, Sam."

*I fear it's already too late.* Sam pushed that thought away and stood up. "You're right. I won't. Ernie wouldn't want that, and I have responsibilities and a lot to look forward to."

A grin lit Paul's craggy face. "Such as marriage to a fetching Irish lass?"

Lucy's beautiful visage rose in Sam's mind, and he couldn't stop his own smile. "Yes. I'm glad I picked her. She's intelligent, strong, and beautiful—exactly the kind of woman I wanted."

"I'm glad to hear it. You deserve to be happy, Sam."

Sam nodded. "Well, I have a little work to do before bed. Goodnight."

"Goodnight, Sam."

As Sam left the reverend's house, a breeze kicked up and an owl screeched from somewhere nearby, no doubt in search of a meal. Sam strolled along the walkway that ran from the parsonage along the side of the church to the main street. As he neared his office, he thought about stopping to see Lucy for a few minutes. She'd been going to spend the evening at Greta's, working on some sewing.

Deciding his paperwork could wait until morning, Sam cut across the street to the tiny house Greta called home. Normally, Greta was a frugal person, but she'd paid extra for the yellow paint that now covered the house. It was a warm, sunny color that brought to mind spring days and rays of golden light.

Sam mounted her low porch and knocked on the door.

Greta opened it and smiled at him. "Dr. Slater, to what do I owe the pleasure, as if I don't know?"

Sam chuckled. "Yes, I've come to see Lucy, but you know I'm always happy to see you."

"Ever the gentleman. Come in, please. May I offer you some coffee or tea?" Greta asked, showing him into her parlor.

Lucy looked up from her sewing. Her smile of welcome distracted Sam for a moment.

"Uh, yes, Greta. Whichever is easiest would be fine," he said. "Hello, Lucy. How is your work going?"

"Very well, thank ya," she said. "How are you doing?"

Sam took off his black Cutter hat made by a new company by the name of Stetson. It was a young enterprise, only three years old, but already word of their exceptional hats was spreading. When he'd accompanied Ernie on a cattle drive to Texas the previous year, he hadn't been able to resist buying it, even though it had cost him quite a tidy sum of money.

He sat in a straight back chair close to Lucy and rested his hat on his lap. "About as well as can be expected. I won't pretend that I'm not deeply wounded by Ernie's death. If he'd merely suffered a heart attack or stroke, I could bear it better." Sam saw Ernie's sightless eyes, the stab wounds in his stomach and the single slice across his neck again, saw the life-blood that had flowed and dried on Ernie's skin and clothes. "It's one thing to kill in war, terrible as that is, but to kill in cold blood." He shook his head.

"'Tis sometimes hard to contemplate how people can do such evil to each other," Lucy said.

Sam nodded. "True, but I shouldn't talk about this in front of ladies."

Her nostrils flared and Sam knew he was about to be chastised again. "Sam, I'm not some young girl afraid of any unpleasantness. I might be a woman, but I'm strong enough to deal with such things. Kindly remember that."

A smile played around his mouth as he inclined his head slightly. "Duly noted. You'll have to pardon my gentleman's upbringing."

An answering smile curved her lips. "You're forgiven. Now, what did yer examination reveal?"

"Not much, I'm afraid," he replied, raking a hand through his hair. "I didn't find a single clue on his body or clothes. The wounds were made with a common blade, there were no bruises from hands holding him down, either. Nothing to help Josh in his investigation."

The sympathy in her eyes warmed him. "Ye tried yer best. That's all any of us can do. I'm sure Josh will bring the culprit to justice."

Greta entered the parlor with a tray of tea and blueberry scones. "Listen to your intended, Sam. She's a wise young woman. You know Josh, he won't give up."

"Yes. You're both right, but let's change the subject if you don't mind." Sam took the cup of tea Greta held out to him. "I've had enough sadness for one day. Let's talk about happier things."

~

LUCY'S HEART went out to Sam. The deeper brackets around his mouth and the fatigue in his eyes showed the toll the situation was taking on him. It had been hard for her to see Ernie lying on the ground, bloody and broken, but it had to be infinitely worse for him. Determined to help him, she set out to cheer him up.

"Well, ye'll be happy to know that I'll be ready for our weddin' on Sunday. Greta is going to help me with any last-minute dress alterations," she said.

"That's very good news," Sam said. "I look forward to seeing you in it."

Greta chuckled. "She's going to be breathtaking, and no, you can't see it before the ceremony."

"I don't doubt she will be."

Lucy's cheeks heated as she caught Sam's appreciative gaze. She hid her shyness by taking a sip of tea. It was unsettling and exciting to have a man look at her that way. Men had looked at her with lust, but there was nothing nefarious in Sam's eyes.

"We'll need to ready the house for Lucy."

"What do you mean?" Lucy sat her cup on a stand next to her. "The house looked very ready when I visited yesterday."

Greta gave her an indulging smile. "Dear girl, a woman wants to make a house her own once she marries. You'll have your own ideas about decorating it, I'm sure. However, I'd like to offer my help, if you like."

Lucy saw the wisdom in accepting Greta's assistance. Although she'd aided her mother in running their home, she had no idea what she wanted her own to be like. She'd been too busy helping to care for her younger siblings and performing endless chores to allow herself the freedom to dream about such things. But now…

"I'd be grateful for yer help," she said.

The mantel clock struck nine, startling them all.

"Goodness, I didn't realize it was so late," Lucy commented and began gathering up her sewing. "I should be on my way and get out of ya hair for the night, Greta."

"Nonsense, it was wonderful to have some company other than Darcy Wainwright's. She's a dear, but does go on about the most tedious things," Greta responded.

Sam stood up, a wry smile on his lips. "Yes, Mrs. Wainwright has a rather dry personality about her. I'll see you home, Lucy."

"I'd appreciate it," Lucy said.

After bidding Greta goodnight, they stepped out into the muggy night air. Sam offered Lucy his arm and she accepted it.

Glancing up at Sam, Lucy asked, "What drew you to this land, Sam? It seems an odd choice for a refined man such as yer self."

"Well, once the war was over, I was ready for a change."

Lucy frowned. "Yer said that once in your letters, but you didn't say much more than that."

His jaw tensed, and he looked up at the three-quarter moon overhead for a moment. "There's only so much of death and carnage a man can take, and I'd had more than my fill. Being a battlefield doctor is a grisly business and often my best efforts weren't good enough. I did my duty and was glad to serve my country, but once the war ended, I wanted to practice a different kind of medicine."

"I can understand that, but I'm sure there were plenty of hospitals to work for, or perhaps open your own practice in a city," Lucy inquired.

Sam chuckled softly. "You are a very determined woman, Lucy."

She smiled. "So I've been told."

Sam stopped, and Lucy halted beside him. "Have you ever wanted a completely different life? To do something new and challenge yerself?"

Lucy enjoyed his surprised expression when she laughed and took one of his hands. "Only every day since I was a lass of fourteen!"

Her pulse did a funny little leap when he kissed the back of her hand. "And tell me, fair Lucy, what are your dreams?"

Taken aback, Lucy could only stare at Sam. No one, not even her best friend back in Buffalo, had ever asked her what kind of future she wanted. Her parents were too busy supporting their large family to discuss their children's individual dreams. Lucy was so accustomed to keeping her desires to herself that it took her a few moments to find her voice.

"Ye'll laugh." She tried to pull her hand from Sam's, but he held onto it.

"I promise not to," he said.

Lucy drew herself up and met his eyes. "I've always been good at designin' clothing and would love to own my own boutique." She forced a laugh. "A silly dream, I know. Don't worry. I intend to honor our marriage and perform all my wifely duties to the utmost."

An odd look passed over Sam's face, and Lucy thought she'd angered him. "Lucy, I know you're probably used to the kind of men who expect you to be focused on seeing to a husband's needs before her own, but I'm not like those men. I want you to be happy, and if designing clothing makes you happy, so be it."

Once again, Sam had surprised her. She narrowed her eyes, suddenly suspicious. "Are you just testin' me?"

He squeezed her hands and smiled. "No, I mean it. I'm straightforward about my thoughts and feelings, and I don't believe in playing mind games. You'll always know where I stand."

Lucy relaxed, the tension leaving her shoulders. "I'm glad to hear that."

They resumed walking.

"We don't know exactly when little ones will come along," Sam said. "So, you'll have time to work on your designs and make clothes."

"Thank ya," Lucy said as they arrived at the Inn. "Both for walkin' me home and being so considerate."

They halted at the door.

"You're welcome. I have some patients to check on tomorrow morning, but how about we meet here for lunch?" Sam asked.

"I'd like that."

They fell silent, just gazing at each other for a couple of moments. Then Sam leaned down and pressed a kiss to her cheek. Her breathing quickened at the feel of his warm lips on her skin.

When he pulled back, he said, "Goodnight, Lucy."

"Goodnight, Sam."

She gave him a brief smile and headed inside, chiding herself for being disappointed that he hadn't kissed her. There would be plenty of time for that, especially once they were married. Going to her room, Lucy readied for bed smiling with anticipation to see Sam the next day.

# CHAPTER 4

"Are you sure you don't mind?"

Lucy and Sam stood in his kitchen the next afternoon. They'd come out to his ranch so he could introduce her to his ranch hands, who hadn't been working near home the other day. However, they hadn't been there very long before a man had come galloping up to the house and announced that his teenage son had gotten stomped by a bull and needed help.

"Of course not, Sam," Lucy replied. "Go and don't worry about me. Do whatever you must to help the lad."

Sam smiled and kissed her hand. "All right. I'll be back as soon as I can."

Lucy nodded and watched him jog over to the barn, his medical bag in hand. She felt a rush of pride over finding such a kind, intelligent man. When Sam disappeared into the barn, Lucy turned her attention to the house. Taking a notepad, measuring tape, and a pencil from her purse, she started jotting down things she wanted for the house as she walked through it.

As she entered her room, she noticed movement when she looked out of the window that faced the driveway. Peering out of it, she saw someone standing at the end of the lane. She waited for them to approach the house, but they didn't. An uneasy feeling washed over her, and she stepped away from the window.

Going to Sam's room, she looked out the window. The figure was still there, only a little closer now. However, they were still too far away to tell if it was a woman or a man. Lucy was just about to go look out of a parlor window, when the lurker seemed to melt from sight.

She waited, but no one reappeared, either there or from anywhere outside the house. Putting her nervousness down to not being accustomed to being so alone, Lucy shrugged off her misgivings and went back to work.

~

AN HOUR LATER, Lucy was startled when someone knocked on the front door. She was in the pantry, taking stock of the supplies they were going to need. Hurrying to the door, she opened it, but no one stood on the other side of the threshold. She poked her head outside, but the porch was empty.

Stepping out onto the porch, Lucy scanned the yard and beyond, but didn't see anyone. The same feeling of dread flowed through her as before. Turning around, she stopped cold when she saw a small piece of paper fluttering in the breeze from a slightly raised nail in the wooden siding by the door. Swallowing her fear, she reached out and plucked the paper from the nail.

A note had been scrawled across it in pencil. *Get out while you can.* Lucy looked around again, her gaze stopping at every tree and scanning the buildings within her line of sight. Seeing nothing strange, Lucy went back in the house and locked the door.

She battled back fright as she closed and latched the windows and secured the kitchen door. It was another warm day, and it was going to get hot in the house. Better to be hot and alive instead of dead, though. She settled on a chair in the parlor where she could keep watch through a window. She looked at the note.

Its warning was clear, but why did someone want her to leave? She'd only been in Spruce Valley for two days. What kind of threat could she possibly be to anyone? So far, she'd only met six people and she certainly couldn't have offended them in such a short span. Could it have something to do with Ernie?

That didn't make sense since she'd never met the man. No, it must be some sort of cruel prank.

Her blood beginning to simmer, Lucy stood up, crushing the note and stuffing it in her dress pocket. She stomped to the kitchen door, fuming, not only at the person who'd written the note, but at her own cowardice.

Squaring her shoulders, she unlocked the door and yanked it open. A shadow fell across the threshold. Lucy stepped back, looked up, and screamed.

~

TURNING down the lane to his ranch, Sam was jerked from his thoughts by a woman's high-pitched scream. The sound sent a chill racing up his spine. Knowing the screams must be coming from Lucy, he spurred Atlas forward and the big equine lunged into a gallop.

Arriving at the house, Sam slowed his mount and slid from the horse's back before it had completely stopped.

Running toward the house, he saw the kitchen door standing open, but he couldn't see inside.

"Lucy? Lucy!" he shouted, mounting the porch.

"Sam!" she screamed. "Stay back! He'll kill you!"

"Listen, my dear, I've told you that I'm Sam's frie—"

"Liar!" Lucy cried as Sam burst into the kitchen. "You wrote this dastardly note, and now ye've come to kill me!"

Sam's heart thudded against his ribs and then started to slow as he recognized both the cultured male voice and man standing in the middle of his kitchen.

"Lucy, he's telling you the truth," Sam said. "He's not here to kill anyone."

He hated the fear and anger in Lucy's wide-eyed, silver gaze. Her cheeks were crimson from the force of her emotions. She bravely wiped away a tear with one hand and brandished a large knife in the other. She looked like a beautiful, sooty-haired goddess, bent on protecting others and meting out justice.

Her gaze moved from the would-be assailant to Sam. "He's not? Are you sure? Because I know a snake when I see one, and this man is a snake indeed."

Sam caught the twinkle in the man's midnight eyes but hid his own amusement in the face of Lucy's terror. "Lucy, I promise that he's my friend and he won't hurt either of us. You can put the knife down."

Lucy's gaze flicked back and forth between the two men. Slowly, she placed the knife on the counter but never took her eyes off the man.

Sam moved over to stand beside Lucy and put an arm around her shoulders. "Lucy, let me introduce you to Gray Jenkins. He's my foreman and a close friend. He lives in the bunkhouse along with two of my other hands. Gray, this is my intended, Miss Lucy Magee."

Gray swept off his gray cowboy hat and executed a deep

bow to her. "It's a great pleasure to make the acquaintance of such a beautiful and brave woman such as yourself, Miss Magee."

Lucy glanced up at Sam and he gave her an encouraging smile. Then she stepped away from Sam and held out a hand to Gray. "Pleased to meet ya, sir. I'm sorry for threatening ya with a knife, but you frightened me when you just strolled in here and approached me the way you did."

Gray took her hand and gave it a gentle shake. "That's quite all right. I'm not unaccustomed to being threatened, but I must say you're the most beautiful attacker I've ever met."

~

LOOKING in Gray's onyx eyes, Lucy's fear dissipated at the sparkle of humor in them. His handsome, angular features and the dimple in his left cheek were quite arresting and Lucy doubted that Gray ever lacked for female company.

"I see yer a flatterer," she teased. "I guess I'll have to keep my eye on yer."

Gray chuckled and released her hand. "Perhaps. Sam will have to make sure you're kept satisfied so I don't have a chance to swoop in and steal you away."

"Don't worry," Sam said smiling. "I intend to keep Lucy satisfied in every way."

Lucy's cheeks pinkened as his gaze roamed over her quickly before returning to her eyes.

"I'm sure you will," Gray remarked. "Well, I can give you my report later. I'll go settle in and find the others. See you tonight?"

Sam nodded. "I'll find you when I get home."

"Very good." Gray touched the brim of his hat. "Miss

Lucy. It's been a pleasure to meet you, and I look forward to getting to know you. Good day to you."

"Good day, Gray." Lucy watched him walk out the door, his dark brown duster fluttering behind him. "He's quite the character," she said once he was out of earshot.

"Yes, he is. I've been friends with him since the moment we met," Sam said. "He's one of those people you instantly like."

Lucy arched an eyebrow. "I might've if he hadn't scared the bejesus out of me. He waltzed in here like he owned the place and I thought he was the one who wrote this note."

She took the crumpled piece of paper from her skirt pocket and handed it to Sam. His jaw clenched as he read it and his eyes darkened with anger.

He turned the paper over and then back around. "There's nothing distinguishing about this paper. Did you see the culprit?"

Lucy hugged her middle. "I'm not sure. I was looking around and saw someone standing down at the end of the drive. It looked like a man, but I couldn't make out any features. Then they were gone, and I thought they went on their way.

"After a bit, there was a knock on the front door, but no one was there when I answered it. That's when I found the note. Then Gray showed up. I thought he'd left the note and meant me harm."

Sam moved closer and put his hands on her shoulders. "I'm sorry that you were frightened. I won't let anything happen to you, Lucy."

Sam's presence was comforting, and Lucy's fear abated somewhat as she looked into Sam's eyes. She believed that he would fight to keep her safe, but what happened when he wasn't around? Their ranch was as remote as many of the others, and if the ranch hands weren't nearby, she'd be vulnerable to anyone who meant her harm.

However, she didn't want to appear weak, so she didn't voice her fears. "I know. I'm sure it's just a prank of some sort." She forced a smile, hoping it looked genuine. "Most likely some youngster who thought it would be funny to scare a newcomer."

The right corner of Sam's mouth lifted. "That's possible. There are some scalawags around here, but I think it would be a good idea to teach you how to shoot a shotgun and pistol."

Lucy's pulse leaped at the thought. "Do you really think that's necessary?"

Sam nodded. "Yes. If no one else is around and a coyote or other predator shows up, you'll have to protect the livestock. We'll have a short lesson with the shotgun this afternoon."

Her palms grew damp at the thought of holding a dangerous weapon, but she saw the sense in Sam's words. "All right. But first, I'll make us a nice lunch with the things I brought with me."

Sam's eyes twinkled as he smiled. "I'm finally going to get to see what was in that big basket, hmm?"

Lucy turned away from him, giving him a coquettish smile over her shoulder as she moved to the counter on which the large wicker basket sat. "Aye. Why don't you go tend to something and I'll call you when it's ready?"

Sam's warm chuckle erased her lingering fear. "All right. I have something I can occupy myself with while you do that."

"Good. Off with ye then."

Lucy watched with amusement as Sam just shook his head and left the kitchen.

~

SITTING at his small desk in his bedroom, Sam looked out the window as he mused about what had happened to Lucy. Although he'd tried to reassure her that she was safe, he was more concerned than he'd let on. Was Ernie's murder connected with the warning note left for Lucy, or was someone else responsible? Either way, why would they threaten her?

Sam put down his pen and drummed his fingers on the desk as he considered how he was going to keep Lucy safe. He couldn't be with her all the time. He had patients to see and work around the ranch, too.

Pulling out his accounting ledger, Sam went over his budget. If he was careful with his funds, he could afford to hire someone to guard the ranch when he had to be away. The more he thought about it, the more Sam liked the idea. It would give them both piece of mind and they would only need a guard until Josh caught the murderer.

Lucy called him for lunch, and he smiled at the sound of her pretty, musical voice. He let her know he was on his way, straightened his desk, and went to join his future bride.

~

LUCY PUT her fork down and stared across the round table at Sam. "You want to hire someone to guard me?" The last bite of her lemon pound cake stuck in her throat a little as anxiety tightened her stomach. "Do you really think that's necessary?"

He wiped his mouth with a linen napkin. "Probably not, but I'm not going to take any chances. Like they say, better safe than sorry."

"Who will you hire?" Lucy took a sip of tea, hoping it would calm her.

Leaning back in his chair, Sam replied, "I'm not sure. I don't have any experience hiring guards, but I'm sure Josh can recommend someone."

To cover her disquiet, Lucy rose from the table and started gathering their dishes. "I'm sure he can."

She took them over to the sink and placed them in a pan of hot water. After adding some cold to it, Lucy wet a cloth and turned back to the table, intending to wipe it off. Sam pushed her back from it and stood up.

Her heart beat a little faster as he approached her with a half-smile. "Lucy, I'll make sure you're safe, so you can stop worrying."

"I'm not worried."

His smile broadened, stirring her ire.

"I'm not," she insisted, arching a haughty eyebrow.

Sobering, Sam said, "Lucy, you came here to marry me and even though we're not married yet, your welfare is my responsibility. I take my responsibilities very seriously, so when I say that I'll keep you safe, you can have complete confidence that I will."

The earnestness in his eyes bolstered Lucy's sense of security. "I believe ya and the idea of a guard does make me feel better."

Sam's smile returned, mesmerizing her with the way it enhanced his rugged features. "Good. Now, I'll help you clean up and then start teaching you how to shoot."

Even though thinking about shooting again made her nervous, Lucy admitted that it also excited her. As they worked in companionable silence, Lucy both looked forward to, and dreaded, the coming lesson.

# CHAPTER 5

The light of pride in Lucy's silvery eyes and the pretty pink flush in her cheeks sent desire flowing through Sam. Both of them had been surprised at how well Lucy had shot and that she'd enjoyed it so much.

"Just a few more shots," Lucy pleaded, as the breeze toyed with her ebony hair that had come loose from her long braid.

Sam grinned at her enthusiasm. "Not right now. We have to save some ammunition."

"All right," she agreed with a dejected expression. "I'm sure bullets are expensive, and we don't want to run out."

The flicker of fear in her eyes made Sam sober. "Right." He took the shotgun from Lucy and cradled it in the crook of his right arm. Putting his left arm around her shoulders, he guided Lucy toward the house. "You did very well for your first time. You'll be a crack shot before long."

Their close proximity enabled him to catch Lucy's scent. She smelled like sunshine and lavender and he found the scent more intoxicating than the expensive perfumes some women wore.

"Thank ya. It was fun. I'm not afraid of guns now," Lucy responded. "I appreciate ye teaching me."

Her shoulder against his side felt nice and Sam was glad that she didn't object to his affectionate gesture. He gave her a gentle squeeze and then allowed his arm to fall away so she didn't become uncomfortable. "It was my pleasure. Is there anything else you need to do here?"

Lucy met his gaze. "No. I'm finished with my list."

Sam chuckled. "I'm sure it's a long one. I know this place needs a feminine touch."

Her smile drew his eyes to her lips. "Not very long."

"Well, get whatever you can from the mercantile and put it on my account. They also have catalogues there to order from," Sam said.

Lucy nodded. "All right. I'm a frugal person, so you don't have to worry about me spending all your money."

"I appreciate that," Sam said. "But I want you to have the things you'd like. I want to make you happy."

As they mounted the porch steps, Lucy said, "I'm here with a handsome man who just showed me a very nice afternoon and it's a beautiful sunny day. I'm already happy, Sam."

He gave a short laugh, pleased by her compliment. "So, you think I'm handsome, do you?"

She sent him a bright smile. "Ye know you're handsome, Sam. I'm sure you've had plenty of women tell you that."

"A few have mentioned that," Sam teased, moving closer. "I'm glad I meet with your approval."

Her eyes widened as he cupped her cheek. "Ye certainly do."

Brushing his thumb over her cheek, Sam said, "Good.

And you're the loveliest woman I've seen in a long time, Lucy." He slid an arm around her waist, pulling her lightly against him. "May I kiss you?"

~

Lucy's heartbeat leapt in her chest as Sam tightened his embrace. The feel of his hard torso against her body created an unfamiliar heat inside that had nothing to do with the warm day. His expression had sobered, and his eyes reflected desire.

She placed her hands on Sam's chest and enjoyed the firm muscles under her palms. Her eyes settled on his sensual lips and her pulse rose as the urge to kiss him overtook her.

"Yes, you may kiss me."

Sam lowered his head toward her, and Lucy's eyes fluttered shut as he brushed his mouth against hers. Her lips parted on a tiny gasp and she slid her arms around his neck. She felt Sam's hands splay over her back and gooseflesh broke out over her shoulders.

She followed his lead when he slanted his mouth over hers and deepened the kiss. Her senses were filled with Sam as he held her closer and intensified his kiss. Reason intruded in her mind as she remembered that they were standing outside in plain view.

With a gentle push on Sam's chest, Lucy broke the kiss, staring into his passion filled eyes. The hungry way he looked at her made her want to resume their kissing, but it wouldn't be proper for several different reasons.

"I'm sorry," Sam said, but he didn't seem very contrite. "I just couldn't help myself. You're so beautiful."

Lucy flushed at his praise but smiled. "It isn't that I

didn't enjoy it, because I did. Very much. It's just that we're not married yet."

Sam tucked an errant lock of hair behind her ear. "Just because we're not married doesn't mean we can't do some sparking."

Lucy's brow puckered in confusion. "Sparking?"

"That's what the people around here call kissing and hugging," Sam said with a chuckle. "There's a line I won't cross, but I won't hide the fact that I'm attracted to you."

His nearness strongly affected Lucy, which was disconcerting. One part of her wanted him to take her back in his arms and the shyer part of her urged her to step back. "I'm glad ye are, and I'm attracted to ye, too."

He seemed to read her uncertainty. With a nod, he moved away. "That certainly bodes well for a marriage since I'd like children."

His statement shouldn't have embarrassed her but thinking about the act of child-making sent heat surging into her cheeks. "Aye," was all she could manage as Sam opened the kitchen door and held it for her.

As Lucy passed him and entered the kitchen, she kept her eyes averted. She started gathering up the things she wanted to take back to the Inn with her to hide her discomfort. However, at one point, she glanced up to find Sam looking at her with an amused gleam in his eyes. Ignoring it, she continued her work and was soon ready to leave.

~

"What a damn shame. I hope Josh catches the miscreant soon," Gray commented as they sat in Sam's parlor that evening.

"I'm sure he will, but I just don't understand who'd want

him dead. I'm glad Drake agreed to take over as my shepherd until I find a replacement."

Ernie's eldest son was a serious, taciturn young man, but he possessed keen intelligence and a kind heart.

Gray grunted. "Yes, he's a good lad. Why doesn't he want to take the job permanently?"

Sam smiled at the picture Gray made. He sat in a royal blue wingback chair in a pair of worn black trousers, white shirt, and a worn gray cowboy hat balanced on his crossed legs. He leisurely puffed on a black pipe and smoke wound toward the ceiling in lazy wisps. Gray was an odd pairing of sophisticated gentleman and ranch hand.

"Drake plans to leave for California in August and is saving up some money before he goes. He's going to join a friend out there to look for a gold claim," Sam replied.

"It's best they're not waiting long, then. I've heard that some veins are drying up."

Sam turned around, stretched his long legs out on the sofa and rested his head on the arm. "He also wants to start out before the snow flies."

"That's smart, as is your choice in a bride."

Sam grinned over at Gray. "I wondered when we'd get around to that."

"She's feisty, beautiful, and intelligent. She'll do well out here once she gets used to things," Gray commented. "She's been a city dweller, so it might take her a little time to adjust. Plus, I doubt she's done much farming."

A wry smile curved Sam's mouth. "Which was something we discussed in our correspondence. She's used to hard work and I warned her that life here can be harsh and crude. I was completely forthcoming about there being no fancy city trappings and not much society life outside of church events. I made it clear that it might be a little lonely here, but she said it would be a nice change from living in an overcrowded apartment where she had to share a bed with one of her sisters."

Gray's eyes lit with humor. "And now she'll share a bed with you, which shouldn't be a hardship."

Sam laughed at his comment. "No, it won't, but I've agreed not to rush her. I hardly think she'll be ready for intimacy so soon."

Gray uncrossed and re-crossed his legs. "Some men aren't so considerate, but it doesn't surprise me that you are. Your decency is one of the reasons I like you."

"That's ironic coming from a reprobate like you."

"We balance each other out, Sam. You're the good guy everyone likes, and I'm the bad guy everyone likes," Gray quipped.

Sam's mood soured as he thought that he wasn't always a good guy. Shrugging off the negativity that tried to worm its way under his skin, he said, "I know the ladies certainly like your dark charms."

"Mmm. That and it seems as though American women have a fondness for foreign accents," Gray responded. "I confess to using mine to my advantage."

Sam said, "I agree that we Americans do like hearing a foreign tongue. Lucy's brogue falls nicely on the ear."

"That it does," Gray agreed, taking a last puff on his pipe. He knocked out the ashes into the ashtray on the coffee table and stood. "Well, tomorrow comes early, and I don't want my boss to get put-out with me for starting late, so I'll bid you goodnight."

Sam chuckled at his teasing remark. "Goodnight, Gray."

He watched his friend leave the room and heard the kitchen door shut. Although he was tired, he didn't feel sleepy. Rising, he went to the kitchen, locked the door, and poured a finger of whiskey into a glass. He took it to his room and sat down at his desk.

Picking up a tablet on which he'd been writing a medical article he was going to submit to a journal, he did some editing and added more to it. However, even while he worked, Lucy kept popping into Sam's mind.

When he'd started searching for a bride, he hadn't planned on finding a woman like her. He'd hoped to connect with a pleasant woman with whom he could have some stimulating conversation, but Lucy was so much more than that.

As he finished his article and started getting around for bed, Sam smiled as he recalled the brave way Lucy had faced-off with Gray that afternoon. So much backbone! Sam knew that she wouldn't be a pushover and would keep him on his toes, but he looked forward to it. His last thought before sleep claimed him was that being married to Lucy would never be boring.

~

LUCY'S HEART lurched as her eyes snapped open but was unsure what had woken her. She'd fallen asleep sitting up in the overstuffed chair by her bed. The book she'd been reading slipped off her lap and the sound of it hitting the wooden floor startled her again.

A noise outside her door made her turn her head sharply to the left. Was someone in the hallway? As far as she knew, she was the only guest at the Inn, but perhaps someone had come in after she'd gone to bed. She waited, but the sound didn't come again.

Thinking she'd imagined it, Lucy stood and was just about to relight the candle by her chair when the unmistakable sound of a footstep in the hallway froze her in place. A furtive noise at the door caused her pulse to rise. Quiet footsteps faded from outside her door and then all was silent again.

Fighting to keep her fingers from shaking, Lucy lit a match and held it to the candlewick. As a flame grew, illuminating the room in dim light, she gathered her courage and moved toward the door. On the floor just inside the room lay a small piece of paper.

Lucy's breathing grew shallow as she bent down and picked it up. Taking it closer to the candle, she turned the paper over and read, "The longer you stay, the more danger you're in. Leave!"

Shock turned Lucy's legs weak and she returned to her chair before she fell over. She stared at the note for several moments before looking at the door. Although there was a strong lock on it, Lucy felt far from safe.

Should she go downstairs to Bill's apartment, off the kitchen, and alert him? Or make a run for Josh's house next to the jail? Fighting back tears of fear, Lucy decided against leaving her room. That would make her vulnerable since she didn't know her enemy's identity and she didn't have a weapon.

She wished she had one of Sam's pistols. The only weapon she had was her large sewing scissors. After retrieving them from her sewing bag, she lit a second candle and settled back in the chair to keep watch. Thinking about Sam helped calm her a little and occupied her mind with something pleasant. Despite growing drowsy, she spent most of the night dozing fitfully before dropping off into a deep slumber near morning.

~

"LUCY? Are you up? It's Sam."

Being woken by the now familiar, friendly voice of her future husband was a far more pleasant experience than the one Lucy had had last night. She stood quickly and laid her scissors on the lampstand beside the chair.

"Oh, um, one moment, Sam," she called to him.

Rushing to the mirror, she looked at her hair, relieved that it wasn't too messy. She re-braided it, washed her face and hands, and straightened her dress.

Once presentable, she pulled the door open and smiled up at Sam. His bulk filled the doorway and she felt safe now that he was there. Although she would've liked to hug him, she refrained.

"Good morning," he said. "You slept rather late. Are you feeling well?"

The way his eyes roamed over her was the gaze of a physician assessing a patient and the frown that formed on his mouth said he wasn't happy with what he'd found. "You have dark spots under your eyes."

Not prone to lying, Lucy couldn't bring herself to tell Sam a falsehood. "I'm sure I do. I didn't sleep much."

"Why not? Is something wrong?" he asked, concern deepening his frown.

Lucy tried to see past Sam into the hallway but couldn't. "I know this isn't proper, but we're going to be married soon, so what does it matter?" Stress and fatigue turned her tone sharper than she'd intended.

"What's not proper?"

"Please come in and shut the door," she replied. "I must show ye something."

Sam arched an inquisitive eyebrow, but he did as she'd asked.

Lucy retrieved the note from the lampstand and held it out to Sam.

NOTING the way Lucy's features tightened with anxiety, Sam's scalp prickled in warning as he took the paper from her. His eyes lingered on her for a moment before dropping to the note in his hand. Fury surged through him as he finished reading it, and he crushed it in his fist.

"Tell me exactly what happened," he requested, forcing himself to stay as calm as possible.

The sheen of tears in Lucy's eyes turned Sam's anger white-hot and he almost turned and punched a wall. However, she was scared enough already, and that kind of behavior wouldn't do either of them any good. Sam concentrated on keeping his anger at bay as he listened to Lucy recount the events of the previous evening.

When she finished, he said, "I'm so sorry, Lucy. I never imagined anything like this would happen when you came here."

She came closer and looked up at him with compassion in her eyes. "I know, Sam. It's not yer fault. Do you think this has something to do with Ernie?"

He blew out a frustrated breath. "I don't know, but I can't rule it out. We need to get married right away. I don't want you here one more night by yourself."

The way Lucy's eyes bulged out almost made him smile. "What? The wedding's not until Sunday. You said the preacher wouldn't be here until then."

Sam did smile then. "I know, but Paul and his wife got back sooner than they'd expected, so he can perform the ceremony now." He reached out to trail the backs of his knuckles down her soft cheek. "I couldn't bear it if something happened to you, Lucy. I need to know that you're safe, but I can't do that if you're not with me."

Lucy bit her bottom lip and Sam wanted to kiss her, to

savor her taste and make them both forget about Ernie's death and threatening notes.

"I don't know." She took a step away from him. "I know the ceremony isn't going to be lavish, but to be in such a rush…"

"I understand," Sam said. "I wish with all my heart that it didn't have to be this way, Lucy, but you can't move in with me until we're married."

"Aye, I know." She shook her head. "It isn't that I don't want to marry ye, Sam. Don't think that. But a woman likes at least a little romance about such an important affair."

Sam gave her a sheepish smile. "And believe it or not, so do some men, myself included." After thinking a moment, he said, "I know! I'll hire whoever Josh recommends as a guard and they can stay in one of the other rooms here to make sure you're safe until Sunday. That way we won't have to rush, and we'll have some peace of mind. What do you think?"

Her bright smile made Sam glad that he'd suggested it.

"I think that I'm lucky to be marrying such a smart man."

He laughed. "I certainly try to be. Now, let's go downstairs so you can get some breakfast while I go talk to Josh. When I come back, I thought it would be nice to go out to the herd and have a picnic."

A frown flitted over her face before she put on a brave smile. "I would enjoy that.

Sam nodded. "Are you ready to go down?"

Lucy grabbed her drawstring purse from a wooden peg by the door. "Ready."

Sam would've offered his arm to her, but the hallway was narrow, so they had to walk in a single line. He led the way down to the dining room and seated her at a table. "I'll be back just as soon as possible. Enjoy your breakfast."

"I'll be here," Lucy quipped.

Sam chuckled. "You better be."

Lucy gave him a cheeky smile. "Don't be gettin' bossy, sir, or ye'll find yourself without a bride."

With a slight bow, Sam said, "I'll keep that in mind," and left Lucy to her meal.

# CHAPTER 6

Sitting on a blanket in the shade of a tall maple tree that afternoon, Lucy couldn't remember the last time she'd felt so uncomfortable. Meeting Drake had been a strange experience. She'd never encountered anyone like him, and she wasn't sure what to say to him.

Her awkwardness around him had nothing to do with his mixed heritage. Rather, it was his quiet, reserved personality that unnerved her. Except when spoken to, Drake didn't engage in conversation. The scornful glances he shot Lucy's way did nothing to reduce her disquiet.

Once Sam had concluded his business with the shepherd, they'd retired to the cool spot and prepared their picnic lunch. With her belly filled with the delicious food Bill had prepared for them, Lucy relaxed against the maple tree and watched Drake and his dog, Scruffy, separate a few sheep from the rest of the flock.

Drake let out a short whistle and Scruffy circled the small group of sheep they'd been gathering.

"Tis Drake always so austere?" Lucy asked.

A small smile curved across Sam's lips. "Most of the time. But it's worse right now. Drake tends to withdraw even further when he's upset. He knows I'm always supportive, but it's rare that he seeks me out."

Sympathy rose in Lucy, and she felt bad for thinking such critical thoughts about the young man. "My da and I aren't close, but I'd still be sad if we lost him. Even though I'm far from home, I still feel a connection to him."

"I understand that. You might think I'm odd, but I do believe that our souls are connected to those of our loved ones. I think we can still feel each other even if we're separated by many miles," Sam responded. He took her hand. "I'm sure that we'll grow to be close like that over time."

His touch sent her pulse skipping. "I hope so."

Approaching hoofbeats interrupted them. A man rode up to their picnic area and pulled his horse to a stop. He dismounted and joined them under the tree. The sober expression on his handsome face told Lucy that something serious had happened.

Sam rose to his feet. "Hello, Mason. This is Miss Lucy Magee." He helped her stand up. "Lucy, Mason Crawford."

Mason smiled as he shook hands with Lucy. "Pleasure to meet you, ma'am."

"Likewise," Lucy responded.

"What brings you?" Sam asked.

Once again, a frown settled on Mason's face. "I wish my visit was about something pleasant, but I'm afraid I'm bringing you bad news."

Sam's left eyebrow arched. "Oh?"

Mason glanced at the flock of sheep. "One of our hands found three dead ewes this morning. Their throats were cut, and they were just left there."

Lucy's eyes widened. "Why would someone do such a thing?"

"I don't know," Mason responded. "But I thought with what happened to Ernie, I'd better warn you. I don't know if it's related or not. I already told Josh about it."

"I'm sorry to hear of your trouble," Sam said. "I hope the culprit is caught. It might have something to do with Ernie, but to what purpose? I can't understand what anyone would have against him. As far as I know, he's never been involved with any shady characters."

Mason shook his head. "You'd know better than me. I didn't know him all that well. Just in passing."

"My father kept to himself a lot."

They all jumped a little. They hadn't noticed that Drake had joined them.

His dark eyes glittered with anger. "Many of us do because most people aren't kind to us."

Sam hated that he was right. The Red Dog family and the others in their village several miles west of Spruce Valley were tolerated by some, befriended by a few people, or treated with disdain and hate by the rest. Sam couldn't blame Drake for being bitter.

Mason's expression turned sheepish. "I'm sorry about that Drake. I hope you know that Sam and my family are your friends."

Drake nodded once. "Yes. You were always good to my father, Sam. He thought well of you. Thank you for your kindness to him and our village."

Sam gestured at the flock of sheep. "If it wasn't for him, I wouldn't have this ranch, or a successful operation. He's the one who got me started and took such great care of the sheep. That's why I made him my partner." He gave Drake a speculative look. "I know you're planning on going to California, so I suppose I can't tempt you to stay by offering you the same deal as Ernie and I had?"

One of Drake's dark eyebrows lifted. "Have you thought about this? Are you sure?"

"I'm positive. Outside of Ernie, you're the best man for the job," Sam said. "You already know the herd, the routine, and you're knowledgeable about sheep care. You're dependable and work hard. So, the partnership is yours if you want it."

"I'll think about it," Drake said.

Sam smiled. "That's all I ask."

Mason turned to Drake. "Be careful out here. It might be a good idea to have someone else stay with you. You can take turns keeping watch."

Sam thought it was a good idea. "I agree. I'd be happy to pay a second shepherd. Do you know anyone who would be suitable, Drake?"

"My brother is a good shepherd and has a good dog, too," Drake replied.

"The job is his if he wants it," Sam said.

A small smile tugged at Drake's mouth. "I will not give him a choice."

Sam chuckled. "Something tells me that Robert doesn't dare argue with big brother."

"It's is true," Drake agreed.

He gave them all a curt nod and returned to the flock.

Lucy watched him go with a mixture of curiosity and relief. The man made her uneasy, but she wanted to know more about him. She decided to ask Sam more about Drake sometime.

"Well, I best get back home," Mason said. "It's been a pleasure meeting you, Miss Magee. You'll have to come to visit us and meet the family. They're all curious about you. Jenny, my wife, is the schoolteacher. Sam says you're an educated woman. Jenny would enjoy visiting with another book-smart lady. Come over anytime."

Lucy beamed at him. "I would like that very much. Thank yer."

Mason touched the brim of his hat. "You're welcome."

He mounted his horse and headed back the way he'd come.

"He's very nice," Lucy commented.

"Yes, he is," Sam said. "His family are good people. His parents and aunt and uncle are the original settlers of Spruce Valley. This whole valley and the mountains in the distance are full of spruce trees."

"That makes sense," Lucy said as she repacked their picnic basket.

Once they finished cleaning up, Sam stowed their things in the buggy and helped Lucy into it. He climbed in and sat looking at the flock of sheep that grazed on the rich, green grass.

"'Tis peaceful" Lucy remarked.

Sam nodded. "Yes. I just hope it stays that way now."

So did Lucy, but as they drove back to Sam's ranch, a shiver of trepidation ran through her. She suspected the killer wasn't done causing trouble for the citizens of Spruce Valley.

~

SITTING in the sheriff's office later that afternoon, Sam told Josh about Lucy's nocturnal visitor and gave him the wadded-up note.

Josh unfolded it and smoothed it out on his desk, which was just an old wooden table. A couple of dime store novels were stuck under one leg to keep it level and scars criss-crossed its worn surface. Concern was etched on his face as he got up and went to a large wooden crate that sat on a table by one of the two windows in the front part of the building.

With amusement, Sam watched Josh rummage around in the crate, pulling out file folders until he found the one that he wanted. Unlike his own tidy filing system, the sheriff's disorganized method of records keeping confused Sam. It amazed him that Josh knew where anything was. His house was much the same way, with stacks of newspapers and books lying all over the place.

Josh took out another small piece of paper from a file and came back to his desk. Sam recognized the first note that someone had left at the ranch and his temper started to rise.

Laying the notes side-by-side, Josh examined them. "The writing matches. The letters are formed the same way."

Sam rose and joined Josh, looking over his shoulder at the notes. "You're right. Both are printed, not written in cursive."

Josh rubbed his chin. "Could be that whoever wrote them isn't all that educated. Everything is spelled right, but the printing is kinda crude."

Sam nodded. "Which should help us narrow down the suspect list."

Josh grinned up at him. "Us? Are you fixing to be a deputy?"

"No, no." Sam held up a hand in protest. "I'm perfectly happy being a doctor and rancher. I don't need a third occupation."

"Too bad. I could use one," Josh commented. "Anyway, I'm going over to the station to look at Damon's records. People are always signing IOU's and such. I might find a handwriting match."

"That's a great idea," Sam said. "I didn't think about that."

"That's why I'm the sheriff and you ain't," Josh teased. "Now, get out of here so I can go do my job."

~

"DON'T BE NERVOUS," Greta said.

Lucy tried to relax as she sat beside Greta on the seat of her buggy. Greta's gelding, Topper, stood patiently waiting for instructions. Seeing that her knuckles had turned white from the force with which she held the reins, she loosened her grip.

"I'm sorry. It's just that I've never driven or ridden a horse before," she said. "Back home, we walked everywhere unless we had a few extra coins to spare on a cab. That was rare, though."

Greta nodded. "I understand, but as you can see, things are far away from each other here. Walking would take forever, and it's just not practical."

Lucy knew that Greta was right. "I see what ye mean."

Greta cleared her throat. "Also, it's not a good idea to walk for long distances alone. Sometimes unsavory characters come through the area, and they may be lonely for the company of a woman. They may avail themselves of the opportunity to take advantage of a woman out by herself."

A chill ran through Lucy as she thought about the day she'd arrived in Spruce Valley. She'd walked at least a couple of miles by herself in the pouring rain. Lucy tried not to think about what might have happened if a disreputable character had happened upon her before Sam and Josh had arrived. She saw the wisdom in Greta's statement. Determined to be as self-sufficient as possible, Lucy straightened her spine and took up the reins in a more confident manner.

"All right, then. I'm ready for my lesson," she said. "I refuse to be a victim, and I don't want Sam to worry about me when he can't be around."

Greta patted her shoulder. 'Atta girl. We'll make an expert driver out of you in no time."

Lucy smiled. "I don't know about that, but I want to be as good a driver as possible."

"Well then, let's get started, shall we?"

With an emphatic nod, Lucy said, "Let's."

Greta began instructing Lucy, showing her how to talk to Topper as well as guide him with the reins. The gelding was responsive and didn't require a heavy hand. Greta had Lucy stay at a walk the whole way through town to allow her to become accustomed to the horse's movements, and to get the hang of maneuvering the horse to the right or the left.

As they left town, Greta smiled at Lucy. "You're doing very well, my dear. You seem to be a natural at this."

Lucy chuckled. "You're very kind to say so."

Greta responded with a small snort. "No, I only give credit or praise when it's truly due. Otherwise, how will one learn the proper way to do anything if their mistakes are praised? Besides, telling you that you're doing well when you really aren't is a lie, and I hate lying and deceit. I refuse to engage in such behavior."

The stern way Greta spoke piqued Lucy's curiosity, and she wondered what might have happened in Greta's past to make her so rigid concerning the subject. However, it was none of her business, so Lucy kept her questions to herself. Instead, she returned her attention to the task at hand.

"You're right," she said. "I can't learn properly that way. Thank you for your honesty and for taking the time to teach me."

"You're welcome," Greta said. "I'm sure Sam would've gotten around to it at some point, but I thought that I could start you off in the meantime. I believe that women should be as self-reliant as possible, and out here a woman must be able to get along without a man. This is especially true for ranchers' wives. There are times when they must be able to run the ranch while their husbands are away on cattle drives."

Lucy hadn't thought of that and she wondered if Sam ever went on cattle drives. If so, that meant that she would be in charge of the day-to-day operations of the ranch.

"Of course, you won't have to worry about that since Sam has a reliable foreman and good ranch hands. He doesn't like to leave his patients in the lurch, so he doesn't usually go along on the cattle drives."

"I won't lie, I'm relieved to hear it," Lucy said. "At least until I become more settled here, I would prefer to not be left alone like that."

Greta instructed Lucy on how to guide the horse around a sharp bend in the road before saying, "That's perfectly understandable, but I don't think you have to worry about that. Sam will never leave you alone with what's going on, so don't fret."

"I'm glad," Lucy said.

Their conversation turned to more pleasant things. They discussed Lucy's upcoming wedding and her worries disappeared as anticipation grew within her to marry her handsome doctor.

# CHAPTER 7

Lucy smiled to herself as she dressed for bed that evening. It had been a long day but very productive. Greta had taught her how to collect eggs from the chicken coop, how to milk cows, and how to unhitch and re-hitch a horse to a buggy.

Then they had made a list of pantry items that Lucy needed to stock up on, so that everything would be in place when the ranch became her home and she and Sam began their life together. Lucy took her responsibilities as a wife seriously, and she would make their home as nice as possible.

She was just about to change into her nightgown when someone knocked on her door. Fear made her heart lurch and she was leery about answering the door. However, it might be Sam stopping by for some reason, so she moved to the door and asked, "Who is it?"

"Hello, Miss Magee. My name is Grant Carlson, the man Sam sent to guard you."

Lucy was still cautious. "What's the code word?"

"Pink bow," came the reply.

A smile lit Lucy's face and she opened the door. A man of average height with light brown hair stood in the hallway. Although he was rather ordinary-looking, his dark blue eyes were filled with intelligence, and his bearing bespoke a man who was confident. There was an alertness and vitality about the man that assured Lucy that Mr. Carlson would keep her safe.

"How do you do?" she greeted him.

"Just fine, thanks for asking. And yourself, ma'am?"

"I'm very well, thank you. I appreciate you coming. I must confess that it does bring me comfort."

Grant smiled, which revealed a dimple in his right cheek and made him look more handsome. "I'm glad to hear it. That's the idea." He pointed to a chair that sat in the hallway. "I'll be right out here if you need anything."

Lucy frowned. "That chair doesn't look very comfortable."

"That's all right. It'll keep me awake," Grant replied.

"I have an extra pillow you could use to cushion the seat," Lucy suggested.

Grant shook his head a little. "I appreciate your kindness, ma'am, but I'll be fine."

"Are ya sure?"

"Yes."

Upon his assurance, Lucy bid him goodnight and shut the door. As she readied for bed, a feeling of peace came over her. Knowing that Grant was guarding her gave her a sense of security, and when she laid down in bed, it wasn't long before she fell into a deep slumber.

SAM MOPPED sweat from his brow as he came out of Olivia Carstead's bedroom. Her midwife, Julia Simmons, had sent Olivia's husband Richard to fetch Sam when complications had arisen. The baby had been breach, and Julia hadn't been able to turn the infant to the proper position.

Since he was friendly with the Crow tribe, Sam had developed good relationship with a few of the midwives in the village. They were adept at turning babies, and he'd traded some quality material for lessons in their methods.

They attempted massage techniques first, only using internal manipulation as a last resort. Sam was relieved that he'd mainly been able to turn Olivia's baby with massage. He'd only had to manually turn the infant the last couple of inches to finish aligning it with the birth canal.

Once it was in place, the baby had slipped out with a minimum of effort on Olivia's part. It was a good thing, because she'd been weak from all the unproductive labor before he'd arrived.

He descended the stairs and entered the Carstead's parlor. Richard sat stone-faced on the couch and looked up when Sam walked into the room.

Sam gave him a reassuring smile. "You have a healthy little girl, Richard, and Olivia is doing just fine.  She'll need to rest as much possible for a couple of days, but she'll recover quickly."

Richard stood up. Relief and joy spread across his features and his pallor improved. "A daughter. I'll bet she's as pretty as her ma. I sent for my sister.  She said she'd come stay with us for a week or so once the baby came."

"Good," Sam said. "I'm sure she'll be a big help."

Richard held out a hand to Sam and they shook hands. "Thanks for everything, Sam. I can't tell you how much I appreciate you coming."

Sam smiled. “Well, that’s what doctors are supposed to do.”

Richard’s gaze lowered and he shifted his stance nervously. “I don’t get paid until Friday. The baby came a little early, so we didn't have the money put aside yet.”

This didn’t come as a surprise to Sam. Few people around Spruce Valley were of moderate means and rarely had enough money between checks to save any.

It was one of the reasons Sam had gone into a business that would keep his head above water. He wasn't going to get rich practicing medicine in the small town, but he hadn’t moved there to make money.

“Friday is just fine, Richard. There’s no rush. Just enjoy your little one.”

“Thanks again,” Richard said.

Sam nodded, clapped the man on the shoulder, and took his leave.

Putting Atlas into a brisk trot, Sam's mind turned to Lucy. He hoped she was having a good day. When he'd checked in with Grant, he'd been relieved to hear that all had been quiet overnight.

Grant had informed Sam that Lucy had gone out to the ranch with Greta to do some more work. It made Sam feel good that Lucy had such a keen interest in making their house homier.  She was also so beautiful, and Sunday couldn't come soon enough for Sam. He wanted to hold her in his arms and show her how wonderful passion could be. Although he never asked her, Sam suspected that Lucy was a virgin based on the hesitant way she kissed him.

He would take his time on their wedding night so that he didn't scare her, and he would also give her as much pleasure as possible. The thought of making love with Lucy made his temperature rise a little, and Sam pulled his thoughts away from that. Instead he wondered what she was doing right then.

At dinner last night, her excitement over all she'd accomplished yesterday had amused him. Her account of her first time milking a cow had left him in stitches, and Sam was looking forward to many such conversations throughout the coming years. How wonderful it would be to have her presence in their house, hear her laughter, and hold her close every night…

A shot rang out, the unexpected sound making Sam jerk the rains and Atlas veered to the left. Sam pulled Atlas to a halt as anger turn his blood hot. He looked around for the inconsiderate shooter but saw no one.

"Who's there? Come out here!" he demanded.

Silence.

Sam's temper rose. "Fine. Stay hidden. But be more considerate and refrain from shooting so close to riders on the trail."

A second shot was fired and this time the shot was so close that Sam could hear the bullet whiz past his head. Sam had seen enough combat to know when someone was shooting at someone on purpose. The events of the last few days came back to Sam. He knew that the shooter might very well be the person who had left the two notes for Lucy, and Ernie's murderer.

Sam didn't waste time trying to speak with the shooter. He put his heels to Atlas' sides and clicked to him. The big horse sprang into motion, snorting as he caught Sam's urgency.

Crouching low over Atlas's neck, Sam gave the stallion his head. Atlas's strides lengthened and they sped away. Two more shots were fired, but Sam didn't bother looking back. He urged Atlas to increase his pace and they flew down the road.

When no further shots were fired, Sam slowed Atlas to conserve his energy. He listened closely, but he heard no horse hooves behind him on the road, nor did he hear any noise coming from the woods that lined both sides of the road.

Had he outrun the culprit. Was there more than one? Could it be a team working together? It was possible, Sam supposed, but what was their motivation? He'd been sitting still, giving the shooter an easy shot. Unless the culprit was blind or a terrible shot, there was no way they couldn't have hit him. That meant that the responsible party had intended to miss.

Had someone with a sick sense of humor just been toying with him? It was possible, but Sam doubted it. After everything that had happened, Sam didn't believe that was the case. However, he didn't waste time pondering it. Reaching safety was more important right now.

With that in mind, he alternated Atlas's gait between a canter and a trot. He was going to stop in town, which was on the way, so that he could tell Josh about the incident. Then he would head home to make sure that Lucy and Greta we're safe, even though he knew that Gray would be on the lookout for anything suspicious. As he made his way along, Sam prayed that no harm would befall anyone at home.

~

Lucy and Greta were in the parlor trying to decide what material to make curtains with. Since the walls were cream colored, almost any print would work. Lucy had bought three different kinds of cloth: a pretty blue, white and gold floral pattern, a solid heavy dream brocade, and a deep maroon with silver stripes.

“I can't make up my mind,” Lucy said. “I don't want

them to be too feminine. That would most likely make Sam uncomfortable." She stood back to consider again while Greta held up first the maroon material against the wall, and then the blue flowered cloth.

"I'm just not sure," she said.

"Well, you might have to ask Sam for his opinion in that case," Greta said.

"Yes, I think I will."

A horse trotted up to the house and Lucy looked out the window. Sam was dismounting Atlas and Lucy smiled at how handsome he looked. His blond hair was tousled and windblown and his shirt was rumpled, but he still made her heart beat faster.

He was virile and strong, and Lucy had never encountered a man like him before. She couldn't believe that some pretty woman hadn't snared him before now, but Lucy was glad that no one had. It was her good fortune to have found someone like him.

He wound Atlas's reins around the hitching post near the kitchen and walked toward the porch. The determined set to his jaw and his swift strides made Lucy concerned.

"Sam's home," she said. "He doesn't look happy. I hope nothing went wrong with Mrs. Carstead's delivery."

Greta echoed her sentiments as they went to the kitchen. Sam was just coming through the door when they entered the room.

His eyes roamed over both women. "Is everything all right?" he asked. "Has there been any trouble today?"

A prickle of fear raised goosebumps along Lucy's arms. "Nay, Sam. All is well. What's happened?"

He raked a hand through his hair, messing it up even more as he crossed the room to the two women. "There's no way around telling you. I had a nasty experience today."

His tense expression set Lucy's nerves even more on edge. "Are ye hurt?"

Sam shook his head. "No. I'm fine."

"Thank heavens," Greta said. "Now, tell us what happened."

Gathering his thoughts, Sam debated giving the women a gentler version of events, but downplaying the danger might put them in more jeopardy. Plus, Lucy and Greta weren't the kind of women who had to be protected from unpleasant subjects.

Opting to tell them the truth, he recounted his story. By the time he was finished, both women's eyes were huge with shock.

Lucy put a hand to her throat. "Who would do such a heinous thing? Why would anyone want to hurt you?" She inhaled a sharp breath. "Do you think it's the same person who's been leaving those notes?"

"What notes?" Greta asked.

Sam and Lucy exchanged a glance. He nodded in answer to Lucy's silent question, so she filled Greta in on the situation.

"Good heavens!" the older woman said. "It can't be a coincidence. The two things must be related."

"I agree," Lucy said.

Crossing the kitchen to a cabinet, Sam took out a small decanter of bourbon and a tumbler. "You'll have to pardon me, ladies, but I need just a touch to steady my nerves. It's not every day that someone shoots at me."

He poured a finger into the tumbler and took a sip before returning the decanter to its place.

Lucy went to him. "I'm not offended in the least, Sam. Who could blame you after being through something like that?"

Greta echoed her sentiments.

"Thank you both for being so understanding," Sam said with a tight smile.

"Of course," Lucy said.

Sam took another sip of his drink and then paused before he swallowed as a thought occurred to him. What if it hadn't been a prank? Could they have followed him home? He hadn't heard a horse behind him, but if the culprit knew him, they wouldn't have to give chase.

Fighting back panic, Sam downed the rest of his bourbon and set the tumbler on the counter. "I have to speak with Gray. I'll be back. Stay inside."

~

LUCY LOCKED the door behind Sam and turned to face Greta. Her own fear was reflected in her friend's eyes.

"I'm sure Sam will get to the bottom of it," Lucy said. "It'll be fine."

Greta gave a little nod. "I'm sure you're right. Now, let's do something to stay busy until Sam comes back. There's no sense letting time go to waste since there's a lot to be done."

"I think that's a fine idea," Lucy said, picking up a bolt of white eyelet material. "I think this will make very nice curtains for the kitchen. Do you?"

"Oh, yes. If we put some gathers in them, they'll look pretty…"

As the women went back to work, they tried to combat their anxiety over the situation but weren't completely successful. They knew it was serious, and no amount of work could keep their worry at bay.

While they measured material, Lucy prayed that Josh would figure out who was behind all of this. She also hoped that it would be accomplished by their wedding day, which was fast approaching.

*Please, Lord, don't let anything ruin our special day,* Lucy thought. *I want to look back and remember it as a time of joy, not fear. I pray that You will grant us at least that one day of peace.*

# CHAPTER 8

It seemed as though Lucy's prayer had been answered. No further incidents occurred, and she hoped that all the unpleasantness was over.

One day while she was shopping in Frost's Mercantile, she met Jenny Crawford, Mason's wife. Lucy liked Jenny right away and invited her to have tea with her. They went to The Eatery, which was situated at the rear of the store.

Lucy found the feisty, intelligent redhead amusing. It was also nice to talk with a woman who was as educated as she.

Nell, the waitress at The Eatery, came over to their table, and Jenny introduced her to Lucy. They exchanged pleasantries. Lucy thought that although mildly attractive, Nell appeared to be a rather sober soul, almost listless, in fact.

Nell then proceeded to take their order, and Lucy thought that the process was rather odd.

"What do you recommend, Nell?" Jenny asked.

All at once, Nell's demeanor changed. Her face lit up and her eyes sparkled, and Lucy wondered if the woman who'd approached their table had been swapped out for an identical twin.

"Today we have a very nice shepherd's pie with a tasty, flaky crust. Emmet also made applesauce and Ella baked cherry and custard cream pie."

Jenny smiled. "Then I'll have the shepherd's pie and the cherry pie for dessert."

"You won't regret it," Nell assured her. "And for you Miss Magee?"

Lucy wondered at the hope in Nell's eyes and glanced at Jenny, noting the conspiratorial smile on her lips. "Um, well, I've had lunch already, and I don't think I could eat the shepherd's pie." She glanced at Jenny again, then back at Nell. "Perhaps ye could recommend something a bit lighter that would go well with a cup of tea?"

Nell's smile returned. "We have a dandy jelly cake that would be very nice with tea."

"That's what I'll have, then," Lucy said. "Thank you for your help."

"You're welcome, miss. I'll get your order in right away."

Lucy and Jenny traded smiles as Nell hurried off.

"Not many people realize it, but Nell has a keen mind," Jenny said. "Most people here order the same sort of thing when they come, which bores Nell. She needs more of a challenge, and she likes seeing the patrons enjoying something different."

"Oh, I see," Lucy responded. "I wasn't sure what to do at first, but I'm glad I followed your lead."

Jenny's eyes glittered with mischief as she whispered, "My husband calls me a witch because I can convince people to do things."

Lucy giggled. "Can ye cast spells?"

Jenny pressed a hand to her mouth to muffle her laughter

and shook her head. "Perhaps. Beware, or I may cast a spell on you."

They laughed over their silliness but sobered when Nell returned with a large silver tray. She placed a very pretty porcelain teapot with a pink rose design on it and two matching teacups on the table. With a smile that was a trifle smug, Nell began fixing their tea.

The other women watched in fascination as Nell performed a proper tea-making ritual with flair and confidence. When she was done, she sat a perfect cup of tea in front of each of them.

Lucy took a sip of hers and looked at Nell. "This is lovely, Nell. It's clear that yer an experienced tea maker. No disrespect to the Inn, but this is the best cup of tea I've had since I came here."

Nell beamed at her. "Thank you for saying so. I'm glad you like it."

"That I do," Lucy said. "Where did you learn to make such fine tea?"

A mysterious smile curved Nell's mouth. "That's a story for another time. I have to get back to work. I'll be back with your food soon."

She was gone before they could respond.

"That's a little peculiar," Jenny remarked. "I wonder what else she's hiding, not that it's any of my business, of course."

"Nor mine," Lucy agreed. "Still, I can't help being curious. It's not just anyone who can make tea like this." She took a sip. "It's as good as my ma's and she was makin' it from the time she was a young lady."

Jenny also sampled hers. "Yes. I grew up around society ladies and worked as a governess for a wealthy family. This is as fine as any I've ever tasted."

Lucy refrained from commenting further because she

didn't want Nell to overhear them discussing her. She also didn't want Jenny to think she was a busybody. "Well, perhaps one day, she'll tell us her story if we're patient."

Jenny murmured her agreement and changed the subject. "Your wedding day is almost here. Are you excited to be marrying the handsome Dr. Slater?"

Lucy's cheeks turned pink as she smiled. "Aye. I never imagined that I'd be marryin' such a good man. I can scarcely believe it."

"I understand what you mean. I'm fortunate to have found a man like Mason. He's kind, decent, and hard working."

Lucy grinned. "Not to mention pleasing to the eye."

Jenny laughed. "He certainly is. When I first saw him, I wouldn't have been surprised it he'd introduced himself as Adonis."

Nell returned with their orders, and the ladies continued conversing about Lucy's upcoming wedding as they ate their meal. Lucy thoroughly enjoyed her jelly cake, impressed by the moist, flavorful layers. The slight acidic taste of the raspberry jelly meshed well with the sweetness of the cake, which had a bit of a spicy bite to it.

By the time they were finished, Lucy's spirits were high, both from Jenny's entertaining company and the delicious fare. She and Jenny made plans for her and Mason to join Lucy and Sam for dinner at the Inn on Friday evening.

Jenny said, "Mason and Sam can amuse each other while we go over your wedding dress after dinner."

Lucy eagerly agreed. "Instead of going home in the dark, why don't you and Mason spend the night at the Inn?" she suggested.

Jenny smiled. "That's a great idea. Then I could help you dress for the wedding."

"Do you think Mason would mind?"

A gleam entered Jenny's eyes. "Don't worry. I have ways of convincing him."

Lucy chuckled. "I think he may be right about you using witchcraft."

They paid their bill and parted ways. Lucy walked to Sam's office. He was with a patient, so she stayed in the small lobby. With the natural pine walls and two windows, it was a nice space, but like their home, it was plain and needed some sprucing up.

Looking around, Lucy envisioned sheer curtains and pretty green drapes that could be drawn in the winter to help insulate the room. The small black pot-bellied stove wasn't in use right now but come fall, it would need to be kept going much of the time. Sam had explained to her that it wasn't unusual for them to have light snow and freezing temperatures by the middle of October, so a fire would be necessary.

The door to Sam's examination room and office area opened, and a young woman holding a baby exited it.

Sam followed them. "Just give him half a teaspoon of that medicine twice a day and his belly will be just fine, Mrs. Harrington."

"Thank you, Dr. Slater," Mrs. Harrington said.

"You're welcome." Sam spotted Lucy. "Allow me to introduce you to my betrothed."

The introductions were made, and the two women exchanged pleasantries.

Lucy said, "You have a beautiful baby boy."

Mrs. Harrington smiled down at the infant. "Thank you. He's eight months old now, and he's the apple of our eye."

"I can see why. He's darling."

Mrs. Harrington thanked her again and went on her way, leaving Sam and Lucy alone.

"All done with your shopping?" Sam asked.

Lucy lifted her large basket a little. "Yes. I found everything I need."

"Good. I'm afraid I have patients to see the rest of the day, but would you care to dine with me this evening at the Inn?" he asked.

Lucy lifted her chin. "Only if you allow me to pay. Ye've bought me several meals, and I feel that I should reciprocate."

Sam considered that for a moment. It went against his upbringing for a woman to pay, but the stubborn set to Lucy's jaw made him realize that arguing with her would be futile. "Very well. Does six o'clock suit you?"

"That'll be just fine."

He moved closer and Lucy's pulse leapt. "May I have a taste to tide me over until then?"

Kissing Sam had been a heady experience and Lucy wanted to feel it again. She nodded as he cupped her face. His hands were warm and gentle as he tipped her chin up. Warmth spread through Lucy as he lowered his head and pressed his lips to hers.

It felt so natural to wind her arms around his neck and lean into Sam. Lucy's breathing quickened when he embraced her waist and slanted his mouth over hers, deepening the kiss. Lucy loved the way his hard torso felt against her body, and she could've gone on kissing him forever. But all too soon, Sam gentled the kiss and broke it.

She noted that his chest rose and fell rapidly as he rested his forehead against hers. "Do you have any idea what you do to me?"

His voice held a husky quality that sent a shiver through Lucy. "I think it's the same thing you do to me."

He smiled and kissed her cheek. "I was hoping we'd be attracted to each other, but I didn't expect it to be so strong. Is it just me?"

Lucy sighed as his lips grazed her earlobe. "No, Sam. It's not just you."

Sam kissed her cheek again and stepped back from her. "I'm glad to hear it. I think it's best if you leave now while I can still resist kissing you again."

Lucy wanted him to take her back in his arms, but she knew he was right. "Aye. I'll see you this evening."

Sam gave her a slight bow. "This evening."

Lucy smiled at his gallant gesture and exited the office.

# CHAPTER 9

It had rained during the night, but the day of Lucy's wedding began with bright sunlight and fresh air. She woke to the scent of coffee and bacon, but anxiety hit Lucy and, although it smelled delicious, her stomach rejected the idea of eating. Rising from her bed, Lucy went to the washstand, poured some water in the basin, and splashed her face with it.

She dried it with the towel hanging on a nearby peg and took several deep breaths. Although she'd been looking forward to marrying Sam, now that the day was here, doubt assailed her. What if she wasn't a good wife? What if Sam wasn't what he seemed?

Stories of disappointed brides were sometimes in the newspapers back home. As she went to the tiny closet in her room, she dismissed the idea that Sam would change once they were married. Too many people had told her that he was a fine man for it not to be true.

Someone knocked on her door.

"Just a moment," she responded, donning a robe on her way to answer it. "Who is it?"

"It's Jenny. I've brought you some tea."

Relief flooded Lucy and she rushed to open the door. "God bless you," she said, admitting Jenny inside.

Jenny smiled and set a small tray with a little teapot and two cups on the dresser. "I remember how I felt on my wedding day. I thought some tea would help settle your nerves."

"I'm grateful to you."

Lucy stirred a little sugar and cream into her tea and took a sip. The hot brew slid down her throat and started soothing her. She closed her eyes and sighed. Her eyes reopened when Jenny chuckled.

"You remind me of Mason when he drinks his first cup of coffee," she said.

Lucy smiled. "There's nothing so lovely as nice hot tea first thing in the morning."

"And what a lovely morning it is, too," Jenny remarked, going to the window. "Especially for a wedding."

Lucy took another sip to combat a little stab of anxiety. "Aye." She looked at Jenny. "Tell me, did ya ever doubt coming here to marry a man ya didn't know? Is Mason still the man you first married?"

Jenny sipped her tea and then shook her head. "No, he's not. He's even more wonderful than I thought he was when we first met. You have nothing to fear, Lucy. Sam is very respected here, and if I had any doubts as to his character, I'd tell you."

Her friend's words went a long way to allay Lucy's fears. "Thank you. I feel better about that now, but I still worry that I won't be a good wife. There's so much about ranching that I don't know."

Jenny smiled. "I also grew up in a city and I never did

any sort of manual labor outside of a bit of cooking. Luckily, I had Cecilia to teach me, and I'm quite good at many things now. You will be, too. I'll teach you and so will Greta. You'll be proficient in no time."

"I hope so." Lucy took a deep breath. "Well, enough of that. I'd better start getting ready. I don't want to be late and I want to look my best."

"Don't worry. By the time we're done, you'll look like a princess."

Lucy laughed and started getting dressed.

"You look so handsome that you'll make her swoon."

Sam smiled at Gray's reflection in the mirror he stood before. "I don't know about that, but I do still fill out a suit nicely. It's been a long time since I wore one."

Gray turned him around and adjusted his tie a little. "Not much call to wear a full suit out here when you're gallivanting around the countryside to treat patients."

"You're right about that. I'd wear one out every week, and I don't have the funds to constantly replace them," Sam agreed.

Stepping back, Gray raised an eyebrow. "You'd have more money if you stopped taking chickens and the like as payment."

Sam fixed him with an irritated look. "What am I supposed to do when people just don't have the money? I can't ignore their suffering, Gray."

"Yes, I know."

"I'll continue to build my practice, but I don't care about becoming rich. As long as the ranch brings in enough money to offset any financial loss my profession might cause, I'll be happy," Sam said.

"You must remember that you also have a bride to support now, Sam. She's relying on you to provide for her needs."

"I'm aware of that. I won't let us end up in the poor house," Sam responded. "Where is all this doubt coming from? I certainly don't need to hear it on my wedding day."

Gray's smile was tinged with remorse. "You're right. Forget I said anything." He consulted his pocket watch. "We should leave now."

Sam nodded and grinned. "I'm not the only one who looks dashing. You'll draw many female eyes today."

"I'm counting on it," Gray said, chuckling and smoothing down his black suit jacket.

Sam laughed and shook his head. "You'll never change. Come on. Let's go."

Gray followed Sam outside where his horse and buggy awaited them. As he climbed in and took up the lines, Sam sought to quell the uncertainty his conversation with Gray had created. He wasn't rich, but he could give Lucy a good life, couldn't he?

His mind turned toward his finances and his doubt faded as he thought about the money he had saved up. There was no bank in Spruce Valley and running to the one in Helena wasn't practical, so he had his money stashed under a floorboard in his room.

There was plenty there to take care of their immediate needs and pay his hands. Sam shrugged off his unpleasant thoughts as Lucy's lovely face rose in his mind. Anxious to wed the wonderful Irish woman he was coming to care for a great deal, Sam clicked his tongue to the horse and started the trip to the church.

THE BRAND-NEW SPRUCE VALLEY CHRISTIAN CHURCH stood at the end of Spruce Street, the main road through town. The bright white building was an attractive structure with two stained-glass windows on either side of the front door and three more on each side. It had been built low to the ground to accommodate some of the elderly members of the congregation who had difficulties navigating steps.

There was only one low step onto the natural pine landing before entering through the red door into the small vestibule. Five rows of pews made of oak took up most of the sanctuary, but a small altar and three short pews for the choir were situated at the front of it.

As he entered it, Sam inhaled the scents of fragrant wood and the linseed oil that had been used to polish the pews and other things.

Paul stood at the altar, a fond smile on his face as Sam and Gray approached. "Well, Sam, ready for your big day?"

Sam nodded. "Yeah. I'm very lucky to be marrying a woman like Lucy."

"She is indeed a fine specimen of the fairer sex," Paul said. "I think you're well-matched."

"Thanks, Paul. I appreciate that." Sam looked toward the door. "I hope it won't be long before she arrives."

Gray chuckled. "Impatient, are we? Perhaps you're thinking of the wedding night."

Sam gave him a sharp glance and a disapproving frown settled on Paul's features.

However, this had no effect on Gray, who just shrugged. "Don't act like it hadn't crossed your mind, Sam."

Sam's scowl deepened. "This isn't the place or time to discuss that."

Gray grinned. "My apologies," he said, but didn't sound contrite in the least.

Choosing to ignore him, Sam asked Paul how he liked

the church and they talked about other town matters while they waited.

~

SITTING behind Mason and Jenny in their buggy, Lucy fought back panic as the church came into sight. It wasn't far from the Inn, but Jenny had insisted that Lucy wasn't going to risk getting her dress dirty by walking. As she watched the married couple, it was easy to see the love they shared, and Lucy prayed that it would be the same for her and Sam.

*No, it will be,* she told herself in a stern tone. *Stop acting like an igit and more like the mature, confident woman ye are.* Her emotions in check, she started looking forward to the wedding, and grew eager to see Sam.

They stopped before the church and Mason helped both women out of the buggy. Lucy smoothed her dress and clutched the pretty spring bouquet of flowers Jenny had bought for her at Frost's store. She held it to her nose and inhaled. The floral fragrances further calmed her nerves. Mason had graciously agreed to walk Lucy down the aisle, and she was glad for his strong arm as they stepped into the church.

Someone had gone ahead of them, and Wade Bannon, whom Lucy had only met yesterday, began playing a pretty song on his harpsichord.

After a few moments, Mason smiled down at her. "Ready?"

Lucy clutched his arm a little tighter and squared her shoulders. "Aye, I am."

Mason led her into the sanctuary and the guests who'd gathered stood. Murmurs of admiration of Lucy's appearance rippled through the crowd, but the only person's opinion she cared about was Sam's.

Her gaze came to rest on him and her breathing quickened. He looked splendid in the deep navy suit that made his blue eyes look even more vivid. His blond hair was combed back, and he was clean-shaven, emphasizing his strong jaw. His gaze roamed over her and heat rose in her cheeks as she saw desire in his eyes. Relief that he found her appearance pleasing made her feel buoyant.

Paul smiled at her and began the service. "Dearly beloved, we are gathered here today in the sight of God to witness the union of Mr. Samuel Slater and Miss Lucy Magee." He looked at Mason. "Who gives this woman to be wed?"

"I do."

"Very well."

With a grin, Mason handed Lucy off to Sam. "Be good to her."

Lucy's pulse skipped as Sam's warm hands closed around hers.

Sam sobered. "I will."

During the brief ceremony, Lucy concentrated on her vows, but it was difficult when Sam was holding her hands and meeting her gaze. He seemed to fill her vision, and she almost forgot that they were in a church and that they had an audience. When Sam slipped a gold band on her finger, she felt an odd sense of homecoming.

Her mother had taught her to listen to her intuition, and she heeded that advice now. *You've found your destiny*, a voice whispered in her mind. She watched Sam slide the ring home and smiled up at him as happiness flowed through her.

They might not be in love, but they liked and respected each other. Their attraction to each other was evident, too. Lucy was honest and admitted to herself that being that far along in their relationship was more than she'd expected, and it gave her hope that perhaps love would come.

When Paul pronounced them man and wife and gave Sam permission to kiss her, a jolt of awareness ran through Lucy. He lowered his head and pressed his lips firmly to hers. The kiss they shared couldn't be called chaste, but it was still respectable. Sam drew back before Lucy was ready for the kiss to end, and the heat in Sam's gaze said that he felt the same way.

Paul presented them to the congregation, and they walked up the aisle while the congregation applauded.

As they emerged from the church, bright sunlight shone down on them, and it seemed to Lucy that it was an omen for their future.

# CHAPTER 10

Later that afternoon, as she rode beside Sam in the buggy on their way to his ranch, it struck Lucy that it was now her home, too. She and Greta had brought the rest of her belongings out the day before, leaving just what she'd need for today in her room at the Inn. Her single small suitcase was stashed at the back of their seat.

Nerves fluttered in Lucy's stomach as she thought ahead to the wedding night. Sam had told her that he didn't expect her to be ready to engage in relations, but she wondered if it was wise to delay consummating their union. The thought of it filled her with uncertainty and excitement in equal measure. A couple of her married cousins had educated her about what happened in the marital bed. However, being told and participating in the act were two very different things.

To distract herself, she turned her attention to their surroundings. A pair of squirrels scurried up a tree, chattering as they went. Several crows flew overhead, calling out to each other in their raucous voices. However, even as she noted all of this, she was still acutely aware of Sam's presence beside her.

"Did you enjoy the reception?"

Sam's voice made Lucy jump a little. "I did. It was lovely. Did you have a good time?"

He grinned. "Yes. The food was delicious, but my favorite part was the dancing. Especially the songs where I was able to hold you closer."

"Aye. That was my favorite part, too," Lucy agreed.

His half-smile sent her pulse skipping along. "Glad to hear it."

Lucy glanced at the large basket that sat behind the seat. "It was kind of everyone to send food home with us. There's so much of it. We should share it with our ranch hands, so it doesn't go bad in the heat."

"About that. A few weeks ago, I ordered an icebox for us. It should arrive next week sometime," Sam said.

Lucy stared at him agog for several moments before speaking. "Sam! Iceboxes are terribly expensive! You shouldn't have done that. Ye've already spent so much on outfitting the kitchen so nicely."

Sam took her hand and kissed it. "Lucy, I promise you that if I hadn't had the money, I wouldn't have spent it. It's a practical purchase as well as adding efficiency to our lives. Eddie Carmichael started an ice delivery business last winter and I think we should take advantage of his services. He travels into the mountains close by where there's plenty of ice to harvest. It's actually turned into quite a lucrative endeavor for him."

Lucy's mind started running through all the ways an icebox would improve their food storage. Milk and cream would stay fresh longer, as well as meat and desserts. It would be more convenient than running to the spring house every time she needed something.

"Do you want me to send it back?"

She snapped her gaze to his. "Of course, not! I was just surprised. Don't you dare return it!"

Sam's rich laugh rang out and he squeezed her hand. "I'm just teasing you. I wouldn't do that. It would cost an arm and a leg to ship."

Lucy nodded emphatically. "Right, so we'll be keeping it."

Sam chuckled and released her hand so he could turn their horse into their driveway. As they arrived at the barn, one of the ranch hands who'd stayed behind to do the daily chores approached them.

"Hello, Doc. Mrs. Slater. Congratulations on your nuptials."

"Thank you, Will," Sam said.

"I'll be happy to take care of the horse and buggy for you," Will said. "You newlyweds shouldn't have to do chores on your wedding day."

"We appreciate it," Lucy said.

They exited the buggy, and Lucy took the food basket while Sam grabbed her suitcase.

"Will, there's plenty of food here. I'll fix you a nice plate for supper," Lucy said. "It's only fair that you celebrate our day with us."

A broad smile spread across Will's face. "I'd enjoy that, ma'am."

"All right, then. Come to the house in about half an hour."

Will touched the brim of his hat and led their horse away.

"That was very nice of you," Sam said, offering his arm to Lucy.

She tucked her hand into the crook of his elbow, and they started toward the house. "I want your ranch hands to like me and I want to get to know them. It's important to be on good terms with them."

"I'm of the same mind. I find that happy employees work harder than those who are treated poorly," Sam commented. "That said, if any of the men become overly friendly with you, be sure to tell me."

Lucy raised an eyebrow as they reached the kitchen door. "I'll tell ya, but not until I've taken care of the problem myself."

With a haughty air, she opened the door and went inside, while Sam grinned and followed her.

~

LUCY STOOD at the kitchen sink, washing the plates that Will had brought back once he'd finished with them. She started when strong arms slipped around her waist.

"Hello, wife."

Lucy smiled upon recognizing Sam's voice next to her ear. A rush of emotion ran through at hearing him use that term for the first time. "Hello, husband."

Sam drew her back against him and nuzzled her neck. "That has such a nice ring to it."

"Aye, it does." The contact with his strong body made her stomach flip pleasantly.

"This is our wedding night. You shouldn't be doing dishes."

"I know, but I just couldn't leave them until morning."

Sam chuckled. "Spoken like a true homemaker. Tell me, Lucy, how much did those Irish brothers of yours corrupt you?"

Lucy grinned as she rinsed the last dish and started drying it. "I don't think I should answer that question. You might be shocked."

"Mmm. A lady of mystery. Tell me this much, did their corruption include playing cards?"

Lucy set the plate aside and turned in his arms. "Why don't ya get a deck and we'll find out?"

He flashed a grin at her, pressed a firm kiss to her lips, and left the kitchen. She smiled and glanced at the cabinet where Sam kept his bourbon. Did she dare? Deciding to risk it, she got out two tumblers and the liquor. She set them on the table and sat down to wait.

Sam returned with a deck of cards, a tablet and pencil for keeping score. He pulled up a chair and sat down.

Lucy saw him glance at the decanter and tumblers. "I don't imbibe often, but today is a special day, so I see nothing wrong with have a wee bit."

"I assure you that I don't think less of you for it."

"Thank you. While I'm being honest, I've also never gone further than kissing a few men," Lucy said. "I'm not a loose woman, but I have taken that small liberty."

Sam grinned. "Frankly, I'd be surprised if someone as beautiful as you hadn't been kissed before. I suspected as much, since you're so good at it."

Her face turned pink as she laughed. "I'm glad ya think so."

"I do. I like this rather naughty side of you. Makes me wonder what other secrets you may be hiding."

Lucy sent him a coy look. "Nothing too scandalous, but I might have a few more surprises for you."

"I look forward to discovering them." He lifted his glass. "I'd like to propose a toast."

Lucy said, "I agree. To what shall we toast?"

"A bright future filled with happiness, good health, and prosperity."

"And as many babies as the Good Lord blesses us with," Lucy added. "*Sláinte!*"

"*Sláinte!*"

They clinked their glasses together and downed the half-finger Lucy had poured for them. Warmth spread through Lucy, making her smile.

Sam held out the deck to her. "You cut."

Lucy did and asked, "What are we playing?"

"You tell me."

After a moment, she replied, "Gin rummy."

"Aha. I had a hunch you were a card player."

"Aye."

Sam dealt the cards and the game began. They played for the next hour and a half, exchanging good-natured barbs and laughing. Lucy came out the victor, winning most of the hands, and Sam admitted defeat.

As he gathered up the cards, he said, "I'd say that you excelled in your card game education. You're a formidable opponent."

"Aye. I don't mean to sound conceited, but my brothers don't like to play me much anymore because I rarely lose."

Sam's eyebrows lifted. "Really?"

"Really."

"Did you let me win?"

"Nay. I don't believe in doing that," Lucy replied.

"Good. I prefer to win on my own merits, not because an opponent throws the game out of pity."

Lucy rose from the table, took their glasses to the sink, and put the bourbon away. "Your integrity is one of the things I like most about you, Sam."

She returned to him and surprised them both by sitting on his lap. Yes, the alcohol had perhaps relaxed her inhibitions a bit, but Lucy was honest with herself and admitted that she wanted to be close to Sam. Since they were married now, there was no shame in being physical with him.

Sam slid his arms around her waist. "What else do you like about me?"

Brushing a golden lock of hair from his forehead, she replied, "I admire your intelligence and sense of humor. Your kind and generous, and so very handsome."

He smiled and Lucy's pulse skipped. "It's good to know that you think so highly of me."

She trailed a fingertip down his cheek and traced his lightly stubbled jaw. "If I didn't, I wouldn't have married ya. I would never settle for any man who didn't meet my standards."

His eyes darkened with desire. "I'm very fortunate to have met them."

Feeling his strong body pressed against hers excited Lucy, and she wanted to kiss him. Running her hand around to the back of his neck, she urged him closer. He obliged and her eyes closed as he claimed her mouth in a kiss that spread heat through her body. Sam held her closer, and Lucy wound her arms around his neck, inviting him to deepen the kiss. He melded his mouth to hers, making her breathing quicken as he caressed her back.

Sam allowed himself to become lost in Lucy. He drank deeply from her soft, pliant lips and reveled in the way she felt in his arms. The whiskey on her lips only enhanced her delicious taste and he couldn't get enough.

Lucy's hair was still up in the beautiful braided bun. Sam started pulling out the pins holding it in place and placed them on the table. He wanted to see her ebony tresses free and loose around her shoulders.

One became snagged and he pulled a trifle too hard. Lucy let out a soft yelp and broke the kiss.

"Sorry about that," Sam said with a wry smile.

"That's all right."

Sam took a deep breath. "Perhaps it's for the best. I was carried away again."

Goosebumps spread over his shoulders as she threaded her fingers through the hair at his temples. "There's no need to apologize. We're married now."

"Yes, but we agreed to take things slow since we're not well acquainted yet."

Hesitation flitted across her face and her brow puckered as her eyes met his. "I know that's what we decided, but I've changed my mind."

Although Sam wanted to make love with Lucy, he was concerned that she was making a hasty decision. "I don't want you to rush into anything and then regret it."

Lucy cupped his cheek. "I know my own mind, and I won't regret it."

When she pressed her lips to his, Sam's resistance faded away. The passionate way she kissed him convinced him that she was truly ready to become husband and wife in every way. Gathering her close, Sam stood with Lucy in his arms, and carried her to his bedroom.

He set Lucy on her feet and took her face in his hands. "Are you absolutely certain?"

Resting her hands onto Sam's chest, Lucy's gaze didn't waver as her eyes met his. "I'm positive, Sam. Make love to me."

Hearing those words sent heat surging through his veins and he couldn't refuse her request. He wanted her too much. Pulling her against him, he kissed her with urgency, unable to hold back any longer. Unwilling to break contact with Lucy, Sam kicked the bedroom door shut.

Amid heated kisses and whispered words of affection

and passion, they were carried away on a powerful current of sensual pleasure. The moon was low on its zenith before they were sated and drifted into a contented slumber, still wrapped in each other's arms.

# CHAPTER 11

The aromas of coffee and frying sausage woke Sam the next morning. Opening his eyes, he discovered that he was alone in his bed. He surmised that Lucy must be cooking breakfast as he stretched. Rising from the bed, he dressed in an older pair of black trousers and a gray shirt. He combed his hair and headed for the kitchen. His stomach rumbled as the smell of food grew stronger.

Entering the kitchen, he saw Lucy stirring some kind of batter in a bowl. She caught sight of him and the smile that lit her face made his heartbeat throb in his chest. She'd pulled her hair back on the sides, but otherwise, it cascaded down her back. The memory of how silky it felt when he'd buried his fingers in the gorgeous locks hit Sam like a hammer and he wanted to drag her back to bed.

"Good morning," she greeted him. "Did you sleep well?"

The mischievous sparkle in her eyes made Sam laugh. "I certainly did. How about you?"

"Very well, indeed." She went to the stove where a

second frying pan sat. "How many pancakes would you like?"

Sam's mouth watered as he looked at the other pan that contained browned sausage links. "I'll start with four and go from there."

Lucy started pouring batter into the frying pan. "I'm glad you have a good appetite. I'm used to cooking for a lot of people."

Sam came over and filled his coffee cup from the pot. "Well, I'll do my best to keep you in practice for when we have a big family of our own."

Lucy smiled up at him. "Aye. I don't think I'll forget how to since I'll be cooking for the ranch hands, too."

A confused frown settled on Sam's features. "For the ranch hands?"

Lucy nodded. "I understand that it's my responsibility to cook for them, and I'm sure they'll be glad for some good food instead of the things they make for themselves."

Sam wasn't aware that Lucy knew so much about the ranch hands. He realized that he had little idea what the men ate. Gray was a fairly competent cook, and he often made a meal for him and Sam. "You're planning to cook for them?"

"Of course. Don't other ranch wives feed the men?"

Sam took a sip of coffee and smiled at how good it tasted. It was much better than his. He got back to the matter at hand. "Who told you that?"

Lucy glanced at him before flipping a pancake. "Greta and Jenny. You don't seem to approve of the idea."

Her tone made Sam tread carefully. The last thing he wanted was to argue the morning after their wedding. "It's just that we don't have a cookhouse."

His mouth watered as she placed a big stack of pancakes and sausage on a plate. "Not yet, but our table is plenty big enough since we only have four hands. We can build a cookhouse later when we have more money, but for now, they can eat here."

Carrying the plate she'd handed him to the table, Sam realized that other than Gray, he didn't know his employees very well. In fact, there were days when Sam didn't see any of the hands, even on paydays. Sam gave Gray the money, and he doled out the wages. Wouldn't it be a good idea to know more about his men? Especially with all the disturbing events lately?

As he sat down, a chill ran through Sam. Could one of the men be behind it all? As he took a sip of coffee, Sam decided to talk to Gray to get his opinion on the matter.

He looked at Lucy. "You're right. The men should eat with us. I'll tell Gray that they're to come to breakfast the day after tomorrow." He gave her a seductive smile. "We may not be able to take a honeymoon, but I'd like you to myself a little longer."

Lucy filled her plate and came over to the table. Before sitting down, she planted a lingering kiss on his lips. "I like the way you think. Now, eat your breakfast before it gets cold."

Sam chuckled. "Yes, ma'am."

OVER THE NEXT FEW DAYS, Lucy started settling in and making their house a true home. Sam had surprised her with a brand-new sewing machine, which they'd set up in her old room. All her belongings had been moved to her and Sam's room.

On the second day, after she'd cooked for the ranch hands, she finished cleaning up from breakfast and made new curtains for the kitchen. She'd decided on a blue floral print that was pretty, but not too feminine. As she brought the curtains out to the kitchen, Sam arrived home. He'd gone to his office to see a few patients.

"Oh, good. You can help me," Lucy said when he entered the kitchen.

He smiled and kissed her cheek. "Hello to you, too."

Lucy chuckled and kissed him back. "Hello. How were your patients?"

It had been a frustrating afternoon for Sam, but just the sight of Lucy washed much of his irritation away. Her eyes sparkled with good humor, and her pretty smile made him want to kiss much more than just her cheek.

"I've had better days, but that's over now."

Lucy's brow creased. "What happened?"

Sam blew out a breath and went to the sink to wash his hands. "Sometimes I wonder why people seek out treatment when they won't heed my instructions."

"That doesn't make much sense," Lucy agreed. "Did they say why they didn't listen?"

Sam leaned a hip on the sink as he dried his hands. "Zacharia Welliver is a rather stubborn old man and he seems to just like complaining. He has bunions, but he won't soak his feet with the salts I've prescribed."

"He sounds like my father. Ya often have ta challenge him before he'll do something," Lucy said. "Or make him think it was his idea all along."

Sam shook his head. "I'm afraid I'm not much good at that sort of thing."

Lucy sent him a coy look. "That's what ya have me for. What does he do for a livin'?"

"Well, he used to be a furniture maker, but his bad feet have made it hard for him to do that sort of work anymore."

"Does he have a shop?"

"Yeah. It's not far from the station. Why?"

Lucy looked over at one corner of the kitchen. "We need

a corner china cupboard. I'll pay him a visit when I go to town with ye tomorrow."

Sam cocked an eyebrow. "You're going to see him?"

"Aye. We women have a way of bringin' men around to our way of thinkin'."

The alluring way she looked at him sent his blood through his veins faster. "Oh, yes. I know what wily creatures females are."

Lucy's pretty laughter filled the kitchen. "Da used to say the same thing to Ma." She patted Sam's arm. "Don't worry. I'll make Mr. Welliver see the light. Just leave it to me."

Although he was curious about how she was going to handle Zachariah, Sam knew that she wasn't going to tell him. He'd have to wait to find out. "All right, but don't let him overcharge you for the cupboard."

A sly smile curved her mouth. "Don't worry, Sam. Ma and Da taught all us children how to haggle. Mr. Welliver won't pull the wool over my eyes."

"I don't doubt it." Sam eyed the material laying on the table. "What's all this?"

"They're the curtains I made for the kitchen today. Will ya help me hang them?"

Sam nodded. "I'd be happy to. You'll have direct me, though, because I haven't the foggiest notion how to go about it."

"It'll be my pleasure."

Sam grinned as she started instructing him on the proper way to hang the curtains. As they worked, he discovered that she was quite particular about how it was done. He learned more about hanging curtains than he'd ever wanted to, but he also had a good time.

When they finished, Sam stood back, going over their work with a critical eye. Although he didn't know the intricacies of sewing or drapery, Lucy's café-style curtains rivaled anything he'd ever seen. They brightened the room, yet they weren't offensive to his masculine sensibilities.

The bottom panels could be drawn at night for privacy but opened during the day to admit light. They also added a touch of elegance, and Sam was proud to have married a woman with such talent.

"You do very fine work, indeed, Lucy. With your kind of skill, I predict that your future dressmaking business will be a success," he said.

Her proud smile warmed Sam's heart. "Thank you. I'm so happy that you like them."

"I do. Very much."

"I appreciate your help," Lucy said.

"You're welcome."

Lucy admired the curtains for a moment before moving to the stove. "I have a chicken in the oven with roasted potatoes and carrots."

Sam's mouth watered as her words made him aware of the savory aromas filling the kitchen. "It smells delicious."

"It won't be ready for a while. Would you care for something to tide ye over?"

Sam was about to respond until he saw the gleam in her eyes. Her tempting smile whet his appetite, but not for food. A different type of hunger assailed him as she exited the kitchen. She hummed a faint tune as she walked down the hallway. It beckoned to him and he was powerless to resist its pull. It was only a few moments before he followed his wife.

A COUPLE OF DAYS LATER, Lucy woke near dawn. A feeling of unease slid through her as she glanced at the window. The sky outside had just begun to lighten, the color somewhere between indigo and blue. Her gaze turned to Sam, who still slept. She smiled for a moment before getting out of bed, careful not to disturb Sam. He hadn't gotten home until late the previous evening and he needed his rest.

Lucy donned her robe and left their room. She yawned as she padded out to the kitchen to start the fire in the cookstove. Once she had it going, she put a kettle on to heat while she went to dress. Tiptoeing into their room, Lucy was glad to see that Sam still slept. The first golden rays of dawn lit the room, illuminating his handsome face.

She watched him the entire time she donned her undergarments and a deep-blue cotton dress with white lace at the collar and wrists. It wasn't the prettiest dress, but Lucy was learning that function was more important in her new life than fashion. You couldn't gather eggs or milk a cow in a fancy gown. Once she was dressed, she pulled her hair back and wound it into a low bun. Finished, she headed back to the kitchen.

The kettle wasn't quite ready, so Lucy decided to go gather the eggs. Debating what to make for breakfast that morning, she got her egg basket and opened the kitchen door. Horror at the scene before her froze Lucy where she stood.

Three mutilated sheep lay on the porch. Pools of still congealing blood spread out from under their bodies, seeping into the floorboards. Their wide, staring eyes conveyed the fear they'd felt before being slaughtered.

The egg basket fell from Lucy's loosened grasp. Her breathing became ragged as she stared at the carnage. It was several moments before she reacted. A scream rose from deep inside her and burst forth, cutting through the early morning quiet.

Sam jerked awake at the sound of a woman screaming. His heart started pounding as he sat up, looking for Lucy. The screaming continued, growing louder. He jumped out of bed and ran through the house, dressed only in his union suit. Entering the kitchen, he found Lucy standing in the kitchen doorway.

When she screamed again, he rushed to her and looked over her shoulder to see what was frightening her so much. A jolt of shock rushed through him as he saw the dead, bloodied sheep on the porch.

He wrapped his arms around Lucy from behind. "Sweetheart, it's all right. Shh. I'm here. It's all right."

With a sob, Lucy turned and wrapped her arms around Sam so hard it made him grunt. He held her close, caressing her back and reassuring her.

After a few minutes, she quieted and sniffed before pulling back to look up at him. Her eyes swam with tears and her nose had turned red.

"Oh, Sam, who would do such a thing?" she asked.

He cupped her face. "I don't know, but we'll get to the bottom of it. Come away from here."

Lucy nodded and let him lead her to the table. He pulled out a chair for her and she sat down. The kettle started whistling, but it didn't seem to register with her. Sam took it off the stove and fixed a cup of tea with a small dose of whiskey in it. He could give her a sedative if necessary, but he hoped the alcohol would help calm her nerves.

"Stay here and drink this. I'll deal with…that," he said.

Her expression blank, Lucy nodded and took a sip of the hot tea. A slight grimace crossed her face, but she took a second sip. Sam left her to finish her drink and stepped outside. Looking over the sheep, he saw that their throats had been slit and their stomachs slashed open.

Hot rage burned through Sam as he gazed at them. Not

only had the culprits killed three good ewes, but their new lambs were now orphans. They would have to be hand fed. Worse than all of that, though, was the blatant attempt to scare them. It rankled further to know that they'd succeeded. Lucy was in shock over the incident.

A breeze rose and something on one of the sheep's back fluttered. Avoiding blood, Sam moved closer and saw that the object was a note. Snatching it from the pin that had been stuck in the ewe's thick wool, he read it.

*This land is cursed. No good will come to whoever stays here. Move on before someone gets hurt.*

Although tempted to crush the note, Sam refrained. Taking a couple of deep breaths to quell his anger, he folded it and tried to put it in his pocket, but then realized that he wasn't dressed. Scrubbing a hand over his face, he rose and went inside.

Lucy had finished her tea and although pale, her tears had stopped, and she appeared to have gathered herself. He had no wish to upset her again, but it was necessary to show her the note.

Sam sat next to her and held it out to her. "This was left on one of the ewes."

Lucy raised questioning eyes to him before taking it. Her mouth thinned and color rose in her cheeks as she read the missive. Her nostrils flared as her chest rose and fell rapidly. Sam jumped when she slammed a fist down on the table, hard enough to make her empty cup rattle where it sat.

"I'll not have it! I won't tolerate cowardly evildoers skulking about, killing our sheep and leavin' them on our stoop!" She glared at Sam, her eyes blazing like lightning flashing through rolling gray clouds. "They're just tryin' to scare us, scare *me*, is more like it." Lucy stood and paced to the door, throwing it open.

Sam followed her when she strode out onto the porch,

passing the carnage with only a quick glance. "Lucy, where are you going? Come back inside until we get this cleaned up."

Ignoring him, Lucy shouted, "Whoever you are, whoever is responsible for this, your wastin' your time!" She pointed at the porch. "It'll take much more than a few dead sheep to scare me. I'm not a woman of faint heart! Nay, I've more courage in my wee little finger than the whole lot of you put together!"

Sam doubted that the criminals were anywhere near the ranch, but he admired Lucy's courage, nonetheless. "While I agree with you on that, wife, I believe you're wasting your breath. I doubt the miscreants hung around."

Lucy turned to him with a haughty expression. "I'm not daft, Sam. It just made me feel better."

Sam laughed and took her by the shoulders. "That's my feisty Irish lass. You're one of the bravest women I've ever met. Now, would you please go back inside? I'll go get Gray, and one of the other men, and we'll get this cleaned up."

Lucy planted her hands on her hips. "We might as well butcher these three. No sense letting the meat or wool go to waste. I'll go change into my old clothes, and we can get started."

She rose up on tiptoe, pressed a kiss to his cheek, and went inside. With an amused shake of his head, Sam went to go find Gray.

# CHAPTER 12

Later that morning, Sam and Gray were on their way to see Drake when they met him halfway there.

As they all reined their mounts to a stop, Sam noted the dark expression on Drake's face. "I see that you already know what happened this morning."

Drake gave him a brisk nod. "I'm not sure exactly what you're talking about, but three ewes are missing. I know because three lambs kept trying to nurse from ewes that aren't their mothers."

"How do you know they're not their mothers?" Sam asked.

One side of Drake's mouth lifted. "The ewes refused these other lambs, which they do when the lamb is not theirs."

"Oh, I see."

Sam made a mental note to endeavor to learn more about raising sheep. He'd left such matters to Ernie and Gray, but he felt a little embarrassed that as the owner of a sheep ranch, he didn't know such a simple fact about sheep behavior. His consternation grew when he noticed Drake and Gray exchange an amused glance.

He sat a little straighter in his saddle. "If you two are done making fun of me, I'd like to fill Drake in about what happened at home this morning."

"Yes, of course," Gray said, but he didn't sound contrite at all.

Sam ignored his annoyance and related the incident to Drake. The young man stayed silent during the story and didn't speak for a couple of moments after Sam had finished.

"Did anything odd happen last night?" Sam prompted when Drake's silence stretched on.

Drake shook his head. "No. The sheep weren't restless, and the dogs didn't raise a ruckus, either." Anger flared in Drake's eyes. "Whoever did this knows our dogs, and how to move sheep so they stay calm."

"Who was on duty last night?" Gray asked.

"Me. It was quiet all night."

"And you didn't fall asleep even briefly?"

Drake bristled at Gray's question. "I was awake all night. I don't shirk my work."

"Gray wasn't suggesting you did," Sam said. "Staying up all night is hard. It wouldn't be surprising if you dozed off a little."

"Well, I didn't," Drake insisted.

"All right. I believe you," Sam responded. "We need to list everyone who knows the herd and is familiar with the dogs."

Gray said, "That may be a long list. Ernie had a lot of friends who used to visit him. I'm sure the dogs were familiar with them, too."

Sam sighed. "I know, but we need to start somewhere. Lucy was scared to death this morning. I won't stand for her being upset like that. Josh needs a list so he knows who to interrogate." He looked at Drake. "Come to the house. The three of us can work on it together, and I'll take it to Josh."

Drake nodded. "Good idea."

The three men turned their horses around and took off for the ranch.

~

JOSH'S GAZE moved down the paper over the list of names that Sam had brought. He scratched his head. It was going to take him a month to talk to all the people on it. He hadn't socialized with Ernie much, so he hadn't realized he knew so many people.

He blew out a breath and looked over at Sam. "Seems like Ernie knew half the town."

Sam smiled. "Those are just the people we know about."

"It's a lot of people to talk to."

"Well, I'm thinking that we can probably cross off the women and children," Sam said.

Josh shook his head. "No, we can't. They may not have done the deed, but it's possible that they're witnesses, or that they overheard something."

"Oh. I hadn't thought of that."

Tapping the badge on his chest, Josh grinned. "That's why I'm the sheriff and you're not."

Sam chuckled. "Too true. How will you go about narrowing down that list?"

Rubbing his jaw, Josh went over various options in his mind. A crafty smile spread over his face. "I know exactly what I'll do."

"Care to share?" Sam asked.

"Not yet. I have to work out a few details."

"Very well. I'll leave it in your capable hands." Sam rose

from the chair on the other side of Josh's desk. "Keep me posted."

"You know I will. Hey, it might not be a bad idea to have Grant stay at your place to keep watch on Lucy when no one else is around."

Sam had been thinking much along the same lines, but he wasn't sure he could afford to pay another employee. He'd have to go over his finances again. Then there was the issue of convincing Lucy. She was a proud woman, and he had a hunch that she would balk at the idea of having a bodyguard. After her shouted challenge to the miscreants, she'd set about sheering and butchering the sheep.

Sam might not know a lot about sheep behavior, but he was proficient at butchering. He'd instructed Lucy on the process and she'd caught on quick. They'd kept out a nice piece of roast, put some in the smokehouse, and stored some in barrels to salt cure. They'd have plenty of meat for a while, and Lucy had stated that she knew many ways to prepare it so that they didn't become bored with the mutton.

Coming out of his musings, Sam said, "That's a good idea. Any idea where I can find him?"

"Well, he always has lunch at the Inn, so I'm guessing that's where he is now."

Sam thanked Josh and went on his way. Before heading to the Inn, he stopped at his office. He kept two identical sets of financial ledgers—one at the office and one at home.

When he first started his practice, Sam had had a weather resistant box made with a slot in the top. He'd mounted it next to the door and tied a pencil and small tablet to it so people could leave him a message when he wasn't there. He checked the box and was glad it was empty.

After reviewing the ledger, he determined that he could afford to offer Grant a small stipend along with room and board.

That decided, he went to the Inn and was glad to find Grant just finishing his meal.

"Hello Grant. Mind if I sit down?" he asked.

"Not at all." He motioned to a chair.

Sam took it and asked, "Are you employed right now?"

Grant replied, "Not right now.. Why?"

"I was wondering if you would guard Lucy. I wish it was more, but the most I can afford to pay you is two dollars and forty cents per week along with room and board."

Grant took a sip of coffee and leaned back in his chair. "That's acceptable. I could save up for a new horse since I wouldn't have to pay for lodging." His brows drew together. "My horse got pneumonia on the way here a couple of weeks ago and couldn't be saved. I was on my way to Helena. No one has been going there as of late, and I don't have enough funds to buy a quality horse that has good stamina."

Sam nodded. "Yes. A good horse is a necessity for anyone traveling long distances."

"I could walk, but a man walking alone is much more vulnerable than a man riding alone," Grant commented. "It would also take me much longer to get there."

"Right." Sam sighed. "We had an incident this morning, which prompted me to offer you this position."

"What kind of incident?" After Sam's brief rundown of the situation, Grant asked, "When would you like me to start?"

"Is tomorrow too soon?" Sam asked. "You're welcome to come get settled this evening, if you like."

Grant finished his coffee before answering. "I'll take you up on that. Then I could start first thing in the morning and get acquainted with the other men."

"I'll be in town until late this afternoon. I have my buggy, so you could ride home with me."

Grant smiled. "Much obliged, Sam."

Sam stood. "Happy to do it, and thanks for agreeing to help us."

The men bid each other farewell and Sam left to go tend a few of his shut-in patients. As he made his rounds, Sam felt lighter in knowing that Grant would keep Lucy safe. He only hoped that his new wife would agree with the plan he'd already set in motion.

~

LUCY'S EYES glittered with anger as she looked at her husband. Her face grew hot and she planted her hands on her hips. "You did *what*?"

Sam pursed his lips for a moment before replying. "You heard me. I hired Grant for security of the ranch."

A derisive snort escaped Lucy as she moved to the stove. "Ya hired him to babysit me, is what ya mean." She turned her attention to taking the mutton roast out of the oven. "I can take care of myself, Sam. You taught me how to shoot, and I keep my derringer in my skirt pocket now. Plus, I'm good with kitchen knives." The smile that tugged at Sam's mouth irritated Lucy further. "Do ye find that funny?" she challenged.

Sam sobered. "No. Well, maybe a little. I know how fierce you are. You kept Gray at bay with a knife, but the fact is that I doubt you could fend off more than one man. Grant will be here to give all of us peace of mind."

His sincerity soothed her ruffled feathers a little. "So, he won't be here just to watch over me?"

"I won't lie to you. That will be his main priority, but only when the rest of us can't be with you. Other times, he'll be patrolling and guarding the ranch," Sam replied.

Lucy lifted the roaster from the oven and was happy with

the way the meat looked. As she tested the potatoes and carrots to make sure they were done, she thought about the situation. Although it rankled that Sam thought she couldn't defend herself, she admitted that he was right about not being able to fend off more than one attacker.

She replaced the lid and started setting the table. Sam still stood there, waiting for a response.

When she was done with the dishes, she said, "I suppose it's not a bad idea to have Grant here. Maybe he can catch whoever is doing all this."

Stepping closer, Sam put his hands on her shoulders. "Precisely my thinking. I need to know that you're safe, Lucy. I care for you a great deal, and I'd be devastated if something happened to you. I'm your husband. It's my duty to protect you."

The concern and affection in his eyes melted Lucy's anger away. "I care for you, too, Sam. I'm sorry I was testy. I hate to admit it, but knowing that Grant is watching over me will give me some peace of mind."

Sam slid his hands up to cup her face. "Good. Thank you."

His touch stirred Lucy's senses and a shiver ran through her as he stroked a thumb over her cheek. Her lips parted when his eyes lowered to her mouth. She now craved his kisses and caresses, and Lucy found herself daydreaming about making love with Sam.

The need to kiss him grew. She rested her hands on his chest and rose on tiptoe as he dipped his head. Their lips touched and instant fire flared inside. She pressed against him and slid a hand up to play with the hair at the nape of his neck. His growl of pleasure increased her ardor and she wanted to drag him off to their bedroom.

A rap on the door made Lucy squeal in surprise, and she pulled out of Sam's embrace. She giggled at his wicked smile as she straightened her apron. "That'll be the men. I'm sure they're famished. Would you please answer the door while I finish supper, Sam?"

"As you wish, milady," Sam replied.

Several men filed over the threshold when Sam opened the door. Jensen Davis, a grizzled, white-haired old-timer, smiled at Lucy and took a seat.

On the first day, Lucy had informed the men that they weren't to wait to sit down until she did, since she would be finishing up getting the food to the table. Although they'd agreed to that, they still insisted on waiting to begin eating until she sat down.

"Miss Lucy, the good smells coming from the house have been making my mouth water all day," Tom Barker informed her.

Lucy smiled at him as she sat a large bowl of potatoes on the table. "I hope it tastes as good as it smells."

Tom appeared to be somewhere in his thirties. His hazel eyes crinkled at the corners and his close-cropped, light brown hair stuck up in some places. "I'm sure it's even better," he remarked.

Lucy was surprised to see Grant enter the kitchen next. He looked at Sam, who just shrugged sheepishly. Apparently, her husband had already decided the matter of hiring Grant and talking to her had just been a mere formality.

She flashed an angry look at Sam but gave Grant a warm greeting. "It's very nice to see you again, Grant. It's grand to have you with us."

Grant's gaze moved between her and Sam, and he gave her a wry smile. "It's good to be here, ma'am, but I take it that you're a little surprised to see me."

"Just a tad, but it's a nice surprise," Lucy assured him.

"Methinks someone may be in the doghouse," Gray quipped, bringing up the rear.

Lucy pretended not to hear him as she turned back to the stove to retrieve the roast. Sam offered to take it to the table, but she ignored him and placed it in the center herself. He must've taken the hint because he sat in his customary seat at the head of the table.

Gray insisted on helping her finish up, and she thanked him warmly. The look of consternation on Sam's face gave her great satisfaction, as did the way Gray seemed to delight in needling his friend. She even allowed Gray to seat her, which turned Sam's expression even darker.

"Now then, would you please say grace for us, Jensen?"

The older man was taken aback by her request. "Um, well, sure, I guess. It's been a mighty long time since I did, so you'll have to pardon me if I fumble around a bit."

"You might be a bit rusty, but I'm certain ye'll do a fine job of it," Lucy said.

Jensen cleared his throat a couple of times. "Dear Lord, thanks for these fine vittles and the hands that made 'em. We're grateful for Miss Lucy's food, which is a heap better than the slop we been eating. Amen."

Lucy had to keep her head bowed a few moments longer to hide her amusement over Jensen's crude prayer. Raising her head, she said, "Thank you, Jensen. T'was very nice."

Jensen's self-conscious smile had a touch of pride to it, and Lucy was glad she'd asked him to say grace. "You're welcome, ma'am."

"Now then, let's eat before it gets cold," Lucy said.

The men didn't have to be told twice. Their plates were soon filled, and silence descended over the table for several minutes while everyone tucked into their meal. Lucy glanced at Sam a couple of times but didn't speak to him.

Lucy disliked being cross with Sam, but she couldn't help it. It hurt that he'd already made the decision to hire Grant before he'd talked to her. He'd been trying to placate her by discussing it. She'd thought he was different than most other men who thought that women were empty-headed creatures. Those men believed that the female of the species was incapable of intelligent thought concerning anything except domestic matters.

It didn't take long for the food to disappear, which was a great compliment to Lucy. She enjoyed cooking for the ranch hands, and liked their company. Their banter amused her, and the stories they told about each other kept her entertained.

Throughout the meal, Lucy kept a pleasant demeanor, but inside she seethed with anger and frustration. She was relieved when supper was over, and the group broke up. The ranch hands each bid her goodnight and left, leaving her and Sam alone.

Lucy busied herself cleaning up the kitchen. She put water on to heat for washing the dishes.

"All right. Let me have it, Lucy," Sam said as she turned back to the counter.

She kept her attention on her work, scraping the few scraps left on plates into a small bucket. "Let ya have it? What for?"

"You know perfectly well what for."

Lucy darted a glance at him. "You mean for discussing something with me *after* ye've already made the decision for me? Or maybe it's for treatin' me like I haven't got a brain in my head? For being just as boorish and condescending to women as any other man?"

Sam's sigh drew her eyes to him. "Lucy, be reasonable. I was just thinking of your safety."

Incensed, Lucy speared him with a hard gaze. "Don't take that tone with me, Samuel Slater."

He lifted an eyebrow. "And what tone would that be?"

"Like I'm being daft or that I'm being difficult. Tell me

something, would you treat a man the way you treated me today?" she inquired. Sam's gaze wavered and Lucy pounced. "Aha! I'm right. You wouldn't have gone behind their back and then tried to placate them! But ye'll do it to a woman."

"Lucy, please try to understand—"

"I understand just fine," Lucy interjected with an angry gesture. "I'm not stupid. I know that I wouldn't be able to fend off a man with sheer strength alone, but I do have a gun now. Even so, it's a good idea for Grant to be here, I know that.

"But you could've done me the courtesy of truly consulting me before just bringing Grant home. Instead, you made a pretense of it, almost as if you were mocking me. How would you feel if I did something like that to you?"

Sam sighed and rubbed the back of his neck. "I wouldn't like it at all. I'm sorry that it seemed like I slighted you, but it really was a matter of convenience. Grant doesn't have a horse right now, so it was easier if he came home with me. "If you had absolutely rejected the idea of hiring him, I would've taken him back into town. But if you did agree, then he would already be here so he could start tomorrow morning. I was just being practical."

The water on the stove started to boil. Lucy poured some into the big metal bowl she used to wash dishes while she thought about what Sam had said. She saw his logic and her irritation lowered a notch or two. Maybe Sam really hadn't meant to hurt her feelings. He'd never treated her with anything but kindness since they'd met.

"Perhaps you were, but you didn't mention that Grant was already here."

"A gross omission on my part, to be sure. I apologize."

Lucy narrowed her eyes at his conciliatory tone. "Do you mean that, or are you just trying to get back in my good graces?" Sam opened his mouth to answer but she held up a finger. "When Da angered Ma, they'd fight like wild cats, and then he would storm out of our flat," Lucy said. "Hours later, or perhaps the next morning, he'd come back and apologize. Sometimes he meant it, but most of the time he was just telling Ma what she wanted to hear, so she'd forgive him and get the fight over with.

"She usually gave in, even when she was in the right, just to create peace. I love Da. He's a good man, but he was of the mind that women should be obedient to their husbands and fathers.

"I believe women should respect men, but only when those men deserve it, Sam." She lifted her chin, her gaze never wavering. "Until today, I thought you a very rare man. Honest, loyal, and kind. The sort of man who valued a woman for more than her body or homemaking skills. A man I could always respect and trust. But now I wonder if I was wrong to hold ye in such high regard. So, which kind of man are ya, Sam? One like my father, or the kind I believed ya to be?" Sam saw the distrust in Lucy's eyes and it disturbed him. He knew that he had to proceed with caution. His instincts told him that this was a pivotal point in their relationship. Lucy spoke the truth about how many men—and most of society—viewed women. As she had, Sam had believed that he had a more enlightened view of the fairer sex, but the way he'd handled this situation made him wonder if he was more like his friends than he'd thought.

Putting himself in Lucy's place, he saw how his actions could be viewed as less than honorable. His motives might've been well-intentioned, but he'd handled things the wrong way. Lucy had a pleasant, witty disposition most of the time, but he was learning that there was an underlying, ironlike strength in her.

They were still newlyweds, still getting to know each

other. He had to make a choice, the most important one in his life thus far. Did he want to spend the next several decades in a marriage marred by distrust and discord, or one blessed with love and happiness? Did he want to be less of a man than a woman like Lucy deserved, or did he want to be the man to whom she was proud to be wed? A man she could love and trust to keep not only her person safe, but also her heart?

His decision made, Sam rose from his chair and straightened his spine. "Lucy, from henceforth, I promise to never lie or go behind your back about anything again. Without trust and respect, a relationship, especially a marriage, cannot flourish. It will wither and die.

"I won't condemn either of us to that fate. Even if it angers you or hurts your feelings, I'll be completely honest about everything. No secrets, no dishonesty shall lie between us. This I vow to you now and forever more."

Lucy drew in a long breath and tears welled in her eyes. She didn't speak for long moments, but despite the torturous seconds that ticked by, Sam didn't rush her. Putting pressure on Lucy would be counterproductive, and most likely turn her from him.

As she searched his face, Sam tried to convey that his words were genuine, not a worthless promise.

At long last, Lucy started to smile. "I believe you, Sam." She tilted her head a bit as her smile turned teasing. "I'm going to hold you to that promise, too. We Irish take vows deathly serious."

Relief and happiness washed through Sam, making him grin. "As do I. Am I forgiven?"

Lucy sobered. "That depends."

"On what?"

"Whether ya help me clean up the kitchen or not."

Laughter burst forth from Sam and he reached her in

three long strides. Sliding his arms around her waist, he held Lucy close and kissed her cheek. "If it'll keep me in your good graces, I'll wash dishes every night."

Lucy poked his chest and moved out of his arms. "Don't get carried away. I have a feeling I'll have to rewash more than a few."

Following her to the sink, Sam rolled up his sleeves. "I'll have you know that I'm no stranger to doing dishes, madam. I did them quite well when I was in the military."

Lucy let out a scoffing noise. "We'll see if a soldier can do dishes as good as me."

Sam stepped up to the sink and gave Lucy a smug smile. "Prepare to be amazed, Mrs. Slater."

# CHAPTER 13

A week later, shouts from outside startled Lucy and Sam awake. Lucy scrambled out of their bed and rushed to the window, Sam right behind her. Peering out, she gasped when she saw the unmistakable flicker of fire reflecting off the front of the barn.

Sam swore, snagged a pair of trousers from the back of the chair near his side of the bed, and shoved his legs into them. "I'll go see what's going on. Please go no further than the porch, Lucy. I'm not sure what we're dealing with yet."

Lucy wrapped a robe around herself while he put his boots on. "Aye. I'll put on some coffee and start pumping water into the big stew pots. No doubt it'll come in handy, either for fighting the fire or for you menfolk to clean up with."

Sam nodded and jogged through the house to the kitchen. Unlocking the door, he ran outside to find that the bunkhouse was on fire. He saw Grant filling buckets of water from the outside pump as fast as possible. Tom and Jensen ran them to Gray who threw the water on the flames.

Sam didn't waste time asking questions. There would be time for that later. Right now, they had to save the bunkhouse. He ran back into the kitchen, passing Lucy on the porch. Grabbing one of the big cast iron pots, he started cranking water into it. His strong muscles enabled him to pump fast and it was full in just a few pumps.

"Keep filling pots!" he shouted to Lucy as she entered the kitchen.

She nodded and rushed to the sink.

As fast as he could without sloshing water out of the pot, Sam hurried to the burning corner and threw the water at the base of the flames. A moment later, Gray did the same and it squelched some of the flames.

They fought the fire for the next twenty minutes before all the visible flames were out. They kept soaking the burned area for another fifteen minutes, to make sure that there were no smoldering embers inside that could reignite later. Finally satisfied, Gray called a halt to their efforts.

"Good work, everyone," he said. "We'll know a little better in the light of day, but I think the repairs will be minimal."

"I'm not worried about that," Sam said. "How did the fire start?"

Tom rubbed his stubbled chin, leaving a sooty smear behind. "I don't know. We were all asleep and the smell of smoke woke me up. I woke the other fellas, and when we ran out, we saw that the bunkhouse was on fire."

Jensen said, "I don't mind tellin' you, it gives me the heebie-jeebies thinking that we mighta burned up if Tom's nose hadn't worked so good."

Sam held up a lantern, inspecting the burned section. "I know that you men couldn't have caused the fire since you were sleeping, and it started on the outside. Someone lit this fire. Looks like they might have used alcohol or turpentine to get it started."

The other men looked it over and agreed with him. Lucy joined them, her brow puckered with worry. Sam told her their thoughts on the origin of the fire.

"So t'was arson, then," she responded with a shiver.

Sam put an arm around her. "Yes, but no one was harmed. We're all safe and sound."

Anger rose in him as he saw a tear escape the corner of her eye, leaving a trail as it slid down her face. Whoever was terrorizing them had to be stopped, but how could they do that when the culprits committed their crimes under the cover of darkness, when no one was about?

Stifling his fury, he kissed Lucy's forehead. Grant was there to guard Lucy during the day, so he couldn't stay up all night keeping watch. However, Sam didn't have the resources to hire another guard. Their budget was already strained.

"Why are they doing this to us?"

Lucy's question echoed Sam's thoughts.

"I know they want the land, but why? There must be other land they could buy. Why do they want this ranch so badly?" she asked.

"Mebbie there's gold or some sort of treasure buried on it," Jensen suggested.

Tom snorted. "I doubt that, so don't go getting any grand ideas about going on a treasure hunt, old man."

Jensen squared his shoulders. "Watch who you're callin' old, sonny boy. And it ain't that farfetched to think that someone buried something on the land way in the past and now someone's discovered it's here." His eyes bulged out. "Or it could be the Injuns. Mebbie there's an old grave site here and it's sacred to them."

"I don't think there's treasure on the land," Gray said.

"But your notion about an Indian burial ground does have some merit. Perhaps you need to have another discussion with Drake, Sam."

Sam hated to think that Drake had held back on him about such a thing, but it could explain why they were going to such extreme measures to get rid of them. "All right. I guess it couldn't hurt. I'll ride out there tomorrow and see what he has to say."

"I think that's a good idea," Lucy said. "We have to get to the bottom of this. I wonder if Josh has had any leads?"

Gray said, "I must go to town tomorrow. I'll track him down and tell him what's happened."

Sam nodded. "Well, I guess there's nothing more to be done here. We might as well try to get a little shuteye."

"You all go to bed," Grant said. "I'm going to keep watch."

The other men offered to split the duty with him, but Grant refused. "There's no way I can go back to sleep tonight. No sense in anyone else losing sleep. Go on. I'll be fine."

As Sam walked back inside with Lucy, he thought about his impending visit to Drake in a few hours. He was fond of the young man, and it pained him to think that Drake might know who was responsible for all the problems at the ranch and hadn't told him. As much as Sam wanted the criminals caught, he hoped that Drake wasn't familiar with them.

~

THE ANGER SHINING in Drake's eyes as they sat at his campfire the next morning made Sam feel guilty for inquiring if anyone in his tribe might harbor any ill will towards him. Although he'd asked the question in the most diplomatic way possible, the implication was still the same.

Drake looked away from Sam, out over the flock of sheep. The sun was still low on the horizon, spreading golden light on the fields as it inched higher in the sky. His jaw clenched before he took a sip of coffee.

"I'm not trying to accuse anyone, Drake," Sam said.

Drake's gaze found Sam's again. "Aren't you? If I was a white man, would you be asking me this?"

His response echoed Lucy's question about whether he'd treat a man the same way he did a woman. It annoyed Sam to realize that in both cases, the answer would be no. The flaws of how society had shaped his worldview became glaringly obvious at that moment, and he didn't like it.

"I suppose not, but it's unlikely that a white shepherd who worked for me would be trying to scare me off my land." Sam rubbed his forehead. "You have to look at it from my perspective, Drake. I have a wife to think of now. Lucy is new here and has no income of her own. It's a good thing that whoever shot at me was only trying to spook me, or else she'd return to being an unwed woman in a strange place. Her welfare is the most important thing to me."

Drake said, "I understand, but why do you think we might be involved?"

"I know that you have ancient burial ground around here. Are there any on my land?"

"No."

"Are you sure?"

"Yes."

Drake's firm tone reassured Sam that he was being truthful. Of course, he'd never known Drake or any of his family members to lie. Dishonesty was abhorred among the Crow and many other tribes.

If there were no sacred sites on his land, then no one in Drake's tribe had any reason to threaten him. Sam hadn't believed there was anyone within the Indian village who felt such animosity toward him, especially because he'd tended to many of their sick and had always been respectful towards them.

With a wry smile, he said, "I'll confess that I was half-hoping you knew someone who might be the guilty party. It would be one step closer to catching them and ending this."

"It's always easier to blame others who are different than you."

Sam cut a sharp glance at Drake. "That's not what I meant. I'm looking for clues anywhere I can find them. I just can't imagine anyone who has anything against me. Can you?"

Drake finished his coffee and sat his cup on the ground beside him. "No. I haven't heard anyone speak against you."

With a groan of frustration, Sam stood up. "Let me know if you do. I have a couple of patients to check on. Thank you for the coffee and for all your hard work. I'll bring your pay in a couple of days."

Drake grunted his agreement and Sam took his leave.

~

The following evening, the church was packed with people. The previous day, Josh had announced that there would be a special town meeting, but he'd purposely omitted the reason it was being held. A lot more people were guaranteed to show up just to satisfy their curiosity.

A low hum of conversation filled the sanctuary as Josh walked to the altar and mounted the steps to the pulpit. He let out a piercing whistle that got everyone's attention, and the room quieted.

"Good evening, folks," he said with a friendly smile. "It's good to be here with you, but I wish it was for a different reason. As some of you know, I'm investigating ongoing crimes against our good doctor and his wife. So far, Sam's been shot at, someone has killed a bunch of their sheep, and threatened Mrs. Slater."

Murmurs of surprise and anger rippled through the crowd.

"And night before last, their bunkhouse was set on fire with four men inside it!"

The voices grew louder at Josh's startling announcement and he had to quiet them again.

"Now, I'm not gonna stand for good people being harassed like this. So, be warned, if the guilty party is in this room, I'm gonna catch you."

Everyone started looking around at each other in surprise. Josh took the opportunity to assess each person, searching for any traces of guilt in their expressions. However, what he found was shock and a little mistrust as the crowd conversed.

After a couple of minutes, Josh held up a hand. "All right. Quiet down, please."

Although a hush fell over the room, an air of disquiet remained.

"Now, I know that most of you around here are good, kind people, but there's someone among us who's trying to scare the Slaters off their land. Someone who's killed livestock and committed attempted murder twice," Josh said. "However, it's not just the Slaters who've had problems. The Crawford family has had some sheep slaughtered as well.

"Most of our fine citizens are ranchers and farmers, so this is an issue that affects a lot of us. If you have any information about these crimes, even if it's only a rumor, let me know and I'll follow up on it. All right. That's it for now. Thanks for coming out and have a pleasant evening."

Although an affable fellow, Josh was also astute and cunning. As the meeting broke up, he took note of who approached both of the families he'd mentioned to express concern and support. He watched the expressions and body language of the people who left right away for any signs of hostility against the Slaters or the Crawfords.

A few individuals stood out, but none that seemed overly suspicious. Although Josh was sociable with everyone who spoke to him, he observed them closely. However, none of them exhibited any odd behavior.

By the time he took his leave, Josh was convinced that unless they were excellent actors, the culprits weren't still present in the church. Disappointment weighed on him as he realized that he still had his work cut out for him, but he wouldn't give up until he'd caught the varmints.

# CHAPTER 14

After the fire, Lucy hadn't argued with Sam when he requested that she not leave the ranch alone. Thinking about how close the ranch workers had come to being gravely injured, or even killed, filled her with fright and anger. Knowing that Grant was always close by made her feel safe, and staying busy helped keep her mind off the scary incident.

So, Lucy finished making curtains for the parlor and both bedrooms. She scrubbed and polished all the floors, making them gleam, and she started making a wedding circle quilt for their bed. In the mornings after breakfast, she practiced her riding and was proud when the men complimented her on her progress. Feeding the men also kept her occupied. She baked bread and churned butter daily to have with the meals, and she made a couple of cakes.

But even with all this activity, Lucy was going stir-crazy by the end of the week. She was in desperate need of some female company and wanted to catch up on what was happening in town. Friday morning, she completed her morning chores and made breakfast as usual. However, Grant wasn't present.

Sam informed her that he and Jensen had taken supplies and the week's pay out to the shepherds, but that they'd be back soon. As soon as Sam had departed for his office, and the other men went outside to resume their work, Lucy started cleaning up the kitchen. As she did so, she mentally went over her chore list for the day.

When she got to the third item, she realized that she'd forgotten to ask Sam to bring home yeast and corn starch the day before. There wasn't enough of either to make bread that day or to thicken the stew she'd intended to cook. Hopefully Grant would be back soon so she could go to town to pick some up.

When he didn't return by nine o'clock, she went in search of Tom or Gray, but found both of their horses gone. "They must be out moving the steer herd to another pasture or mending fences," she thought. She waited another half hour, but still no Grant or Jensen. Frustration grated on Lucy's nerves. If she didn't get her ingredients soon, she'd be forced to make something else for supper, and she didn't want to have to alter her plans for the day.

Lucy stood at the kitchen sink, drumming her fingers on the counter as she mulled over the situation. If she left now, she could make it to town and back with enough time left to carry out her original plan. But she'd promised Sam she wouldn't go alone.

Her fist clenched in anger at their tormentors. How long was this going to go on? What if it took months for Josh to bring in the criminals? Or what if he never caught them? She refused to live out the rest of her life in fear, hiding like a frightened mouse.

Her mind made up, Lucy retrieved her small money pouch and her derringer, and secured them inside her skirt pockets. On her way out, she snatched her hat from the row of pegs by the kitchen door and headed for the barn. Once she'd saddled one of their geldings, she mounted and put it into a fast trot.

Although she remained alert for any sign of danger, Lucy enjoyed the ride. A storm had rolled through the area last night, washing away any humidity. The cool, fresh breeze felt good against her cheeks and the air smelled of grass and flowers. Birds flitted back and forth in the trees, singing to each other.

Lucy's spirits lifted. "All right, Buck," she said to the horse. "Let's have a wee run, shall we?"

She urged the bay quarter horse gelding into a lope and laughed as the scenery sped by. Once she'd grown accustomed to the pace, she tapped her heels against Buck's side, sending him into a fast canter. The spunky horse snorted, enjoying the run as much as Lucy.

After a few minutes, Lucy pulled him back down to a trot and patted his neck. "What a nice lad ye are, Buck. Thanks for such a fun time."

Buck whickered low in his chest and bobbed his head a couple of times as if to say, "You're welcome."

As soon as she arrived in Spruce River, Lucy went to the mercantile, intent on getting her goods and returning home as quickly as possible. She'd inform Sam about her trip into town when he came home that night, but she didn't want to run into him while she was in town.

She greeted Mr. Frost, a large, middle-aged man with graying dark hair. He was a pleasant sort, and they were soon engaged in conversation for several minutes before she got on with her shopping.

"There you are!"

Lucy turned around at the sound of Jenny's voice, smiling at seeing her friend again. "Here I am."

Jenny linked arms with her. "Come have a cup of tea. I've been so busy that I haven't had the chance to come see you."

Lucy said, "I'd love to, but I'm in a bit of a hurry—"

Jenny tugged her in the direction of The Eatery. "We'll make it quick then. Just one cup."

"All right," Lucy agreed. "I'll finish my shopping and meet you in just a few minutes."

"Good. I'll get us a table," Jenny replied.

Wasting no time, Lucy picked up the remaining items she needed and put them in her saddlebags. She found Jenny sitting near the back of the restaurant, which suited her fine since it was away from the windows.

She'd no sooner sat down than Nell arrived at their table with a tea pot and teacups. She'd also brought a plate of assorted cookies. Lucy exchanged pleasantries with the waitress before Nell had to go serve other patrons.

As she poured their tea, Jenny asked, "Have there been any further incidents?"

"No, thankfully," Lucy replied. "I'm hoping that they'll give up since they can plainly see that we have no intentions of leaving. I'm not going to let anyone run me out of my home, and neither is Sam."

"I'm so glad to hear that." Jenny frowned. "I can't figure out what they want. Is it just the land itself?"

Lucy laughed. "I've been wondering the same thing. I thought maybe there was some sort of buried treasure around the place or something. I've spent a lot of time going over the house for any hidden compartments and looked around the property, too. But I didn't find anything."

"Well, it is valuable property," Jenny commented. "They must want it very badly to be going to such lengths."

"Aye, but they're not going to get it. Between Josh, Grant, and the other men, they'll be caught."

"You're right. Now, onto more pressing matters. Is married life still treating you well?" Jenny teased.

Lucy laughed and the two women started conversing about their respective husbands. Talking about something other than her troubles was a boon to Lucy and before she knew it, almost an hour had passed. After her third cup of tea, she announced that she had to leave.

"Well, thank you for such a nice time," Jenny said.

"Nay, thank you for the tea and conversation." Inspiration hit Lucy as she stood. "I'd like you and your family to come to Sunday dinner this week. In fact, we'll make it a party. I think we can all do with a bit of fun."

Jenny's face lit up. "A splendid idea! I accept, and so will my family."

Lucy chuckled. "I have a feeling that they won't have a choice."

"Right you are."

Nell came to clear off their table.

"Nell, would you like to come to my party on Sunday?" Lucy asked.

Nell's mouth opened in shock and she almost dropped the teapot she'd just picked up. "Me, ma'am? Come to your party?"

"Yes. I'd love for you to come." Lucy touched Nell's arm. "Please say you will?"

Nell's face turned pink, but she offered her a shy smile and nodded. "I'd enjoy that very much."

"Good! Do you know where our ranch is?" Lucy asked.

"Yes," Nell said. "What time should I arrive?"

"How about two o'clock? That'll give people plenty of time after church," Lucy replied.

Jenny's eyebrows lifted. "People? How many are you inviting?"

Lucy said, "Well, I'd like to invite Pastor Paul and

Annette, the Frosts, Greta Royal and Bill Eckert. I might decide on a few more, but that's it for now."

Giggling, Jenny said, "I wonder what Sam will say when you tell him."

Lucy lifted her chin. "I don't much care. I'm the lady of the house and it's my right to throw parties, one of the few things that a woman doesn't seem to need a man's approval for. Ladies, it's been so good to see you. I really must be off. Thanks again for a nice time."

The other women bid her good day and Lucy walked back through the store. She found Damon stocking the candy near the front counter and invited him and Maggie to her party. That done, she hurried out to Buck, secured her full saddlebags, and got underway.

~

As Buck carried her towards home, Lucy hummed and sang to her horse since they were the only ones on the road. Although she didn't have the most pleasant singing voice, she enjoyed it and Buck didn't seem to mind that she sometimes got off-key.

She kept the gelding at a trot most of the way because she needed to get home as soon as possible so she could get supper started. It would be a bit late as it was. She didn't feel bad about it, though. After all her hard work that week, she was due a little bit of fun.

Her mind turned towards the party and she wondered what she should wear. She couldn't wear one of her old dresses, and the event wouldn't be the kind to which one wore high fashion. Something in-between would be appropriate. Two of her dresses would suit, and she debated which one to choose.

She became so focused on planning the party that she

didn't notice a rider approaching from the rear until the hoofbeats were quite close. Buck whickered a greeting to the other horse as Lucy turned in the saddle to see who it was.

A prickle of alarm spread over her shoulders when she saw a man with a blue bandana over his face closing in on her. She'd rarely seen men around town cover their faces, and since it had just rained last night, the road wasn't dusty enough to warrant wearing a bandana.

That combined with the cruel glint in the man's dark eyes turned Lucy's surprise to fear. She didn't bother greeting him, just tapped her heels to Buck's sides. He shifted into a lope, but the stranger was quicker in commanding his mount. The big chestnut rammed into Buck's shoulder, causing him to stumble.

Knocked off balance, Lucy grabbed the saddle horn to keep her seat, but she felt hands snag her shoulders. The next moment, she was yanked from the saddle. Her scream was cut short when she collided with the ground and hot pain shot through her right shoulder. She lay dazed, looking up at the sky.

She shrank back when the man came into view.

Menace gleamed in his eyes as he loomed over her. "You're coming with me. Don't scream or try any funny business if you want to live. Got it?"

Trying to remain calm, Lucy nodded. Her attacker grabbed her upper arms and hauled her to her feet. His actions hurt her throbbing shoulder, but she gritted her teeth against the pain.

He shoved her towards his horse. "Get on."

As she walked to the chestnut, Lucy remembered the gun hidden in her skirt pocket. Rubbing her shoulder, she moved her right hand down to the pocket and slipped it inside. Hope rose in her breast as her fingers curled around the small handle. Gripping it firmly, she gathered her courage and pulled it out, using her body to shield it from the thug's view.

She might not have enough brute strength to ward of her attacker, but she had a gun and surprise on her side. When the man's hand settled on her shoulder, she whirled around, aimed the gun at his stomach and pulled the trigger. He roared in pain as the bullet ripped through his abdomen.

Lucy screamed and shoved him away. He reached for her, but then clutched his stomach and fell to his knees. Nausea rolled through Lucy at the sight of blood seeping from between his fingers. Ignoring it, she thrust her weapon in her pocket and ran to Buck, who had stopped a short distance up the road.

As fast as her injured shoulder allowed, she pulled herself into the saddle and kicked Buck into motion. He caught her fear and lunged into a gallop. Lucy took gulping breaths to calm herself enough to guide the speeding horse.

The scenery flashed by, but Lucy didn't pay attention. She was intent on getting home and willed their lane to come into view. Tears of fright leaked from her eyes and were whisked away by the wind, created by their swift pace. With sheer determination, Lucy kept panic at bay. She glanced behind them a couple of times and was relieved to see that they weren't being pursued.

After what seemed like an eternity, their ranch came into view, and Lucy slowed Buck enough to make the turn without mishap. She urged Buck into a dead run again, riding him right up to the house where they skidded to a stop. Exhausted, Lucy could only sit on the gelding and try to catch her breath.

~

SAM ARRIVED home to an empty house. He'd finished with

his patients and there were a few things around the ranch he'd wanted to get done that day. When he saw that Lucy wasn't in the kitchen, he searched the rest of the house, but didn't find her. He checked the garden, but there was no Lucy.

A sense of foreboding overtook him as he jogged to the barn. There was no one there, either. His unease grew when he saw that Buck's stall was empty.

"Lucy, you little fool," he muttered.

Intending to go after her, Sam was just exiting the barn to fetch Atlas from the paddock when Buck and Lucy raced past the barn. He watched the horse come to an abrupt halt, but Lucy made no move to dismount. Sam ran across the drive, reaching them in moments.

Buck stood with his head lowered, his lathered sides heaving from the heavy exertion. Lucy clung to the saddle horn, her forehead resting on her hands and her breath coming in gasps. He reached up and laid a hand on her arm, startled when she cried out and tried to hit him.

"Lucy, it's me! Sam."

"Oh, Sam!"

Lucy launched herself at him and her momentum almost knocked Sam down as she slid from the saddle and into his arms. She embraced him hard, squeezing him tight. Sam held her close as she trembled against him.

"Shh. It's all right now. You're safe, Lucy."

He kissed the top of her head, trying to comfort her by continuing to murmur soothing words and rub her back. It took a couple of minutes for her to calm down.

Drawing her away from him a little, Sam cupped her chin and made her look at him. "What happened, Lucy?"

The terror in her gray eyes tore at Sam. "I, there was a man, and we ran. I used my gun."

Sam's heart leapt. "You used your gun?"

She nodded vigorously, her ruined bun bobbing with the motion. "We were coming back from town. Me and Buck." She swallowed hard. "He attacked me. He was going to kidnap me." Her eyes squeezed shut tight. "I shot him in the stomach and got away."

Fear, anger, and relief sent Sam's blood pressure soaring and he couldn't speak right away. He cleared his throat and called on his doctor's detachment so he could find out exactly what had happened.

"Lucy, take a couple of deep breaths—"

Lucy pulled away from him and ran in the house. He followed her into the kitchen where she went straight to the cabinet and took down the bourbon decanter. "Lucy, now's not the time—"

"Oh, no, Sam. If ever there was a time, it's now!" She grabbed a tumbler and poured some of the alcohol into it. "I've never shot someone before." She took a gulp of the whiskey, grimaced and poured more.

Sam crossed the room and took the decanter from her. "I understand, but getting drunk won't help. Trust me." He pointed at the table. "Sit down here and gather your wits while I take care of Buck. Then you can tell me the full story."

He strode from the house, doing his best to control his emotions lest he scare Buck. Lucy's foolhardy actions weren't his fault. Sam patted the gelding's sweat-slick neck as he gathered the reins and turned him towards the barn. He kept the pace slow, giving Buck time to cool off a little, and himself time to calm down.

# CHAPTER 15

Lucy sat down at the table, but was right back up again, too full of nervous energy to remain still. She sipped her drink and paced around the kitchen, trying to come to grips with what had just happened. Was it real? She knew it was, but it was hard to believe. It was all so surreal.

She'd never thought she'd ever harm another human being, but she had. She tried to wall herself off from it, telling herself that she'd only acted to protect herself. But guilt slipped in through the cracks, filling her mind. Although her would-be kidnapper had put her life in danger, she had to know if he was all right.

Rushing from the house, she made it halfway to the barn before encountering Sam. She stopped in front of him and took his arm. "Sam, we have to go back to him. He needs help."

"Lucy, we're not going back there," Sam said. "Let's go back to the house and talk."

Lucy refused to move. "We have to. He's injured. You have to help him."

Sam's jaw clenched and anger filled his eyes. "I think the whisky has gone to your head. You're not thinking clearly. It's understandable after what happened."

Hot tears burned Lucy's eyes. "What if he died or he's dying? I might be a murderer!" She shook her head. "I can't live with that, Sam. Please!"

The sound of a galloping horse interrupted their conversation. They turned to see Grant coming in their direction. He rode up to them and dismounted.

"Lucy! There you are!" he said. "Are you all right? I was on the way home and found the signs of a struggle. There was blood on the road."

Lucy grabbed his arm. "Was he still there?"

"Was who there?" Grant asked, taking her hand.

"The man I shot. Did you see him?"

Grant's eyes widened. "You shot someone?"

"Let's all go to the house and talk about this," Sam said. "I don't know the full story yet."

The former soldier jerked his chin towards his horse. "I'll put Sully away and be right there."

Fuming because they wouldn't listen to her, Lucy started for the house, barely resisting the urge to stomp the whole way there.

Sam caught up with her. "I don't know why you're angry."

Lucy bit her cheek to keep from speaking. She just kept walking with her eyes focused on their house. If he didn't understand her feelings, she wasn't going to spell it out for him when it was so obvious. His condescension was infuriating. Remaining silent was the best course of action, lest she say things she'd regret.

Sam put his hand on her shoulder, but she shrugged it

off. Normally, she craved his touch, but she didn't welcome it right then. She was relieved when he didn't make a second attempt. Reaching the house, she went right to the stove, filled it with wood and got the fire going again. Then she put the kettle on.

"I have blood on me and I'm dirty. I'm going to clean up and change," she announced, and went to their bedroom.

Her right shoulder protested as she undressed. Looking at it in her dressing table mirror, she saw that a bruise had formed on the front of it. It was tender to the touch and the area was slightly swollen.

Sadness stole through her when she realized Sam hadn't asked if she was hurt. He was too angry and obstinate to bother, it seemed.

She put on a robe and went to the small washroom. Taking a bath would be wonderful, but it would have to wait. She washed off and combed out her hair, securing it with a ribbon. Going back to the bedroom, she decided to spare her shoulder and not bother wrestling with a corset. Instead, she put on a shift, a couple of petticoats, a camisole, and one of her thicker robes. It was a little warm, but comfortable.

Finished, she returned to the kitchen. By this time, Grant had arrived and was sat at the table with Sam. The kettle had just started to whistle.

"Would either of you like a cup of tea?" she asked, taking the kettle off the stove.

"Don't go to any trouble, Lucy. Seems like you've been through a terrible ordeal," Grant replied.

"'Tis no trouble. I'm making some for myself." She cut a glance at Sam. "I want to be clear-headed when I tell you my story."

Sam sighed. "I shouldn't have said that about the whiskey. I'm sorry, Lucy."

Lucy didn't respond as she fixed their drinks. Once

she'd served them, she sat down and looked at the two men in turn. "I know that you're both angry with me for going into town on my own, but there was no one around to go with me. I waited until almost ten-thirty, but Grant and Jensen weren't back yet, and Tom and Gray weren't here, either."

Regret filled Grant's expression. "I'm sorry about that. It took us a little longer than expected because Jensen's horse threw a shoe and turned up lame. It was slow going to get him home."

"It's all right," Lucy said. "You didn't know that was going to happen."

"Why did you go to town?" Sam asked.

"I needed some cooking supplies I'd run out of," Lucy replied. "So, I saddled Buck and away we went. I went right to the store. I was just going to get my things and get right back home, but I ran into Jenny. It was so good to see her. We had a couple of cups of tea, and then I left."

Sam smiled. "I'm sure it was nice to see another female face after only having us men to talk to."

Lucy responded with a curt nod and took a sip of tea. "I left town, and I'd gotten about halfway home before it happened..." She took her time recounting the event, wanting to give as much detail as possible. It could be useful in catching the crook. "And so, we raced the rest of the way home. Buck has a lot of heart and he was so brave. Is he all right?"

"Yes. I cooled him off and rubbed him down. I gave him a little extra hay for all his hard work," Sam answered.

"Good. Thank you."

Grant stretched his legs out in front of him and crossed his arms over his chest. "It's my fault this happened. I shouldn't have gone this morning, but I wanted Jensen to show me where the herd is located right now. I should've checked to see if you needed to go to town, Lucy. I'm sorry."

Lucy shook her head. "I wouldn't have known right then. It wasn't until I went to make bread that I realized I was out of yeast and a few other things I needed. It's not your fault, Grant."

"That's kind of you, Lucy, but I promise that it won't happen again."

"Speaking of that, you can't guard me forever," she said. "We don't know if or when these scoundrels will be caught. I refuse to be a captive in my own home. I won't live my life always looking over my shoulder or afraid to be alone. I think I've proven that I can handle myself." She felt a twinge of nausea and took another sip of tea to calm her stomach. "Even though I feared for my life, I'm not proud that I shot a man. I'm glad that he was gone when you came through, Grant. That means that he wasn't injured badly enough to prevent him from leaving, or that someone helped him."

Sam grunted. "Most likely one of his cronies. They're probably watching the ranch, but I'm also sure they're keeping watch in town. The guy you encountered must've followed you from there."

"Not necessarily," Grant countered. "They could also have a hiding place along the road into town. The woods provide great cover and it would be almost impossible to see someone hiding in a small thicket. We could've passed their hideout lots of times and never knew it."

A chill swept through Lucy at the thought of someone spying on her, just lying in wait for the chance to attack her. Her alarm must have shown on her face because Sam took her hand. Despite being upset with him, she didn't pull her hand from his comforting grasp.

He lifted her hand and pressed a kiss to her knuckles.

"Darling, I know you're frightened, but we won't let anything else happen to you. And be assured that these men will be caught. Josh is working tirelessly, and he won't rest until they are. Neither will the rest of us."

Lucy pulled her hand from his and stood up. "Don't you see? I'm not the only one in danger. They almost killed Grant and the rest, and all of you ride around alone. You've already been shot at, Sam! We can't all ride around together in a posse or something."

Sam also rose. "I know that, but we can take every precaution possible until these thugs are apprehended. One of those precautions includes you not going to town on your own."

Lucy's hands clenched. "So, it's all right for you to go traipsing all over the countryside by yourself, but I can't even go into town? That's not fair, Sam. You didn't stay home or hire a bodyguard after you were shot at."

Sam's expression tightened. "It's different for me. I'm a doctor. I have patients to take care of and I'm the only one around here who can help them. It's a risk I have to take."

"I see." Lucy's nostrils flared. "You're a big, important man, so you get to defy these brutes and do as ye like. But poor, little me, a lowly housewife is forced to cower at home, like a good little wife should."

"That's not what I meant."

Discomfort spread over Grant's features. "I think I'll just give you two some privacy. Lucy, I won't be going anywhere tomorrow so I'll be at your disposal all day. I'm real proud of you, though, and I'm even happier that you're all right. Good night."

Lucy stopped him. "I'll be fixing supper in a bit. It'll just be something simple, but—"

"No, no. The boys and I can fend for ourselves tonight. You get some rest."

She barely resisted sighing as he went out the door.

"Lucy, now that he's gone, let me look at your shoulder."

Lucy's eyes flew to his. "How did you know?"

His lopsided smile made her heart flutter, even though she was angry. "There's not much I don't notice about you, sweetheart. I could tell from the way you were holding yourself that it hurt. You're also wearing a robe, which is easier to put on than a corset."

"Well, aren't you the smart one?" she snapped. "It's fine. I'll put some cold compresses on it and some liniment, and it'll be better in the morning."

"Please don't fight me on this," Sam said. "You could have a bone bruise or a slight fracture."

Knowing that he wasn't going to give up, Lucy stomped off to their room. She'd have to undress partway for him to examine her shoulder properly, so it wasn't a good idea to stay in the kitchen in case someone came to the door. Her mood wasn't improved by the fact that she was almost certain that she heard him chuckle as he followed her.

Once in their room, she undid her robe and took off her camisole. She untied the string at the neck of her shift that held it on her shoulders, and lowered the right side low enough to bare the joint. Looking up at Sam, she saw desire ignite in his eyes. With great effort, she ignored the sensual pull he had on her.

As his gaze lowered to her shoulder, Sam's expression grew concerned. With gentle hands, he examined her, apologizing each time she winced as he manipulated her arm.

When he finished, he drew her shift back over her shoulder and tied the string. "I don't think anything is broken, but the end of your collarbone near your shoulder is bruised and there are signs of a sprain. I'll draw you a hot bath to soak in. That and the liniment will help keep it from stiffening up too much overnight, but it's going to be very sore tomorrow."

Lucy groaned. "But I have so much to do!"

"You can do light chores to keep it flexible, but I'll take care of the milking and gather the eggs," Sam said. "Now, I'll go put water on to heat for your bath. Why don't you sit in your chair in the parlor, and I'll make you some willow bark tea to help with the pain."

How was she supposed to stay angry at him when he was being so kind? "Fine. I appreciate your help, but we're not done talking about this."

The amusement in his eyes made her angry again. "I didn't think for a moment that we were."

"Good." She put on her robe, turned on her heel, and left the room.

# CHAPTER 16

Pain lanced through Lucy's shoulder, waking her up. She groaned and opened her eyes. A throbbing burn filled her injured joint and she wished she could go back to sleep until it was healed. Sam had advised her against lying flat overnight, and she was glad that she'd listened to him. She could only imagine how much worse she'd feel if she hadn't.

"Good morning."

She moved her neck to the left in increments, testing to see how far she could turn it. It was a little sore, but she could stand it.

Sam sat on the edge of the bed, holding a breakfast tray. "It's not as good as your cooking, but I made you some breakfast."

A plate of scrambled eggs, bacon, and toast that was a little on the burnt side sat on the tray. There was also a cup of tea and a glass of milk.

Lucy's stomach gurgled, announcing that it was empty. "It looks wonderful."

Sam set the tray on the bureau and helped her sit up straighter. "I hope it tastes as good as it looks. Drink the tea first. It's willow bark for the pain."

She drained the teacup, anxious to feel better. Famished, she made quick work of the rest of her breakfast. When she finished, she relaxed back against the pillows, replete and content.

Sam took her hand. "Let me know how your pain is in a little while. I have some laudanum if you'd like it."

"I may take you up on that," Lucy said.

"As your doctor, I'm ordering you to rest today. There's nothing pressing that needs your attention, and we men can take care of your chores. Gray is going to cook supper, so everything is well in hand."

Although she hated not performing her duties, Lucy knew that she couldn't milk the cows or tend the garden. Gathering the eggs might also be tricky if the hens got cranky, which a few of them sometimes did. And washing clothes was completely out of the question.

She sighed. "Aye. Resting is best. I'll heal faster if I do."

"Right you are. That said, I don't want you to be bored. Would you like to read one of my books, or maybe work on your embroidery?"

Lucy thought about her options. "Reading would be fine. Choose for me. I'll also need my sketch pad and pencils. I could work on some designs. But I'd also like to talk to you about an idea I had for Sunday. I invited a few people out to the ranch for dinner Sunday afternoon in hopes of brightening up our spirits with a party."

Sam was a bit surprised that Lucy had invited people over to their home without first talking to him about it. But after everything they'd been through, a party didn't sound like a bad idea. After all, Lucy could probably use the company while she recovered. On the other hand, he wasn't sure if it was safe for people to come out to the ranch right now.

"When I go into town later today, I'll be sure to let everyone know whom you've invited to at least come out as a group," Sam reasoned. "I don't want to scare anyone, but they do deserve to know what's been going on." Lucy nodded her head, wondering if they should just cancel the party till things settled down at the ranch. But the more she thought about it, the more she reasoned that there was no reason to let these mysterious criminals win.

"I would appreciate that very much," Lucy replied as she looked up into Sam's eyes. "I have invited Jenny and her family, as well as Nell, Bill Eckert, and also the Reverend and his wife."

Sam smiled as he stood up. "Then I'll be sure to speak with them this afternoon. Alright, I'll go get the other items you need right away." He took the tray from her and left the room.

In a few minutes, he returned with the requested items and a cup of coffee. He set the drink on the nightstand beside her and put the other things on her lap.

Lucy smiled at his thoughtfulness. "Thank you. I need to take care of my morning business, though."

Unlike some men who would be embarrassed by her statement, Sam took it in his stride. "I should've thought of that. Sorry." He moved the things he'd just placed on her lap and drew the covers down. "Take your time and let me help you."

Lucy swung her legs off the bed and sat on the side. Other than a twinge, her shoulder didn't protest, but as she stood up, fire spread through the injured area, making her gasp. Sam was right there to steady her, and she was grateful for his support.

"Will you need help?" he asked, accompanying her down the hall to the washroom.

Lucy replied, "I think I can manage, but would you mind waiting in the hall in case I can't?"

"Of course, not. I'll do anything you need me to, Lucy."

She gave him a small smile and went into the washroom. Completing her toilet was somewhat difficult, but she gritted her teeth and got through it. However, by the time she opened the door, she was in agony.

"I'm ready for that laudanum now," she said.

"I thought that might be the case. I'm glad I didn't give it to you right away, though. It might have made you unsteady on your feet."

Sam helped her back to their room and resituated her in bed. She noticed a small medicine bottle and a spoon on the nightstand. Once she'd taken a dose, she washed the bitter liquid down with a couple sips of her coffee. Even though it was lukewarm now, it helped get rid of the awful taste.

"I'll be right at my desk working on a few charts if you need anything," Sam said.

Lucy chuckled. "You don't have to babysit me, Sam. I'll be all right if you have something else to go do."

"Actually, working on charts is exactly what I need to do. I'm a little behind, and keeping accurate records is important to me." A hint of mischief shone in his eyes. "But I will say that having you to look at from time to time will make the job quite pleasant."

Laughter bubbled up inside Lucy and she pressed a hand to her shoulder. "Don't make me laugh. Go on with ye, then. Do your work and leave me in peace."

Sam leaned down and pressed a kiss to her forehead. "As you wish. The medicine should be kicking in anytime now."

"Good. I'm all for it."

"I'm going to get some coffee. Would you like more?"

Lucy nodded and felt a little dizzy. The laudanum had begun to take effect. "No, thank you." She covered her mouth when she started to yawn. "I don't think I'll be awake for much longer. The medicine is quite powerful."

"Sleep then, sweetheart. I'll wake you for lunch."

Although she tried to respond to him, Lucy's eyelids were too heavy. Even before Sam exited the room, she'd drifted into slumber.

~

When Sunday came, Lucy was feeling a little bit better. There was still lingering pain, but nothing like it had been a few days before. Planning this party had been the only thing that had really brought Lucy any joy lately. Her and Sam were still disagreeing from time to time, and despite what she said, she felt that Sam still didn't hear her. So, instead of arguing, Lucy had put her mind to making this party a success.

Sam had gone into town to attend services while Lucy stayed home to make sure all the food was ready by the time people started to show up after church. Lucy wasn't sure if she was ready to ride into town just yet, and though she regretted not being able to attend church, she figured some alone time from Sam would do her some good.

Lucy was pleased with herself for having baked a custard pie, along with several rolls with different flavors inside like peppered chicken, beef and tomatoes, and also mined meat. It reminded her of growing up within her Irish family and hoped to showcase some familiar dishes of her childhood now that she had the hang of cooking. Boiled potatoes and sauerkraut were amongst the other dishes, and by the time Lucy had set everything on the dining table, people were starting to arrive.

"Oh, Lucy, you look darling," Jenny Crawford said as she came into the house with her husband. "My goodness, doesn't it just smell lovely in here."

"Thank you, Jenny," Lucy said as they embraced carefully. Lucy was still trying to avoid bumping into anything with her sore shoulder.

"Sam told us what happened when you rode home the other day," Jenny continued. Lucy looked up to see Sam coming into the house with the Pastor Paul and his wife. They were chatting idly, so Lucy didn't try to interrupt them.

"Aye, it was quite an unfortunate event," Lucy agreed. "Come and fix yourselves something to eat." Lucy took the time to visit with all the guests as Nell and Bill Eckert came in as well. It was nice to talk to so many people when all she had to speak to was Sam and the cattle hands. It was good to be surrounded by other people, and also a few more women.

Even though they were in the same space, Lucy and Sam hardly said anything to one another. It appeared as though they were both trying to be on their best behavior in front of all their guests. But every time Lucy would laugh, Sam couldn't help but smile at his wife, thinking she had one of the most beautiful laughs in the world. And when Sam would start to describe something with much enthusiasm, Lucy was reminded how passionate Sam often was about his work and helping other people.

By the time the sun was setting, and everyone had enjoyed the dinner and conversation, along with Gray and the other ranch hands, the guests started to depart. Sam had wanted everyone to return to town before it got dark and insisted that they all travel together.

"Oh, come now, Dr. Slater. Don't be such a worry wort," Mr. Crawford said as he escorted his wife from the ranch home. The guests chuckled at the comment and Lucy felt justified in the way she felt in being kept at home. She raised her eyebrows at Sam but he didn't want to acknowledge her right now. Instead, he saw that everyone was settled before they departed.

When Sam entered the ranch house once more, Lucy was already busy doing the dishes. The house was empty save for the two of them and now Sam wondered what they were going to do. Thinking he best help his wife, Sam took dishes into the kitchen and started to help Lucy dry and put them away. As they worked together, neither one of them said a word. Lucy wanted the freedom to go where and when she pleased. And Sam was trying to do his best to hold his tongue so as not to upset her anymore. For now, he tried to at least be grateful that they'd had a pleasant evening together even if it had been by talking with other people.

~

THREE DAYS LATER, Sam and Lucy were on their way into town. The atmosphere between them was frosty at best. Sam's jaw ached from clenching it so hard to keep angry words at bay.

They'd argued about Lucy's desire for independence and were at a stalemate. Before he'd planned to leave that morning, Lucy had suggested that he take Grant along for protection. His hackles had risen over the implication that he needed it.

When he'd refused, she'd pressed him on why she had to be accompanied but he didn't, and their disagreement had escalated.

Lucy had then announced that since Sam was going to town, he could take her with him. She wanted to pick out some material and order some if the mercantile didn't stock it. She planned to stay in town to get to know people and drum up some business.

They'd agreed to meet at Sam's office at four o'clock and come home. Supper would be a simple affair since Lucy wouldn't get home in time to prepare a more involved meal by a reasonable hour.

Sam was relieved that her shoulder was feeling better, but that also meant she was returning to her more spirited self. Even though he was fuming on the inside, Sam kept an eye out for danger. Someone could be lurking anywhere —in the bushes, behind trees—there were so many places for unscrupulous characters to hide.

In a way, he was glad for the silence between him and his wife. He was able to listen to what was going on over the clip-clopping of their horse's hooves and the buggy wheels. Engaging in conversation would've reduced his level of concentration.

He glanced at Lucy. She sat staring straight ahead with a stubborn set to her jaw. Her hair was swept up into a high bun. Inky tendrils had escaped and fluttered against her pretty neck. Her cheeks were pink, no doubt because her temper was still running high.

Sam's hands tightened on the reins as he stifled the urge to kiss the nape of her neck and work his way around to capture her lips. Even though he was upset with her, his attraction to Lucy was even more powerful. Due to her shoulder injury, they hadn't made love in several days and he missed that close connection between them.

Holding back a sigh, Sam faced frontwards again and wondered how to resolve the situation.

"I know that I'm not supposed to be privy to our financial matters, but how much am I allowed to spend today?"

Sam frowned at her cool tone of voice. "I've never refused to divulge that information, Lucy. I'll be happy to go over the books with you. As for a spending limit, is fifteen dollars sufficient?"

Her head whipped around and her eyes met his for the first time since they'd left home. "That's far too much, Sam. I'll not spend more than ten at the most."

"All right. That's up to you. I just thought it would help you stock up on material in order to start your business."

A smile started to form on Lucy's mouth, but then she pursed her lips and looked away. "Don't think your generosity will placate me, Sam."

The frostiness had returned to her voice, which aggravated him. Why couldn't she see reason? Once again, he clenched his teeth to hold in the retort on the tip of his tongue.

~

"WHY CAN'T he understand my point of view?" Lucy lamented.

After a busy morning of shopping, she was ready for lunch. She'd decided to go to the Inn to catch up with Greta. The older woman had just sat down with her to eat her own meal.

"Men don't have to adhere to the same set of rules, so they don't understand our struggles, Lucy."

Lucy's cutting of her chicken grew more aggressive. "'Tis the problem. The double standard makes me angry—no, makes me furious."

Greta eyed her. "That chicken is already dead. You don't have to kill it again."

Lucy smiled and softened her motions. "I'm sorry. It just vexes me sorely."

"I can tell. Sam isn't an unreasonable man. Surely you can work this out?"

Tears gathered in Lucy's eyes. "Aye, but not when it comes to this. I know he's trying to keep me safe, and I appreciate it to a certain point. I think that I proved that I can defend myself. What was the point of learning how to shoot if I have to cower and hide?"

Greta sipped her coffee for a few moments before responding. "Lucy, I've been around for a lot more years than you, and one thing I've learned is that men will usually not respond in a positive way to a woman who shouts or argues a lot."

Frustration gripped Lucy. "What am I supposed to do, then? Nod and smile and do whatever he says whether I want to or not?"

Greta raised her eyebrows. "I didn't say that. There are more effective ways of dealing with men and making them see things from your point of view."

"Not where I come from," Lucy said. "If Ma didn't yell and shout at Da, she would've never gotten her way about anything."

Greta reached over and patted her arm. "Well, there's no need for it to be like that between you and Sam. I believe you should be independent, but I have to agree with Sam somewhat. You shouldn't tempt fate just to prove a point."

Lucy wanted to stab the chicken with her fork. "And what happens if these igits are never caught? How long do I wait before I start moving about freely and living my life? As it is, Sam doesn't even want me walking out to the barn alone, but he and the other men can cavort around the ranch and all over God's creation all they like. Nice as it is, I refuse to be stuck in my house for the rest of my life!"

Greta glanced around the room. A couple of diners looked their way. "Please lower your voice."

Lucy blushed and looked down at her plate. "I'm sorry. I didn't mean to cause a scene. How do I get through to Sam? I tried this morning, but it was no use."

"I don't mean to pry, but how did you go about it?"

"I suggested that he should take Grant with him for safety." She couldn't hold back a smile. "He didn't like that at all."

Greta put her fingers to her mouth to muffle a laugh. "I'm not surprised. Men are prideful creatures and they like to think that they don't need protecting, that they're strong enough to deal with any enemy. Almost any man will get angry when his manhood is threatened, which is what you did."

Lucy finished her chicken. "I grew up with prideful men, so I understand. I was trying to show Sam how it feels to have someone suggest that you're not competent at something."

"Your reasoning is sound, but the way you went about it is where you went wrong."

Defeat weighed on Lucy, and her shoulders slumped. "I guess I might as well just accept that men will always be in charge of women. I'll never be anything but a piece of property."

Greta reached across the table to squeeze her hand. "I know it's frustrating, but change takes time. I believe that someday women will be their own masters. We must help the cause along any way we can. However, certain methods are more effective than others."

Lucy managed a small smile. "I wish I shared your optimism. You said I went about it wrong. What should I do?"

"You have to show Sam that you're capable of protecting yourself. I know that you were successful against the man who attacked you, but that may not always be the case. Practice and become proficient with a weapon. Don't argue with Sam. When you become skilled enough, challenge him to a friendly competition and show him that you have no need for a bodyguard any longer."

Hope rose in Lucy's heart as she thought about Greta's

advice. The more she mulled it over, the clearer she saw the wisdom in her suggestion. "I think that's a splendid idea. That's exactly what I'll do. Thank you so much."

Greta patted her hand and stood up. "Happy to help. I must return to work now. I'll talk to you soon. I'm very curious to know how you make out."

"I promise to keep you up to date on my progress," Lucy said.

The two friends said goodbye.

As Lucy walked over to the mercantile, she decided on a course of action. Walking up to the counter, she greeted Damon.

"Back again, I see," he said.

Lucy smiled. "Aye. I need to purchase ammunition for a pistol and a rifle."

The surprise on Damon's face was comical. "You're buying ammunition? Is it for Sam?"

"Nay. It's for me."

Damon arched an eyebrow and seemed reluctant to give her the supplies. But when she fixed him with a hard stare and cocked her head a little, he started gathering the requested items.

"That'll bring your total today to thirteen dollars and ten cents."

Even with buying several bolts of material and the ammunition, she was still under the allotted spending limit Sam had given her.

"Thank you. Please put it on our account," she said. "We'll be by shortly after four o'clock to pay for everything and pick it up."

"Will do."

"Thank you, Mr. Frost. Ye've been very helpful today, and I appreciate it."

The big man grinned. "It was my pleasure. Always enjoy helping out a pretty lady."

Lucy laughed when he gave her a wink and left the store.

~

RIDING HOME THAT AFTERNOON, Sam was more confused than he could remember. Lucy's mood was the complete opposite from that morning. When she'd arrived at his office, she'd given him a peck on the cheek before he'd locked up. On the way to the store, she'd inquired about his day. They'd picked up her purchases and started for the ranch.

Now, she chatted about what a nice day she'd had and told him about having lunch with Greta. She'd also run into Pastor Paul, and they'd had a nice chat. While Sam was enjoying their conversation, he was baffled by her buoyant mood.

"When we get home, I'll make us some nice sausage, gravy, and biscuits. There's also the shoofly pie I made last night," Lucy commented.

"That sounds delicious. I'm starved. I'd be happy to help, if you like."

Lucy shook her head. "I'll be fine. It feels good to be up and moving about after being still for so long."

"I know what you mean, but please don't overdo it. I'd hate to see you relapse. Watching you be in so much pain was very difficult."

"I appreciate your concern. It's quite wonderful having my own personal doctor." The teasing smile she sent him made his blood run faster. "I think perhaps a thorough examination is in order later on. What do you think?"

"I think that could be arranged." Sam shook his head the

next moment. “Am I talking to the same woman I came to town with this morning?”

Lucy’s eyes sparkled as she laughed. “Aye. ‘Tis.”

“Are you sure? Because she was quite put out with me.”

“I know, and I’m sorry. I just realized that there’s no sense arguing about this anymore. All that matters is catching these thugs. I’ll do my part by staying out of the way and heeding the advice of those who are experienced with this sort of thing.”

Sam was still dubious. “Is this a trap of some kind? I find your quick capitulation a little suspicious.”

“I promise that it’s not a trick, Sam. It’s just not important enough to keep fighting about,” she replied with a shrug.

“That sounds more like resignation than agreement.”

“’Tis neither,” Lucy said. “It’s acceptance of something I can’t change right now. I have more important things to do than drive myself crazy over it. Such as starting my business.” She slid over and tucked her hand in the crook of his arm. “I can’t wait to start cutting patterns and making clothing.”

It warmed Sam’s heart to see her so excited. “I’ll help in any way I can. Eventually, you might need your own shop in town. More women are coming West all the time. This area will become more populated before too long. People will need fashionable clothing.”

Lucy rested her cheek against his shoulder. “I want to make affordable clothing. Anything from gowns and suits, to everyday clothes.”

Sam kissed the top of her head and inhaled the scent of roses in her hair. She’d bathed last night, and she smelled wonderful. “You’re wise to offer those kinds of products. They’ll sell well. Both the town residents and travelers passing through will purchase them.”

The rest of the ride home was spent discussing Lucy's plans for her future business venture. Sam was impressed with her business acumen and promotional ideas. He was fortunate to have married such an intelligent woman.

When they arrived at the ranch, Sam helped Lucy carry her purchases into the house, which they stored in the spare room. Then he went to take care of the wagon and horse while she started dinner. While he worked, he thought about the change in Lucy's attitude.

Her acceptance of the situation was a good thing, but it was obvious that she was still unhappy about it. However, he'd take her acceptance over obstinance any day. Once he was finished rubbing down their horse, he put it in its stall and headed for the house, looking forward to spending the evening with his beautiful wife.

# CHAPTER 17

Grant rubbed his jaw, indecision stamped on his face. "I don't know about this, Lucy."

"I already know how to shoot, but I need to improve. I'd also like to learn how to use a knife."

They stood in the kitchen. Everyone had gone for the day, leaving them alone.

"I don't like it," Grant said.

Lucy planted her hands on her hips. "If a man asked you to teach him to use weapons, would you?"

Grant's expression darkened. "That's not fair, Lucy."

"I disagree. It's very fair. I—" She broke off as Greta's advice echoed in her mind and she changed tactics. "Let's be honest. Josh is a highly skilled lawman from what I understand, but there's no guarantee that he'll find the people responsible.

"How long am I to be guarded? You're planning to leave once you have enough money to buy a horse. What am I to do if these criminals haven't been caught by then? I must be able to defend myself."

Grant motioned for her to sit at the table and joined her. “Lucy, I won’t leave until they’ve been apprehended.”

“What if it takes six months, or even a year?” Lucy countered. “What if someone breaks into the house during the night while Sam is out on an emergency? You’ll be out in the bunkhouse, and if I’m not able to scream, you won’t know that I’m in trouble. What then?”

Grant frowned. “I see your logic. It’s true that I can’t be with you every minute of the day and night, but—”

“And what if someday when we have children, I need to protect them from something or someone?” Lucy had to work hard to keep her voice even. “Sam said this can be a harsh land filled with danger. He told me that women have to be more self-reliant than women back East because the men can’t always be around. It’s important for me to be proficient with weapons.”

Grant looked out the window with a thoughtful expression on his face. Lucy didn’t push for a response. It was wash day, so she took the large basket of dirty laundry outside and sat it by a huge metal tub.

Grabbing a pail, she went back inside and started pumping water into it. Grant still sat at the table, looking deep in thought. She let him alone and continued her work.

When the bucket was full, she started for the door with it. Grant rose and took the bucket from her, but he still didn’t speak.

All through his assistance in readying the washtub, he remained silent. Right before Lucy started to wash the clothes, Grant finally spoke. “I’ll teach you. You’re right. I’ll be leaving as soon as possible, and it will ease my conscience to know that you’re well trained in defense and shooting.”

Lucy wanted to jump up and shout her triumph to the

sky, but she settled for beaming at Grant. "Thank you so much. This means more to me than I can truly tell you."

"You're welcome. I need to write a letter. I'll be right back. I can work on it while I sit here with you," he said.

"All right."

It turned out that Grant didn't get his letter written after all. He'd sat close by her and started it, but after the third time she'd stood up to hang an item on the nearby clothesline she'd strung between two trees in the yard across from the kitchen, he couldn't abide his inefficiency and started helping her.

Lucy washed and rinsed the clothes and he hung them on the line. The work went quicker, and they finished in good time. All the while, Grant had kept careful watch over his charge.

As she handed Grant the last shirt, she said, "Thank you for helping me. I have a little free time before lunch. How about a little lesson, and then I'll make us something nice to eat?"

Grant chuckled. "You sure don't waste time. Might as well."

Lucy stood up and started tugging one of the heavy tubs towards the side of the lawn where it was all right to dump it, but Grant jumped in to help again.

"Let me do this. These are heavy. It's easier for me to do it."

Proud though she was, Lucy's shoulder was still tender and lugging the heavy tubs would aggravate it. It already ached from using the washboard. "That's fine. I'll put these things away and be back with a gun and ammunition."

Grant pointed at the paddock. "I'll set up some targets there since none of the horses are out right now."

"Sounds like a good plan," Lucy said, and went on her way.

"THAT WAS some pretty shooting today, Miss Lucy."

Sam stopped chewing a bite of roasted chicken and looked at his wife.

"Thank you, Jensen, but I was only following Grant's instructions."

Grant speared a piece of potato with his fork. "Instruction will only get you so far. It's what a person does with new knowledge that matters. You paid attention and then put what I taught you into practice. You worked hard and did very well, so be proud of yourself."

Sam asked, "You've been target practicing today, Lucy?"

"Aye. In between my work I had some free time, so I asked Grant to teach me."

Although he looked a bit sheepish, Grant met Sam's gaze. "I thought we might as well put the time to good use, and it won't hurt for her to be able to shoot well."

Sam forced his voice to remain neutral. "I did give Lucy lessons, which is why she was able to fend off that lout who attacked her." That wasn't what he'd meant to say, but his tongue seemed to have a mind of its own.

"Right. The groundwork you laid with her really shows. You got her off to a solid start," Grant said.

Sam arched an eyebrow. "A solid start?"

"That's right. Lucy did well today, but there's still a lot I can teach her."

A note of challenge had entered Grant's voice and Sam didn't like it at all. "Such as?"

"She needs to be able to defend herself in close quarters in case her derringer would jam, or if her assailant would get the gun away from her," Grant replied.

Sam laid down his silverware. "She's not a soldier. She doesn't need that kind of training."

"She's also right in this room, lads." Irritation laced Lucy's words. "I'd appreciated it if you didn't talk about me as if I wasn't here."

"I'm sorry, Lucy. I didn't mean to be rude. I was just surprised," Sam said. "I thought we'd settled this yesterday."

"I was attacked and almost kidnapped." Lucy's hand tightened around her fork. "If I hadn't had that gun, God only knows what would've happened to me. I won't be a victim again, so with or without your permission, I'm going to learn how to better defend myself."

Anger burned in Sam's gut, not because of her assertive behavior, but because she wanted to learn from Grant instead of him. Jealousy was a foreign emotion for Sam, but the green-eyed monster was alive and well in his mind just then.

He chastised himself for his juvenile thoughts, but it was hard to quash them. Grant was an honorable man and more experienced in combat. While Sam had been treating injured soldiers, Grant had been out on the battlefield, right in the thick of the fighting. Sam's logical mind said that Grant was the better man for the job, but his pride was making it difficult to remain objective.

There was also the fact that Lucy had gone behind his back about this. She'd never mentioned that she was going to ask for Grant's assistance. Was this some sort of revenge for yesterday? Looking in Lucy's eyes, he detected no malice, but her expression was defiant.

Tom shifted in his seat and Sam became aware of the other men again. He was embarrassed enough and had no interest in having an audience witness an argument between him and Lucy.

He wiped his mouth and laid his napkin on the table. "I think this is a discussion best had in private, Lucy. If you'll all excuse me, I have some work to do."

Without another glance at his wife, he left the table and went to their room.

~

POUNDING on the kitchen door had Sam bolting up in bed. That kind of knocking almost always signaled something awful had occurred. He rushed from the room, jogging out to the kitchen. His gun sat on the table. He grabbed it and approached the door.

"Who is it?"

"Let us in, Sam."

Recognizing Gray's voice, Sam unlocked the door and admitted him into the kitchen. The fear in Gray's eyes set Sam's nerves on edge.

"Get your bag and come to the bunkhouse. It's Grant," Gray said.

"What happened?"

"We'll tell you out there. Hurry."

Sam turned around as Gray departed and almost ran Lucy over. He hadn't heard her come up behind him.

"What happened to Grant?" she asked, moving aside to allow him to pass.

Sam hurried down the hall to their room. "I don't know. Gray didn't say. Just told me to get my bag." He snatched it from where it sat on his desk. "Please start boiling water, Lucy. I have a feeling we're going to need it."

"Aye. Unfortunately, I think you're right." Lucy put a hand on his arm. "I'll help in whatever way I can, Sam. Just tell me what you want me to do."

Sam's smile was grim. "Thank you."

Calling on his ability to hold back his emotions during medical emergencies, Sam headed for the bunkhouse, preparing himself for the worst.

WHEN SHE TOOK HOT, wet towels and cloths to the bunkhouse, terror struck Lucy at the sight of Grant lying bloody and beaten on his bed. Sam and Gray had removed his shirt and blood oozed from two knife wounds: one in his right ribcage and one to the left side of his abdomen. Both looked deep and lethal. Lucy felt a little woozy at first, but she rallied, refusing to faint over some blood and let Grant and Sam down.

Lucy walked over to a square wooden table in the middle of the bunkhouse. The men's beds were set up in a horseshoe pattern, with Grant's being the one to the left of the door.

"Everything is here, Sam," she said. "Jensen, will you please light your campfire?"

The older man's face had turned ashen and Lucy thought that some fresh air would do him good. They didn't need him passing out on them.

"Sure thing," Jensen said, looking relieved to get out of there. He wasted no time leaving.

"What happened?" Sam asked, as he gave Grant a large dose of laudanum. The former soldier was barely able to swallow it.

Gray replied, "We went to Handy's. Tom and I became engaged in a game of poker. Grant went to do the necessary out back of the saloon. The next thing we knew, he came staggering in the door and collapsed. From what we could gather, three men attacked him and left him to die."

Lucy's burning anger was mirrored on Sam's face. "They have to be involved in what's going on around here. Hopefully he'll be able to tell us who they were when he wakes up."

Tom sat down on his bunk. "If I find out who they are, I'll kill them."

Gray rested a hand on his shoulder. "No, you won't. The guilty parties will face justice, but not at the hands of vigilantes. Understand?"

Tom looked like he was going to argue for a moment, but then nodded.

Lucy was glad. There had been enough violence and bloodshed. It had to end somewhere. She moved closer to Grant, forcing herself to watch what Sam was doing. She had to become accustomed to this sort of thing. No doubt she'd witness many medical emergencies in the coming years.

"How can I help?" she asked.

"Can you keep pressure on his stomach while I work on the rib puncture?"

"Aye."

Lucy took over for Sam, and he moved over to further examine the other wound. Grant let out a weak moan when she pressed a fresh towel against his abdomen. She blinked back tears at the thought of causing Grant pain, but she knew what she was doing was important, and that it could save his life.

"I don't believe this stab hit anything vital," Sam said. "It doesn't seem like the lung has been punctured. I'm going to cauterize the wound to stop the bleeding."

Gray opened Sam's bag. "I'll heat your knife."

Lucy blanched at the idea but didn't let up on her test. Gray took the knife outside to heat in the flames of the fire Jensen had started. Several minutes later he returned with it. The blade glowed red-hot.

Sam poured whiskey onto a clean cloth and wiped the injured area with it. "Lucy, keep up that pressure. Gentlemen, hold him down and keep him as still as possible. I'll make this as quick as I can."

The men moved into position and Lucy steeled herself for what was coming.

Gray put a leather strap between Grant's teeth. "Bite down, lad."

Despite his glazed over eyes, Grant heard Gray and gave a slight nod.

Sam's eyes moved between those gathered around the bed. "Here we go."

Sam pressed the knife blade across the wound. Grant stiffened and let out a muffled cry as the scent of burnt flesh filled the bunkhouse.

Lucy closed her eyes against the nausea that churned in her stomach. Grant writhed under her hands, and she followed his movements, keeping the pressure on his stomach steady. She opened her eyes when Grant relaxed and fell silent. "What happened?"

"He passed out," Tom said.

Sam started bandaging the burn site. "It's a blessing. He's going to be in a lot more pain before we're through. That stomach wound is going to be much more difficult to deal with."

Sympathy flooded Lucy, strengthening her resolve to help in any way possible. Grant had been good to her and she considered him a friend.

Sam moved closer and smiled at Lucy. "Let's see how this is doing."

Lucy cautiously removed the towel, which was almost soaked with blood. More started flowing from the wound at an alarming rate as soon as she took the towel away.

"His artery has been damaged. I need to repair it," Sam said.

Lucy's heart hammered in her chest. "Can you do it here?"

Sam replied, "I've repaired far worse and in far worse

places. But I have to be quick and I might need your sewing skills. Do you think you can help?"

Fear clogged Lucy's throat, making her reply almost a whisper. "You want me to help perform surgery?"

The intense way Sam stared into her eyes scared her even more because it indicated that he was dead serious. "If need be, yes. I hate to pressure you, but time is of the essence. Can you help me?"

"You did a beautiful job with all the curtains, Miss Lucy. I reckon you could help the doc patch Grant up just as good," Tom said with a wink.

Lucy was about to berate him for making light of the situation, but Sam's chuckle stopped her.

"You might even make him a little prettier," Gray chimed in.

The right corner of her mouth quirked up as she caught on. Using humor to deal with difficult situations wasn't a strange concept to Lucy. Looking down at Grant lying so still on the bed, his hair soaked with sweat, she knew that refusing wasn't an option.

"Aye. I'll help. Just tell me what to do."

"Good. Let's begin."

Though Sam's statement was curt, the pride shining in his eyes bespoke his admiration and approval of her. She wondered how he could be proud of her for one form a bravery but not for another. Knowing this was no time for such thoughts, she locked them in a mental box and began following Sam's instructions.

~

THE SURGERY WAS a harrowing ordeal despite the short time it took. While he'd been unconscious, they'd moved Grant onto a makeshift operating table made from long wooden boards laid over wooden sawhorses. Lucy had covered the boards with two old horse blankets for cushioning.

Several lanterns were hung around the table to give them as much light as possible. Sam instructed Gray on how to administer chloroform to Grant. He'd ordered the expensive anesthetic several months ago and was now glad that he had. It meant that Grant wouldn't be subjected to the agony of an invasive surgery while being completely aware of what was occurring.

Sam monitored Grant and waited to make an incision until he was certain that he was fully under. When Grant remained motionless, save for his breathing, Sam went to work. Although he wished that he had an operating theater with all the new medical equipment available, Sam was used to performing surgery in difficult circumstances. Compared to treating wounded soldiers on the battlefield, performing an operation in a bunkhouse was a luxury.

Although Sam had an excellent education and was a skilled surgeon, he felt a little inadequate. There were new procedures he didn't know about, and he worried that he wasn't up to par for what Grant needed done. Abdominal surgery was a tricky business even in the best conditions, let alone their current one.

Lucy's gasp as blood gushed from the new incision almost made him glance at her. "Lucy, I know this is all shocking to you, but please don't make sudden noises or bump me. It wouldn't take much for me to nick something vital.

"I'm so sorry." Lucy's words were heavy with regret. "I'll be very careful, Sam."

"Thank you."

Sam instructed Lucy to soak up blood with clean linen cloths while he worked. His excellent grasp of anatomy enabled him to find the two damaged blood vessels. He repaired the first one without much difficulty, but the second one was difficult to reach, since he had large hands.

He glanced at Lucy, relieved to see that although her face was pale, she was avidly watching him. "Lucy, do you see this vein that's been cut?"

She leaned closer and nodded after a moment. "Aye."

He moved his index finger a fraction. "This is the other part of it. Do you think you can sew them together?"

Her mouth dropped open as she gaped at him. "I've never done anything like that. What if I do it wrong and kill him? I couldn't bear it."

Sam smiled reassuringly. "I felt the same way the first time I operated on someone. It wasn't easy but knowing the patient would certainly die if I didn't at least try motivated me.

"You have smaller hands than me, Lucy. If we can't get this bleeding stopped, Grant will die. I'll guide you the entire time. Will you try for his sake?"

The fearful expression on her face made Sam afraid that she was going to refuse, but then she squared her shoulders and pulled herself together. "I'll do my best. Don't let me kill him, all right?"

Her determination and use of humor made Sam even more proud of her. "I'll do my utmost to not let that happen."

At her brisk nod, Sam began instructing Lucy. He was impressed by her deft handling of the needle and thread. If her sutures were a bit clumsy, it was only because she was nervous, not because she wasn't capable.

With more practice, Sam felt confident that she could out-suture many surgeons. When she'd successfully tied off the vein, he couldn't resist kissing her cheek. "Well done, my love. I'll take over now. It's imperative that we get him closed up now."

Lucy turned white and he knew what would happen next. She nodded and fled from the bunkhouse. The sound of retching reached him as he worked, but he couldn't stop to go check on her. Her reaction was completely understandable. To be thrown into major surgery without any prior medical experience was beyond daunting, but Lucy had borne up well under the strain.

Before long, he finished closing and stepped back from his patient. "You can stop with the chloroform now, Gray."

Gray took the handkerchief away from Grant's face and sat the bottle of anesthetic on the table. It was almost gone. "Looks like you finished in the nick of time."

Sam sighed as he started washing and rinsing his hands and forearms in the large basins of hot water. Lucy had returned at some point, prepared the basins and started cleaning up the area.

Looking over, he saw her changing Grant's bed and felt a rush of intense emotion roll through him as he watched her. Love so powerful, so raw, suffused his heart and he could hardly restrain himself from blurting it out. It wasn't at all the right time, so he kept it locked inside. But at the earliest possible time, he would tell his stunning wife that he'd fallen in love with her.

~

Lucy had been frequently bathing Grant, trying to cool him off. He'd woken a couple of times, but Sam had given him more laudanum, so he'd remained asleep most of the time.

She agreed with Sam's strategy. If Grant rested, he would heal faster because he wasn't moving around, putting pressure on his injured areas. Sam was confident that Grant would make a full recovery from his wounds, but the infection posed a dire threat to him.

Her eyes were gritty from exhaustion, but Lucy refused to leave Grant's side. She felt a deep responsibility to him. Having her hands inside his body had created an intimate connection to him, and she was scared that her participation in the surgery had been inferior and that he would perish as a result. Sam had assured her several times that she'd done a splendid job, but she was still doubtful.

Drawing the covers down until Grant's torso was revealed. Lucy carefully bathed his shoulders and arms, making sure to avoid his bandaged midsection.

Just as she finished, Sam came in. "How's he doing?"

Lucy sighed. "His fever has not broken. Isn't there something more we can do?"

Sam held up a jar. "Actually, there is. I had Tom ride out to Drake's village to visit their medicine woman. The Crow have many remedies that white people don't. This poultice is to be spread on his feet and his feet should be wrapped up. They use it to reduce fever and drive out infection. I also made a tincture of honey for him to drink, which is very good for healing and helps to relieve inflammation. Once his pain level starts to decrease, we can switch to willow bark tea. I don't like to keep patients on laudanum any longer than necessary because it's addictive."

"I'll put the poultice on," Lucy said, starting to rise. She swayed on her feet a little.

"No, you won't. You need to sleep," Sam said. "You're no good to Grant if you collapse. You also need to eat."

"I'm fine," she insisted.

Sam put an arm around her shoulders and guided her towards the door. "No, you're not. I'm going to get you something to eat and then you're going to bed."

Lucy didn't have the strength to argue. She let Sam take

her to the house where he fixed her eggs and bacon. Until she took the first bite, she didn't realize that she was so famished. Her breakfast disappeared in a flash and she washed it down with the cup of tea Sam made her.

A huge yawn gripped her as she rose from the table. She went to their room, stripped down to her shift and fell into bed. She fell asleep so fast that she never remembered Sam pulling the covers over her.

# CHAPTER 18

Riding up to the Slaters' house, Josh dismounted and tied his horse to the hitching post there. Gray had tracked him down at the Inn to let him know that Grant was awake, so he'd come right away. He hoped that Grant could give him some information about his attackers.

Although he'd gotten a few leads, none of them had panned out so far. As he walked towards the bunkhouse, Lucy came out.

"Morning, Josh."

Josh removed his hat. "Morning, Miss Lucy. How are you?"

The fatigue in her face couldn't quite be erased by her smile, but she was still beautiful. *Sam's a lucky man,* Josh thought.

"I'm fine, thanks, and you?"

He nodded towards the bunkhouse. "I'll be better if Grant has some useful information for me. I want to catch these ba—um, dirtbags," he amended. Although he was frustrated, he remembered his manners at the last moment.

Lucy's eyebrows drew together. "I hope he does, too, but he's still weak so please don't tire him out more than necessary."

"I'll keep it as brief as possible," Josh promised. "How is he?"

"Better now that the infection is subsiding, but he still has a long recovery ahead."

"Well, he's a strong fella, and he's got the best people looking after him. I'm sure he'll be back to his old self in no time," Josh responded.

Lucy smiled. "I hope so. I pray that he doesn't have any setbacks."

"Same here," Josh agreed. "Well, how's about I get on with it so he can go back to resting?"

"Aye. That would be good."

Josh followed her into the bunkhouse and looked around, noticing that it looked a little nicer than the last time he'd been there. Dark blue curtains hung at the windows and a new braided rug covered the floor in the middle of the room. Everything looked clean and tidy.

"Lucy insisted that the place needed some sprucing up."

Josh turned at the sound of Grant's voice. He sat in bed, propped up by several pillows. He looked haggard and pale, but his eyes were clear and he was lucid—all good signs.

"I'd say she was right." Josh took a chair from the table, moved it over to Grant's bunk and sat it down by it. "Certainly does look nicer in here."

Grant shifted his position a little. "Agreed."

Josh sat down. "What do you remember about the attack? Don't leave anything out. Even the tiniest detail might be important."

"I've had a lot of time to think about it, and most of it is very clear to me," Grant said. "I went with Gray and Tom to Handy's. They got into a poker game, but I didn't join in since I'm saving up money. I watched for a little while and then went to the outhouse.

"When I came out, three men approached me. I knew they were up to no good just from the way they moved. I backed up against the outhouse to protect my back and drew my pistol. I gave them every opportunity to back out, but they wouldn't."

Josh leaned forward in his chair a little. "Did you recognize any of them?"

Grant shook his head. "No. It was dark and I'm still new around here. But I did see the guy's face who did this to me, and I can identify him."

Excitement flooded Josh, but he kept a level head as he pulled a small notepad and pencil stub from his shirt pocket. "Please describe him to me."

Grant obliged, telling Josh every detail he could remember. "While we were struggling, I noticed that he had a scar that ran from the left corner of his upper lip almost to his nose."

That made Josh sit up a little straighter. "Are you sure about that?"

Grant grimaced as he shifted in bed a little. "Positive. Why? Does that mean something to you?"

"Based on that last tidbit and the rest of your description, I'm positive that I know who the guy is," Josh replied.

"Who?" Grant asked.

"The brother of a fella I hauled off to prison several months ago. Andy Franklin was abusing his wife and kids. He's locked up in Helena now," Josh said. "The Franklins have always been jealous of Mason Crawford's family because their land is so fertile. The Franklins' place is mainly rocky soil that doesn't yield many crops."

Lucy asked, "Do you think it's the Franklins who've been threatening us?"

"I think it's a real possibility. Your land is just as good quality as Mason's." Josh stood up. "Looks like I'll be taking a ride out to their place to have a talk with them. I didn't know that any of the other Franklins were around since Andy's wife took the kids and moved back East." He held out a hand to Grant. "I'm real glad to see that you're on the mend. Thanks for all the information."

Grant shook his hand. "Happy to help. Let us know what happens."

"I sure will."

Lucy followed Josh out to his horse. "Why do you think those men attacked Grant? It's me and Sam that they're after."

As he unwound his horse's reins from the hitching post, Josh considered his words carefully. He didn't want to scare Lucy, but he felt that she deserved his honesty. "They went after Grant for a couple of reasons. Hurting or killing Grant might drive you folks to get off this land, but if it didn't, at least he wouldn't be around to get in their way."

Lucy's eyes widened, but she didn't look away. "What you mean is that he wouldn't be here to protect me anymore."

"That's right. So, until I bring these guys in, be extra careful," Josh responded. "They're getting more desperate, so there's no telling what they'll try next. Understand?"

A fierce light lit her eyes. "Aye. I understand and I'll be prepared if anyone tries something."

"Lucy, don't go looking for trouble," Josh said. "I don't want you or anyone else getting hurt."

"I won't go looking for it, but if someone brings trouble to us, I won't run from it," Lucy told him. "This is our land, our home, and I'll be darned if anyone is going to run us off. Be careful, Josh."

"Yes, ma'am, and you do the same."

She gave him a curt nod and headed back to the bunkhouse. Josh watched her go for a moment before mounting up. As he trotted his horse to the main road, Josh admired Lucy's bravery, but he hoped she'd heed his warning. The Franklins were not people to trifle with.

SAM KEPT Atlas at a lope the whole way home from Mrs. Stavros's ranch. He'd been checking on her granddaughter, Elise, who'd broken her arm last week. The rambunctious six-year-old had been playing with her older brother near the creek. They'd been skipping rocks and had tussled over a very nice, smooth specimen.

Their two mongrel dogs hadn't liked their arguing and had tried to break it up. When they jumped on the kids, all four of them had tumbled into the shallow creek. Poor Elise had tried to break her fall and had broken one of the bones in her forearm in the process.

Once he'd ascertained that Elise was coming along well, he'd said his farewells and went on his way. He wasn't far from his ranch when he heard gunshots in the distance. They were relatively close, which made his heart lurch in fear. Was someone attacking his ranch?

His alarm abated somewhat when he realized that the shooting was coming from a different direction. He listened for a moment and knew that this wasn't someone doing some target practice. Somewhere to his right, a gunfight was in progress.

Sam looked in the direction of home for several moments. Although he wanted to get home to his wife, he couldn't ignore the fact that someone might need his help. With a click to Atlas, he put the big horse in motion, speeding towards the unknown danger.

~

Following the gunfire, Sam was surprised that it led to the Franklin ranch. He'd been told that it had been empty since Andy's wife and children had moved away. If that was the case, who was having a shootout there?

Sam brought Atlas to a halt at a thin stand of trees before the place and proceeded on foot from there. With great caution, he approached the faded, graying barn that had seen better days. He made it to the back of it and cringed when he heard at least two guns fire.

The sound had come from the direction of the house. Sam chanced a peek around the corner of the barn and saw Eddie Murtaugh hiding behind the stone well that stood between the house and barn. A bullet ricocheted off the well, making Eddie jerk.

Swinging his gaze to the right, Sam saw Eddie's brother Sawyer standing behind a big oak tree, aiming his rifle at the house. He fired and the bullet shattered a glass pane of one of the front windows.

Eddie and Sawyer Murtaugh often acted as deputies for Josh, and Sam surmised that they were doing so now. But who were they after? Had they chased some criminal here, who was now holed up here?

Sam examined the area before creeping along the side of the barn towards Eddie's hiding place. Eddie saw Sam and grinned. The Murtaugh brothers were known for their bravery, cunning, and for liking fights a little too much. Staying low, Sam ran over to another tree that stood near Eddie.

"What's going on?" he asked between gunshots.

Eddie said, "We've got Titus, Art, and maybe Zeb Franklin pinned down in there."

Sam arched an eyebrow. "Why? What did they do?"

"Josh is pretty sure that they're the ones who've been

after you and yours," Eddie replied. "Turns out that Grant recognized the guy who stabbed him, and he fits Titus's description. Josh just wanted to talk to them, but as soon as we got here, they started shooting at us."

Rage built inside Sam until the landscape took on a red tinge. He gripped the handle of his revolver as he contemplated blasting his way into the house. The next moment, he rejected that idea. He needed more information before charging into the situation like a bull in a china shop. Doing that could get him killed. His thirst for revenge would have to wait to be quenched, since he had no intention of making Lucy a widow.

"Where's Josh?" Sam asked.

"He's over there by that old wagon."

Sam looked where he pointed and saw his friend hunkered down behind the rickety structure. Josh shouted for the occupants of the house to lay down their weapons and come out. He was answered by a volley of shots.

When it subsided, Sam sprinted to Josh's position, cringing when a bullet hit the ground two feet away from him. Gaining the safety of the wagon, he crouched by Josh and smiled. "Looks like you're all having fun."

Josh grunted. "What are you doing here?"

"I was on my way home and heard all the shooting. Eddie says you have the suspect of Grant's attack holed up in there."

"That's right. I'd bet my last penny that Titus Franklin is behind all this. I don't put anything past that polecat," Josh said. "There are a couple of other guys with him, but I'm not sure who they are. I recognized Titus's voice, though. I didn't know he'd come back to town, but I guess he did."

Sam had to clamp down on his anger again. "So, they're the ones who've be after us. What's your plan?"

"Well, just like you do with rats, I'm gonna smoke them

out. Robert Red Dog is out back, putting that part into motion."

Shortly after Josh spoke, the sound of breaking glass reached them, followed by a lot of shouting. The two men raised their heads just high enough above the wagon to be able to see the ramshackle white house. Smoke started coming out of one of the front windows and the yelling turned into coughing.

The front door opened, and four men rushed from the house, guns blazing as they made a break for the barn.

"I hope you're a good shot, Sam," Josh commented. "We could use you."

The thought of aiding in the apprehension of the men who'd terrorized his wife and almost murdered Grant filled Sam with satisfaction. He cocked his gun. "It'll be my pleasure to help bring these goons to justice."

"Glad to hear it. Let's go."

Josh stood up and shouted, "Titus! You and your men surrender now, and no one has to get hurt!" One of the thugs shot at Josh, who ducked. "I'll take that as a no. All right. I guess we're going to do this the hard way."

Things got even crazier and bullets were exchanged with dizzying speed. Sam joined in the fray and didn't feel bad when he shot one of the guys in the leg. The man lay screaming until another gunshot hit him in the chest, forever silencing him. Sam had been taught to save lives, not take them, but he felt no sadness that the man was dead.

Somewhere to his and Josh's right a man screamed.

"I don't see Sawyer anywhere," Josh said. "I'll bet he got that fella. Time to get the rest."

Josh left their hiding place, running towards the barn. As Sam followed him, he saw a man step out from behind a bush. He acted before he truly registered his actions. Sam raised his gun, took quick aim and fired. His shot connected with the guy, who twisted to the left from the force of the bullet's impact and crumpled to the ground.

Several other shots echoed off the buildings before everything went quiet.

"Eddie! Sawyer!" Josh shouted as he approached the criminal Sam had shot. "Are you fellas all right?"

"We're fine!" Sawyer called back as he joined Josh and Sam. "Can't say the same for these sidewinders, though."

Sam walked over to his victim and looked down at him. An ugly scar marred the man's features. "Is this Titus?"

"Yep. That's him," Josh answered. "Looks like you spared me having to make a trip to Helena, Sam."

Sam holstered his weapon and crouched next to Titus, making sure he was dead. "You're right. He's gone."

All the others had also been killed.

Josh congratulated his deputies on their excellent work, and they moved the deceased into the barn. The sheriff said he'd have the undertaker come out for them as soon as he got to town.

"I'll bet it feels good to know that you guys are safe now, Sam," Josh said.

Sam smiled. "Thanks to you."

Josh shook his head. "No, it wasn't just me. If it wasn't for Grant's description, I'd still be scratching my head. Well, why don't you get home to that wife of yours and I'll finish up here."

Sam didn't argue with Josh about it. He thanked him and the Murtaugh's again, mounted Atlas and urged the gelding into a canter. He couldn't wait to tell Lucy that their nightmare was over. He also couldn't wait to tell her how he felt about her. With a smile on his face, he sent Atlas galloping for home.

As they stood in the kitchen, Lucy listened to Sam's story with a mixture of relief, fear, and anger. She was happy that no one else would be hurt and that she didn't have to constantly be on the alert any longer, but the way Sam had placed himself in danger made her furious.

"So, it's over," he said, resting his hands on her shoulders. "No more danger, or reason to live in fear. Everything is fine now."

Lucy pulled away from him. "Fine! You think everything is fine now?"

The confusion in Sam's expression only made her angrier. "Yes. The threat is past. Why are you so upset?"

Lucy held back angry tears. "You berated me for having the audacity to want to protect myself by learning how to shoot better, but it's perfectly all right for you to go rushing into a gunfight! You could've been killed, Sam!"

"Lucy, it's not the same thing at all," he said.

"Why, Sam? Explain why it isn't?"

Sam put his hands on his hips. "Because I'm a former soldier and I've fought in battles. You haven't."

"I may not have fought in a war, but I've fought a battle!" Lucy shouted. "How could you go do something like this? What would I have done if…?" She couldn't finish. Her vision blurred from the tears she could no longer keep at bay, and she realized that she was no longer angry with Sam because of their ongoing disagreement. No, she was enraged with him for a much different reason.

"Lucy, I'm fine. Not a scratch on me. Calm down, sweetheart," he said.

"Don't tell me to calm down like I'm some child, Sam." She pointed towards the bunkhouse. "There's a man lying inside there who almost died several days ago—a seasoned soldier, mind you. If that can happen to him, it could've happened to you. Losing Grant would be terrible, but if something happened to you, it would be so much worse. Promise me you won't do something so foolish again."

His gaze softening, Sam cupped her face. "Lucy, I'm here and I'm not going anywhere."

Lucy grabbed his shirt, fisting her hands in the fabric and shaking him. "You have to promise me not to be so reckless. I love you too much to lose you, Sam!"

Sam went still, his eyes locking on hers. "What did you just say?"

Lucy shook him again. "I said that I love you, you big igit!"

Her next words were cut off when Sam wrapped his arms around her and claimed her lips in a searing kiss. Lucy didn't bother protesting. Her emotions were running too high and she needed the reassurance of his embrace. She rose on tiptoe, kissing him back with abandon.

The way his hands roamed over her back felt so good and desire unfurled inside her. It wasn't just a physical craving, though. Her heart wanted him as much as her body did. She released his shirt, resting her palms on his chest. She whimpered in protest as he broke the kiss.

He took her face in his hands. His intense expression rendered her speechless. "I love you, too, Lucy. I love you so much, and the only reason I didn't want you learning about weapons and such was because I was afraid you'd get hurt. I couldn't bear to lose you any more than you could withstand losing me. So, if you're going to continue being angry with me for helping Josh today, I get to be angry with you."

Tears of happiness trickled from Lucy's eyes. "Do you mean it? Do you truly love me, Sam?"

He stroked her cheeks with the pads of his thumbs. "I mean every word I just said. I love you, Lucy. My heart is yours. Do you really love me?"

Lucy nodded. "Yes, Sam. I love you so much."

Sam crushed her to him, and she went eagerly into his embrace. Then she pushed against his chest, needing to settle this thing between them before giving in to the joy surging through her.

"What's wrong?" Sam asked, his breathing a little ragged.

"I don't want to fight anymore. Let's both promise each other to be as careful as we both possibly can and not to take unnecessary risks," she said.

A smile curved his lips. "I don't want to fight, either. I think your idea is a good one." He sobered a little. "But I do think you're right. It's also a good idea for you to learn to shoot better, but I want to teach you."

Lucy blinked in surprise. "You do? I thought you didn't think it was appropriate because I'm a woman."

"I realize how asinine that was of me, Lucy. How could I deny you the right to protect yourself, or other people if necessary?" Sam responded. "It would be irresponsible and cruel of me to do that. So, I want us to practice together. How does that sound to you?"

Lucy wound her arms around Sam's neck. "It sounds wonderful."

"Good." Sam kissed her cheek and whispered, "There's something else that sounds wonderful to me."

A shiver ran through her when Sam's warm breath tickled her ear. "What would that be?"

"Actually, I'd rather just show you."

Lucy laughed when he took her hand and pulled her after him, down the hall and into their room.

# EPILOGUE

Loud guffaws of laughter and Lucy's pretty laugh rang out across one of their fields. Several targets had been set up and Lucy and Sam's practice session had evolved into a friendly competition. Sam shook his head as he looked at the can that now lay on the ground. She'd shot it and four others off the fence in quick succession. He knew when he'd been bested.

"All right. I concede victory to my beautiful wife. I'm man enough to admit when I've lost." He dropped a kiss on her forehead. "Congratulations, my love."

"Thank you, Sam. I think I've had enough for today. I'm starving. I'll go finish supper. It won't be long until we eat, so don't dawdle in cleaning up." She gave Sam a cheeky smile and started for the house.

Sam laughed and started gathering up the various weapons they'd been practicing with. Gray and Tom helped him take the guns to the house where he locked them in a gun cabinet. He washed up and went to the kitchen where Lucy was just pulling two shepherd's pies out of the oven.

She'd already set the table and she placed the pies on the trivets that sat each end of the table. "Would you please put the bread and butter on the table, Sam?"

"Of course."

He'd just completed the task when the men came in the door. The meal commenced and Sam closed his eyes in appreciation as rich, savory flavor flooded his mouth. Lucy's excellent cooking was only one of the reasons he was blessed to be her husband. He often found himself wondering how he'd lived without her for so long.

When the meal ended, he helped her with the dishes and then they retired to the back porch. They looked out over the paddock, watching the horses in the far pasture.

"Sam, do you love me very much?"

Sam looked at Lucy. "Of course, I do. I love you more than life."

"I'm so glad. If there was more of me, would you still love me?"

A laugh escaped Sam. "Are you worried that you'll get fat for some reason? I doubt that will happen, but if it ever did, I'd still desire you as much as ever."

Lucy took his hand and kissed it. "I'm so glad to hear you say that because by February, there's going to be much, much more of me."

Shock shot up Sam's spine and he stared at her. "What are you saying, Lucy?"

Her smile was sweet and a little nervous. "I'm with child, Sam. We're going to have a baby."

How had he missed it? Looking back, he now realized that there had been no interruption of their lovemaking. He passed a hand over his face as he laughed. "Some doctor I am. I've been so wrapped up in you that I didn't realize you missed your cycle."

The blush that stained Lucy's cheek brought out a rush of love for her. "Are you happy about it?" she asked.

Taking her hands, Sam drew Lucy over onto his lap and encircled her waist with his arms. "How could I not be? I love you, and I can't wait for our baby to come."

Relief showed in her eyes as she smiled at him. "I'm so relieved. I was afraid you'd think it was too soon."

He pressed his lips to hers, enjoying their softness. "It's not too soon at all."

"I can't wait, either. We'll have to get the nursery ready before too long."

Sam chuckled and held her closer. "It'll be several months before the baby is due. We have plenty of time."

This started a good-natured argument which involved a lot of laughter. As the sunset turned into twilight, they made plans for their baby, and looked to the future with happiness and hope that the coming years would bring only good things. And if strife hit, they would face adversity together and never forget the love they'd found with one another.

The End

# THE RANCHER'S UNEXPECTED PREGNANT BRIDE BOOK 2

# CHAPTER 1

Martha knew she needed to be patient, breathing shallow so as not to raise anyone's suspicions. Even though it was roughly three o'clock in the morning, and she was dreadfully tired after the horrible hand of fate she'd been dealt, she wasn't going to allow herself to rest even a few minutes for fear of missing her chance.

As Martha stood by the door, peering through the crack, the smell of sweat and beer heavy in the air, she listened intently to the sounds around her. She could hear the drunken older man on the bed beside her snoring softly, thankfully too drunk to do with her what he had paid Max for, having passed out before anything could happen. So drunk that she'd been able to shimmy off his clothes and assemble her disguise, plotting her escape the moment she'd successfully changed her outfit.

Martha listened to the bar room below, silence seeming to ring out. She could still see lantern-light from the bar itself, and she wondered if Max was still awake, perhaps counting his money from the busy Saturday night. Martha knew she would eventually need to make a move, before being forced to do unimaginable things with complete strangers. With that thought in mind, she decided the chance to escape was now.

Martha quickly opened the small room's door and stepped outside into the hallway, closing the door firmly behind her. She kept her breathing calm as she started towards the stairs that led down into the bar room. After that, she'd just have to pass the bar and get out the front door without anyone noticing her.

Wearing oversized boots, Martha stepped carefully down the stairs, being sure not to make too much noise. She wore a large cowboy hat, hoping the rim would cover her face when she bent her head down. Her long auburn hair she'd rolled and fitted into the hat, hoping the burnt orange strands of her hair wouldn't betray her. The jeans she wore felt like two tents strapped around her legs, secured only by a belt she'd fiddled with to fit her hourglass frame. The western shirt she wore tucked into the jeans was thankfully big enough to hide the fact that she was a woman. All in all, Martha felt she fitted in with the type that had come into the saloon that night, and she hoped no one would think twice about her leaving.

When Martha finally made it to the bottom of the stairs, the stench of the place was that much stronger, and her breath quickened when she noticed a few drunken patrons passed out at a few tables, barely visible from the single lantern left alight in the saloon. She skirted around the bar room as best she could, careful not to bump into any chairs or tables, her bright blue eyes scanning the room constantly in the dim light. As Martha made it from that room towards the main bar, her eyes darted to the front door, although not before spotting a satchel on the bar.

She knew she should just make a run for it. No one

seemed to be awake, and she didn't know how long the drunks in the bar would be asleep before waking. Surely the older man upstairs would be furious once he realized he didn't get his money's worth. But Martha couldn't deny her curiosity: she made two quick steps to the bar, peered into the satchel, and, confirming the contents, slung it over her shoulder and made due haste to leave the place behind.

Not being very familiar with the small town she'd been taken to, Martha didn't stop to check anything out. With only the full moon to guide her, she marched past the last few buildings on the main street and followed the road heading out of town. No matter where the road took her, no matter how long she had to walk to reach the next town, it would all be better than the hell she'd just been dumped in by the man she thought she loved.

# CHAPTER 2

Gray Jenkins sat at the breakfast table with his bosses, Sam and Lucy Slater, and the two other ranch hands, Jensen and Tom. When Sam had put in an ad for a mail-order bride, Gray never thought Sam would attract someone like Lucy, someone strong-natured and not afraid to speak her mind. It was Lucy who started the tradition of having meals in the ranch house, giving Gray a break from serving everyone in the bunkhouse. Lucy was sure a good catch, with her black hair and piercing, stormy eyes. Not that Sam wasn't a good-looking gentleman, but Gray had never had much faith in the concept of mail-order brides. The thought alone made him smirk at the irony of it all.

"So, Gray, have you received any interesting letters lately?" Sam Slater asked with a small smile, taking a rather large bite of his food. He'd be rushing off into town to manage his office and no doubt long list of clients. Being the only doctor in town, Sam always had plenty of patients.

"Not recently, no," Gray responded carefully. His

response nevertheless caused smirks and small escapes of laughter to commence. It was no secret that Gray was well acquainted with the women in the area, and that it was never difficult for him to find company for an evening. But at the age of forty-five, and after seeing how happy Sam had become after marrying, he knew that he had better give marriage a chance before it was too late. "I'm sure if they could accompany the ad with my photo, there'd be no shortage of responses."

"Don't ya worry, Gray. Your many other amiable qualities are sure to attract a large response to your ad," Jensen said carefully, trying to imitate the sophisticated way Gray often spoke due to his British heritage. Since Jensen was an old-timer, his quip was that much more humorous, causing everyone, include Gray, to laugh.

"I appreciate your support, old man," Gray returned as he slapped Jensen on the back.

"I would say you're not far behind Jensen," Tom pipped in, a man in his mid-thirties with often disheveled brown hair.

"And I'd watch your words there, my boy, because I can still run laps around you any day of the week," Gray responded quickly, causing Tom to focus on his food because he didn't want to get on the wrong side of his boss. While Sam Slater was the owner of the ranch with both steers and sheep, it was really Gray who ran the operation, and both Jenson and Tom knew that.

Lucy's sweet laughter rang out over the banter before she said, "Ye've always been a charmer, Gray. Just be honest in yer letters and I'm sure it won't be hard for ye to find a bride."

Gray smiled as he turned his gaze upon Lucy. "If I can be as lucky as Sam in finding a bride like you, Lucy, then I'll be doing just fine."

"Oh, there ye go pulling on me heart strings," Lucy replied as Sam reached over and squeezed his wife's hand. Ever since they'd discovered three months ago that Lucy was expecting, she'd been overly emotional and quick to shed a few tears. Gray noticed the way Lucy's eyes teared up as she gazed into her husband's, and he hoped that one day a woman would look at him like that. Most of the time women just looked at him with lusty eyes, and though he enjoyed an evening with company, Gray wanted more in his life than just a string of one-night stands. It was time he found his one and only.

After breakfast, Sam headed out of the door after embracing his wife, while Tom and Jensen got to work on the ranch. Having been a cook himself, and knowing that Lucy was expecting, Gray took a few minutes to help Lucy clean up after breakfast. After what she'd endured last year, he'd become slightly protective of her as well.

"Thank ye, Gray, for all yer help. Greta comes by every once and again to help me tidy up on days I just don't feel that great, but I think I'm starting to regain some of me energy again," Lucy said as she washed the dishes and Gray dried them.

"It's no trouble at all," Gray said.

Lucy regarded him: a tall man with onyx eyes and broad shoulders that made him intimidating to those who didn't know him. His handsome, angular features and the dimple in his left cheek were quite arresting. Though his dark brown hair was peppered with grey, he was no less alluring to the female kind.

"Gray, yer going to make a woman very happy. Ye work hard here on the ranch, and if yer willingness to help is any indication of how ye'd treat yer wife, I don't think ye have anything to worry about, despite yer past pursuits with women," Lucy spoke up.

Gray smirked as he looked down at her. "I think your emotions are going to your head," he quipped as he finished his task and picked up his duster from the peg by the door.

"Yer just afraid to show a woman yer soft side, Gray. All ye know is how to swoon a woman. Now ye'll have to learn to win over her heart," Lucy called from the kitchen, not bothering to follow him out the front door but just hollering away. She just didn't feel up to it today.

Donning his grey cowboy hat as he pulled on his duster, Gray stepped out into a spring morning, the bitter cold of winter finally seeming to have left Spruce Valley, Montana. The rising sun felt warm on his face as he made his way towards the barn. He could almost smell spring's fresh fragrance on the wind, though the wildflowers had yet to start rising. It had been ten years since he came to this valley, joining Sam Slater five years ago when he started up the ranch business that Sam knew nothing about. It was Gray's knowledge of steers, paired with the late Ernie Red-Dog's experience with sheep, that had made the ranch so successful. And with Ernie being killed the year before, his son Drake had thankfully taken over the task of watching over the sheep herd down the road on his own little homestead.

While Sam focused on being a doctor, Gray managed the ranch. He enjoyed the solitary work that kept his body in great shape. But sometimes he did feel lonely of a woman's touch, even though it was something he could easily seek after. But would a woman honestly consider him for a husband? He was older, lived in a bunkhouse, and though he had saved much of his fortune over the years he wasn't all that sure what a woman would expect of him as a husband.

Gray sighed as he got to work, more intent now on making repairs to the outer fence than worrying about a potential wife. After all, he hadn't received any responses to the ad he'd put in the paper four weeks ago. Perhaps he finally had to settle for the fact that he'd never marry, never have kids, and simply grow old and lonely as a ranch hand, much like Jensen had done. Putting on an emotionless mask as he was skilled at doing, Gray cleared his mind and saddled his horse, focusing only on his work.

# CHAPTER 3

Four weeks on the road had done Martha good. After making it to the first town when she successfully escaped hell, Martha had been able to rent a small room at an inn, and with the help of the inn owner, Betty, Martha had been able to recover and regain her strength. Once Martha had rested, bathed, and purchased a horse and riding clothes, she'd taken to the road again, intent on getting as far away from Wisconsin as possible.

Martha knew that travelling alone on the open road was dangerous for a woman. That was why she carried a small pistol in a saddlebag that hung on the front of her saddle, in close proximity to her in case she'd need it real quick. And though she was always on watch for other travelers on the road – or worse, the men she was running from – Martha was enjoying traveling and living on her own.

Granted, Martha had been on her own ever since she was nineteen when her father had passed away, leaving her a small ranch in Wisconsin. After selling all the cattle, Martha had taken work as a waitress at a small restaurant, enjoying the social aspect, though she disliked smelling like food all the time. And with it being a small town, Martha knew everyone, and knew that there were no eligible gentlemen in the area. That was probably why she fell so hard and fast for Jared.

He had been like a breath of fresh air in an old, dusty town. He came in for a local rodeo and quickly won her heart with the sweet nothings he whispered in her hair as he held her, promising a better future as his wife, a life on the road as they went to rodeo after rodeo. It sounded like an exciting life to Martha, who saw no future of her own. And it didn't hurt that Jared was a handsome man with light blond hair, sparkling blue eyes, and a body like a god. Martha had been shown many aspects of Jared's body, and had become intent on marrying him. And though he had shown her passion like she had never known, with his steamy kisses and the gentleness with which he made love to her, Martha now knew that it had all been a ploy to destroy her.

She pushed the disturbing thoughts from her mind as a town appeared on the horizon. She urged her mare into a canter, intent on making it to the next inn before dark. Having passed into Montana a few days ago, she worried less about being found by her ex-fiancé and the devil of a man he'd sold her to, and started to think more about her future. She was tainted in terms of marrying material. She'd be considered "spoiled goods" to any gentlemen. So she was intent on reinventing herself and getting away from the bad memories of her past.

Martha approached the town of Helena and found it to be a bustling place. She'd never seen a place so big and was thrilled with the possibilities this town could hold for her. She felt her confidence return to her as she rode down the main street at a trot, looking at all the shops and stores in the setting sun and finding the local inn easy enough. With her mare, which she'd named Chestnut after its coloring, situated in the local livery stable, Martha took her saddlebags towards the inn.

"Good evening, my dear. How can I help you?" asked a young gentleman when she entered the inn and approached the check-in counter. He was tall, with light brown hair and deep blue eyes. Though he appeared charming, he was the type of man Martha now stayed away from. And by the way his eyes roamed over her figure, she knew she'd have to be as lacking in charm as possible in order not to give this guy the wrong idea about her.

"I'm looking for a room to rent for the night. I'll be wanting a hot bath and dinner to be brought to my room," Martha said sternly, with little warmth in her voice as she narrowed her eyes at the man.

The man seemed startled by her reply and stammered, "Certainly. Can I get a name for the reservation?"

"No," Martha replied with little hesitation.

"Oh, I see," the man stammered again, trying to figure out how a woman as beautiful as she could be so cold and demanding. Yet the man recognized the type: this was a woman who was running from something. "I have a room upstairs and could have our housekeeper assist with the bath and dinner."

"I'll take it," Martha replied in turn, looking forward to setting down her saddlebags and being able to unbraid her long hair. When the man told her the total cost, Martha fished out a few bills and passed them across, causing the man to raise his eyebrows. "That's for the room and your discretion," she explained as she took the key and made her way upstairs without a look over her shoulder.

As soon as she was in her room, a pleasant and clean space with a connecting water-closet, she dropped her bags on the ground near the four-poster bed and started pulling her hair from the long braid. Though the braid made it more comfortable for riding, she often preferred her hair down and flowing freely. Just as she was done with her hair, a knock came at the door. With an eye on the saddlebag that held her pistol, she moved towards the door.

"Who is it?" Martha called through the door.

"Cynthia, ma'am. I've brought you a dinner plate," called a woman from the other side of the door.

Martha unlocked the door and opened it a crack, confirmed that Cynthia was who she said she was and that she was alone, and then opened the door all the way to let the woman in. Cynthia was an older woman, her hair pulled back into a tight bun, most likely the most comfortable arrangement for her type of work, and set the plate on a nearby table. The aroma alone made Martha's stomach rumble.

"I'll let you enjoy that for a bit, and then I'll have Freddy, my nephew, bring up the tub. I'll have hot water along in no time." Cynthia chatted away, her kind eyes putting Martha at ease.

"Thank you, Cynthia," Martha replied in kind, sitting down next to the table, her mouth watering at the sight of fried chicken steak and mashed potatoes. Riding all day always made her hungry, especially when dinner was her largest meal of the day, and being alone, she rarely worried about table manners, despite the way she'd been raised.

"My pleasure, my dear. I've also brought the daily paper in case you fancy something to read," Cynthia said as she set the paper down next to the plate of food, before leaving the room.

Martha rose swiftly and locked the door, then sat again to devour her food. The taste was divine for such a simple dish, or perhaps she'd simply been that hungry. After she'd finished and wiped her mouth and hands, she turned to the newspaper, happy to have something to do till Cynthia and her nephew returned with a tub.

She flipped through the pages, noting the local crime reports and pleased to see that things seemed calm around the area. She read through a few ads for employment, but found nothing that suited her, which was fine for the moment since she still had quite a stash of money to tide her over. With a smirk on her full lips, she then read over the mail-order bride ads. She always found them amusing – and sometimes sad, when an ad sounded desperate.

As Martha glanced through the paper, she couldn't deny that a certain mail-order bride ad had caught her eye. The author was an older gentleman, a ranch hand who lived in what sounded like a quiet town called Spruce Valley. Martha smiled at the description of the man. "I look better in person," the ad read. Martha was curious to know why a man with stable employment and good humor hadn't found a wife already. She wasn't about to give her heart to someone again, but perhaps someone to live with, someone who could offer her protection, would be worth marrying in any case. She'd certainly not make the mistake of falling in love. She couldn't risk that kind of heartache again.

Though Martha had never heard of Spruce Valley, the fact that the town was in Montana seemed like fate had dealt her a good hand. Surely, she couldn't be that far away. When a knock came at the door again, and she was able to confirm the identity of two on the other side, she allowed Cynthia to enter along with her nephew, Freddy, who carried the tub with little effort. But despite his good looks, and obvious strength, Martha didn't have eyes for him at all, which seemed to please Cynthia. And once the older woman had the tub filled, she left Martha alone once again, saying they'd return in a bit to remove the tub.

After ridding herself of the riding dress, petticoat, shift, and boots, Martha slowly eased herself into the hot water, letting out a soft sigh. The water helped her sore muscles relax, which was much needed after several days of riding. She took the time to wash her hair, ridding herself of the grime of the road. She felt pleasantly clean by the time the water started to cool.

As she soaked in the tub, her mind drifted back to the mail-order bride ad. She thought of what the author might look like, what the body of an older gentleman of forty-five would look like after working so many years as a ranch hand, helping to raise cattle for his employer. After daydreaming about the author's features, Martha pushed the fantasy out of her mind. She instead focused on the logical aspects of such a match. Protection, security, a decent income … yes, these were the only sensible aspects of marriage, because she knew from experience that true love didn't exist.

As Martha got out of the tub and dressed in an evening gown, not quite ready for bed, she found writing paper in a nearby desk and started penning a response to the ad. Surely it wouldn't hurt to write back and perhaps secure some sort of decent future for herself. Not wanting to ever be discovered by her past, she signed her letter Mary Carter instead of Martha Walters. Indeed, the Martha of the past was truly dead. Now she could be whomever she wanted, as long as it allowed the demons of her past to stay there.

When Cynthia and Freddy came to collect the tub and dump the water, Martha handed Cynthia the letter, along with a bill, asking for it to be posted first thing in the morning. Cynthia had the same reaction as the young man downstairs who had checked her in. Her eyes grew large and she nodded her head several times.

"Yes, ma'am, I'll make sure this gets posted at sunrise,"

Cynthia said with a curtsey before leaving the room. Martha smiled as she locked the door for the last time tonight. She was happy to surprise these people with the large tips she gave them. She felt like she was doing some good with a horrible man's money.

With nothing left to do, she readied herself for bed and brought the newspaper with her as she blew out the lanterns in the room and got under the comforter. She spent some time outlining the ad with her finger, and memorizing the words. She silently prayed that this Gray Jenkins would turn out to be her savior from the horrors of her past. Or at least provide her with a better future.

## CHAPTER 4

"Gray!" Sam called from the parlor as soon as the man walked through the doorway for the evening report.

"I'm coming, I'm coming," responded Gray as he hung up his duster by the door before strolling into the parlor, sitting in his favorite wing-back chair by the fireplace, removing his pipe from his pocket and preparing it for an evening smoke.

"You know, I don't think I like the idea of you smoking in the house with Lucy expecting," Sam said casually, looking at the ranch hand that was in many other ways very gentleman-like.

Gray gave Sam a curious look as he lit his pipe, took a long draw, and let out the smoke. "And why is that, Sam?" he asked, his brows knitted together.

"Well, you know. The smoke isn't good for the baby," Sam reasoned.

This made Gray chuckle as he pointed the pipe at Sam. "My friend, I'm not blowing smoke right into Lucy's or the baby's face. Lucy isn't even in the room," Gray countered, rolling his eyes at the thought of how protective Sam had become of Lucy ever since he confirmed she was expecting. His retort caused Sam to cross his arms in annoyance.

"Fine. But I hope this lady doesn't mind that you smoke," Sam said, changing the subject as he withdrew a letter from his suit pocket and handed it to Gray. The older man puzzled at what Sam was referring to as he took the letter and analyzed the elegant hand in which the letter was addressed to him.

Gray didn't know what to think of the letter. First, he was surprised that someone had actually written to him. Second, the address came from the inn at Helena. It made him wonder what the woman had written about, and if this woman was someone he had been with before. He'd been with plenty of women, from Spruce Valley to Helena, and wondered if someone he had been with had recognized his name from the paper and had decided to try to play husband and wife with him.

"Well, aren't you going to open it?" Sam pushed, as curious as Gray about what the letter contained. Gray ignored him for a minute as he took off his cowboy hat, set it aside, and ran his fingers through his hair.

"It's addressed from Helena," Gray started, flipping the letter over and then back again as he looked at the delicate way the letters had been written.

"I did see that. I didn't think your ad would run this close to town," Sam said, seeing how this could be a possible disaster given Gray's womanizing ways in the round-about areas.

"Nor did I. What if it's from someone I know?" Gray wondered out loud as he placed his pipe in his mouth and used both hands to open the letter carefully.

"Only one way to find out," Sam said as he moved forward on his chair.

Gray finished opening the envelope and pulled out two sheets of writing paper.

*Dear Gray,*

*I hope you don't mind my informal greeting. I figure since this isn't a business letter, I didn't need to be so formal. My name is Mary, and I'm not originally from Helena. I originate from a boring, small town in Wisconsin that I put behind me earlier this year in pursuit of something a little more exciting than a life as a waitress at a stinky restaurant. I love cooking food, I just hate smelling like it.*

*I've been travelling on the road these past four weeks, trying to find a new place to settle down and grow some roots. I found your ad in the paper and decided it wouldn't hurt to write since it seems that Spruce Valley isn't that far from Helena, and I figured it could be a decent place to check out. Though, as your ad stated, Spruce Valley is also a little town, I've come to find that any new place is a lot more exciting than the place I used to live. And with no family left, I'm free to roam and go wherever I'd like. However, travelling on the road can get very tiring after a while, and I look forward to being settled once again.*

*To give you an idea of what I look like, I have what they call an hourglass body. My hair is auburn, and very long. My eyes are blue, and I've been told are quite bright in the sunlight. I have a mare whom I've named Chestnut, who seems to enjoy being on the open road and has been a great companion these past few weeks.*

*I'm competent in all things domestic and would make any man a good wife, but I'm looking for someone who is more mature and knows what they want in life. Though I'm twenty-nine, I'm not worried about our age difference in any aspect. As a ranch hand, I'm sure you're fit enough to take on a woman like me.*

*Well, that's enough of that. If this letter interests you at all, reply. Whether or not it leads to anything, I plan to stop through Spruce Valley in a few days just to see what it's like.*

*Sincerely,*
*Mary Carter*

GRAY SMILED as he folded the letter back up and tucked it into his jean pocket, turning his attention back to his pipe. Sam looked at him from the edge of his seat, clearly on tenterhooks. This made Gray smile even wider as he let out a puff of smoke.

"Come on, man. What did the letter say?" Sam demanded, though careful not to raise his voice too loud to disturb Lucy in the other room. She'd come down with a headache and he didn't want to wake her with his outburst. But he was dying to know what was in the letter.

"I don't think Mary would appreciate it if I shared all her details with another man. But either way, I'm sure you'll get to meet her soon," Gray responded cryptically, enjoying torturing his employer.

"What? What does that mean?" Sam said, wanting to throttle the man. "At least tell me something about her."

Gray thought about it for a moment, taking his pipe out of his mouth and tapping the contents onto a nearby ashtray that Sam kept just for him. "She has a mare named Chestnut," he settled for, smiling wickedly as he stood.

"For Pete's sake, that's not what I meant," Sam protested, crossing his arms and leaning back into his chair like a scolded child.

"That I know, my good chap. Now, if you don't mind, I

have a letter to write to Miss Mary," Gray said as he stood, donned his hat, and made his way towards the front door.

"But what about the evening report?" Sam called. The only response he got was the sound of the front door shutting, and Lucy calling down the hallway for him to stop shouting. With a heavy sigh, Sam stood and made his way to the bedroom and his wife. He was intent to rid her of her headache and tease her about Gray's letter from this Miss Mary. Sam knew that what little information he had been able to get from Gray, his wife would learn tomorrow after breakfast.

# CHAPTER 5

"Calvin' time is right round the corner," Jensen said the next day between bites of lunch. The men were seated on the front porch of the ranch house, eating sandwiches that Lucy had prepared, along with fresh lemonade.

"I agree, Jensen. I feel like any day now it will be a round-the-clock watch on the herd," Gray agreed before taking a long sip of his drink. He wanted to get back out in the pasture and start counting how many cows were currently expecting, and then meet up with Drake and Robert, the shepherds down the road, and see how many extra hands they were going to need this season with the newborn lambs.

"Sounds like ye fellows are going to be extra busy these next few weeks," Lucy piped up as she came onto the porch and offered them some oatmeal cookies she'd made that morning. Lucy seemed to be craving the sweet treat, since she'd made some every day that week.

"Right ye be, bonnie lass," Gray said, imitating Lucy's

accent. Though she didn't look it, Lucy was Irish through and through, but her accent had diminished over the years.

"That will be quite enough of that, my good sir," Lucy replied, giving Gray a taste of his own medicine. Tom and Jensen laughed at the bantering before thanking Lucy for the meal and heading back out towards the pasture.

Gray got up to follow them, but Lucy asked, "Are ye going to tell me about her?"

Gray sighed heavily as he put on his grey hat. He should have assumed Sam would say something to his wife. Gray fixed his onyx eyes on Lucy, standing well above her, as he said, "Only if you do me a favor first."

Lucy smirked as she crossed her arms over her chest. "And what kind of favor are ye asking of me?"

Gray shrugged his shoulders, trying to act casual about it all. "If you take my letter into town and have it posted, I'll tell you the little I know about Mary during supper," he offered, his smile growing as he watched Lucy roll his eyes at him.

"We have a deal, ya bloke," Lucy responded, flashing her eyes at Gray as though she'd gotten the better end of the deal. Little did he know that Lucy already had plans to go into town and get more baking supplies. She also wanted to take some cookies to Greta to thank her for her help during the beginning of her pregnancy.

Gray chuckled as he handed Lucy the letter he'd written last night in his bunkroom. And with that he stepped off the porch and made his way towards his horse, intent on finishing his tasks before super. He also wanted a distraction from thinking too much about Mary. He had so many questions and was hoping to soon get some answers, either through their correspondence, or perhaps in person.

Lucy looked over the letter as she readied herself to go.

Tom had already promised to have the buggy ready for her, so all she needed was her beaded drawstring purse and grocery basket before she was set. She wished she could open and reseal the letter so she could learn what Gray had written to this mysterious Mary. Lucy could only hope that Mary was someone who could do Gray some good, provide him the type of happiness she'd found with Sam. With that happy thought she set out towards the barn, Gray's letter safely tucked in her basket.

*Dear Mary,*

*Thank you for your letter. I found it both interesting and amusing, and I'm glad you already feel comfortable being less formal in our letters. I can imagine you riding the open roads, your auburn hair glowing in the spring sunshine like a beacon. I'm sure when you come to Spruce Valley, you won't be hard to spot. When we meet, you'll be able to hear my British accent, something I could never hide even if I tried to.*

*I'm glad to read that you don't particularly mind our age difference. Let me reassure you that I'm quite fit and able for my age. With that being stated, I want you to know a bit more about myself than a simple ad could describe. Everyone who knows me can tell you I'm charming, humorous, and, quite frankly, was a womanizer. The last bit I used to be proud of, but now that my life has progressed and I've seen the way Sam and Lucy are happy together as a married couple, I've learned that there is more in life than just a warm body to hold at night.*

*I know the best way to form a business relationship is with complete honesty, and I'm sure that it works the same way with a romantic relationship. I want to be completely honest with you as we move forward. I'm a great romancer, but have little experience in the relationship department. However, I'm a very committed man and would never cheat on you if we started courting. I might have a tainted past, but I've always been a gentleman.*

*Now I have some questions for you. I find it interesting that you've been roaming these past few weeks, and though you've stated you're just looking for a new start, that usually means something happened in the past to cause a person to leave what was familiar. I don't mean to pressure you by reading between the lines, but let's just say that with age comes wisdom. I've done my share of roaming and know what it's like. Let me just add that you can tell me when you're ready.*

*I look forward to meeting you, Mary, and getting to know each other. Because frankly, you can only learn so much about a person through letters. Let me know when you'll be passing through town and I'll come to meet you, and even invite you out to the ranch to meet everyone. Calving season is approaching, and I'll be extremely busy keeping an eye on the herd in case any of the cows are going to need assistance with the birthing. It's quite a special time of year, to be honest.*

*Well, that's enough for now. Till next time,*
*Gray*

MARTHA READ and reread the letter a handful of times before setting it aside on the table in her hotel room. Her emotions ran the gauntlet as she thought of what Gray had stated. He sounded charming and alluring in his description of her and in the fact that he had a British accent. When he wrote about his past with women, it made her stomach clench. She didn't want to end up with someone who was going to be with other women behind her back. But she figured that might be the case if she was never able to give her heart completely over to a husband. And then, when Gray hinted at the real reason behind her travels these past few weeks, she knew that he was a very intelligent man.

At first Martha didn't know quite what to do about his letter. She was intrigued by Gray, for sure, but would he understand her past as much as he was expecting she'd accept his? It seemed that if he was going to be open and honest with her, then she should be the same with him. What she knew for sure was that this wasn't something to discuss in a letter. And with Gray giving her the opportunity to talk to him about her past when she was ready, she felt less pressured.

Martha picked up the cup of tea she'd had delivered to her room after lunch and took a sip, already thinking about her response to Gray. She was enjoying the lemon tea when a strange feeling took her. She set the teacup aside and rested her hand on her stomach, worried that her lunch wasn't settling well with her. And when the pain became unbearable, she stood and moved quickly to the water closet, her stomach contents coming back up again. After a few minutes, Martha washed her face and walked slowly back to her chair, hoping the sickness would leave her. She started to think that it was time to move on.

After pausing here for a few days, she was itching to get back on the road. She'd spent the last week cooped up in the hotel room, not wanting to be spotted by anyone who might know Jared or Max. She had gone to the general store very early in the morning, just to stock up on some necessities she'd need while travelling; but she'd taken all of her meals in her room, and now she was feeling a little antsy.

Moving over to the writing desk, Martha pushed back

her long auburn hair, which she'd allowed to flow freely when she was alone in her room. There was no need to put it up when she had no plans to socialize with anyone. Taking out a sheet of writing paper, she began constructing her response to Gray. Within an hour of posting it, she planned to make her final arrangements to get back onto the road. And by the time she arrived in Spruce Valley, Gray would have received her letter, no doubt.

"Time to take a chance on a better future." Martha spoke to herself as she began writing. Though she felt bad for using a false name when Gray had been so honest about his past, Martha was at least confident that she would tell Gray the whole truth about herself before they tied the knot. Her stomach fluttered at the idea of being married before the end of the year, but she knew that anything was better than being sold as a slave to be a saloon girl.

Martha managed to finish the letter before her nerves got the better of her. The moment it was sealed, she made her way down to the front counter to have it posted and to announce that she was leaving the inn.

"You'll be sorely missed," the young man replied on hearing Martha's announcement.

"How can I be, when I was never here?" Martha replied with a wink.

"Of course, miss," the man said with a nod of his head.

And with that she returned to her room, changed from her day gown into her riding clothes, making sure to braid her hair for the journey, and gathered her saddlebags to make the trip to the livery stable to collect Chestnut.

The moment Martha was on the open road again, heading to Spruce Valley having received directions from the stable boy, she finally felt like she was able to relax. Away from the town, and the increased population, she felt free and in control of her life.

"Spruce Valley, here I come!" Martha called to the wind, the sweet smell of spring on the air as the wind whipped by her as Chestnut galloped down the road. The sun was still high in the sky, and she knew that by the time the day ended she'd be closer to hopefully settling down for good.

# CHAPTER 6

Scruffy barked as he noticed a familiar rider coming up the lane to the homestead. He barked a few times and ran over to his owner, Drake, letting him know that they had company. After taking Sam up on his offer, Drake had remained on his late father's property, turning what was once a shepherd's shed into a decent homestead. Now Drake looked after a decent-size herd of sheep with Scruffy, assisted by his younger brother, Robert, and his sheepdog, Monty.

"Good day, to you," Gray called as he neared the pasture where Drake and Robert stood carefully watching the flock, particularly a group of ewes that the sheepdogs had separated from the rest of the herd, no doubt keeping an eye on them just like he and the other ranch hands were keeping an eye on the cows for newborn calves.

"Hello, Gray," Drake said, approaching the pasture gate as Gray dismounted his horse and flipped the reins over the fence. Drake, the eldest, was a serious, taciturn young man, but he possessed keen intelligence and a kind heart. He and his brother were of mixed heritage, their father being a descendant of the Crow Indian tribe, not too far from town. It was their father, Ernie, who had taught Sam all there was about cattle drives, taking care of steers, and even a herd of sheep. It had allowed Sam to diversify his income when being a doctor alone couldn't pay the bills, and thankfully it had allowed Gray a stable job. Now both of Ernie's sons took care of the sheep operation while Gray focused solely on the steers.

"I've come to see how the lambing is coming along," Gray explained as he hopped the fence and joined the men in the pasture. Drake was impressed by Gray's agility for an older man. He smirked as he turned his eyes to the few lambs that had already been born.

"Things are good here. The weather is warmer than we expected, so the late nights are not so terrible. Sometimes March can be very bitter this time of year, making the birthing season that more difficult," Drake said, knowing that Gray would carry his message back to their employer.

"We are feeling the same way with the cows. But we know that it has just begun. Sam and I are wondering if you two will need any more assistance out here, especially at night," Gray stated, looking out over the sheep and glad he was only responsible for the steers. He couldn't imagine assisting in the birth of such small animals, especially when the sheep would need shearing soon after the lambing season was over.

"We have been taking turns." Robert spoke up. "And our sheepdogs do a good job of letting us know if any of the ewes are stressed out." Drake was the more softly spoken one, always getting straight to the point, whereas the younger brother Robert was more outspoken and a lot chattier. "Drake's been watching over the herd most of the night and I've just come to relieve him. I don't think we'll need any more help."

Drake regarded his brother for a second before turning his dark eyes back on Gray. "I agree with my little brother that at this time things are manageable. But we'll let you or Sam know if that changes," he said, his tone stern.

"I have no doubt of that, my dear fellow. Good luck to you, then. I best be getting back to the ranch. I don't mind leaving Tom to watch over things, but sometimes Jensen worries me," Gray admitted as he walked back to his horse, Drake following after him.

"Jensen is getting older. But with no family of his own I doubt he'll retire," Drake reasoned.

"I have the same fear," Gray replied, hopping back over the fence and mounting his horse. Gray gave Drake a nod, who grunted in return before he turned his horse back towards the lane that joined the main road. Gray was glad to hear that Drake and Robert were having no trouble with the sheep this year, but he wondered if he and Tom would be having difficulties with the new calves, especially since it was true that Jensen was just getting too old to be a ranch hand anymore.

By the time Gray had made the hour-long trip back to the ranch, the sun was already setting. Once he'd put his horse away in the stable, having brushed the stallion down and filled his food bag, Gray made his way towards the ranch house, hoping that dinner was still in full swing.

"Well, it's about time you showed up," Sam said good-heartedly as Gray came through the door, hung up his duster, and pulled off his hat, setting it on the peg over his duster.

"The work never seems to end at this time of year," Gray retorted, and sat down next to Tom at the dinner table, quick to fill his plate with the pot roast Lucy had made. "Looks amazing as always, Lucy."

"Thank you, Gray," Lucy replied in kind. Gray couldn't help but smirk when he noticed an oatmeal cookie beside Lucy's plate.

"How are Drake and Robert holding up?" Sam asked once Gray got settled at the table.

"They seem to be doing just fine. When I told them about the offer of an extra hand, they declined. It seems those two are just like their father. I'm sure glad Drake took up your offer instead of heading out to California to chase some gold-digger's dream," Gray said before taking a few large bites of his food. He was famished, but knew he still had a long night ahead of him.

"I agree with you one hundred percent on that. I wouldn't have known what to do if Drake had decided to leave last August like he intended to. And the fact that his brother has joined him with watching over the sheep – why, I feel quite lucky that fate has dealt us such a good hand," Sam said as he reached over and squeezed Lucy's hand. She smiled back at him before pushing her plate away and eating the cookie. Gray dared not comment on it since he didn't want to hurt Lucy's feelings, but he couldn't help but smile at the scene.

"What's got you all smiles over there, young man?" Jensen said, seeming to catch on to what Gray saw and looking for a way to poke fun at him, as he often did.

"Oh, just thinking of boss man and his misses. What a great pair they make," Gray quipped, not willing to take Jensen's bait tonight. Jensen rolled his eyes as he turned his attention back to his food.

"That's so sweet of ye, Gray," Lucy said, tears in her eyes as her emotions started to get the better of her. At this point Gray was trying to contain the bubble of laughter that was threatening to spill over. "I know that before too long you'll have a special someone in yer life, too," she added.

Gray just nodded his head, unable to speak, but his mirth was immediately squelched when Jensen stood and quickly left the ranch house, not bothering to take his plate to the sink as was his custom. Gray watched him go and then sighed, guessing what was irritating the old man.

"What's got into him?" Sam asked, standing to go after the older man. Gray raised his hand to stop him.

"Sometimes Jensen gets like this, especially during the calving season," Gray explained as Sam sat back down at the table. "Jensen has no family of his own. No wife. No children. Don't think he's not happy for you and Lucy, because he is. But I'm sure sometimes he regrets not going after a wife like he has steers all these years. Cattle drives is all Jensen knows, and I'm sure he wished he knew about the other fine things in life as well as a good day's work." It wasn't hard for Gray to say these things, for he felt the exact same way. There was silence around the table as everyone reflected on this.

Eventually Tom got up from the table and bade the others a good evening, saying he was going to go watch over the herd tonight. Gray just nodded his head in agreement, knowing he'd relieve him in a few hours. Gray now took the opportunity to speak to his employer about what Drake had spoken about earlier.

"Though Drake and Robert are doing fine this lambing season, I think it wouldn't hurt to hire another ranch hand for the steers. I'm afraid Jensen isn't cut out for this type of work anymore. He can't assist with the birthing, and he can't stay up all night like he used to. I'm not saying let him go, because God knows that man has nowhere else to go. But it might be time we started looking for someone else to help out around here," he said in all seriousness.

Sam let out a deep sigh as he looked over at Lucy, knowing that Gray spoke the truth. He was sure the re-evaluation was going to pull at Lucy's heart-strings, and he could see the tears in her eyes. Lucy pushed back a lock of her black hair, trying to hide the fact that she was rubbing the tears from her eyes.

"I can talk to Josh about it in the morning. I'm sure the Sheriff will have a recommendation for us. I would hire Grant again if he hadn't taken up the position of assistant deputy, but I'll have to think of someone else," Sam said as he started thinking about who might be able to help out, if only temporarily. He could check in with one of the Murtaugh brothers, Eddie and Sawyer, and see if either one of them were in need of a job. The brothers often acted as deputies for Josh, but now that the Sheriff had a full-time deputy, Sam wasn't sure what the brothers were up to nowadays.

"I'll leave that to you, boss," Gray said as he rose from the table. He took the dishes to the sink, bade the couple a good night, and putting back on his coat and hat, made his way out to the bunkhouse.

Gray wasn't surprised when he entered the building to see darkness behind Jensen's door. He was sure the old man wanted to be left alone. Gray went to the lantern hanging in the common room and blew it out before making his way to his own room. Stripping down to his long underwear, he fell into bed, knowing that a few hours of sleep would do him good and help him make it through another night. Though he hoped that Sam could hire another ranch hand before too long, Gray's mind was now filled more with thoughts of Mary.

He knew it wouldn't be too long before they actually met in person. He felt reaffirmed in placing a mail-order bride ad after watching Jensen this evening, when the other man's bitterness got the best of him. Gray knew that Mary might be his only shot at finding a wife since he hadn't received any other letters, which wasn't surprising considering his age. But after telling Mary about his past with women … he only hoped he hadn't scared her away.

Gray sighed, closing his eyes tight, and praying that some day he'd be as lucky as Sam when it came to finding a great wife.

# CHAPTER 7

After the two-day ride to Spruce Valley, thankfully with no more sickness, Martha was excited to see what the little town was all about. Leading Chestnut down the main road at a slow walk, she eagerly looked around. There were a few establishments that lined the main road, the largest being Frost's Mercantile, according to the sign that hung out over the front porch. Martha led her horse over to this establishment, curious to see what she'd find inside.

Stepping in through the front door, Martha took her time looking over the goods, pleasantly surprised to find the store both very tidy and containing a large variety of items she wouldn't have expected in a small town. It was undeniably a lot better than the little store she was used to back in Wisconsin.

"Can I help you look for anything?" a large, middle-aged man with graying dark hair asked as he approached her.

"No, sir. Just looking. But I do smell something rather heavenly," Martha said as she looked past the man to what seemed to be a small restaurant at the back of the store.

"Indeed, and you'll find more than one thing delicious at the Eatery. Emmet and Ella are great cooks, and Nell's a fantastic waitress. You can't go wrong," the man enthused, seeming very pleasant.

"Why, I do appreciate the recommendation, Mr …?"

"Frost, and this is Frost's Mercantile, which I manage with my wife," the man explained. "And you might be?"

Martha couldn't help but smile at Mr. Frost's way of turning the conversation back to her. "My name is Mary Carter," she said slowly, the name still unfamiliar to her tongue. "I've just arrived from Helena and I'm quite famished."

Mr. Frost regarded the young lady, her beautiful auburn hair done back in a simple braid, allowing her bright blue eyes to shine without hindrance. Mr. Frost couldn't remember seeing her before, and since he knew all the families in the area he was quite curious about Miss Carter's sudden appearance.

"And what brings you to the little town of Spring Valley? I hadn't realized that the stagecoach had already run today," Mr. Frost said as he gazed out the window. His shop also served as the local depot, so he was always the first in town to meet newcomers.

"I rode in on my mare, actually," Mary explained with great confidence. She pointed to Chestnut outside, her reins wrapped around the fence post.

"My goodness, I've never heard of a lady travelling that far on her own," Mr. Frost exclaimed.

"Fear not, good sir. I'm hoping to make Spruce Valley my new home. There is a certain gentleman I've been corresponding with that I also hope might become my husband," Martha said in a soft tone, giving Mr. Frost a wink.

Mr. Frost chuckled, as he understood Martha's reasoning. "A mail-order bride, then?" he said, to which Martha nodded in reply. "Well, then, let me be the first to welcome you to Spruce Valley. Perhaps I could give you directions so you can go meet your intended?"

"Perhaps," Martha replied simply as she gave the man a smile before moving past him to the restaurant. She wasn't about to give away such sensitive information, since she wasn't even sure that her letter to Gray had arrived yet. She didn't want anyone knowing she was here to meet him and perhaps tip him off that she'd arrived. No, she'd rather he came to her.

Martha settled down at an empty table, pleased to see that the restaurant wasn't too busy. A woman who she could only assume was Nell approached the table. "What can I get you, my dear?" she asked as she handed Martha a menu.

"Could I start out with a cup of tea?" Martha asked as she opened up the menu.

"Certainly," Nell said, and turned from the table. It appeared to Martha that Nell wasn't the most social, and after her own years of experience working as a waitress, she knew that personality was a big part of the job. She also didn't bother looking over the menu, intent as she was on getting Nell's recommendation because the waitress always knew what was best.

Martha gazed around the room looking at the other patrons. She never felt uncomfortable eating in a new place because she never stayed in one town or another for very long; but since she hoped to make Spruce Valley her new home, she couldn't help but feel curiosity about the other patrons. Surely after a while she'd come to know everyone in town, much like she had when she was a waitress in Wisconsin. She watched those around her, trying to imagine what their stories were.

When Nell returned with a teapot and cup, Martha was impressed by her pouring of the tea, which seemed to be quite a ritual. "Your tea-pouring skills are quite impressive," Martha commented as she picked up the cup of tea, taking a small sip.

A smile came to Nell's face as she regarded the new girl. She'd never seen the woman before and was curious about her. It was rare that ladies came to dine at the Eatery alone. "Thank you, ma'am. Now, do you know what you want to eat?" she asked.

"What would you recommend?" Martha asked, delighted by the taste of the tea; it was perhaps the finest cup of tea she'd had in as long as she could remember. Martha could imagine herself coming to the Eatery for the tea alone.

Nell seemed pleased by Martha's question, given the way she smiled enthusiastically. It was like a new person had magically appeared in Nell's place. Martha could instantly tell that Nell appreciated being asked for once, instead of told. "Well, Emmet made an excellent meatloaf today that I would highly recommend. And Ella baked a fresh apple pie this morning. It smells heavenly back there," Nell enthused.

"Well, then, that's what I'll have. Thank you," Martha replied.

Nell stuck out her hand. "My name's Nell," she said.

Martha returned the woman's gesture, shaking her hand. "Mary Carter, pleased to meet you."

"The pleasure's mine," Nell replied, and then hurried away to place her order. Martha smiled as she sipped her tea, glad to have met two new people in such a short time since arriving in Spruce Valley.

By the time Nell had returned with a plate of meatloaf and mashed potatoes, paired with a small plate of pie, Martha was quite famished. Trying her best to be ladylike, she dug into her food, not evening noticing that someone had taken a seat at the table next to her and was watching her with amusement. It wasn't until the young man cleared his throat that Martha looked up and realized she was being watched.

"I beg your pardon," she said as she picked up the napkin and dabbed her full lips. "I didn't know I had an audience."

"Was my fault. I shouldn't have been staring," the man replied with a smile. Martha observed the man for a moment as she took another sip of her tea. He had rather sharp features, and his warm brown eyes held intelligence. She then noticed the lawman's badge pinned to the front of his western vest and could only assume the man was either a deputy or the sheriff himself.

"It's rude to stare, you know," Martha replied, taking a bite of the apple pie and closing her eyes for a moment as she enjoyed the sweet taste. But this only caused the young man to laugh at her. She narrowed her eyes at him then, being rather put out by having her meal interrupted.

"I'm so sorry," he said as his mirth subsided. "You're quite right about me staring, but it's not to often that Spruce Valley sees any new young women in town. I was simply curious, and then amused that someone as petite as yourself could eat that much."

"I don't know if I should be offended or take that as a compliment," Martha replied as she turned her focus back on her pie, trying to enjoy the rest of her meal.

"Sheriff Josh Ryder, at your service, ma'am," the man finally came out with. He tipped his Stetson towards her and she nodded in return.

"Mary Carver," Martha replied, becoming accustomed to the new name.

"Well, Miss Carver, what brings you to this fine little town?" the Sheriff asked. Martha figured it was only his job that caused him to be so curious and nosey, and therefore she couldn't fault him for that. After all, it wouldn't hurt to befriend the local Sheriff if she did run into trouble in the future.

"I'm looking to start fresh in a new town, and I've been corresponding with a possible husband-to-be," Martha explained, finally finishing her pie.

The Sheriff's brows rose at this news, followed by him leaning forward and whispering, "And who might the lucky fellow be?"

Martha couldn't help but chuckle and lean forward as well, whispering back, "You'll have to wait and find out." The look on the Sheriff's face made her laugh: he was obviously put off by her response.

Nell came by then and took the Sheriff's order as Martha laid a few bills on the table, knowing it would cover the cost of the food and then some. Martha stood and nodded towards the Sheriff before she made her way out of the restaurant, waving at Mr. Frost as she left the general store. Her next goal was to find the local inn and get some rest, the great meal already causing her to feel exhausted.

~

As Josh watched the young lady with fiery auburn hair leave the Eatery, he couldn't help but think that whoever the man was who was going to be her husband was a very lucky man. Mary was beautiful, for sure, with her shapely figure, her piercing blue eyes, and a look about her that just seemed wild. And the witty way in which she spoke to him made him tingle all over. He couldn't wait to meet a woman like her one day.

While Josh was enjoying his food and speaking with some of the locals who had come in for lunch as well, he was pleased to see Dr. Sam Slater come into the Eatery. Josh wanted to discuss the matter with someone who might know which men in town were currently looking for a mail-order bride, and since Dr. Slater knew everyone in town, and was a close friend of his, he was certain Sam would know.

"Sam, come join me," Josh called out, waving his hand in Sam's direction.

"Thanks, Josh. How's the day going?" Sam asked as he took a seat at the Sheriff's table and quickly gave Nell his order, who went off to the kitchen without another word.

"It's been pleasantly quiet these last few days. But I have a feeling that might all be changing as I just met this fiery young lady a moment before you walked in. Did you notice her as you walked in." Josh asked, folding his arms over his chest as he watched for Sam's reaction – a habit of his.

"No, Josh, I didn't see who you were talking about. I just popped in for a quick bite to eat before I get back to the office. Mayor Delphine is coming in for her physical and I don't want to keep her waiting if I can avoid it," Sam explained.

"You're a smart man, Sam. I respect Mayor Delphine for everything she's done for this town, but she can get after you if she needs to, if you know what I mean," Josh said with a chuckle.

"That I do know," Sam replied.

"So, do you know any men around town who are currently writing to a mail-order bride? This Mary Carver explained that she was looking for a new start and had been writing to someone she called a 'possible husband-to-be'. That sounds like a mail-order bride to me," Josh said.

Sam choked on his glass of water as he listened to Josh. The Sheriff had to lean over and slap his friend's back a few times till the coughing subsided. "Did you say her name was Mary?" Sam asked as he wiped his mouth on a napkin.

"Yeah, she said her name was Mary Carver. Do you

know her?" Josh asked, knowing that Sam had met Lucy through letters.

"I don't know her, but I do know that Gray Jenkins has been writing to a Mary and said that we might be meeting her soon. Gray hasn't shared a whole bunch about her, but I didn't think she'd be arriving so soon. Gray didn't say anything about it," Sam explained as their food was served.

After he'd thanked Nell, Josh asked, "Do you think Gray even knows that Mary is in town?"

Sam shrugged as he dug in to his food. "If he doesn't, he will soon enough, I'm sure."

Josh just nodded his head in agreement, digging into his own food, loving the taste of the meatloaf. Josh wasn't much of a cook, so he often came to the Eatery to enjoy a good hot meal. As he ate, he thought about Mary, and why she might be looking for a new start. Surely the woman had some sort of past. And if she was willing to come all this way to marry Gray, someone Josh knew was much older than him and Sam, then surely Mary must be desperate. In any case, Josh thought Gray was a very lucky man.

# CHAPTER 8

Martha checked into the Honeywell Inn, having been welcomed warmly by Bill Eckert, the owner. The inn wasn't very large, with only four rooms to rent, but it was a neat and clean place with a decent-sized dining room, and Bill explained that her room had a water closet attached. Bill was very proud of this fact, enthusiastically talking about how his place was the only one in town that had indoor plumbing.

"I surely appreciate the consideration," was the only thing Martha could think to reply to this charismatic young man. Bill was tall and appeared to be a few years older than her. He had wavy brown hair that was parted to the side in a stylish way; his deep blue eyes were something a young lady could get lost in, and Martha wondered why this man, who ran a successful establishment, wasn't married yet.

"Certainly, Miss Carver. If you need anything, don't hesitate to come down and ask. My apartment is just down this hallway, and dinner will be served later this evening. Mrs. Royal will be by later this evening to check on you.

She's quite a friendly older woman, a widow, so don't be surprised if she talks a mile a minute," Bill explained as he handed Martha her room key. She found his character assessment amusing, considering how fast Bill was talking now.

"Thank you, Mr. Eckert," she replied as she picked up her saddlebags from where she'd placed them by her feet when she'd checked in, and now, with them slung over her shoulders, she made the journey upstairs and to her room at the end of the hallway.

Martha was pleased to find her room comfortable and clean. She dropped her bags at the end of the bed: a decent size for a small room. Martha peered into the water closet as she stretched her arms, glad she wouldn't have to walk to an outhouse to relieve herself in the middle of the night. This March had been thankfully warm, but she still didn't want to be outside at night in a new town. Anything could happen in a small town like this.

For the first time in a long time, Martha felt a sense of excitement in her. She knew that whether or not she hit things off with Gray she was going to stay in Spruce Valley. She settled into a wing-back chair near the window where she could look down on the main street. She thought about how long she'd been running, and since she hadn't run into anyone from her past in the past four weeks she was starting to believe that perhaps she didn't need to worry about her past any longer.

Martha turned her gaze towards her saddlebag with all the money in it, and the other with the pistol. Though she hadn't seen a bank yet, she knew she'd have to find a safe place for her things. Staying at the inn would be a temporary option until she could either find a small apartment to rent, or perhaps an empty house to buy. She started daydreaming about the type of house she would one day want when her eyes began drift shut, and soon she was snoring softly in the chair.

~

As soon as Sam finished with his patients for the day, he debated whether to run home and tell Gray about Mary, or head over to the Honeywell Inn, where she was no doubt staying, and inquire of her himself. Knowing that the second of the two choices would be too forward, and would possibly land him on Gray's bad side for butting into his personal business, Sam settled for preparing his horse, Atlas, for the journey home. Once he had Atlas out of town, he set the draft horse at a fast pace, eager to get home and share the news of what he'd discovered from the Sheriff.

When Sam arrived at his ranch, he was lucky to find Gray coming in from the pasture on his own horse, looking worn out. Sam followed him into the barn, intent on getting Atlas settled quickly in the hope of having a word with Gray before he went to get some rest in the bunkhouse.

"How's it going today?" Sam called as he followed the man out of the barn. It was obvious that Gray was in a hurry.

"Had to assist two cows, and it was a long and grueling process. I thought for sure I was going to lose a momma at one point, but she pulled through in the end," Gray said in a grave voice, obviously exhausted.

"Well, I think you should rest up for a few hours and then head into town for dinner. I hear Bill is making something special tonight at the inn," Sam said with a smile. Even though Gray was exhausted, he knew his foreman would perk up at this news.

"Until you get us another ranch hand, I won't be leaving till birthing season is over," Gray said with a direct look at

Sam as the man followed him into the bunkhouse, irritating him further.

"But what if I knew that a certain young lady by the name of Mary would be dining there tonight and would no doubt like some company from a certain fella?" Sam said, enjoying Gray's reaction as the man spun on his heels and looked at him with wide eyes.

"What do you mean? How do you know it's my Mary? Did you talk to her already?" Gray asked without taking a breath. He felt he had come alive again at the mention of the young woman.

Sam chuckled as he placed his hands on his hips. "I never thought I'd see you get this wound up over a woman, Gray."

"Enough jerking me around. Tell me what you know, dammit," Gray said, getting annoyed again.

"Calm down, man. All I know is that a woman had lunch at the Eatery today before I got there, and Josh introduced himself to her and she introduced herself as Mary Carver, saying she was new in town and had been writing letters to be a mail-order bride. I can only assume she's staying at the inn, and since she ate at the Eatery she probably won't be going there again tonight," Sam explained as Gray ran his fingers through his hair.

"That's a lot of assumptions considering you didn't talk to the girl yourself," Gray said as he started to pace the floor of the bunkhouse, unsure what his next move should be.

"Well, I know we've been stretched thin here, but I want you to take the night off. Get some sleep, then head into town. I'm sure I could help Tom and Jensen while you're away," Sam offered, the words coming out of his mouth before he had really thought about them.

"You? Help out at the ranch? No offence, Sam, but you'd

probably just get in the way," Gray said with a smirk, not believing what he'd just heard.

"I'm a ranch owner, I should know something about cattle and get some hands-on experience from time to time. I'll bring a chair out with me and Lucy can watch me mingle with the cattle. I'm sure she'll find it amusing," Sam said, wanting to include his wife. He was always keen to keep an eye on her since she was expecting.

"Have it your way, boss. I'm just glad to be having a night off. That, and I can't wait to hear about Tom and Jensen's reaction when you step out with them," Gray said as a rumble of laughter overtook him.

"Laugh all you want, Gray, but I bet I could surprise you," Sam said as he shook her head and left the bunkhouse. As the two men parted ways, Sam couldn't help but look forward to the experience, and the looks on everyone's faces when he explained to them what he was up to – and, equally important, what Gray would be up to this evening.

# CHAPTER 9

Martha was startled by the sound of someone knocking on the door. She was surprised to have fallen asleep in the chair and quickly smoothed back her hair, and, as she rose from the chair, her skirt, too, to look more presentable. Habit caused her to call to the person knocking, and when an older female voice replied, Martha cracked open the door.

"Hello, dear. I'm Mrs. Royal. But you can call me Greta. I have some lovely jasmine soap for you if you care to have a bath," the woman said. Martha smiled and let the woman – tall, thin, with green eyes – into her room.

"Thank you, Greta, that would be lovely," Martha said as she took the soap from the woman and shut the door behind her. Greta began fussing around the room, taking the saddlebags towards the wardrobe.

"Do you have anything that needs to be pressed or laundered?" Greta asked as she unclasped the first bag. When she peered into it, she let out a gasp. Martha looked up from where she'd set the bar of soap in the water closet, to see

Greta looking into the saddlebag that contained all her money. Martha moved swiftly towards the woman and took the bag from her as she watched Greta's face flush.

"I'm so sorry, ma'am. I'm just so used to helping young ladies get settled in, I didn't even think to ask," Greta said quickly. Martha knew there was no point in getting angry with the woman since she already seemed so embarrassed.

"Please, Greta, you did nothing wrong. Here, let me show you the dresses I have that could use a good wash," Martha said as she set the saddlebag in the wardrobe and turned Greta's attention to the bag that contained her few dresses. She hadn't travelled with much, intending to purchase what she needed once she settled down.

Martha spent the next few minutes unpacking her things with Greta. She couldn't remember the last time she had done so, and it felt divine to think that she soon would have a place of her own again where she could put away all her things and never have to worry about moving again. She felt more determined than ever to find a place of her own – and perhaps share it with someone like Gray. For now, though, she pushed the thought out of her head as she looked over her riding dress.

"I think I should get a new dress for tonight. I'm tired of wearing this riding dress, and since I'm giving you the rest of mine, I should probably find something a little more elegant for dinner," Martha said, looking towards Greta for her input.

"I think that's a grand idea, miss. Families often come to the Honeywell Inn to dine with the travelers. Bill is such a great cook that others come by just for dinner. You could try Frost's Mercantile to see if they have any ladies' wear in stock, although most ladies either need to sew their own dresses or order them from a catalogue," Greta explained.

Martha sighed, knowing that settling in a small town

would have some drawbacks. Her hometown did at least have a lady's boutique, and she wasn't sure what she'd find at a general store that doubled as a depot and restaurant.

"I think I'll go see what Mr. Frost has. Hopefully Mrs. Frost keeps a decent stock," Martha said hopefully.

"Good luck with your shopping," Greta said as she moved towards the door with the bundle of laundry in her hands.

"Greta," Martha called as she watched the woman open the door.

"Yes, miss?"

"I can count on you to keep what you saw a secret, correct?" Martha asked, wondering if she needed to keep the saddlebag on her person.

"Of course, miss!" Greta exclaimed. "No one will hear a word from me, you can count on that."

Martha nodded her head and gave the older woman a smile as the door shut. Alone once again, she took a few deep breaths before crossing the room to the wardrobe and pulling a few bills from the bag. She tucked them into her skirt pocket, and picking up the room key, left the room and locked it tightly behind her. This was the first time anyone had discovered how much money she was travelling with, and she really hoped that she could trust Greta. Saying a quick prayer, she left the inn and headed back to the mercantile.

~

"How about this one, dear?" Mrs. Frost asked as Martha looked at the small selection of gowns that were currently in stock. She had to admit that Mrs. Frost did have good taste and kept an elegant selection of gowns, as well as gowns for everyday use. But tonight Martha wanted to wear something besides riding clothes or a plain gown. She wanted to dress up for dinner and finally start feeling more herself again. Mrs. Frost held up a green satin dress with pretty lace designs sewn into the hem. "This one will surely enhance your features with that beautiful head of red hair."

Martha chuckled as she took the gown from the woman, a petite lady with long white hair, the kind that looked beautiful with age. Mrs. Frost had it done up in a chignon, which only seemed to make her more charming. "I think you're absolutely right, Mrs. Frost," Martha agreed as she held it over her body, thinking that it would be a close fit to her size. She wouldn't know, though, until she tried it on.

"I think it will be a pretty sweet deal, Sawyer," came the voice of a man. Martha looked down the aisle she was standing at the end of with Mrs. Frost. She saw two young men, both with light brown hair; the one she thought had spoken was taller than the other, while the slightly shorter one had overly broad shoulders.

"I don't know, Eddie. I like Sam and all, but you know how Gray is. Aren't you afraid of working for him? And what happens after calving season is over? We will be right back where we are now," the other said as he stopped and looked up at the taller man.

"Sawyer, it's not like there are many job options right now. Josh hired Grant as his full-time deputy for his background and experience, and the local farmers aren't going to need any additional help to harvest this season. We need to learn new skills if we are going to survive," the first man said, his voice soft, although where Martha and Mrs. Frost stood, they could easily hear the whole conversation.

"I'll take the gown, Mrs. Frost," Martha said as she handed it over to the woman.

"Perfect. I'll take it to the front counter and ring it up when you're ready," Mrs. Frost said before she moved away and headed back to the front of the store. Gathering her courage, Martha approached the two young men.

"Excuse me, gentlemen. I don't mean to eavesdrop, but I overheard you speaking about a man named Gray. Are you by chancing speaking of Gray Jenkins, of Slater's Ranch?"

The two stopped talking and turned their gaze towards her, both of them surprised that such a beautiful woman would be coming up to them. They both gave her a goofy smile that made Martha a tad uncomfortable. Perhaps she shouldn't be so friendly to strangers.

"Why, yes, miss. We're talking of Gray Jenkins. Certainly a fine young lady such as yourself wouldn't want anything to do with like a guy like Gray. This is my brother Sawyer, and I'm Eddie Murtaugh," Eddie said as he extended his hand towards her. She simply dipped her head, and Eddie quickly put her hand down.

"I am indeed curious about Mr. Jenkins and would care to understand your opinion," Martha replied, hoping to perhaps learn the true nature of Gray before she met the man. But the way these brothers were looking at her gave her the idea that perhaps she'd made a wrong choice there. She could practically feel Sawyer undressing her with his eyes.

"Well, I can say that many women are curious about Gray but never seem to stick with him very long, if you now what I mean. He's not the long-term relationship type, which is why he's an old, lonely man now. I'm sure I could give you more to be curious about," Eddie said as he winked at her.

Martha refrained from rolling her eyes as she turned to leave. When she felt a hand on her arm, she lashed out and slapped her assailant. She turned to see Eddie's surprised face as he held his hand up to where she'd slapped him. Sawyer gave her a quizzical look as he stared at her.

"Please, don't ever touch me again," Martha stuttered, and she left in a worry, paying Mrs. Frost for her dress without another word, and then making haste back to the inn.

Martha didn't stop to say hello to Bill at the front counter and practically ran up the stairs to her room, taking so long to unlock her door that she almost threw the key to the floor in frustration. Closing her eyes and taking a steadying breath, she finally unlocked the door and stepped inside, closing the door and locking it again before pocketing the key. She felt like crumbling to the ground, but made it to the bed where she laid out her new gown, and then slumped down into one of the chairs.

She took several minutes to steady her breathing as she thought about how she had reacted in the store. It was so natural to strike out that it frightened her to think she had acted so coldly. Surely if she had just told Eddie to remove his hand he would have done so, but she hadn't even thought about that. All she had thought was that she needed to escape the situation as quickly as possible.

"Get a hold of yourself, Martha," she chastised, knowing that she needed to bring her nerves under control. Deciding it would do her some good to take a nice long, hot bath before dinner, she rose and made her way back downstairs to order up the tub.

# CHAPTER 10

Gray pulled his horse back into a trot as he neared town. It had been a while since he'd made the trip, usually only coming in seeking a warm body for the night or a good time at Handy's, the local saloon. This time he was heading to the inn with hopes of meeting the woman he'd exchanged letters with. Gray wasn't yet sure how to feel about the idea of Mary, or what he'd learn about the woman once they met in person. Could she have lied about who she was? Perhaps this Mary wasn't even the one he'd been corresponding with, and the whole thing would be a huge misunderstanding.

Gray tried to get his emotions under control as he neared the inn, dismounted, and tied the reins to the hitching post out front. He could hear plenty of voices coming from inside as dinner seemed to be underway. Taking a deep breath, he put on his mask of emotions and went in.

Strolling in, Gray smiled as he neared the front counter, spotting Greta manning the counter. "Good evening, beautiful. How is my favorite widow this evening?" he asked.

"Oh, Gray, you charmer. What brings you to the inn tonight? Meeting some lady or another?" Greta said with a knowing smile.

"I'm sure hoping to, Mrs. Royal. I hear there's a young lady named Mary staying at the inn and might be dining in tonight?" Gray questioned, hoping Greta could either confirm or deny what Sam had told him.

Greta stilled as she thought of Mary, that young girl who looked so innocent and not Gray's usual type. Everyone knew that Gray was a womanizer and often older, lonely women flocked to him. She wasn't sure what intentions Gray had with the young woman she had met earlier. Feeling protective of the girl, Greta narrowed her eyes at Gray.

"And what would a bad guy like you want of a good girl like Mary?" Greta asked as she folded her arms over her bosom.

Gray smiled his charming smile as he leaned over the counter towards her. "It might be hard to believe, my dear, but Mary and I have been writing letters to each other. Mary is my mail-order bride," he said in a low voice, not wanting anyone to overhear them. Greta was clearly surprised, as she playfully slapped Gray's arm.

"Why would a man like you be interested in marriage? Not like that thought ever crossed your mind before," she replied, not believing a word he had just spoken.

"Well, you see, Mrs. Royal, you of all people would understand that there comes a time in one's life when you just don't want to be lonely anymore. And all the great women I've crossed paths with in the past weren't exactly looking for a husband, if you know what I mean," Gray said, his mask seeming to fall away as he spoke honestly with the older woman.

Greta softened as she reached out her hand and laid it on Gray's, sympathetically. She'd give anything to have Mr.

Royal back in her life again, and couldn't imagine going through life having never met or married him.

"She's already seated in the dining room," she said as she pointed towards the room. "I think she could use some company as well, Gray. She didn't look to happy this evening, not like earlier."

"I'll see what I can do, Mrs. Royal. Thank you," Gray said with a tip of his cowboy hat. He straightened, then and moved towards the dining room, looking over the crowd of people.

~

MARTHA WAS FOCUSING on her dinner of pork roast and green beans, not really paying anyone much attention because she wanted to be more cautious around strangers. She'd let her guard down earlier, having been overly excited about the idea of settling down, and felt that had probably led her to be the person whom the town was gossiping about this evening. Martha could hear those around her whispering intently, when someone sat in the seat across the table from her, drawing her attention.

She gasped as her bright blue eyes met dark onyx. The man before her had very broad shoulders and probably stood taller than her, should he be standing up. But he was staring at her from across the table they now shared. After noticing the slight greying of his hair around the temples, and the dimple in his check when he smiled at her, obviously enjoying her reaction, Martha had a pretty good idea who was sitting across from her.

"It seems the saying is true," she started with, reaching forward to gather her water and take a long drink.

"And what saying would that be, my dear?" Gray asked

as he leaned forward, having loved the surprised look on Mary's face.

"Speak of the devil and he shall appear," Martha said with a smirk, meeting the man's eyes once more. Gray let out a laugh, a pleasant sound that Martha thought she might never tire of hearing.

"So, you've been talking about me all day, and you think I'm a devil," Gray said, his smile charming and alluring. Martha couldn't stop staring at him, his handsome features not what she was expecting from a man over a decade older than her. She was pleasantly surprised, indeed.

"I might have spoken with a few about you, indirectly. And I don't know if I should consider you the devil or not. You sure have the charm of one. Now I'm curious to see if you have the heart of one," Martha replied before she'd truly thought about what she was saying. Gray noticed the way she seemed to reflect on something; the way a streak of sadness ran through her eyes as she momentarily looked away. And when Mary turned her gaze back on him, she smiled brightly, as if trying to cover up some sort of emotion.

"Well, Miss Carver, I can assure you I'm a perfect gentleman and would never treat a woman poorly or force her to do something she doesn't want," Gray said, lowering his voice and speaking with complete honesty.

Martha could tell his words were sincere, and she wondered just how much she might have given away through her poor choice of words. It seemed that even when she was trying to flirt she couldn't completely get rid of her pain, or her past.

"Well, Mr. Jenkins, I'm sure you'll prove that in time," Martha replied as she held her hand out to him. "It's a pleasure to have finally made your acquaintance."

Gray took her hand firmly in his and placed his lips to

her knuckles, taking his time with the kiss as his eyes locked with hers. Martha felt a spark race through her from where Gray had placed his lips on her skin, filling her with warmth all over. She withdrew her hand then, trying not to appear as startled as she felt. She'd never had that kind of reaction from any sort of kiss before.

"Please, Mary, call me Gray. After all, we've already decided not to be so formal," Gray said, reminding her of their letters.

"Of course, Gray. Have you eaten?" Martha asked, not wanting to appear rude by eating in front of his man.

"I have not, but please don't wait on me. I'll order once the server comes around," Gray said, pleased to see that Mary wasn't someone to be shy around food. "What you have looks delicious."

"It is," Martha confirmed as she took another bite. It would be best for Gray to understand just what type of woman she was: not someone to wait around to eat just because it was considered ladylike. Between bites, Martha took the time to ask, "Did you happen to receive my last letter?"

Gray watched her, noting her full lips and thinking how much he'd enjoy kissing them. Her question brought his eyes back to hers. "I did not. No, it was Sam who told me he suspected you were in town. Sam heard from Sheriff Ryder that a mysterious woman with fiery red hair had rode into town."

Martha couldn't help but smile at the description of herself, and also at the fact that some small-town characteristics were the same no matter where she travelled. "I'm guessing Spruce Valley doesn't get many visitors," she said as she pushed aside her finished plate just in time for dinner to arrive at the table for Gray.

"You're correct in thinking such. But it's also not every

day that an unknown young woman rides into town by herself," Gray confirmed before taking a bite. He enjoyed the savory taste of the pork roast, pleased to find the pork still juicy and not dried out. He noted that the rub used to season the pork was excellent and decided that he'd have to ask Bill what his recipe was. Bringing his attention back to Mary, he saw her watching him carefully.

"Well, needless to say, I'm not like most women," was all Martha was willing to say at this time. This was neither the time nor the place to be speaking freely of her past.

"I'm sure that's one of the many things I'm going to like about you," Gray said encouragingly between bites. Mary smiled, and Gray thought her eyes became even brighter. He'd never thought that placing an ad in the *Matrimonial Times* would bring someone as beautiful as Mary to him. Now he just hoped he could keep her and actually start a meaningful relationship with a woman. Surely he could start fresh with her.

Hearing the British accent in his voice, Martha asked, "So, what brought you to America from England?" She watched as his eyes softened, as though in memory.

"Well, as you can imagine, living in England and travelling out West are completely different experiences. I was tired of the same boring life every day, and, wanting to pave my own way in life instead of having to live the life given to me, I left everything in England behind and came to America intent on using my hands to make my fortune," Gray explained.

Martha couldn't help but laugh as she shook her head. "That's a whole lot of words to explain absolutely nothing," she said.

Gray winked at her as he finished eating. "As you can imagine, my dear, there is something in my past I was running from, but I don't care to discuss it over dinner," he explained. Martha nodded her head, agreeing fully. "Now, since we are both done, would you care to join me for a stroll? The night air isn't too chilly."

Martha raised an eyebrow at Gray, a smirk on her lips, as she considered the offer. A spark of energy went through Gray as she gave him that look. He found her positively divine as she wondered whether or not to join him on a night walk. They had only just met and had exchanged very few letters, so he understood her hesitance. But she looked so lovely in her emerald gown that he wanted an excuse to continue enjoying some time with her, away from prying eyes.

"I'd love to accompany you, Gray. I could certainly use some fresh air," Martha finally agreed, rising with him after he set a few bills on the table. "Thank you," she said as she took the arm he offered her.

"The pleasure is all mine, Mary. After all, I can only imagine the financial burden you've been under after travelling for so long," he said as he led her from the dining room and out of the front of the inn. Martha felt like she could breath easier once they were a few yards away from the inn. And though the air was a bit chilly that evening, Martha hardly noticed because she felt so warm being so close to Gray.

"Before I left Wisconsin, I sold my family's land, never planning on returning again. I had a decent amount from when my father passed away, and I also sold the cattle, not intending on keeping the family business. I worked as a waitress and made a decent wage. So, all in all, I have plenty to get by on. Granted, it won't last forever, so I hope to find some sort of employment before too long," Martha explained, not wanting to share the bit about the stolen money she had hidden away in her room at the inn. Tonight was not the night for those types of details.

"Well, Mary, I'm not sure what you're hoping to do, but Spruce Valley isn't a large place," Gray said, trying to think if he knew of any open positions.

"I'm not too worried about it right now," Martha confessed as she walked close to him. "I hope to become more acquainted with Spruce Valley and the people here, and hopefully find my own place to stay."

The more time Gray spent with Mary, the more curious he became. Since she was more concerned with a place to stay than with employment, he wondered just how well-off she was. They walked in silence for a while as they wound through the town. Martha noticed several empty stores and wondered what types of business Spruce Valley could benefit from. *She* could certainly use a women's boutique, and having a local bank would make things more convenient for her, instead of keeping her money in a saddlebag.

"Well, I'll be busy for a while since we're right in the middle of calving season, but once things die down a bit at the ranch I'd love to help you get settled. Sam and Josh know practically everything that's going on in this town, besides Mayor Delphine herself, so I'm sure we can help you find a place," Gray said, smiling down at Mary. She returned his smile as they made their way back to the inn. Gray found himself not wanting the night to end. He couldn't remember the last time he had enjoyed the company of a woman without the intention of spending the night together. He realized this kind of company was something he'd been missing out on for a long time, and he didn't want to let Mary go.

"I appreciate your kindness, Gray. Most people here seem to be quite friendly," Martha said; but then she thought about Eddie and Sawyer.

Gray noticed the way her brows furrowed, and couldn't

help but ask, "Has anyone not been friendly to you since you got into town?"

"I wouldn't say unkind, really," Martha said as she stood outside the inn, her arm still resting on Gray's. "But the Murtaugh brothers were a bit forward when I ran into them today at Frost's Mercantile. Mrs. Frost helped me pick out this beautiful gown and I overheard them talking about coming to work for you on the ranch. When I heard your name, I inquired of you, but they seemed more interested in knowing why I'd asked than answering my simple question about their opinion of you. And since you might hear it from someone else, I'll just come out and tell you: when Eddie stopped me from leaving, probably to flirt with me, I slapped him. To be honest, I think it startled both of us. It was just a reflex, to tell the truth. But I'm sure I hurt his feelings."

Gray suppressed a laugh at the thought of Mary slapping Eddie, but he could tell that she was embarrassed by the whole thing by the way she spoke quickly and averted her eyes from him. He squeezed her hand, drawing her attention back to him. Martha noted the dimple in his cheek and the way his eyes swam with humor, causing her to smile in return. "I would have paid to see you give one of the Murtaugh brothers a good whooping. I'm sure Eddie deserved it," Gray said.

Martha just shrugged her shoulders as she finally let go of Gray and neared the front door, knowing she should go inside and settle down for the night. But he caught her hand and drew her back to him. Even though he knew he was being forward, he didn't want to miss the opportunity to leave a good impression on Mary. And as she looked up into his eyes, Martha wondered if he was going to kiss her. This was the part she had been dreading when it came to the idea of being courted by a man.

Noting the fear in her eyes, Gray dropped her hand. "I

hope you have a pleasant evening, Mary. If things go well, I'll visit you again tomorrow evening. With the Murtaugh brothers coming to work with us in the morning, I'm sure I could get away for a bit," he said, instead of wrapping his arms around her and planting a soft kiss on her lips. No: Mary would have to be won over with words tonight instead of his normal charms.

"I'd like that, Gray. I hope you have a good night as well," Martha replied. She tried to give him a genuine smile, but Gray could tell it was contrived, by the way it didn't reach her eyes. She turned away from him then and went inside the inn, not stopping to chat with Greta as she ascended the stairs and went to her room.

Gray stood for a few minutes before he turned away from the inn and went over to his horse, his mind deep in thought. He had enjoyed his evening with Mary, finding her both humorous and charming, and he was pleasantly surprised by her beauty. But he could tell that she was hiding something. Still, he would give her all the time she needed to open up to him, especially if she was willing to give a man like him a chance of a happy, married life.

# CHAPTER 11

The next morning, after enjoying a light breakfast in her room, Martha thought of her evening with Gray. She was surprised how handsome he was, and by his gentlemanly character. She had loved to listen to his British accent and had thoroughly enjoyed the feeling of him next to her as they had walked through town together. When the idea of love crossed her mind, though, she dashed her thoughts to pieces, knowing she'd never allow herself to become that vulnerable with a man again.

Instead, Martha turned her thoughts to the task at hand. She wanted to go out and see if she could learn anything from anyone about a possible apartment or house to rent. Having dressed in one of the freshly laundered gowns Greta had delivered to her that morning, she pinned back her long auburn hair, allowing it to flow down her back for the most part. She felt refreshed and ready to take on the day as she left her room, locked the door behind her, and headed out of the inn.

"GOOD MORNING, BOYS!" Gray called as he stepped down from the front porch of the ranch house, having enjoyed an early breakfast with the Slaters. Tom had just come in from the pasture and had gone straight to bed, and Jensen was still in bed, so Gray had enjoyed hearing about Sam's experience in the pasture last night, and also the way Lucy had laughed when she gave details of Sam's panicked reaction to a cow giving birth. They had spent the morning laughing while Sam simply scowled at his best friend and wife. Now Gray met the Murtaugh brothers out front as they arrived at the ranch.

"Morning, Mr. Jenkins," Eddie said he approached the intimidating man with Sawyer. He sure didn't like the cold stare Gray gave them, but Eddie wasn't going to pass up an opportunity for employment, and he knew that Dr. Slater was one of the wealthiest men in town.

"I hope you two are ready for a full day's work," Gray said, pointedly looking at Eddie. The young man didn't like the way the older man was looking at him, and prayed he wasn't in over his head when it came to trying his luck at ranch work.

"Yes, sir." Sawyer responded for Eddie, giving his brother a strange look. He wasn't sure how Eddie had gotten on Gray's bad side, but he could tell something was up by the way Gray was staring at his brother.

"Well, then. Saddle up and let's get to it. We need to get the herd moved to the far pasture and separate the expecting cows from the rest. I expect full cooperation today, fellas. You have to be fully focused and ready to follow my commands at a moment's notice," Gray said sternly, fixing his gaze on Eddie, who seemed to visibly slink back from his stare. "And if I ever hear of you laying a hand on Mary

Carver again, she won't be the only one slapping you in the face."

Eddie's eyes grew wide and Sawyer let out a snicker. Gray ignored them as he saddled his horse and made his way to the pasture gate, the brothers quick to mount their own horses and follow. "Guess you insulted the boss man's girl," Sawyer whispered to his brother as they passed through the gate, but Eddie didn't respond and only scolded his brother, his gut telling him that Gray was going to work him hard for nothing more than flirting with a young lady. How was he supposed to know that Gray could be interested in a woman for more than just a warm body to hold at night? Things were certainly going to be interesting for Sawyer and himself.

~

After stopping in at all the local businesses and introducing herself, Martha felt strangely fatigued, though she didn't think she'd done that much, and decided to stop at the Eatery for a something small to eat and a cup of tea. She'd met Zachariah Welliver, the furniture maker, the Reverend Paul Gibbons and his wife, Annette, at the church, Grant Carlson, the Sheriff's deputy on his rounds around town, and Jenny Crawford, the local schoolteacher on her way to the schoolhouse. It had been a wild morning visiting and talking with so many people, and though they had all been quite friendly, Martha still hadn't heard of any leads about places she could rent right away. She was starting to feel a little hopeless as she went into Frost's Mercantile and headed to the back of the store to find an empty table to sit at.

"Hello, Mary. How are you doing today?" Nell asked as the older woman came around to her table.

Martha smiled at her as she took a deep breath. "I am

doing okay, Nell. I've been trying to meet as many people as I can this morning, trying to find someone who might know of a place I could rent," she explained as she accepted a menu from Nell, not really intending on using it.

"Oh, that must be exciting. It sounds like you plan on staying a while, then," Nell said with a smile.

"I do hope to make Spruce Valley my new home. I'm just hoping there will be opportunities here to make it worth it," Martha confessed as she set down the menu. "I'll just have a cup of the wonderful tea you make, and whatever small snack you'd suggest."

This made Nell smile even more. "Certainly, my dear," she said as she headed off towards the kitchen.

"Excuse me, miss. I couldn't help but overhear you talking about opportunities here in town," an older woman said from two tables over. Martha looked towards the voice and watched as the plump woman, who looked to be seventy-ish, approached her and took a seat at her table. "Mrs. Delphine Stavros."

Martha shook the woman's hand. "Mary Carver, pleased to meet you. If I've heard correctly, you're Spruce Valley's Mayor."

Mrs. Stavros smiled widely as she nodded. Her dark brown hair was pulled back into a bun, and though she smiled, she had a sense of authority around her. "That would be true. My husband, Anton, was Mayor for several years, and when he died I took the position over since no one else wanted it. I like to think that I'm serving in my husband's memory as he would have done for this fine town," Mrs. Stavros explained with a pleasant smile.

"That's very noble of you," Martha replied as she eyed the woman. "And yes, you overheard correctly. I'm looking for new opportunities here in Spruce Valley. I just arrived yesterday and hope to get settled as quickly as I can."

Mrs. Stavros raised an eyebrow at Martha, a small smirk on her lips. "And what brings such a beautiful young lady as yourself to this fine town?" she asked.

"Well, I've been corresponding with Mr. Jenkins, and after meeting him last night for dinner I plan to stick around and see where things lead. Besides, I have nowhere else to go and Spruce Valley looks like as good a place as any to settle down and grow roots," Martha explained, having a feeling it was easier to come straight out with the truth with the Mayor instead of beating around the bush. Mrs. Stavros didn't look like the type of woman who liked to be led around.

Mrs. Stavros considered the young girl's words for a moment, as Nell returned with a pot of tea for the both of them and a small plate of sugar cookies. The women thanked her as she left, then turned their attention back to each other.

"Mr. Jenkins is a lucky man to have attracted such a beautiful young lady. I didn't know he was the marrying type," Mrs. Stavros said as she tried to think whether she had ever seen Gray in a serious relationship.

"Gray has been quite honest with me about his past, and his genuine sincerity is what makes me think that he could be a worthy husband," Martha said pointedly, hoping this woman hadn't come over to cause her any trouble. Since Gray was known as a womanizer, it wasn't unlikely that she would come across someone who would oppose the idea of Gray ever being a worthy husband.

"I agree that Gray has always been a gentleman whenever we've met in social situations. I'm Dr. Slater's neighbor, so I've run into the ranch hand from time to time. And since we are the only two Brits in the area, it's nice to visit with a fellow countryman," Mrs. Stavros explained as she took a sip of her tea, enjoying as always the fine tea Nell made. She could tell that Martha enjoyed it too, by the way she smiled after she took a sip.

"I'm glad to hear your good opinion of the man, considering you are the Mayor," Martha replied. She was starting to see just how small Spruce Valley really was. Only two days in town and she'd already met some of the most important people there were to meet.

"Indeed. And I think anyone would be lucky to catch Gray's eye. He's always been a charmer, but deep down he's as manly as the rest of them: in need of someone to love and to have someone love him in return," Mrs. Stavros said with a far-off look in her eyes. Martha could only imagine she was thinking of her late husband. Mrs. Stavros then refocused her eyes on her. "So, what kind of opportunities are you looking for besides finding a husband?"

Martha smiled as she set aside her teacup. "Well, I'm wanting to find a place to stay that isn't the inn. Though Mr. Eckert is a nice host and Mrs. Royal is the kindest housekeeper I've ever met, I look forward to having a space of my own. Besides that, I will want some sort of employment before too long. I have means, but they won't last forever," Martha explained, figuring the best person to talk to about these matters had to be the Mayor.

Mrs. Stavros nodded her head in understanding as she thought about current possibilities for the young lady. "I see. Well, there aren't any vacant houses at the moment. Spruce Valley is mainly made up of farmers and ranchers outside of town, and those who live in town have built their own houses and businesses to sustain themselves. In the past, my husband had other buildings put up, in hopes of new businesses coming to town, but it just hasn't happened yet. I would suggest considering having your own home built," Mrs. Stavros explained.

Martha felt dejected at the idea, for she was hoping to move into a place sooner than later. She didn't want to wait months for a home to be built and have to continue living at the inn. That would force her to spend all her money faster than she'd intended to.

"Of course," Mrs. Stavros continued, "if you and Gray do decide to marry, I'm sure you'll want to build a house together."

Martha pondered this, never having thought of the possibility before. "I guess you're right, Madam Mayor," she replied as she took another sip of tea.

"Please, dear, call me Delphine. "Madam Mayor" sounds like a pompous title. I'm human, after all," Mrs. Stavros said with a contagious smile.

"Delphine it is. Well, I guess I can wait to see how things go between Gray and myself. Till then, I'm sure Mr. Eckert won't mind me staying for a bit longer than I'd intended," Martha settled with, wondering what else she was going to do with her time if she wasn't out looking for a place to stay. She knew that Gray would be working hard at the ranch and wouldn't be in town till that evening.

"You seem to be a woman of action, someone who likes to be moving and doing," Mrs. Stavros observed as she watched Martha look around in the room as though deep in thought.

Martha smiled as she nodded her head. "Indeed. I've been travelling these past four weeks since I sold my family's ranch and decided to relocate. After all, with no family there was nothing keeping me in Wisconsin. But with nowhere to go and nothing to do, I feel a bit restless," Martha explained.

Mrs. Stavros was surprised to hear more about Mary's past, but she wasn't going to pressure the young woman to tell her more. She knew what it was like to want to move on after the death of a loved one, and if it hadn't been for the vacant Mayor's position, Mrs. Stavros wouldn't have known what do to with herself. Her daughter Elena was a delight to visit with, especially given that Mrs. Stavros had four grandchildren to play with during her visits, but everyone wants a purpose in life that gives it meaning. For Delphine, that purpose had been helping to run the town in her husband's name.

"What would you think of accompanying me to Dr. Slater's ranch? I've been meaning to pay Mrs. Slater a visit, since she is expecting and I care to know how she is faring these days," Mrs. Stavros offered, knowing that any young lady being courted by a man would take any opportunity to see her beau as often as she could. That, and it would also give her the opportunity to see where Gray spent most of his time and the people he spent his time with.

"That's very kind of you, Delphine. I'd love a chance to see the ranch and continue meeting the locals. Having come from a small town myself, I know how important it is to meet everyone and make acquaintances," Martha said, happy that this new opportunity had arisen. She didn't want to appear like she was spying on Gray, but she couldn't deny that it would be pleasant to see him sooner than planned.

"I'm sure Lucy would love to meet you, too. With her being so far along, she doesn't make it into town as often as she did, and I'm sure she could use the company," Mrs. Stavros said.

The two finished their tea and cookies, and soon headed out of the Eatery together, Mrs. Stavros leading Martha to her buggy in front of the mercantile. Together the pair headed out of town, Mrs. Stavros filling Martha in on everything she knew about the place: how it first started many years ago, and little titbits about all the townspeople. Martha was certain that she was going to enjoy hearing all she could from Delphine, and as they continued on their way, her pulse started to race at the prospect of seeing Gray in action on the ranch.

# CHAPTER 12

When Mrs. Stavros announced that they were pulling down the lane to Dr. Slater's ranch, Martha craned her neck this way and that to see everything she could. A small, one-storey, white clapboard ranch house stood a little way down the lane on the right. A large red barn had been erected farther down the lane, with wooden fencing running out from the back of it. Several horses grazed in the pasture, and she could make out the shape of cattle in the distance. The sight made her feel like she was coming home, as she remembered similar details of her life growing up while her father raised a small herd of cattle. So many sights and smells reminded her of her childhood and her father, bringing tears to her eyes. But she pushed it all away as she continued to look around.

A sea of prairie grass stretched away as far as Martha could see, meeting the dazzling blue sky above the horizon. Maple and birch trees dotted the ranch, and there was a white bunkhouse on the left of the driveway. She assumed this building was where all the ranch hands lived, including

Gray. And with it being the middle of the day, she assumed Gray would be out in the pasture. So she was pleasantly surprised to see him stepping down from the front porch of the ranch house with a small group of men. But her heart thudded in her chest when she noticed the Murtaugh brothers.

As Mrs. Stavros brought the buggy around to the front driveway it drew the attention of everyone out front. Martha looked over at Gray and smiled, their eyes locking as he smiled in return, placing his hands on his hips. The stance filled Martha with warmth, as it did to see a man looking at her like that. She'd never felt like this before.

"Why you two just gawking? Help those ladies down from the buggy!" Gray barked, directing his attention towards Eddie and Sawyer. The two brothers jumped into action, Eddie running around the buggy to help Mrs. Stavros down before taking the reins, while Sawyer helped Martha alight from the vehicle. As the women approached the porch, the brothers made quick work of leading the buggy to the barn to settle the horse.

"My, my, Mr. Jenkins, I do believe I've never seen those two move as quickly as I just witnessed," Mrs. Stavros commented as she looked back over her shoulder at the barn.

"Let's just say that I've put the fear of God in them,' Gray said.

Mrs. Stavros then went into the house, leaving Gray alone with Martha.

'I have ensured that Eddie will not be bothering you again, Mary," Gray said as he took a step closer to her.

Martha blushed as she looked up into his onyx eyes. "Why, thank you, Gray. It always makes a lady feel nice to know there's a man out there willing to protect her."

Gray winked at her. "Well, you have a man right here willing to do just that for you."

This only made Martha blush even more as she looked up into Gray's charming face. She never imagined she'd feel this way around a man again, but there was something in the way Gray looked at her, all mixed in with his sincere words, that almost had her believing she could honestly trust him. But then she remembered what had happened to her the last time she'd trusted a man, and her silly feelings quickly left her.

"I thank you again, Gray. If you'll excuse me, I told Mrs. Stavros I'd meet Mrs. Slater and visit with them for a bit," Martha said quickly, and dipped her head before heading into the ranch house.

Gray sighed as he watched her go, not moving till the door was closed in front of him. It frustrated him to see how quickly Mary had shut him down, but he couldn't fault her. It was obvious to him that something was haunting the young lady, and he was going to give her time to not only get used to him and a new town, but also to the idea of opening up to him.

He stepped off the porch and made quick haste to catch up to the Murtaugh brothers, enjoying putting those two through their paces as they learned what it meant to be a ranch hand.

~

"It's such a pleasure to finally make yer acquaintance, Miss Carver. Gray's been teasing us with small details of ya from yer letters, so I can't tell ya what a relief it is to finally meet ya," Mrs. Slater said, her Irish brogue obvious to Martha. From looks alone – she had long black hair and blue eyes – she didn't look very Irish, but her words made it quite obvious.

"You're too kind, Mrs. Slater. Thank you for welcoming

me when you weren't expecting Mrs. Stavros to be bringing along a visitor. You have such a lovely home," Martha commented, more curious to know what exactly Gray had said about her to his employers. They sat in the parlor, Martha in a wing-back chair close to the fireplace. This made Lucy smile because she knew that it was the seat that Gray took to every evening to give his daily report to Sam.

"Bein' so far from town, I do love receiving visitors. And since I'm so far 'long, it makes it hard to travel into town. So this is quite a pleasant surprise. Ye are most welcome any time you fancy a trip to the ranch," Lucy said as she poured tea and handed the Mayor and Martha a cup.

"Thank you, Lucy. I do appreciate the tea. How have you been faring lately?" Mrs. Stavros asked. As the two ladies chatted about Mrs. Slater's condition, Lucy describing the uncomfortable aspects of pregnancy (though she was quite joyful to be expecting), Martha looked around the house. It was finely furnished, and she could surmise that the Slaters were well off. As she thought of the house she'd like one day, Martha reasoned that she'd have Mrs. Slater help her with the decorating since her house was so nicely done.

"So, Miss Carver," Mrs. Slater said, drawing Martha's attention back to the conversation, "what do you think of Spruce Valley so far?"

Martha smiled as she set down her cup. "To be honest, it reminds me a bit of home. I come from a small town in Wisconsin and I've missed the small-community feel of home. I've only been in town for two days but feel I've met some wonderful families. I know how important community is in a small town, so I want to meet everyone I can," Martha explained, causing everyone to chuckle. They all understood the importance of this in a close community.

"Granted," Martha continued, "the only down side is how quick word spreads in town. Why, I just arrived yesterday and already I've been able to meet Gray without having to say hardly a word."

Another round of laughter ensued before Mrs. Slater said, "I do have to agree with that, Miss Carver. My dear Sam was just full of enthusiasm as he talked about bumping into the Sheriff at lunch and learning about yer arrival from Josh. Sam just couldn't wait to tell Gray. Some things ye just can't avoid in a small town."

Mrs. Stavros nodded her head and mentioned, "I met Miss Carver at the Eatery today. I overheard her and Nell talking about opportunities in town."

Mrs. Slater sighed as she turned her gaze back to Martha. "That has been a wee bit of a problem, hasn't it? There doesn't seem to be enough jobs to go around. I was hoping I could start my boutique before to long," she said with another long sigh.

"Are you hopeful of opening up a women's boutique?" Martha asked, thinking it would be a wonderful idea.

"Aye, Miss Carver. My family is from Buffalo, New York, and there are some things I miss about home and living in a big city. I've always had an interest in fashion, and I still have plenty of family back in New York who keep me updated on the latest. I'd want to bring the latest to Spruce Valley and give women the opportunity to have dresses for nice occasions, and more durable, fashionable fabrics for everyday gowns," Mrs. Slater explained. The way the woman was smiling told Martha just how passionate she was about the idea. "But alas, I don't have the ability to go into town and make things happen now."

An idea sparked inside of Martha, and as a woman of action she was ready to begin then and there. "Mrs. Slater, I think Spruce Valley could absolutely use a women's boutique. And with your connections in New York, plus your experience, I think you'd make a wonderful businesswoman.

I'd love to help you bring this idea to reality, seeing as I need employment of my own; quite frankly I like to have something to keep myself busy with. I have my own horse and can come out to the ranch to run the business side with you, and then manage the store in town till your little one comes along and you feel up to coming into town yourself," she said, her excitement showing in her voice.

Lucy's blue eyes grew huge as a large smile crossed her face. "Ye'd really do that for me? I mean, I'm not sure what I'd be able to pay ya right away, there would be all sorts of things to figure out," Mrs. Slater said as she pushed back her hair, trying to keep her composure even though she was rather excited about the idea of someone helping her make her dream come true. With her dear husband at work each day, she really didn't have someone to talk to about her fashion ideas, and having another woman to work with would be fantastic.

"I'm not to worried about pay right now, Mrs. Slater. I would be happy just to help you get set up and we can worry about those details later," Martha said, her mind already racing to remember the various empty store fronts she'd seen earlier in town. She wondered which one would be best for the boutique.

"Please, Miss Carver, call me Lucy. After all, it seems we'll be more than just acquaintances soon 'nough," Mrs. Slater said with a wink.

"Thank you, Lucy," Martha replied, feeling a bit guilty about giving her false name to so many good people. But she knew it was for her own safety, and instead of thinking about her past Martha turned her thoughts to the future as the three women started talking about the boutique and the business side of things.

After a while, Mrs. Stavros stood and announced, "I really must be getting home, my dears. It's been a lovely visit. Miss Carver, I presume you can make your way back to town on your own?"

"Absolutely, Mrs. Stavros. I'll make sure Mary gets back this evening. Or I should say that Gray will ensure Mary's safe return," Lucy said with a chuckle.

"Then I leave her in your capable hands, Lucy. Till next time," Mrs. Stavros said as she made her departure. Martha couldn't help but blush, but quickly turned the conversation back to the boutique, pleased to be having such a wonderful project to work on, and also a good excuse to stay longer in the hopes of visiting with Gray soon enough.

# CHAPTER 13

Gray was beat by the time the sun was setting over the ranch. He rode in alone from the pasture, having already dismissed Eddie and Sawyer for the day. Though those two had experience working as deputies – and causing a bit of trouble themselves in town with the young ladies – the Murtaugh brothers were nonetheless hard workers. And even though they were green ranch hands, they proved to learn real quick and be fast to follow orders. Gray could actually endure calving season knowing he had two fresh hands to work with.

He led his horse into the barn and then worked on taking off her saddle and brushing her down. Jensen came in. He had a rather large smile on his old face, as though he was waiting to tell Gray something pretty amazing.

"Have out with it, old man. I don't have time to dawdle," Gray said as Jensen continued to watch him, his arms crossed, with that smile on his face.

"Oh, it's nothing, really. But the misses has had such fine company today – a young lady with beautiful fiery red hair,"

Jensen said teasingly, giving Gray a wink when the man turned towards him, closing his horse's stall behind him.

"I'm glad to hear that Lucy and Mary have been keeping each other company. I didn't expect her to have stayed so long when I ran into her after lunch," Gray said with a smirk as he saw Jensen's face relax into a scowl. Gray couldn't help but laugh as he said, "Sorry to ruin the surprise."

Jensen shook his head and threw up his arms as he left the barn. Gray followed after him to the bunkhouse, intent on cleaning up before heading to the ranch house. He didn't want to smell like cattle while trying to impress Mary.

As Gray was washing in the water closet, he heard Jensen say, "It's sure getting crowded around here with all these young people movin' about."

Gray stuck his head out and said, "Don't you worry, old man. There will always be room for you here."

As Gray finished cleaning his face and arms, he heard Jensen take a long sigh. He stopped what he was doing then and walked over to where Jensen was sitting, in what was the common area of the bunkhouse; just sitting, with his arms crossed and his eyes towards the fireplace that kept the building warm in the winter.

"What's bothering you, old man?" Gray asked as he sat down in a chair next to Jensen.

It took the older man a few seconds before he opened his mouth. "Seeing the Murtaugh boys on the ranch makes me worried that I won't be needed here any longer," he said softly, not moving his eyes from the fireplace. Gray nodded his head, understanding the man's point of view.

"Jensen, there is one thing I can guarantee you, no matter who comes and goes on this ranch: you, my good sir, will always have a place here. I know the Slaters don't say it, but you're like family to them, to all of us. Hell, I bet you'd make a fine grandpa once Lucy's baby comes along," Gray said, a twinkle in his eyes at the thought of Jensen playing with a baby.

Jensen's eyebrows rose at the thought of that, as he finally looked over at Gray. "Ya really think so?" he said softly, never having really thought about it before.

"Absolutely, my dear fellow," Gray said as he slapped Jensen's back good-naturedly. "You belong here just as much as those cattle out in the field do. And even when the day comes that you don't have the strength to pull yourself up into a saddle anymore, the Slaters are still going to want her hear."

Gray enjoyed the way the old man nodded his head, a smile on his face once more. With that, he left the man to his thoughts and went to change into some fresh clothes.

"Miss Carver, it's been a pleasure to have you in our home this evening. I can't tell you the last time I saw my dear Lucy this excited," Dr. Slater said as Martha and Lucy sat at the dining table with him. They were enjoying a cup of coffee after the dinner Martha and Lucy had prepared for the ranch hands. Martha was a little disappointed that Gray hadn't come in from the pasture yet, but Dr. Slater had assured her that she could stay till they had visited with Gray. Martha felt like it was a lifetime ago since she'd ridden out with Mrs. Stavros to visit with Lucy. She had no idea that she'd enter into a business with the woman. But after spending the afternoon with her, she was so excited at the idea of opening a boutique that she hadn't wanted to leave.

"The pleasure is all mine, Dr. Slater. I would have never thought that coming to Spruce Valley would bring such a good hand of fate," Martha replied as she set her coffee cup aside. She felt pleasantly comfortable after helping Lucy prepare a large meal for everyone. She wasn't used to cooking for so many people and found the experience educational. Lucy had spent part of the afternoon talking about what it had been like coming to Spruce Valley herself as a mail-order bride and having to learn so much about living in the frontier. Martha could understand the woman's plight, if you weren't used to rising early and making most of what you needed. She also had suppressed a laugh when Lucy explained how she had to learn to ride a horse and drive a buggy from Greta. Martha would have loved to see that.

"Please, call me Sam. I only allow patients to call me Dr. Slater anyways," Sam said as he took a long drink from his coffee.

"Very well, then," Martha replied.

"Mary, where do ye plan to stay while yer in town? I know that the Honeywell Inn is pleasant enough, but it's not a long-term solution," Lucy said, another thought coming to mind as she remembered how stuffy her room had been while she was staying there. It also held several bad memories, so she couldn't really imagine Mary being there for any longer than was needed.

"Well, that's what I started my day off doing. I visited with anyone I came across in hopes of meeting more people from the community, and to inquire about somewhere that might be available for rent. Unfortunately, nothing's available right now. There aren't any homes or apartments in town. So for the time being I'll be staying at the inn," Martha explained, not quite ready to bring up Mrs. Stavros's point that perhaps she'd be building a new home with Gray one day, if they did decide to marry.

Lucy look towards her husband, whose eyes twinkle with humor, seeming to already know where his wife was going with the conversation. She smiled at him, happy to see his approving look, before she turned back to her new business partner.

"With us going into business together, it's not sensible to have ya riding back and to town every day to conduct affairs. I think it would be best if ye stayed here with us till ya found yer own place. Then we could work together easier. Besides, I could use an extra hand around here, with me gettin' larger by the day," Lucy said, this time surprising Martha with an idea of her own. Martha was delighted by the offer, never having expected such kindness before.

"And you would have some of the same creature comforts as the hotel. We're the only other ones in the area to have indoor plumbing, and I even have an icebox. Keeps the groceries fresher longer," Sam said, seeming to boast, but Martha smiled nonetheless as Lucy giggled at him.

"Well, it sounds like I'd be quite foolish to refuse such an offer. I'd be happy to help you around the house, Lucy, and I'd be willing to pay expenses. I have a mare named Chestnut who I would be bringing with me, and I'm not going to be a freeloader, either," Martha said, a bit of sternness in her voice. She didn't want the Slaters to think that she'd ever abuse their hospitality.

"With ye starting the boutique for us, I'm sure we can work out some sort of agreement until ye find yer own living arrangements," Lucy said with a wink as she took another sip of her coffee.

Martha smiled, still having a hard time believing how fast her life was changing. And with that thought, the front door opened and in came the man she'd been hoping to see all day. Gray left his duster and hat at the door before he came into the dining room and took a seat next to Mary.

"Evening, ladies. Sam. How's the day been?" Gray asked, giving Martha a wink that brought a blush to her cheeks. She looked away from his warm eyes and focused on her coffee again.

"Spectacular!" Lucy said as she jumped right into everything she and Martha had been discussing. She was left quite winded by the time she'd finished, but she never stopped smiling excitedly the whole time she talked. Gray chuckled as he looked over at Mary, pleased to see how excited the two were, and to hear that Mary had found some sort of employment already, as long as the business was a success.

"And we've invited Mary to stay with us until she's settled elsewhere. I agree with Lucy that she could use an additional hand during the day, and the ladies will be able to conduct their business easier as well," Sam explained, giving Gray a pointed look. Gray smiled, but Sam could tell that he wasn't as thrilled about the idea as he'd thought he would be.

"I'm sure you'll be more comfortable here with the Slaters than at the inn. And I know for a fact that Lucy will keep you busy," Gray said, turning his attention back to Mary.

She smiled up at him before saying, "I plan to come out tomorrow with Chestnut and my things. But would you mind giving me a ride back into town tonight?" Martha knew she could have asked Sam to hitch up the buggy and take her into town, but she was hoping to spend a little more time with Gray in private.

"I'd be happy to assist you back into town," Gray said, before turning to Sam. "Mind assisting me with hitching up the buggy, Sam?"

Sam was puzzled by the request, knowing that Gray was fully capable of doing it himself, but he appeased the man nonetheless. "Sure thing, Gray," he said as he rose and leaned over to give his wife a kiss on the check.

"I'll meet you out front when you're ready, Mary. Lucy,

have a good evening," Gray said as he nodded to the ladies and left the ranch house with Sam in tow.

"Care to explain why a tough guy like you needs the help of a lowly doctor such as myself?" Sam asked as he followed Gray into the barn.

"Sam, what happens when Mary is living with you and the misses and things don't work out between her and me?" Gray said, spinning on his heel to look at Sam once they were alone in the barn.

Sam stopped and thought about it a moment, suddenly seeing Gray's perspective. "I honestly didn't think about that, Gray. She seems like such a sweet girl that I couldn't imagine you two not getting on together. She's full of energy, and she and Lucy really do have good plans for this boutique. She seems like a hard worker and seems very self-reliant. She told us about her leaving home and travelling all this way on her own," Sam said, hoping he hadn't offended his foreman and close friend.

"Sam, I have no doubt that she's all of those things and more. But I can tell that she's hiding something from her past, something that causes her to be hesitant any time we're about to have a moment. It's like she's scared to open up to me, and until she can be as open and honest as I've been with her, I can't guarantee that things are going to work out for me and her," Gray said with his hands on his hips, looking at the younger man.

Sam just nodded his head as he led a horse from its stall and towards the buggy. Gray didn't need the help, but he appreciated it at this moment. "I really do hope things work out between the two of you. I know it's a little early to tell, but you deserve to be happy, Gray, you really do," Sam said as he stood back to let Gray finish hitching up the buggy.

"I appreciate the words of support, Sam," Gray said as he finished up the work. Sam even held open the barn doors for him so he could drive the buggy up to the front porch where Mary was waiting for him. When Gray stopped in front of the ranch house, he hopped down and quickly moved to the other side of the buggy to help Mary into it.

"Thank you," Martha said as she got settled into the buggy. She waved at Sam as Gray then drove the buggy away from the ranch. It was pretty dark out, but the light from the moon was enough to light the way. With the surrounding area being wide open, it was easy to get around at night as long as it wasn't too cloudy out.

"So, it seems like you've had a busy day," Gray commented, hoping to enjoy the ride into town with Mary.

"I feel like I've been living in a dream all day. I ran into Mrs. Stavros at the Eatery, and one thing led to another and she was taking us out here to the ranch to visit with Lucy. Then we talked business, Mrs. Stavros had to leave, and then we were getting dinner ready. It's like the day flew by, but so much happened at the same time that it's all rather hard to believe," Martha explained, still surprised by it all.

Gray chuckled as he looked down at the woman, her blue eyes seeming to shine even at night. He loved the way they sparkled in the sun, but at night they seemed absolutely dreamy. He thought about leaning down and kissing her, but wanted to wait until he could make sure she was ready for that sort of thing. "I'm sure glad to hear you've had a good day. I sure had fun ordering those Murtaugh boys all over the ranch. But I have to say, they're good workers even though they are absolutely green," Gray said with a shake of his head.

Martha laughed as she thought of how fast Eddie and Sawyer had moved to help Mrs. Stavros and herself down from the buggy the moment Gray had given the command. "Well, I'm sure glad to hear they're not giving you any trouble and actually being of some use," Martha replied as she stared up at the sky, loving the view of all the stars. It was one of her favorite things to do at night because it made her feel like the sky was so large that anything was possible. Gray stole glances at her, thinking how beautiful she was and hoping that she was the one he'd been waiting for his whole life. But when he thought about her past, Gray knew that sooner or later they'd have to talk about it.

# CHAPTER 14

Gray and Martha chatted idly, talking about Spruce Valley and all the people Martha had met that day. Gray joked about some of those people, and loved hearing the sound of her laugh, which seemed musical to him. When they came into town and headed towards the inn, he was enjoying himself so much that he didn't want the night to end. But he knew he needed to get back to the ranch and get some sleep, and more importantly find something to eat because he'd missed out on dinner. But when Gray noticed a small commotion outside the inn, he feared that his night wouldn't be over for some time.

"Oh, thank heavens, there you are, Miss Carver!" Bill Eckert exclaimed as Gray pulled the buggy up to the inn. Outside, Bill stood with Sheriff Ryder and Mrs. Royal, who looked quite pale and frightened.

"What's the matter?" Martha asked as Gray came around and helped her down from the buggy.

"I came to do my rounds in the rooms when I found your room door broken open and your things thrown around the room. I've feared the worst for you, Mary," Mrs. Royal explained, visibly shaken. Bill had an arm around the older woman, seeming to try to keep her calm.

"We were just giving a report to Sheriff Ryder before I sent Mrs. Royal home for the evening," Bill explained. "I was telling him how a young man came earlier this morning looking for a young lady matching your description, Miss Carver; but I didn't tell him anything, I swear. I don't know how he got past reception and into your room, if that is who done it."

Martha paled, fearing the worse. She swayed a little and Gray quickly steadied her, bracing her around the shoulders with his strong arms. Gray's warmth and grip around her brought some clarity to Martha's panicking mind. She didn't say anything, just stared ahead at Mrs. Royal, who seemed terrified.

The Sheriff finally spoke up. "Gray, why don't you take Greta home and I'll assist Mary with collecting her things."

Gray didn't want to leave Mary, but he knew that Josh probably wanted a minute alone with her to question her. He looked down at Mary and said, "You gather your things and I'll take you back out to the Slaters. Once we explain, they'll understand."

Martha just nodded her head, missing Gray's warmth as he stepped away from her and helped Greta up into the buggy. Then Martha went inside the inn with the Sheriff and Mr. Eckert.

"This way, Miss Carver," Mr. Eckert said, leading the trio through the inn and upstairs to the rooms. As Martha took each step up, her heart beat faster and faster as she prepared herself for what she was going to find once she stepped into the room. As they neared the room, she could make out the mangled door that splintered into the bedroom. It appeared as though someone had rammed it.

Mr. Eckert stepped aside to allow Martha to enter first, and she placed her hand over her mouth once her eyes turned to the carnage in the room. Everything in the small room had been flipped over, torn apart, completely destroyed. As Martha stepped a few feet into the room, she surveyed the damage, thankful that she hadn't been present when the intruder came looking for her. Given the mayhem all around her, she was certain that, had she been in the room, she'd be dead by now.

"So, Bill, you said that no one noticed the break-in until Greta came upstairs to check on Miss Carver?" the Sheriff asked. Martha was making her way over broken furniture and torn bedding to reach the wardrobe, praying beyond hope that her one saddlebag still lay at the bottom. The doors of the wardrobe had been ripped off, as though the intruder had been in a rage, and nothing of hers now remained in it. Nothing but broken remnants.

"That's correct, Sheriff," she heard Mr. Eckert say as tears welled in her eyes. "I had Greta go check on Miss Carver this morning when the gentleman came asking about a young lady fitting Mary's description. When Greta said that Miss Carver was out for the day, I didn't think anything of it until this evening. Before Greta went home I had her check again, and that's when she saw what had happened. I can't believe it since I've been here all day, but with no other guests at the moment, I had no reason to go upstairs and check. I have no idea when this could have happened."

By now Martha was in shock and had started to tremble. Folding her arms around herself, she held onto herself as her eyes darted around the room. Not only were all her things either destroyed or missing, including the saddlebag with all the money in it, but she had a suspicion that she knew who had come looking for her.

Finding her voice, Martha asked, "What did this

gentleman look like that came asking after me?" She turned her eyes towards the two men as they regarded her for a moment, clearly worried about her current state of mind.

"Well, he was taller than me, had very fair blond hair. He was wearing a western shirt and jeans, nothing fancy or out of the ordinary. He seemed friendly enough and didn't seem too upset when I lied to him about there not being a young lady here at the inn. I'm not sure how he found out," Mr. Eckert said as he started to ramble. The Sheriff was starting to worry about the fright everyone had had, but he also needed to do his job.

"Does that sound like anyone you know, Miss Carver?" Josh asked, observing Mary closely as she spoke.

Martha fixed her watery eyes on the Sheriff, doing her best not to cry or get overly emotional. After all, she'd been fearing this day ever since she ran away, and now that the day had come, she really shouldn't be surprised. She always knew in the back of her mind that her stealing that money would come back to haunt her, no matter how much good she tried to do with it.

"Yes, Sheriff, I do. His name is Jared Mathews. He's my ex-fiancé," Martha explained. She knew the Sheriff would want more details, but she felt that could wait right now. After all, it was so late at night and she was suddenly feeling very exhausted.

"And do you believe that your ex-fiancé may want to cause you harm, Miss Carver?" the Sheriff asked, not liking the sound of where this burglary could be leading.

"Yes. I can think a few reasons why he'd want me dead," Martha said plainly, the tears finally spilling over onto her checks as the trembling increased.

All of a sudden, Gray was in the room, coming to her and wrapping his arms around her. Martha allowed the man to comfort her even though she felt she should have never come to Spruce Valley. How foolish she had been to think that she could ever settle down. The moment she found herself actually happy about the future was the moment her past came to haunt her.

"Shhh," Gray whispered into her hair as he held her tightly to his chest. "Everything is going to be okay. Let's get you back to the ranch and settled for the night."

Martha allowed Gray to lead her from the disaster of the room and back out into the chilly night air. She heard the Sheriff mention something about coming to speak with her tomorrow, but she didn't pay it any attention. She just wanted as far away from the inn as possible.

After helping her up into the buggy, Gray was quickly in the driver's seat, leading the horse out of town and down the main road towards the ranch. This time, they didn't say anything, although a million things ran through Martha's mind as she tried to reason what her next step was going to be. Would Jared continue coming after her now that he'd gotten the money? Had Max sent him after her? Would she ever be able to escape them? When a fresh set of tears started to escape her eyes, Martha did her best to quiet her sobs the best she could.

Gray felt for the young lady, unable to imagine what it would feel like to have all your few possessions taken from you. He put an arm around Mary, pulling her close to him in hope of bringing her some sort of comfort. Gray felt a fury build up inside him towards the man that had caused Mary so much grief. It was becoming clearer to Gray what Mary may have been running from in the past, and he felt an undoubtable need to protect her.

As he led the buggy back to the ranch, he was starting to feel very determined about ensuring Mary's safety moving forward. Never had he felt this strongly about any woman before; though he'd spent very little time with Mary, he couldn't deny his feelings. One way or another he was going to make sure that he had Mary by his side for the rest of his life.

"Come now, Mary. We're almost home," Gray said softly, surprising them both as he used the term "home" instead of "the ranch". But he didn't regret saying it. Martha wrapped her arms around him, placing her head against his chest, allowing Gray to hold her close. "I'll not let any harm come to you, Mary. I promise you I'll always keep you safe."

Martha let the tears continue to fall, not because of the shock she'd experienced, but because of the relief that those words brought her. She was surprised when she felt the need to express her feelings for Gray. She had wanted to tell him "I love you", but quickly realized that it would be silly for her to say such a thing. Surely she couldn't be in love with this man already, even with his willingness to offer her protection? And though she had written to Gray with the intention of marrying him, she was still uncertain if she could ever love a man again. Martha was confused about the way she was feeling, but she knew one thing was for certain: she didn't want to let go of Gray.

When he stopped the buggy in front of the ranch house, Martha finally moved away from him. He was quick to come around and help her down, and with an arm around her shoulders he led her into the house.

"How did everything go this evening?" Sam called from the parlor, having stayed up to hear both Gray's evening report and any other interesting details of his and Mary's ride back into town. Honestly, he was dying to hear what Gray thought of the young lady after getting to spend some genuine time alone with her. But as Gray came into the parlor leading Mary by the shoulders, Sam quickly stood, concerned to see Mary so upset.

"She was robbed, Sam," Gray said as he led Mary to his favorite chair by the fireplace and eased her down into the seat.

Martha didn't look up at Sam, feeling embarrassed about having to return sooner than expected, especially after how kind the Slaters had been to her. To bring this sort of trouble to Spruce Valley and to this ranch made her feel guilty. Jared could be very well watching her now and she felt the need to flee the house before anyone got hurt. For now, though, she needed to gather her wits about her.

"When we reached the inn, Josh was outside with Bill and Greta. They explained that a man had come looking for Mary this morning, and later on her room was turned upside down. I don't think she was able to salvage anything," Gray explained, pulling a chair over to sit next to Mary, and slipping his hands into hers.

Sam couldn't deny the pleasure it brought him to see the way Gray was caring for Mary. The poor girl looked quite frightened, and he was glad that Gray had had the forethought to bring her back to the ranch. He just wished it was under different circumstances.

"I'm so sorry to hear this. Of course, Mary, you are welcome here. Lucy has already gone to bed, but I'm sure she'll be pleased to see you in the morning," Sam said kindly, taking a seat across from the couple. As he watched the two of them, both taking the time to look into each other's eyes, he was certain that they would indeed make a wonderful couple.

"Thank you, Sam. I'm indeed in your debt," Martha said softly, the trembling in her body seeming to return. She tried to hide it by letting go of Gray's hand and folding her own hands tightly together. But Sam noticed, his keen doctor's experience allowing him to see Mary more as a patient now than a house-guest.

"Gray, let's get Mary to the spare bedroom. I'm going to go prepare some laudanum to help her sleep tonight," Sam said, rising again and leading them to the spare bedroom once Gray had pulled Mary to her feet. He left them for a short while to prepare the tonic. Alone, Gray took a moment to turn down the comforter before leading Mary to the bed and easing her down upon it.

"I can manage, Gray. You don't need to fuss over me like a child," Martha said in a shaky voice, trying to smile as she looked up at Gray, his onyx eyes seeming to shine in the dim light.

"I know I don't need to, Mary. But I want to," Gray said as he approached her, and, tilting her head towards his by lifting her chin, he placed his lips gently upon hers. Martha was shocked by the kiss, but she didn't move as she felt his warm lips on hers. It was soft and kind, neither needy nor demanding. It was so unlike anything she'd ever experienced before that all she did was focus on the feeling of how it made her feel and the warmth it seemed to fill her with. When Gray pulled away, it took Martha a second before she opened her eyes. She saw the way that Gray smiled kindly at her as he ran his fingers through her hair. He finally stepped away when they heard Sam coming back down the hallway to the room.

"Here you go, Mary. This will help you sleep," Sam said, noticing that her checks were now flushed. He had a suspicion that it had something to do with her and Gray being alone together for that moment; Gray's smile on his face was rather obvious, but the two made no mention of what had transpired between them as Mary took the medicine.

"Well then, I'll see you in the morning, then. Have a pleasant night, Mary. Gray, I would like a word within the parlor a moment," Sam said, nodding to Mary as he drew

Gray from the room. Gray waved at Mary before closing the door behind him.

"Well, that sure was unexpected," Sam commented in a hushed tone once the two were in the parlor and away from the bedrooms. Gray plonked down in his chair and looked over at Sam, wishing he had his pipe on him. He ran his fingers through his hair, unable to get the thought of kissing Mary out of his mind.

"I knew she was running from something," Gray said as he finally took a deep breath and leaned back in the chair. "A young lady doesn't just up and leave because she's bored of where she lives and feels the itch to roam. A man – sure, I'd buy that story. But even with her father having passed on, surely she had no reason to leave everything she knew and was familiar with behind."

"And even with all of this happening, how does it make you feel about her?" Sam asked, unsure of how Gray was going to handle a young lady with such a mysterious past.

Gray looked up at Sam and a smile crossed his face. "I'll be honest, Sam, I kissed her in there. And it was unlike anything I've ever felt before. I've kissed my fair share of women, but nothing compared to that," Gray said, his smiling growing bigger as he admitted what he felt.

Sam couldn't help but smile and shake her head at Gray, not because he was surprised, but because he was relieved. It takes a certain type of man to take on a woman with a heavy past, and Gray proved that he could be a true gentleman even when he was also a hard-working ranch hand. Now they just had to discover what sort of past Mary was running from, and what they might be up against next.

"Why don't you go on and get some rest, Gray. Mary will be fine here and you can come check on her in the morning. I'm sure Josh will be out before too long, and I'm sure we'll have more answers as well," Sam said, knowing that it was getting rather late. He didn't want to be away from Lucy longer than he needed to; he felt his own need to put his arms around his wife and feel her close to him.

"You're right, Sam. Well, I'll see you in the morning, then," Gray agreed, standing and shaking hands with Sam before leaving out through the front door. Sam let out a long sigh as he blew out the lamps that were left on in the house when he'd waited up for Gray to return. He just wasn't expecting all of this to happen, and he sent up a silent prayer as he walked back to his and Lucy's bedroom, pleased to hear the house quiet once more.

# CHAPTER 15

When Martha woke the next morning, her head was pounding, and as she opened her eyes it took her a moment to remember where she was. She lay still for several seconds, taking deep breaths and watching the sunlight dance around the room. It was a very stylish room, smartly designed, and the bed was rather comfortable, more so than the one at the inn had been. Memories of last night flooded her mind, and with it returned the fear that was sharp in her chest. The need to flee arose in her again and she worked very hard to tame those thoughts. After all, Chestnut was still at the livery stables back in town, and she now had no money to run with. No, Martha would have to face this day no matter what it would bring.

She sat up when she heard a knock on the door. Pulling the covers up over her chest since she only wore her chemise, she called for the person to come in. She was surprised when the door opened and Lucy popped her head in.

"Morning, Mary. I wanted to come in and check on ya," Lucy said, coming into the room and closing the door behind her. Then she crossed the floor and sat on the edge of the bed, taking Martha's hand in hers.

Martha tried to smile but failed, and focused instead on holding back her tears. "I just feel so embarrassed," she finally got out in a small voice. Saying how she felt out loud made it that much more difficult to hold back her tears. Lucy simply rubbed her hand, trying to comfort her new friend.

"Ye have nothing to feel embarrassed for, Mary. It's not like ya ask' that man to ransack yer room. And Sam and I already invited ye to come stay with us, so it's not like yer inconveniencing us or anything," Lucy said encouragingly. "And with me not fitting most of me gowns anymore, I'm sure we can find ya something lovely to wear today."

Martha couldn't help but smile as Lucy coaxed her from the bed and towards the wardrobe on the other side of the room. Opening the doors and drawers, Lucy picked out a lovely cream-colored day dress for Martha to wear, along with accompanying garments.

"You're too kind, Lucy," Martha said as she took the clothes and brought them over to the bed to lay them out.

"It's nothing at all, my dear," Lucy said with a wink. "Now, when yer ready, there's a certain man whose waiting for ya. But take yer time. The water closet is just across the hallway."

With that, Lucy left the room, giving Martha time to dress. Once she finished, she opened the door slowly, and seeing no one in the hallway, crossed to the water closet, taking her time to finish getting ready for the day. As she stood there pinning back her hair, not wanting to fuss to long with it, a feeling of sickness overtook her. Thankful to already be in the water closet, Martha vomited, sweat coating her forehead by the time it finally passed.

When the sickness left her and Martha washed her face, she took several deep breaths, trying to figure out why she'd been feeling so fatigued lately and been vomiting off and on. She wanted to speak to Sam about it right away – and then a thought sneaked its way into her mind. She did some quick thinking and adding up of recent weeks. Looking at herself in the small mirror in the water closet, her eyes grew big as she realized she hadn't had her monthly. Martha put her hand over her mouth as she fought the urge to cry as her worst fear came to mind. Surely it couldn't be true … could she be pregnant with Jared's child? After taking a deep breath, she opened the door and finally made her way to the main room.

Breakfast was well underway when she entered. Gray watched her as she came into the room, and moved down the bench to make room for her. She forced a smile at him as she took a seat and busied herself with fixing herself a plate. She wasn't hugely hungry but she knew that eating something would be important. She just wished she'd risen early enough to help Lucy with the meal; but she appeared well enough this morning, her laughter ringing through the air as they listened to Jensen tell a story about when he'd first learned to be a ranch hand.

"Sounds like Eddie and Sawyer." Gray spoke and then he took a long drink from his coffee. "Those two are so green that I'm surprised they made it through the day without spooking the cows or falling off their horses."

More laughter rang out, and for a moment Martha was able to forget all her worries. That was until Sam spoke up. "How'd you sleep last night, Mary? Any nightmares?"

Martha inwardly cringed as she tried to keep the smile on her face. "I slept fine, Sam, thank you. I appreciate the medicine." She felt like everyone was staring at her then, but Gray was quick to speak up.

"Time to move out, boys. I don't want to be sitting around when the Murtaugh boys show up. Jensen, I'm letting you take over things today. Surely there is no one better than you to show those two what to do," Gray said, standing from the table as he gathered his plate. Martha simply focused on her food, trying to eat something even though her stomach was in knots. She was pleasantly surprised when Gray stopped back at the table and placed a kiss on her cheek before continuing out the front door after the two other ranch hands. Martha's cheeks burned as she blushed, giving her face a fiery appearance, much like her hair.

"Well then, I'll leave you two ladies to it. I should be heading into town before my first patient of the day shows up," Sam said as he rose from the table.

"Sam," Martha called as she thought of something. "Could you bring Chestnut, my mare, back to the ranch with you this afternoon? I didn't have a chance to get her last night and I don't think I'll be going into town today."

"Certainly, Mary. I'd be happy to," Sam replied, bending over to give Lucy a kiss before he collected his doctor's bag and headed out of the house too.

"Well then, since we seem to have the house all to ourselves, why don't we make some oatmeal cookies," Lucy suggested happily. Martha chuckled as she set to work with the woman, busying themselves with chores and housework, chatting idly about the boutique and what they'd like to accomplish first. It was enough to keep Martha's mind off of worrying about possibly being pregnant.

~

Gray had thoroughly enjoyed his morning watching

Jensen bark orders at the Murtaugh Brothers while they were out in the field with the cattle. It seemed to breathe life into the old man to have something purposeful to do during the hectic calving season, and he was pleased to see the two young men following orders without issue.

When Gray noticed someone coming up the lane to the ranch house, he rode with haste to see who it was, intent on keeping his promise to Mary to always protect her. Though he'd had a good morning of working hard, his mind hadn't been very far from thinking about Mary and the kiss they'd shared the night before. As Gray got closer to the ranch house, he noticed that the rider was the Sheriff and figured he'd come by to ask Mary more questions about last night. Though Gray had his own questions, he was waiting for the best time to talk to Mary about them. But since Josh was here, he figured that now would be as good as any time with Jensen and Tom in the field with the two greenhorns.

"Afternoon, Sheriff," Gray called as he tied his horse's reins to the front porch post while the Sheriff rode over to him.

"Hello, Gray," Josh simply said as he dismounted. "I've come to ask Miss Carver some questions."

"I expected as much. I plan to join you," Gray explained as he led the man up the porch and into the house. They immediately smelled the aroma of baking and could only imagine that Lucy had made another batch of oatmeal cookies.

"Oh good. Now I won't have to eat them all meself," Lucy said as she came into the front room to see who'd come to visit. She'd gotten used to people coming and going in the ranch house, but she still never forgot the training Grant and Sam had given her when it came to using a gun. Granted, she didn't know how much help she'd be in her current state. "Mary and I made some cookies this morning and I've already had three!"

Gray chuckled, even more so when he saw the confused look on Josh's face. Gray led him to the parlor as Lucy disappeared and came back with Mary and a plate of cookies. Now understanding what Lucy was referring to, Josh took a cookie and thanked the ladies. He also watched Mary as she went and sat down next to Gray, who smiled at her.

"Good afternoon, Sheriff Ryder," Martha said, turning her focus back on him. Though she knew that the Sheriff had come to question her, it was also nice of Gray to take time out of his day to be with her too. Plus, it would make it easier to share her story with him, so that he would also come to understand her past as well.

"Afternoon, Mary. How are you doing today?" Josh asked, noticing how well she looked compared to last night.

"I'm fine, thank you," was all Martha said, waiting to take the Sheriff's lead.

"Well, I'm glad to see you are doing better. I'm sure last night's events gave you quite a fright," Josh said, observing Mary closely.

"Indeed, Sheriff. I wasn't expecting anything like that to happen," Martha replied.

"Certainly. Now, Miss Carver, I have some interesting facts to share with you. Later last night, I was called down to Handy's – that's the local saloon in Spruce Valley. There had been some sort of ruckus there and a fight broke out over a card game. Unfortunately, a man was shot and killed. When I arrived to see what had happened, the man I found dead was a young man I'd never seen before, but he matches the description Bill gave of the man who'd come questioning about you," Josh explained, watching as Mary's eyes grew large with the news.

"Are you telling me Jared is dead, Sheriff?" Martha

asked, her voice very soft. She didn't want to give up hope just in case the man he'd found dead wasn't Jared.

"If the details Bill gave me were correct – a tall man with blond hair, wearing a western shirt and jeans – then that would be the case. But unfortunately I'm going to need you to come to town and confirm the identity of the body," Josh said, hating to request such a thing from a young lady who was already shook up.

Martha took a deep breath as she nodded her head. "Absolutely, Sheriff. I'd need to know for myself anyways that it was him," she said, tears coming to her eyes. "I hate to say it, but it would surely bring me some peace to know that man was dead."

Lucy was surprised to hear her say this, wondering what she meant by those strong words. But it was Gray who spoke up next. "What did he do to you, Mary?" he asked softly, taking her hand in his. Martha didn't look at him, but enjoyed the feeling of his hand in hers. Since Jared was most likely dead, and the money now gone, Martha knew that she could leave out some details of her past and never have to speak or think about them again.

"I was a waitress at a restaurant in my hometown, so I met everyone that came in and out of our little area. A rodeo had come to town, and with it a bunch of different people. That is how I met Jared, one day at work when he came in for a meal right before the rodeo began. He was such a charmer, and his looks didn't hurt either. He was the first person I ever fell in love with, and after the rodeo ended he asked me to marry him," Martha began, still not meeting anyone's gaze as she talked. Instead she focused her eyes outside the window like she was watching her memories flash in front of her.

"I'd always wanted to leave that town behind, especially since my father had passed away and I didn't have any other family. I had a few friends, but there was no one I was willing to stay for. So I sold mostly everything I owned, including the ranch, and prepared to leave with Jared the next day. It was that night I found him in bed with another woman," Martha said, knowing she wanted to leave out the part where she was dumped in a hell-hole and sold as a slave. Her story didn't show Jared in any better light than what really happened, and by the time she realized that Gray was holding her hand tightly, she could only guess that her audience believed her.

"So I continued with my plan to go on this great big adventure that I'd had in mind when I agreed to leave with Jared; but after so many weeks I grew tired of it all. That's when I replied to Gray's ad in the paper and decided to make Spruce Valley my new home," Martha finished, hoping to be done talking about the whole situation. Surely with Jared dead, she no longer needed to worry about her past.

"I see, Miss Carver. Well, I certainly give you my sympathies concerning your plight. Mr. Mathews got what was coming to him when he chased you down and ransacked your room," Josh said, truly sorry for this young lady. But if Gray's actions had been any indication of his feelings, then Josh wasn't overly worried, feeling in his gut that Mary would be in good hands moving forward in her life.

"Thank you, Sheriff. I appreciate your kind words," Martha said. She let go of Gray's hand, then squared her shoulders. "I'd like to confirm the identity sooner than later. I want to get that part over with."

"Of course, Miss Carver. If you'd follow me back into town we can get this business over with," Josh said as he stood, placing his Stetson back on his head. Dealing with dead bodies was always the worst part of the job. But the sooner Miss Carver identified the corpse, the sooner everyone could move on.

"Would you like me to hitch up the buggy and take you into town?" Gray asked, wondering if she'd ever seen a dead body before. Then he chastised himself for such a foolish thought, knowing that both her parents had passed.

"I wouldn't want to inconvenience you, Gray. I know you must be getting back to your work and the other ranch hands," Martha reasoned, hating to take up any more of Gray's time. But he just smiled in return, a smile that seemed to melt the ice around her heart and make her head reason that perhaps she really could love again, especially now Jared was dead.

"I'll meet you out front, Mary," Gray said as he stood and followed the Sheriff out the front door.

"I'm so sorry for ya, Mary. I can't imagine what ye must be feelin' right now," Lucy said as she placed her hands on top of Martha's. She squeezed her friend's hand back and gave her a weak smile.

"To be honest, Lucy, it gives me much relief. I escaped his wrath and fate took care of the rest. I know it's not right to speak ill of the dead, but I'm glad that Jared Mathews is gone. He was a vile creature and I aim to make sure that the man that was shot is him," Martha said, with a stern edge to her voice.

"Well, yer a brave soul, Mary. Run along, then, and I'll see you after a bit," Lucy said, removing her hand and leading Martha out the front door. Lucy surprised her by embracing her, and when Martha looked into her eyes, she saw tears building. "Ah, don't mind me. I get a little emotional sometimes, that's all."

"I'll be back soon," Martha said with a smile as she descended the porch stairs and allowed Gray to help her back up into the buggy. She felt like she'd spent too much time riding around in the buggy with Gray, but she couldn't deny how happy she was to have him during this time in her life. Though it was rather strange to be riding into town to confirm the identity of her ex-fiancé with her prospective fiancé beside her; and while it also felt rather grim, Martha still couldn't suppress the small upwelling of happiness it brought her. Even with the chance that she was expecting.

# CHAPTER 16

After taking care of things in town, with Martha confirming that the dead body was indeed Jared and adding to the Sheriff's report her statement of the events that transpired, she was looking forward to returning to the ranch with Gray. She had been so thankful to have him with her during the whole ordeal, and he'd been very patient with her when the sight of the body had brought her to tears. Now that they were heading out of town, Martha felt like she could breath again.

She was focusing now on what she planned to do for employment so she could replace the things that had been destroyed. She wouldn't be able to build a place of her own till she had saved quite a bit, and she didn't know how long the Slaters would allow her to stay with them. With a little one on the way, she didn't imagine it could be very long. Martha sighed deeply as she tried to figure out what she was going to do. If she was expecting a little one in a few short months, she would have to secure her future and that of her child.

"A penny for your thoughts?" Gray spoke up, noticing the way Martha looked anxious and confused. But that all seemed to go away as she looked up at him and smiled. That sight alone made him want to lean over and kiss her silly. But he refrained, genuinely curious as to what she was thinking about.

"Well, in the end, Jared really did take everything from me, and I don't think I'll be getting any of it back. I know I need employment, and I don't know how long the Slaters will allow me to stay with them. Getting the boutique open and running it with Lucy will take time since she's expecting … and now that I'm penniless I may need to start looking for other work," Martha explained, knowing that her situation didn't really paint her in a good light for Gray. She wondered what he thought of her now that all of this had happened. The thought caused her to look away from him: she had starting to feel ashamed all over again.

"Don't," Gray said, putting the reins in one hand so he could use the other to pull her chin up to him, forcing her to look at him. "I can see the anxiety in your eyes, Mary. But I'm telling you that you don't have to worry. Now, all your problems can't be solved today, but rest assured I won't let anything happen to you. We can do this together."

"Together?" Martha said softly, her eyes growing wide at the thought. Could Gray really still care for her after learning so much about her past? But the guilt overthrew any joy she could feel, knowing that there was still plenty she could tell Gray about herself – including her real name. Her face softened as she looked into his onyx eyes, wishing she could simply believe in his words and not feel so much turmoil inside of her.

"I know we haven't known each other that long, Mary, but I can't deny these strong feelings I have about you. You're beautiful, brave, funny, and, most importantly, open-hearted. If you can accept a man like me, someone whose always been considered the bad boy in town, then there is no reason why I wouldn't accept you for who you are," Gray said, a moment before he lowered his lips to hers, claiming her mouth in a hungry kiss that was full of passion and wanting. Martha wrapped her arm around his torso, pulling herself closer to him to deepen the kiss. She'd never wanted anything more than to forget the guilt and just feel the love for this man that was waiting to take hold of her. She wanted to create a new life with Gray, one not full of fear of the past, and she was practically desperate to make that happen.

They quickly parted when they felt the buggy wheel roll off the edge of the road, causing Gray to jerk and lead the horse back into the middle. Martha couldn't help but laugh as she stayed close to Gray, her arm still wrapped around him. Soon they were laughing together, both surprised at how their emotions had gotten the best of them.

"For now, Mary, we just take it one day at a time," he said, leaning his head against hers.

"Alright, Gray. I can do that," Martha replied, for now just enjoying the feeling of him close to her, allowing her, in this moment, to forget about the past or the future.

~

WHEN THEY GOT BACK to the ranch, Martha headed into the house while Gray took the buggy to the barn to unhitch the horse and get back out to the pasture to help wrap up the tasks for the day. He missed being around his woman, but knew he'd already spent too much time away from his work to justify staying close to her the rest of the day. Gray enjoyed that thought – *his* woman – as he went about his work.

Martha, on the other hand, was all over with her

emotions. She couldn't deny any longer that she had strong feelings for Gray – but how was he going to react when she told him her real name and why she'd lied to everyone? She knew that she couldn't really move forward until she completely confessed her past. And what would Gray say when she told him her fear that she was pregnant. As she thought about the passionate kiss she'd shared with him earlier, she knew that she couldn't wait much longer to tell him the truth before they became any more serious in their relationship. There were so many promises in Gray's words that she felt she had to do right by him, no matter what.

Martha was busy helping Lucy tidy up the house and prepare dinner when she noticed a few figures out of the corner of her eye. Thinking they must be the ranch hands, Martha moved over to the window and gasped when she saw instead three Indians nearing the ranch house.

"Lucy!" Martha called as she ran to the kitchen. "Tell me you have a gun in this house. There's three Indians coming up to the house."

"Oh Mary, I'm so sorry, me dear. Ye must not be used to Indians and I didn't tell you about the local tribe here that Sam is friendly with. I'm sure they're just Red Dog's friends," Lucy said, trying to be reassuring. "They can be quite a fright when yer not used to seeing them." She patted Martha on the shoulder, who was still somewhat stunned but had the nerve to follow Lucy to the front door as a knock came upon it.

When Lucy opened the door, three tall Indian men stood on the other side. And as Martha watched Lucy smile at them, she tried to not look as frightened as she felt. Not only were they tall, intimidating, with long, flowing black hair and dark eyes, but they also wore nothing more than breech-cloths, although one had on a few necklaces that seemed to be made out of horsehair and small bones.

"Hau, Lucy Slater. I've come with my sons to bring you payment for the sheep," the man in the middle said, his eyes shifting between Lucy and Martha. "I hope we are not interrupting."

"No, Bright Star, yer always welcomed. I'm glad to hear that Drake and Robert Red Dog delivered the sheep to ye," Lucy said, stepping back and allowing the men to enter the house, something that caused Martha to tense. She had no idea that the Slaters did business with Indians, and she'd never met one before. "May I introduce ye to Miss Mary Carver."

When Lucy said her false name, Martha shifted her eyes to the ground as she nodded her head. She didn't want their eyes on them. But when the older man spoke again, the one that Lucy had called Bright Star, she couldn't help looking up at him as he said her name. "Miss Mary Carver, I am pleased to meet you. May you know my sons, Running Bear and Sky Bird."

Martha looked over at the two Bright Star had introduced, and nodded her head towards them, watching as the two younger men regarded her. It made her feel uneasy, the way they watched her, and she was even more surprised when Bright Star began to laugh.

"Forgive me, Miss Mary Carver, and my sons. We have never seen anyone with such beautiful red hair before," Bright Star explained, making his sons look away from Martha and instead begin to look at their own feet. Martha then understood that their father had embarrassed them. "Your husband will surely be a lucky man."

This made Martha blush, as she realized that Bright Star was flirting with her, which then caused Lucy to laugh. "You'll be pleased to hear that she is being courted by Gray Jenkins," Lucy said, humor in her eyes.

Bright Star raised his eyebrows as he regarded Martha

again. "But Miss Mary Carver, Gray Jenkins has seen many seasons. Surely my young sons would be of more interest to a beautiful young girl such as yourself," he said, a smile on his lips. Martha couldn't help but laugh then, especially when one of the sons grunted in response to what his father had said.

"As kind an offer as that is, Bright Star, and though I mean your sons no dishonor, I do quite enjoy Gray's company," Martha said in Gray's defense. She was at least more at ease now that she'd seen how well Bright Star spoke English and his quick humor.

"Well then, on to other matters. Lucy Slater, we bring you moccasins that my younger sister made, in hopes of bring your relief during your pregnancy," Bright Star said, motioning to one of his sons, who pulled out a pair of moccasins from the small satchel he carried and handed them over to Lucy.

"These are very beautiful, Bright Star. Please tell Red Feather I said thank you," Lucy said as she felt the fur inside the moccasins, and then handed them to Martha to feel. She was surprised by how soft they were, and thought they'd feel lovely on the feet.

"I also bring this knife that I made myself this past winter when the nights were long and cold," Bright Star said, unsheathing a knife from his side and handing it carefully to Lucy, the hilt being made out of what looked like bone. "The handle is made from buffalo bone, and the knife from iron ore that I had treaded the summer before. It's good for cutting and slicing many things."

"Yer very talented, Bright Star. I will show Sam when he gets home later today, but I don't know if I'll let him have it," Lucy said, causing them all to chuckle as she laid it carefully on the dining table. "Can I offer ye any tea?"

"No, Lucy Slater. We must be returning to our camp. I

want you and Sam Slater to know how grateful we are to have the extra meat till we can go buffalo hunting," Bright Star said as he motioned to his sons, who made their way to the front of the house once again.

"Of course, Bright Star. We are happy to do business with the Crow Tribe. If I wasn't expecting, I'd come visit the next time Sam pays ye a visit," Lucy said as they all stepped out onto the front porch.

"When your little one comes along, please bring it to the camp. I'll do a special blessing for your child, Lucy Slater," Bright Star said before turning to Martha. "It was nice to meet you, Miss Mary Carver. Gray Jenkins is a lucky man." He winked at her then, making Martha blush as the Indians stepped off the porch and made their way down the lane, Lucy standing and waving at them as they left.

"Well, that was rather unexpected," Martha commented as the two went back inside the house. She let out a heavy sigh as she began to chuckle. "I never expected to ever be flattered by an Indian." She and Lucy laughed together as they began preparing for dinner.

# CHAPTER 17

Martha had gone out to the pasture to watch the cattle roam as the sun was setting. She'd enjoyed helping Lucy with dinner and was so pleased when Sam had returned to the ranch with Chestnut in tow. She was undoubtedly grateful for everything the Slaters had done for her. She enjoyed laughing over dinner as Lucy told the story of the Indians coming to visit and how terrified Martha had been. She'd even enjoy teasing Gray when she told him about Bright Star offering his sons as a possible husband. They all enjoyed the banter that passed back and forth between everyone, making Martha feel like she was a part of a family again.

She'd never had a large family, but she missed the way she'd laugh with people she cared about. Her mother had passed away when she was little, but her father always made her feel a part of a family, making her laugh and feel loved. She was glad to be a part of something like that again. But deep down inside, she knew that if it was going to last, she'd have to come clean with all of them.

Martha turned when she heard footfall behind her. She smiled as she looked up at Gray coming towards her, the setting sun shining off his hair, making him appear to have a halo. He looked angelic in that moment, despite his womanizing ways in the past. There was nothing Gray had shown her thus far that convinced her otherwise.

"I wondered where you'd run off to," Gray said as he joined her, leaning against the fence as he cast his gaze over the pasture. He spotted several newborn calves, and felt a sense of pride in knowing he helped those little animals come into this life.

"I just needed a bit of fresh air. I sort of needed to catch my breath after all that laughing I did," Martha explained as she followed his gaze, smiling as she watched the mama cows fuss over their newborns.

Gray chuckled as he thought of the jokes that had been told. "Yeah, it's not normally that rowdy. But you seem to bring the best out in us," he said as he looked down at Mary, his heart filling with pride for her as well. He was truly proud to think of her as his woman, and in turn he began to think about how much longer he'd wait before he proposed. It was obvious to him that they had great chemistry, and he loved everything he'd learned about Mary, even though she'd had some hard patches in her life when it came to love. And despite all that, she'd seem to be opening up to him and try for love again.

"You're too kind, Gray," Martha said, her smile slipping away as she turned back towards the pasture and leaned up against the fence. She sighed, knowing that now would be as good a time as any to talk to Gray about the truth.

"I've seen that look before, Mary. I have a feeling you're about to tell me something that's been heavy on your shoulders. Let me just say now that there isn't nothing in your past that would make me stop feeling the way I feel about you, even if you tell me you're not a virgin," Gray said, trying to ease whatever was bothering her.

Martha smiled for a moment before saying, "What? Are you telling me that you are?"

They both laughed at that, but Martha's smile soon slipped away again. "Just tell me, Mary," Gray urged, coming close to her then.

"Gray, my name's not Mary," Martha started with, figuring that was one of the biggest lies she'd told yet. Gray's eyes narrowed at her and he stilled, running what she'd said through his mind once more. "My name is Martha Walters. Ever since I ran away, I've been telling people my name is Mary Carver so that I wouldn't be found. But I guess that didn't quite work out."

Gray didn't say anything as she talked. He was stunned by this news even though he understood why she'd lied. She had been trying to hide from her ex, and a new name would help. "But why didn't you at least tell me the truth … Martha?" Gray asked, her real name unfamiliar on his tongue.

"Needless to say, I have a hard time trusting anyone, after what I went through," Martha continued. "And it's a lot more than what I told Sheriff Ryder this morning." She went on to tell him everything. How not only had she'd fallen in love with Jared, sold everything, and left with him, but how she'd been sold by Jared to a heinous man named Max and been expected to serve him and the patrons of his saloon. Her voice became strained as she told Gray how she'd escaped, and the money she'd stolen to pay her way these last four weeks.

The whole time she spoke, Gray didn't say a word. He simply watched her as she told him everything, a new person seeming to appear right before him. Martha wasn't just brave – she had risked her life to be where she was today. But the more she talked, the more he began to fear. First, if Jared was able to find her, who was to say that this Max guy mightn't, too? And second, if she could lie this much to him and others, did that mean she would lie to him in the future to try to cover up other things she'd do?

Gray's demeanor darkened right before her eyes. She could tell that what she'd just told him wasn't settling all that well. Martha didn't blame him, because she knew it was a lot to take in. She knew the risk of telling him would possibly undo everything he felt for her. And by the almost angry look he gave her, she was certain that any future they might have had was now over with.

"Why did you tell me all of this now?" Gray asked, his voice shaking with all the emotion he was feeling. Half of him wanted to pull her into his arms, and the other wanted to tell her to never talk to him again.

"Because you deserve to know everything there is about me, Gray. I have strong feelings for you and wanted you to know all this before things become official between us. In your letter you stated how you wanted complete honesty, and you'd been so honest with me that I felt so guilty keeping any of this from you. And to make matters all the worse, since this morning I've feared that I might be pregnant. I've been feeling awful in the mornings and I haven't had my monthly," Martha explained, looking down at her feet.

Gray considered her words as the shock of it all rolled over him, looking off in the distance before focusing back on her again. "So you were intimate with Jared, then?" Gray asked softly, seeing the way she trembled before him. He wanted to wrap his arms around her but didn't know if that would be the right thing to do. It was one thing to want a wife. It was another to want to become a father so soon after marriage.

Martha just nodded her head, unable to look up at Gray as she confirmed one of the most horrible aspects of her past: the fact that she hadn't waited till she was married to give that special part of herself to someone else.

"I need some time to think about all of this, Martha. It even feels strange saying your real name. And the Slaters are going to need to know as well, especially if this Max comes looking for you, and his money," Gray said in an even tone, trying to keep his composure. Speaking those words made him think of something else Martha hadn't explained yet. "And how much money are we talking about anyways?"

Martha swallowed hard as she looked away, unable to meet Gray's eyes. "About fifty thousand dollars in large bills," she said softly.

Gray felt like the wind had been knocked out of him. He was surprised that Martha was still alive given the sheer amount she'd been carrying. If Max hadn't tracked her down yet, he was going to do everything in his power to get that kind of money back. And if Jared had already found her, Gray was quite certain Max would, too, if he hadn't already.

"And you don't have it anymore, correct?" Gray asked, hating to see Martha this upset again. But he couldn't let his feelings dictate his actions right now. No, right now he needed to keep a level head about him.

"No. Jared took it when he raided my room and destroyed my things," Martha confirmed, still not looking back into Gray's eyes.

"Well then, we better go tell the Slaters together," Gray said, knowing that his employers would need to know the type of threat they could be under with Martha being such a large target for what she'd done. However, he still wasn't going to allow any harm to come to her. He held out his hand towards her, but she didn't take it.

"I just need another few moments, Gray," Martha said, folding her arms around her.

"Sure, I understand," he said, stepping back from her before turning and heading back towards the ranch house.

Martha watched him walk across the lawn and go back into the house. She feared having the conversation with the Slaters and wondered if they'd kick her out, knowing that she could be putting them all in potential danger. Surely Sam wouldn't allow such a thing to happen to his expecting wife.

Wanting to seek comfort and strength before she went into the ranch house, Martha headed towards the horse barn, ducking inside the door and seeking out her mare in the dim light of the setting sun. The light was so poor that even though she found Chestnut easy enough, she didn't hear or see the person who snuck up behind her and struck her on the back of the head until she was unconscious.

# CHAPTER 18

Gray paced the parlor waiting for Martha to arrive to talk to the Slaters with him. He wasn't about to tell her story for her, but he had let Sam and Lucy know that they needed to talk to them. At first Sam was excited at the prospect of Gray sharing the news that he'd proposed, even though it seemed a little soon; but by the grave way that Gray looked, Sam knew it wasn't good news. Lucy had put on a kettle of tea, and when it began to whistle she went to get it from the stove.

"I'll go see if she's okay," Gray said. He looked over at Sam before quickly leaving the ranch house once again. He went back to the spot he'd last seen her, the night having set in and the dark making it hard to see clearly. When he didn't find her near the pasture, he went to the barn and lit a lamp. Holding it above his head, he looked around and found her mare still in her stall, so he knew that Martha hadn't left. But when he looked down at the floor, he gasped to see blood near the mare's stall.

Moving quickly, Gray ran back to the ranch house,

cursing himself for ever leaving Martha alone, especially after everything she'd told him about this Max fellow. Bounding up the steps, he barged in through the front door and went straight to the parlor, telling Sam and Lucy in a hurry everything Martha had told him, plus the fact that he now suspected that she'd been kidnapped.

"I'll ride to town and warn Josh. Gray, ride to the Indian camp and tell Bright Star. He's the best tracker I know and will surely help us," Sam said as he rose. He then turned to Lucy and kissed her softly. "Go get Tom and Jensen to come stay up at the house while we're away. Sleep with the shotgun tonight and make sure to give Tom and Jensen a pistol from the safe."

"Don't ye worry about me. Just go out there and bring that girl home," Lucy said with tears in her eyes at the thought of someone harming Mary … Or rather Martha, she corrected herself.

"I will, my dear, don't you worry about that," Sam said as he followed Gray out the front door, both men ready to take action.

~

As Martha came to, she felt sore all over. The back of her headed pounded and her arms and legs felt stiff. When she tried to open her eyes, she was blinded by the light around her. Blinking back tears, she was able to discover that the light was only from a single candle, yet it hurt her eyes immensely. She didn't try moving but simply looked around her, realizing she'd been taking from the barn and tied to a chair in a small cabin she didn't recognize. She tried to keep her breathing steady, but she was truly scared.

"Looks like my little darling is awake," came a chilling voice from across the room. Martha hadn't seen him in the shadows, but as Max leaned forward in his chair, she could see the candlelight highlighting his face. Just like the first time Martha had met the man, when she had at first thought Jared had just taken her to a random saloon for a drink and dancing, Martha thought Max looked quite handsome, with his black hair parted to the side and his moustache grown long enough that he could twist the ends. But it didn't take Martha long to realize that Max was really the devil disguised as a gentleman. One moment she'd been having the time of her life, and the next she been abandoned and sold by her lover. Looking into his eyes now, Martha feared for her life.

"Now that you're awake and we have no one to bother us, let's get down to business," Max said as he stood up and crossed the little room, standing above her so that Martha had to look up at him, the action causing her head to swim with pain. "Where is my money, you piece of filth?" He spat on her, making Martha recoil. She felt disgusting just being in his presence.

"Jared took it when he tore apart the room I had been renting at the inn in town. It was gone when I returned, so I figured he had it," Martha explained. She wasn't expecting him to lash out and strike her, so when he did, she cried out in shock and pain.

"You can scream all you like, Martha dear, because no one is around for miles to hear you. And unless you want me to hit you again and give you a real reason to scream, I suggest you tell me the truth," Max said as he knelt down in front of her. "Jared didn't have the money on him when I shot him dead. After my men searched him, his horse, and the filthy room he'd been sharing with a whore, they found nothing. So, unless he buried it somewhere, you must still have it."

The room swirled as Martha tried to look into Max's

eyes, but she was having a hard time staying conscious after that last hit. She wanted to vomit and pass out at the same time and wasn't sure she had the strength to do either. "I don't know where the money is, Max, I swear. I promise I'll pay you back, just let me go," Martha said softly, wishing there was some way she could escape this hell all over again. She tried to focus on Gray's face to give her comfort, but it only brought tears to her eyes as she thought about the fact that she'd probably never see him again.

"It would take years for you to pay back what you stole from me, you wench. So, you can either tell me where the money is or I'm going to end you right here," Max said, his voice rising until he was practically yelling at Martha. He slapped her again, this time sending backwards the chair in which she was tied, and as her head collided with the floor she thankfully slipped into unconsciousness again.

# CHAPTER 19

"Are you sure this is the place?" Gray whispered to Bright Star. The Indian nodded his head as they all fixed their eyes on the structure in front of them, a dim light glowing from within. They were crouched down together in the tall grass surrounding the abandoned cabin Bright Star had led them to. Behind them were Sheriff Ryder and Sam, both intent on helping them out on this mission. When Gray had reached Bright Star at the Crow Indian Camp, Bright Star had listened intently to Gray's plight and had agreed to aid the man. And since Bright Star was known as the best tracker in camp, he'd left with Gray as soon as the rancher had finished explaining what had happened.

They'd started their search at the barn, and with his years of experience tracking wounded animals, Bright Star had been able to lead the small search party to an abandoned cabin in the woods – or at least believed it was abandoned. Josh was already making mental plans to have the cabin dismantled once they'd successfully rescued Martha. Having been filled in on Martha's full history, he was as intent as Gray on rescuing the young woman. He couldn't imagine being betrayed like Martha had by the one she thought she'd loved.

"Looks like there's only one way in," Josh said softly, only seeing a front door and a single window. He didn't know who owned the property, but he assumed the cabin had been created for hunting in the winter: just enough shelter to provide a man the bare minimum while away from home.

"I agree," Sam joined in, his pistol in one hand and his medical bag in the other. He didn't know what condition they were going to find Martha in, but he was intent on keeping the promise to his wife to bring the woman home.

"Josh and I will go in the front. Sam and Bright Star, hang here in case we need back-up," Gray said, his eyes searching the only window for signs of Martha, silently praying she was still alive. He didn't want to think about what might have happened to her since he'd last seen her by the pasture. It felt like an eternity ago.

"When you're ready, Gray," Josh said, moving up close to Gray as everyone took their positions. Gray wasn't a gunfighter, but he was ready to do everything that was possible to rescue the woman he'd fallen in love with. That thought alone fuelled his determination to see Martha well again, and, more importantly, in his arms where she belonged.

Gray and Josh moved slowly up to the front door, listening for any sounds around them. They didn't know how many men were in the cabin or if anyone was patrolling the grounds round about. They stood still by the door for a moment, trying to hear anything that would give them an advantage, but when the night's silence was pierced by Martha's screams, Gray lost all patience and kicked in the door, firing a warning shot at the ceiling as he barged into the small room, Josh right behind him.

Upon hearing the gun firing, Max darted behind Martha and crouched there as though she was his shield. He held a knife up to her neck as his eyes darted back and forth between the two men who'd ruined his torture session, something he quite enjoyed doing in his spare time.

"Drop the knife or you're dead," Gray shouted, trying to aim his gun at the man who held his precious Martha at knife-point. He didn't want to accidently shoot Martha, but the man wasn't giving him an easy opening.

"Back off or the girl dies," Max replied with a sneer, his cold voice sending chills down the spines of the other men. They both understood that this evil man wasn't lying when he made that threat.

Martha's vision swam as she tried to focus on Gray's face. She'd lost all hope of being rescued when Max had woken her once again, the pounding in her head growing more severe with every passing second. Martha felt the cold steel across her neck and did her best to keep her head up, even though it felt like it weighed a hundred pounds. She struggled between staying conscious and not slicing her own neck on the blade. Either way, she prayed that it would all be over soon.

"Just give up now, you vile scum. The cabin's surrounded and you're not getting away with kidnap and attempted murder," Josh shouted, growing anxious with every passing second. They were at a standoff, with Martha's life hanging in the balance.

Suddenly, gunfire rang out from the distance, a bullet piercing the only window, making Max shift his position, his line of thinking being that the attack was now coming from outside. But the moment the man moved, Josh and Gray took their shots, too, moving forward as Max hit the floor hard. Josh was on him within a second, sending another shot into the man's right arm to prevent him from firing back at them. When Max tried to stab Josh in the ankle with the knife boot he'd unsheathed, Josh jumped out of the way and sent another bullet into the man, finally ending all movement.

Gray ignored the kidnapper and turned his attention to Martha. Tears streamed down her face as he whispered comforting words to her, despite the two further gunshots that rang out beside them. Sam and Bright Star had come in now, and Sam was quick to help Gray get Martha untied. Collecting Martha in his arms, Gray walked her out of the cabin, Sam close behind him as he started to examine her.

"Let's get her to the clinic in town. It's closer," Sam said, unable to see Martha's wounds clearly in the dark. "You get her into the buggy and I'll drive."

Gray didn't reply but did as he was told. His biggest concern now was to get Martha to safety and allow Sam to make sure she'd live through this ordeal. If Martha died on him now, Gray was certain he'd live the rest of his life a very sad and angry old man.

~

THE FIRST THING Martha realized as her mind came out of the darkness of her subconscious was that she was warm. She took a deep breath; the smell of wildflowers was close by. It reminded her of spring, which helped her remember that it was March and that there shouldn't be wildflowers in bloom right now, and then that triggered her last memories of Max torturing her to death.

Her eyes shot open and she tried to sit up from where she was lying, but the pain in the back of her head made it hard for her to focus her eyes or gain balance. She felt a pair of hands on her, urging her to lie back down. She fought against the hands until she heard her name from a familiar, comforting voice.

"Martha, you need to lay down. You must get some rest," Gray said, his touch warm on her skin where he pressed his hands into her shoulders, forcing her to lie back down and relax.

"Where am I?" she asked, the words hard to say because her mouth was so dry, as though she'd swallowed a spoonful of dirt before falling asleep.

"You're safe, Martha. After we rescued you, Sam and I took you back to Sam's clinic. You're there now, resting after sustaining several head injuries," Gray explained, speaking slowly and softly, his words causing fear to run through her again as she remembered the way Max had hit her over and over again.

Martha felt Gray's hand on her head then, gently tipping her head up as he placed a cup to her lips, allowing her to drink deeply of the water. When she'd finished, he laid her down again gentle as a feather. Martha swallowed several times and then took a deep breath as she struggled not to cry or get upset. Her head already hurt as it was, and she was still trying hard to focus on Gray. She looked towards him but only saw the blur of a figure.

"What happened to Max?" she asked, not remembering much after Gray and Josh had stormed the cabin. She didn't want to think about the vile man ever again, but the fear wouldn't allow her to be free yet.

"He's dead, Martha. Josh killed him after Max tried to stab him. You won't ever have to worry about him again," Gray said, taking her hand as the tears finally came down her checks. She felt relieved to know that Max was dead and wouldn't be able to hurt her again. "Shhh, my love. You don't have to worry about him now."

Through Martha's tears, she was still able to hear Gray clearly. "You love me?" Martha asked between sobs, having a hard time believing anyone would love her after everything she'd been through.

"Yes, Martha," he said, coming closer to her. "I love you, and I'm never letting you out of my sight again."

Before Martha could say anything in returning or declare her own deep feelings for the man who'd captured her heart, she felt Gray descend upon her, his lips capturing her as his free hand wiped away her tears. He was gentle and Martha was hungry for more, but the pounding in her head wouldn't allow her to lift her head and press harder against Gray. Sensing her discomfort, Gray pulled away.

"I love you, too, Gray. I never thought I could ever love a man again after the betrayal I experienced, but I know that what I feel for you is like nothing I've ever felt before. I feel safe with you, Gray, and I want to spend the rest of our lives together," Martha said slowly, wishing she could see more clearly. "But what if I'm pregnant, Gray? Surely you wouldn't want to take on a child that isn't yours?"

Gray took a deep breath as he squeezed Martha's hand again. "I'm so glad to hear you return my feelings, Martha. And yes, I love you even if you are pregnant. I want to have children with you Martha, and I think the sooner the better," he said, the smile apparent in his voice.

Martha cried happy tears as she clung to Gray, feeling happier than she had in years. But then she frowned, becoming frustrated with her lack of sight. "Gray, is Dr. Slater nearby? I'm having trouble seeing and I don't understand why," she said, reaching out towards Gray till she could at least touch his face.

"Of course, Martha. You just rest here. I'll go get Sam," Gray said, placing a light kiss on her forehead as he let go of her hand and left her side. Martha took several deep breaths as she closed her eyes and opened them again, hoping that her vision would clear and she'd be able to see Gray's face again.

After a while, she heard footsteps near the small bed. She tried to look over at who was approaching her but still failed to see clearly. It was a little disturbing, but she relaxed once she heard Sam's voice.

"Good morning, Miss Walters," Sam said, the humor apparent in his voice.

"Hello, Sam," Martha replied as she felt Sam approach her, his hand gentle on her shoulder as he moved her hair this way and that, as though inspecting her head.

"You've taken a nasty beating, Martha," Sam said, analyzing the bruising that had formed across her scalp, the sides of her face, and the swelling on the back of her head where she sustained multiple blows to the head. "Do you feel any pain?"

"Yes, Sam. My head feels like it's pounding," Martha admitted.

"I'm going to prepare some laudanum to help ease the pain, but only a little bit since we're all pretty sure you're pregnant," Sam explained, and Martha soon heard the opening of a bottle and the clanking of a metal spoon against the glass. When she felt it pressed against her lips, she parted them and drank the bitter medicine quickly, praying it would work fast. "It's going to make you sleepy and you'll probably fall asleep soon, but that's okay because you need your rest. We won't know if there is any permanent damage to your eyes until you've rested for a few days. For now, try to rest and not worry about anything. You have a guardian angel beside you who's informed me that he's not leaving your side till you're full recovered."

They chuckled as Martha felt the effects of the laudanum kick in. She felt it easier to laugh now, even though the effort caused her head to swim. Her vision continued to blur until her eyes were closing, and as her breathing became steady, she felt someone take her hand. She focused on the texture of the calluses of the man's strong hands as she fell back to sleep.

# CHAPTER 20

It had taken Martha a week in the clinic until she was fully recovered from the beating she'd endured. Sam once told her that it was a miracle that she'd not only lived but had very few injuries besides severe bruising. With time, her vision had cleared and she could see properly again. She had spent her time praying words of thanks and thinking about how she'd live each day to the fullest, never taking a moment for granted.

Now back at the ranch house with the Slaters, Martha was almost feeling her old self, despite the morning sickness. She enjoyed working with Lucy every day, whether it was housework, ironing out the details of the boutique, or talking about their pregnancies. Already Lucy had written her family contacts back in Buffalo, New York for advice on the latest fashions and fabrics that would be suitable for pioneer women. It wouldn't be long before Lucy had everything she needed to start filling her boutique with the things the women of Spruce Valley desired. It was up to Martha then to find the perfect store front and start getting it ready.

Though Martha no longer had a cent to her name, she was happy to work with the Slaters in return for the things she needed. And one of the biggest perks of going into business with Lucy and staying with the Slaters was that she got to see Gray on a daily basis. Even though they'd confessed their love for each other, they were taking things slow so they could enjoy this newfound feeling for each other. Gray reasoned that he wanted to court Martha properly with no fear or lies to get in the way of what they wanted to build together. And every day that Martha got to spend some time with Gray was what she considered Heaven must be like.

She was doing the lunch dishes while Lucy was lying down for a nap, fatigue seeming to get the best of her during this last portion of her pregnancy, when Martha heard a knock on the front door. Drying her hands on her apron, she left the dishes and went to the door, and was pleasantly surprised to see Greta on the step. But as Martha looked the widow over, her eyes grew wide as she realized what Greta had slung over her shoulder.

Martha quickly pulled Greta inside, fear clenching her chest as she looked at the woman with confusion written across her face. "Mrs. Royal, where on earth did you find that saddlebag?" Martha demanded as she led Greta into the parlor and sat her down in a chair, Martha's chest rising and falling as she tried to control her breathing.

"Please don't be displeased with me, Miss Walters, but you have to understand that I didn't steal it. After that man came asking for you, I knew that I needed to get it to a safe place. I'm sorry I wasn't able to rescue all your things, but I knew that this would be important to you. And with you ending up bedridden for so long, I knew that wasn't the best time to tell you. But now that you're settled and well, I thought you'd be happy to know that I kept it safe for you and never once opened it," Greta said in a rush of breath, almost too fast for Martha to follow. As the two women sat together in the parlor, their eyes locked as Martha tried to process everything Greta had said and done for her, and Greta prayed that Martha wouldn't be angry with her. In fact, Martha couldn't help but laugh.

"My dear, Mrs. Royal, I just can't believe this!" Martha said, taking the saddlebag as Greta pushed towards her. Martha unclasped the buckle and peered inside. The mounds of cash were still there as though she'd never parted with them.

"Are you angry, Miss Walters?" Greta asked after a while, wondering if the large smile on Martha's face was a true sign of how she was feeling.

"No, Mrs. Royal, I'm not angry with you at all. You have done the kindest thing imaginable for me. I don't know how I can ever repay you," Martha said, feeling overjoyed and overwhelmed at the same time. She'd never expected to see this money again.

"Well, let's just not tell Bill that I took it from your room, or I'm afraid he'd have to fire me," Greta said, so seriously that Martha couldn't help but laugh again. She pulled the older woman into a tight hug, doing her best not to squeal in delight so she didn't wake Lucy.

"You must stay for dinner, Mrs. Royal. I will make you whatever you wish and we shall have tea and cake while we wait," Martha said enthusiastically as she slung the saddlebag over her shoulder and led Greta to the kitchen, intent on treating her like a queen that day. Greta simply chuckled as she followed the young lady, unable to deny her.

# EPILOGUE

Martha was trying to keep her composure as Lucy fanned both their faces at the same time with extra pew fans they'd found in the pastor's office. They were waiting for Sam to meet them in the room to let them know that the wedding was about to begin.

"I can't believe it, Lucy. It all still feels like I'm living in a dream and I'm afraid that at any moment I'm going to wake up," Martha said as she took deep breaths to settle her nerves.

"Ye have nothing to feel nervous about, Martha. Gray is lucky to have ya as a wife. Ye are everything a man could want in a woman, and a whole bunch more," Lucy said enthusiastically, even though the heat of the day was starting to get to her. "Where in the world is that husband of mine?"

As though Sam had been waiting to be summoned, he opened the door in the next moment as the "Wedding March" began to play. "Who's ready to marry a feisty ranch hand?" Sam said with a smile, causing the ladies to chuckle.

"Behave, ye," Lucy said as she walked past her husband

carrying a small bouquet of roses. She looked radiant in a pale green gown that made her pregnant figure very flattering, especially with its layers of lace. Lucy gave Martha a wink as she stepped out of the room and down the aisle of the church, heading towards the altar, where Gray stood with Bright Star and Josh at his side.

"You look beautiful, Martha," Sam said, his voice taking on a serious note. "Gray is truly lucky to have a woman like you."

Martha beamed up at Sam, so happy that he'd agreed to walk her down the aisle, after everything he'd done for her and Gray. After all, it was he who told Gray about her arrival, which had been perfect, since her last letter had never arrived in Spruce Valley. "It is I who is lucky, Sam. After everything I went through to arrive to this moment, I am lucky to even be alive," Martha said, turning her eyes back to the open door. Just a little further down the aisle and she'd be able to see Gray.

"Well then, let's get you married so you can begin the rest of your life as Mrs. Jenkins," Sam said with a smile. Martha simply nodded as she allowed Sam to guide her forward.

Gray was standing at the front of the church, his heart pounding in his chest as the wedding music had begun. With the entire town appearing to have shown up for the occasion, the building was rather warm, and he was afraid to ruin his new suit by sweating too much. He took deep breaths, his eyes forward as he waited to catch sight of his bride.

He couldn't believe how much he'd come to love Martha, even when she didn't have a penny to her name. And then, what seemed like a moment later, she had become one of the wealthiest women in the area. It was only to him that she had confessed what Greta had done with the stolen money and how the older woman had returned it to her. The news had been so unreal, that if it hadn't been for Martha showing him the money, he would have never believed it. Together, with their two fortunes, they were able to have a decent-sized house built down the lane from the ranch. It was close enough to the ranch for Gray's work, and Martha could continue working with Lucy; but Martha would also be a little bit closer to town so she could run their new women's boutique.

Gray had also taken the time to finally tell Martha the truth about why he'd left England. As a member of a wealthy family, he'd been expected to run the family business after his father died, but he'd run away from home to marry a young lady who had captured his heart. But when this lady only showed interest in his money, and since he'd lost his inheritance when he'd chosen to elope with her, she'd left in minutes after he'd explained their future prospects. Heartbroken, and now penniless after being raised a very wealthy person, he'd fled to the Americas to make his fortune, intent on never loving again.

Gray's own story of love and betrayal had brought him and Martha closer together, allowing him to feel that it was finally the right time to propose. The night before Martha and Lucy's boutique had opened, Gray had surprised Martha at the shop and knelt before her, offering up his heart and a small token of his affection: a beautiful silver ring with diamonds embedded in the band. Martha had been surprised and overjoyed by Gray's proposal, and when they shared the good news with the Slaters, Lucy had insisted on making Martha's gown, even this late on in her pregnancy.

Now, Gray looked ahead as Sam and Martha came into sight, but Gray only had eyes for his bride. Dressed in a gorgeous flowing white gown, Martha appeared to be an angel coming his way. It fit her figure perfectly despite her growing stomach; her auburn hair was done up in an intricate design with pins embossed with pearls. Pearls decorated the front of the gown as well, making her shine before him.

"Who presents this young lady to this man?" Reverend Paul said as Sam placed Martha's hands in Gray's.

"The Slaters," Sam replied, winking at Gray before he went to join his wife in the pew.

Martha and Gray stared into each other's eyes as they tried to listen to the Reverend's words, but they became more focused on the feeling of their hands together, and their eyes, which were locked in a state of love and adoration. When a soft chuckle rang through the air, Gray refocused and had the Reverend repeat the vows so he could say them correctly. Martha did the same, and as Reverend Paul introduced them to the attendees, Gray was quick to draw Martha to him and give her a long, passionate kiss that received many hoots and hollers from the crowd.

Leading his wife down the aisle to the open church doors, Gray couldn't believe that the time had finally come for him to take that step in life where he'd become a husband, and perhaps one day a father. Though he had a few grey hairs, he knew that his age wouldn't stop him from loving Martha ever day as though that day was their last.

~

After a warm reception at the Eatery, Martha and Gray returned to their home, the first time either one of them would be sleeping in the new place. Having worked with Zachariah Welliver, the local furniture maker, they had everything they needed to enjoy their first night together as a married couple.

As tradition requires, as soon as Gray had stopped the buggy out front, he'd helped Martha down and then gathered her into his arms, carrying her over the threshold of their new home. "Welcome home, Mrs. Jenkins," he said, setting her down and pulling her into a lingering kiss.

"Why, thank you, Mr. Jenkins," Martha said before kissing him back, loving the way his strong arms wrapped around her.

"How about you go get comfortable upstairs and I'll put Chestnut in the barn," Gray said, his voice husky as he placed a kiss on her forehead.

"Okay," Martha said shyly as she finally let go of her husband. He stood there a moment, simply watching his wife in her beautiful gown, before heading back outside to take care of the mare.

Gray couldn't believe how lucky he was to have a woman like Martha in his life. Though they'd overcome much together by confessing their own histories to each other, Gray couldn't deny that he felt a love for Martha unlike anything he'd ever felt before. He worked quick with settling Chestnut for the night so he could return to his loving wife.

As Martha waited for Gray to meet her in their room, she took her time looking around, slowly taking the pins from her hair and laying them down on the dresser that was across from the four-poster bed. Everything felt so new to her that it almost seemed that none of it was real. She sighed as her hair was finally free of all the pins, allowing her to relax a bit. But as she tried to unbutton her gown by herself, hoping to be in her sleeping gown by the time Gray returned, she began to get frustrated.

Hearing his footsteps coming down the hallway, she stopped struggling, knowing that she would have to wait for his help. Her heart began to race as Gray approached their bedroom door, and she knew that she was about to face the rest of her life with this man, in their new home, starting in their own bedroom. For a moment, Martha could envision the rest of their lives together: having children, raising them together, watching them grow up, and then growing old together. Martha was smiling even before Gray came into the room, creating a beautiful scene for him to see as he stepped into their room.

With her long auburn hair flowing down her back, Martha looked even more gorgeous to Gray. She looked wild, but more importantly, she looked happy. Without speaking, Gray went to her, collecting her in his arms as he kissed her fondly. After a moment, as they both became very warm, Gray looked into Martha's eyes and said, "Mrs. Martha Jenkins. For the rest of my days on this Earth, I will always love you. And every night, no matter what the day has brought, we will come to this room together, united, of sound mind and of one love."

"Gray, I look forward to our life together. I look forward to the sound of small feet on the floor, days spent around the kitchen table laughing and playing with our children – but I also look forward to the years we simply spend together, just the two of us," Martha said, running her fingers through his hair, loving the feeling of being so close to him for the rest of her life.

Gray lowered his head to her then, capturing her in a kiss that would represent their strong love for each other, and the many promises left untold that would help pave the way for their happy future together – no matter what happened next.

The End

# THE LONESOME COWBOY'S ABDUCTED BRIDE: BOOK 3

# CHAPTER 1

The late summer air ruffled Eddie's hair as he sat astride his horse in the back pastures. He was watching over the herd as they roamed and grazed, mindful of any predators that might be lurking from a distance. With the wide-open spaces of Montana stretching as far as the eye could see, it was easy to spot people coming and going, but more importantly, if a coyote or mountain lion was wandering about.

Eddie smiled to himself as he ran his hand through is light brown hair. It had been almost a year and a half since he'd come to work for Dr. Slater on his cattle ranch. For the first time in his life, he was finally feeling his feet on solid ground. He had a stable income for once, a place to rest his head at night, and three home-cooked meals he could look forward to each day. His bosses were considerate men. Where Dr. Slater had a great sense of humor, his foreman, Gray, was very straight to the point. Although, he often proved that he had a solid funny bone in him.

Together with his brother, Sawyer, they lived on the

ranch in the bunkhouse, learning the way of the cowboy. Much had happened in their short time on the cattle ranch. The eldest ranch hand, Jensen, had passed away during a brutal winter. He was an old-timer who had done his job well for many years. But the Montana winters were always daunting. Cold winds, piles of snow, and days where you couldn't leave the house because of the freezing temperatures. This past winter had been no exception and had unfortunately taken a toll on Jensen. When he did pass away, it had taken days before they were able to dig a proper grave and hold a small service for the feisty man.

The Slater Ranch had lost a great soul, but it had also gained two little ones. Lucy Slater had given birth to a redheaded little girl that looked just like Lucy. They'd named her Francene after Dr. Slater's mother. Eddie couldn't help but laugh over how doting Francene's parents were. Dr. Slater had become a very worrisome parent while Lucy let the little girl toddle all about the house. The love between Dr. Slater and his wife had only grown stronger, and Eddie wouldn't be surprised if Lucy would be expecting again soon.

In addition to the bunch was Gray and Martha's son, Samuel, which had been a hilarious announcement since Dr. Slater thought Gray had named his son after him. But in fact, it was to honor Martha's father. However, Dr. Sam Slater still teased Gray about it endlessly. Together, Lucy and Martha enjoyed raising their little ones together, as well as managing their women's boutique in town. Now, Eddie couldn't help but shake his head at that. He always thought that women were better off at home, raising children and taking care of the cooking for the family. It was different to see two women working, minding the children, and taking care of a household. Though, Gray had gone back to helping with the cooking; before Lucy had come along, he'd been the ranch's cook and had reclaimed that title again with the women working in town.

Eddie sighed as a strong summer breeze swept over the open pasture. It was quite early in the morning and already the day felt hot. He let his hand fall from the reins to his saddle bag at his side as he double-checked the amount of water he had in his canteen. Then, he pulled out a date and handed it to the furry fellow on this shoulder.

"Looks like it's going to be another hot day, Jack. We should probably go post up in the shade," Eddie said to the brown capuchin monkey that sat on his shoulder, where he resided most of the day. The monkey simply chattered in return as he ate the date. Eddie made his way slowly through the herd, guiding his gelding through the cattle to a shady tree in the distance. The moment Eddie had guided his horse underneath the long branches, Jack climbed off his shoulder and up into the tree before Eddie could dismount.

"Hey, don't get stuck up in the tree again, Jack. The last time that happened you didn't come down for three days and got stuck in a rainstorm. Looked like a drowned rat to me," Eddie called up into the tree. Jack simply bared his teeth at Eddie, something Eddie considered to be some sort of smile. There was much about Jack he was still trying to learn, but he enjoyed having the monkey around simply to see what he would do next.

As Eddie settled back against the trunk of the tree, his eyes switching between the moving cattle and Jack above him, he recalled the night he'd gotten Jack. It had been a wild night at Handy's. He and Sawyer were up to their usual antics of trying to impress the ladies. But he'd settled down at a poker table when he realized that there was a traveler trying his luck at the game. The thing that amused Eddie the most that this British man had a monkey on his shoulder. Wanting to learn what the monkey was all about, Eddie had taken a seat at the table, much to the chagrin of the other players. Eddie was known for his poker skills, but he wasn't interested in money that night. He'd never seen a monkey before and wanted to know the traveling man's story.

As Eddie had begun playing round after round, trying not to draw to much attention to himself by winning every hand like normal, Eddie had learned from the British man that he'd bartered for the monkey from a group of Chinamen. At the time, the fellow had wanted to take the monkey back home to England with him. But the more Eddie watched the monkey sitting ever so obediently on his master's shoulder, the more Eddie had wanted the furry animal himself. Eddie had then started to play the game seriously, intent on pressuring the British fellow to give up the monkey. He'd played the man all night, and finally had left with the monkey in hand.

"What in the world do you plan to do with a monkey? You can't even eat it if you change your mind," Sawyer had said when he'd shown his brother the furry thing.

"I'm going to train it just like a cattle dog. He'll help me keep an eye over the cattle," Eddie had said with a wide grin. He'd learned all he could from the British man about raising Jack successfully, but the man had been so angry about losing his pet that Eddie hadn't learned very much. Therefore, there had been a major learning curve for Eddie.

Furthermore, Dr. Slater and Gray weren't too happy with Eddie bringing a monkey back to the ranch. Eddie quickly learned to keep Jack on a leash after the monkey had gone on a tangent and ripped Lucy's curtains. Lucy had to admit that Jack was cute, but it was no longer allowed in the house. Gray had been worried that Jack would spook the cattle instead of keeping them in line, and it had taken a lot of convincing to the foremen to allow Eddie to keep Jack in the bunkhouse. But even though Jack was very cute and could do a few amusing tricks, he had a wild side to him that often got on everyone's nerves.

But to Eddie, Jack had been the friend he'd been looking for. Though he loved his brother Sawyer, Eddie felt like they were headed in two different directions. Eddie longed to settle and put down roots, while Sawyer was always ready for the next adventure. Though Sawyer was a silent fellow, he loved the thrills of life. That's why together as brothers they were often asked to be assistant deputies for Sheriff Josh Ryder because they worked well together and often loved a good chase. They were great shots under pressure and often worked great together, even though they bickered here and there. Sawyer loved the adrenaline of chasing down bad guys, but Eddie had come to realize that there was more in life than a good thrill.

As Eddie sat looking over the herd, trying to keep an eye on Jack at the same time, he started to think about what he wanted most in life. Though he loved having Jack and got to work closely with his brother, he knew there was more to life than that. After coming to stay on the ranch, he'd gotten to see firsthand what married life was like. Lucy and Dr. Slater were a great match, even though Lucy had been a mail-order-bride. They'd created a wonderful life together and obviously loved each other.

The same could be said for Martha and Gray. Even though there was a large age gap between the two, they still loved each other dearly. So much so, that even though Samuel technically had a different father, Gray still loved and raised him as his own.

After watching the two couples closely for the last year and a half, Eddie started to think that perhaps now was the time to start thinking about finding a wife of his own. He knew that it would be difficult since he knew most of the women in the area more personally than he should. And after seeing how successful both Dr. Slater and Gray had been after finding mail-order-brides, Eddie started to consider doing the very same thing.

It was a thought that often came to him during the hot hours when he needed something to keep his mind busy, or he would focus too much on the heat. He continued to go back and forth over the idea since he didn't know if he was the type of person that would interest a lady. Though he had an established position at the ranch that paid well enough, he didn't have his own home. And to make matters more interesting, he had a pet monkey that often caused more trouble than good. He wasn't very confident in the idea of finding a match, and therefore had put off physically placing an ad for some time.

"There you are!" called Sawyer away in the distance. He rode over to where Eddie was resting in the shade. As his brother approached, he stood and shielded his eyes from the sun to get a better look at his brother. Where Eddie was tall and lengthy, Sawyer was shorter with broad shoulders. But they both had light brown hair and blue eyes.

As Sawyer guided his horse underneath the tall branches to reach the shade, Jack jumped down to a nearby branch, startling Sawyer.

"I swear, one of these days I'm going to shoot that damn monkey," Sawyer said as he tried to shoo Jack away with his cowboy hat. Jack simply bared his teeth and screeched with laughter.

"Come on. You can't deny that you love Jack just as much as I do," Eddie reasoned.

"That's only when Jack is teasing someone else," Sawyer said. "Speaking of, Mrs. Lucy says lunch is ready. I'll take your spot for a bit."

"Much appreciated," Eddie said as he pulled himself back up into the saddle of his gelding and clicked his tongue three times to tell Jack it was time to go. But Jack remained where he was in the tree, looking down at Eddie with pleading eyes.

"Looks like the fellow wants to stay with his uncle," Eddie said with a smirk as he turned his eyes to Sawyer. He watched as Sawyer rolled his eyes before shrugging his shoulders.

"Never thought I'd be a monkey's uncle," Sawyer said as he dismounted. Eddie couldn't resist laughing as he clicked his heels against the gelding, sending the horse into a canter.

As Eddie traveled across the pasture to the ranch house, Eddie thought that things were a lot different than either one of them could have ever imagined. They had steady employment, a roof over their heads, and were saving their money instead of spending it all every weekend at Handy's. At least, Eddie knew that he was saving most of his pay now and hoped that his brother was doing the same. Eventually, Eddie wanted space of his own. And perhaps one day he'd finally meet a woman he'd want to settle down with.

As Eddie made his way towards the ranch house, he kept contemplating if now was the time to write that ad.

# CHAPTER 2

Fiona Wilkins found refuge from the Boston heat by lounging in the drawing room. It was much cooler in that part of the house as it was positioned on the opposite side from where the sun was. The room had been positioned precisely in this manner for her mother, Mrs. Melisa Wilkins, so she could entertain guests during the warmer months. But since her mother was out visiting friends, that meant that Fiona could find peace and quiet in the cooler room until her parents made her do something else.

Fiona sighed with boredom as she set aside the novel she had been trying to read. It no longer interested her since she'd read it three times. Her parents often didn't let her purchase novels because they were afraid the books would tarnish her mind. But it was one of the few pleasures in life that Fiona treasured. She had a small collection of western novels that she could lose herself in. Though she hid them underneath her bed, she considered them one of her prized possessions. But since her parents didn't often let her shop alone and were always very watchful of Fiona and her decisions, she hadn't been able to purchase a new novel in months.

"Good afternoon, Miss Fiona. Here's some lemonade and cucumber sandwiches I put together for you," Mrs. Dickens said as she came into the drawing room wheeling a tea cart towards her.

"How lovely, Mrs. Dickens. Thank you so much for thinking of me," Fiona said, brightening up. The housekeeper had always been very mindful of Fiona's needs and Fiona considered the older woman one of her closer friends. Fiona's earliest memories had been of Mrs. Dickens and she didn't know how else she had managed to survive without the woman since her parents were more concerned about their social appearance than their daughter.

"Of course, darling. The last thing I want is you getting overheated on this hot day. I'd invite you to join me in the kitchen today if it wasn't so warm. It seems your parents are gone for the afternoon and I could teach you how to make those croissants you always love, but it's just too hot today," Mrs. Dickens said, rambling on like normal.

Fiona simply smiled in return as she took a long drink of her lemonade before taking a bite of the cucumber sandwich. Fiona hummed with pleasure as she ate. "These are delicious, Mrs. Dickens. Did you use the cucumbers from the garden?" Fiona asked.

"Indeed, Miss Fiona. I know your mother wasn't keen on you having a garden, but I think it's done you some good to have something to do outside," Mrs. Dickens said with a chuckle. Fiona couldn't help but join her.

"My goodness, the look on Mother's face when I told her I wanted to learn how to garden. That was precious, for sure," Fiona replied as they laughed together about it.

"I know you'll marry well-off, Miss Fiona, but I'm so

proud of you for pursuing the things that interest you the most," Mrs. Dickens said, as she took a hold of the tea cart and began wheeling it out of the drawing room. "You just call if you need anything."

As Mrs. Dickens left the drawing room, Fiona let out a sigh and leaned back against the settee, tucking her feet under her in a very unladylike fashion. If her mother had spotted her doing such a thing, then she would surely be scolded for the behavior. But when her parents were not around, Fiona did her best to do as she pleased.

Though she did love her parents dearly, sometimes she thought of them as very overbearing. And since she'd turned eighteen-years-old, they'd been pressuring her even more. Where Mrs. Wilkins was constantly bickering with Fiona about how she acted and dressed, Mr. Wilkins was constantly hosting dinner parties with every prestigious family in the area that had an eligible son to showcase to Fiona. Every gentleman Fiona had been introduced to since her eighteenth birthday had been more boring than the next. None of them had offered Fiona even a morsel of interest as they all planned to follow after their fathers in the world of business.

Even though Fiona did enjoy all the finer things in life, she was deadly bored of socialite life. She didn't care about balls or dinner parties, the latest fashions, or gossiping with other ladies her age. Instead, she longed for the adventurous life of the heroines she read about in her novels. She dreamed of traveling out West and seeing how people really lived and survived each day. The untamed West called to her both night and day– it was what had inspired her to start gardening. It was a crucial skill that all the heroines had to learn to do, and she thought she might try her hand at it. Now she had a bountiful garden full of all sorts of vegetables that Mrs. Dickens had been using in her cooking. Fiona had even learned how to make a few dishes when her parents didn't know about it.

Fiona knew that her Western dreams were simply just that. She had many fantasies that she knew would never come true. The likelihood of her father allowing her to travel out West was a non-existent one. Just suggesting that they take a trip as a family would probably cause her mother to faint from shock. She knew her mother despised anything that was dirty or difficult. She was born a socialite and would always enjoy this type of lifestyle. But Fiona craved something more than city gossip and fancy clothes. She wanted a life that was more meaningful than getting married, living in luxury, and having babies.

Fiona tucked back a strand of her honey colored hair as she leaned her head back on a plush pillow. She closed her blue eyes as she stretched out her legs before her. Her mind floated to what she pictured to be wide-open plains, a light breeze blowing around her as she looked as far as she could see of the countryside. She could listen to birds chirping all day long as the city faded away from her mind. She was standing in her garden and watching the horizon as she waited for her cowboy to come home from the fields, having watched over their cattle all day. She would then make something delicious for herself and her husband for dinner, and then they would…

Fiona was pulled from her daydream as the drawing room door was pulled open and the butler, Mr. Bentley, came walking quickly into the room. Fiona opened her eyes and sat up just as he said, "Miss Chantelle is here to see you," before the young lady herself came floating into the room as though she owned the place. Fiona quickly stood and smoothed down her blue silk dress, hoping she didn't look to disheveled from lounging about all day.

"Oh, Fiona, darling. You must be beside yourself with

grief," Chantelle said as she came into the room, sashaying her hips in a dramatic way as she handed Fiona a newspaper. Fiona smiled at Mr. Bentley and dipped her head, dismissing him as he swiftly left the room, sliding the door shut.

"I simply do not know what you speak of," Fiona said in a calm voice as she sat once more. Chantelle took a seat close to her as she smoothed down her muslin dress. Fiona would agree that muslin would have been more comfortable on a hot day like today, but her mother insisted she wear silk, in case she had a visitor. At this moment, Fiona thought her mother had been correct in that demand.

"Look at the engagement announcements, darling. You will surely be shocked to read who Miss Genève has been engaged to," Chantelle said in a very dramatic voice. Though the lady was two years younger than Fiona, she liked to act well beyond her age. Since their mothers were close friends, Chantelle took it upon herself to visit with Fiona, and often without a previous announcement or invitation. And since Fiona was quite used to these types of visits, she simply did her best to please her guest and bide her time before she could find a way to escape.

So, Fiona opened the newspaper and made her way to the announcements until she found Genève's name. "It seems that Mr. Prescott has offered his hand in marriage to Miss Genève. That sounds pleasant enough for her," Fiona said, as she folded the paper once more and looked up at Chantelle.

"You must be filled with such anger to learn that Mr. Prescott overlooked you and instead made his offer to that lowly Genève," Chantelle said with such passion that Fiona was certain that the woman had rehearsed this speech many times before visiting her. Fiona instead remained calmed and refrained from rolling her eyes.

"No, Chantelle. I am not moved at all by the announcement. I had no attachment to Mr. Prescott, and I can't think to reason why you would think I would," Fiona said, as she set the newspaper aside and served Chantelle a glass of lemonade. At least it gave her a moment of silence as they both took a long drink.

"Why, it's all your mother has spoken of all morning. She explained how close you two had become and that she thought he would propose to you rather soon," Chantelle explained. Now Fiona was angry as she learned the source of the rumor. She wanted to throttle her own mother for being so flighty.

"Well, my dear, you've heard it from the horse's mouth. I had no attachment to Mr. Prescott and can be truly happy for Genève," Fiona said, as she handed Chantelle a plate with a few cucumber sandwiches on it.

"No thank you, darling. I'm trying to watch my figure. I shall be attending the ball this Saturday and don't want to eat anything that I might regret later," Chantelle said as she refused the plate. Fiona simply set it back on the tea cart and tried to keep her composure. She had forgotten about the ball and now dreaded it even more than when she'd first heard of its existence. She feared what type of gown her mother had chosen for her to wear, and the men her father would force her to meet.

"What do you plan to wear to the ball?" Fiona asked, knowing the question would occupy Chantelle for some time and remove them from their current topic of discussion. The question worked like a charm, and for the next half hour the ladies talked about Chantelle's dress and the gentlemen she hoped to entice.

"That all sounds quite lovely, my dear. But you must excuse me. This heat has done dreadful things to my nerves and I must go lay down now so I can have my strength for this Saturday. But I do appreciate you stopping by to look after me and to bring me a paper," Fiona said in her most kindly voice, as she stood, paper in hand, using it to cover up the novel she'd been reading earlier.

"Of course, darling. I should probably do the same. What a fantastic idea," Chantelle said as she stood. "Do tell your mother I stopped by." And with that, Chantelle sashayed out of the room like a queen.

Once Chantelle left the house, Fiona let out a long sigh as she left the drawing room and took the stairs up to her room. It would be warmer in her room, but at least she wouldn't be disturbed. The house was rather large with multiple rooms that were often left vacant. The house had been designed for guests and events, but besides the routine dinner party, the house saw little life. It was a dull thing to Fiona who saw the house as wasted space. But once she made it to her room and locked the door behind her, she found that this was the safest place in the whole world.

She tucked her novel safely underneath her bed and set the paper on her writing desk before stripping out of her silk gown. She felt much more comfortable in her simple under garments, and in the privacy of her own room with the door locked, she felt comfortable enough to wear what she wanted.

"Women of the West only wear chamise and day gowns," Fiona mumbled to herself as she put the silk gown away in her wardrobe of silk gowns. The sight almost disgusted her knowing the cost of it all. The amount alone would pay for her ticket out West. Letting out another sigh, Fiona sat down at her writing desk and started to flip through the paper. She was hoping to find something of interest when she stumbled across the matrimonial section.

Though she did intend to marry one day, she hadn't really put much thought into it since her father was always pressing her to meet one gentleman or another. The thought of marrying hadn't been something to cause her dread most of the time, but as she saw the recent wedding announcements, she wondered how many of these matches were made out of love. If Fiona was ever going to marry, she was certain she'd only say, "I do," if it was to someone she really loved. There hadn't been a man yet that had made her think she could possibly love someone one day. She wondered if she would ever meet someone that could capture her heart like the heroines in her novels.

As Fiona read through the paper, her eyes were caught on a particular set of bold letters: "Mail-Order-Brides Wanted for Cowboys," the heading read. Fiona's heart did a flip as she started to read over the announcement. It was an advert explaining how an agency was looking to match young ladies to cowboys out West who needed a wife. And with the West having a limited number of women, it wasn't unusual to see these types of ads. But there was something about this one that interested Fiona. She'd always wanted to meet a real cowboy, and she knew she wouldn't marry a gentleman of Boston. Then perhaps she could meet someone out West and truly have a reason to go?

A smile came to Fiona's lips as she withdrew a piece of writing paper and began to respond to the ad. She'd have to bribe Mr. Bentley to post it for her without her parents ever finding out. It wasn't very hard to do since the older man had a soft spot for a heart. She hadn't been this excited since her last novel arrived in the mail unnoticed. As she wrote her letter to the advertisement, she listed everything that she wanted in a husband and explained that she'd be willing to travel West to meet her husband-to-be.

After Fiona had written her letter and sealed it up, she looked at it for a long time. With this letter, she could be changing her entire future. She couldn't possibly be put into correspondence with a real cowboy that she could possibly fall in love with one day, could she? But even if she did agree to go and meet him, would her father ever let her? Would she need to run away from home to seek a better future for herself? As Fiona sat and thought about what she'd honestly be able to do in leaving Boston behind, she started to reason with herself. But in the end of a long mental debate, Fiona knew she had to do something in order to avoid living a very long dull life.

## CHAPTER 3

Eddie felt nervous as he sat at the dining table of Dr. Slater's home. The other ranch hands had moved on for the night after dinner had come to an end. He'd told Sawyer to go on without him, asking him to make sure Jack got fed and hadn't destroyed the bunkhouse while they'd come into the ranch house for dinner. Sawyer had given him a puzzled look, but hadn't asked any questions. Now, Eddie sat at the table with Dr. Slater since Lucy had gone to put Francene to bed.

"Something tells me you want to talk about something," Dr. Slater said, after an uncomfortable moment of silence.

"Yeah, there is," Eddie said as he let go of the deep breath he'd been holding in his chest. "I wanted to talk to you about placing an ad in the East for a mail-order-bride."

Dr. Slater looked at him with wide eyes as he seemed to consider what he'd just said. Then, a small smile started to creep onto his face. Eddie couldn't help but smile as well. He felt silly for talking to his boss about such a thing, but there were only two men that he knew of that had mail-order-brides. And since Gray wasn't the personal feelings type of guy, he'd picked the good doctor to talk to. That, and he was certain that Dr. Slater would keep his secret until he was ready to share it with the others.

"Well, Eddie, I'd sure love to help you. When I first met you and your brother, I thought you two were both a pair of hellions that would never be tamed. But I've seen you truly transform this last year, and I think marriage would suit you well. Though, I don't know how many young ladies would love the idea of sharing a home with a monkey," Dr. Slater said, causing them both to laugh heartily.

Eddie nodded his head as his mirth subsided. "Yeah, I reckon there are a few things about me that most young ladies would turn up their noses to. But I don't want to date anyone from our little town. I'm hoping to meet someone from out of state, if possible," Eddie explained.

"Something tells me you're in the same situation as Gray was," Dr. Slater said with a wink. Eddie could only nod his head since he knew that both he and Gray, along with Sawyer, had been womanizers for a long time.

"That would be true, Doc," Eddie replied. He wasn't ashamed of how he'd lived his life. But he also knew that he didn't want to be Gray's age when he decided to consider a wife and kids.

"Well, how about we write something up tonight, and if you like it, I'll take it in to town with me and post it with Mr. Frost? Ever since Mayor Stavros was able to commission a telegram line to Frost's, he's been biting at the bit to send telegrams as often as he can," Dr. Slater said.

Eddie thought about the offer for a moment. Originally, he'd only intended to talk to Dr. Slater about the idea. The fact that his boss was offering to help him write the ad made him feel a little nervous. But he knew that this would probably be his only way to meet a potential wife, unless the good Lord placed a woman in his path somehow.

"Sure, let's do it," Eddie decided with a smirk.

"That's the spirit. Let me go get us some writing paper," Dr. Slater said as he quickly rose from the table. In the meantime, Eddie tried to think about what his ad would say. What did he want most in a wife? Should he really be all that picky? And what should he say about himself in order to inspire someone to reply to him? By the time Dr. Slater returned to the table with writing paper in hand, along with a quail and ink, Eddie had some sort of idea of what he wanted the ad to say.

"Now, the key to these things is being honest and genuine," Dr. Slater said as he began to write. "You're a hard-working young man with a stable income and fairly good looks."

"Why thank you, Doc. You're not too bad looking yourself," Eddie replied with a chuckle.

"I'm serious, Eddie. The ladies are going to want to know what you look like and what type of guy you are like," Dr. Slater tried to say in a serious tone, though a grin crept at the corner of his mouth.

"Well, I'm a cowboy with a monkey. Make sure that's in there, too. Don't want anyone being surprised if they come out to meet me," Eddie said. He knew that having Jack could be a deal-breaker for most women, but he hoped that there would be someone out there who would love him despite how ornery Jack could be sometime.

"Yes, I think that would be wise. And it will definitely set you apart from all of the others," Dr. Slater agreed as he finished writing the ad. "Alright then, let me know what you think."

As Eddie took the paper. He looked over the words, feeling embarrassed for what he was about to say. "Forgive me, Dr. Slater, but could you read it to me? I was never really good in school," Eddie said sheepishly.

Dr. Slater took back the ad and looked at Eddie for a good moment or two. "Eddie, you can read and write, can't you?" he asked.

Eddie took a deep breath and let it out before replying, "Just a little. Pa took us boys out of school to run the farm when he and Ma both got sick from the flu. They died soon after, and Sawyer and I have been working to survive ever since. There wasn't much time for learning after that," Eddie explained. He knew that he could have taken the opportunity to learn to read and write instead of chasing after women. But he hadn't thought it very important until now.

"Well, I'll read this for you, Eddie, but it's the last time. From now on, in the evenings you're going to have to learn to read and write if you're going to get yourself a mail-order-bride," Dr. Slater said in a firm voice.

"Yes, sir," Eddie replied, knowing there was no point in arguing with the doctor. With that agreement, Dr. Slater read him the ad. Afterwards, Eddie agreed to it, knowing that it was very accurate.

"Well, wish me luck," Eddie said in parting, as he left the ranch house and headed for the bunk house. The night was dark and cool, a refreshing feeling. And as Eddie glanced up at the stars above, he prayed that he'd meet his future wife one day soon.

~

"Boring. Boring. Dull. Not likely to happen," Fiona mumbled to herself as she looked through the ads the agency had sent her after they'd received her inquiry. So far, she'd been able to hide her correspondence from her parents after offering to pay Mr. Bentley five extra dollars a week to ensure her mail was delivered to her room instead of left on the mantel in the hallway for when her father returned from his office every afternoon. And now she read through her second batch of mail-order-bride ads without much luck.

So far, she'd read several ads about cowboys wanting a woman to cook, clean, raise children, and keep his bed warm at night. They all sounded rather odious and didn't really pique her interest because she was looking for adventure. She didn't want to be someone's live-in servant. Fiona wanted a chance at a real life, and someone to truly love.

Fiona almost took the ads and prepared to rip them up into tiny little pieces so she could dispose of them later without having her parents happen upon and read them, when the last ad caught her attention. The title read, "Cowboy With A Monkey."

"What in the world?" Fiona said as she flattened out the ad and began to read.

'Montana cowboy is seeking a bride from the East. He's a hardworking man with stable employment and a great sense of humor. Has light brown hair and blue eyes that dazzle. But the best part is that Eddie has a pet monkey that can do all sorts of fun tricks. This unique cowboy won't be single for long, so send your letters right away.'

Fiona was giggling by the time she finished reading the ad. She could hardly imagine a cowboy with a pet monkey that could do tricks. She had to admit that this Eddie character was more amusing than any other ad she had read, and probably more charismatic than any gentleman she'd ever been introduced to. As she sat there, she started to bite her lower lip as she tried to decide what to do. She could certainly tear up this ad with the others. But would there ever be a more interesting ad? Knowing that most of them had been rather dull, Fiona decided to save this ad. And as she started to tear up the others, she grew excited about the idea of writing to Eddie right away.

"WHO'D you get the letter from, little brother?" Sawyer asked, as they walked towards the barn after having lunch up at the ranch house. Lucy had just come home from her morning shift at the boutique with Francene, bringing home the mail with her. And though Lucy had been kind enough not to pester Eddie about the origins of the letter, since everyone knew how nosy Lucy could be, it seemed that his older brother wouldn't give him the same treatment.

"I have to open it first," Eddie responded as he pocketed the letter. Though he was curious himself to know who the author of the letter was, he hadn't told anyone besides Dr. Slater that he'd placed an ad for a mail-order-bride. He didn't want to share the news with anyone until it was certain that he'd met someone worth sending for. Until then, he wasn't going to give up hope, or allow anyone to stir up his emotions, either.

"Well, aren't you going to open it now?" Sawyer asked as they mounted their horses. But all Eddie did was whistle for Jack, causing the monkey to come running to him from up in the rafters of the barn. The monkey swung down with his tail and landed on Eddie's shoulder. Then with a click of his heels, he sent his gelding to a canter towards the open gate. Not wanting to respond to his brother's question, he made quick work of separating himself from the other man, wanting to seek a moment alone in order to read the letter in private.

As he worked on the far side of the field, keeping an eye on the cattle and making sure the herd was together, he finally took the time to pull the letter from his back pocket. But like Jack often did, he jumped down on the saddle, thinking Eddie had pulled some food from his pocket, and quickly took the letter from Eddie's hand and jumped down to the ground with it.

"Jack, no! Bad monkey! Bring me back that letter," Eddie called as he turned his horse around. As Jack scurried across the ground, dodging between the feet of the cattle and disappearing into the herd, Eddie did his best to follow the monkey, trying not to scatter or disturb the cows. Eventually, Eddie had to dismount and follow the monkey on foot.

"Jack! Jack, get back here!" Eddie called out between whistles he used to summon the furry animal. But nothing seemed to work until he came to the shady tree he often sat under on hot days. It was also the same tree that Jack often seemed to get stuck in. And it was here that Eddie found the monkey high in the trees, eating the corner of the letter.

"Damn monkey!" Eddie cried out as he kicked the tree as hard as he could. The tree shook, scaring Jack to the point where he dropped the letter and clung to the tree. But Eddie was also hollering in pain from where he'd stubbed his toe. By the time the pain had subsided, the letter had finally drifted down to him from the tree above, where Jack remained, clutching one of the top branches.

"That's what you get for stealing from me, Jack! You can stay up there for days for all I care," Eddie called up to the tree. Eddie picked up the letter from the ground then and inspected it, seeing small tears in the envelope and an entire corner wet from where Jack had tried to eat it. Muttering to himself, Eddie pocketed the letter once more and walked away from the tree, needing to find his horse and regroup the herd from where he had scattered it earlier.

Once things seemed to be calm again, Eddie looked around him to be certain he was alone before extracting the letter again, and finally opening it. Inside were three sheets of writing paper, both front and back. He was surprised by the length of the letter, and as he looked down at the fancy cursive letters, Eddie groaned with frustration. He'd been so excited to read the letter, having been practicing every night with Dr. Slater, that he hadn't thought of having to deal with cursive. But as he pressed the letter to his face, hoping to see better, he only groaned louder with frustration.

"Damn it!" Eddie hollered as he folded the letter carefully and placed it back inside the envelope. Now he'd have to wait even longer to discover the contents of the letter.

"I'M SORRY, Eddie. I think Sam got stuck in town with a patient. But if ye want, I can help ya if ye need it," Lucy said as she rocked Francene to sleep in the rocker that Dr. Slater had commissioned Zachariah Welliver, the local furniture maker, to create for Lucy. Eddie had come into the sitting room after dinner had been cleaned up, hoping to figure out when the doctor would be home so he could help Eddie read the letter with him. And now he was faced with an even harder decision. Tell Lucy why he needed help reading the letter and who the letter was from, or, have to wait until tomorrow night to discover what the letter said. Not being a very patient man, Eddie took a seat in the chair next to Lucy as he pulled out the letter.

"I've been working very hard with Dr. Slater to improve my language skills," Eddie said carefully. "But the letter I received today is in cursive. I'm not experienced with this type of language and was hoping Dr. Slater could help me."

"If ye don't mind, I could read the letter to ya," Lucy said, her Irish accent still very apparent even after her time away from her Irish family. And despite being born into an Irish family, she had long black hair. It was her accent that gave her away each time.

"It may be sensitive, Mrs. Slater. You see, Dr. Slater helped me place an ad in the paper," Eddie explained nervously. Lucy seemed to have understood his meaning because her eyebrows rose as her mouth formed an 'o'.

"I see," she said as she rocked the baby in her arms. "Well, I believe that will be up to ye. I won't tell anyone what the letter says, but the young lady who has written ya might be upset if someone else reads her letter."

"Oh, I didn't think about that," Eddie said, feeling more defeated than before. "Then how am I going to be able to read it?"

Eddie watched Lucy as she rocked in the chair, looking off in the distance as though thinking hard about the situation. "Well, either ye have someone read it to ya, or, ye learn how to read cursive real fast," Lucy said with a smile, as she focused her eyes back on him.

Eddie sighed heavily as he thought about the two options. He could either learn the contents of the letter quickly, but risk upsetting the author of the letter. Or, he could take the time to learn the necessary skills to read it himself.

"Well, I don't want to risk messing up my chance at marriage before I've even begun. I'll learn how to read cursive," Eddie decided, even though he hated to think how long that would take. Lucy smiled at him as though she approved.

"It seems we should get started right away then," Lucy said. Eddie smiled kindly, even though he disliked the idea of having to learn another form of writing. But as he looked down at the letters on the front of the envelope, his motivation was sparked to learn more about the young lady who had taken a chance on him and write him three whole sheets of writing paper.

# CHAPTER 4

After waiting for weeks for a reply from Eddie, Fiona was starting to get discouraged. Since she'd replied to a mail-order-bride ad, she hadn't received any other ads from the agency in the hopes that she would be successful with Eddie. But without receiving a response from the cowboy with a monkey, Fiona reasoned that it was time to inquire with the agency once more to hopefully correspond with someone else.

"Maybe it wasn't meant to be," Fiona mumbled to herself.

"What is that, dear?" Mr. Wilkins spoke up from the head of the table. Fiona had forgotten herself once more and had spoken out loud when she had meant to keep her thoughts to herself. She was surrounded by her father's closest friends, their families, and of course, their eligible sons.

"I was just commenting how wonderful the meal is, and the pleasant company we have this evening," Fiona said with a smile she hoped would be convincing.

"Ah, how nice of you to say," Mr. Wilkins said before turning the conversation back to his business partner.

"Fiona dear, why don't you tell Mr. Leanly how you've been spending your time volunteering at the children's orphanage," Mrs. Wilkins spoke up, startling Fiona since she'd never stepped foot in an orphanage before.

Fiona forced a smile onto her face, willing to play her mother's game. "Indeed, Mr. Leanly," Fiona said, as she turned her eyes to the gentleman that had been purposefully sat next to her in an effort to capture her interest. "The children's orphanage has a lovely plot of land behind the building that they've been using to garden. I help the children with their vegetable garden, teaching them what plants are best to grow this time of year since summer is coming to an end." There were gasps around the table, yet Fiona kept a smile on her face.

"Are you saying, Miss Fiona, that you enjoy gardening? That you're knowledgeable in it?" Mr. Leanly asked in a shocked voice.

"Indeed, sir. I do love to garden. There is a small vegetable garden here that I enjoy cultivating. There is nothing better than tasting the vegetables from your own hard work," Fiona said proudly. If her mother was going to start telling lies about Fiona in front of a room full of socialites, then she was going to make sure she not only embarrassed her parents, but used truths to combat lies. The last thing she'd ever be considered is a liar.

"If I didn't know better, I would say you were a pioneer woman," Mr. Leanly said with a chuckle, causing the others to join him. But as Fiona looked towards her mother, she could see she was not laughing with the others and that her face had turned a shade of red.

"Why thank you for such a lovely compliment, Mr. Leanly," Fiona said, even though her eyes were locked with her mother's. She even laughed with the others when this comment seemed to stir everyone's mirth.

For the rest of the meal, Fiona was left alone. She didn't receive any more encouragement from her parents to speak during the meal, and after her declaration that she manually worked earth to grow vegetables, she instantly became less attractive to every eligible gentleman in the room. But it was no matter to Fiona. She preferred it this way since she would never marry a man who couldn't accept her for who she truly was. And she'd be damned if she was going to be told she couldn't do what she loved by her husband. It was bad enough that she was constantly told what she couldn't do by her parents. She would never tolerate that from her husband.

When the meal had come to an end and the dinner guests had left for the night, Fiona was making her way up the stairs when her mother came walking quickly after her. "You ungracious little girl. How could you embarrass your father and I like that?" she called up to Fiona who had stopped to face her mother. As Fiona stared down at her mother, she squared her shoulders.

"How could you say such a lie about me? I have never been to the children's orphanage. It would be easy to discover that you and I were lying about such a thing. Did you think that one of the families at dinner more than likely volunteers their time there as well? I was not going to lie any more than I needed to," Fiona said in a stern voice.

And before her mother could get in another word, Fiona continued. "Mother, I am not a little girl any longer. I am of age and will not tarnish my reputation any more than you two have already." Fiona then turned and continued up the stairs as her mother continued to call up to her.

"Mr. Crane has asked your father for permission to marry you," Mr. Wilkins then said. Fiona froze on the stairs, her heart beating fast in her chest as she turned around and looked down at her mother, her face red with embarrassment.

"Mr. Crane is twice my age," Fiona replied.

"Yet he's a wealthy man who is sure to make you happy," Mrs. Wilkins shot back.

"Wealth doesn't make a person happy, Mother. Compassion, love, and honesty do," Fiona said as she took a few steps down the stairs towards her mother.

"Those are things of fairytales," Mrs. Wilkins scoffed. "Your father will allow Mr. Crane to marry you if you don't obtain any better suitors."

"But I'm the one who gets to agree to the marriage. Not you, or Father," Fiona said, her anger building.

"Not in this family, you don't. You'll listen to whatever your father tells you to do, and that's final," Mrs. Wilkins said in a high-pitched voice, which was her attempt at yelling at Fiona. She then turned on her heels and walked away quickly. As Fiona stood and watched her mother make her way to Father's study, she knew that the woman would have cross words with her husband. Fiona wasn't going to stick around to hear her parents argue once again. Instead, she turned back around and marched up the stairs, then walked quickly down the hallway until she reached her room.

Once the door was securely locked behind her, Fiona crumbled to her knees as her emotions overtook her. Tears streamed down her face as she sobbed, praying beyond hope that she would find a way out of this mess. She couldn't believe her parents could be so heartless about her future. The image of Mr. Crane rose in her mind. Just the thought made her stomach churn with unease. He was not only much older than her, but also a very round fellow with a sleezy reputation. Even if his income far exceeded her father's, she would never marry him for all the money in the world.

A knock on the door forced Fiona to settle her nerves so no one would hear her sobbing. "It's just me, Miss Fiona," came Mrs. Dickens voice. Fiona quickly wiped her eyes on the back of her hand as she stood and went over to the door. She unlocked it and pulled the door open, eager to get out of the tight-fitting gown her mother had insisted she wear this evening.

"Let's get you ready for bed," Mrs. Dickens said, as another chambermaid came in to assist Fiona. In no time at all, Fiona was stripped of her gown and petticoats and helped into a nightgown. It felt refreshing to not be in so many layers, and after she'd been wiped down with a cool, damp cloth, she felt much better.

"There you go, Miss Fiona. All better," Mrs. Dickens said as she shooed the chambermaid out with Fiona's laundry to tend to. "And if I remember correctly, Mr. Bentley brought up some mail for you," Mrs. Dickens added as she pointed to Fiona's writing desk.

Fiona had been so overcome by her nerves that she hadn't even noticed the letter. But as she looked towards her writing desk, where a candle had been lit and set beside it, she could clearly see a letter postmarked from Montana. She couldn't help but smile as she turned back to Mrs. Dickens.

"Thank you, Mrs. Dickens," Fiona said.

"My pleasure, Miss Fiona. Anything you need, you just let me know," Mrs. Dickens said in a more serious voice. Fiona wondered about the meaning of her words as the woman curtsied and left the room. Fiona locked the door once more before taking a seat at the writing desk.

Fiona picked up the envelope and ran her fingers gently across the printed letters. They were neatly written, and she couldn't help but smile as she looked at her own name. Then, she looked at Eddie Murtaugh's written name and smiled even more. Just when she'd given up hope, she had finally received a letter from him.

Carefully opening the envelope to preserve Eddie's postal address, Fiona pulled out a sheet of writing paper. At first, she was a little disappointed because she'd written such a detailed letter. But she soon reminded herself that a short letter was better than no letter at all. So therefore, she pressed the letter flat to her writing desk as she began to read with excitement.

*Dear Miss Fiona Wilkins,*

*Please forgive me for my late response. Your beautifully written letter took me longer than anticipated to read since I am not familiar with cursive words. But after receiving help from a good friend to learn cursive writing, I then did enjoy your letter, over and over again.*

*You shared with me so many details about your life in Boston that I can understand why you'd want to leave it all behind. Having been without parents since my brother and I were very young, we've had to work hard for everything we have today. There is a sense of pride that comes from forging your own destiny. And though I know several businessmen and women who work hard, it sounds like if you are born into wealth, then you have a higher chance of taking it for granted.*

*I'm glad to hear you enjoy gardening. It's a fundamental part of living so far from town. People in our community have to do this for themselves since supplies are limited. Though Mr. Frost keeps a good stock at his mercantile, one can't rely on stagecoaches to make routine stops in our town to deliver more supplies. Therefore, everyone in Spruce Valley maintains their own gardens, and large ones at that.*

*You asked good questions about Jack, my pet monkey. He's a wild one, for sure, but has a kind side to him as well. He often sleeps at the foot of my bed and will keep me company on long cattle drives. He is liked by many on the ranch, even though he's not allowed in the ranch house after he tore at Mrs. Slater's curtains. He keeps reminding me that he's more a wild animal than a pet. But I wouldn't trade him for the world.*

*I know you wrote a lot about your life in Boston and how you don't really care for it. I want to reassure you that there are two mail-order brides here in Spruce Valley, and actually live here on the ranch. Mrs. Slater —Lucy— is a mail-order-bride, and so is my foreman's wife, Martha. So, you'll be in good company here. Lucy and Martha now manage a women's boutique in town, even though they both have small children. I guess times are changing and women are becoming more independent.*

*Well, it seems I'm rambling now. I look forward to your next letter and promise to respond quicker next time.*

*Eddie Murtaugh*

By the time Fiona finished reading the letter, she had a wide smile on her face. She read the letter three times over before she pulled out sheets of writing paper and began to write her own response. It was late at night, but she didn't care. She was filled with such excitement to have received Eddie's letter that she wanted to respond right away. She knew it would take some time for Eddie to receive her letter because of the wide distance between them, but she knew the sooner she wrote the letter, the sooner it would arrive.

As Fiona finished her letter and addressed it to Eddie in Spruce Valley, Montana, she sat for a while and looked at the address. She'd have to find a map to discover where Spruce Valley was, and even investigate how to travel there. The idea of traveling by stagecoach sounded dreadful, but perhaps the train went close enough to the small town that she wouldn't have to worry too much about travel arrangements. Fiona was so filled with thoughts that she didn't know how to best organize them, or what type of action she wanted to take. But as she thought about Mr. Crane once more, she knew that no matter what, she was going to leave Boston behind.

# CHAPTER 5

Eddie was putting his horse in the stable after a long day out under the sun. For the end of summer, it was sure hot. He'd even kept Jack in the bunk house with plenty of water because he was afraid of fatiguing the monkey or allowing him to stay outside for too long. And with the heat, it had also meant hauling extra water from the stream to ensure none of the cattle were getting dehydrated.

"Good work out there today," Gray said, as he came riding into the stables on his stallion.

"Thanks, boss. The heat was killer, but I'm confident the cows have plenty of water 'til tomorrow," Eddie replied as he brushed down his horse, not wanting the beast to feel sweaty with matted hair all night. Not too long after that, Sawyer came riding in with Tom Barker, the other ranch hand.

"Fences are secure, boss. The repairs were pretty minimal and no signs of wildlife," Tom reported as soon as they dismounted.

"Then it seems I'll have good news for the boss man

tonight," Gray said with a chuckle, as they all finished bedding down their horses for the night. Then, they made their way into the ranch house for dinner.

"Honey, I'm home!" Gray called as soon as he stepped over the threshold of the ranch house. Eddie chuckled with the others, but Martha was soon crossing the main room to shush him.

"Samuel just fell asleep," Martha chastised her husband, who was quick to close the space between them, wrapping his arms around her and planting a passionate kiss on her lips.

"I'm glad to hear he's well," Gray said when he broke their kiss. Eddie just shook his head as he took a seat at the table. It was another reminder of how badly Eddie wanted something like that in his own life.

"Here's the mail for you, Eddie," Dr. Slater said as he came into the room. He handed Eddie a small pile of letters, which Eddie quickly tucked underneath his leg. He pretended that it was nothing but could feel Sawyer's eyes on him.

As the dinner progressed, Eddie did his best to join in with the conversation where he could. He was eager to look through the letters to see if any of them were interesting. He'd been enjoying his reading and writing lessons with Dr. Slater in the evenings and felt more confident about responding to any possible letters. However, he hadn't received any interesting letters since he'd received Miss Fiona Wilkins' letter.

Eddie was anxious and in a hurry by the time dinner was done. He stuck the letters in his back pocket as he helped clear the dishes and clean up after dinner. He was heading back to the dining table to read his letters and hopefully respond to one, when Sawyer came up to him and spoke in a low voice.

"When are you going to tell me about these letters you keep getting?" Sawyer asked as he narrowed his eyes at Eddie.

Eddie was silent for a moment as he bid goodnight to Tom, Gray, and Martha as they left the house. Dr. Slater was known for retiring to the sitting room, and Lucy had taken Francene to rest for the night. When the coast was clear, Eddie turned his focus back to Sawyer.

"It's nothing yet, Sawyer. I'll let you know when it's serious, though," Eddie said, hoping his answer would please him enough.

"Are you plotting some sort of big move? What do you have in the works?" Sawyer asked as he stepped closer to Eddie.

"Sawyer, it's nothing like that. I enjoy working here at the ranch. Besides, if I was thinking of something else, you'd be the first to know," Eddie said as he looked at his brother with a puzzled expression. Usually Sawyer wasn't this paranoid.

"Yet it seems you've told the Slaters what you're doing," Sawyer said, as he looked over his shoulder where Dr. Slater was sitting in the other room in his favorite wingback chair.

"That's because the Slaters have helped me improve my reading and writing skills. Can't send and receive mail if you can't read and write," Eddie explained.

"But why won't you tell me what's going on?" Sawyer pressed. Eddie stared into his brother's eyes. He could either continue to push his brother away, or he could finally tell him everything.

"Dr. Slater helped me place a mail-order-bride ad in the papers back East. Mrs. Slater helped me learn cursive so I could read and respond to a letter I had received. And now I have a whole pile to go through, it seems," Eddie said point-blankly. Eddie watched as his brother took the time to process everything he had just said. Then, Sawyer doubled over as laughter riddled his body.

"Shut your trap, Sawyer. You're going to upset Mrs. Slater if you wake the baby," Eddie said as he slapped his brother on the back of the head, shutting him up real fast.

"I'm sorry, Eddie. I thought you were in some sort of financial trouble and that's why you kept getting all those letters," Sawyer said, as he wiped the laughter tears from his eyes.

"Well, now you know the truth. Can I get some peace and quiet to read these letters? It's still hard to read so much," Eddie said, as he sat down at the table and pulled out the pile of letters, setting them before him.

"Do you need any help?" Sawyer asked.

"I don't think so. I figure your reading skills are as miserable as mine," Eddie said as he looked at the address of the first letter, and then started opening it.

"True. I don't read so well, but I can listen to what you think of the letters if you want someone to talk about them with," Sawyer offered, as he sat down at the table across from Eddie.

Eddie observed his brother for a moment. Normally Sawyer would have teased Eddie pretty good about something like this. Especially anything that related to women. But it seemed that Sawyer was being genuine with his offer.

"Sure, why not," Eddie agreed as he opened the first letter. "Most of them are pretty ridiculous, I'll tell you. Either dull as a doornail, or older women looking for a young man."

Sawyer chuckled as he folded his arms over his chest. "A bunch of old maids hoping to get lucky later in life," he said. Eddie simply nodded his head as he began reading the letter slowly, making sure he could understand it without issue.

"I don't think I could take on four kids right now," Eddie

said as he set the letter aside and turned his attention to the next one. When he recognized Fiona's name, he opened the letter as excitement shot through him.

*Dear Eddie,*

*I hope you don't mind that I use your first name. I like to think with each letter we are truly getting to know one another on a first name basis.*

*The weather in Boston has finally started to cool. It's a blessing since the days have been so dreadfully hot. I'm sure more so in Montana while being outside all the time. But even when it's hot, I do enjoy cultivating my garden or helping Mrs. Dickins with the cooking. I'm sure my parents would love me to learn how to play the piano or spend my time volunteering in the community to attract wealthy gentlemen as suitors, but I thoroughly enjoy creating things with my own hands. I even had Mrs. Dickens show me simple needle work like mending clothes. I take pride in seeing what I can do myself.*

*My parents have been pressuring more and more to marry. They've even threatened to arrange my marriage. So, since I am now of age, I know that I have the right and privilege to pave my own way in life. I'm not sure why I'm writing to tell you this, but I've always believed that a relationship of any kind should be based on compassion, trust, and honesty. If we are to ever become a match, I want you to know everything there is about me, and what motivates me to take action.*

*I'm sure I sound like a spoiled brat sometimes, wanting to leave this life of luxury behind and move out West. But you see, I find no pleasure in any of it. Perhaps it's simply because of the type of parents I have, or the pressure of society I currently feel. But I can't help but think that life is simpler in the West. No big cities, no one judging you for your wants and dreams. When I think of possibilities, I think of anywhere but Boston.*

*Now it seems that I am the one rambling. I've just experienced a dreadful dinner party and my emotions are still running high. But I shall post this letter the day after receiving your last one. I look forward to your next letter to read what has been happening in your life lately. How is Jack doing? Tell me more about the people of Spruce Valley.*

*Fiona Wilkins*

*P.S. I've also included a photo of myself that was used in the papers when I was debuted into society this past spring.*

As Eddie read the letter slowly, he couldn't help but smile. He found Fiona's letter quite humorous because he couldn't imagine a socialite enjoying things like gardening, cooking, and fixing clothes. But he could understand Fiona's perspective of feeling pride by creating with your own hands. Eddie was proud of the type of work he did and always felt good at the end of the day for having earned a living by doing the best work he could do.

Eddie then took the black and white photo that Fiona had included with her letter. A faint smile clung to her luscious lips as she looked straight at the camera. Her eyes were mesmerizing, even in the photo. Her hair had been curled and pinned up behind her head, accentuating her long neck. She appeared tall with a slim figure, but not in an unpleasant way. Eddie thought she looked rather delicate, but her letter showcased just how fiery she could be.

Eddie then passed the photo to Sawyer as he folded up the letter and tucked it into his shirt pocket. He planned to respond to Fiona right away, as soon as he read through the rest of the letters.

"Wow. She's definitely not a Western woman," Sawyer replied, as he handed the photo back to Eddie.

"Yes. It's clear that she's from a wealthy family, but she's been very honest and up front about herself and her family. You'll be surprised to know that she can cook, garden, and fix clothes," Eddie said with a chuckle.

"Why in the world would a young lady raised by a prestigious family be interested in those things? Surely she has loads of servants to do that sort of thing?" Sawyer reasoned.

"She explains that she enjoys creating things with her hands, that she takes pride in what she's able to do for herself," Eddie replied. He didn't want to share any intimate details with anyone about Fiona's letters, to respect her privacy. But he was enjoying speaking about her to his brother.

"Well, I guess it's a good thing that she understands how to do some things. She might not have been raised out here in the prairie, but there are plenty of skills that a young woman needs in order to get by," Sawyer said as he stood from the table. "Well, I'm getting some sleep. Tomorrow waits for no man."

Eddie simply nodded in agreement as Sawyer left the ranch house. He felt better having shared his secret with his brother, and talking to him about Fiona also made him feel good. As Eddie looked down at the other letters, he decided it would be best not to even bother with them. He had a good feeling about Fiona and wanted to pursue writing her, even if it meant having to have his ad run again in the paper, at a later time, if things didn't work out. As he looked down at her photo in his hands, Eddie hoped that he'd found the one.

~

FIONA HAD JUST RETURNED from a tea party with her mother and had made quick work of going straight to her room to avoid any further conversation with the woman, when Mrs.

Dickens came into her room. Fiona turned towards her, ready to let her know that she wasn't needed, but she watched as Mrs. Dickens locked the door. Then, the older woman took a letter from her apron pocket and handed it to Fiona.

"Mr. Bentley asked me to hold onto this for you 'til you returned from afternoon tea," Mrs. Dickens explained. Fiona took the letter and saw that it was from Eddie. She smiled as she traced her fingers around the letter. She couldn't wait to read it. But as she looked back up at Mrs. Dickens, she could tell that the woman was worried.

"What is the matter, Mrs. Dickens?" she asked. She set the letter aside, wanting to give the woman her full attention.

"Mr. Crane stopped by while you and your mother were out. It seems that you'll soon be married," Mrs. Dickens said with tears in her eyes. Fiona was instantly filled with dread as her stomach tightened. She looked away from Mrs. Dickens as tears of her own started to fill her eyes.

"What am I going to do?" Fiona said softly to herself, not intending to direct the question at Mrs. Dickens.

"Don't you want to marry a man such as Mr. Crane?" Mrs. Dickens asked.

Fiona laughed in mockery. "The man is twice my age and quite repulsive. I will never marry such a man," Fiona replied. A faint smile came to Mrs. Dickens' mouth and she couldn't help but smile as well.

"What do you want to do, Miss Fiona?" Mrs. Dickens asked carefully. Fiona looked to the letter on her writing desk and knew that there was a whole world of possibilities waiting for her outside of Boston.

"I will not remain in my parent's home if they are going to force me to marry someone I don't love, let alone respect. If I have to, I'll run away," Fiona said, squaring her shoulders.

"I don't blame you for wanting to go, Miss Fiona. But where would you go?" Mrs. Dickens asked.

"There is a place called Spruce Valley, in Montana. I've heard that it's lovely and a good place for women to choose their own destinies," Fiona explained.

"That's an awfully far place to go," Mrs. Dickens said. "But your parents surely wouldn't think to look for you there."

Fiona nodded her head, thinking that would be true. Then, she wondered just what Mrs. Dickens would do if she did decide to run away. "And if I did flee to Montana, would you tell my parents?" Fiona asked.

Mrs. Dickens smiled kindly at Fiona as the older woman closed the distance between them and took Fiona's hands in hers. "I've been with you since the day you were born, Miss Fiona. I've watched you grow up into a very fine woman that any mother would be proud to have. And though I am not your real mother, I like to think I've cared for you as such. And as a motherly figure in your life, I want what is best for you. I will miss you dearly, but I like to think that you'd write me when you got settled," Mrs. Dickens said with fresh tears in her eyes.

"Oh, Mrs. Dickens. How could I ever leave you behind? Surely you'd want to come with me?" Fiona asked as she fought back the tears that threatened to spill from her eyes.

"No, I am far too old to be setting off on any adventures. You must go on this trip alone and make a way for yourself. Just tell people you're a married woman returning home from visiting your family in the East. I bet I could even find you a ring to wear if you needed it," Mrs. Dickens said as she let go of Fiona's hands and wiped away her tears.

"Now then. It seems we have much to do to get you ready to travel. And I'm afraid we don't have much time to do so. If I heard correctly, the wedding itself should take place in a fortnight," Mrs. Dickens said.

Fiona was shocked to discover that her wedding would be so soon when her parents hadn't even told her, nor had she agreed to such a thing. Fiona was burning with anger as she considered it all. How could her parents expect her to truly go through with the wedding when she would never agree to such a thing?

"I'm not sure how to get started, Mrs. Dickens. Surely my parents would discover my plans if I tried to shop for the trip, or even make my own traveling arrangements?" Fiona queried, worried she could actually escape before the day of the wedding.

"Don't worry, my dear. I'll get everything settled for you. Mr. Wilkins won't even know a thing 'til you are long gone," Mrs. Dickens said with a pleasing smile. "But for now, you better keep out of sight. I'm sure your parents will want to tell you the news yourself. Try to act surprised and not upset too much. I promise you, I won't let you marry Mr. Crane."

"Oh, thank you dearly, Mrs. Dickens. I don't know how I would have survived this long without you," Fiona said before Mrs. Dickens unlocked the door and stepped out into the hallway. Fiona quickly locked it after her and sat down at her writing desk. She was overcome with emotions as she looked down at Eddie's letter. She desperately wanted to open it, but her mind was racing so fast concerning her own situation, that it took her some time to calm down before she could open the letter and read it.

*Dear Fiona,*

*Thank you for writing your last letter in print. It made it much easier to read and I appreciate your consideration. I'm sorry to hear that your parents are pressuring you so much into marrying. I can't imagine that and can only admit that there is much about your lifestyle that I may have a hard time understanding. Life here in the West is very different because everyone must grow or raise their own food and make what they can. There are only a few businesses here, so we have to make do with what we have.*

*This time next year, I hope to start building my own home. I enjoy the bunkhouse and the comradery of the other ranch hands, but one day I want to be able to sit out front on my own front porch and watch the sun set. I want a place I can feel excited about returning to each day. I don't know if I ever want to start my own ranch, but I do know I want my own plot of land. It doesn't need to be very big, just big enough for me and my future family.*

*I'm only twenty-five, but I do know what I want in life. I think my brother Sawyer is starting to think the same way. He was so paranoid about why I was receiving so many letters. I was at first embarrassed to tell him that I put in an ad for a mail-order-bride, but getting to talk to him about it, and about you, made me feel really good. I like to think that I'm making good choices for my future and that includes taking chances.*

*Thank you for the photo you sent with your letter. I can honestly say you're a beautiful woman. Any man would be honored to have you as their wife. I wish I had a photo to send back to you, but I've never had the chance to be photographed. Perhaps that's something else I can look forward to in the future as well.*

*I hope this letter finds you well, and I'm glad to hear the weather in Boston is cooling down. Things are still hot here in Spruce Valley, but I'm sure fall weather is right around the corner. I look forward to your next letter.*

*Eddie Murtaugh*

## CHAPTER 6

The train whistle blew, signaling the train would soon be leaving the station. Fiona stood on the platform, her hands intertwined with Mrs. Dickens as they looked at each other with tear-filled eyes. It had been a week since Mrs. Dickens had told Fiona the news about her arranged marriage and they were able to put into place this plan for Fiona to flee Boston. Mrs. Dickens had made all the travel arrangements for Fiona. It had taken some time to purchase the proper traveling clothes and things Fiona would need to get settled in Spruce Valley, but Fiona was now ready to make the trip.

"I knew the day would come when I would have to say goodbye to you," Mrs. Dickens said in a shaky voice. "There's writing paper in your trunk. Make sure to write to me as soon as you are settled, and not a moment later."

"I will, Mrs. Dickens. I will let you know that I am well and safe, and hopefully I'll be writing to let you know that I am happily married to a man I actually love," Fiona said with a smile as tears streamed down her face. She didn't realize how much she loved the older woman until she had to say goodbye.

The whistle blew a final time, signaling its departure. Fiona quickly let go of Mrs. Dickens hands and stepped up onto the train as it started to move. She stood on the narrow stairs, waving to the woman as the train started to pull away. She was filled with so much pain in her chest to be leaving her behind, but since today was the day that her mother planned to take her to get fitted for her wedding dress, she knew she couldn't wait any longer.

As the platform disappeared from sight, Fiona finally made her way into the passenger car. In the hopes of trying to fit in and not stand out as a socialite, Fiona's ticket was for a common seat instead of an entire cabin to herself. With a limited amount of funds, she'd have to make smart decisions moving forward.

The further the train pulled away from Boston, the more excited Fiona became. She was able to eventually settle her nerves and clear her face of tears as the sun started to rise. It was a brand-new day, and the first of many days until she would reach Spruce Valley. She would be able to take the train all the way to Montana, but eventually she'd have to rent a stagecoach to take her straight to Spruce Valley. And even when she got there, she wasn't certain what she would do when she arrived or how she would get in touch with Eddie. She knew that he worked on Dr. Slater's ranch, so she figured that would be enough information to help her locate him.

Fiona tried to picture Eddie in her mind as the train made its way. She had taken a seat next to the window and was able to watch the scenery come alive with the morning sun. Fiona wondered if Eddie being tall meant he was taller than her, which she hoped he was, even though she was a tall woman herself. She even wondered what it would be like to go on a real date with him instead of having to attend a dinner party and have their meeting arranged by her parents.

Fiona rubbed the golden band on her wedding finger, a tool Mrs. Dickens assured would help her stay out of trouble. She didn't want to attract any unwanted attention by traveling alone. Appearing as though she was a married woman would help others hopefully respect her. But as she looked down at the wedding band, she wondered what it would be like to be married to a cowboy like Eddie.

But all that Fiona knew for sure was that the further and faster the train made its way away from Boston, the happier she would be. Shortly after hearing the news from Mrs. Dickens, her mother and father had summoned her into the drawing room to explain to her that Mr. Crane had asked for Fiona's hand in marriage. That not only had her father accepted the offer, but also the business investment that Mr. Crane was willing to donate to his company. She'd been appalled to have been sold in such a way but had done well to keep her emotions under control. She didn't let her parents see her disapproval, knowing that Mrs. Dickens would help her escape. Instead, she had accepted the news with grace before returning to her room.

For the next few days after speaking with her parents, Fiona had done her best to avoid them as much as possible and spoke very little at dinner. There was even one point when her father asked if she was feeling well because she'd become very lifeless around the house.

"Yes, Father. I am healthy," Fiona had replied, without even looking at her father as she enjoyed the butternut squash soup that she'd helped Mrs. Dickens prepare that day.

While she'd been avoiding her parents, she instead had spent every available moment with Mrs. Dickens. The older woman was doing her best to prepare Fiona for living as a pioneer. Fiona had to quickly learn to cook basics such as bread, rolls, and meats. Though she often became flustered when cooking, Fiona had never given up. She was doing her best to learn as much as she could in such a small amount of time.

During the evenings, Fiona would sometimes think of the things she would miss the most. Mrs. Dickens had explained that indoor plumbing wasn't common in the West. Fiona had learned this from her Western novels but hadn't really put much thought to it. Now, however, she was facing all sorts of things that she hadn't considered until planning on physically leaving her home. She knew it would be difficult to adjust to a completely different lifestyle, but she knew that anything would be better than being forced to marry Mr. Crane.

After an hour of traveling by train, Fiona was starting to feel rather relaxed. She didn't mind the constant rocking of the train as it made its way. She rather enjoyed seeing the forests and countryside, wondering if any of it would be like Montana. She'd never traveled outside of Boston before and thought that everything she was seeing was like traveling to a completely different world. She imagined that this is what every heroine in her books had felt when they began their journey. Fiona couldn't wait to see what the train would pass by next.

~

EDDIE WAS HEADED into town with a package from Lucy to be delivered to the boutique. She'd finished adjusting a dress for Mayor Stavros after taking it home to finish, and now wanted to make sure the Mayor had it as soon as she needed it. Eddie was more than happy to run this errand since things seemed to be going smoothly at the ranch. Just yesterday, he'd been in town with the wagon to pick up food and other supplies for the ranch. He hadn't received a letter from Fiona, so he was hoping today would give him another chance to stop by the mercantile to see if any new mail had come in on today's stagecoach.

As Eddie made his way into town with Jack resting on his shoulder, he made quick work of going straight to the women's boutique to drop off the dress. As he dismounted in front of the store, which was situated along with the other businesses on the main street, he handed Jack a date in the hopes of keeping him occupied so he could quickly drop off the gown, and then head over to Frost's to check on the mail.

"Good afternoon, Eddie," Martha said happily as Eddie walked into the store. He didn't quite enjoy the boutique because it always smelled overly flowery. But he reasoned that it was the type of thing that women liked. He set the package down carefully on the counter.

"Mrs. Slater sent me into town with the Mayor's gown. Said she finished it last night and needed to have it brought into town as soon as I could get it here. So off I went," Eddie said with a chuckle. Jack then barred his teeth and screeched at Martha as he tried to laugh along with his master. The sound startled the other ladies in the boutique and Eddie quickly reached up and pulled Jack down from his shoulder and cuddled him in his arms.

"Thank you, Eddie. That was very kind of you. I hope you have a good day now," Martha said quickly as she escorted Eddie out of the store.

"I'm sorry Jack frightened your customers," Eddie said softly once they were outside the store. "Jack was just laughing."

"I know, Eddie, but most don't understand the sound a monkey makes when it laughs. You two go on with your business and get back to the ranch. I'm sure everyone would agree that Jack is cute, but he's still an animal," Martha said in parting. She then quickly returned to her boutique and began chatting with the customers.

Eddie sighed as he placed Jack back on his shoulder and gave him another date. "Come on, Jack. We best be quick," Eddie said in a melancholy voice. Seeming to understand his master, Jack hugged the side of Eddie's face, causing him to chuckle.

"Don't worry, I still love you," Eddie said as he stroked the monkey's soft fur before pulling himself back up into the saddle of his gelding and making his way further into town.

Frost's mercantile was a center place for Spruce Valley. It not only served as the general store, but also the stagecoach depot and a café in the back called The Eatery. Mr. Frost and his wife were great people and always made patrons feel welcomed. And now that the mercantile housed a telegram machine, it had become quite a busy place.

As Eddie stepped into the mercantile, he quickly received a few puzzled looks with Jack hanging onto his shoulder. It was well known that Eddie now owned the British man's monkey. With Spruce Valley being a very small town, Eddie knew that everyone already knew. But knowing and seeing seemed to be two completely different things. To Eddie, it seemed that Jack scared most people away. And since Eddie often left Jack at home with either Sawyer or Tom, he rarely brought Jack into the mercantile either. But with the other ranch hands busy today, Eddie had little other choice.

"Afternoon, Eddie. Afternoon, Jack," said Mr. Frost from the front counter. Eddie made his way quickly there to hopefully pick up the mail and go before Jack had a chance to do anything naughty.

"Afternoon, Mr. Frost. I've just come in to see if there is any mail, and perhaps see what kind of dried fruit you might have in stock," Eddie explained as he raised one hand around Jack, in case the monkey decided to act up. Thankfully, Jack took it as a sign of affection and wrapped his monkey arms around Eddie's head.

Mr. Frost chuckled as he pulled out the mailbox and started flipping through it. "One letter for Mr. Eddie Murtaugh," Mr. Frost said as he pulled out the letter and handed it to Eddie. Eddie quickly pocketed it as he pulled a few coins from his pocket. "And let me get you a bag of dates. I know how much Jack loves them."

"You would be correct, Mr. Frost. He loves them so much he thinks they're treats since he normally just eats bugs," Eddie explained.

"My, my. I would have never known. I bet he keeps the bunkhouse clean of any pesky things, then," Mr. Frost said as he filled a small sack full of dates.

"That he does, sir," Eddie replied as he looked around the general store. There seemed to be a good number of people in the store today, and they all appeared to be keeping one eye on Jack.

"Here you go, Eddie," Mr. Frost said as he handed him the sack of dates. Eddie set the change down on the counter before he accepted the dates.

"Thank you kindly, Mr. Frost. You have a good day now," Eddie said as he turned to leave. But then he came face-to-face with one of the women he used to run around with. Not that he was the only one who often did.

"Well, well. If it isn't Eddie Murtaugh, the handsome Murtaugh brother," Nicky said as she licked her lips. "Oh, and what a cute pet." As she reached out to touch Jack, Eddie took a step back.

"He doesn't like to be touched by strangers, Nicky. Now if you don't mind, I have to be getting back to Dr. Slater's ranch," Eddie said as he tried to step around Nicky, but she placed her hands on her hips and used her elbows to block his way.

"So, you're working as one of Dr. Slater's ranch hands now? I never pictured you to be a hard-working type of fellow. I thought you and your brother liked to chase bad guys with Sheriff Ryder?" Nicky said in a sultry voice.

"We've both put that type of life behind us now, Nicky. We'll help out Sheriff Ryder any time, but I like where I am at now and would very much like to get back to work, if you don't mind stepping aside," Eddie said as he narrowed his eyes at Nicky, catching her off guard. She stepped aside as she shook her head at him.

"I always thought you were polite towards women," Nicky said as she raised her voice. Not wanting any trouble, Eddie simply gave her one hard look before making his way to the door.

Eddie sighed heavily as he stomped towards his horse. He wasn't proud of the fact that he'd slept around with a few women in town and prayed that it wouldn't come back to haunt him one day. But if Nicky was going to act this way towards him in the future, he worried about it hurting his chances of marrying in the future.

As Eddie made his way out of town at a canter, he gave Jack a date from the sack to help keep him calm as they made their way back to the ranch. Jack ate the date with his tail wrapped securely around Eddie's neck. It didn't hurt Eddie but instead allowed Eddie to receive some form of comfort from the monkey. He had known the moment after seeing Jack in Handy's that the monkey was special, and he was glad that Jack was proving him right from time to time.

Once he was out of town, Eddie slowed his horse to a walk so he could retrieve the letter he'd received. As he pulled it out of his back pocket and looked at the address, he was pleased to see that it was from Fiona. But as he looked at the postmark, he was a bit concerned to see that it had been posted in Indiana. Eddie quickly opened the letter and began reading as fast as he could.

*Dear Eddie,*

*My letter will no doubt come as a surprise. By the time you receive this letter, I will most likely be much further in my journey than Indiana. I left Boston a few days ago after the news came to me that I had been put into an arranged marriage with a man twice my age. My beloved housekeeper, Mrs. Dickens, helped me arrange all my traveling plans and the things I may need while living out West. You see, I've run away from home and I'm now making my way to Spruce Valley. I don't want you to feel pressured, because this is my choice. But I hope we can meet in person and see how our relationship will develop from there.*

*I'm excited to meet everyone you've written about in Spruce Valley. I'm sure to arrive by stagecoach and get to meet Mr. Frost first, like you've mentioned in a previous letter. I'll be sure to book a room at the Honeywell Inn, and then come to see you from there. I look forward to meeting you, and to creating a new life for myself in Spruce Valley. I know it will be hard to adapt to living in the West, but I know that any future I create for myself will be better than being married to Mr. Crane.*

*I don't have many skills, but I feel prepared for living as a pioneer woman. I'm sure as I travel, I can think deeply about my abilities and what I may be able to do for employment. If you know of anyone hiring, I look forward to learning about it once I arrive. I'm determined, and I think that's the best thing I can offer someone right now.*

*Well then, I shall be seeing you after a bit.*

*Fiona Wilkins*

. . .

As Eddie folded the letter and stuffed it back into his pocket, he turned his horse around and started back towards town. If Fiona would be arriving in the foreseeable future, then he would have to let a few people know so that when she was spotted, she could be properly directed.

When Eddie made it back to town, he made his way straight to the Sheriff's Office. He and Sheriff Josh Ryder had been good friends ever since childhood. Josh's father had taught both Eddie and Sawyer how to shoot rifles and pistols, and was one of the reasons Josh often called after the brothers any time he needed back up when tracking down criminals. Sometimes Eddie missed the thrill of chasing someone down with Josh, but the peace he felt when on cattle drives couldn't be beat.

After dismounting and tying the reins to the front post, Eddie took Jack inside the building that Josh used for work. As soon as he stepped through the door, Josh startled awake from where he'd fallen asleep at his desk. Eddie couldn't help but chuckle as he took a seat across from Josh's desk. Josh tried to smooth back his brown hair.

"Morning, Sheriff," Eddie said with a smile. Jack jumped off his shoulder and plopped onto the desk, his eyes spotting Josh's sheriff badge pinned to his vest.

"Yeah, yeah," Josh said as he took off the badge and handed it to Jack. The monkey liked shiny things and held it in his hands to inspect it. "What brings you by, Eddie?"

"Well, there is a certain young lady making her way to Spruce Valley that I want you to be on the watch for. Her name is Fiona Wilkins," Eddie said. That bit of news seemed to wake Josh as he looked wide-eyed at Eddie.

"I didn't know you knew anyone outside of Spruce Valley," Josh said with a smile.

"Well, as I'm sure you can deduce, she's a mail-order-bride. She's coming early after having run away from her parents in Boston who had just arranged for her to marry a man twice her age," Eddie explained.

"Sounds a bit dramatic to me, Eddie. Sure you want to get mixed up in some rich family's problems?" Josh asked.

"From her letters, I can tell that Fiona is a fierce woman who isn't willing to let anyone tell her what to do. Sounds like the perfect woman for me," Eddie said with a smile, as Jack started to tap the badge against the desk.

"Alright there, Jack. Give me back the badge," Josh said as he extended his hand towards the monkey. Jack barred his teeth and screeched before jumping back up onto Eddie's shoulder. "Hey now, it isn't funny."

"Actually, it's hilarious," Eddie said with a chuckle as he traded a date for the badge with Jack, and then handed the badge back to Josh. "Anyways, what has you so exhausted?"

"Well, there's been a run of train robberies from here to Massachusetts. Every sheriff anywhere close to a train station has been telegrammed and warned about the robbers' identity. I've been putting my brain to work, gathering as much information as I can, and thank God we have a telegram machine here in town now, or I would have never known about it," Josh explained as he rubbed is eyes. "I think it's time for some coffee from The Eatery."

"Sure looks like you could use some," Eddie said as he stood with the Sheriff. "And I best be getting back to the ranch. I didn't expect to be gone this long, but as soon as I received Fiona's letter, I just knew I needed to let someone else in town know about it."

"No problem, Eddie. If I get word of her arrival, I'll let you know," Josh said as he came around the desk and shook hands with him. As the two left the Sheriff's Office, they parted ways. And with Jack securely back on his shoulder, Eddie mounted his horse and made his way back towards the ranch once more.

# CHAPTER 7

By the time Eddie made it back to the ranch, he was brimming with excitement. It had finally hit him that someday soon, he would be meeting Fiona. He tried to figure out in his head how many more days it might take for Fiona to reach Spruce Valley, since the closest train station was two days away by stagecoach. But eventually Eddie stopped trying to figure it out and simply felt more excited than he had in years.

When he got back to the ranch, he made quick work of letting Mrs. Slater know that the task was finished and that the dress had been delivered to the boutique. He also couldn't help but share the good news with her that Fiona was traveling to Spruce Valley.

"Oh my word, what good news! I'm sorry to hear that she was forced to choose between marrying and leavin', but sometimes a woman has very little choice when yer born into wealth. Anyways, I'm just so glad for you, Eddie. I'll talk to Sam about having Fiona stay here when she makes it to town," Mrs. Slater said happily.

"Oh no, I couldn't put that kind of burden on you and Dr. Slater. Fiona already knows that there's the Honeywell Inn in town," Eddie said. He was glad that Mrs. Slater could share in his enthusiasm but didn't want his boss to go out of his way for him.

"Well, we both know how much I dislike the Honeywell Inn, even though Bill is a great man and runs a good business," Mrs. Slater said with a sigh. "I'm going to talk to Sam about it tonight and we'll let ye know."

"I appreciate the consideration, Mrs. Slater. I better get back out there though," Eddie said as he dipped his head and quickly left the ranch house before Jack had a chance to cause any trouble.

After making sure Jack was secure in the bunkhouse (since his little furry friend had been out in the sun all day already), Eddie mounted his horse and took off into the pasture, excited to share the news with everyone else.

"No kidding!" Sawyer said in reply when Eddie found him. Gray and Tom pushed the cattle to another pasture that had grown tall grasses.

"Just received her letter today. I have no idea when she'll be arriving, but I made sure to let Josh know since he stays in town and always knows what is happening," Eddie explained.

"That's a good idea. Josh won't let her wander around aimlessly," Sawyer agreed.

"No kidding. The moment Martha arrived in town, Josh practically told everyone. Sam made it home just in time for me to get dressed and head into town to surprise her for dinner," Gray said, shaking his head as the others laughed.

"I happened to mention it to Mrs. Slater as well when I got back to the ranch. She said she's going to talk to Dr. Slater about allowing Fiona to stay with them. I think that would help her feel more at home," Eddie said. He was concerned about Fiona and how she was currently feeling since she had felt pressured to leave her home so unexpectedly. He only hoped that she was enjoying her travels and wouldn't run into any trouble.

"Well, if for some reason the boss man isn't keen to the idea, I'm sure Martha wouldn't mind having Fiona stay with us," Gray said as he kept an eye on the cattle. Eddie was surprised by the offer but nodded his head in agreement.

"Thanks, Gray," Eddie said as they began to focus on the work at hand.

As Sawyer and Eddie moved around to the other side of the herd to ensure that none of the cattle were disappearing between the two pastures, Eddie could tell that Sawyer wanted to say something. But he didn't speak up until they were a bit further away from the other two.

"So, what do you think about a city girl coming all the way out here to avoid getting married?" Sawyer asked Eddie in a soft voice as they rode side-by-side.

"I do have my worries about it, Sawyer. She wasn't raised in this type of lifestyle and might realize that living with her parents is a better deal than this. Perhaps she'll get all the way here and want to go home and marry a rich man when she realizes how harsh the West can be," Eddie said as he voiced his fears.

"That's understandable, Eddie. I mean, look at Mrs. Slater. She came from a big city, too, but she adapted with time. Though, Dr. Slater is better off than most. And Greta does come to help Mrs. Slater from time-to-time with the housework. Hell, even Gray has been cooking more and more meals with the woman working at the boutique while raising two young children," Sawyer said. Sawyer was always the more logical of the two of them, and he appreciated his perspective on the matter.

"I think it will come down to her passion and motivation

to be out here. I really do hope none of my fears come true, but I think I'll have to keep a level head about all of this. After all, she may get here and we may not even like each other in person," Eddie said with a shrug of his shoulders.

"I'm glad you're thinking about this matter, Eddie. But also, don't lose hope. It's okay to get excited about meeting a woman," Sawyer said with a smirk.

"Yeah. The first woman I actually want to date and not just enjoy between the sheets," Eddie said with a chuckle.

"You're the better brother for sure, Eddie," Sawyer said, causing them both to laugh loudly.

"Hey, you two! Knock it off!" Gray called over the cattle, causing the Murtaugh brothers to quiet down and get back to work. But Eddie couldn't stop feeling excited inside.

~

FIONA WAS FEELING UTTERLY DREADFUL. After a week and a half of traveling by train, she was racking her brain to try to remember why any of the heroines in the novels she'd read had described traveling by train to be a thrilling experience. For the first few days, Fiona had learned a lot about train travel. First, the train stopped often, sometimes giving passengers a chance for a short break and to stretch their legs. But Fiona was so afraid of not reaching the train in time before it left again that she rarely left.

Furthermore, she found that after a while, looking at the scenery became boring. She continued to see the same things over and over again and she was certain that the entire world was covered in forest with areas of civilization mixed into it. Fiona had tried to enjoy the one novel she'd brought with her, but found that it no longer appealed to her. She was seeing firsthand what it was like to go on an adventure. And sometimes it was quite unpleasant.

The food on the train was often stale, salty, or simply uneatable. When she got up the courage, she would scurry off the train during stops to find some fresh bread and cheese to enjoy. But the further away the train traveled from major cities, the less variety and fresh foods Fiona found.

Fiona had gotten used to relieving herself on the train, though it was always a scary moment because the train was always moving and shaking. When fresh water was available, she tried to soak her handkerchief in some and wipe her skin down the best she could in the changing room. She found that it was easier to wear the same two traveling gowns she'd brought with her. But as the train neared Montana, she decided to wear one of her nicer gowns that she'd decided to keep as a memory to her old life.

Though traveling by train had been odious from time to time, the thing Fiona enjoyed the most was getting to know all the people in her compartment. All sorts of people from various social classes were traveling out West for one reason or another. Some were returning West after visiting family in the East, much like the story she told everyone she met. Others were on their first trip out West in hopes of striking it rich in a gold mine, or starting their own homestead. Fiona always enjoyed hearing the stories that were motivating, that detailed why they were leaving it all behind and taking a risk in an unknown land. These stories were very similar to what she was feeling and currently experiencing.

Just two days left on the train before Fiona would be able to finally disembark and start the rest of her journey by stagecoach. The hours seemed to stretch out and Fiona was feeling rather restless. Even in one of her nicer gowns that smelled of home, Fiona couldn't seem to get comfortable. She had walked up and down the train cart a few times and tried to strike up conversations with a few people she'd come to know, but alas, she became rather bored. Even with the scenery having changed from forest to open fields, little seemed to entertain Fiona at this point. That is, until the train was suddenly stopped.

"My word, why has the train come to a stop?" said an older man, sticking his head out into the aisle as though he could see through the many passenger cars to the front engine.

"Do you think there is something wrong with the engine?" queried the woman next to him. There were various whispers of concern until shouts could be heard from towards the front of the train. When gun fire was heard next, everyone slunk back into their seats and became very quiet.

"Just do whatever they tell you to," whispered the woman sitting across from her. She held a young boy in her arms and was using her hands to shield his eyes and ears. Fiona went to ask who the woman was referring to when the front of the train car was opened suddenly, and a tall man with a bandana tied around his face stepped through with a pistol held high.

"Toss your valuables in the aisle and no one will get hurt!" the man yelled, his voice muffled by the way the bandana covered his mouth. A cowboy hat covered his head, only allowing his eyes to be seen on his face.

Everyone in the car started to throw their things into the aisle. Purses, watches, wallets, money, and jewelry were quickly flung in hopes of not being shot in return. Fiona tossed her purse in with the fray before pulling off her wedding band. She went to throw it but couldn't possibly part with Mrs. Dickens' present to her. So instead, she tucked it up her sleeve in the hopes of it not being discovered.

"You there. Surely someone dressed as fine as you still have more to donate," the man said to Fiona as he pointed his gun at her. She was instantly shocked into silence as she stared at the gun, her heart beating fast in her chest. All Fiona could manage to do was shake her head rapidly in hopes of conveying that she had nothing else on her.

"Come now, don't give me any trouble. Best to just give it up," the man said as he grabbed Fiona by the arm and pulled her to her feet, so he could check where she'd been sitting. But as the man continued to hold onto her arm in a rough manner, instinct took ahold of Fiona and she lashed out at the man, smacking him in the face.

"Take your hands off me! I've already given you my purse with all my precious things in it. Take the things and get on with you," Fiona shouted as she stepped away from the man. The robber glared at Fiona as he rubbed the spot on his face where he'd been struck.

Another robber then came onto the train with a large burlap sack in his hand and started to quickly pick up everything that had been tossed into the aisle. But when he saw his partner standing there with his gun pointed at a woman, he spoke up. "Hey, what's going on?" This man was shorter than the other and seemed to be experienced at his task as he continued to collect the items and toss them into the sack.

"She's just being feisty, is all," the robber with the gun said as he continued to glare at Fiona.

"Well, she's a woman. What do you expect?" the robber on the floor said as he picked and scooped up every valuable thing.

"I'll have you know that I'm the daughter of Mr. Mathew Wilkins of Boston. And once he hears how you robbed me, I'll ensure both of you are hanged for assaulting me," Fiona said in her anger. Her face turned red as she stared back at the man who held a gun at her. She was frustrated and tired of traveling by train, and the little money she had left was being taken by someone else. But as both robbers came to stand in front of Fiona, she suddenly felt very stupid for opening her mouth.

"So, yer a daughter of a rich father, are you? Seems to me that you are the most valuable thing on this whole train, then," the man with the gun said. The way his eyes wrinkled told Fiona he was smiling under his bandana.

"Been a while since we've had a hostage. A pretty thing like her would be fun to have around," the smaller man said. Then, without warning, both men quickly grabbed Fiona's arms and started pulling her down the aisle towards the open door.

"Take your hands off me! Let go this instant! Help! Someone help me!" Fiona shouted, as she pulled and fought against the two men. She tried to become a dead weight in their hands, going limp and trying to curl up on the floor, but they continued to wrestle with her until she was being pulled down the narrow steps to the ground. Furthermore, it shocked Fiona to the core that no one was coming to her rescue.

Tears were streaming down Fiona's face as she was pulled to her feet and quickly bound around her hands. A handkerchief was tied around her head and mouth to gag her from talking. Her kidnappers dragged her over to a group of horses that was being tended to by a man Fiona assumed was a criminal as well. The other robbers in the posse were quickly descending the train with similar burlap sacks that seemed to be full to the brim. As the others gathered around Fiona, the two that had kidnapped her quickly explained the situation.

"Great job," said a man with a very deep voice. "We'll return to camp and send someone into town to post a telegram to Mr. Wilkins. Something tells me we're all about to become very rich." There were whoops and cheers to the news from the other robbers. Then they all saddled up. Fiona was pushed up into a saddle and forced to ride with her legs on either side of the saddle. She turned red in the face as her stocking legs became apparent for the men to see. Never having been on a horse before, Fiona gripped onto the saddle horn with all her strength as the reins were taken up by her tall kidnapper.

Fiona held on for dear life as the horses were put into a fast trot across the open plains and away from the train. The rhythm of the running horse was so foreign to Fiona that she was afraid that at any moment she'd be thrown off the beast. She tried to rock her hips with the momentum of the horse, but it wasn't long before her rear end was becoming very sore and she did not know how much longer she could take such a beating.

In the distance, she could hear the train's whistle once more, signaling that it was departing. The posse of robbers was already long gone, to the point that no one could possibly save her now. She tried to keep her emotions under wraps because she was mostly concentrating on not falling off the horse. She squeezed her legs each the side of the horse, doing her best to stay on the saddle all the while gripping the saddle horn. But she couldn't help but think what would possibly happen to her next.

After a while, a thick wood line came into view, and the robbers slowed the horses to a canter, leading them one by one through a narrow parting in the trees. It was like being transported into a whole other world as the open plains faded away and the thick forest of North Dakota quickly surrounded them. Fiona was trying to focus on her breathing, taking deep breaths trying not to hyperventilate as the sun seemed to disappear. It was much darker and cooler in the forest as Fiona listened to the sounds of chirping birds. She could see squirrels and chipmunks running along tree branches and up and down tree trunks.

If it had been under any other circumstance, Fiona would have found the forest very majestic. But even though she was taking in different sounds, sights, and smells of the earthy forest, her mind was still focused on the robbers in front and behind her. The horses followed a narrow trail that seemed to be well-known by them. Fiona moved her hips to the movement of the horse, trying to follow the motion of the saddle. Her body was so tense that she started to silently pray that soon they would be able to dismount, even if that meant the next horrible part of her abduction would commence.

Fiona didn't know what would become of her, or if her father would even send money for her after she'd run away from home. She was scolding herself horribly for speaking up on the train and wished she'd just followed the advice of the woman that sat across from her. She could be on the train right now if she'd just tossed the gold wedding band onto the floor with the other precious things and turned away from the robbers. But no. She'd opened her mouth and let her emotions get the best of her. And now she would probably pay for doing such a ridiculous thing.

And the worst part of it all seemed to be the fact that she'd probably never get to meet Eddie in person, if she did get out of this mess alive.

# CHAPTER 8

Eddie was laughing with the others at dinner time as Martha teased Gray about being over protective of Samuel during a picnic at lunch that day. His gut hurt from laughing so much, and he had to cover his mouth with his hand in order to settle his laughter.

"My goodness. Sam is the same way. We were riding into town to have Francene's medical checkup at the clinic and he insisted on holding her the whole way," Mrs. Slater said, as another round of laughter sounded about. Everyone found it hilarious that the two fathers were so protective of their children that at first, no one heard someone knocking on the door.

"I'll go get it," Tom spoke up when the knocking sounded again. He quickly got up from the table to answer the door and Eddie returned to eating his food. He wanted to hurry up and be done so he could get back to Jack in the bunkhouse. The other night, Jack had gotten into the cupboards and tossed all the extra plates and cups onto the ground. And, not liking to keep Jack cooped up in his room, he wanted to go check on the pet monkey as quickly as possible.

"Evening, folks," Sheriff Ryder said as he came into the dining room. "Sorry to bother you all, but Eddie, I need a moment with you."

Eddie looked up from his plate with concern as he focused on his friend. He quickly finished chewing the food in his mouth to take a sip of water before standing from the table to follow the Sheriff into the other room.

"Everything okay, Josh?" Eddie asked in a soft voice. He was nervous because Josh had only asked to talk to him and not Sawyer.

"Eddie, you remember me mentioning those train robbers a few days ago?" Josh said as he rubbed his chin. It seemed that Josh hadn't shaved for days and had started to grow a shadow of a beard. As Eddie really looked at Josh, he could tell the man was exhausted.

"Yeah, I remember," Eddie replied.

"I just got a telegram from Frost. It's from a sheriff in North Dakota, right on the territory line of Montana. It explains that another west-bound train was robbed," Josh explained.

Eddie was silent for a moment as he tried to process what Josh was really saying. "You think it could be the same train that Miss Fiona is riding on?" Eddie asked.

"I'm sure of it, Eddie. The telegram explained that a young girl was taken hostage after she threatened the robbers, because her father is Mr. Wilkins of Boston. The passengers who witnessed the kidnapping have explained that the robbers plan to hold her as a hostage," Josh said softly.

Eddie was so taken back by the news that he was silent for several minutes. He just stared at Josh, waiting to wake up from this nightmare. But after he pinched himself hard in the leg, he realized that he wasn't sleeping, and that Fiona was in real trouble.

"Her family should be notified right away," Eddie said, as his mind started to spin towards taking some sort of action. His thoughts were split between imagining what Fiona was going through and how he was going to save her.

"They've already been sent several telegrams," Josh reassured.

"Where in North Dakota was the first telegram sent from?" Eddie asked, mentally making a list of all the supplies he'd want for this rescue.

"Medora. That's the station the train pulled into next after being robbed," Josh explained.

"Then that's where I'll go first. From there, I should be able to find something that will lead me to where the robbers are keeping Fiona," Eddie said, walking out of the room to let the others know that he had to leave immediately. But Josh grabbed him by the collar of his shirt and tightened his grip on him, forcing Eddie to stop.

"Now hold on there, lover boy. You can't just go running off into the night without a solid plan," Josh said as he forced Eddie to look at him. "Plus, you're going to need back up."

"And who's going to back me up?" Eddie asked.

"I am, dummy," Sawyer said as he stepped into the room. "I've been listening to the whole thing in the hallway."

"But what about the ranch? We can't both lose our jobs," Eddie replied as Josh let go of him.

"But we also can't allow a young woman to die in vain. She was coming out here to meet you and we have a responsibility towards her," Sawyer said in a stern voice.

Eddie stood for a moment before he nodded his head. He agreed that he felt responsible for Fiona, since it was his letter that told her of Spruce Valley, influencing her to come here when she needed to flee her home. He just hated the idea of losing their jobs over it. Even if they did rescue Fiona, what kind of life could he offer her if he didn't have solid employment? Reconciling that was a problem he'd have to address later, Eddie made his way into the dining room to tell the others.

"Sorry to do this, Dr. Slater, but Sawyer and I have to head out. The train Miss Fiona was traveling on has been robbed, and she's been taken as a hostage," Eddie said. He knew there was no point mincing his words and the ladies gasped in shock at the news.

"You can't just leave, Murtaugh. You need to have some sort of plan," Gray spoke up.

"That's what I told them," Josh said as he came into the dining room after the brothers.

"We'll figure it out as we go. But we have to get to North Dakota as quickly as possible," Sawyer said.

"You're going to need more than just gun hands against an unknown number of robbers," Gray retorted.

"And it wouldn't hurt to have a doctor with you," Dr. Slater added.

"And probably a good tracker," Martha spoke up then.

Eddie was dumbfounded as he looked to everyone in the room. He couldn't believe what they were implying. He felt so overwhelmed with support that tears started to pool in his eyes.

"Yeah, I think that is a great idea," Eddie said in a shaky voice.

"I'll get dinner cleaned up," Tom said as he stood from the table. "I'll try to pack some supplies for the road."

"I'm going to get the children put to bed. Martha, ye might as well stay here for the time bein'," Mrs. Slater said as she stood from the table with Francene on her one hip, and collected Samuel and rested him on her other hip. She toddled from the room to get the little ones ready for bed.

"Martha and I will ride over to the Crow Tribe camp and speak with Bright Star. We will try to convince him to come with us as well," Gray said, as he helped Martha to her feet.

"And I'll start getting my medical bag ready, along with the guns," Dr. Slater stated. Eddie was in awe as everyone was quick to help and take action. So many people were moving in different directions that at first, Eddie didn't know which way he should go.

"Gray, I'll join you and Martha. Bright Star should hear the news from me, after all," Eddie said as he followed the couple onto the front porch. "Sawyer, make sure to check up on Jack!" His words were followed by a grumble from his brother.

"Well, come on then," Gray gestured over his shoulder, as they made quick haste of getting to the barn and hooking up the horses to the wagon. Thankful for a full moon to guide their way, Gray snapped the reins, sending the two horses into a fast pace as Martha sat next to him on the wagon's board bench and Eddie sat in the back. As the night wind whipped his face, he prayed that Fiona was alive and well.

~

Several fires still burned brightly as Gray, Martha, and Eddie entered the Crow Indian camp. They were quickly halted by the sentinels, but once they saw the families faces, they let the wagon pass on into camp. The news of their arrival quickly spread through the camp, and soon Bright Star and his two sons, Running Bear and Sky Bird, were coming to greet them as they climbed down from the wagon.

"It is good to see my favorite redhead," Bright Star said

to Martha in way of greeting. She laughed as his two sons grunted in response.

"It is good to see you as well, Bright Star. But I'm afraid that our visit is not one of leisure," Martha said regretfully.

"Is Samuel Jenkins well?" Bright Star asked quickly, concern on his face.

Gray chuckled as he shook his head. "No, Bright Star. The little one is well. I'm sure because of your great blessing for the children this past spring," Gray assured.

"Bright Star," Eddie spoke up. "We've come to ask for your help. You see, there is a young woman who was riding on a train to come to Spruce Valley. We are meant to meet one another in hopes of marrying. But her train was robbed, and she has been taken hostage. I plan to ride straight to North Dakota to hopefully locate her and bring her to safety."

Bright Star looked at Eddie with much concern on his face. Then, he looked to his two sons. "My sons, I feel compelled to help this young woman, much like I did for Martha Jenkins last year. Would you two accompany me, or do you wish to stay with our tribe?" Bright Star asked his sons. Eddie felt relief that Bright Star would agree to come with them, but feared what his sons would say as they regarded one another.

"The tribe needs able men to help prepare for the journey south for the winter. We will leave to follow the buffalo in just a few short weeks," Running Bear said as he focused on his father.

"I agree, Father. I know that the tribe will not remain in Montana for much longer as summer fades to fall. It will be hard enough losing one great warrior to this cause," Sky Bird said in agreement with his brother.

Bright Star nodded his head as he looked at Eddie for a

moment. "Nonetheless," he spoke up. "I must go and do this thing. I feel the Great Spirt would have me go."

"Very well, Father," Running Bear said in a soft voice. "Let us prepare you for this journey, then."

"Good. I shall join you at the Slater Ranch before the rising sun. Go and sleep, for tomorrow morning we shall ride hard," Bright Star said in a voice that held great authority. Gray, Martha, and Eddie nodded their heads as Bright Star turned and made his way back through camp with his sons close by. Without any further words, they all climbed back into the wagon and Gray guided the horses around and back towards the main road.

"I don't think I'm going to be able to sleep tonight," Eddie spoke up from the back of the wagon.

"Well, you're going to have to try. You're no good to anyone if you don't get some rest," Gray said over his shoulder, as he steered the two horses back towards the ranch through the dark. Even though no one could see him, Eddie nodded his head. He tried to put his mind to focusing on everything he would need for the journey and how fast he could gather supplies together tonight so they could all leave in the morning. But his heart pounded in his chest as he thought about Fiona and what type of circumstance she might possibly be in.

"Please, Lord, watch over Fiona," Eddie whispered into the night as he looked up into the sky, watching the stars intently.

~

IT HAD BEEN three days since Fiona had been taken hostage from the train. The robbers had taken her deep into the woods where their camp was situated between several rocky formations. There was a small gap in-between the rock wall that allowed enough room for their horses, their bedrolls, and a central firepit. After arriving at this camp, Fiona had been lowered down from the horse and taken over to a post on the far side of the camp between the tallest parts of the rock formation. Her bound hands had then been tied to the post and the gag in her mouth removed. It was a relief to have the handkerchief off her head and mouth, but as she looked around the camp, she knew that escaping would be almost impossible.

As Fiona watched the others around her move about, she saw how they hid the burlap sacks deep into pits in the ground that were easily covered up by a wooden door and then disguised by fall leaves and branches. The horses had a place where they were tied up to other hitching posts and fed from feed bags and a central water trough. There was a small shed in the back of the clearing that looked to be a place to store supplies. Here, the short man who had been collecting everyone's valuables from the train, went to start gathering things to cook with.

Fiona watched everything going on around her as the five robbers all seemed to have some sort of job to do now that they were back at camp. Fiona didn't dare say anything else that might get her into trouble. She knew now to keep quiet and simply look for a way out of this mess.

In all the days they'd been at camp, none of the robbers had removed their bandanas or cowboy hats while they were around her. She reasoned that this had something to do with the fact that they were trying to keep their identity from her. It was this little fact that gave her hope that one day soon she would be released. But she hadn't heard any of them speak about sending a telegram to her father, or if a reply had been received. In fact, any time the robbers did speak, it was in hushed voices, so Fiona couldn't hear anything they were saying most of the time.

Three times a day, Fiona was brought a small cup of water and some sort of gruel to eat. It tasted rather horrible, but Fiona knew that she needed to keep up her strength and therefore needed to eat whatever was given to her. This was often the time of day when the robbers would begin to tease her.

"I bet a princess such as yerself has never eaten poor man's food before," the tall robber laughed, causing the others to laugh with him.

"That's right. I bet all that rich people eat is fish eggs and snails," another said, their laughter continuing.

"That's a good one, Smitty," said the short one, as he spooned more gruel on a plate for the others. But the group quickly went quiet as they stared at him. Even from a distance, Fiona could see the way they glared at the shortest robber, especially the man the robber had called Smitty.

"Ah, I'm sorry," the short one said in a soft voice as he looked between Fiona and Smitty. But Fiona quickly turned her eyes to the ground and looked at her slippered feet as though she hadn't heard anything. They all chastised the short man for several minutes, taking the focus off her as she quickly ate her food and finished drinking her water.

And so the days passed in this manner. She spoke very little and watched everything that happened around her. At night, she hardly slept. And during the day, she sweated in the heat. Still being dressed in her finest gown and several petticoats, she felt much warmer than she would have if she'd remained in her traveling gown. But there was nothing to be done of it now. At night she was thankful for the layers, because the air would turn very cold and she was never given a blanket to keep warm.

The only time she was unbound from the post was when she needed to relieve herself. One of the robbers would come over to her, untie her, and lead her out of the camp and into a small grove of trees. There, she had to hike up her skirts and carefully take care of her business. She already smelled of sweat and dirt. She didn't want to add to her smell and therefore was careful of what she did.

During the day, sometimes she would stand and move her legs in hopes of staying active. She knew that sitting all the time would do her no good. It also gave her something to do while she watched the robbers in the camp. Sometimes, some of the men would leave with the items they'd stolen in the burlap sacks. She assumed they were trying to sell or trade the items in exchange for more supplies. And even though the shortest robber always had enough to cook with, his food always tasted of ash and dirt. It was awful, but filling enough.

"Boss, when are we going to move on?" complained the tallest robber. Fiona focused in on the two men, wanting to know as much as she could about their current situation.

"Not until we hear back from the mister. If he doesn't agree to pay the two-thousand dollars, then we'll dump and run," the boss of the robbers said in his deep, dark voice.

"The longer we stay, the easier it will be to get caught," another robber said in an uneasy voice.

"I'm not stupid, ya hear me?! I've been running robberies and taking hostages since you were still a wee little thing. If you want out, go on then," the boss man said in a loud voice, causing the others to observe the two of them carefully. In Fiona's opinion, things were getting tense at camp. Pairs were talking in soft whispers and often everyone was keeping an eye on the boss man. Fiona wasn't quite sure what was going on, but she had a horrible feeling in her stomach.

Fiona silently prayed all day and night, hoping that no matter what happened next, she'd at least be free from this hell. She was starting to regret ever leaving Boston and wished she'd just stood up to her parents when they tried to marry her off. Perhaps if she'd taken to finding a decent husband more seriously, she would at least have been able to choose her husband instead of having to settle for Mr. Crane. As Fiona kept her eyes locked on the robbers around her, she feared not only for her life, but whatever future she could have once all of this was over.

# CHAPTER 9

The open plains shot past Eddie as he sat on the bench of the covered wagon, the dirt road stretching far beyond and behind him. Jack, for the most part, stayed perched on Eddie's right shoulder, his monkey tail wrapped around his shoulders. And sometimes he'd sit on his lap and try to position himself inside Eddie's vest. Eddie was thankful for the comfort of the small animal close to his chest as he tried to keep his nerves under wraps.

The wagon rumbled along the road with four other horses running beside it. Dr. Slater, Gray, Josh, and Bright Star rode Indian ponies that Bright Star had brought from the camp for them to use, insisting that they would be faster than any of the horses they owned at the ranch. The only downside was that they all had to learn how to ride bareback very quickly. Having been on the road for two days already, it helped that Dr. Slater, Gray, and Josh quickly learned the best way to ride the Indian ponies so they could make it to North Dakota without needing to rest for very long.

With Eddie and Sawyer taking turns leading the team of

horses that pulled the wagon with supplies, they were able to travel as quickly as possible on horseback. With every new morning, Eddie was motivated once again to reach Medora in North Dakota, and start gathering clues as to where Fiona might currently be held captive. He'd never traveled this far from Spruce Valley, but he kept reminding himself that this adventure would be worth it if it resulted in finding Fiona safe and sound.

"Alright, fellas," Josh said as they started to near Medora near nightfall on their third day of traveling. They slowed down to a canter so they could talk amongst themselves. As they neared the town, they knew they would be seeing other people more frequently on the road.

"I'm going to head into town with Dr. Slater and Eddie. I'll meet with the local sheriff and we'll collect all the information we can. Gray, Bright Star, and Sawyer, I want you guys to find a place to set up camp for the night. We don't want to spook anyone since we have Bright Star with us. Gray, once camp is set up, come into town and let us know," Josh said in his authoritative voice. Bright Star chuckled and took no offence to Josh's plan. Their group knew that not everyone accepted Indians as civilized people, unlike those in Spruce Valley had come to do.

"Switch me spots then, Eddie," Gray said as he pulled his Indian pony to a stop by tugging on his mane. Eddie then stopped the wagon and encouraged Jack to stay with Sawyer. He knew that having the monkey in town would only cause problems.

"Hey there, little buddy," Sawyer said as he took Jack and put him on his shoulder. Eddie couldn't help but smirk as he saw Sawyer warming up to Jack. Then, when Eddie was ready, he quickly hopped onto the pony like Bright Star had taught them, while Gray climbed up onto the wagon and picked up the reins.

"We're all set then. We'll see you all in a bit," Dr. Slater said with a nod, as he tapped his heals into his pony and set off with Josh and Eddie.

Eddie was brimming with excitement and uneasiness as they made their way into the town. He'd been looking forward to this moment for the last three days as his body was filled with worry for Fiona. He couldn't wait to get to hear what the local sheriff had to say about the situation and if any progress had been made in finding Fiona. He just hoped that they would be met with friendliness as they sought out the sheriff.

"Looks bigger than Spruce Valley, that's for sure," Josh said as they came onto the main street of the town. Businesses lined the street as locals walked up and down the boardwalk. In the distance, they could see the train station that was currently empty. Eddie figured that the railroad had brought a lot of business to Medora and thought something like that would really benefit Spruce Valley. But for now, all that Eddie was concerned about was finding the sheriff.

"I reckon we'll find answers in there," Dr. Slater said as he pointed to a wooden door that had a giant sheriff's symbol painted in yellow on the front of it.

"Don't ever let me do something like that," Josh said with a sigh as they made their way over to what looked to be the sheriff's office. As they dismounted from the Indian ponies, they had to tie rope around the beasts' necks and secure them to the hitching post in order to keep them situated. Then, they walked up to the door as Josh knocked heavily on it.

"Come in!" called a man from inside. Josh opened the door for them and stepped in first. As Eddie brought up the rear, he closed the door behind him and looked around the office. It looked rather modern with whitewashed walls, polished wooden floors, and a mirror hanging on the wall. It was more a sitting room than a sheriff's office.

"Good day, gentlemen," said an older man as he stood from his desk and moved around it with a bright smile on his face. "Have you come for my autograph?"

Eddie refrained from laughing as Josh moved aside his duster to show the man his sheriff's badge.

"Sheriff Miller, my name is Sheriff Josh Ryder. My deputies and I have just come from Spruce Valley in Montana after receiving your telegram about the train robbery and the young lady that was taken hostage," Josh explained. The older man looked puzzled as he looked at Josh, and then at Dr. Slater and Eddie.

"Well then, why have you come here?" Sheriff Miller asked.

"Because Miss Fiona Wilkins is my bride-to-be," Eddie spoke up. It wasn't completely true, but it was one of the reasons why Miss Fiona had started to make her way to Spruce Valley.

"Forgive me, young man, but Mr. Wilkins never telegrammed me anything about a fiancé all the way out here," Sheriff Miller said with a critical eye on Eddie.

"That is because Miss Fiona didn't share with her parents that she was becoming a mail-order-bride. It was the reason she was on the train heading to Montana," Eddie further explained.

"I see, then. Well. We haven't heard anything from the robbers, yet Mr. Wilkins has let me know that he received their telegram about a ransom amount and a time frame. But that's all I know," Sheriff Miller said as he went around his desk once more and took a seat in the chair. Josh, Dr. Slater, and Eddie all gave each other a look of uncertainty before Josh turned back to the other sheriff.

"Sheriff Miller, what is the ransom amount and when is the deadline?" Josh asked.

"The robbers have asked for two-thousand dollars to be delivered by next Monday," Sheriff Miller replied in a grave voice.

"But that's only three days away!" Eddie exclaimed.

"Indeed, son. That's why I'm a little surprised you are all here because there has been no word from Mr. Wilkins on whether or not he's on his way to pay the ransom," Sheriff Miller said.

"But what are you doing about it all?" Dr. Slater asked quickly.

"What can be done? These robbers have been pillaging trains for months. No one has been able to find them, and if Mr. Wilkins isn't willing to pay the ransom, then what can I do about it?" Sheriff Miller said with a shrug of his shoulders. Eddie was brimming with anger as he glared at the older man.

"How far back was the attack on the railroad?" Josh asked. By the way his jaw was clenching, Eddie could tell that the man was furious as well.

"About three miles east along the railroad," Sheriff Miller said. Then, Josh turned and began to leave the building without another word. "Hey! Where are you going now?" the sheriff asked.

"We're going to go rescue Miss Fiona, like you should have done already," Josh spat at the older sheriff before opening the door so hard that it slapped against the building, scaring a few people who had been walking by. Dr. Slater and Eddie followed quickly after Josh as he untied his pony and mounted. He then turned the pony in the direction they had come, forcing Dr. Slater and Josh to make haste.

"What's the plan, Josh?" Eddie asked as they caught up with him.

"We wait to regroup with Gray once he comes into town and leads us back to camp. In the morning, we'll follow the train tracks to where the scene of the attack was, and hopefully there, Bright Star can lead us to the robber's camp," Josh explained.

Eddie rode silently with the others back out of town. As they followed the road once more, they eventually happened upon Gray as the sun was setting. After filling him in on the situation, Gray shook his head in disgust.

"I can't believe the sheriff hasn't done anything. Sounds like he's a bit showy but doesn't actually do the work," Gray said as he began to lead them away from the road and into a nearby tree line.

"No kidding. Makes me appreciate you even more," Eddie said to Josh.

"Don't thank me yet, Eddie. We still have a lot of work ahead of us, and a very short time to find Miss Fiona," Josh said in a serious voice. Eddie simply nodded his head, knowing what the sheriff said was very true.

Once they'd reached town, Eddie had been so optimistic that they'd have a bigger lead on where to go next. But it seemed that their adventure was only just getting started.

~

It was early in the morning when Fiona awoke. She was freezing from another cool night without any protection from the elements. She was in a tight ball on the ground as she tried her best to keep warmth in her body. But she felt rather cold and stiff this morning, and as she sat up, she felt lightheaded and stuffy. She could instantly tell that she had some sort of sickness and would not recover properly from being left out in the woods without any protection.

As Fiona's head eventually cleared, she looked about her

and realized that the group of robbers were still asleep. Smoke drifted up from the firepit in the center of the men, but it was clear that no one had risen to put more wood on the fire. As Fiona's eyes moved from each one of the sleeping robbers, she watched their chests rise and fall in a deep slumber. Thinking that she needed to escape before she died out in the middle of nowhere, she started to pull at the ties that bound her.

Having been tied up for almost a week now, the cords had become loose around her wrists. She pulled at them without making any sound as she wiggled her wrists through the ties. Fiona breathed a sigh of relief as her left hand pulled free and she used it to pull her other hand through. For a moment, Fiona rubbed her wrists together as she looked towards the sleeping robbers once more. Fiona knew that she couldn't wait much longer, so she stood up onto shaky feet, hiked up her skirts, and started to move around the outer parts of the camp to the narrow opening in the rocks.

As Fiona moved slowly, doing her best not to make a sound, she kept shifting her eyes between the narrow opening and the robbers, who were still asleep. She prayed fervently that none of them would wake so she could be gone long before the first one arose. Fiona didn't know where she would go after she escaped, but she reasoned that anywhere was better than here. And with the gold ring still hidden in her dress sleeve, she figured it would fetch her enough money to make her way back home.

Fiona's heart was pounding so hard that she could hear her blood rushing through her ears. She was terrified yet determined to escape. And as she made it to the narrow rock opening, she turned her back on the camp and began to make her way out. However, she didn't make it far before she tripped over a line of rope she hadn't seen in the foliage of the forest. The moment her foot made contact with the rope, a rattle of empty bottles sounded from above.

"Someone's coming!" shouted one of the robbers, causing fright to fill Fiona's body. She grabbed her skirts and pulled them up high as she moved over the hidden rope and took off into the forest. Fiona had no idea where she was running, but with fear running through her veins, she simply knew that she needed to get as far away from the camp as possible. She wound her way through the trees, hoping they would provide her enough cover to not be seen.

"She went this way!" called someone from behind her, causing a spike of fear to be wedged into her heart. She now knew that they had discovered she'd escaped, and would be tracking her immediately.

Hoping to lose them in the forest, Fiona started running more to her right. She figured that going in a straight line would be too obvious, so she adjusted her course and ran for her life. Her heart pounded in her chest from the exhaustion of sprinting and her breath came in hard gasps as she tried to breathe in air. Sweat covered her body from running and from the sickness that had set in, shivering throughout the night. Now, her body felt like it was on fire as she ran for all that she was worth.

Yet despite her best efforts, she cried out in surprise as one of the robbers cut her off on horseback, forcing her to stop and fall back as she tried to turn and run the other way. She tried to scramble to her feet, but the robber was faster. As the man approached her, she tried to kick him away, but her body was very weak by now.

"Oh no you don't, Miss Wilkins. You don't go free till daddy pays up," came the dark voice of the leader. Fiona began to cry then as the man made quick work of binding her wrists once more, the rope feeling tighter than before. "But I must say, you have more fight in you than I would have ever imagined," he laughed as he pulled Fiona back onto her feet. He then tied another rope to her wrists before pulling himself up into his saddle, using the additional rope to pull her behind him.

Fiona felt hopeless and exhausted as she was forced to walk all the way back to camp. As time passed, she realized just how far she'd been able to run, and it taught her just how large the forest was. Even with the distance she'd been able to gain from the camp, she'd still not seen a way out of the forest.

Tears streamed down Fiona's face as she was pulled back into camp. Even with their faces covered by bandanas, she could see the hatred in the robbers' eyes. She knew she should be afraid of how they would treat her from now on, but she was so tired and exhausted that she didn't have any more strength to be fearful.

The moment she was tied back to the hitching post, Fiona collapsed to the ground. Her chest rose and fell as she tried to catch her breath. Her body ached all over, and though she felt hot and sweaty, she began to shiver from exhaustion.

"She doesn't look so good, boss," said the tallest robber as they all crowded around her. Fiona closed her eyes, trying to block them all out from her reality. No matter how hard she tried to breathe, it felt like her lungs weren't receiving enough oxygen. She even reasoned that she would soon die from having tried to run as hard as she did.

"Serves her right for trying to escape. If she dies, she dies," said the boss in his dark voice. Fiona listened as the robbers all walked away, some mumbling to themselves.

It was a long time before Fiona was able to breath easily. She lay on the ground on her side, her arms shielding her face from the rising sun. She kept her eyes closed, knowing that there wasn't anything for her to really see at the camp.

Fiona listened to the coming and goings of the robbers but paid them no attention. Even when one came to give her the morning meal, Fiona didn't bother with it. She was too exhausted to even raise her head and drink the water.

Eventually, Fiona blissfully passed out. She reasoned a fever had taken hold of her.

# CHAPTER 10

The moment the sun had peeked over the horizon, Eddie was instantly awake. He lifted his head from his bedroll to see a fire burning in the central pit that had been constructed last night. His eyes traveled to see that Bright Star was already awake and tending to the fire.

As Eddie moved out from his bedroll, Jack uncurled himself from the bottom and made his way out as well. Eddie smirked as he watched the monkey stretch and move around the fire as though he was warming himself. Then, he scurried back to Eddie for his morning meal.

"I never knew that anything like Jack existed. He reminds me of a small child," Bright Star said in a soft voice. The others were still sleeping, and though Eddie was eager to get moving this morning, he didn't want to disrupt their much needed rest.

"The moment I saw him, I just knew I wanted him for a pet," Eddie replied as he picked Jack up and set him on his shoulder whilst the monkey enjoyed pieces of dried fruit. Eddie made quick work of rolling up his bedroll and sticking it in the wagon before taking care of his business. Once he came back to the fire pit, Jack was eating his second date, and Eddie started on making some sort of breakfast.

"May I hold Jack?" Bright Star asked as he extended an arm towards the monkey.

"If he'll come to you," Eddie replied as he shifted over towards the Indian. He moved his right shoulder towards Bright Star, trying to encourage Jack to move off his shoulder and towards the Indian's extended arm. Jack made a few clicking noises with his mouth as he turned his head to the side and looked at Bright Star. When the Indian returned the noises, Jack found this fascinating as he unwound his tail from Eddie and hopped over to Bright Star. Eddie chuckled as he watched the Indian and the monkey exchange clicking sounds. Eddie started to prepare breakfast.

"It's too early for such racket," Josh said, rolling over from where he was sleeping on the ground, looking over towards Bright Star and Jack.

A chuckle rose up from Gray as the man continued to lay on his back with his eyes closed. "That is because you don't have children yet, Josh. When the little ones come, you'll be awake at all hours of the night," Gray said as he raised his arms over his head and stretched. Slowly, everyone woke and rolled up their bedding before joining at the fire. By then, Eddie had finished frying some lard in a cast-iron skillet to cook a few eggs and salt biscuits.

"Not bad, Eddie," Gray said as he dug into his food. Eddie knew that was a compliment coming from a man who often cooked.

"I learned from the best," Eddie retorted as they all focused on their food. Gray had taught him much about cooking over a fire when they'd been working on a cattle drive last fall. Eddie wouldn't say he was a good cook, but he could make edible food that filled the belly.

The moment they were finished eating and had everything cleaned and put away in the wagon, it was time to get ready to move out. Eddie approached Bright Star then, thinking it was time to retrieve Jack, who surprisingly had been on his best behavior whilst with the Indian.

"Come on, Jack," Eddie called after using his signaling whistle for the monkey. But as Eddie watched Jack, the monkey remained on the Indian's shoulder.

"Do you mind if Jack travels with me today, Eddie Murtaugh?" Bright Star asked with a kind smile. Eddie was surprised that Jack hadn't come to him when called, and that the Indian was taking a liking to his monkey. He wasn't sure how he felt about it, but for now he saw no harm in it, since their main focus was finding Miss Fiona.

"I don't mind, Bright Star," Eddie decided. He nodded to the Indian before pulling himself up into the driver's seat of the wagon.

"Alright folks. Here's the plan," Josh announced. "We'll ride out to the railroad and follow the tracks east for about three miles. Everyone, be on the lookout for any signs of something out of place. The littlest detail can be a huge lead. Once we make it to the place where the robbery took place, we'll fan out and look for signs of their escape." Josh spoke in a loud enough voice that everyone could hear him. There were words of agreement as Dr. Slater doused the fire with a bucket of water before tossing the bucket in the back of the wagon and mounting his own pony.

When they were all set, they followed Josh's lead. It took a while to leave the forest behind, and once they reached open plains once more, they set off at a fast pace. Dust and dirt filled the air as the ponies raced forward with the wagon trailing behind. Eventually, Eddie had to put on a bandana to shield his face from most of the dust.

As they continued, eventually they came up to the train

tracks. They turned their progress east, following the tracks away from the town. With every passing minute, Eddie was filled with more determination to succeed. From time to time, his eyes would spy the terrain ahead and scan the horizon. The path the train took covered mostly open plains, but to the right of them was a large forest that seemed to go on forever. As Eddie took in the scenery, he prayed that Fiona was somewhere close.

Eddie slowed down the wagon as Josh raised his hand in the air, signaling for all of them to stop. When they came to a halt, he slid off the back of his pony quickly and dropped to the ground, closely observing the ground with his fingers. A second later, Bright Star was at his side with Jack still placed firmly on his shoulder. Eddie watched as the monkey held onto Bright Star's long black hair as the Indian moved with speed and agility.

"I can see scattered footprints here, Bright Star," Josh spoke up. Eddie watched as Bright Star nodded and began to follow the footprints away from the train tracks.

"Someone was dragged through the dirt and appeared to put up some sort of fight," Bright Star said as he walked. "And here there was a group of horses."

Eddie tied the reins to the board of the wagon before jumping off to quickly follow Bright Star. He looked to the ground to where the Indian was pointing to see several hoof prints in the dry ground. Though it had been over a week since Fiona had been kidnapped, the lack of rain had allowed the prints to remain in the brush. Eddie followed the direction of the hoof prints and eventually his eyes rose to the forest in the distance.

"Seems to me that they took off into the forest over there," Eddie said as he pointed towards the tree line.

"Very good, Eddie Murtaugh," Bright Star said with a smile. Jack screeched and bared his teeth as he laughed in his own way. This surprised Bright Star and he looked at the monkey with concern. Eddie couldn't help but laugh as he shook his head.

"That's Jack's laugh, Bright Star. He thinks you were telling a joke by the way you smiled," Eddie explained. Once Bright Star understood, he laughed as well. Yet this only caused Jack to laugh in return, and soon the two were laughing at each other.

"Alright, that's enough monkey business, you two. Bright Star, I'm putting you in the lead. Let's follow these tracks and see if we can't find Miss Fiona before sundown," Josh said as he shook his head and went back to his pony. Eventually Bright Star's mirth subsided, and everyone readied once more to move forward.

The thought of getting to see Miss Fiona by sundown set fire to Eddie's determination. With his pistol on his hip, Eddie was ready for anything. He and Sawyer had aided Josh several times in the past, and just like Sawyer had said before, there was a certain thrill about chasing down bad guys.

"Are you ready for this?" Sawyer asked with a smile as Eddie climbed back up onto the wagon.

"Absolutely," Eddie replied with a grin, right before he snapped the reins and sent the horses forward with a jolt. Together as a group, they raced into the forest as Bright Star led them forward.

~

FIONA FELL into a world of dizziness and uncertainty. Her body was riddled with pains and aches, her skin felt like it was on fire and she continued to shiver as though freezing. For what seemed like days, Fiona was mostly unconscious, always dreaming of trying to run very far away from the robbers but never seeming to get very far. Yet when she was awake, she kept her eyes closed because she was too dizzy to open her eyes. Her breathing always came in short gasps, as though she truly had been running while she slept. At one point, she felt someone help her up into a seating position and coaxed her to drink some water. But the moment she was laid down again, she quickly passed out once more.

It was in this state that Fiona began to dream of something different. She heard gun fire ringing in her ears, followed by the sound of shouting, chaos, and screams of agony. Fiona felt like she could feel fear all around her as she only focused on freeing her hands and running away once more. But whatever sickness had befallen her had a tight grip on her body. She no longer had the energy to run and simply lay on the ground.

Fiona reasoned that she would die soon. The thought brought tears to her eyes as shouts sounded all around her. She heard the frightened neighs from the horses and truly felt sorry for them. But she thought that soon it would all be over. She would fade away into death and no longer feel the pain that riddled her body. She regretted never seeing her parents again, and more so she hated herself for ever running away from the safety of her home. She even wished she'd married Mr. Crane so she didn't need to experience this painful death.

When everything went silent around her, Fiona figured she'd died. There was silence and blackness all around her, even as she continued to struggle to breathe. Then, she felt the bounds around her hands cut free and arms encircle her as she was pulled from the ground and carried away. Fiona risked all logic and forced herself to open her eyes. For a brief moment, she saw that she was being carried by a man with light brown hair and bright blue eyes. He looked down into her eyes. She smiled, thinking she was being carried away by the most beautiful angel in Heaven. Feeling relief like never before, Fiona closed her eyes once more and drifted away.

~

It had taken some time to follow the horse tracks through the dense forest. But when a large formation rose in front of them, Josh had signaled for them to stop and dismount. After tethering their ponies and horses, they had crept close together to speak softly.

"I bet you everything I'm worth that their camp is inside of that," Josh whispered. Bright Star nodded in agreement as he pointed towards it.

"We need to move in carefully," Dr. Slater spoke up. "We have no idea how many are there or how much gun power they have. My biggest concern is safety at this moment."

"And don't forget traps," Sawyer spoke up. "If they are all in there, there must be something out here to warn them of people coming up onto them. They might have a scout or something else to warn them."

"Good point, Sawyer. We need to approach slowly and carefully. Keep your eyes on the ground for possible traps and ropes," Josh said as he nodded his head.

"I shall go ahead and scout out the area. I have the eyes for seeing hidden things," Bright Star said in a confident voice. Josh simply nodded his head, but before Bright Star could move away, Eddie quickly spoke up.

"Shouldn't you leave Jack behind?" Eddie asked softly.

Bright Star looked at him and smiled. "Don't worry, Eddie Murtaugh. Jack is a good boy and will not be any trouble," Bright Star replied. Eddie forced himself to nod his head, even though he was worried about moving forward with Jack. The monkey was a comfort, but also quite unpredictable.

Eddie watched with the others as Bright Star crept forward. At one point, he removed a large knife from its sheath on his leg. The blade glinted in the few rays of sunlight that passed through the tree's canopy. Eddie could tell that it wasn't just any old knife. He assumed that it had been designed for the purpose of taking lives quickly.

Eddie felt like he was sitting on pins and needles as he waited for Bright Star to return. He wasn't sure how long they had waited, but he could feel sweat collecting on his forehead. At one point, he lifted his arm and wiped the sweat from his brow as he tried to settle his nerves. He was anxious to move forward and see for himself if there was anything within the rock formation.

Eventually, Bright Star returned to their group with a serious expression upon his face. "There are indeed people inside the rock formation. Upon a closer look, I could spot a campfire and several men inside. I counted at least five of them," Bright Star explained.

"And what about Miss Fiona?" Eddie quickly asked.

Bright Star nodded his head again, but his eyes were dark with concern. "I did spot a young lady through the narrow opening. She was lying on the ground and did not look very well," Bright Star explained in a grim voice. Fear instantly pierced Eddie's chest, so much so that he even raised his hand to grip the front of his shirt.

"We need to move quickly then," Dr. Slater spoke up. "We can't wait much longer if she needs medical attention."

"Agreed," Gray said as he pulled his pistol from the holster at his side. Josh did the same, signaling for the others to prepare themselves. Eddie was itching to move as he pulled out his gun and rested his trigger finger on the side of the barrel, gripping the handle firmly.

"There are many trip ropes along the way. Be mindful to step over them or we'll lose the element of surprise," Bright Star warned as he gripped his knife and turned back towards the robbers' camp. As a group, they all crept towards the rock formation slowly. As they neared various trip ropes, Bright Star pointed them out and they all made their way over them cautiously.

When they came to the narrow passage into the rock formation, Eddie was able to see just a glimpse of the camp. He could see a group of horses and smoke rising from a campfire. Josh raised his hand for all of them to see and when he counted to three with his fingers, they all stood and rushed the camp.

Time seemed to slow in an instant as they all ran through the narrow opening, their guns aimed at the first person they came across. Shouts of surprise filled the air as the robbers were quick to collect their guns and try to take aim. But with the surprise ambush, they were able to fire their guns before the robbers could defend themselves. Cries of pain followed the sounds of gun fire as they were quick to disarm the robbers and begin tying them up.

When the gun smoke settled, Eddie felt relief that none of their team had been shot after one particular robber had been able to get a few bullets out before he was taken down. Though none of the robbers seemed to have been killed, it looked like a few of them had serious gunshot wounds.

"I'll get them patched up and then we'll head back to town," Dr. Slater said as he stood and ran for the wagon to collect his medical bag.

As he left, Eddie seemed to remember why they were all here. The thrill of the gunfight faded, and Eddie quickly looked around for Miss Fiona. Just like Bright Star had described, he found Miss Fiona on the far side of the camp. Her hands were tied together and a lead rope connected her hands to a hitching post. She lay unconscious on her side with her arms stretched out in front of her.

"Bright Star! Your knife!" Eddie called. The Indian was to his side in a moment. Jack was still on his shoulder but had been gripping his hair tightly in fear. Bright Star quickly cut the rope around her wrists and Eddie pulled it apart. A moment later, Eddie pulled Miss Fiona into his arms and quickly took her away from the camp.

As Eddie carried Miss Fiona towards the wagon, he could tell that something wasn't right. Her skin was hot to the touch and sweat was all over her skin. Yet, as he held her close to his chest, he could feel her shivering.

"Dr. Slater!" Eddie called as he came across the doctor collecting his medical supplies. "She has a fever." Eddie carried her to the back of the wagon and met the doctor there. Holding her in his arms, Eddie held her still while Dr. Slater started to check her over.

"Definitely has a fever, and a bad one, too. She's already starting to shake. We need to get her out of these clothes. The layers are probably not helping at all," Dr. Slater said as he hopped onto the wagon and started to clear a space. "We'll get her laid out here once it's comfortable enough."

Sawyer and Gray came walking back to the wagon, leading a robber each ahead of them. Once they reached the wagon, they tied the robbers to a lead rope off the wagon and then came to help Eddie with Miss Fiona. Together, they were able to use their bedding to make a comfortable space in the back of the wagon where Miss Fiona could rest easily as they made their way back to town.

"Since I'm a doctor, Eddie, it's best if I do this next part by myself," Dr. Slater said. "Just stand guard for me."

Eddie nodded as he hopped out of the wagon and stood behind it with the flap drawn closed, while Dr. Slater made Miss Fiona more comfortable. Petticoats were soon tossed out the back of the wagon, followed by her gown. As the gown was tossed aside, Eddie noticed something gold sailing through the air. As he heard it clank to the ground, Eddie moved quickly towards it until it stopped rolling and was still. Eddie bent down and picked up the small gold ring, wondering why Fiona would have such a thing.

"Alright, you can join me again, Eddie," Dr. Slater called. Eddie pocketed the ring and pulled himself back into the wagon as he folded back one of the flaps to let in sunlight. "Now, I'm going to have you start washing her skin with this clean cloth and buckskin of water. She needs to be cooled down, but not suddenly." Eddie looked down at Miss Fiona. She was undressed down to her chamise. A light blanket covered her, but Eddie blushed nonetheless. He'd been with plenty women before, but had never looked upon a woman this exposed without permission.

As Dr. Slater hopped down from the wagon to start patching up the robbers so they could all head back to town, Eddie did what the doctor had instructed. He took the clean cloth and soaked it with water from the buckskin and began to wash Fiona's face, neck, and arms. Her skin felt so hot to the touch that he feared she wouldn't recover. His anger grew towards the robbers as he wished he could just finish them off right here and now. But he forced himself to stick to his task in the hopes of saving Miss Fiona's life.

Eventually everything was set to head out. With the robbers bound and gagged, they were saddled onto their horses and tethered behind the wagon. The goal was to reach the town by nightfall in an effort to find better medical care for Miss Fiona. Eddie allowed Sawyer to drive the wagon as he remained in the back with Miss Fiona, helping to keep her from swaying too much as the wagon was moved forward.

Eddie was so focused on Miss Fiona's face, praying that

she would wake up soon, that he paid little attention to what was going on around him. Eddie felt the rocking of the wagon as they started out of the forest, and as he held Miss Fiona's hand in his, he took in her features. Eddie had to admit that Miss Fiona was a beautiful young woman. The photo she had sent him did little justice to her actual beauty. She had golden hair with a hint of redness to it that made her appear fierce. Her face was defined with high cheekbones, and he could tell that she was taller than most women. He smiled, thinking that she would match him well since he was much taller than his brother. As Eddie looked to her luscious lips, he reasoned that he would very much enjoy kissing her.

But as the convoy of horses, ponies, and the wagon made its way out of the forest and back to town, Eddie only hoped that Miss Fiona would recover from this nightmare.

# CHAPTER 11

Fiona was certain that she was dead. She was surrounded by a bright light, a feeling of comfort all around her. She felt warm, but no longer felt the burning heat in her skin. She was lying down, relaxed in a plush cot. She could smell the scent of flowers nearby and reasoned that she was about to open her eyes to Heaven. But when Fiona finally mustered up the strength to open her eyes, she instead found herself in a small room with white walls. A window was nearby and had the shutters were propped open. A light breeze came into the room from the window, bringing with it the scent of flowers.

As Fiona slowly turned her head and looked about the room, she soon spotted a young man sitting in a wicker chair in the corner. His head was slumped down as he slept, but she instantly recognized him. He had been the one that had been carrying her in the forest. She remembered his light brown hair and how beautifully blue his eyes had been. She was certain he was an angel, but now, as she looked at him properly, she wondered who he really was.

He was unlike any man Fiona had seen before. As she looked over his rugged attire, she figured that he could be the image of all the cowboys she'd ever read about in her novels. He wore a western shirt with a tan vest overtop. Jeans covered his legs and boots stuck out of the bottom. Fiona saw the pistol in the holster on his side, as well as rope on the other. She wondered why this man would be armed, and for a second she feared that perhaps this man could in fact be one of the robbers.

Panicked, Fiona tried to sit up quickly, but the moment she did so her head was flooded with pain. She raised her hand to her forehead as she tried to stifle the cry she was about to release. Her breaths came in heavy gasps as she felt a sickness rise up in her.

"Hey, you shouldn't be up. You need to lie down and rest," came a male voice beside her. Fiona opened her eyes slightly and saw those beautiful blue eyes once more. The man had a gentle expression on his face as he came to sit on the edge of the cot. Softly, he used his hand to ease her down onto the cot once more.

"I'm Eddie Murtaugh," the man explained, causing Fiona gasp with surprise.

"Eddie? From Spruce Valley?" Fiona asked. But when she spoke, she began to cough as her throat was very dry. Eddie quickly gathered a cup of water from a nearby table and helped her drink it all.

"Easy now, Miss Fiona. Yes, I am Eddie from Spruce Valley. Once our sheriff received the telegram that you'd been taken hostage, my friends and I set off immediately to come rescue you. I'm just sorry we didn't reach you sooner," Eddie said in a soft voice.

"I don't remember much after I tried to escape. I had become so weak by the time they recaptured me that it was hard to stay conscious," Fiona explained as she rested her head back down on the pillow.

"You're safe now, Miss Fiona. We are back in Medora. You've been asleep for the last three days as you've recovered from a terrible fever," Eddie explained. As Fiona looked up at him with surprise, he only looked at her with kindness.

"What about the robbers?" Fiona asked, fear finding its way into her mind again.

"They were captured and brought to the town's jail. You won't ever have to worry about them again," Eddie explained. Fiona released a long sigh at the relief of knowing that the robbers had been captured.

"And what about my parents? Is my father here yet?" Fiona asked. She desperately wanted to return home as soon as possible.

"Your father has been sent a telegram, but we've heard no word from him yet," Eddie said with a grim expression.

"What do you mean? If I've been resting for three days, certainly he should have replied to the telegram by now?" Fiona asked in disbelief.

"I agree, Miss Fiona. I'm not sure why there has been no word. However, now that you are awake, I'll send another telegram to let your parents know that you are alive and well. But we'll be leaving for Spruce Valley as soon as you are strong enough to travel," Eddie assured.

"Spruce Valley? But I want to return home," Fiona said before she realized she shouldn't have. She instantly saw the pain in Eddie's eyes and regretted saying those words. She had hoped her father would have come for her by now and she could tell Eddie, upon her departure, that she would rather return to Boston than risk being kidnapped again.

"I understand why you would want to return home, Miss

Fiona. After what you've been through, any young lady would want to return to what she is familiar with. I'm sure your first experience with the West hasn't been a pleasant one," Eddie said with his eyes averted from hers. Fiona felt guilty for causing him pain after everything he'd done to save her.

"I'm sorry, Eddie. I'm sure that is disappointing for you to hear," Fiona said, her eyes feeling heavy once more.

"Think nothing of it, Miss. We'll get you well before long and you'll at least get to see Spruce Valley before you go home," Eddie said in a cheerful voice. But Fiona had no strength to reply as she drifted off to sleep once more.

~

Eddie sighed deeply as he rubbed his fingers through his hair. He was relieved to see that Fiona had woken for a short time but felt saddened to hear that she wanted to return home. After everything she'd gone through to escape her home, he couldn't understand why she would want to return. But as Eddie sat on the edge of her cot in the small medical clinic that was in Medora, he could reason that she was frightened still by everything she'd experienced. He couldn't judge her for wanting to return home, but simply hoped that she'd change her mind once she felt better.

After Eddie made sure that she was resting easy, he got up from the cot and made his way out of the room. At the front of the clinic, he let the nurse know that Fiona had been awake for a time and that he was leaving to let his companions know. She thanked him for staying with Fiona since the clinic had become rather full lately. Eddie simply nodded as he left the clinic and went down the road to the local inn.

Dr. Slater and Josh had decided to stay in town for two reasons. One, because Dr. Slater wanted to keep a watch over Fiona as she recovered. And two, because Josh had instantly become famous from coast to coast after the news was telegrammed across the country that he and his deputies had jailed the infamous train robbers. Josh had been invited to dinner with both the sheriff of Medora, as well as its mayor. Josh was a hero now and was being recognized as such. And therefore, it wouldn't have been wise for Josh to stay with the others outside of town where they had made camp until they could all start the journey back to Spruce Valley.

As Eddie walked down the boardwalk towards the inn, he tried to gather his nerves. He was looking forward to letting the others know that Fiona had woken up for a time and that her fever was gone. But his stomach tightened in knots over the fact that she wanted to return home. Eddie felt grim indeed as he entered the inn, and found Dr. Slater and Josh in the dining room where lunch was being served.

"Eddie, it's good to see you," Josh said with a smile. He'd been enjoying the publicity, but once he seemed to recognize Eddie's face, he quieted down and motioned towards the chair next to him.

"Has something happened to Fiona?" Dr. Slater asked as Eddie sat down.

"Fiona's fever broke in the night and she just woke up. We talked for a few minutes before she fell asleep again. I helped her drink some water, explained that she was safe, and that her kidnappers were in jail," Eddie explained.

"Well, that sounds fantastic. So why do you look so grave, Eddie?" Josh asked.

"She wants to go home. She doesn't understand why her father hasn't come for her, and I explained that we would be traveling to Spruce Valley as soon as she is well enough to travel. I fear that this whole experienced has frightened her so much that she's willing to return to the life she once ran from," Eddie explained grimly.

"I can't blame her, Eddie," Dr. Slater spoke up. "She was in a bad way when we found her, and God only knows what she went through when she was kidnapped. She didn't have any bruising and didn't look to have been forced upon, but there are other ways to torture a lady. She could now be malnourished. She was probably forced to sleep out in the open."

Eddie nodded. He could understand why Fiona would want to return home as quickly as possible. "I get that, Doc. I just wasn't expecting it, is all," Eddie said in a somber voice.

"Well, she'll come home to Spruce Valley, and I'll telegram her father to let him know that she is awake and well and will be coming back with us. I doubt she'll want to stay alone in Medora," Josh reasoned.

"Was the same thing I told her as well," Eddie commented. "Well, I'm going to ride out and go visit with the others. I'm sure she'll be awake by supper time and will be as hungry as a bear after winter."

"I'll go stay with her until you return, Eddie," Dr. Slater said.

"I appreciate it, Doc. I appreciate everything you two have done," Eddie said as he stood.

"Don't you worry one bit, Eddie. Go spend some time with your monkey and brother, and we'll see you after a bit," Josh said. Eddie nodded and smiled at the joke before he left and made his way back to the main street to collect his Indian pony.

As Eddie trotted out of town towards the place where the others had been camping out, Eddie tried to see the bright side of the situation. Fiona had been rescued and she was currently recovering from having a severe fever. Eddie understood that it would take some time to mentally recover from being kidnapped, and he only hoped that Fiona would be able to live the rest of her years in happiness. But the thought of her returning home did something to Eddie that he'd never felt. Having only been with her for a short time, he felt like he would miss her after working so hard to meet her.

Eddie prayed that no matter what happened next, Fiona would finally be able to feel safe again.

~

IT TOOK another three days in the clinic to feel like she had the strength to travel again. Fiona enjoyed the company while she rested in the small room she'd been assigned. She was able to meet everyone that Eddie had written about in his letters. And she learned for herself just how humorous Dr. Slater and Gray Jenkins could be when they were together. Eddie explained at one point that she would get to meet Bright Star during their journey to Spruce Valley, because they were worried that the locals wouldn't accept the Indian in town. Fiona had to admit that she looked forward to meeting this man and thanking him for everything he'd done to rescue her.

As time went on and Fiona regained her strength, she enjoyed her time alone with Eddie. They talked about all sorts of things but were careful not to mention her time with the robbers. Everyone had been kind enough not to bring up the subject around her. Instead, Eddie described what it would be like to travel to Spruce Valley with the others, that she'd be able to ride up front in the wagon with him, or if she wanted to, she could try her luck with horseback riding.

"I'm not sure if I would be any good at it," Fiona said, though she thought riding a horse might be some fun.

"Well, we all recently had to learn how to ride bareback. I think Bright Star is a good teacher, and we would all make sure you didn't get hurt. I doubt that we'll be traveling at the same pace that we did coming up here," Eddie assured.

The one thing that Fiona was learning about Eddie was that he was a very kind and considerate man. He was not only handsome, but the very sight of him made her smile. As she waited for her body to feel strong enough to travel, she looked forward to talking to him each day. Though, every time he did come to visit with her, she always asked him if he'd heard back from her father.

Fiona was overcome with so many emotions every time Eddie shared the disheartening news with her that still there had been no word from her parents. A part of her wondered if they were currently traveling by train and therefore hadn't received the messages. But when Sheriff Ryder had sent a telegram down the trainline as a sheriff on the lookout for her parents, there had still been no reply. Fiona was starting to think that her parents did not truly care about her and if returning home was the answer anymore.

However, Fiona did her best to put that out of her mind because first she would be traveling to Spruce Valley. From there, she would have to determine her own future. With the extended invitation from Dr. Slater to join him and his family during her stay, Fiona knew that she had much to look forward to. She would be traveling with a group of armed men who would protect her from any danger, and there was much about Spruce Valley that she looked forward to discovering.

On the morning of their departure, Fiona rose from her cot in the medical clinic and put on the traveling gown that the nurse had lent her. She disliked the fact that she owned so few items and had to borrow clothing from other women. But she reasoned that this was the way things were done out West. There weren't women's clothing stores on every corner like she had been used to in Boston.

A knock on the door sounded, and Fiona called to the person to come in as she finished pinning back her hair. Though she often had it curled and pinned for her, Fiona had been taught how to braid her hair by the nurse in order to keep it out of her face. Eddie came into the room carrying a bouquet of wildflowers.

"Good day, Fiona. I picked these for you on my way into town this morning from the camp," Eddie said as he handed Fiona the small bundle. She was surprised and happy as she accepted the flowers and inhaled their sweet aroma.

"Why thank you, Eddie," Fiona said as she held onto them. Fiona looked around the room and realized she had no other things to collect. "I guess I'm ready to be off." Fiona was further surprised when Eddie extended his arm to her in a very gentlemanly fashion. She smiled as she took his arm and allowed him to lead her out of the clinic.

"The others are waiting for us just on the outskirts of town. It shouldn't be a long walk," Eddie explained, as they left the clinic after a quick goodbye to the nurse and resident doctor. Though it was far from the nearest city, Fiona had to admit that the medical care she'd received had been excellent.

"I think a long walk will do me good. I've been cooped up for so long that I shall look forward to any amount of exercise," Fiona replied. She was also enjoying being so close to Eddie as they walked at a leisurely pace.

"When we reach the others, I have a surprise for you as well," Eddie said with a smirk.

Fiona smiled up at him, enjoying his handsome features. "You seem to be full of surprises this morning, Mr. Murtaugh," Fiona said with a chuckle.

"I will admit that I always enjoy impressing a young lady," Eddie replied.

"Then I shall consider myself lucky to be the current

young lady in your sights," Fiona said, surprised at how easy it was to flirt with Eddie. She'd never acted this way towards a man before and couldn't reason why she felt so comfortable with it now.

"Miss Fiona, you are the only woman in my sights," Eddie reassured her with a serious tone of voice. Fiona smiled at Eddie with a simple nod of her head. She knew she shouldn't encourage Eddie since she still thought of going back to Boston. Her future was so uncertain that she didn't want to commit to starting a relationship with Eddie when she wasn't even sure how long she'd be in his company.

As they traveled out of town, Fiona quickly spotted a covered wagon in the distance that was surrounded by several horses. But as they drew closer, she realized that they weren't just any horses. They were Indian ponies that were currently being ridden bareback, just as Eddie had described. And on one such horse was a tall Indian man with long black hair with bits of gray weaved through it. He wore a buckskin tunic and leggings, and his feet were dressed in moccasins. Fiona had read about Indians several times before, but never thought she'd ever get to see one, let alone meet one.

As Fiona and Eddie drew closer to the group, they were greeted warmly. "Good day to you, Miss Fiona. It's good to see you out and about on this fine day," Dr. Slater said.

"Thank you, Dr. Slater. I have much thanks to give to you for keeping such a close watch on me," Fiona replied.

"Just don't be thanking him the whole way home. His ego is already this big," Sheriff Ryder said, holding his hands up far from each other.

"This coming from the sheriff that is currently full of himself," piped up Gray.

"Hey! It's not every day that you get to bring in a gang like that," the sheriff retorted. Just the mention of the robbers caused Fiona to stiffen.

"Well, let's get ready to move out. First, Bright Star. May I introduce you officially to Miss Fiona Wilkins," Eddie spoke up. Fiona was thankful that Eddie had changed the subject so quickly. He then led Fiona over to where the Indian was positioned upon the pony. And as Fiona drew closer, she realized that a monkey sat on his shoulders.

"It is nice to meet you, Fiona Wilkins. I am proud to have accompanied these fine men to rescue you," Bright Star said in greeting.

"Thank you very much, Bright Star, for all that you've done. I hope one day I will be able to repay you," Fiona said. And though she didn't mean to be rude, she couldn't help staring at the monkey that seemed to be staring back at her as well.

Eddie made a clicking noise next to her and as Fiona turned her head to see what he was doing, a moment later the monkey was scurrying down from Bright Star's shoulder, finding a new position on Eddie's shoulders. Fiona was so surprised that she stepped away from Eddie quickly as she and the monkey came face to face.

"Don't worry, there's nothing to be afraid of," Eddie reassured her as she stared wide eyed at the monkey.

"Forgive me, Mr. Murtaugh. The monkey is just surprising, is all," Fiona said, regaining her composure. After taking a deep breath, Fiona stepped forward and reached out her hand towards the monkey. It made cute sounds as Fiona petted the monkey's fur, which she found surprisingly soft.

"His name is Jack, and it takes everyone a few minutes to get used to him," Eddie said reassuringly.

"Except me, of course," Bright Star said with a laugh.

"Yes, Bright Star. Jack has taken quite a liking to you," Eddie said as he looked towards the Indian.

"Alrighty folks, let's get a move on. Home is not close by," Sheriff Ryder spoke up. Eddie then escorted Fiona over to the wagon and pulled back the cover to reveal the inside. As Fiona's eyes fell upon her suitcases, she could hardly believe her eyes.

"How did you ever retrieve them?" Fiona asked in disbelief.

"While you were resting, I inquired with the train depot. The suitcases were amongst others in the lost and found with your name on the handles. They were easy enough to locate, and I kept them in the wagon 'til you were recovered," Eddie explained. "You'll be able to ride comfortable back here. There's plenty of blankets to sit on and you'll be able to lay down if you need to."

Fiona was still shocked as Eddie helped her up into the wagon. He showed her the best place to position her foot and she climbed onto the wagon with ease. She was surrounded by supplies as she got into the wagon, but she found the pile of blankets Eddie had pointed out and sat upon them to get as comfortable as she could. A moment later, Eddie was rounding the wagon and pulling himself up onto the driver's seat before slapping the reins to get the horses moving.

It took a second for Fiona to get used to the movements of the wagon. It was much like riding on the train, but much more jarring every time one of the wheels would hit a rock or bump in the road. Fiona reminded herself that a little bump here and there was better than what she had to endure a few days ago. It wasn't the most comfortable way to travel, but Fiona was simply glad to be traveling.

As they traveled along the main road, the sun continued to rise in the sky. Fiona took the time to open her suitcases and look over the contents to see if most of her things were still intact. She was pleased to discover that all her things had been left alone in the suitcase, including her traveling gowns and personal things. She found her novel and placed it in her lap before closing the suitcases back up, pushing them to the side. Even though she'd read the novel a dozen times before, she felt excited to read it again, simply because she had the freedom to do so.

Fiona was very thankful for having been rescued, and as she continued to sneak glances at Eddie from over the top of her book, she was especially grateful to have met him in the process.

# CHAPTER 12

Traveling to Spruce Valley had several ups and downs for Fiona. She enjoyed the company during their days of travel, getting to laugh and joke with many of them. Fiona was made to feel at ease and comfortable in the way she was respected, since she was the only female traveling in the group. She was certainly enjoying the scenery as the wagon rolled along the road, delivering sights of hills, forests, and open plains.

But at night, the nightmares would come again and again. Tucked safely in the wagon with several layers of bedding and blankets, Fiona would toss and turn in her nightgown. Images of pain and fear would rush through her head as she tried to fight off invisible assailants. And when she would wake with a start, she'd quickly sit up and take several seconds to realize that she was safe in the covered wagon. Fiona would have to sit still for a while, listening to the sounds of the night. She'd look towards the front of the wagon and out into the open sky to see stars shining. It would be a while before she tried to sleep again, but she took some comfort in knowing that she was surrounded by several brave men. Even if some of them snored loudly at night.

One morning, Eddie invited her to ride up front on the bench of the wagon. "But what about Sawyer?" Fiona had asked.

"I didn't get much sleep last night and wouldn't mind stretching my legs out back there," Sawyer spoke up in his defense.

"Well, alright then," Fiona agreed, standing steadily to her feet as the wagon rumbled down the road. She'd gotten used to the feeling of the wagon's movements and took small steps in order to switch places with Sawyer. Once she neared the bench, he hopped into the back of the wagon as though it was standing still, and then helped her up onto the bench.

"Thank you, Sawyer," Fiona said with a sigh of relief when she was safely sitting on the bench. Sawyer nodded in return as he made his way towards the back of the wagon and started fashioning himself a comfortable spot to lay down on.

"Seems like Sawyer isn't the only one whose been having trouble at night," Eddie spoke up as he moved closer to her. His eyes stayed on the horses and the road ahead, but he seemed attentive to her as well.

Fiona sighed as she looked out into the distance, enjoying the scenery as the morning sun made its progression through the sky. "Is it that obvious?" Fiona asked, worried that her nightmares had woken someone else.

"We heard your frightened cries last night," Eddie stated. "I did rise to check on you, only to see you were dreaming. Bright Star wants to do a cleansing ceremony on you tonight, if you'd be willing?"

Fiona looked at Eddie then, a feeling of both embarrassment and curiosity came over her. "What does this ceremony entail?" she asked.

"The way Bright Star explained it is that you'll get to sit comfortably while he prays over you," Eddie explained.

Fiona thought about it and reasoned that it didn't sound terrifying. "I could use all the prayers I could get," Fiona reasoned. Eddie smiled and nodded his head.

"I always enjoy seeing Indian ceremonies, so I think you'll enjoy it," Eddie reassured. "Dr. Slater suggested that you could use some laudanum to help you sleep."

"I would rather not use anything that I could get addicted to. I've seen businessmen blackmail doctors into giving them more," Fiona said.

"I'm sure Dr. Slater wouldn't let something like that happen, but I respect your reasonings. I simply don't want you to suffer any more than you already have," Eddie said. Eddie's words surprised Fiona. She looked to him and watched him for a long moment. A smile crept onto his face as he turned his eyes to her.

"Why you lookin' at me like that?" he asked.

Fiona blushed as she realized she was staring. She looked away as she said, "Because I'm surprised by your gentleman-like characteristics. I never thought a cowboy could possess such kindness as you've shown me," Fiona said, her head lowered. She was further surprised when she felt Eddie's hand gently tilt her head towards him.

"You deserve all the kindness in the world, Fiona, after what you experienced in North Dakota, but also back in Boston. No one should ever have to experience what you've gone through, and I hope that spending time in Spruce Valley will be a comfort to you," Eddie explained as their eyes locked. Fiona was so lost in his gaze and touched by his words that she was hardly aware of herself as she leaned towards him.

However, Eddie broke their eye contact as he quickly looked back to the horses and moved them to the left to keep the wagon on the road. Him breaking their eye contact was like being pulled from a magical spell. Fiona took several deep breaths as she realized she was about to kiss Eddie. She had no idea where these deep feelings had come from. She reasoned that she was simply recovering from being kidnapped and any amount of kindness felt almost surreal to her.

Having regained control of her emotions, Fiona knew she had to be more careful around Eddie. After all, she still planned to return to Boston.

~

Eddie had enjoyed spending the day talking with Fiona. Getting to make her laugh seemed worth all the effort since her laugh often sounded like music to him. Every once and a while, Jack would come over to him from where he enjoyed riding with Bright Star. During those times, Fiona spent time petting Jack's fur and feeding him dates. Eventually, Jack moved over to Fiona's shoulder and she would giggle and talk sweetly to the monkey.

Sometimes, Eddie liked to think that Fiona was coming to Spruce Valley to be with him. She was not only beautiful, but had a sweet spirit that Eddie found lovely. He didn't like to think that she'd be gone from his life when her parents arrived to take her home. Eddie wasn't certain that they would ever come since there had been no word from them, but he knew that returning to Boston was Fiona's current plan for the future.

That night, as they made camp off from the road, they sat around the fire to enjoy one of Gray's cooked meals. For being a Boston socialite, Fiona had adapted well to traveling on the open road. She hadn't complained about having to sleep in a wagon or eat rustic food, since ingredients were few. She easily talked with everyone and could guess that her experience in social settings afforded her the ease of speaking. And Eddie felt proud when she even included Bright Star in the conversation.

As the meal came to an end, and Sawyer and Josh went off to take care of washing the dishes in a nearby stream, Eddie was sitting next to Fiona talking about cattle drives when Bright Star approached them. He kneeled in front of Fiona, which seemed to surprise her a moment.

"Fiona Wilkins, I would like to perform a cleansing ceremony on you now. I believe it will help settle your spirit so that you may move forward and away from the darkness of your past," Bright Star explained. Eddie watched Fiona's expression as she looked at the Indian. She looked nervous, but eventually she nodded her head with a small smile.

Bright Star smiled in return as he rose once more and tossed a satchel into the fire. A pleasing smell of herbs filled the air as Bright Star started to chant and sing. He removed a large feather from his hair and started to fan the smoke from the fire around Fiona. He began to stomp his feet to the rhythm of the song he was chanting.

Everyone watched with respect and interest as Bright Star performed the ceremony. It was as though nothing else in the world mattered, as they listened to his chanting and watched the way he danced and fanned the smoke from the fire. As Eddie shifted his eyes to Fiona, he saw how intently she was watching Bright Star too, with tears in her eyes.

In that moment, Eddie wanted to do everything in his power to take all the fear away from her. He wanted to protect her with his very life and ensure that she never felt this type of pain again. Eddie mindlessly stroked Jack's fur as he watched the performance with the monkey sat on his shoulder, thinking that he needed to do something to convince Fiona to stay in Spruce Valley and give their relationship an honest chance.

As Bright Star's ceremony came to an end, the night seemed to fill with a deafening silence. Sawyer and Josh had returned from their chores and had stood on the outside of their circle as they watched and listened. It was Fiona's voice that eventually broke the trance they had all been in.

"Thank you, Bright Star. You have a wonderful voice and you dance very well," Fiona said.

Bright Star smiled keenly in return as he nodded his head. "You shall make a great wife one day, Fiona Wilkins. If you are ever in need of a husband, I have two sons who would be honored to have you as a wife," Bright Star said. His words startled Eddie, thinking that Bright Star was offering one of his sons to Fiona. As she laughed, he wondered what was so funny.

"Thank you, Bright Star, but I am not in need of a husband at this moment. And I would not consider a man whom I have not yet met," Fiona replied, her mirth subsiding.

"Well then. We shall come visit you at the Slater's Ranch during our visit to Spruce Valley, and perhaps then we could convince you otherwise," Bright Star said with a wink, replacing the large black feather into his hair once more. Then, he took a seat around the fire next to Dr. Slater as the two struck up a conversation.

"How did you enjoy the ceremony?" Eddie asked as he drew Fiona's attention back to him. Fiona reached out and petted Jack as she gathered her thoughts.

"It was like being hypnotized," Fiona said. "It was wonderful to see and filled me with a lot of peace. I have never been prayed over like that before and I am grateful to have had the experience."

Eddie smiled at her, thinking she had the perfect response. He had felt the same too, and wondered if the others had felt it.

"I was certainly not expecting Bright Star's offer," Fiona said in a soft voice, as she began to giggle once more. Eddie joined her as he nodded his head.

"He did the same thing to Gray's wife when she first came to Spruce Valley. It seems that Bright Star is constantly on the lookout for a decent wife for his sons. The Crow Tribe has a small camp on the outskirts of Spruce Valley. There is a small number of them now compared to what they used to be. Soon, they'll travel south for the winter to follow the buffalo herd," Eddie explained.

"It will be sad to see him go," Fiona said softly as she turned her eyes back to the fire. Eddie wasn't sure what to say in response. A part of him wondered if she had considered staying for an extended period in Spruce Valley. He certainly hoped so..

~

THE NEXT MORNING brought a wave of excitement for Fiona. Not only had she slept soundly for the first time in what felt like weeks, but this would be the day that they finally arrived in Spruce Valley and the Slater Ranch. Fiona was looking forward to being surrounded by four walls again instead of out in the open. She'd enjoyed the nice weather and getting to see the stars as she laid down, but the thought of sleeping in a real bed since she ran away from Boston was something she was desperately looking forward to.

Fiona had been back and forth with her thoughts over what she would do for her future. A part of her desperately wanted to return to Boston, hoping to please her parents enough to allow her to marry someone she at least liked.

And the other part of her—the part that was healing more rapidly with every passing day—wanted to rediscover her courage and strength once more in order to make her way in the West. Either way, she was excited to meet Mrs. Slater and Mrs. Jenkins, since they'd both been mail-order-brides from the East.

Fiona was sitting up front with Eddie once more, having passed up her opportunity to ride one of the Indian ponies. She felt like she wasn't quite ready to start riding yet, but Eddie had started to show her how to lead the wagon. With the reins in her hands, and Eddie sitting very close to her, he instructed her on how tight to hold them, how to steer the horses, and how to tell them to pick up their pace.

"Relax your arms," Eddie guided. "You don't want to go stiff and lose strength in your arms." Fiona smiled as she tried to relax. She'd never done anything like this before and found steering the four large horses to be thrilling. It was an easy enough task, but Fiona feared doing something wrong.

"When we get home, I can show you how to unhook the horses from the wagon so that you can learn for yourself how it's done. So, if you ever need to ride into town, you can at least take the wagon," Eddie offered.

"It seems I'll have to learn a lot once we reach the ranch," Fiona reasoned as she kept her eyes to the road ahead of them.

"Yes. But you won't be alone. You'll have Mrs. Slater and Mrs. Jenkins, who will be eager teachers. I'm confident that if I can learn to read and write from the Slaters, then you can learn a few things about living in the West from them as well," Eddie said with confidence.

Fiona was certainly appreciating his tone of voice. He always seemed to be so positive, and though Fiona had many fears about her immediate future, she took comfort in knowing she would be close to Eddie through it all.

The sun was high in the sky when the first sights of the Slater Ranch came into view. Fiona craned her neck this way and that to see everything she could. A small one-story, white clapboard ranch house stood in the distance. A large red barn had been erected farther away with wooden fencing running out from the back of it. Several horses grazed in the pasture and she could make out the shape of cattle in the distance. The sight made her feel excited to be seeing a real Western home. She couldn't believe that she was finally arriving at their destination at long last, and the thought of not having to travel any longer brought tears of relief to Fiona's eyes.

A sea of prairie grass stretched out as far as Fiona could see, meeting the dazzling blue sky above the horizon. Maple and birch trees dotted the ranch and there was a white bunkhouse on the right of the driveway that seemed to stretch on forever. Fiona assumed that Eddie stayed in the bunkhouse with the other cattle hands and seeing how close it was to the main house, she knew that she'd be able to see Eddie plenty.

"Home sweet home," Dr. Slater said as he urged his pony forward. Gray was right on his heels as they seemed to race each other towards the house. Fiona chuckled as she watched them race across the prairie, practically leaping off their ponies before dashing inside the house where a choir of happy voices sounded.

"Well fellas, it's been a real pleasure. Fiona, welcome to Spruce Valley," Josh said as he tipped his hat towards her and then made his way towards the barn.

"It is good to be back," Sawyer spoke up from the back of the wagon.

"Yeah, I would agree with that. It's been fun traveling, but nothing quite beats home," Eddie replied.

"I will need to take the ponies back to camp and prepare

for our journey south," Bright Star spoke up. Eddie pulled the wagon to a stop in front of the ranch house.

"Thank you again, Bright Star, for helping us when you are so close to leaving Spruce Valley. I shall think of something to bring you when you return," Eddie spoke up.

"Perhaps Jack would like to accompany me south for the winter?" Bright Star asked. "That way he will not have to worry about the fierce cold weather."

Fiona noticed the surprised look on Eddie's face as he looked towards the Indian. He even held Jack close to him as he regarded the other man.

"I will have to think about that, Bright Star. You make a valid point, but I am very fond of Jack and would surely miss him," Eddie replied. Bright Star only nodded his head and grunted as he led his pony in the direction of the barn. Fiona sat with Eddie for a moment before the ranch house doors swung open and two ladies came strolling out.

"Welcome, welcome!" called the one with long black hair. She had dazzling green eyes that Fiona found lovely. She also realized that this woman was dressed in the sophisticated manner with which Fiona was used to back in Boston.

"My name is Mrs. Lucy Slater. And this is my business partner, Mrs. Martha Jenkins," the black-haired woman introduced. Eddie quickly hopped down from the wagon and came around to help Fiona down as well.

"Mrs. Slater, Mrs. Jenkins. It's a pleasure to meet you both. My name is Miss Fiona Wilkins, from Boston," Fiona said as she dipped her head towards the two married women.

"Fiona, we are so glad to finally meet you. Eddie has told us so many wonderful things about you from your letters that I feel like we know you already," Mrs. Jenkins spoke up. She had lovely red hair and bright blue eyes that shone with kindness.

"I will admit that Eddie spoke highly of both of you as well. I am pleased to finally get to meet you," Fiona replied.

"And we are so glad the whole business is behind ye. It seems that mail-order-brides can't seem to catch a break when coming to Spruce Valley," Mrs. Slater commented. "When I first came here, there were these nasty men harassing us because they wanted the ranch."

"And I certainly brought trouble with me," Mrs. Jenkins added.

"Does Spruce Valley get much crime?" Fiona asked, frightened at the idea of having to deal with robbers again.

"No, dear. It was all very circumstantial. My goodness, we are probably frightening you. Come on in and let's get you settled. The little ones are eager to meet you and there is a water closet you can use to bathe and whatnot," Mrs. Jenkins said as she came to Fiona and took her hand, leading her up the front porch stairs.

"I'll bring your stuff inside in a bit," Eddie called after her. Fiona turned and waved at him, giving him a smile before she was led inside the ranch house.

Fiona hadn't expected the ranch house to look so modern. There were several elements that reminded her of her home in Boston. There was a formal dining room, sitting room, and in the back was the kitchen. A large stove rested in a spacious kitchen. Fiona was even surprised to see an icebox.

As Fiona was taking in all the finery, she saw Dr. Slater and Gray in the sitting room, playing with two children on the floor like two overgrown children themselves. One girl, who was slightly older than the boy, ramped on the two gentlemen, climbing on their backs and riding them like horses as the men crawled around on the floor. Fiona couldn't help but laugh at the sight since she knew both these men to be quite serious at times.

"Ye'd never think that Sam and Gray would act like this with the children," Mrs. Slater said with a shake of her head.

"Well, I'm sure they've missed them," Mrs. Jenkins said as she continued to lead Fiona through the house. She was led down a hallway and shown the water closet, then the spare bedroom. "I stayed in this room when I first came to Spruce Valley as well," Mrs. Jenkins said as Fiona walked around the room. It was stylishly decorated with a large bed that looked very inviting. There was a dresser and a writing desk in the room with beautiful curtains that hung over the window. As Fiona peeked through, she could see plenty of people coming and going. She even spotted Eddie in the distance.

"This is a very lovely room," Fiona said as she turned back to the two women. "I am very thankful, Mrs. Slater, for your hospitality. I've very much looked forward to arriving and not having to be out on the open road any longer."

"Please Miss Fiona, simply call me Lucy. We are both big city girls, but things are much less formal here," Mrs. Slater replied.

"Yes, and simply call me Martha. I like to think we'll make quick friends," Mrs. Jenkins added. Fiona simply smiled because she didn't want to be rude in stating that she didn't plan to stay in Spruce Valley longer than when her parents would surely come to get her. Her inner turmoil was still raging over what she should do about her future. But for now, she was simply thankful to be out of a wagon and surrounded by four walls once more.

Just then, Eddie came walking into the room with her two suitcases. He set them down easily at the foot of the bed like they weighed nothing. He certainly continued to surprise Fiona with his skills, and for a moment she couldn't help but wonder what it might feel like to be wrapped up in those strong arms. Pulling her eyes away from Eddie, she smiled pleasantly at the two women who seemed to be watching her keenly.

"Thank you, Eddie. I appreciate your help," Fiona spoke up, before she completely lost all sense of manners.

"Of course, Fiona. I'm glad to help. But I'll be off for a while. There is much unpacking to do, and I told Bright Star I'd help him return the ponies to his tribe for everything he's done for us," Eddie explained. "I left Jack with Sawyer if you need a friend." He winked at her before leaving the room. Fiona couldn't refrain from blushing as she watched him leave the room.

"Well, we'll let ye get settled," Lucy said with a smile. "Take your time, and feel free to use the water closet across the hallway."

"We'll go put on some hot water so you can take a bath. I know that's what I always wanted after being out on the road for days," Martha spoke up. The two ladies then left the room, Martha closing the door behind her.

It had been so long since Fiona had been by herself that it almost felt strange. There had been a time when she'd enjoyed spending hours alone in her room. But as she stood and looked around the quaint space, she couldn't help but feel an immediate sense of loneliness. She didn't like the feeling at all and quickly went to work on putting her things away in the dresser before selecting a nice dress and under garments to change into. Her nice house slippers had been ruined, so all she had was one set of traveling boots. Fiona reasoned it would have to do for now.

Taking her things to the water closet, Fiona was pleasantly surprised by the space of the room. A large cast iron tub was fashioned into the room, along with the flushing commode. It reminded her much of home, and Fiona was once again thankful that the Slaters had offered to house her.

With no money to her name, Fiona wasn't certain how long she would be able to survive on her own in the West.

After taking care of her business and hanging up her nice clothes, Fiona opened the door and ventured back into the kitchen with the intention of helping with heating the hot water. In Boston, the water in her house had been heated by a central boiler and then piped to the water closet. But from the novels Fiona had read, she understood that things were done differently in the West when boilers weren't a common thing to have.

"I hope ye've found everything to yer liking," Lucy said as Fiona came into the kitchen.

"Yes, very much. I am pleasantly surprised that a Western home has a water closet," Fiona admitted.

Lucy chuckled as she lifted a lid on a large pot and checked to see if the water was bubbling yet as wood burned from within the stove. As she replaced the lid, she fully turned to Fiona. "When I came to Spruce Valley almost two years ago, there was much about this ranch house that surprised me. Sam certainly spoils me," Lucy said.

Two children came toddling into the kitchen then as Martha led them by the hands. "The men are going to go get things settled. Seems they'll be busy 'til dinner time," Martha explained. "But in the meantime, we shall certainly have a nice visit. Fiona, may I introduce you to Francene Slater and Samuel Jenkins."

Fiona smiled at the children as she bent down to greet them. "It's a pleasure to meet you," Fiona said as she waved at the children. Francene seemed a bit shy, but Samuel was quick to break from his mother's grasp and wrap his little arms around Fiona. She laughed as she picked up the boy and rested him on her hip.

"Why hello there," Fiona said as the two chuckled

together. Samuel then grabbed onto Fiona's braided hair and began playing with it.

"Oh, Samuel likes to play with hair, unfortunately," Martha said as she came to retrieve her son.

"Don't worry, Martha. I'm not worried about my hair at this point. He could not do any more harm to it than the open road has," Fiona said as she handed Samuel to Martha.

"Well, the water seems to be ready. Help me carry it to the tub and ye'll be all set to have a nice, long bath," Lucy spoke up. Fiona was quick to help the woman lift the large pot from the stove using several hand towels. Together, they carefully carried it down the hallway to the water closet while Martha kept a close eye on the kids. Once the hot water had been poured into the tub, Lucy was able to carry it once more by herself.

"There ye go, my dear. Feel free to use whatever ye find in the cupboard," Lucy said before heading back down the hallway.

As Fiona closed the door, she released a long sigh. She was so excited to take a bath that she quickly discarded her clothes right onto the floor and stepped into the tub. She exhaled deeply as she lowered herself into the water. With a bar of soap she'd found in the cupboard, Fiona planned to scrub every inch of her body thoroughly. It wasn't just the grime of traveling for days that was bugging Fiona, she also wanted to rid herself of every bad thing that had happened to her since she left Boston.

Tears stung her eyes as she lathered up the soap and began to wash her body. She eventually unbraided her hair and plunged her head underwater. The hot water did wonders for her skin and hair but no matter what she did, she couldn't seem to stop the tears from sliding down her cheeks. Fiona clasped a hand over her mouth as the sobs came. The last thing she wanted to do was alert someone to the pain that was coursing through her body. She tried to focus on washing her hair instead of the memories that seemed to flash through her mind.

It was a long while before Fiona was able to get in control of her emotions once more. The water had started to turn cold as Fiona finally got out of the tub, pulled the plug at the bottom, and dried herself off with a towel. She felt better than she had in days and was thankful for the opportunity to bathe. After dressing once more, Fiona used her comb to brush her long hair, and when she was done, she decided to simply tie back the top part to keep her hair out of her face. She reckoned that if this town was less formal, she could visit with others with her hair down.

After taking her soiled clothing back to her room and storing them in her suitcase until she could find the time to properly wash them, Fiona then made her way back down the hallway to the main part of the house. There, she found Martha and Lucy busy in the kitchen while the two toddlers sat on the floor playing with wooden blocks. Fiona was amused as she watched the children stack blocks on top of each other, as though they were competing with who could build the tallest tower.

"I bet you are feeling better," Martha spoke up, drawing Fiona's attention to her. Fiona smiled as she nodded her head.

"It's amazing what a simple bath can do to help wash away days of road grime," Fiona said.

"I hope yer hungry, Fiona. We plan to cook a feast in honor of yer arrival," Lucy said happily.

"Oh, I don't want you two going to any trouble," Fiona said quickly, surprised by the generosity.

"Nonsense. I'm sure everyone is starving from Gray's simple cooking," Lucy replied.

Fiona chuckled. "He's not a bad cook with what he had

to work with. I've certainly eaten worse," Fiona said, remembering the food she was forced to eat while she'd been kidnapped. The very thought seemed to settle Fiona into remaining quiet.

"Well then, why don't you give us a hand? I'm sure we could teach you a thing or two about cooking," Martha suggested. Fiona focused on the woman and mustered up a smile.

"I've been taught to cook a few dishes, so I'm certain I could be of good help," Fiona said proudly.

"That is a blessing to hear, for sure. When I first came to Spruce Valley, I'd never cooked for meself before. Yer already more well off than I was when first becoming a mail-order-bride," Lucy said happily. Fiona couldn't help but smile at the woman's words. She knew it was better to keep a happy expression on her face instead of telling them that she didn't know if she'd stay in Spruce Valley for long.

As Fiona worked alongside the two women, she quickly realized how lovely it was to be around them. Fiona had missed female companionship and thought that Martha and Lucy would make wonderful friends. As they worked together to prepare dinner, Fiona also looked forward to visiting with Eddie once more.

# CHAPTER 13

By the time dinner was ready up at the ranch house, Eddie was certainly looking forward to sitting down and enjoying a home-cooked meal. It felt like weeks since he'd had a proper meal, and though he had to credit Gray for being able to put together some good meals, he couldn't deny that he looked forward to some of Mrs. Slater's home-cooking.

Eddie was also looking forward to getting to spend some more time with Fiona. They'd had plenty of opportunities to talk over the last few days since traveling from North Dakota, but he knew that things would be different now that they could both settle down. Eddie would be returning to work tomorrow, and Fiona would no doubt begin to find her own way in Spruce Valley. He only hoped that she would decide to make this place her home instead of a temporary place to be.

After helping Bright Star take all his ponies to camp, Eddie bathed thoroughly, using a new bar of soap, in the stream that ran along the eastern part of the ranch. He was hoping to make a good impression on Fiona once she saw him all cleaned up. He even took the time to shave and dress in his best clothes. At least, the clothes that were the cleanest. After traveling for countless days, Eddie didn't have too many pairs of clean pants and still hoped to show Fiona that he could clean up well.

"Somethin' sure smells better," Sawyer joked, as Eddie came into the bunkhouse to drop off his road clothes. Sawyer was sitting at the main table with Jack in front of him, feeding the monkey dates.

"You should try bathing some time. You'd be surprised how much better you could smell, too," Eddie said with a chuckle as he ducked into his room, deposited his clothes beside his bed, and then walked back out to the main room.

"I think me and the monkey are going to head down to the stream in a moment," Sawyer replied.

"Well, you two better hurry. I'm guessing dinner will be done shortly," Eddie said as he made his way towards the door.

"You're just in a hurry to go see a certain young lady," Sawyer said with a chuckle. Eddie stopped walking for a moment to face his brother.

"I won't deny that I am looking forward to seeing Fiona. I know we've spent all this time together, but I can't help but think that things will be different now that we're not out on the open road," Eddie admitted.

Sawyer nodded his head as he stood and stretched. Jack quickly scooped up his date and climbed on top of Sawyer's shoulder for a personal ride.

"You're probably right, Eddie. She's been through hell and is finally getting to be in one place for more than a day. It might take some time, but I'm sure Fiona will come around to you," Sawyer said, trying to be reassuring.

"I sure hope so. She's talked about returning to Boston after everything she's been through," Eddie confessed with a deep sigh. Sawyer seemed shocked to hear this.

"I can't believe she'd go back after what her parents put her through. You told me how she was practically being sold off to be married to a man twice her age," Sawyer said with heat in his words. Eddie could tell that the news was rallying him up.

"I think she's just scared, Sawyer. So scared that she isn't thinking clearly. All she knows is that she was safe in Boston," Eddie tried to explain.

"The way she described her life in Boston, it didn't sound like she was safe there, either," Sawyer said as he pushed past Eddie and out of the bunkhouse. Eddie took a few minutes to collect himself. Though he knew his brother was the quieter of the two of them, Sawyer didn't shy away from speaking the truth to someone when he felt they needed to hear it. Eddie only hoped that Sawyer would keep his thoughts to himself while Fiona took time to make the decision for herself.

Eddie then made his way from the bunkhouse towards the main house. The sun was starting to set, and Eddie was certainly looking forward to a good meal and a restful night. Though his bed wasn't anything fancy, it would surely feel better than sleeping on the ground with nothing but a bed roll. As Eddie walked up the front porch steps, he could hear happy chatter coming from inside the house. He couldn't help but smirk as he opened the front door and stepped in.

Eddie shut the door behind him as he came into the house. Heavenly smells filled the air as he made his way into the dining room. Gray and Dr. Slater were already seated at the table with their kids on their laps. Fiona had just set a plate on the table, and Eddie's stomach grumbled at the sight of mashed potatoes and gravy. But what really caught his eye was Fiona's good looks. She looked radiant in her pale blue gown, her hair pulled back from her face –he was definitely attracted to her tall, slim frame. But more than that, he simply enjoyed being around her.

"Good evening, Eddie," Fiona said as she came closer to him.

"Hi there, Fiona. You are sure looking fine this evening," Eddie said as he gave her his best smile. He noticed the blush that quickly spread across her checks, and he felt a deep desire to kiss her. But knowing that she was still uncertain about returning to Boston or staying in Spruce Valley, he knew to keep his hands to himself.

"Thank you, Eddie. You look practically transformed," Fiona said with a light chuckle.

"It's amazing what a bath and a shave can do for a man," Eddie said, joining in with her laughter.

"Hello, Eddie. Good to see you back," Martha said as she came carrying another plate of food from the kitchen.

"Good to see you, too, Mrs. Jenkins," Eddie said, his stomach starting to grumble again as Mrs. Slater then came by carrying a large platter of roasted turkey. "My goodness, that all looks amazing."

Fiona laughed, her hand coming up to cover her mouth as she did so. "Well, you best go save your seat at the table. There is more where that came from," she explained before following the ladies back into the kitchen.

"I heard that Miss Fiona helped prepare the meal," Dr. Slater said as Eddie came to sit next to him near the head of the table.

"I believe it. Fiona explained how she'd learned to cook a few things from her housekeeper," Eddie said, as he remembered some of what Fiona had written about.

"A woman who knows how to cook is an important

quality in a wife," Gray added as he bounced Samuel on his knee, causing the young boy to cry out with laughter.

Eddie only nodded his head, not wanting to talk about marriage right now. There was so much uncertainty surrounding Fiona right now that he didn't want to get his hopes up. He'd have to be patient and see where things went after today.

As the others gathered for dinner, with Sawyer and Tom joining them from the bunkhouse, everyone settled around the table. Dr. Slater said grace for the meal, giving thanks for their safe return. Then, everyone filled their plates as stories started to be shared about what had been happening around the ranch and Spruce Valley while they'd been gone.

"I about had a heart attack when the paper arrived with the news of Sheriff Ryder. Is it true that you guys all helped to bring in those train robbers?" Tom spoke up as they ate. With Fiona having sat next to Eddie on the bench at the table, he noticed when she went still at the mention of the robbers.

"It is true, Tom, but let's not talk about that here at the table," Eddie quickly spoke up before anyone else could. He said this in such a stern voice that he hoped that everyone caught his message.

"It's been rather busy at the boutique since you've all been gone. Everyone's been coming in to find out when you all would be home again. Even the men have come in hoping to hear of something," Martha spoke up.. "I never thought we'd ever get men at the shop!"

"I couldn't stop laughing after Mr. Frost left the boutique. Ye should have seen how large his eyes became when he noticed the lady's undergarments," Lucy said with a chuckle.

"Fiona, you should come into town with Lucy and I

tomorrow. With the men all returned, we'll have time to show you around," Martha offered.

Eddie was thankful for the turn in the conversation and watched Fiona as he waited to hear her reply. She smiled as she nodded her head. "I would love to see the town. Eddie has written so much about it that I think I'd enjoy putting faces to the many names," Fiona replied. Eddie was relieved to see her so eager and excited. He certainly didn't want her to be fearful anymore.

By the time all the food had been happily eaten and many compliments had been given to the women for a job well done, everyone was quick to retire for the night. The Jenkins' headed to their own home the moment the dining table was cleared. Tom and Sawyer volunteered to wash the dishes so that Dr. Slater and Mrs. Slater could put their daughter to bed together. It gave Eddie the chance to invite Fiona out onto the front porch so they could have a private moment together.

"I feel as though I could sleep the week away," Fiona commented as they stepped out onto the front porch together. Eddie pulled the front door closed behind him before joining Fiona on the steps. She looked up at the sky, the night clear and the stars bright.

"I feel the same way. But there is much work to get caught up on. Morning will certainly come too soon," Eddie said as he looked up at the stars with her.

"A part of me feels guilty for bringing you all away from your work and families," Fiona said as she kept her eyes to the stars. Eddie looked down at her and, feeling brave, reached out with his hand and titled her head towards him so he could look into her beautiful blue eyes.

"Never, ever feel guilty about what happened, Fiona. We were all very willing to come to your rescue. The moment we got word, we left Spruce Valley immediately. Don't ever feel bad about what happened because it wasn't your fault in the least," Eddie said as they gazed into each other's eyes. Even with the darkness of night, Eddie could see the tears that were collecting in Fiona's eyes. He moved his hand so he could draw Fiona to him, wrapping his arms around her, holding her close.

Eddie ran his hands through Fiona's hair as she began to cry against his chest. Her hands rested on his chest as her shoulders shook as she let out all the pain she'd been holding in. Eddie was willing to stay with her for as long as it took for Fiona to feel calm and safe again. He was enjoying holding her in his arms and wished to do so for the rest of his life. And even though Fiona was indifferent about staying in Spruce Valley, he was glad to have this moment alone with her.

After a while, Fiona leaned back from him, allowing them to look at each other once more. Eddie smiled down at her, resisting the eager to kiss her.

"I'm so sorry for crying all of a sudden. It's just, I've felt lost in this deep inner turmoil and I simply couldn't help myself when you talked about your willingness to come rescue me. My own parents have done little to right the wrong that was placed against me that it's hard to believe that complete strangers would do such a thing for me," Fiona said, her hands still resting on his chest as he held her close to him.

"I hope that, if anything, you can see that there are real, kind people here in Spruce Valley who are eager to not only be your friends, but help you create a life for yourself," Eddie said, his hope rising once more that perhaps Fiona would decide to stay.

Fiona smiled up at him as she nodded her head. "I can already tell that Lucy and Martha are wonderful women, and so brave for raising two little children while managing a business. It's such an unheard thing that they really do inspire me," Fiona admitted.

Eddie could not deny that the two married women were very courageous. "I think Western women have more freedoms to create their own future. Society here isn't quick to judge because we are all doing our best to survive and make a life for ourselves," Eddie said. "I know this could be a good place for you to create whatever life you wanted."

As Eddie looked down at Fiona, he silently pleaded that she would reconsider ever returning to Boston. But as Fiona pushed away from Eddie, forcing his arms to fall once more to his sides, he felt a yearning to feel her in his arms once more.

"You've been awfully kind to me, Eddie, considering everything that has happened. And I shall always be grateful to you and your friends for rescuing me. I'm certain that I wouldn't even be alive right now if it wasn't for your efforts," Fiona said, her head turned away from him. "But now, I'm so uncertain about the future. It's hard to make any right decision."

"I understand, Fiona, I really do," Eddie said quickly. "My brother and I wandered since we were very young. It wasn't until last year when we were offered this ranch-hand job that we finally had a place to call home. Stability isn't something I've ever had 'til now. I know what it feels like to feel lost and unsure of what to do about it. So, take as long as you need to make that decision for yourself."

Eddie then took Fiona's hand and kissed the back of it before releasing it again. "I hope you sleep well, Fiona. I'm sure we'll see each other tomorrow. I look forward to hearing what you think of town," Eddie said as he stepped off the front porch stairs and started to make his way to the bunkhouse. If he didn't leave right away, then Fiona would certainly see his own tears at the thought of having to say goodbye to her if she did decide to return to Boston after all.

~

Fiona watched as Eddie walked off the porch and headed towards the white bunkhouse. She stood watching him, her arms wrapped around her body as she thought about how it felt to have his lips on her hand. It was a very gentlemanly gesture that Fiona appreciated, and there was something about that kiss that sent warmth radiating throughout her body. Fiona could only imagine what it would feel like to have his lips on hers. But before Fiona's thoughts could get the best of her, she turned away quickly and went back into the ranch house.

As Fiona made her way towards the hallway, she spotted Dr. Slater in the sitting room as he rocked his daughter to sleep. He was humming softly as he rubbed her back, her little eyes fluttering closed. Fiona couldn't help but smile as she looked at the picture of the two together. She also couldn't help but think what type of father Eddie would be. With the kindness he'd shown her, she could easily imagine Eddie being much like Dr. Slater in his affection and concern towards his own child.

After nodding to Dr. Slater and receiving a similar gesture in return, Fiona made her way down the hallway to the spare bedroom. She was looking forward to sleeping in a real bed. After closing the door behind her, she made haste in getting ready for bed, crawling under the thick comforter. It felt amazing to be able to lay her head down on a real pillow and feel the blankets around her. The bed was exceptionally comfortable, and Fiona knew that it wouldn't take long to fall asleep.

Ever since Bright Star had performed the cleansing ceremony, Fiona had finally been able to sleep through the night without being woken by nightmares. She would be forever thankful to Bright Star and the other men who had come to her rescue. As she lay in bed, she tried to think of a way she could personally thank them, or do something in return for what they'd done for her. They'd left their homes, families, and responsibilities behind in order to come to her rescue. No matter what she decided to do for herself, Fiona was determined to pay back their immense kindness.

As Fiona thought about her future, she tried to think about what her best option would be. Returning to Boston seemed like the sane thing to do. She missed the familiarity and safety she knew her home in Boston provided. She'd never experienced any sort of crime before, though she knew it existed in Boston. She was certainly missing the ease of her life back in that large city. Fiona tried to think if her life in Boston had really been worth running away from.

It took thinking of Eddie and comparing him to Mr. Crane for Fiona to start to remember what it had been like back in Boston. Though being kidnapped and almost dying had been very traumatic, her mind started to return to what she'd been facing whilst living with her parents. She started to remember the feeling of shame and despair after learning what her parents had planned for her. She knew that if it hadn't been for Mrs. Dickens, she'd have been married to Mr. Crane by now and forced to live underneath his roof.

Fiona pushed those fearful thoughts aside as she tried to think about her current situation. She was penniless and only had a few belongings that she could call her own. Her purse had been stolen and as far as she knew, nothing had been recovered from the robbers. She'd lost everything precious to her, to include the gold ring Mrs. Dickens had given her. Fiona knew that if she was going to stay in Spruce Valley, she would need to find some sort of employment. But what could she possibly do? She'd never worked a day in her life for payment, and knew only how to garden, do a bit of cooking, and mend simple clothing.

As Fiona closed her eyes, she willed herself to sleep. There was no point in worrying about her future right now. For tonight, she could simply sleep, and in the morning she would be able to see for herself all that Spruce Valley could actually offer her.

# CHAPTER 14

By the time morning had come, Fiona was feeling more well rested than she had in years. She was quick to dress and get ready for the day. She didn't want to hold anyone up since she knew that Lucy and Martha would be traveling to town early that morning. After dressing in a simple gown Fiona could feel proud of, and having brushed and braided her hair, Fiona made quick work of her personal business before joining the Slaters.

"Good morning, Fiona. Yer looking well," Lucy said as she greeted Fiona in the kitchen. She was balancing Francene on her hip as she flipped flapjacks in the frying pan.

"Morning, Lucy. Here, let me take over on the stove since you have the little one," Fiona offered, as she took the wooden flipper from Lucy.

"Thank ye, me dear. Sometimes it can be a handful to cook for the crew and get ready to head into town for work," Lucy said with a sigh. "Women should be blessed with an extra set of hands when they give birth." Fiona laughed with Lucy at the very thought.

"Well, while I'm here, I want to earn my keep. You just let me know what you need help with, and I'll make sure to do it," Fiona reassured.

"I'll more than likely take ye up on that offer. I love managing the boutique in town and making all sorts of women's clothing, but I fear I'm lacking in my other duties here at the ranch," Lucy admitted as she bounced Francene around the kitchen, the little one becoming fussy. Fiona made quick work of finishing the flapjacks and brought them to the table for Lucy so she could feed her daughter. Fiona returned to the kitchen and began to fry the rest of the batter as the others soon joined them for breakfast.

By the time everyone had come to sit at the table,, Fiona had managed to not only finish cooking the flapjacks, but had sausage and bacon cooked and ready for serving. Fiona found it interesting that all of Dr. Slater's employees shared three meals a day with his family. She was starting to see that he was not only a kind person, but also a kind and considerate employer.

"Thank ye, Fiona, for helping out this morning," Lucy said as Fiona settled into a chair next to her. Across the way were Eddie and Sawyer, and the other cattle hand that Fiona had met as Tom.

"It was no trouble at all. It feels good to be doing something productive again," Fiona admitted.

"Well, with Sam havin' to leave early this morning to get to town and see his patients, I certainly appreciate it," Lucy replied as she fed Francene small pieces of flapjack and sausage.

"Grant's already out in the pasture. I plan to bring him something to eat after this," Sawyer spoke up.

"There is plenty to be done, that's for sure," Tom spoke

up. Fiona watched as he ate his breakfast as quickly as possible, making Fiona fear that he'd choke. Fiona took her time eating, having a hard time breaking the habit of eating small bites at a time.

"Well ladies, thank you again for a wonderful meal. I'll be seeing you after a bit," Eddie said as he also quickly finished eating and stood from the table with the other ranch hands. Fiona watched him go, and right before he stepped out of the house, he looked back at her and gave her a wink. Fiona couldn't help but smile as Eddie left the ranch house. She was able to watch him from the window as he scurried after the others towards the barn.

"I think he likes ye," Lucy spoke up as she slowly rose with Francene, who needed a good scrub from the messy way she had eaten her breakfast.

"I think Eddie is just trying to be kind," Fiona said as she tried to do her best to quickly finish eating now that the men had departed. Lucy chuckled as she carried Francene out of the room.

"I'd say the man's in love," Lucy called from the other room. Fiona was shocked by this comment and stopped eating to ponder her words. Fiona listened to the sound of running water and a fussy Francene. Fiona guessed that the young one wasn't pleased about being washed. As Fiona looked out the window and watched Eddie ride out of the barn on a horse after the other two, she wondered if the man could have developed feelings for her already. And if so, how did she feel about that?

Fiona pushed the thought from her mind as she finished eating, then gathered all the dishes to be washed. By the time she and Lucy had finished cleaning up after breakfast, Martha was coming through the front door with Samuel in her arms.

"You ladies ready to head into town?" she asked.

"Absolutely. I can't wait to see everything," Fiona said in an excited voice.

"Well, come on then. I have the wagon out front," Martha said. Fiona eagerly followed Martha out of the ranch house with Lucy and Francene right behind her. Lucy climbed into the back of the wagon with the kids where they sat upon several hay bales. It took a moment, but Fiona finally found her footing on the wheel of the wagon in order to pull herself up and onto the front driver's bench.

"Yer already acting like a true Western woman, Fiona. Ye can get into a wagon all by yerself," Lucy said as she held the two small children on her lap as Martha flicked the reins and spurred the two horses forward.

"I've had a bit of practice these last few days as I rode in the covered wagon with Eddie and Sawyer," Fiona explained.

"That must have been an adventure all on its own," Martha commented with a chuckle.

"I cannot deny that," Fiona said as she joined in with Martha's laughter. "I quickly had to get used to sleeping in the wagon, riding in the wagon, and sometimes entertain Jack when he seemed to get moody and bored."

"Me goodness, does that monkey get under me nerves! Jack once tore down all me curtains in a fit," Lucy said in an exaggerated voice.

"Jack once got cranky and started banging all the pots and pans together in the back of the wagon. Sawyer had been resting and caused him such a fright that I thought I'd never stop laughing," Fiona recalled. They all laughed over the thought, causing both the toddlers to join in with their laughter. When their mirth subsided, Fiona added, "And I think Bright Star has become quite fond of Jack. He even offered to take Jack south with him."

"I think that is a mighty fine idea. I can only imagine

how that monkey might get in the way of you and Eddie properly courting," Martha said. Her words caused Fiona to go stiff with fear. She hadn't told anyone else besides Eddie that she was seriously thinking about returning to Boston. She only felt disheartened because she hadn't heard anything from her parents.

Seeming to notice her silence, Martha said, "I know you just got here, Fiona, but don't feel pressured about making any decisions right away. Eddie isn't going anywhere."

"And yer more than welcome to stay with us 'til ye can get settled," Lucy added. Fiona was truly touched by their kindness that at first, she didn't know what to say. Then an idea came to mind.

"The only thing I know I need to get settled is some sort of employment. I'm afraid I lost all my money on the journey out here when the robbers took everything," Fiona explained. She didn't like to speak about anything related to what she had experienced, but it was the truth.

"Well, you're more than welcome to help us out at the shop. Having one more eye on the children would be a great help," Martha said.

"And I could use all the help I can get at home with feeding so many mouths. Yer a good cook, Fiona," Lucy added to the conversation. Fiona couldn't help but smile proudly.

"Thank you, Lucy. That means a lot to me since I was raised to never have the need to cook my own meals. I find pride in being able to take care of myself," Fiona admitted.

"As you should, Fiona. There is nothing more enjoyable than being an independent woman," Martha said.

"And I know how to mend clothing as well," Fiona added, as she remembered the needlework she'd been taught by Mrs. Dickens.

"That's fantastic. We're always getting clothes in the shop to fix," Martha said enthusiastically.

The three girls chatted the whole way into town. Fiona soon discovered that it was a good hour's ride to town, but the scenery was absolutely beautiful. Pine and oak trees dotted the horizon as wildflowers bloomed along the main road. They passed several other ranches and houses that the ladies were eager to tell Fiona about. The weather wasn't too hot in the early morning hours, but with few clouds in the sky, she reckoned that it would become warm as the day went on.

As the wagon rounded a bend in the road, Fiona caught site of town. There was a single main street that was lined with several businesses and stores. Fiona saw the Honeywell Inn, and across from it was the Sheriff's office. At the end of the street on the left was Mr. Frost's mercantile, and the church on the right. Behind that, Fiona could spot livery stables.

"It's not much, but it has everything you might want," Martha said as she led the wagon down the road,. She then stopped the wagon in front of the women's boutique.

"I think it's a quaint place, indeed," Fiona said as she stepped down from the wagon and went around to help Lucy and the children dismount. Then, they made their way to the front of the shop were Martha unlocked the door and ushered everyone inside.

Fiona was pleasantly surprised by the feminine decor of the shop, as well as the quality of the dresses she started to examine on the rack.

"I can tell you're from Boston, Lucy," Fiona spoke up as she turned to the woman. They had started straightening up the shop and pulling out mirrors and chairs for customers to use while visiting.

"I tried to design the shop based on me memory of other boutiques in the big city," Lucy admitted.

"You've done a justifiable job of that. It reminds me much of what I'm used to in Boston," Fiona admitted.

"Lucy designs and makes all the clothing while I take care of the paperwork," Martha said, as she stepped behind a central counter and pulled out a ledger book to show Fiona all their current orders.

"It seems you two are very busy," Fiona exclaimed as she read several lines.

"We've started to receive business from neighboring towns because Lucy is such a good seamstress," Martha explained.

"But we could use someone to greet the customers, keep an eye on the children, and tackle all the mending work," Lucy said as she steered Francene from a mannequin with a long gown that the little one was trying to pull over.

"Well, since I'm here, put me to work," Fiona said eagerly.

As the day progressed, Fiona got to mending the clothes that had been brought in for such work. Fiona sat at a chair and small table with all the needle and thread she could need. She focused on the work, but also on the children as Lucy worked mostly in the back of the shop, making gowns for various women in the community and from neighboring towns. Fiona had never felt this proud before as she tackled the pile of clothes that needed patching up or fixed in some way. She had envisioned herself doing some sort of work when she left Boston, and she was glad to be able to use the skills Mrs. Dickens had taught her to help the other ladies.

When lunch time rolled around, Martha agreed to stay behind while Lucy and Fiona took the children to The Eatery. Fiona had been so focused on her work that the morning seemed to pass by so quickly. But as she prepared to walk down the road to the small café at the back of the mercantile, she bent down and collected Samuel into her arms from where he'd been playing with a wooden toy horse.

"Come along, young man. We need to get something in that belly of yours," Fiona said as she tickled his tummy. The small boy giggled happily, causing Fiona to smile in return.

"Motherhood becomes ye," Lucy said with a wink as she picked up Francene and then made her way to the front door. Fiona blushed at the thought of having children of her own. She hadn't considered it before but assumed that with marriage, soon came children.

"You two have fun," Martha called as they left the boutique and headed down the boardwalk towards the café.

As they walked, Fiona enjoyed looking into the windows of the other shops. There was a furniture store with several beautiful pieces displayed in the window, but as Fiona continued on, she realized that many of the store fronts were empty.

"It seems that this town has room for more," Fiona commented.

"Sometimes I worry about this town. Sam explained that it used to be bustling when the local mine was opened and producing. But when the mine ran dry, everyone either left or had to find different employment," Lucy explained. As they walked, Fiona spotted the medical clinic amongst all the empty buildings.

"I sure hope that things continue to get better. I'm sure the town has benefited from having a women's boutique," Fiona said, trying to stay positive.

"I can agree with that, Fiona. I can't wait to see what happens next," Lucy said as she led them into the mercantile. There, Fiona was able to meet Mr. Frost and his wife, a very chatty couple. Then, Fiona and Lucy dined with the children at The Eatery were Fiona was introduced to Nell, the waitress, and was able to have the finest cup of tea of her life.

"My goodness, that is lovely," Fiona exclaimed after she had tasted the tea that Nell had expertly poured.

"I told you it was good," Lucy said with a chuckle. As the meal progressed, a very important fact popped into Fiona's head.

"Lucy, I don't have any money to pay for my portion of the meal," Fiona said in a soft voice, leaning towards the other woman.

"I have enough, dear. With ye helping out at the boutique, I can cover our lunch," Lucy reassured. It was relief to hear, since Fiona wasn't sure what she was going to do about covering her expenses unless Lucy started to pay her for her work. But with everything the Slaters were willing to do for her, she didn't dare ask for pay.

As the day continued, Fiona couldn't wait to return to the ranch and tell Eddie all about her first day working in town with the other ladies.

~

Eddie wiped the sweat from his brow as he looked at the setting sun. It had been a long day out in the pasture as he helped move cattle, repair fences, and made sure to survey the other pastures for their progress on degrowing grass for the herd to be moved. As the summer faded to fall, it would be time to drive the best of the herd to market west, in Idaho. Just the thought of being on the road again after returning to Spruce Valley didn't settle well with Eddie. He wanted to spend every moment he could with Fiona while he still had the chance. That is why he had something special planned for them tomorrow, if he could get permission from the boss.

"Gray!" Eddie called as he rode in from the back pasture and made his way towards his boss.

"Yeah, Eddie?" Gray replied as Eddie came riding over to him. Gray had been keeping a close eye on the herd after hearing reports of wolves in the area.

"Do you care if I'm absent around lunch time tomorrow? I want to take Fiona out for a picnic," Eddie said, trying to keep confidence in his voice.

Gray smiled at him as he turned his eyes to Eddie. "So, you're going to try to take Fiona out on a date, are you?" Gray asked.

"Yes, sir, I am. I think it would be nice," Eddie said with an assertive voice.

"Well, make sure you let Mrs. Slater know. She makes the best picnic baskets," Gray said, turning his eyes back to the herd.

Eddie smiled as he said, "I'll make sure to do that, Gray. Thanks." Then he steered his horse and made quick work of getting back to the barn so he could put his horse away and get ready for dinner. After changing out of his work clothes and washing quickly with a wet cloth, Eddie changed into some clean clothes before taking Jack to his room.

"Now behave yourself, Jack. If you're good, I'll bring you something special to eat," Eddie said, as he handed the monkey two dates. The monkey jumped up and down on his bed as he screeched happily about having been given two dates at once. Eddie couldn't help but laugh at the monkey before he left the room, closing the door firmly behind him. Then, he walked quickly from the bunkhouse to the ranch house.

"Howdy, folks," Eddie called into the house as he

entered. He made his way to the dining room to see that he was the first of the ranch hands to arrive.

"Hey there, Eddie. How did the day go?" Dr. Slater asked as he came into the dining room with Francene in his arms.

"Busy. There was plenty of work to get caught up on," Eddie said.

"I understand completely. I feel like every patient of mine came in today for their check up," Dr. Slater said with a sigh. "I'm not complaining about the good business, but I'm exhausted."

Eddie and Dr. Slater chatted for a while about ranch work as Sawyer and the rest of the ranch hands filed into the ranch house. By then, the ladies had started to bring dinner out to the table.

"Let me see that fellow," Gray said to Martha as he came into the house, reaching for Samuel. The little boy squealed with delight as he went to his father. As Eddie watched the interaction, he couldn't deny that he wanted that connection with a son or daughter one day. With that line of thinking, he looked towards Fiona as she sat across from him at the table. Their eyes locked until Dr. Slater spoke up and addressed Fiona.

"So, Miss Wilkins, what do you think of our small town here in Spruce Valley?" Dr. Slater asked.

Fiona's eyes moved from Eddie's as she smiled at the doctor. "I had a lovely time in town today. I think the women's boutique is marvelous, and there are several quaint shops in town," Fiona said with enthusiasm.

"Do you think that Spruce Valley is suitable for a woman from the East? Sheriff Ryder and I are always discussing ways that the town could be improved to hopefully attract more women to come here. There are plenty of men, but very few eligible young ladies," Dr. Slater explained.

"Honestly, I think it depends on the young lady. I myself have never needed to do the things I must do now, in order to live comfortably. But I don't mind cooking, cleaning, and mending my own clothes. I find satisfaction in making something with my hands that others can enjoy," Fiona replied. Her words filled Eddie with so much pride, he felt that he might burst.

"It's hard for me to imagine a woman not being raised to know how to do those things," Tom spoke up before he took another bite of food.

"Oh, don't mind him, Fiona," Lucy said, making a shooing motion towards Tom. "He doesn't understand what it's like to live in a city." Fiona laughed then, the sound of her laughter a delight to Eddie.

"I agree that I could not imagine my acquaintances coming to live in a place like Spruce Valley. I think if you are born into wealth, then you become quite used to it and will more than likely seek it out in the future," Fiona said.

"But not ladies like us," Lucy added quickly. "We were born to pave our own way."

Dr. Slater then raised his cup in an effort to propose a toast. "To city women making a living in the West."

"Hear, hear!" Eddie called with the others as they toasted together.

"I surely would have it no other way," Lucy said, as she looked lovingly at her husband. Eddie watched them, thinking he wanted to experience that type of love with someone one day. And as he looked across the table, he caught Fiona's beautiful blue eyes once more and yearned to be able to have a real chance with her.

As the dinner progressed, the ladies happily chatted about their day in town. It seemed to Eddie that Fiona was really starting to fit in and had been a huge help at the shop today. He only hoped that good days like today would convince Fiona to stay in Spruce Valley.

When the dinner was over, Eddie volunteered to help clean up. He wanted to find a moment to be alone with Fiona so he could ask her to accompany him on a picnic for lunch. Eddie carried dishes into the kitchen and started to scrub them, then Fiona dried them.

"I was wondering, Fiona, if you had plans for tomorrow?" Eddie asked as he cleaned a plate and handed it to her.

Fiona seemed to think about his question for a moment before saying, "I only thought that I would accompany the women to town again tomorrow to work at the boutique. I thought about posting a letter to Mrs. Dickens as well."

Eddie nodded as he remembered the housekeeper that helped Fiona escape Boston. "I was wondering if you might consider coming with me instead for a picnic," Eddie offered.

"Oh! I'll pack ye two a wonderful basket," Mrs. Slater said as she came into the kitchen, having heard what Eddie had asked. Eddie watched as Fiona blushed as she quickly dried the next dish and put it away.

"You don't mind, do you?" Fiona asked with concern in her voice.

"Not at all," Mrs. Slater assured. "Martha and I can look after things for a day."

"Well, if it's alright with you, I'd be happy to go on a picnic," Fiona said happily. Eddie felt relieved to hear Fiona's response. He was honestly looking forward to it. He quickly finished washing the dishes and helped to put them away.

"I'll be back in the afternoon to help you saddle up, and we'll go out to an empty pasture for lunch," Eddie said, smiling at Fiona.

"You mean I'm going to have to ride a horse?" Fiona asked, clearly surprised.

"You'll have to learn how to ride sooner or later. I'd be happy to teach you," Eddie said with a chuckle.

"I look forward to it," Fiona replied, squaring up her shoulders. The look of determination on her face made Eddie want to kiss her soundly on the mouth. But instead, Eddie bid her goodnight and made his way back to the bunkhouse. For the first time in his life, Eddie was looking forward to a picnic with a beautiful lady.

# CHAPTER 15

Fiona was filled with excitement as she arose the next morning. She'd often daydreamed of riding a horse, much like the heroines in her novels. And the idea of getting to learn today from a handsome man was a thrilling thought of its own.

After Fiona dressed in one of her nicer traveling gowns, she made her way into the kitchen to help with the morning meal. She found Lucy and Dr. Slater talking in the kitchen in hushed words, and hating to disrupt a private conversation, she loudly cleared her throat as she came into the room.

"Oh, good morning, Fiona. How did ye sleep?" Lucy asked, quickly breaking her conversation the doctor as she looked towards Fiona.

"Very well, thank you," Fiona said. As she looked to Dr. Slater, she could tell that he was concerned about something. "Is everything alright?"

"Fiona, Sheriff Ryder stopped by …" Dr. Slater started to say when Lucy butted in.

"And wanted to see how ye were doing. We reassured

him that ye are settling in here at the ranch just fine," Lucy said with a smile. She then went over to the stove where what looked to be eggs and bacon were cooking.

"Well, that's awfully nice of Sheriff Ryder to be checking up on me," Fiona said as she joined Lucy in the kitchen. Fiona jumped right in to helping Lucy prepare the first meal of the day but couldn't help but wonder what Dr. Slater had been about to say. It was obvious to Fiona that Lucy didn't want her to know right now, and she was fine with that. She was so excited about riding a horse today that she didn't want anything to ruin her first experience of it.

As Eddie and the others came into the ranch house, Fiona helped set the table. She smiled at Eddie, wishing it was already the afternoon. She couldn't wait to try her luck at riding a horse, and she couldn't deny that she liked the idea of Eddie showing her how to do it. All through breakfast, Fiona couldn't help but keep catching Eddie's eye, causing them both to smile at each other.

When breakfast was finished, Fiona volunteered to wash the dishes so Lucy and Francene could head into town with the kids. Lucy took a moment to pack Fiona a picnic basket that she could take with her later in the day.

"There's cheese and bread, and some apple pie I baked a few days ago. Surprised it was still in the ice chest," Lucy said as she set the picnic basket down on the counter for Fiona.

"Thank you so much, Lucy. I'm going to tidy up around here and try my hand at doing laundry," Fiona said with a kind smile. Lucy chuckled at her enthusiasm.

"Just be careful with boiling the water for the wash all by yer own. I know yer familiar around a kitchen. I just want ye to be careful on yer own," Lucy said with concern in her voice.

"Don't worry, Lucy. I'll make sure to go slow. I'll take

the wash outside and hang everything up to dry when I think I've finished," Fiona said, trying to reassure her new friend. The idea of having a true friend dawned on Fiona, and she thought she could never be happier.

"Well then, I shall see ye later," Lucy said as she picked up Francene and carried her out the door.

It had been a while since Fiona had been completely alone, and before her thoughts could run away with her, she quickly finished cleaning the dishes before gathering all the laundry.

Fiona quickly learned that washing one's own laundry was a timely process. But since she had very few clean garments and dresses, she was glad to have the opportunity to clean her clothes. After heating the water and dumping it in the washing pan, Fiona sat on a stool outside in the fresh air, and used the soap to wash her clothes thoroughly before hanging them up to dry.

By the time Fiona was done washing her clothes, she made her way back inside the house to see what else she could tidy up. But as she entered the kitchen, she found Eddie standing at the front of the house.

"Hey, there you are," Eddie said with a smile.

"Yes, I was out back washing my laundry," Fiona admitted with a smile.

"How'd that go?" Eddie asked with a smirk.

"I managed my own, thank you very much," Fiona replied as she tilted her head up.

Eddie chuckled as he shook his head at her in a playful way. "For a city girl, you could certainly pass for a Western woman," Eddie commented.

"Well, I'm certainly glad I could impress you," Fiona said in a flirtatious tone. She then picked up the picnic basket Lucy had prepared that morning. "Shall we be off?"

"Absolutely. I have a pleasant mare saddled and ready

for you," Eddie said as he moved towards her and took the picnic basket from her hands. For a moment their hands brushed up against one another and Lucy couldn't help but imagine what it might feel like to be wrapped up in his strong arms once more.

Fiona focused her mind as she followed Eddie out of the ranch house. Tied to the front hitching post were two horses. Fiona recognized Eddie's gelding from yesterday and then turned her eyes to the chestnut mare that stood on the other side of him.

"This is Missy," Eddie explained as he led Fiona over to the mare. "She's a softy and should be suitable for your first horse."

"She's beautiful," Fiona said as she came to the side of the mare. She let her fingers graze across the horse's neck.

"Well, let's get you up into that saddle," Eddie said as he set down the picnic basket and neared Fiona. "You'll want to put your foot into the stirrup and push down with all your weight to lift yourself up into the saddle. Unfortunately, there isn't a sidesaddle in the barn, but you'll find riding this way to be more comfortable in the long run."

"I trust you," Fiona said lightly. For a moment, Fiona and Eddie stood smiling at one another before Fiona lifted her foot and placed it into the stirrup.

"Now, reach up your hand here and grab the saddle horn, and the other on the back of the saddle. Don't be afraid to climb up there. Missy knows what's going on," Eddie encouraged.

Knowing that Fiona simply had to go for it, she placed all her weight into her foot and pushed with all her might in order to pull herself up into the saddle and swing her leg over the horse. As she did so, she felt Eddie's strong hands guiding her up into the saddle, causing her to blush deeply.

She'd never been handled so by a man and found Eddie to be both strong and gentle.

"Well look at you, Miss City girl," Eddie said with a chuckle. Fiona smiled with happiness as she shifted her weight in the saddle whilst holding on to the saddle horn.

"It's like learning to sail a boat," Fiona admitted, as she slid her other foot into the stirrup and tried to find her balance upon the horse.

Eddie chuckled. He untied the reins from the hitching post and handed them to Fiona, then retrieved the picnic basket and got on his own horse. "You'll be riding like you were born doing so by the end of the day," Eddie said with confidence, as he turned his horse away from the house. Fiona stilled her nerves as she followed Eddie's lead and pulled on the reins to steer Missy away from the ranch house and towards the gelding. Missy seemed to know which way to go as she followed closely after the other horse at a steady trot.

"I can't believe I'm riding a horse," Fiona said as she caught up to Eddie. The two horses trotted easily beside each other as Eddie led them along the white fence that enclosed the cattle pasture.

"You look good doing it, too," Eddie said with a wink. Fiona couldn't help but laugh as she looked down at her legs to see that they were slightly exposed from her dress, being raised up to accommodate riding in a saddle.

"That's because I'm rather scandalous in this position," Fiona replied.

"No, you look good because you look fearless, Fiona. I'm certainly proud of everything you've been able to accomplish since leaving Boston," Eddie said with pure seriousness in his voice.

"I don't know about being fearless, Eddie," Fiona

reasoned as she looked at the scenery that stretched far in front of them.

"You've overcome a lot, Fiona. And it takes a certain type of woman to recover from what you went through. Any man would be happy to call you his wife," Eddie said in the same serious tone. Fiona went silent for a moment at the mention of being a wife. She knew that, originally, she'd come to Spruce Valley with the intention of not only avoiding being married to an odious man back in Boston, but to also give a relationship with Eddie a try. As they traveled together at a leisurely pace, Fiona couldn't help but observe Eddie and think that he would be a wonderful husband.

After a while, Eddie encouraged Fiona to increase Missy's pace. Putting her fear of falling aside, Fiona followed Eddie's directions thoroughly, and soon Fiona could feel the wind rushing by her as the horses trotted at a fast pace over the open prairie. Never had Fiona ever felt so free as she felt riding the strong horse beneath her, galloping happily.

Eventually, Eddie slowed his horse and Fiona followed suit. Up ahead, Fiona could see a single large oak tree that seemed to have been there for years. Eddie led her over to that tree, and after he dismounted and tethered the horses to the tree, he helped Fiona ease her way down from the saddle. As Fiona felt Eddie's strong hands on her waist again, she couldn't deny that she did enjoy the feeling.

With her feet firmly planted on the ground once more, Fiona found a decent place to sit and together, they settled down under the oak tree and enjoyed the lunch that Lucy had prepared.

"I can't believe how peaceful it is here," Fiona said at one point. They had been looking out over the open fields as a light wind blew across the grasses and wildflowers.

"I can only imagine how different it all is from being in the city," Eddie commented.

"It's very different, but in a good way. Certainly, things are more difficult here, but not impossible. I think more people would move out West if they realized how beautiful it was here," Fiona admitted.

Fiona noticed that Eddie went silent then, and she turned to look at him only to discover that he'd been watching her. She didn't know what to say and sat there looking at him, thinking him the most handsome man she'd ever met.

"Fiona, are you still thinking about returning to Boston?" Eddie asked. As soon as he said the words, guilt crashed over Fiona. She was starting to feel foolish for ever having said such a thing.

"I don't think it is realistic that I'll go back. I haven't heard from my parents and I don't have the funds to make the trip back," Fiona explained. "But even if I did, after coming here and getting to know the area a little more, it reminded me of everything that I ran away from in Boston. I would be foolish to return there simply so I could live an easier life. That doesn't mean I'd be any happier."

As Fiona looked up at Eddie after she finished talking, she was surprised by how happy he looked. She couldn't help but smile at him in return.

"I can't tell you how happy it makes me to hear that you won't return to Boston. I was hoping beyond hope that you would decide to stay," Eddie said.

Fiona blushed again as she looked away from Eddie and instead on the wildflowers nearby. "It would be foolish to go back to Boston after realizing how wonderful it is here. Lucy and Martha have been the kindest ladies to me, and the fact that they were willing to offer me employment so quickly just goes to show what type of people they really are. I never had any real friends in Boston, but I believe I could here," Fiona said.

"Yeah, the Slaters continue to surprise me with their generosity. I truly enjoy working for them, but sometimes I dream of owning my own ranch, even if it's just a small herd of cattle," Eddie said.

"Really? What else do you dream about?" Fiona asked as she looked back at him, eager to know what his plans were for the future.

"Well, I'd like to own some land and build a decent house upon it. Eventually, I'd like a small herd of cattle that I could tend to and take to market each year. And I'd very much like to have a wife and a few kids, too," Eddie said as he looked at Fiona with much intensity. Fiona couldn't deny the pointed way in which he talked to her, and she was starting to suspect that he had strong feelings for her.

"That is an amazing dream, Eddie. I hope you're able to achieve it one day," Fiona said. As they finished their picnic and began to make their way back to the ranch house, Fiona wondered what her dreams were. What did she hope to obtain one day? But as she and Eddie returned to the ranch house after having a very pleasant picnic together, Fiona almost fainted from the sight of the two people standing on the front porch of the ranch house.

~

AS EDDIE RETURNED to the ranch house with Fiona, he noticed two older people standing on the front porch. At first, Eddie assumed that they were patients of Dr. Slaters' who had come to his home in the hopes of catching him at home. But the closer they got to the ranch house, the more Eddie could see the fancy clothes they were wearing. And as Eddie looked to Fiona, he noticed how pale she'd become as she noticed them, too. It didn't take long for Eddie to realize who these two must be.

When Eddie stopped his horse in front of the porch, the couple turned to see them, their mouths falling open as Eddie dismounted, then helped Fiona down from her horse. She quickly straightened her dress and tried to smooth it.

"It's going to be okay, Fiona. I promise," Eddie whispered, taking her hand in his, giving it a gentle squeeze before leading her onto the porch.

"Never in my life would I expect my daughter …" rose the voice of the older woman that Fiona resembled, to some degree. Her words were cut short as the man beside her raised his hand, silencing her instantly.

"Fiona, dear. We're glad to see you well," said the man. Eddie felt Fiona's grip tighten on his arm and he patted it to reassure her.

"Father, Mother. May I introduce you to Eddie Murtaugh. It's thanks to him and his friends that I'm alive right now," Fiona said in a voice that Eddie found rather odd. It lacked the warmth that Eddie was used to.

"Mr. Murtaugh, my many thanks for saving my daughter," said the man as he extended his hand toward Eddie. Eddie was quick to shake his hand, not wanting to be rude.

"It was my pleasure, Mr. Wilkins. The moment the news reached me, my friends and I set off to North Dakota to rescue Fiona," Eddie said, hating to bring up the fact that Fiona had ever been in such grave danger.

"Well, we'll be pleased to bring her home safely with us. We'll be leaving for the train depot in the morning," Mr. Wilkins said in a happy tone. But his words sent a shiver of fear running through him. And before Fiona could say anything, Eddie was quick to speak.

"Mr. Wilkins, I'd like to ask your permission for Fiona's hand in marriage. She is a wonderful woman that I'd be proud to call my wife. She enjoys being here in Spruce Valley, and I desire to bring her happiness for as long as I shall live," Eddie said, mustering every ounce of courage he could. His words clearly shocked Fiona's parents, as they did Fiona herself.

"There is no way …" Mrs. Wilkins started to say, but Mr. Wilkins quickly silenced her once more. Eddie watched as Mr. Wilkins looked from him to Fiona.

"Fiona, my dear. Do you also wish to marry Mr. Murtaugh?" Mr. Wilkins asked. Eddie looked at Fiona then and watched as her eyes searched his. Then, as a smile crept onto her face, Eddie knew what her answer would be.

"Yes, Father. I'd be happy to have someone like Eddie for a husband. He's kind, hardworking, and very devoted to his boss. Eddie's the type of man I know I can trust to the fullest, and who will always encourage me instead of telling me what to do," Fiona said with a fierceness that Eddie had come to admire.

Eddie turned his eyes back to Mr. Wilkins as he waited to hear what the man would say. It was clear to him that Mrs. Wilkins wasn't pleased with what has happening, but Mr. Wilkins appeared to have the upper hand over his wife.

"After you ran away, Fiona, I was so terribly angry at what you'd done. We received such outlandish comments from our acquaintances that I was certain you'd planned to hurt us so. But when the news came that you'd been kidnapped, it didn't matter what anyone said. We came as soon as we could, but by the time we reached North Dakota, you were already gone," Mr. Wilkins explained. "And to see you well off, even riding a horse, it makes me think that perhaps you are better off here, with a man that can honestly protect you."

"I'll never let Fiona come to any harm," Eddie said reassuringly.

"And I'm certain of that," Mr. Wilkins replied. "And therefore, I'd gladly give you my blessing to marry Fiona, as long as she'll be happy the rest of her life."

Eddie couldn't help but smile as he hugged Fiona's arm to him. They looked at each other then, a deep feeling passing between them. Then, Eddie reached into his pocket and pulled out the ring he'd been carrying around ever since he found it. When Fiona saw it, her eyes went wide.

"Where did you find it?" Fiona asked as Eddie slipped the gold band onto her ring finger.

"When we rescued you, I found it and thought it meant something to you," Eddie explained. Fiona rubbed her finger over the gold band, thinking this was a complete miracle.

# EPILOGUE

With her parents wanting to leave for Boston as soon as possible, Fiona and Eddie didn't have much time to prepare for their wedding. But with the help of all their friends, they were able to bring everything together in just two days.

Fiona never imagined when she ran away from Boston that one day, she would be walked down the aisle by her father on her wedding day. But low and behold, here she was now at the open doors of the church with her arm resting on her father's. Having borrowed Martha's wedding dress, Fiona was prepared for her big day. She could hardly believe that she was getting married, but she couldn't be happier.

"Once I return to Boston, I'll have your dowry money sent to you right away," Mr. Wilkins said softly to his daughter.

"Thank you, Father. You have no idea how much this means to me," Fiona said, as she looked at the man she'd loathed for most of her life.

"It's the least I could do after everything that's

happened," Mr. Wilkins replied as the *Wedding March* began playing on the organ. At the sound of the music, Mr. Wilkins led his daughter down the aisle towards her waiting groom.

Fiona's eyes locked on Eddie as she came down the aisle towards him. He was handsomely dressed in a Western suit jacket and tie. They were also borrowed items, but Fiona reasoned that Eddie would look handsome in anything that he wore.

The church was filled with all their friends, and many people that Fiona was certain she would soon get to know as she started her life with Eddie. Even Bright Star had come to attend the wedding with his sons. As he sat next to Dr. Slater, he held onto Jack. Eddie had agreed to allow his beloved pet to travel with Bright Star so the monkey would have a more comfortable winter.

As Fiona reached the alter and came to stand in front of Eddie, her father sat down at the front of the church with her mother. Fiona held onto Eddie's hands as her body was overcome with such happy feelings. Reverend Paul began the ceremony as Fiona leaned close to Eddie.

"I love you," she whispered to him, causing him to smile brightly.

"And I love you," Eddie whispered back. They smiled at each other the whole way through the ceremony, and once they were pronounced husband and wife, Fiona experience a first kiss unlike anything she could have ever imagined. In that one kiss, she felt every ounce of love that Eddie had for her, as well as a promise of what their future together would be.

For the first time in her life, Fiona felt complete. She had found happiness with Eddie Murtaugh, and a home in Spruce Valley.

The End

# THE SHERIFF'S STUBBORN SECRETIVE BRIDE: BOOK 4

# CHAPTER 1

Sheriff Josh Ryder sat in his office, his boots up on the desk as he leaned back in a wooden chair. His arms rested behind his head and his Stetson rested forward to cover his face. He was thoroughly relaxed, enjoying the sound of silence. Things had been pretty quiet in Spruce Valley lately, and that's exactly how he liked it.

Josh was the type of sheriff you could always rely on. Just last summer he'd helped his close friend—and often last-minute deputy—Eddie Murtaugh rescue his mail-order-bride, Fiona, when she'd been kidnapped and held hostage after a train robbery. Josh had a strong sense of duty, and what was right and wrong. Furthermore, he always took his position as sheriff very seriously. But every once in a while, it was nice to enjoy a relaxing spring day with just peace and quiet.

After saving Miss Fiona, Josh had received quite a bit of publicity in the papers from coast to coast. At first, he'd liked all the letters he received for a job well done, even though he had to give his close friends credit. He couldn't have done it without his best friend Dr. Sam Slater, or Bright Star, one of the local Crow Tribe Indians. But he had taken the reward money and put it away somewhere safe, intending to do good with it. A part of him wanted to put down roots and build a small home for himself, and perhaps his future family, right outside of town. It would sure beat the small apartment above the sheriff's office he currently occupied. The other half of him liked how things were going for him and he didn't really want to change anything.

Josh never had the opportunity to find female company in the remote frontier town, even after his fame weaved all about Montana. But he didn't want some random woman warming his bed at night. The more he thought of his best friend, Sam, the more he thought about how happy he'd been ever since he met his mail-order-bride, Lucy, almost three years ago now. Josh couldn't help but smirk the first time he'd met Lucy himself. He and Sam had ridden out of town when the stagecoach didn't show up with his intended, and they found her in quite a predicament with a turned over stagecoach.

Thinking about all the men in Spruce Valley that had found happiness with their mail-order-brides made Josh really think about his future. He knew there weren't eligible women in Spruce Valley who were looking for husbands. He'd even considered placing his own mail-order-bride ad in the hopes of meeting someone who could also capture his heart, instead of just being a good-looking woman. He wanted more from a woman than just another body in the house. He really wanted someone with whom he could connect, and thoroughly enjoy waking every morning with.

A knock on the door pulled Josh from his inner thoughts. He pushed back his Stetson and put his feet back on the floor as his chair rocked forward. Josh called for the person to enter just as the handle was turned and the door was pushed open. Dr. Slater's smiling face popped round the door. He spotted Josh rising to his feet, pushing back his honey brown hair. He rolled his eyes, knowing what Josh had been up to all day.

"I like to think that I didn't just catch the good sheriff napping," Sam said as he came into the office, closing the door behind him. Josh chuckled as he shook his head.

"Let's just say it's our little secret," Josh said with a lopsided grin. "What can I do for you, Sam?"

"Care to join me for lunch at The Eatery? It's been a bit slow at the clinic today and I thought a leisurely lunch would do us both some good," Sam suggested.

"I'm surprised you're not taking the girls out to lunch," Josh said. He was referring to his wife, Lucy, her business partner in the women's seamstress shop, Martha and their latest addition, Fiona, who did all sorts of clothing repairs. They had become known as the mail-order-bride trio around town.

Sam sighed in response to Josh's question. "Well, Lucy and I are not seeing eye to eye right now on a certain matter, so I'm just going to let it be for the moment," Sam explained. Josh grabbed his duster off the hook on the wall and gestured towards the door.

"How about you tell me about it over lunch?" Josh suggested. They stepped out of the office together and Josh fished his keys out of his pocket to lock up, before they made their way up the street to The Eatery. Frost's mercantile doubled as many things: in the back was the small café; in the front was all sorts of goods for sale. But it's also where the mail came in on the stagecoach. And ever since Mayor Delphine Stavros had convinced the state to run telegram lines to the small town of Spruce Valley, Frost's was also where Josh had to go to send and receive telegrams.

"I just don't know what to do, Josh," Sam said as they

walked together up the boardwalk and across the street to the front of Frost's. "Lucy is obviously pregnant again, but she won't listen to me when I tell her she should really be resting more than working. I'm worried about her health, but she's the independent woman she's ever been." Josh sighed heavily, knowing how stubborn Lucy could be sometimes.

"Must be hard being both her doctor and husband," Josh said, trying to put himself in Sam's shoes. It was one of his best techniques when it came to nabbing bad guys. If he could see the world through their eyes, it was always easier to catch them.

"That's the understatement of the year," Sam said as they entered the mercantile. They said a quick hello to Mr. Frost as he stood behind the counter tending to customers. Together they went back to The Eatery, a small café where Nell was the only waitress there and Emmet and Ella, an older couple, managed the kitchen.

"Good day, Nell," Josh said in greeting as they took to one of the open tables. It was starting to get busy and Josh wanted to place his order before it was too late.

"Hey there, Sheriff. Dr. Slater," Nell said with a kind smile. "What could I get you two today?"

"What's Emmet and Ella cooking today that you think I'd like?" Sam asked, remembering his wife telling him that Nell liked to be asked instead of told. And just as expected, Nell's face lit up with satisfaction.

"Emmet's cooked up a flaky and delicious Shepard's pie, and Ella's been baking all morning with her cream custard pie," Nell said excitedly.

"Sounds delicious. I'll take one of each," Sam said as he passed Josh his menu.

"Great choice, Doctor. And you, Sheriff?" Nell asked.

"I'll just take my usual, Nell," Josh said as he handed Nell the menu. She jotted down their orders and nodded to the Sheriff before walking away in a hurry. "How on Earth do you get Nell to like you?" Sam chuckled at the question as he watched the waitress disappear into the kitchen.

"Lucy taught me a long time ago that Nell likes to be asked her opinion instead of being told," Sam explained. Josh's eyes grew large as he looked towards the woman. She was in her late thirties, but still moved like she was a young woman.

"I guess that makes sense," Josh reasoned. "She's been waitressing here as long as I can remember and I'm sure that sometimes things can get quite boring."

"That's the secret," Sam said.

"Speaking of, what secret method do you have for convincing Lucy you're serious about her keeping off her feet?" Josh asked. "It can't be easy managing a business and looking after a two-year-old." Sam nodded as he poured them both a glass of water from the pitcher on the table. He took a sip, thinking of his daughter, Francene.

"Thankfully, Fiona has been a big help. She not only works at the seamstress shop, but she also watches the kids and sometimes comes by to do chores around the ranch house," Sam explained. "But Lucy literally needs to be off her feet. I want her on bed rest, Josh."

Josh ran his fingers through his hair, his way of taking a moment to think seriously about the situation. "Sam, you're just going to need to be stern with Lucy. I know she's a stubborn woman, but this is your wife and child we're talking about," Josh said with all seriousness. Sam looked him straight in the eyes as he nodded.

"And that's why I think you should talk to her for me," Sam said as he leaned back in his chair and crossed his arms. "You have a way of convincing people to do something they don't want to." Josh stared at his friend, not having expected him to say such a thing.

"Though I agree with you, Sam, that convincing bad guys to surrender is one of my skills, we're talking about your wife," Josh said as he pointed to Sam. "*You* need to talk to her."

"But I tried, Josh, and I got no results," Sam pleaded. Josh sighed, always having a soft spot for his friends.

"Fine, Sam. I'll go talk to the woman," Josh relented. A bright smile came onto Sam's face and he couldn't help but smirk to himself.

"Speaking of women, when are you going to get yourself a wife?" Sam asked as their food was delivered to their table. Nell parted with a giggle, having heard Sam's question. Josh scowled at his friend for having been overheard. Spruce Valley was a small town, and the last thing he wanted was to have his business gossiped by everyone in time for dinner.

"I've been thinking about that myself," Josh said once he was sure no one could hear them. He took a few bites of food as he thought of his words. "I'll probably have to post my own ad."

"That's not a bad idea," Sam said as he pointed his fork at Josh. "There is nothing wrong with writing for a mail-order-bride. After all, you know plenty of men who've been successful thus far."

"Don't I know it," Josh said with a shake of his head. "I just hope that if I do start writing to a woman from the East, that she won't be so much trouble as Fiona." Sam chuckled as he returned to his food.

After a few bites he said, "Fiona wasn't trouble. She just stumbled upon trouble."

"You know what I mean, Sam," Josh said. "I just hope that I can post an ad, find a good woman, and settle down."

"Nothing is as easy as it seems," Sam deadpanned. "Just be realistic and open minded."

Josh shrugged his shoulders, unsure of what to say. "I appreciate the advice," Josh managed as they finished up their meal. "Seems I'll go write up this ad and then go have a conversation with your wife."

"Good man, Josh. Always willing to help out around here," Sam said with a grin. He paid for their meal so at least Josh couldn't complain about being treated to a good meal.

As Sam made his way back to the clinic, Josh returned to his office. There, he took out a piece of writing paper and set about writing an ad that he'd have Mr. Frost telegram to the *Matrimony Times* in the East. Thankfully he could trust Mr. Frost to keep a tight lip about his telegram, having sworn before the marshal of Montana to never say a word about what people telegrammed out of Spruce Valley. Not having to worry about the older man telling anyone about his telegram, he only needed to figure out what to write.

What did he want in an ideal wife? He'd always been more interested in a woman's looks that he never thought about what qualities a good wife had. Josh thought about the other mail-order-brides and tried to imagine what had influenced them to write to the men in Spruce Valley. After a while, Josh decided that his ideal wife would have to be thick skinned and able to handle when he needed to go off in the middle of the night to catch a criminal, or help out when asked. His wife would need to be independent and able to look after herself when he wasn't around. With those details in mind, Josh finally drafted his ad. Task completed, Josh made his way back over to the mercantile.

"Here on official business?" Mr. Frost asked as Josh approached the counter with his letter.

"You could say that, Mr. Frost," Josh said as he handed the older man the letter. "I need this message telegrammed out to the newspaper listed on it." Mr. Frost read over the message, and looked back up at Josh with raised eyebrows.

First his face read shock, then a wide grin started to spread across his face.

"It would be my pleasure, Sheriff," Mr. Frost said with glee.

"Alright now, Mr. Frost. I hope you won't have loose lips over this matter," Josh said in a stern voice. He didn't take kindly to being mocked, yet he knew that Mr. Frost was a harmless old man.

"Oh no, Sheriff. You never have to worry about that with me," Mr. Frost said as he settled down from his excitement. "But I do hope you'll keep me posted on the progress," he added with a wink. Josh simply chuckled as he shook his head.

"We'll see about that, Mr. Frost," Josh said as he pushed a few coins across the counter to pay for the telegram. "I appreciate you."

"And I you, Sheriff. Have a good day then," Mr. Frost said. He placed the change in the register before disappearing into the back of the store where the telegram machine was housed. Josh turned from the counter and made his way from the mercantile. He looked down the road leading out of town towards the women's seamstress shop on the far side of the road. He sighed as he made his way towards it, wishing he could simply return to his office for a much deserved nap.

## CHAPTER 2

Emily Middleton laughed as the gentleman across from her said some sort of joke that caused the others in the sitting room to laugh. She was able to follow social cues and began to laugh with the rest of them;, the only thing she was focused on though was the cards in her hands. It was very unladylike to be playing poker with men, but she never turned down a good challenge. Her dear friend Cynthia had invited her to a special luncheon where several eligible gentlemen would be present. And since Cynthia knew how desperate Emily was, she'd invited her as soon as she herself had received an invitation.

As the last card in the river was flipped over, Emily held her breath. She couldn't believe that she'd just gotten a flush. Now all she had to do was keep her cool and hope that her opponents didn't have anything better to beat her. As the final rounds of betting commenced, Mr. Fisher, the man with all the jokes that evening, raised the pot by going all in. The other gentlemen at the table began to fold, obviously defeated. But as it came to Emily's turn to either go all in or fold, she didn't hesitate when she pushed all her chips to the center to be added to the pot.

"Seems like someone's feeling lucky tonight," Mr. Fisher said with a chuckle, another round of laughter circulating through the room. Out of all the women who'd attended as well, Emily had been the only one with enough courage to play with the men. Emily always did enjoy being the center of attention, but she also wasn't going to turn down an opportunity to earn a quick dollar. After all, she had a higher education than most, and a critically thinking mind that often surpassed most of her father's business partners.

"I'm always feeling lucky," Emily replied with a smile as she laid down her cards. Gasps filled the air as they realized she had a flush. All eyes turned to Mr. Fisher as he stared at Emily, his smile quickly disappearing. He flung his cards on the table, showing that he indeed had nothing to beat her. Cheers and applause rose up in the air as Emily smiled victoriously, reaching forward to pull all the chips to herself. With Cynthia's help, the two ladies started to organize the pile.

"Perhaps next time you won't be so lucky," Mr. Fisher remarked as he rose from the table quickly and walked off. He was booed by a few of his friends for showing a lack of good sportsmanship.

"Don't pay him any attention, Miss Middleton. He's just upset that he lost to a woman," Mr. Franklin said to her left. She just smiled kindly at him and stood to her feet.

"I don't plan to, Mr. Franklin," she said. She turned her attention to the others at the table as she declared, "I'm afraid that's all the time I have for today." They all looked very disappointed, especially Mr. Franklin, who had been keen on her all afternoon.

"Won't you join us next week, Miss Middleton?" Mr.

Mathews spoke up then. He was a shy man, but his question showed that he'd also taken an interest in her.

"Absolutely, Mr. Mathews. I wouldn't miss this for the world," Emily said sweetly. With her chip tray in hand, she made her way over to the butler who had been acting as banker. His eyes widened as Emily brought her chips over to the older man, Cynthia close behind her.

"How on Earth did you manage to pull that off?" Cynthia asked her in a hushed voice. Her blonde hair hung around her head in ringlets in a way that made Emily wonder why the young lady hadn't married yet. She was a vision in her blue silk gown, yet she knew that Cynthia wasn't willing to marry anyone unless it was for love.

"That was pure luck, my dear," Emily said as she let out a long breath. "For most of the game I had been able to read them pretty good. But that last round was truly just plain luck."

"Why, I can't believe you just won a thousand dollars," Cynthia said as the butler started counting out the notes. "Do you really think that by next week you'll return again?"

"I doubt I'll be accepted anywhere by next week," Emily said as she took the large stack of notes and stuffed them all into her purse. She'd need to return home right away to hide the money. If her father found out she had it, he'd tear her room apart just to take every penny away from her.

"Oh, Emily. It surely can't be as bad as you say," Cynthia said as she followed her friend out of the room. "You must acquire a husband soon."

"My dear, no one is going to want a penniless woman for a wife once the papers publish that my father just lost everything in a bad business deal," Emily said in a soft voice. She knew that most would still be in the sitting room and she didn't want the dreadful news to run rampant through Atlanta, Georgia before the due time.

"Surely there must be someone here who would love you despite your reputation," Cynthia suggested. Emily stopped her in the hallway then as they made their way to the front door. She turned and addressed her, wanting to put her friend at ease.

"Cynthia, darling, a young lady is nothing but her family's reputation and the friends she has. There is no such thing as true love, I'm afraid. Just good business deals in what we call marriage," Emily said plainly. As she watched her friend's face, she could tell that her words didn't settle well with her.

Cynthia regarded Emily for a moment, having always looked up to the young lady who was taller than her, slimmer with dark black hair and bright blue eyes. She was always the star of every social function, and the type of lady that Cynthia imagined would fall deeply in love with a wealthy man and live happily ever after. It hurt to hear her speak this way now. But after everything she'd had to endure these last few weeks, she didn't blame Emily for becoming so cold-hearted.

"Let's get home before anyone asks about us," Cynthia said as she moved past Emily. They left the manor then, both climbing into Cynthia's carriage. Both their parents thought the other had gone to tea at the other's home, so they needed to return home before anyone became suspicious. With her father now home most of the time, Emily had a harder time getting away from the house. When he'd still been in business, she'd had the freedom to come and go as she pleased since her mother had died in childbirth and her governess was often very lenient, believing women should be more independent.

"What are you going to do, Emily?" Cynthia asked as they approached Emily's house. It was a manor much like the one they'd just left. It was large, historical, and had the most expensive of everything. However, the inside of the house was now rather bare as her father rushed to sell everything he could to keep up appearances. They no longer had friends over and only accepted invitations out. Only Cynthia, her dearest friend, had an idea of what type of hell she was currently living through.

"I don't know, Cynthia, but so far I have a small fortune, should I need it," Emily said proudly.

"Why don't you come to stay with me and my family? I'm sure my parents would understand," Cynthia offered.

Emily shook her head, knowing that would never work. "Once the story hits the papers, no one is going to be very accepting of me, Cynthia. We both know that," Emily said as she looked out the carriage window, the world seeming to pass by as though everything was normal. Like today was just another day.

"We've just been friends for so long that I can't imagine sitting here and watching you suffer," Cynthia said in a pleading voice. Emily looked at her friend then and gave her a reassuring smile.

"Cynthia, no matter what happens, I will be fine," Emily said. She tried to convince herself of her own words, but sometimes feared one day not being able to live the life she'd always had. Somehow, she needed to find a way to maintain her way of life. She was a Middleton and deserved to live as such.

Thankfully, the carriage had come once more to her house and as the footman came down from the driver's seat to let Emily out, she quickly bid her friend farewell. "Till tomorrow," Emily said as she alighted from the carriage.

"Goodbye, Emily. I'll come pick you up again tomorrow," Cynthia promised. She watched as Emily made her way up the lane to her manor, her pale green gown swishing around her legs. She had a hard time imagining her friend in her current situation and prayed that one day she'd find peace.

Emily stepped into her house and was met by an uneasy silence. The majority of the servants having been dismissed, the sound of the door closing behind her echoed throughout the manor. She hated the sound and detested seeing how bare the house now looked. As she made her way to her room, taking the stairs upwards, her footsteps echoed as well, her walking boots clattering on the wooden stairs.

The moment Emily made it to her room, she closed and locked the door behind her. She took her purse and withdrew all the notes and began to stuff them with the others underneath her mattress. She didn't have to worry about her maid finding her small fortune since her lady-in-waiting had been dismissed as well. All that was left was the housekeeper, and the older woman was no doubt so busy with all the housework that she'd hardly have time to enquire after Emily's needs. Therefore, Emily changed out of her own clothes, finding the action quite foreign since she'd always had someone to dress her. With her father's fortune now gone, Emily had to learn to do much for herself. It was another reminder of how hard Emily would need to work to find her a husband who could give her the life she deserved.

Emily spotted a newspaper on her nightstand as she came to sit on the edge of it. It was one of the last pleasures her father had allowed her to keep. Each day Emily looked forward to reading the paper. Before her father had told her about his sorrowful business dealings that had led to all his money being gone, she'd enjoyed reading the paper to read the latest gossip. But now, Emily feared what she might read, knowing that any day now the news would finally be published all throughout Atlanta. As she read each article, Emily received comfort from not seeing her name in it. And as she reached the last page of the paper, where the *Matrimonial Times* was published, she released a long sigh.

"One more day," Emily said as she started to fold up the paper. But as she did so, a particular ad caught her attention. Emily normally didn't pay the *Matrimonial Times* any attention because she always found the ads uninteresting. She wasn't about to leave her home behind for a penniless rancher or farmer. Emily had no experience in labor work and never wanted to have to experience such a thing in her life. But she saw that this particular ad was written by a sheriff and it caught her interest immediately.

"Surely a sheriff would be able to afford my lifestyle," Emily reasoned as she read the short ad. The sheriff was looking for an independent woman who didn't mind his type of work or the demands of having to leave on short notice. Emily figured that she was a very independent woman who could take care of a household. And even though Spruce Valley, Montana wasn't a place she was very familiar with, she figured the sheriff had a decent staff. And when she read the end of the ad and realized that this sheriff was none other than the famous Sheriff Josh Ryder, responsible for bringing to justice the train robber gang, Emily's heart thumped with hope.

"This sheriff has to be loaded!" Emily said as she stood and started to pace with the newspaper in her hand. She couldn't imagine why Josh would want a mail-order-bride. He surely could not be in want of any Western woman, so instead wanted someone from the East that had a lot more class. Emily imagined herself being a sheriff's wife, always attending social functions and being an important figure in the community. Emily smiled, seeing herself as that person.

Sitting down at her writing desk, Emily made quick work of writing a response to Josh. She wrote slowly, wanting to show how well her penmanship was. She needed to stand out from all the other letters that he would no doubt receive. She wrote about her family and position in Atlanta, knowing that Josh would be impressed with her connections and the work that her father used to do. Emily didn't write about her current troubles, wanting to appear as sophisticated as possible to Josh. She also made sure to note how responsible and independent she was, hoping to appeal to every aspect of his ad. And as she started to fold the letter together, she took the only portrait of herself and folded it inside the letter. She hated to let go of one of her prized possessions but knew that she needed to do everything she could to win over this sheriff. Emily liked the idea of leaving Atlanta behind her and starting fresh in a new place. And the idea of being a sheriff's wife greatly appealed to her.

The moment the letter was ready to be posted, Emily took a few notes from underneath her mattress and made her way back downstairs. She'd have to take the letter herself to the postmaster to see that it would be delivered to Josh as quickly as possible. Emily knew that it would take time for the letter to travel, but in the back of her mind she reminded herself that time was not on her side. She needed a plan, and something quick because she knew that any day now her reputation would be ruined in Georgia. But if she could convince Josh to agree to her coming out to Montana so they could be married, then she wouldn't have to worry about what anyone thought about her in Georgia.

"Emily, my dear. Where are you going now?" Mr. Middleton said as he came out of his study. He'd heard Emily come back after her tea party with her close friend, Cynthia Danny, and was curious why she was going out again.

"Don't worry, Father," Emily said with a bright smile, trying to placate her father. He reeked of booze and the thought of him drinking away any penny he had left made her stomach tighten in knots. "I'm just going to mail a letter."

"Alright, my dear," Mr. Middleton said with a nod of his head. The action caused his headache to increase and he yearned for another tankard. "Just, please be careful." He turned from her then and stumbled back to his study. Emily's smile faded as the study door closed. She turned towards the front door then, determined to save herself from her many misfortunes.

# CHAPTER 3

Josh's lopsided grin only grew and grew as he walked out of Frost's. In his hand he had a pile of letters in response to his mail-order-bride ad, and even a few telegrams from prospective wives. Josh couldn't believe that his ad had received so much attention, but the more letters he read, the more he realized that his fame for bringing the train robbers to justice had really spread all over the country. His ego surely doubled in size as he read letter after letter that mentioned his triumph. However, that also was a double-edged sword. It seemed to him that women only wanted to write him because he was so famous, and not necessarily because they were looking for a husband. They simply wanted a reason to write someone so brave and daring.

Josh took all his mail back to his office, intent on weeding through all the letters. The first time he'd received a big batch of letters he had made it his intent to reply to each one to at least thank them for writing. But he soon discovered that it would be both a waste of money and time. So instead, he set his mind to discovering which letters would be worth replying to in order to hopefully meet his future wife. Sitting down at his desk, Josh took the time to at least read each letter and sort them between simple letters of praise and letters that related to his ad.

Once the sorting was complete, Josh had a wide grin on his face. He felt good to have received letters in relation to the good work he and his friends were able to complete. Josh was certainly glad that people riding the train didn't have to fear anymore about that gang robbing them. But Josh knew that the point of placing the ad wasn't to attract praise. So, he took all those letters and deposited them in his desk drawer. He didn't just want to throw them away, so for now they'd rest in his desk.

Next, Josh turned his attention to the letters that were written with the intent of marriage. He sifted through all of them, finding that many of the letters weren't very interesting. He sighed, a little frustrated to not have read one letter that detailed a woman he could really picture as his wife. And just when he thought he was done for the day, perhaps needing a stiff drink to settle his frustration, he happened upon a letter that he'd missed amongst all the others. Almost deciding to put it off till he could pour himself a small thimble of whiskey, Josh finally tore open the letter and was surprised when a small photo fell out.

Josh's honey colored eyes grew large as he looked at the young lady's photo. Though black and white, he could tell that she had a long torso, more than likely making her taller than most women. Dark hair flowed down her back in curls and Josh was certain it was black. And as he looked at the young lady's face, he guessed her eyes were blue. Having spent most of his life observing people and their details, memorizing them to perhaps use them later, Josh had a good idea what this young lady would look like in person. He was captivated by her beauty, but as he unfolded her letter, he hoped her words would also interest him.

*Dear Josh Ryder,*

*I'm sure you're called Sheriff all day long, so I figured you could use a break. My name is Emily Middleton and I reside in Atlanta, Georgia. Like most women of leisure my age, my father is a successful businessman that has lent to my years of education and good upbringing. I'm a lady, through and through, but my closest friend, Cynthia, would say that I'm quite a rebel.*

*Just today I joined a group of like-minded individuals for tea and cards. Most of the women present wouldn't dare play poker with gentlemen, but I'm not like other women. I like to take chances and put my education to the test. I'm pleased to say that I won the final round and took home a very handsome purse. This is not to say I have a gambling addiction, but I do like to push the boundaries on what women can and cannot do.*

*Society here in Atlanta is very overbearing. I wish to travel West, to seek my own way. But I still understand the benefit of having a husband. Your ad interested me because of what you seek in a wife. I'm strongly independent but enjoy socializing with others. I'm content with the idea of seeing you off in the middle of the night for work because you have a very demanding job. I'd be proud to be your wife and support you in your position in the community. But like Cynthia often reminds me, marriage isn't just a business deal. I would be interested in coming to Spruce Valley to see if we are compatible romantically. Surely, we both desire a family at one point, and marriage wouldn't be enjoyable if we did not like one another.*

*Since there is nothing holding me to Atlanta because I am now of age, and my father has always been very supportive of my decisions, I would like to come to Spruce*

*Valley as soon as you agree to the arrangement. I know this seems rather sudden, but I tend to act on gut instinct. And my gut is saying that I need to take a chance on you. Either way, I'm overdue for a trip and could think of this as any other vacation. If things don't work out between us, then there is no need to fret.*

*I hope you approve of the photo I sent with this letter. If you like what you see, reply as soon as possible.*

*Miss Emily Middleton*

Josh was certainly intrigued by the time he'd finished Emily's letter. She not only had beautiful handwriting, but she wrote with plenty of humor and surprise in her letter that he had to read it a few times before he could truly believe what he was reading. He'd never heard of a woman playing poker before and was surprised she would admit to it. She appeared to be a Georgia socialite, perhaps even a debutante, and would be the last person he'd expect to admit to playing poker with other gentlemen. The fact that she'd won only made him chuckle, thinking she must be a force to be reckoned with.

The only part of her letter that concerned him was her eagerness to come to Spruce Valley. Perhaps she really was bored with Atlanta, or there could be a completely different reason. Either way, Josh had a decision to make. As he looked down at her photo, trying to picture the sound of her voice as he thought about the words she'd used in her letter, he knew that he wanted to take a chance on her probably as much as she wanted to take a chance on him. He liked that she hadn't mentioned his publicity in the papers like all the other women had.

Setting Emily's letter and photo aside, Josh pulled out a fresh sheet of writing paper along with his ink and quill.

Then, he set about to writing a response to Emily as he focused on writing as elegantly as she had. Or at least, as legible.

*Dear Emily,*

*I certainly appreciated your letter. Thank you for the photo because it really helps to put a face to the author of such a beautifully written letter. I've received countless letters in reply to my ad, but you are the first one to include a photo and to not have mentioned my experience as a sheriff. It's nice that someone can see me for who I really am and not just my position in society.*

*I will admit that I was surprised that you'd admitted to playing poker. Even here in the West, women wouldn't dare to do such a thing. I can't help but wonder if you'll be trouble for me, but know I write this sentence with a smirk on my face. I am only teasing. I can tell you are a fierce, independent woman. You certainly sound like you'd be able to manage the frequent demands of my position in town. And I think I'd enjoy getting to know the real Emily, too.*

*Your request to come straight away to Spruce Valley is a little forward, I will admit. But if you truly are only looking for a change of scenery, I'm sure the trip won't hurt. When you arrive, we can take the time to get to know one another with no strings attached. I'd be happy to show you around Spruce Valley, though I'm sure it's nowhere as large as Atlanta. I'm not sure how much you know of the West, but it's very different to the East. As an educated woman, I'm sure you'll take it all as a learning experience when you do take the trip to Montana.*

*The one thing I can say about Spruce Valley is that everyone here is really friendly. It's a close-knit community and you'll most likely get to meet everyone real quick. We're always eager to make new friends, and there are several other mail-order-brides here that you could get to know as well. In fact, the three of them now run a women's seamstress shop. There are not many shops in Spruce Valley, but we are not without some creature comforts as well.*

*Really, it's a beautiful place here. Winter has finally passed and the spring air is completely refreshing. Soon, wildflowers will be blooming everywhere. I'd say this is the best time of year to come visit our small little town.*

*Well, I think that's enough rambling. I look forward to getting to know you better and perhaps seeing you after a while.*

*Josh Ryder*

BY THE TIME Josh had finished writing the letter, he knew that it was much longer than what was proper. It would be a pretty penny to mail, and since him and Emily hadn't been officially introduced, his long letter might seem a bit forward. However, he felt very pleased with himself. He liked how it had been constructed and after rereading it, he realized how proud he was of Spruce Valley. Josh knew that it wouldn't compare to Atlanta, but he would be honored to introduce any young lady to this small town in Montana. He couldn't imagine ever living anywhere else and hoped that if Emily did come, that she'd come to love it just as much as he did. He was certain that he could fall in love with a woman as beautiful as Emily, but wouldn't be able to tell till they met in person.

Sealing the letter, Josh took all the other letters and telegrams he'd received that day and put them in the drawer with the others. He'd wait to reply to other letters till he heard back from Emily. He'd also need to have Mr. Frost send a telegram for him to have the *Matrimonial Times* stop his ad. He'd certainly received plenty of responses and didn't need anymore. After all, he was secretly hoping things would work out with Emily because her letter had been so different from the others.

After stopping back into Frost's to mail his letter and send the telegram, he went to the livery stables to collect his horse. Now that he'd replied to a letter, he needed to make a trip out to the Slater Ranch. After talking to Lucy about her needing to rest in bed till she was no longer expecting, she'd in turn struck a deal with him. He needed to keep her up to date on all the happenings in town and also tell her that he'd finally written to a young lady. Always a man who kept his promises, Josh lead his mare out of town towards the ranch to deliver the news to Mrs. Slater.

# CHAPTER 4

Emily paced in the sitting room, feeling her heart pounding in her chest. She had dressed herself in a simple day gown, knowing that she wouldn't be entertaining anyone for a long time. That morning, the papers had finally printed the horrible story surrounding her father. She hadn't seen her father so far that day, but was certain he would know what had transpired already.

Emily was certain what she should do now. With her reputation being tarnished, she didn't dare call on any of her acquaintances. She understood how debutantes acted towards those who had lost everything. She herself had done it before and was certain that this was some type of karmic revenge for the way she'd treated others in the past. She let out a deep sigh, doing her best to settle her nerves. She didn't want to cry but could feel tears pooling in the corner of her eyes.

A knock on the sitting room door startled her, causing her to cry out in fright. She was so on edge that any little thing seemed to unnerve her. Gathering her courage, she called for the knocker to come in. She let out a sigh of relief as Cynthia opened the door and came strolling in.

"Oh, Emily. I came as soon as I could," Cynthia said as she wrapped her arms around her dearest friend. "I'm sure my parents won't be pleased and would scold me for risking being seen with you. But frankly, my dear, I don't give a damn."

Emily chuckled as she held her friend closely. "You never cease to surprise me, Cynthia," Emily said as she stepped back from her friend. "You were once so quiet and shy, and now you are almost as rebellious as I am."

"Why thank you," Cynthia said with a proud smile. They then sat down together on the couch, one of the last few remaining pieces of furniture in the room. "So, how are you doing?"

Emily shook her head as she said, "I simply don't know what I'm going to do."

"Have you heard back from the sheriff you wrote to?" Cynthia asked, trying to remain hopeful for her dear friend.

"I have not. But just in case, I'm packed for the trip. I decided to only pack one trunk. I figured I can order more gowns once I reach Spruce Valley and have become engaged to the sheriff," Emily explained.

"I can't imagine traveling with one trunk," Cynthia said, concerned. "Why don't you let me pay for another trunk to go with you? Surely you still have gowns and things to fill it?"

"I have plenty, Cynthia, but I must think of what I can carry alone," Emily said, always being reasonable. "The train to Montana is almost two weeks long, with a few days by stagecoach to reach Spruce Valley thereafter. I don't want to travel with too many things." Cynthia shook her head, having a hard time imaging traveling for that long alone.

"I wish you had someone to go with you," Cynthia said. "I hate the idea of you being on your own."

Emily gave Cynthia a wicked grin as she said, "Then why don't you come with me? We could both find wealthy husbands in the West." Cynthia laughed then as she shook her head, a sound Emily found pleasing to the ear. It was good to know that at least she could make her friend laugh.

"I'm not as brave as you, Emily," Cynthia admitted. "I might one day gather the courage to play a hand of poker with the men, but I could never leave my family behind."

"I don't blame you, Cynthia. You have a great family," Emily said. "And I'm sure that if my mother had survived childbirth, none of this would have happened." The two sighed together as their eyes drifted around the bare room. Once, the room had held many prized possessions and Emily had always been proud anytime they'd have company over. She always thought this manor was the most elegant of any in Atlanta. Now it was just a shell of a ghost of what once was.

"Excuse me, Miss Middleton," Mrs. Silver, the housekeeper, said as she came into the sitting room. "The mail has just come in." The housekeeper handed the mail over to Emily before turning and quickly leaving. The front door opened and closed then, telling the young ladies that Mrs. Silver had left the house for the last time. Emily knew that she was truly on her own then and couldn't even rely on her father for anything.

"Well, hurry up and see what has come," Cynthia encouraged, pulling Emily from her thoughts. Emily gave her friend a kind smile as she started flipping through the letters. Most were addressed to her father, having been sent out that morning. She could only assume that they were sent with anger and hate, so she set them aside with the intent of perhaps never showing her father. But she did find one addressed to herself. As she flipped it over and saw that it was from Spruce Valley, hope leapt into her heart.

"My goodness, he's written me!" Emily said excitedly as she tore open the letter and read it as quickly as she could. "And he's agreed to my coming to Spruce Valley!" The ladies cheered together as relief flooded Emily. At least now she had some place to go.

"How does he feel about what has happened to your father?" Cynthia asked, eager to read the letter herself. But Emily quickly folded it back up.

"I haven't told him yet," Emily admitted. "I will go to Spruce Valley and see how I like it before I confess everything to him." Cynthia was stunned into silence by her friend's words. She didn't dare believe that Emily had deceived the sheriff.

"Then what on Earth did you tell the man?" Cynthia asked, perplexed.

"I simply wrote that I desired a change of scenery and that Spruce Valley would make for a good vacation," Emily explained, unable to meet her friend's stare. "I wrote that if things didn't work out, then there would be no hard feelings."

"Oh, Emily. But what if things do work out and he proposes? Then you're going to have to tell him the truth of everything and perhaps the truth will hurt too much," Cynthia said, more concerned than ever.

"What does that matter?" Emily said as she looked up finally. "It's not like the sheriff would be marrying me for my money. He no doubt finds me beautiful enough to have for a wife, for I sent my photo with my letter."

"My dear, there is more to marriage than the union of two attractive people," Cynthia said with a sigh. "He'll want to know your true character."

"I have been honest about other things and will do my best to remain honest about my expectations of marriage," Emily said as she stood. "But I must go acquire a train ticket now."

"Emily, don't be cross with me. We shall never see each other again after this," Cynthia said. Emily stopped dead in her tracks, Cynthia's words settling over her. She knew her friend was right and that she shouldn't just turn her back on her.

Emily turned to her friend, a deep frown on her face. "I'm so sorry, Cynthia. I know you are only looking out for me," Emily said as she returned to her friend and embraced her. "I shall surely miss you the most."

"And I, you," Cynthia replied as she held her friend close. She tried not to cry but could feel the tears trickling down her face.

"Now, about this ticket," Cynthia said as she pulled away from her friend and quickly wiped her eyes on her handkerchief. "I shall go down to the station and purchase it for you, and don't you dare try to stop me." Cynthia raised a finger at Emily as she tried to speak up against the idea.

"You should not show yourself in public but instead, slip away in the night. It's the only way to preserve one's image in Atlanta, should you need to return," Cynthia explained. "There shall be so much mystery about your disappearance that there shall be rumors about you for years to come." Both young ladies smiled and laughed about the idea as they embraced once more.

"Fine then. I shall see you off and look forward to your return," Emily said as she walked Cynthia to the front door.

"And I shall make sure to return with some food as well," Cynthia said, looking about the empty house. "I'm not sure what you have left."

"I'm sure I can put something together in the kitchen," Emily said as she tried to reassure her.

"I hope this sheriff staffs a good household," Cynthia said with a sigh. "You truly do deserve the best in the world."

"I hope the same," Emily said as she pulled open the door for Cynthia. It was an action so below her station that she shivered for a moment, thinking how low she'd come from a debutante to someone opening her own door.

"Alright then, I shall be back after a while," Cynthia said with a dark expression on her face. She left the house quickly and hurried down the stairs to her waiting carriage. Emily didn't wait to see her off but instead quickly shut the door, as though people might be lurking around to catch a glimpse of the most sought after debutante in Atlanta who had just fallen as low as you could in this city.

Left alone, Emily finally let the tears that she'd held back all morning fall. She walked towards the kitchen with the sheriff's letter still in her hand. She was thankful that the man was willing to take a chance on her and would hopefully continue to support her way of life, once she reached Spruce Valley. She had a large sum of money to travel with and had done well to sew it into the sides of her trunk, in case it would ever be searched. Emily knew that she would have a little to live on until things could be made official between her and Josh, but she only hoped that their courtship and engagement would be short.

Emily did her best to get her emotions under wraps as she made her way to the kitchen. There, she rummaged around in the pantry till she found some bread, jam, butter and cheese. Emily had never prepared her own food before and found the action rather odd. But, she needed to eat something and this was all that she could find. Sitting down on a stool at the center counter of the kitchen, she ate the food quietly, listening to the silence of the empty house. Emily knew that her hours left in the manor were numbered, and she eagerly looked forward to Cynthia's return. By midnight, she hoped to be on a train headed West.

# CHAPTER 5

The back and forth rocking of the train put Emily's nerves on edge. She didn't like the movement of the train and often fought it, finding herself being slightly tasseled back and forth. Emily was at least thankful that Cynthia had paid for her to have her own private room on the train, but often couldn't find a very comfortable position to sit or sleep on the metal beast.

When she'd left Atlanta in the middle of the night, she'd been excited to leave her old life behind her. She was setting off for the West like many before her, to seek a better life for herself. She was going to meet a famous sheriff whom she was convinced she could seduce into marrying her. Then, she'd have every comfort in life she'd been used to and plenty of social outings with her new husband to enjoy. Emily only had to endure getting to Spruce Valley first.

The first few days of the train ride had been spent staying put in her room. She'd sometimes stare out of the window, eager to see the scenery change. She couldn't wait to see what the West looked like, but for the most part the train's views were of only cluttered forests, broken up by various small towns. Nothing reminded her of Atlanta, and since this was her first time traveling outside the city, she was a bit nervous to see nothing familiar.

After she'd gotten used to the flow of the train, she started to venture out of her room in hopes of socializing with other people. Emily was so used to being the center of attention that she'd started to crave some sort of conversation with another person. Eventually she got over her fear that someone on the train might know her and her reputation in Atlanta. She started taking the time to walk the train, sitting in the public carriages, and sometimes striking up conversation with other ladies traveling. But every time they found out that she was traveling alone without a chaperone, their conversations often stopped. Even when Emily mentioned she was traveling West to be a mail-order-bride to the famous Sheriff Josh Ryder, it didn't give her any leeway. Emily was quickly learning that people in the West valued other things that Emily always thought everyone cherished above others. She now understood the weight and importance for a woman to have a husband more than anything, which Emily found very overwhelming.

Not only was the company poor while traveling by train, but also the food. She dined in the dining cart for every meal since she had the extra cash to do so, but the same old food over and over again started to become very boring. She even thought of getting off the train at the many stops in various towns but feared missing the train's departure, and therefore decided against it. She even started dreading mealtimes because she didn't want to see the same people and menu each time.

Having nothing else to fill her idle time, she often spent most of it resting in her private room, daydreaming about what it would be like to live in Spruce Valley and be married to a sheriff. She imagined all the social gathering they'd attend together since he was such an important person in town. Emily smiled as she imagined herself dancing with the sheriff at charity balls or attending dinner with the Mayor at least once a week. She was excited about the idea of marrying someone so important. And when Josh needed to race from town to go after a criminal, she'd gush to all her friends over how proud she was of her husband. She'd no doubt make many jealous. The thought itself made her giggle with excitement.

Emily would also picture in her mind the type of house a sheriff must have. Since it was the West, she knew that Josh probably didn't own a home quite like the one she grew up in. She didn't think that manors were often seen in the West. But she'd be happy with a two-story home with plenty of spare bedrooms for guests who needed to sleep off a fun night over at their house. Emily would often smile with glee at the idea of throwing dinner parties for all the prestigious families in the area. She only hoped that the cook Josh employed would be skilled in the dishes she was used to. Emily knew that Southern food was very different from the rest of the country, but she'd be willing to help teach any cook about Georgia dishes if need be.

Emily had never really been excited about the idea of marriage. She simply knew that one day she wanted to be married and have a family of her own. The idea of childbirth terrified her because that is how her mother had died. And in Georgia, she'd been reassured by her family's physician that medicine had come a long way since then. But would this same type of medical treatment be available in Spruce Valley? She wasn't certain and would make sure to discuss this with Josh before they started trying for children.

And since Josh was such a famous sheriff, he would certainly aspire to one day become the Marshal of Montana.

Then they could live closer to a large city and have all the creature comforts that she'd been used to. Emily reassured herself that she'd just have to deal with the minimum amenities in Spruce Valley while Josh continued rising up in law enforcement until he had the desired position that would allow them to relax for the rest of their lives. Emily was confident about her future with Josh, and now only hoped they'd one day grow to like each other.

~

JOSH SAT on the front porch of Frost's, his eyes focused on the road heading east out of town. He sat on a wooden bench, one that Mr. Frost had commissioned furniture maker Zachariah Welliver to make, so people could wait on the stagecoach. And as the sun slowly rose over the horizon, Josh sat in front of the mercantile waiting on the stagecoach to arrive for the day.

According to Emily's last telegram, she had already made her way to Wyoming. Josh knew that it wouldn't be much further for her to travel, after about two weeks, he could only imagine what kind of state she would arrive in. Being a Georgian socialite, Josh had a pretty good idea of what type of person Emily would be. She'd be surprised by Spruce Valley and probably compare it to Atlanta. And like the other mail-order-brides that had come before her, she'd either fall in love with the town and its people, or she'd hate it and perhaps come to resent Josh. But that was why she was only coming for a visit. There were no strings attached, and Josh felt quite comfortable with the current arrangement.

Even so, Josh sat on the bench anticipating the stagecoach with much nervousness. He was excited to finally get to meet Emily, even though they'd exchanged very few letters of communication. He had a gut feeling that Emily would be the type of person that he'd enjoy having as a wife. She'd shown him that she could be bold and therefore would at least be interesting to be with. He only hoped that she could deal with a simpler way of life that often required hard work to obtain what you truly wanted in life.

Though Josh had obtained his position in the community at a young age, he'd never turned down a challenge. He was excited to prove to everyone in town that he could be both a good and fair sheriff, but also someone they could rely on. He'd driven out criminals when they'd wandered into town and taken care of anyone else that would cause trouble. Sometimes disputes had to be settled between townsfolk, and he was okay with doing that type of humble work. Josh chuckled as he realized he was playing the middleman between the Slaters, and that was something he could be proud of too. He liked being the one people relied on when they needed help.

Josh hadn't written to his parents in southern Montana about Emily coming to meet him yet. He wanted to see how things went between them first before he wrote home. He'd grown up ranching with his father, but always dreamed of doing more. When a deputy's position had become available close to home, he'd taken it, even though he knew that his father needed the help at home. Josh had done his best to do the two jobs, but eventually ended up hiring someone to help out his father just so he wouldn't feel guilty when he took this sheriff job further away from home. As far as he knew, that ranch hand was still working for his father. It gave Josh some comfort to know that his parents were not on their own when it came to the ranch. He knew that they were getting on in years and one day would need to come stay with him in Spruce Valley.

Josh sighed, not liking the idea of seeing his parents away from the ranch. But he couldn't leave his job here in

Spruce Valley and one day, he would have to convince them to sell the ranch and retire in Spruce Valley. And if he could marry and have a few children before then, he was certain the idea would appeal to his parents more, to be closer to their grandchildren.

All thoughts were pushed out of Josh's mind as dust began to stir on the road in the distance. The spring rains hadn't come, so it was still pretty dry on the roads, causing the dust cloud to rise up behind the stagecoach. The vehicle thundered down the road, the sound of hard-hitting hooves echoing as the stagecoach rumbled into town. It came to a sudden stop before the mercantile and Josh rose to his feet, bounding off the porch to open the carriage door for Emily so the driver could make his fast deliveries to Mr. Frost before continuing on.

"Welcome to Spruce Valley," Josh said as he stuck his head into the carriage. There on the velvet bench was a very road tired Emily. But she smiled happily at the news of finally arriving. She collected her purse and stepped down from the carriage with the help of the man that had opened the carriage door. She marveled at how handsome he was with his light brown hair and honey-colored eyes. The lopsided grin on his face did something to Emily; no man had ever been able to affect her in such a way.

"Thank you for your assistance. Are you valet?" Emily asked as she started to look in her purse for a few coins for the man. He laughed in response as he shook his head.

"No, Miss Emily Middleton. I am Sheriff Josh Ryder," he explained. Emily froze as Josh revealed his identity. She looked him up and down, from head to toe after realizing who he was. He wasn't dressed as finely as she would have assumed for a sheriff and for a moment, was puzzled by his simple Western shirt and jeans. A Stetson rested on his head, so she figured that at least he had good taste in hats.

"Forgive me, Sheriff. The long trip has left me less than presentable," Emily said as she put away her money. The driver dropped her trunk on the front porch of the store they'd come to a halt before, and her stomach tightened to see her own possessions treated so. Josh followed where she was looking and could only assume she was concerned about her things.

"Here, let me get that for you. I've arranged a room for you at the Honeywell Inn," Josh explained as he moved quickly to pick up her trunk. "Is this the only one?"

"Sure is, thank you," Emily replied. She was pleased to see that Josh was so thoughtful, and had planned ahead for her arrival. "I wanted to pack light and figured I'd only bring what I need and perhaps get what else I might need once I arrived."

"That's smart thinking," Josh said as he led her down the road. "The inn is right around the corner." Emily simply smiled and nodded. It felt good to walk after sitting and riding for so long. She took the time to really take in Josh's appearance, finding him very handsome and muscular. He lifted her trunk as though it weighed nothing.

As they walked together, Josh could hardly believe how beautiful Emily was. Though she looked tired from traveling, it didn't seem to take away from her natural beauty. She wore a gorgeous gown that Josh could only assume was made from the finest silks. He liked to think she'd dressed up for this occasion and appreciated that she took the time to do so. Her long, black hair hung around her shoulders in curls that Josh was curious would feel as silky as her gown. But he quickly pushed those thoughts out of his mind because he knew Emily was here to be his potential bride. She wasn't just another warm body to occupy his bed at night.

"Here's the inn," Josh said as he led her inside. "Bill

Eckert is the owner and he'll be able to tend to your needs while you're visiting."

"I look forward to making his acquaintance," Emily replied. Mostly she was looking forward to a nice long bath and getting into a fresh gown. The inn appeared to be very minimal to Emily and she hoped that he had laundry services available.

"Hey there, Sheriff," said a man behind the counter that Emily could only assume was Bill.

"Hello, Mr. Eckert. I've brought Miss Middleton over from the depot to check in," Josh explained.

"Certainly, Sheriff," Bill replied as he turned and plucked a room key off the wall. Emily saw how there was only four and that the key Bill gave her was the only one being used. She figured that Spruce Valley didn't get many visitors. "I assume you'll take that up yourself?"

"Yes, Bill. I can show Miss Middleton the way and take the trunk upstairs," Josh replied, eager to spend as much time with Emily as possible.

"Oh, certainly you have an attendant who could carry the trunk for the good sheriff?" Emily spoke up, not wanting to cause her possible intended any more work.

"No, Miss Middleton. I manage the Honeywell Inn myself," Bill said, slightly embarrassed.

"That's quite okay. I don't mind," Josh said, understanding that Emily was more than likely used to a place where servants and attendants were at most places she visited. Emily thankfully only smiled kindly as she nodded.

"Welcome to the inn, Miss Middleton. I hope you enjoy your stay," Bill said before he left the counter and disappeared into a back room.

"I do hope I didn't offend him," Emily said as she followed Josh upstairs.

"Bill's always been a pretty private man, so don't

worry," Josh replied, trying to reassure her. He figured that Emily would eventually learn that Spruce Valley wasn't like Atlanta at all. It might be a rude wake-up call for her, but he was confident that any independent woman with courage could adjust well to this small town.

"Here we are," Emily said as she found the room at the end of the hall and used the key Bill had given her to open it. She pushed open the door and stepped inside as Josh came through and set her trunk at the end of the bed. It was a small room with whitewashed walls that made the space feel bigger than what it was. It was nicely furnished, though not as nice as she was used to. But compared to the train and the stagecoach, it was a huge improvement.

"Thank you so much for bringing up my things," Emily said as she turned her attention to the sheriff. She flashed him her signature smile and saw the way he smiled at her in return.

"I'm always willing and able to help out when needed," Josh replied, mesmerized by her beautiful blue eyes and how they shined so brightly against her black hair. "How about a bite to eat once you get settled?" Emily's stomach rumbled and they both laughed at the sound.

"Food sounds like a lovely idea," Emily replied. "I just need to freshen up first. Where shall I meet you when I'm ready?"

"The Eatery is a small café at the back of Frost's mercantile. It was the place that the stagecoach stopped at," Josh explained.

"Easy enough," Emily said as Josh made his way towards the door.

"Alright then. I'll see you in a bit," Josh said absent-mindedly as he pulled the door closed. He had a hard time not staring at Emily. She was certainly beautiful and would be turning a lot of heads in town. Josh couldn't help but whistle as he went down the hallway and then the stairs to reach the front of the inn.

"Got your hands full there, Sheriff," came Bill's voice. He'd returned from his small apartment at the back of the hotel and now stood once again at the counter. Josh stopped as he saw Bill at counter and slowly leaned over it, a dreamy look on his face.

"She sure is something, isn't she," Josh said, feeling pretty proud for having met Emily finally. He was certain that Bill would agree with him.

"Pardon me, Sheriff, but that woman only likes a certain type of man. And you're not it," Bill said straightforward. His words made Josh sober up right away.

"What are you talking about, Bill?" Josh asked, a bit annoyed by the innkeeper.

"Sheriff, I've seen it many times before," Bill said with a sigh. "A woman like that wants a man with loaded pockets so she doesn't have to lift a finger." Josh stared hard at Bill, trying to believe what he just heard.

"Look, I get she's from a big city, but that doesn't mean that Emily is the type of woman who would just be looking for a wealthy husband. She's very independent," Josh said, feeling like he needed to defend Emily's honor.

"Please, Sheriff, don't take me the wrong way," Bill said with his hands raised in front of him like he was a criminal surrendering to him. "I'm just looking out for the best person I know in town."

Josh chuckled then as he shook his head and straightened his posture. "Now you're just trying to sweet talk me," Josh said. "But I get what you're saying, Bill. I appreciate you looking out for me."

"Least I could do because you're always looking out for the people of Spruce Valley," Bill said as Josh departed. Josh waved at Bill before leaving the inn. Something about Bill's words rubbed him the wrong way. He could understand that Bill was only watching out for him, but he didn't like the idea of anyone speaking disrespectfully of Emily. He only hoped that he didn't have any more trouble on Emily's first day in town.

# CHAPTER 6

By the time Emily had taken a leisurely bath and dressed in a fresh gown, she was feeling like a completely new person. She'd finally made it to Spruce Valley, and all on her own without needing help from anyone. She felt a sense of accomplishment she'd never really felt before. Sure, she had taught many young ladies the proper way to act and talk during certain social settings, but nothing brought her as much satisfaction as she felt now for having taken care of herself. Now, as she made her way to the bottom level of the simple inn, she was looking forward to getting something to eat with the sheriff.

"All done with the tub, Miss Middleton?" Bill asked as she came down the stairs. Emily flashed him her signature smile and she could see the way his cheeks blushed. Emily was used to this type of reaction but didn't tease Bill any longer.

"I am, thank you," Emily said in parting. As she stepped out of the inn, she turned her eyes towards the mercantile the stagecoach had deposited her at. Emily took her time returning to the store. She took in the town around her, being able to see one end from the other from where she stood. She saw several men riding on horseback and so far hadn't seen a single carriage, or even a wagon. It made her wonder how folks got around without hired carriages. Just the idea of riding a horse didn't settle well with her, and she knew that she'd probably never leave Spruce Valley unless the sheriff had a small carriage for her.

Emily saw that there were a few important businesses in town. She noticed a clinic and felt relief that at least there was a local medical doctor. Emily wasn't surprised that there wasn't a hospital but thought that a clinic might do for childbirth. She also could see a furniture store and a women's seamstress shop at the far end of town. She looked forward to going into the store tomorrow. But for now, she needed a decent meal.

Stepping into Frost's mercantile, she took a moment to wander around the store. She was in need of a few things and was hoping she'd find them in stock. But the more she wandered around, the more she realized that most of the items for sale were food related, or some item needed to make something else. Emily had never been in such a store and wondered if she'd ever need to purchase anything there.

Following her nose, Emily was able to locate The Eatery. Like the sheriff had explained, the café was rather small, but the smells coming from the place made Emily's mouth water. It all smelled like home-cooked food and that was something that Emily could use at that moment. Though there were a good number of patrons, she was able to skirt around the tables till she found Josh's table at the back. His Stetson was lowered over his face as though he'd been sleeping, and she wondered how long he'd been waiting on her.

Emily took a seat across from him, then leaned over the table and flicked back his hat with her fingers. She giggled when she realized he hadn't been sleeping at all.

"You surprised me," Emily confessed as she settled down into her chair.

"That is the whole point," Josh said with a wink. "Everyone always suspects that I'm sleeping and when the crook tries to sneak up on me, I surprise them in return."

"Seems like your sharing a trade secret with me," Emily said as she batted her eyelashes at Josh, trying to get his blood running hotter. His lopsided grin appeared once more, and she felt her own heart starting to beat faster as she took in his handsome looks.

"Why, are you interested in becoming my deputy?" Josh asked, enjoying the way Emily was trying to tease him.

"Certainly not, Sheriff. I can't imagine ever working a day in my life," Emily said with a laugh. But as Josh processed what she'd just said, he couldn't even force himself to laugh with her.

"Well, surely you thought of some employment to occupy yourself with once we are married?" Josh asked, trying to understand Emily's idea of marriage. Emily was surprised to hear this, trying to imagine why Josh would ever think she'd be able to work.

"Honestly, it's not something I've put much thought into," Emily said, trying to keep the peace. She didn't want to argue with the man she hoped to marry on their very first date. "In fact, I'd rather like to hear what your plans for the future are. Do you plan to ever run for State Marshal?" This time, Josh did laugh at the idea of him ever being a marshal.

"I plan to grow old and die in this town, Miss Middleton. Nothing on this earth could ever convince me to leave my position," Josh was able to explain once his mirth subsided. Emily stilled, not liking the idea that her future husband wasn't very ambitious. She was counting on him rising into a higher position that would ensure she'd never have to work a day in her life. But if Josh wasn't willing to be anything other than a sheriff, then perhaps she had to rethink her situation.

"Well, at least tell me what you'd recommend," Emily said as she turned her attention to the menu. "There are many dishes that I'm not familiar with."

"I see," Josh said, noticing the way Emily quickly changed the subject they were discussing. "I would suggest the meatloaf if you've never had it before. Emmet makes an amazing meatloaf, and no one can beat Ella's mashed potatoes and gravy."

"Sounds delightful," Emily said with a smile, even though she didn't think having her food covered in gravy would be very appetizing. Perhaps she could imagine it was like grits and shrimp and still enjoy the dish.

When their waitress made her way to their table, Emily was surprised to see a female working in a café. She'd never dined in a place where a woman worked the front, always having waiters tend to her needs. She smiled at the woman as Josh introduced her to Nell. But the more the two women looked at each other, the more Emily thought she recognized Nell from somewhere long before.

"What can I get you two?" Nell asked in an uneasy voice. Josh quickly picked up on the waitress's tone of voice and started to look between the two of them. He could tell that they recognized each other.

"I'll have today's special, and Miss Middleton would like the meatloaf," Josh explained.

"And some tea, please," Emily added, her memory starting to come back to her.

"Right away, Miss," Nell said as she jotted down her notes and went immediately on her way.

"Do you know Nell or something?" Josh asked once the waitress was far away from the table that she wouldn't overhear their conversation.

"I have this feeling like I've seen her before, but not for a very long time," Emily explained as she watched Nell move across the room. "I almost want to say that she used to be a servant in my house and used to always pour the tea because she was so skilled at making the absolute perfect cup." Josh was surprised and looked at Nell, trying to imagine her working anywhere else but The Eatery. She'd come into town about the time Josh had taken up the position as sheriff.

"You remember why she left?" Josh asked. This was the first time he'd taken an interest in Nell and now he was dying to know her back story.

"I honestly have no idea," Emily admitted. "I simply remember her one day being gone and Father never mentioned where she'd gone."

Josh shook his head as he said, "Who would have thought that two ladies from the same place would have made their way to Spruce Valley?"

"I guess this world is really small after all," Emily said, remembering a literary quote she'd once read. As Nell came around and poured Emily a cup of tea, she remembered the woman more clearly. She didn't mention this to Nell, thinking that now wasn't the time or place to speak about such things, but as she took a sip of the tea, she couldn't help but sigh deeply.

"As delicious as I remember," Emily said as she smiled kindly up at the woman. Nell simply nodded before walking off again.

"Doesn't look like Nell enjoys remembering," Josh observed.

"Yes, I would have to agree with you on that," Emily said.

"Are you saying you're a good observer?" Josh asked, his interest in Emily piquing.

"I wasn't lying when I said I won that poker game," Emily said as she smiled at Josh over the rim of her teacup. "It's easy to play when you're watching the players more than the cards."

"Seems like we should plan a time to play a game or two sometime," Josh suggested, feeling like it was so easy to flirt with her. He could easily tell that she was the type of young lady that was often flirted with and that she could handle her own in a crowd of gentlemen.

"Just tell me when and where and I'll be there," Emily agreed. "I never back down from a good challenge."

"And nor do I," Josh said, feeling like Emily would be the type of woman that would give him a run for his money.

When their food arrived, they settled into mutual silence as they ate. Emily found the meatloaf to be a hardy meal, but one that she could easily enjoy. The flavors were bold and she couldn't deny how hungry she was after eating mostly stale bread and salted meat for almost two weeks. By the time they were done, she had completely cleaned her plate.

"I would have never thought a woman such as yourself could eat me under the table," Josh said with a chuckle. Emily blushed, knowing how much she'd eaten was very unladylike. She was just so hungry that she couldn't help herself.

"I have to admit that I did surprise myself," Emily replied softly.

Josh quickly realized his error and said, "I like a woman who can hold her own and isn't afraid to show her true feelings." Emily chuckled at that response, glad to find Josh so humorous.

"Well, at this time I think I could use a long rest. After being without a proper bed for two weeks, I'm eager to finally get to use one," Emily said as she patted her lips with a napkin and rose from the table. "I'll be sure to come pay you a visit tomorrow at the Sheriff's Office."

"I'd be delighted to see you tomorrow then," Josh replied as he dipped his hat towards her. She winked at him, causing his blood to run warm. As he watched her walk out of The Eatery, turning several heads, Josh thought he was the luckiest man alive to have been given the opportunity to court such a lovely woman. Josh was always more attractive to women with dark hair, and Emily seemed to be the full package, with a tall, slim frame and elegant manners.

But as Josh fished out some money out of his pocket to pay for their meal, Bill's words came back to haunt him. He wondered if there could be any truth to them, especially as he thought about what Emily had said about work. Josh wanted a wife that could be his equal, not some woman he'd have to take care of. He expected his wife to work just as much as he did, and he knew he couldn't support the type of lifestyle that Emily might have been used to back in Atlanta. As Josh waited for the bill, and thought more about his interaction with Emily today, he could tell that there was a chemistry between them but couldn't say if Emily would one day become his wife.

Emily was starting to fret as she returned to the inn. She wasn't completely pleased with everything she'd learned about Josh. She didn't know how much he currently made a year as the small town's sheriff but was certain that it was nowhere near what she'd been expecting. Emily hadn't felt that it was the right time to talk about his current financial situation but felt pressed to do so soon after everything she'd been through with her father. She also knew that at some point she'd have to come clean to the sheriff, if their relationship did start to progress.

As Emily entered the inn, she approached the counter and asked Bill for a few sheets of writing paper. She wanted to write Cynthia right away to at least let her know that she'd arrived in Spruce Valley safely and to share her current insight on the sheriff.

"That will be five cents," Bill said with an uneasy smile. He felt intimidated by Miss Middleton and didn't know how she would react to being asked to purchase the paper.

"Of course," Emily said as she took out a few coins from her purse and gave them to Bill as he handed her the writing paper. "Thank you." With the paper in hand, she turned from the counter and made her way up the stairs to her room. She didn't want Bill to think that she was ungrateful, so she had willingly paid for the paper because she was certain the Sheriff was paying for her room. And since Emily could tell that the inn didn't receive many patrons, she would have to expect Bill to charge her for almost everything.

Emily sighed heavily as she made it back to her room, making sure to lock the door securely behind her. Alone, she felt like she could let her guard down as she let down her hair and allowed it to hang around her shoulders. She took to the writing desk in the room and began to pen her long letter to Cynthia. She figured she'd have to return to Frost's to mail the letter since she hadn't spotted a post office. But Emily didn't worry too much about what she was going to do next. For now, she simply wrote all she'd learned and discovered about Spruce Valley and Josh Ryder to her dearest friend.

Not wanting to worry Cynthia, Emily did her best to

write about everything in a positive light. After all, the small town was a cute little place, and everyone had seemed to be friendly thus far. And, Josh was a very handsome man who was easy to tease. She certainly looked forward to having the opportunity to play cards with him and wondered how daring the Sheriff was when he was supposed to be the main role model for all the town's people. The very thought made her smile as she penned her letter.

Emily even wrote about how surprised she was to see Nell working at the café. Emily described first her shock over seeing a female waiter, and then coming to discover the woman used to work for her father as a servant. Emily wondered if Cynthia would remember her for the woman who made the best cup of tea either one of them ever had. A part of Emily wanted to know why Nell had left her father's staff and came all the way out to Spruce Valley. She always enjoyed a good story and felt like Nell would have a juicy one to tell her, even though the woman didn't look too pleased to see her.

After Emily had finished her letter, she changed into a simple day gown and out of the pale-yellow silk gown she'd worn to simply show-off for Josh. In something a little more comfortable, Emily crawled underneath the covers of the bed and let out a sigh of relief. The bed was small, yet comfortable. It had been so long since Emily had the pleasure of sleeping in a real bed that she felt her body relax immediately. She reasoned that she could possibly sleep till tomorrow, the sun already passing noon.

As Emily closed her eyes and held the pillow close to her body, she wondered what she was going to do about her present situation. If she and Josh did marry, would he really expect her to work? She didn't have any skills that she could turn into some sort of employment, and the very idea didn't settle well with her. After all, she was a Middleton and none of the women in her family had ever worked. But as Emily drifted off to sleep, she couldn't help but wonder what sort of life she could possibly have with the Sheriff, and what she'd be willing to do to obtain stability in her life once more.

# CHAPTER 7

When the morning came, Emily did her best to stay positive. She had plans to visit the women's seamstress shop that morning to have proper gowns made for her, since she had brought so little with her. Shopping for new gowns always cheered her up and Emily was determined to have a good day.

After she rose from bed, Emily did her best to wash up and dress herself. After having to do it for over a month now, Emily was starting to get used to the task. She even had practiced doing her own hair and now wore her long black hair pinned up to the top of her head. With it being spring, she wore light fabrics so she wouldn't get too hot as the day progressed. Viewing her reflection in the small looking glass in the room, Emily felt pleased with her ability to not only dress properly, but also do her hair.

Once Emily felt ready enough for the day, she collected her purse and her letter to Cynthia, then made her way out of her room, locking the door behind her. Emily thought she could get a bite to eat at The Eatery since it was the only restaurant in town. Perhaps she could even meet some of the local townsfolk and maybe even get a chance to talk to Nell about why she left her previous position back in Georgia. She also liked the idea of talking with someone from home.

Emily waved at Bill as he stood at the counter. He seemed to be reading a novel and she didn't want to disturb him. Once outside, she was greeted with the morning sun. Emily had to admit that Spruce Valley was a quaint town. It might not be as flashy as Atlanta, a whole lot more convenient, but there was a small town charm that had settled over the place. In the distance, Emily could hear the sound of a church bell, and she was able to see all the children racing towards it. Emily figured that the church must also act as a school building. Emily had always been privately tutored so the idea of attending school with others intrigued her.

Having nothing better to do, Emily walked through town and approached the church, curious to see the children attending their lessons from the day. As she approached the church, she could hear all sorts of happy chatter as the children assembled and got ready for their day. As Emily walked up the stairs of the church and peered in, the pews were filled with local children of all ages. And at the front stood a woman.

Emily was surprised as she looked all around the church. There wasn't a man present, and Emily had never heard of a female schoolteacher. Spruce Valley seemed to be full of many surprises where women obviously held different positions. Perhaps there were no educated men in Spruce Valley and that is why a woman had been selected for the position.

Seeming to be noticed, the woman at the front of the church shushed the children and gave them their morning math problems for them to figure out on their clay tablets before approaching Emily. She smiled kindly at the woman approaching her, hoping she wasn't interrupting the day's lesson.

"Good morning, Miss. Is there something I can help you with?" the teacher asked kindly.

"Forgive me if I'm interrupting. I've never seen a school like this and was simply interested," Emily explained. "My name is Emily Middleton. I just arrived yesterday."

"Ah, I see. Well, my name is Mrs. Jenny Crawford. I'm the schoolteacher," Jenny explained.

Emily could see that Jenny was far along in her pregnancy and asked, "When are you expecting your baby?"

Jenny chuckled as she ran her hands over her midsection. "It seems like any day now," Jenny explained as she looked down at herself. "I was hoping this little girl or guy would wait till this summer when school is out, but it doesn't seem that way."

"Do you have a teacher to replace you for when you'll be recovering with your baby?" Emily asked, curious to know how the school system worked in Spruce Valley.

Jenny shook her head with a sorrowful expression on it. "I'm guessing you're not from around here because you'd already know that I'm the only schoolteacher," Jenny explained.

"I'm from Atlanta, Georgia," Emily explained. "I was privately tutored so I never had the opportunity to attend lessons with others." Emily looked around the church and smiled to see all the eager students looking her way instead of on their mathematics.

"I see why this would interest you so," Jenny said. "Would you care to join us for the morning lesson?"

"Oh, I wouldn't want to impose," Emily said quickly, surprised by the woman's offer.

"You wouldn't be at all," Jenny reassured her. "It would be good to have another adult in the room to help me keep an eye on the more rebellious ones." Jenny then looked behind her, the students turning around quickly and focusing on their work once more as giggles swarmed across the room. Emily couldn't help but giggle with them.

"I need to mail a letter and grab something to eat first, but then I'll come back to observe for a bit," Emily agreed, thinking it might be fun to help out in a classroom setting.

"Sounds like a plan. I look forward to seeing you again after a bit, Miss Middleton," Jenny said before she turned and began to address the students. Emily stood for a moment and watched as Jenny flawlessly started to review the many math problems she'd distributed for the different ages. Emily was certainly impressed by her ability to teach so many ages at once and looked forward to seeing the students later. But first, she needed food in her stomach.

Emily descended the stairs of the church and made her way back over to the mercantile. There, she visited with Mr. Frost for a few minutes as she asked him to mail her letter. He seemed like he was a very sweet older man who enjoyed talking. Since Emily enjoyed a good bit of gossip, she imagined talking Mr. Frost's ear off when there weren't so many people in the shop. After being introduced to Mrs. Frost, she made her way around to The Eatery to order some sort of breakfast.

Emily waved at Nell as she sat down at a table. It didn't seem to be all that busy that morning, and Emily wondered if that was because not everyone was awake yet, or if she was simply the one seeming to be running behind. Either way, she was looking forward to getting something to eat and perhaps speaking with Nell privately.

"Good morning, Miss Middleton. How can I help you?" Nell asked as she came over to her table.

"What would you suggest, Nell? I'm not very familiar with the cuisine out here," Emily admitted. Nell smirked as she nodded, thinking the daughter of Mr. Middleton was far from home. She didn't understand why Emily was here, and she only hoped it wasn't to see her, in particular. After seeing Emily with the Sheriff, she suspected that Emily had come as a mail-order-bride. But since Nell knew how wealthy the Middleton's were, she couldn't ever see Emily in that position either.

"Scrambled eggs, bacon, and toast are what's most popular. Nothing like the poached eggs and fresh fruit of Georgia," Nell said with her hands on her hips. Emily knew without a shadow of a doubt now that Nell was the servant who used to work for her father. And as Emily looked around the café and saw only one other customer, she dared to ask the question that had been on her mind since last night.

"Nell, what on earth are you doing in Spruce Valley? Why did you ever leave?" Emily asked as she straightened her posture. She wasn't ashamed of her question at all and was dreadfully curious. Nell sighed as she settled into the chair across from Emily, folding her arms over her.

"Miss Middleton, do you really want to hear the truth?" Nell asked. "You won't like it."

"Nell, I don't ever plan to go back to Atlanta so it can't hurt anything now," Emily explained. She wasn't ready to tell Nell the real reason why she had left Atlanta and what had happened to her father's business. But it was easy to say that she never wanted to go back to Georgia. As she watched Nell closely, observing her every moment, she could tell that the woman was surprised.

"Is your father with you? Does he plan to come to Spruce Valley any time soon?" Nell asked as she narrowed her eyes at the young lady. The last thing she wanted was another confrontation with Mr. Middleton.

"No," Emily said as she turned her eyes away from Nell

for a moment. She let out a heavy sigh, wondering whatever would become of her father. He'd never been very affectionate, but she still wondered about him from time to time. Her response only made Nell more curious, but she decided not to press the issue until Emily felt comfortable enough to talk to her about it.

"In that case, I can tell you that the reason I left employment at your household was because your father was attracted to me," Nell explained slowly. "I didn't return his feelings in any way, so when I refused to be with him intimately, he fired me immediately without giving me any references." Emily looked up at Nell then, clearly shocked to hear this. "I couldn't stay in Atlanta after that, in fear of what type of reputation I then had. So I hopped on the train heading West and never looked back."

Emily was stunned by the explanation. She'd never heard from any of the other staff being pressured by her father, and though she could admit that Nell was a beautiful woman, she couldn't imagine her father sinking that low. But after all the shady business deals that her father had made, she shouldn't be overly surprised by his past behaviors.

"I'm so sorry to hear that, Nell," Emily eventually said. "You are the best tea maker I've ever known, and though I'm new to Spruce Valley, I can honestly say I'm pleased to see you again." Nell smiled slightly as she nodded. She was often complimented by her skills at making a good cup of tea.

"But why are *you* in Spruce Valley?" Nell then asked, leaning forward over the table so that Emily could feel comfortable speaking to her. Emily bit her lower lip, wondering how much she should tell Nell. After all, her former servant and come clean to her.

"I'm here as a mail-order-bride for the Sheriff. Let's just

say that my father ruined my reputation, too," Emily explained. Nell raised her eyebrows at hearing this, even more curious than before.

"Well, it's none of my business, but I hope you'll make Josh happy. He's the best of the best, and deserves as much," Nell said as she got up from the table. "I'll go make you a cup of tea and fix you a decent breakfast."

"Thank you," was all Emily said in parting, hopeful that Nell would order her something she'd like. She was eager to eat something so she could return to the church to observe the students. And the idea of being of some sort of use to Mrs. Crawford intrigued her.

Emily couldn't help but think of her father as she enjoyed her breakfast. Egg whites had been separated from the yoke to create a light and fluffy scrambled egg, paired with a few sausage rolls. It was a light breakfast that Emily was used to and appreciated Nell's consideration. After all, she knew so few people in town thus far and could always use a friend. Emily thought how strange her life had turned after learning that her father was now penniless and that she would soon have a tarnished reputation. Even though she'd just arrived in Spruce Valley, she thought of traveling all the way here as something unimaginable. Yet, she'd done it, and survived the aftermath of her father's failing business.

After breakfast, Emily made sure to give Nell a decent sized tip. The tea had been as excellent as ever, and though Emily did not have a large fortune, she felt that Nell deserved to be recognized for her continuous service to her. As they said parting words, Emily left The Eatery and made her way through town and back to the church.

By the time she arrived, the children had been released for a short break from their morning studies. Emily came to stand next to Jenny in the school yard as children raced around, playing tag or hopscotch. It filled Emily with joy to see so many little ones happy. Emily hadn't had much time for playing growing up since her father had made her education a vital part of her upbringing. She'd been groomed since birth to be married off to a wealthy man to continue the Middleton traditions. Now, she felt at a loss of what her fate would actually be.

"So, what brings you to Spruce Valley, Miss Middleton?" Jenny asked after a bit. They'd watched the children play together, but Jenny was very curious about this newcomer.

"I answered Sheriff Ryder's mail-order-bride ad," Emily explained with a kind smile. "I've come to see if we'll make a good match." Jenny looked at her then, surprised by the news.

"I didn't know that the good Sheriff had placed an ad," Jenny remarked. "Well, I'm certainly glad you are here. I always thought that Josh deserved to meet a nice young lady and settle down." Emily chuckled, feeling like that was everyone's opinion of Josh. She was at least glad to hear that he was so well liked.

"Well, we shall see how things go," Emily said.

"And what type of employment are you looking for now that you are here?" Jenny asked. Emily was as surprised by her words as she had been when Josh had asked her the same thing last night. Emily refrained from replying right away, realizing that women worked all sorts of different positions in Spruce Valley. Were all the women expected to work?

"I haven't given it much consideration to be honest. It's a new idea for me," Emily explained, feeling a bit embarrassed.

"That is understandable. After all, you only arrived yesterday," Jenny said, sensing Emily's unease. By the fine fabrics that Emily's light green gown was made from, Jenny assumed that Emily was from a very wealthy family. The idea of working must be foreign to her.

"I am surprised to see so many women in important positions. I was surprised to see Nell as a waiter when I've only seen men in that position, and all my tutors were also men," Emily explained. Jenny chuckled as she rubbed her pregnant belly.

"Then you'll be further surprised to hear that Spruce Valley's mayor is also a woman," Jenny said. She was correct, because Emily was instantly shocked upon hearing this.

"How on earth was a woman elected to such an important position?" Emily asked, very curious to learn this. If a woman could be mayor, then perhaps she could one day also hold a very important position in town.

"Well, her late husband was the last mayor, and when he passed away, Delphina Stavros simply took up his spot," Jenny explained. "She does a fine job and even convinced the telegram company to run lines all the way out here to Spruce Valley. She has a daughter she looks after as well as a few grandchildren, but she does her best to honor her husband's memory." Emily took a few moments to think about Jenny's words, thinking how honorable that was of Mrs. Stavros.

"And none of the men have said anything about the woman mayor?" Emily asked, curious to learn how long Mrs. Stavros had been in the position.

"I'm sure a few have tried, but Mrs. Stavros is a force to be reckoned with. Here I am, a married woman and pregnant, but yet I'm still teaching. She's been mayor for almost a decade now and I don't think any man would dare try to get in her way, and she makes sure that us women aren't bothered by men and their sore opinions," Jenny said with a chuckle. Emily was very curious about the woman and looked forward to meeting her.

Soon after, Jenny called all the children back into the church. Emily joined them and assisted Jenny in instructing the students on their words for the day. Emily particularly liked helping the younger children write their letters and words, encouraging them to sound out each letter in order to read. She enjoyed seeing their smiling faces. Jenny was impressed by the way Emily was interacting with the children and how easily she taught them. An idea came into her mind then and she wondered when she could speak to Emily about it in the near future.

After a while, Emily said goodbye to Jenny and the students. She wanted to visit the women's seamstress shop, and since it might take a while to be properly fitted and for the gowns to be designed, Emily knew that it was better to head over now before the day got away from her. After all, she told Josh that she'd come to visit him as well and wanted to leave room in her day for that. The children said happy goodbyes. Emily promised to come visit again soon as she left the church and walked down the road to the other side of town, till she reached the women's seamstress shop.

As Emily entered, she was pleasantly surprised by the elegant design of the shop. It was clearly decorated for women and reminded her of several other shops back in Atlanta. It was nice to see something familiar, and as she approached a short rack of pre-made gowns, she realized that not only had they been designed smartly, but they were much like the gowns she'd worn back in Georgia.

"Hello," came a woman's voice, drawing Emily's attention to the front counter. "Can I help you with something?" Emily smiled as she approached the woman with auburn hair.

"I've come in to have some gowns designed. I was

hoping for a fitting, then a consultation," Emily explained. The woman smiled kindly at her as she began to observe Emily closely, no doubt sizing her up in her mind already.

"I'd be happy to assist you. My name is Fiona Murtaugh, and I fix and repair garments," the woman explained. "But Mrs. Slater, the owner and seamstress, has taught me how to take measurements. I can do that for you and send them to her since she's on bed rest."

"My name is Emily Middleton. Since the seamstress isn't well, is she currently not taking any orders?" Emily asked, feeling a little deflated at the thought.

Fiona smiled at her as she said, "Well, Lucy is supposed to be resting but that woman can't sit still to save her life. Though she's agreed to stay in bed, she's still making gowns at home with her business partner, Martha Jenkins."

"How nice that all three of you are working together to manage this shop," Emily admitted. "Coming all the way from Georgia, it's nice to see something a little familiar."

Fiona nodded, knowing just how Emily felt. "I'm originally from Boston myself," Fiona said. "I came out here last year as a mail-order-bride and was so impressed by everything that Lucy and Martha have been able to accomplish on their own." Hearing Fiona's words, she was instantly curious about the woman. She remembered how Josh had explained there were other mail-order-brides, but as she observed Fiona closely, she could tell that this young lady was also a socialite.

"The one thing that Spruce Valley has shown me is that women really can do anything. Just now I learned that the mayor is a woman," Emily said. Fiona giggled, covering her mouth with the back of her hand. It was a clear sign that Fiona was from a wealthy family and she was dying to know why she'd come out to the West. Had her family also become penniless? But by the fine fabrics of her dress,

Emily would have guessed that Fiona was still wealthy. Perhaps she'd married a wealthy gentleman as well…?

"Yes, Spruce Valley has lots of surprises," Fiona admitted. "I think that's because the people here are so interesting and hardworking. This might sound funny, but I didn't feel alive until I started working for Lucy and Martha. I might have been raised with every luxury, but my true purpose wasn't discovered until I came here." Emily was startled by her words, trying to imagine ever finding pleasure from working. She dreaded the idea of hard labor and tried to see Fiona's perspective on life. She could only guess that her previous life had been so dreadful that she enjoyed working now that she was in Spruce Valley.

"I'll have to take your word on that, Fiona," Emily said, wanting to turn her attention over to the gowns she wanted to have ordered. She wanted something nice for her day gown, and a few evening gowns for when she would go on dates with Josh or attending other important social gatherings.

"Well, that's enough about me. How about we get you measured, and you can tell me about the gown you'd like to have designed," Fiona said, sensing Emily's restlessness. Emily smiled kindly and nodded as she followed Fiona back to the fitting room.

"I was hoping to have a few gowns made," Emily explained. "I want something nicer for the day and evening."

"Well, there are all types of different fabrics to choose from," Fiona explained as she went about measuring Emily's body with a tape measure. She wrote clearly on a piece of paper, planning to bring it to Lucy that evening on her way home from town. "You'll no doubt want something breathable for everyday wear since the weather is warming up."

"That would be ideal. I just want to make sure it's good quality as well," Emily explained.

"Are these gowns more for show or work?" Fiona asked as she moved around Emily, moving her arms out to the side so she could measure her waist and bust.

"I would say show. I don't work," Emily said pointedly. Fiona suspected that Emily must be new in town. Though she had met most of the townspeople after having moved to Spruce Valley to marry her husband, Eddie, and started working in town, she figured that perhaps Emily had come to visit with some of her family that Fiona had simply not met yet.

"Will you be staying in Spruce Valley for long? I want to let Lucy know how soon she needs to have the gowns made," Fiona said.

"Spruce Valley is my new home," Emily explained. "I've come to be a mail-order-bride for Sheriff Ryder." Fiona almost dropped the measuring tape after hearing this.

"My goodness, how fascinating! I had no idea that the Sheriff had placed an ad," Fiona admitted. "He's one of the kindness men I know. If it wasn't for the Sheriff, I wouldn't be here right now." Fiona then took the time to explain her story and how she'd come to live in Spruce Valley after being kidnapped by train robbers and then rescued by the Sheriff, Eddie, and their close friends.

"Oh, Fiona, I'm so sorry to hear that. It must have been absolutely terrifying," Emily said as she looked Fiona directly in the eyes. She wanted the woman to know she was speaking very genuinely. Emily could also admit that her travels to Spruce Valley were mild compared to what Fiona had to go through to get here.

"Well, that's all behind us now. I don't often think of it because I'm so happy with Eddie," Fiona said with a grand smile. Emily could tell she was speaking the truth and hoped that one day she could also feel that type of happiness.

Emily and Fiona spent almost two hours together as they

went over gown designs and fabric. Emily was enjoying her time with the other mail-order-bride, learning more about her time here in Spruce Valley, but also realizing that the woman had good taste. Emily could easily see herself becoming good friends with Fiona, the woman often reminding her of her own dearest friend, Cynthia.

After their business had come to an end, Fiona took the time to write up the final bill. It was the most expensive bill Fiona had ever written up and figured that Emily also came from a wealthy family. Though she didn't think the gowns would be fitting for life in Spruce Valley, she wasn't going to argue with the woman who was going to pay for the gowns.

"Here you are," Fiona said as she handed the bill to Emily. Emily nodded as she reviewed it.

"Everything looks in order. Have the bill sent over to the Sheriff for processing," Emily said as she handed it back to Fiona. Fiona was startled to hear this, thinking this large bill wouldn't be something Josh could handle. Only a very successful businessman would be able to take care of this. But not wanting to cause trouble, Fiona only nodded. But after Emily left the shop, Fiona couldn't help but have a bad feeling about this situation. Fiona could tell that Emily was a very nice girl, but she didn't want the Sheriff to be taken advantage of.

Fiona gathered her things and left the shop, locking the door behind her. She then quickly made her way to the Sheriff's Office, needing to explain to Josh what had just happened before she would be willing to take the designs to Lucy.

# CHAPTER 8

Josh was seething with anger after speaking with Fiona. He'd done his best not to show his emotions as Fiona came to him and explained how Emily had ordered an expensive bill of gowns and had told Fiona to bring him the bill. He'd taken the bill from Fiona, saying that he'd have to discuss things with Emily before approving the order. Fiona had smiled uneasily at him after agreeing and quickly left him alone since she needed to get back to the shop. And the moment Fiona had left, Josh had tightened his fists so tightly that he tore the piece of paper that detailed everything Emily had tried to order and then leave him with the cost.

Josh did his best to get his anger under control as he thought about how to best handle this situation. He wasn't sure if Emily was trying to test him, but he certainly wasn't going to give in and just waste his savings so that Emily could have some new clothes. He'd need to talk to Emily about this matter right away and hopefully do it in a way that she'd understand that he was never going to tolerate this type of behavior.

As Josh left the Sheriff's Office, he went to look for Emily. He went straightaway to the inn, thinking she'd be there and perhaps resting. But as he started walking in that direction, he saw her in the distance, standing on the edge of town and looking out into the large expanse of land that stretched on for as long as the eye could see. He quickly walked over to her but didn't say anything right away as she leaned against a tree and simply stared off into the distance.

Even though Josh was angry at her, he couldn't deny how beautiful she was. She was wearing a fitting gown that showed off the best parts of her curvy figure. It was her beauty that had instantly intrigued Josh, but he hoped that he hadn't been wrong about her good character.

"Emily," Josh said, pulling the woman out of her daydream. She turned to him quickly, surprised to see him when she'd just been thinking about him. She had been curious about what Spruce Valley looked like outside of town and she'd become preoccupied by taking it all in. She couldn't believe how far and wide the land stretched with not a single building or home dotting the landscape. She was thinking how glad she was to be in town and not stuck in the middle of nowhere.

"Josh, it's so good to see you," Emily said as she settled her nerves and smiled at the Sheriff. "I was so captivated by the beautiful scenery that I lost myself in thought." Josh nodded, understanding because he often enjoyed taking long rides out of town on his mare to simply take in the beauty of Spruce Valley this time of year.

"It sure is lovely out here," Josh agreed. Then taking a deep breath, he withdrew the crumbled-up piece of paper in his pocket and handed it to Emily. "Fiona brought this over to me. To say I was surprised is an understatement."

Emily took the piece of paper and looked down at it to see that it was the bill from the women's seamstress shop. Her brows furrowed as she looked back up at Josh, trying to understand his surprise and why he'd crumbled up the paper.

"Is there some sort of problem?" Emily asked. Josh was very concerned by her words as he tried to think of the best way to explain things to her. He figured that being blunt would be the best thing in this situation.

"Emily, I can't afford to purchase all of these gowns for you. Perhaps one, when it comes time to marry," Josh explained. "If you want new gowns, you'll have to pay for them yourself or have your father send you some money." He didn't like talking to Emily like this, but she needed to have a solid idea of his character. Emily was even more perplexed by his words as she fought to keep her temper at bay.

"Josh, I can't just ask my father for money…" Emily said, knowing that the time had come to tell Josh the whole truth. "The reason I replied to your ad is because my father lost everything in bad business deals. The day I left Atlanta for here, I ran away from an empty home that had been torn down to just a shell. My father was nowhere to be seen."

Josh certainly wasn't expecting this from Emily. He had his suspicions about why she wanted to marry him, or why she had been so eager to come straight away to Spruce Valley, and now the big picture was becoming clear to him. He ran his fingers through his hair, realizing just how much trouble Emily was going to be for him.

"I'm sorry to hear about your father, Emily," Josh said, trying to be sympathetic. "It must have been hard on you, and it explains why you were so eager to come here." Emily nodded, doing her best to keep her tears at bay.

"I didn't mean to be so deceiving, Josh, but I didn't want to tell you some sob story just to convince you to marry me.

I honestly want to see if we'll do well together first," Emily said.

"And if we don't? What will you do then?" Josh asked, his temper starting to rise again. He wasn't keen on the idea that Emily hadn't told him the entire truth.

"I have a small fortune that I brought with me. I don't have a solid plan, but I really am hoping that things will work out between us," Emily said, straightening her posture. "I figured your salary as a sheriff will be suitable for the both of us." Josh shouldn't have, but he couldn't help but laugh at her idea of their married life. He shook his head, trying to figure out what Emily's end goal was with marrying him.

"Emily, I hate to break this to you, but if you want things like new gowns, you'll have to find employment and pay for them yourself," Josh said point blank. "As I'm sure you can tell, women need to make their own way here in Spruce Valley. I'm not some rich man who can sustain your previous way of life."

Emily was trying to keep her composure as she listened to everything Josh was telling her. She couldn't believe what she was hearing. She'd placed so much of her future on marrying the Sheriff and not having to worry about working. But if he couldn't take care of a simple gown order, something her father had no issue paying in the past, then perhaps the Sheriff was as poor as her father was now.

"I've never considered working before, ever in my life," Emily said, tears coming to her eyes. "I honestly dread the idea."

"Well, I understand how this may all seem different to you, Emily. But if things are going to work out between us, then I need to be able to respect my wife. And I can't do that if you're not willing to find some sort of employment to help support our family," Josh said. A part of him felt terrible for being so straightforward with Emily, but the other side of him thought that this type of explanation was exactly what Emily needed if she was going to survive on her own. In her current condition, Josh wasn't sure if they had a future together if she was going to rely on him for everything.

Crumbling the gown order into her hands, she threw it at Josh's feet and quickly walked around him. She hurried back to the inn, tears streaming down her cheeks. She felt embarrassed for having come all this way to be his wife and even more livid at Josh for the way he'd spoken to her. She wasn't some child that needed scolding. How dare he speak to her as such?

Emily was thankful that no one saw her as she entered the inn. And even more grateful that Bill wasn't at the counter. She took the stairs two at a time till she reached the second floor and could disappear into her room. She was breathing heavily from all the fast movement that her chest heaved up and down as she tried to catch her breath. She flopped down upon the bed as she pulled a pillow close to her and buried her face in it, letting out all of her frustration.

Emily cried for what seemed like hours. She was alone, afraid, and completely helpless. She'd placed so much hope and trust in Josh that she couldn't imagine what she was going to do now. She certainly couldn't ever work, even though she saw how many women in the community held important jobs. She'd never been raised to work, only to marry a wealthy man so she'd never have to worry about money. But as she thought about the small fortune she had with her, she knew that it wouldn't be able to sustain her for the rest of her life.

Eventually, Emily was able to calm down. She thought of Josh, thinking how handsome and kind he'd been to her thus far. Though he wasn't willing to sustain her in their marriage, he still had a lot of good qualities. Though she was still furious with him, she couldn't deny her attraction to him. As she drifted off to sleep, she was at battle with her emotions as she thought about how ridiculous the idea of working was.

~

JOSH CERTAINLY FELT terrible as he watched Emily storm off. He wanted to go after her but didn't know what he could say to her at this moment. She needed to understand how important it was that she worked, but it was clear to him that she didn't like the idea at all. Josh picked up the crumpled piece of paper she'd thrown at his feet and put it in his pocket. He hated the idea of breaking her heart or making her feel more miserable than she must already be. Now that he understood why Emily had agreed to come to Spruce Valley and why she was so eager to do so, he tried to think just how upset she had to have been to leave behind everything that was familiar to her to go somewhere completely new with the knowledge she could never return to her home.

Josh sighed heavily as he turned and made his way to the livery stables. He wanted to have a long talk with his best friend but knew that the doctor had already left the clinic for the day. Not wanting to try to talk to Emily right now, Josh collected his mare from the stables before heading out of town and to the Slater Ranch.

Josh always enjoyed the long ride out to the ranch. The road cut through the landscape, skirting around a dense forest before opening up to the never-ending expansion of land. Needing to release his own frustrations over Emily's unrealistic views of their marriage together, he set his mare off at a fast gallop, feeling the wind whipping by his face as the roar of it sounded in his ears. He loved the thrill of riding at such high speeds, sometimes reminding him of previous chases he gave when catching criminals that were trying to get away.

As he approached the ranch, Josh pulled on the reins to slow down his mare. She trotted down the lane to the ranch house, happy to have been able to get a good exercise for the day. Normally Josh took his mare out to do some patrolling around town, but it had been a while since they'd last moved at those speeds. It was exactly what they both needed as Josh pulled the mare to a stop before the house and dismounted, tying the reins to the front hitching post before heading inside.

The Slater household was in complete uproar, as normal. Everyone was sitting down at the dining table, or at least trying to as fathers chased their little ones around in order to get them settled at the table. Josh just shook his head as he took off his Stetson and hung it by the door. Ever since Lucy had arrived at the ranch, she'd insisted on cooking every meal for the ranch hands. And now that two of the ranch hands had married, their numbers had increased, making every meal almost a comical act.

"Good to see ye, Sheriff," came Lucy's voice at the head of the table. Since she'd been on bed rest, she'd been taking it easy. Though she enjoyed cooking, she turned that task over to Gray and his wife Martha. Gray had experience cooking for the ranch hands and often filled in for Lucy, even though he was the foreman and put in long hours at the ranch. But as Josh heard him whistling in the kitchen, Josh knew that the man didn't mind one bit.

"Hello there, Lucy. Care for one more?" Josh said with a chuckle.

"Ah, ye always know yer welcome here anytime," Lucy said with a smile. "And ye can tell me what's been happening in town." Josh stilled then as he thought about Emily. Lucy could see that something was bothering the

Sheriff. And even in all the commotion of the evening meal, Lucy put her focus on her friend.

"Well, me and Emily have come to a crossroads. She gave me some insight today on what she had been expecting by coming out here and getting married to me," Josh said. As everyone came around the table to get ready for dinner, they listened to Josh's story with much concern.

"I can see her point of view, Josh. Remember, I was a debutante meself," Lucy said as she looked towards her husband. He sat beside her on the bench with their daughter on his lap. She'd recently turned two and with that came all the sass in the world. Lucy only imagined what trouble her mother had had with her and her many brothers.

"But surely you didn't come to Spruce Valley thinking that Sam was going to pay your way, even if he is a doctor," Josh retorted as he gestured towards Sam. He simply smiled as he bounced Francene on his knee. She giggled happily as she tried to hang on and eat her food at the same time. Lucy scowled at the two of them, which only seemed to egg Sam on.

"No, ye are right, Josh. I didn't expect Sam to pay me way. I was willing to learn how to cook, clean, and do all sorts of housework in order to support Sam as a doctor," Lucy explained. "It wasn't until Martha suggested it that I started the seamstress shop."

"And now the seamstress shop is able to support two other employees," Martha added as she held her son, Samuel, on her lap. Where Francene had grown up into a daring Irish girl, Samuel was often shy and reserved. She guessed that Gray had been the same way as a child.

"I'm sure Emily only did what she has done a hundred times before," Fiona piped in. "I was surprised, since that sort of thing isn't common around here to order so many gowns at once, but I'm sure Lucy and I have made similar purchases in our youth with the intention of our fathers paying for the bill." Josh sighed, appreciating the women's input. However, it only added to his guilt of the way he'd spoken to Emily. He didn't regret speaking honestly with her, but wondered if he could have said things in a better way.

"Seems to me that the ladies should get together and do a little schooling with Miss Middleton," Gray spoke up further down the table. He was a little busy focusing on eating his food so he could spend the evening with his family as soon as possible, but he felt for Josh. Since Gray was so much older than everyone else, he never thought he'd ever marry. Meeting Martha seemed to be like a dream come true, but it took time to work through her past in order for them to have any future together. And he'd been real hurt when he discovered that Martha had been lying to him during most of their courtship. But in the end, their love for each other had won the battle.

"Hey, that isn't a bad idea," Martha said as she winked at her husband. "Why don't we invite Emily out here to the ranch for a little welcoming party. She'll really get to see what it's like to live in the West when she comes to the ranch." Laughter rang out then as they all knew that it was true.

"I really do like Emily," Fiona said. "And since she was a debutante in Atlanta, she'll enjoy the time to attend a party."

"You always see the best in everyone," Eddie said as he leaned over and kissed his wife on the temple. Fiona giggled and blushed, still getting used to her husband's open way of showing affection to her.

"That is because I know what ugly people look like on the inside," Fiona retorted.

"Then it's settled," Sam spoke up. "We'll have a

welcoming party here at the ranch and hopefully help Emily to see what it's like to live in the West."

"And encourage her," Lucy added. "I think she just needs to see her own potential." Josh nodded, thinking that could be the key to the whole situation. Then a smile came to his lips as he thought of something fun they could all do.

"And we should play cards as well," Josh added. "She's been known to play poker." Laughter rang out again. Sawyer, Eddie's brother, shook his head at the idea.

"I'd be willing to see how good she plays," Sawyer spoke up.

"As would I," Eddie agreed with his brother.

"Well, when I go in to open the shop tomorrow, I'll pay Emily a visit and invite her to the party," Fiona said.

"And perhaps we can invite some other women as well," Martha suggested. "Emily needs to see that women can achieve anything they put their minds to. Mayor Stavros would be a welcome addition."

"That's a good idea, Martha," Gray said, always willing to encourage his wife. After all she'd been through, he always wanted to show her that he supported her. They shared a special smile as they looked deeply into each other's eyes.

When the dinner came to an end, Josh stayed and visited with everyone while the dishes were cleaned. Eventually, Gray and Martha left to their own home not too far away from the ranch, along with Eddie and Fiona who had started building their own home. Most of it was done, but the young couple was taking their time with it. Josh was left with the Slaters. And after Sam helped his wife and daughter to bed, he joined Josh in the sitting room.

"How are you feeling about all of this, Josh?" Sam asked as they settled into the chairs by the fire. It hadn't been lit tonight since the weather was warming up, but instead several lanterns hung around the room as the sun set.

"I'm not sure, Sam," Josh admitted with a long sigh. "I mean, I really am attracted to Emily." Sam chuckled as he nodded.

"Yes, I saw her this morning in passing and noticed that she could easily turn heads," Sam admitted. "But you shouldn't propose just because she's pretty."

"Yeah, Sam, I get that," Josh said, discouraged. "Her letter was just so interesting that I thought for sure she would be the fierce, independent woman I've always been looking for."

"And I'm sure she is, Josh. I mean, she left her home behind to travel here on her own," Sam said. "You do have to give the girl some credit where credit is due." Josh nodded, knowing his friend was right.

"I was just so shocked when Fiona came to me today and gave me that bill. It just drove me nuts," Josh said. "And Bill had mentioned to me after I got Emily settled at the inn that she looked like those type of women that only want a wealthy husband."

"See, now I understand what you've been worried about," Sam said as he pointed at Josh. "You let Bill get in your head." Josh shrugged his shoulders, uncertain if Sam was actually speaking the truth.

"I don't know, Sam. I get this feeling that she thinks working is beneath her and that her husband should do everything for her," Josh said honestly.

"And that's probably all she's ever known or expected out of marriage," Sam reasoned. "You'll just have to show her that there's more to life than just money, and that marriage should be founded on love, not some sort of business deal." Josh nodded, knowing that Sam always gave the best advice.

"Well," Josh said as he stood to his feet. "I just hope that this party will do Emily some good. I'd hate to see her so discouraged ever again." Sam stood as well and shook hands with Josh before he left. As Sam watched his best friend leave the ranch house, he said a silent prayer that things would work out between the two.

# CHAPTER 9

By the time the next morning came, Emily was feeling all sorts of awful. She hadn't eaten anything since yesterday morning and had been too beside herself with worry to even venture out to get something to eat at The Eatery again. Now, her stomach hurt and she knew she needed to eat something as soon as possible to keep up her strength.

Knowing that no one was going to come to her aid, Emily eventually got out of bed and put on a simple gown. Then, she took the time to braid her hair simply so she didn't need to fuss with it. She figured she could change after she got something in her stomach. She wished she could simply ring a bell and summon a breakfast tray to be brought to her and a bath to be drawn. A quick glance into the looking glass showed that she could really use a good wash of her face, since she looked a bit puffy from crying so much.

Taking a deep breath, Emily made her way from the room and down the stairs. At the counter was the always present Bill, and when he looked up from his book and saw her current state, his brows furrowed together in concern.

"Are you feeling alright, Miss Middleton?" Bill asked as he set his book down on the counter. Bill noted how she appeared to have been recently upset and wondered if things hadn't gone as planned with the Sheriff.

"Yes, just waited too long to eat something," Emily admitted. "I'm going straightaway to The Eatery now to order something."

"Well, would you like me to go over there for you?" Bill offered. "Perhaps you should rest for a bit." Emily thought about his offer for a moment and decided she would accept his help.

Pulling a few notes from her purse, she handed them to Bill and said, "Thank you so much. Just order whatever Nell suggests. She always has great recommendations."

"Sure, I'll do that for you and bring it on up as soon as it's ready," Bill said as he took the money and pocketed it. He then placed his 'away' sign on the counter before rounding it and heading out.

Emily took her time returning to her room, happy to have accepted Bill's assistance. She left the door unlocked as she entered her room and took a seat at one of the nice wing-backed chairs. Emily could see out the window to the main street below as she watched all sorts of people walking up and down the road. She sighed heavily, her thoughts returning to everything she'd said to Josh, and what he'd said in return.

*How could I have been so wrong about the Sheriff?* Emily asked herself as she stared almost absentmindedly out the window. She wasn't really focused on who was walking by the inn as much as she wanted to understand how her plan had gone so wrong. Emily had always been perfect at planning and seeing her well thought-out ideas come true. She thought that the Sheriff probably thought she was quite naive and even stupid about what their marriage would look like. And the more she ran their previous conversation through her mind, the more she realized that it was nonetheless true.

When a knock on the door came, Emily called to the person to enter since she assumed that it was Bill returned with some sort of food for her. But as she turned her head and saw that Fiona had just stepped into her room, she was clearly surprised. She instantly felt embarrassed, thinking the woman had come to tell her that she needed to come straightaway to pay for the dresses or have her order canceled. But the closer Emily observed her, the more she thought that she didn't look upset, but perhaps cheerful instead.

"I'm sorry if I'm disturbing you, Miss Middleton," Fiona said, a bit nervous once she realized that Emily looked unwell. Fiona could see the way her cheeks and eyes were puffy, and if she had to guess, she'd say that Emily had been crying.

"No, you're not disturbing me at all. Please, have a seat," Emily said as she motioned to the chair across from her. "You'll have to excuse me though because Bill was kind enough to grab me a bite to eat from The Eatery. It seems I look as bad as I feel." Emily tried to smile, but had a hard time doing so.

"Are you not feeling well?" Fiona asked, wondering if she should go get Dr. Slater.

"Yes, I am well, thank you," Emily reassured her. "I just didn't get much sleep last night and I skipped dinner."

"Oh goodness, you must just feel terrible," Fiona said. She also had the knowledge that she and Josh had shared some unpleasant words but wasn't about to tell Emily that

Josh had talked about it with other people. That would probably only make her feel worse.

"Nothing a good meal can't fix," Emily replied.

"Well, I won't keep you long. I simply wanted to come by and personally invite you to a party," Fiona said with a bright smile. The idea of attending a party piqued Emily's interest as she raised an eyebrow at the woman.

"A party? Well, that certainly sounds like a pleasant affair," Emily said.

"Yes, well, when I told the other mail-order-brides of your arrival, they wanted to throw you a welcoming party. So, we want to know if you'll join us tomorrow afternoon at the ranch?" Fiona explained. At first, Emily wanted to agree right away, but then realized that the location didn't sound like it was in town.

"I'd be happy to attend, and I feel honored to have a party thrown for me. But I'm afraid that I'm not sure how I'd get to this ranch," Emily explained. Fiona only smiled brightly as an idea came to mind.

"Well, we've invited quite a few people from town to also attend. I'm sure one of them would like to give you a ride in their wagon," Fiona said, knowing exactly who she was going to ask to do the errand.

"In that case, I have no reason to refuse," Emily said with a genuine smile.

"Fantastic. I'll let the women know you'll be coming tomorrow afternoon," Fiona said as she rose from the chair. "You'll have to excuse me. I must get the shop opened and let everyone know."

"Alright then. Thank you again, Fiona," Emily said as Fiona neared the door.

"Trust me. It's my pleasure," Fiona said with a bright smile before leaving the room. Emily couldn't help but chuckle as Fiona left. She was so enthusiastic that it was almost contagious.

The next time a knock came on the door, Emily was pleased to see Bill coming into her room with a few plates of food on a large wooden serving tray. Emily's eyes grew wide as she saw everything on the tray. Bill had certainly gone out of his way to make sure she was taken care of.

"My goodness, Mr. Eckert. You've certainly outdone yourself," Emily said as she sat forward. Bill began to place the many plates on a nearby table and the aroma started to make Emily's stomach growl with hunger.

"I'm glad you think so," Bill said as he withdrew Emily's change and handed it to her.

"Keep it. I think you deserve it for an outstanding job well done," Emily said with a smile. Bill only nodded as he pocketed the change, pleased to hear Emily's positive words.

"Well, if there is anything else I can help you with, just let me know," Bill said as he neared the door. "When you're done, I can help you take the dishes back over."

"I'll be sure to let you know," Emily said before Bill left the room. Once the door was closed, Emily threw ladylike tendencies out the window. She ate with gusto and enjoyed a little of everything that Bill had brought her. By the time she had finished, not only was most of the food eaten, but she felt rather stuffed to the gills.

With a heavy sigh, Emily set about cleaning up the room and even taking the time to wash her face and hair with the basin of water that resided in the small washroom attached to her room. It was nothing like the indoor plumbing that Emily was used to growing up, but she was starting to realize that it was important for her to count her blessings instead of comparing everything to what she was used to back in Atlanta.

After she'd cleaned up and changed into a gown that was

more fitting her stature, she collected all the plates, and when she found the wooden tray in the hallway, she used it to pile up all the plates and take them down the stairs.

"Wow, you really look like you know what you're doing," Bill said as he watched Miss Middleton come down the stairs with the tray balanced perfectly in her hand while the other held up the hem of her dress so she could walk with ease.

"Must have been those years of etiquette training my father put me through," Emily said with a smile as she set the tray down on the counter. "I could probably still walk around with a pile of books balanced on my head." Bill whistled in response as he imagined Miss Middleton doing such a thing.

"Looks like you can also pack it away when you want to," Bill said as he gestured towards all the empty plates. He couldn't fathom how a young lady as slim as Miss Middleton could eat so much.

Emily chuckled as she raised her hand to cover her mouth. "That's what I get for going too long without eating," Emily said. "I'll be more mindful in the future."

"Yes, you do need to take care of yourself," came the Sheriff's voice as he walked into the inn. Emily and Bill immediately went silent as they turned to face Josh as he came towards them. Emily's eyes narrowed at the Sheriff and Bill took that as his cue to give the young couple some privacy. He picked up the tray then and walked out of the inn, intent on returning the plates and giving the two plenty of time to talk.

"Can I help you Sheriff?" Emily asked, not overly keen on the idea of entertaining him at the moment. She was still upset with him and fancied herself a light nap.

"Seems like I can help you, Miss Middleton," Josh said as he came to stop in front of Emily. She looked beautiful in her afternoon gown, and Josh had to remind himself to focus on more than just her good looks. "Fiona told me you need a ride out to the Slater Ranch for the party." Emily inwardly sighed as she thought how Fiona must have asked Josh on purpose.

"Yes, I would appreciate a ride out to the ranch. I think what the women are willing to do for me is very kind and I should have no reason to refuse attending a party," Emily said as she straightened her posture.

"Good. I think you'll enjoy seeing a real ranch and spending time with other people," Josh said with a smirk. His lopsided grin did something to Emily that she couldn't deny. She might be angry at him, but she would never be able to lie about her attraction to him.

"I would agree as well," Emily replied. She then turned away from him, thinking their conversation was done. But Josh quickly caught her hand, pulling Emily to a stop. She was surprised by his bold gesture and she didn't know whether to be angry or flattered.

"I never meant to upset you so much, Emily," Josh said in a soft voice. She stared up into his honey colored eyes, seeming to be lost in them. Her previous thoughts of anger drifted away as she was caught in the moment.

"I understand it wasn't intended," Emily eventually managed to say. He dropped her hand then, needing to get back at the office. He wanted to help the other women in planning this party and didn't want to waste any time since it was planned for the following day.

"Well then, I'll see you tomorrow," Josh said in parting. He tipped his hat to her and finally turned away. Walking out of the inn wasn't a pleasant experience for Josh because he wanted to take the time to discover the real Emily, but figured that only time would tell.

Emily watched Josh walk out of the inn, curious about

his motives. She certainly didn't seem to be his ideal wife with her certain ideals of what their marriage would be like, but he seemed to still be making an effort to impress her. Did he expect her to change her way of thinking? Could she really become a working woman and a wife, plus a mother one day? The thoughts alone seemed to exhaust her further as Emily finally made her way back up the stairs and to her room. There, she settled onto the bed with the intent of taking a nap. But the harder she tried to sleep, the more she thought about the handsome sheriff.

# CHAPTER 10

Josh was looking forward to picking Emily up at the inn that day. After spending so much time the day before helping the Slaters and the others plan for this get-together, he was really looking forward to it himself. That morning he'd dressed in his finest suit, the type he only wore for official business. His goal was to impress Emily and show her that he could still be a gentleman, even if he wasn't very wealthy. And so, Josh made his way over to the inn with the wagon he'd borrowed from the Slaters, because he didn't think Emily would be keen on the idea of riding double on his mare.

After he pulled the wagon to a stop in front of the inn, Josh took a deep breath. He really hoped that Emily would enjoy herself today, but also see what living in the West was all about. He hoped that Emily would see from the other women what it took to be successful in this town, and not just the work they did. Emily would have to learn to cook and clean for herself, along with all the other chores that must be completed by hand. If anything, Josh hoped that

Emily would see how satisfying it was to do things for yourself and gain that feeling of self-accomplishment. Perhaps she'd never felt like that before and would soon see that spark of life in the other women today.

Josh entered the inn, thinking about the way he'd reached out and touched Emily the day before. It had been his gut instinct that propelled him to take that action. He'd come to the inn the day before after talking to Fiona, but a part of him really wanted Emily to know that he hadn't given up on her, even if they'd had a disagreement. He knew he'd been a little rough with Emily when it came to his word choice, and now he'd hoped to *show* Emily what he meant, more than just tell her.

Josh dipped his head to Bill at the counter, who sitting and reading a novel. Bill didn't seem to pay him any attention as Josh took the stairs to the rooms upstairs. When he reached Emily's door, he quickly knocked and waited for her to answer. When the door opened, Josh's mouth fell open. Emily had done her hair up, her black hair framing her face in ringlets. She wore a simple gown, one that he'd figured would be used for working that day. It wasn't at all fancy, but she still was as beautiful as ever.

"I picked it up from Frost's yesterday evening when I stopped by for dinner," Emily said as she watched Josh's eyes roam over her from head to toe. She hadn't expected this type of reaction from him because she considered the dress to be rather plain. But it appeared as if Josh approved. "I was surprised that they had in stock a gown already made that fit me, but I figured that it would be good for going out to the ranch."

Josh smiled at her, feeling proud of her for what she'd done. He figured that she felt like it was below her to purchase a premade gown and one so simple. But the fact that she'd done it and actually thought ahead proved to Josh that Emily had the ability to not only think for herself, but think logically enough about situations and the best way to go about them. It was the instinct needed not only in his profession, but also living a long and successful life in the West.

"I think you look lovely," Josh said as their eyes met. "Though, I think you'd make a burlap sack look good." Emily couldn't contain her laughter as she imagined herself only dressed in a sack. She didn't even have time to cover her mouth as she laughed, hugging her middle. Josh thought she was even more beautiful as she laughed freely.

"My goodness, I hope we never have to put that thought to the test," Emily said as her mirth subsided. "But I appreciate the compliment." Emily stepped out of her room and locked the door, placing the key in her purse. She then accepted Josh's arm as he offered it to her and he led her down the stairs. In the lobby they waved to Bill, who still seemed to be too engrossed in his novel to notice them. Little did they know that Bill was simply giving them privacy and as many moments alone as possible. He really did hope that the Sheriff would fall in love, and even though Emily was good looking, that perhaps she'd also show how she could be a good wife, too.

Outside of the inn, Josh helped Emily up into the wagon. She'd never ridden in such a thing before, having always had the pleasure of riding in an elegant carriage. Even the stagecoach had been finely constructed for its fast travels yet comfortable seating for riders. But the wagon was simply made, and the front bench was rather uncomfortable. Emily only hoped that it wouldn't be very far outside of town to the Slater's ranch.

Josh pulled himself up into the driver's seat and quickly took the reins. With a flick of his wrist, he sent his mare into a canter. Emily held firmly to the side of the wagon, not used to the sudden momentum of such a thing. But as they traveled out of town, she got used to the rhythm and eventually loosened her death grip on the wagon.

"Would you like to try driving the wagon?" Josh asked as he closed the distance between them, scooching over on the sitting board and handing the reins to her. Emily was surprised by the offer, never having considered driving herself. She'd always had a driver to take care of that business, but knew she couldn't turn down the offer. She was curious about driving and figured it couldn't hurt.

Emily took the reins in her hands and felt a sudden jolt of fear run through her. What if she did it wrong? What if she got them hurt?

"Easy now," Josh said, his soft voice seeming to pierce through her mind. "Loosen up your grip. She'll know if you're nervous."

"She?" Emily asked, her eyes focused only on the road. She tried to loosen her hands around the leather reins while taking a few deep breaths.

"Yes, Emily," Josh said with a chuckle. "The horse is a mare." Emily's eyes moved to the horse for a second, thinking she'd never really paid much attention to the gender of horses before.

"Alright, now what do I do?" Emily asked.

"Well, you'll want to put some slack in the reins if you want her to pick up her pace. You only tighten them when you want her to slow down or come to a full stop," Josh instructed as he placed his hands around hers. He moved his fingers till slack was applied to the reins, letting the mare know she had more range of motion and could pick up her speed. Soon she moved from a canter to a trot, and then a full gallop. Emily couldn't contain her smile as she listened to the wheels of the wagon thundering down the road, mixed with the sound of the mare's hooves and the feel of the wind whipping by her face. She'd never done anything like this before and found it to be exhilarating.

Josh kept his hands on Emily's so he could help her steer the wagon around the rutted part of the roads. He was enjoying this experience with her. And though he was certain she could figure it all out on her own, he liked the excuse to keep his hands around hers. As he looked down at her, the wagon rolling down the road at a steady pace, he was pleased to see how happy she looked and even excited about such a mundane thing. Josh often took horseback riding for granted since it was the fast way to travel around Spruce Valley. But by the look on Emily's face, he had a solid guess that she would find it very enjoyable and almost thrilling. He smirked, thinking of the idea of horse racing with her one day.

Before too long, they made their way to the Slater's ranch. Emily had enjoyed the thrill of driving the wagon mixed with the beautiful scenery that passed them by. The land seemed to go on forever with only the horizon coming to meet it. Small houses dotted the landscape with various amounts of cattle and sheep grazing in the distance. Emily had never seen livestock before and found them very interesting.

As they came upon the ranch, Josh helped Emily pull on the reins, causing his mare to slow. After growing up in a city, the vast expanse of farmland that spread out before them was a surprise to Emily. She'd gotten glimpses of fields and forests on the trip to Spruce Valley, but she hadn't yet seen a ranch. A sea of prairie grass stretched out as far as Emily could see, meeting the dazzling blue sky above the horizon. Maple and birch trees dotted the ranch and there was a white bunkhouse on the left of the driveway.

A small one-story, white clapboard ranch house stood a little way down the lane on the right. A large red barn had been erected farther down the lane with wooden fencing running out from the back of it. Several heads of cattle grazed in the pasture and Emily found them fascinating, if not strange smelling. Emily looked at it all, finding it quite charming and welcoming. There was a large wraparound porch on the ranch house and based on the size, she figured it would be rather roomy on the inside. She had figured that ranch homes were nothing more than a shack, but this structure completely proved her wrong.

The front door opened, and several women came out quickly to greet her. Emily recognized Fiona and assumed the other two to be the other ladies that worked at the seamstress shop. The short, black haired one had a very large belly, so she assumed that had to be Mrs. Slater, and therefore the other must be Martha Jenkins.

"Welcome, Emily!" Fiona called from the front porch as Josh came around and helped her down from the wagon. Emily couldn't deny that she enjoyed the feeling of Josh's strong hands on her waist as he helped her down. She tried not to show how much she enjoyed the feeling and instead focused her attention on the three women smiling down at her from the porch.

"Hello ladies. It's good to see you again, Fiona, and a pleasure to make all of your acquaintances," Emily said as she joined them on the porch.

"It is a pleasure to meet ye as well, Emily," Lucy said. "Please, come in."

"I'll be right in after I get the wagon put away," Josh called after Emily. She waved at him before following the women inside the ranch house. As predicted, Emily was pleasantly surprised by the lovely ranch house. The majority of the front room housed a large dining room with a decent sized sitting room to the left. Towards the back was a wide and open kitchen where she could smell all sorts of pleasant aromas coming to meet her. She could spot a long hallway to one side and figured that was where all the bedrooms where located.

Two small children ran towards her, seeming to chase after one another as they zoomed through the house. But when they saw that there was someone new in the house, they came to a full stop in front of her, their wide eyes looking up at her with curiosity.

"Francene, Samuel, I'd like you to meet Miss Emily Middleton," Martha introduced. "The party we've put together is for her."

The young girl placed her hands on her hips as she looked up at Emily. "Is it your birthday today?" Francene asked in her very young voice.

"No, it is not," Emily answered with a smile. "But sometimes it's fun to simply have a party for the sake of celebrating." Francene seemed pleased with her response as she resumed a game of tag around the house with little Samuel. They both seemed to be about two years old and full of laughter and light.

"What lovely children," Emily observed as the ladies watched the little ones play.

"They are the joy of me life," Lucy spoke up as she rubbed her stomach. Emily remembered how Fiona had explained that Lucy was meant to be on bed rest till her next child was born. She hoped that she wasn't putting any extra stress on the woman. "Well, let me give ye the tour of our grand house."

Together, the women showed Emily all the different parts of the ranch house. Emily found the house to be warm and inviting. Everything had a purpose, and even though they were practically in the middle of nowhere, Emily found that the house had many modern features such as a water closet and an ice chest.

"Eddie and I are still building our house, but we hope to put in a water closet as well," Fiona said as she saw how Emily marveled at it. "After staying with the Slaters last year when I arrived in Spruce Valley, I was certain I'd never be able to live without one."

"I'm sure it is very difficult to get running water away from town," Emily observed.

"As long as one can access running water below ground, there can then be enough pressure added to the pipes to draw it up," Martha explained. "The home Gray and I built was completely finished when we were able to tap into underground water. My goodness, that was a terrible mess at first." They all laughed at the story and Emily realized how much she missed being with other ladies. There was a need to socialize inside of Emily that she hadn't really satisfied since arriving at Spruce Valley.

"Well, me dears. It seems I've reached my limit," Lucy said as she wrapped her arms around her belly. "I'm going to go lay down for a wee bit and see if I can stitch a gown together."

"Sounds good, Lucy," Fiona said. "We'll make sure to keep an eye on Francene."

"Much obliged," Lucy called back as she waddled down the hallway to what Emily assumed was the main bedroom.

"Speaking of, we should probably get lunch on the table," Martha spoke up, the sound of the children laughing coming from the sitting room.

"What do you normally like to eat?" Fiona asked Emily as they walked back into the main part of the house.

"Oh, I'm not very picky," Emily assured them. "Anything would be lovely."

"Well, let's try our hand at Johnnycakes with some pork and Mormon gravy," Martha said with an eager voice. Emily had never heard of this type of food before but was at least willing to watch. But as soon as the women entered the kitchen portion of the house, Emily was soon enlisted to help out with preparing the meal. Though Emily didn't really feel confident about what she was doing, she was at least happy to have thorough instructions and happy company.

By the time they'd finished the meal, Josh had joined them in the house. He couldn't contain his large grin as he looked at Emily. She was now in an apron and had flour all over her. It was his chuckle that told Emily he'd come into the house. When she looked at him, she gave him a devilish grin that seemed to stop his laughter cold in his tracks. He simply shook his head then as he left to go play with the children in the sitting room. They were all playing blocks and the children would laugh loudly any time Josh would knock over the blocks, pretending to be a burglar. Emily watched him play with the children for a moment, thinking that he'd really make a great father.

When the food was served to the table, Emily put up her apron and joined them. She had to admit that she felt a feeling of accomplishment as she looked at all the food she'd helped make. Even though it was purely based on Martha and Fiona's guidance, she could at least feel proud of helping out. And as she tried everything, she was surprised at how delicious it all tasted.

"Good job, Emily," Samuel spoke up after he'd eaten everything off his plate. She was surprised by the compliment and smiled happily at the young boy.

"Why thank you, Samuel," she replied. Josh was watching her the whole time, thinking he hadn't seen her smile this much since arriving in Spruce Valley. He was happy to see her doing so well on the ranch and was excited to teach her a few things himself.

After they all helped clean up the dishes, Fiona took a plate of food to Lucy while Martha put the children down for their afternoon nap, despite their much protesting. Emily couldn't help but smile as she watched them go down the hallway to the nursery. She hadn't spent much time around children and thought they were utterly adorable.

When Josh took her hand, she almost jumped because she was so focused on everything around her. He smiled at her and tugged her from the house. When they stepped onto the front porch, Emily asked, "Where are we going now?"

"I figured you'd like to see the rest of the ranch and perhaps try your luck at riding a horse," Josh explained as he led her by the hand towards the barn.

"Riding a horse?" Emily questioned, surprised. "Don't you think that learning to drive a wagon is enough for one day?" She was nervous about the idea of riding a horse, but never really liked to back down from a challenge or show fear or weakness. That wasn't her nature because she always enjoyed impressing others, so she did her best to control her nerves as she allowed Josh to lead her into the barn.

"The only way you'll learn to survive in the West is by learning these basic skills as soon as you can," Josh explained. "I know you're an independent woman, Emily. I just want you to continue being so here in Spruce Valley." Emily was certainly touched by his words and figured she'd give it her best shot.

"Alright, so I have my mare saddled and ready for you," Josh explained as he let go of Emily's hand and went into the stable to bring his mare out. "I'll follow behind you on one of Sam's extra horses he keeps just in case. The horse should need the extra exercise anyways." Emily could only watch in wonder as Josh led the mare out to her. She tried not to be nervous as she reached out her hand and let her fingers brush against the horse's neck. She found the horse-hair to be rather soft and soon enjoyed the feeling of petting the horse. The mare seemed to enjoy it as well as she pushed against Emily's fingers.

"I think she likes me," Emily said as she looked at Josh. She saw how close he was watching her and only hoped that she was making a good impression on him.

"Of course, she does," Josh said as he motioned Emily over to him. "Now, I want you to put your foot into the stirrups here and push up with all your might until you can get your other leg on the other side."

"But won't my legs show if I do that?" Emily asked, thinking that it would be rather risky to be seen in such a position.

"Your calves might show a bit, yes. But you can draw your knees up and together if you're worried about it," Josh explained. "Trust me. No one would dare look at your calves while you're with me." When he winked at her, she couldn't help but blush. Taking a deep breath, she tried to focus on the task at hand. She approached the mare and placed her foot into the stirrup while reaching up and grabbing the saddle horn. When she counted to three, she pushed up with all her might as Josh guided her up onto the saddle with his hands. Again, the feeling of his strong hands on her sent a wave of warmth through her. Emily did her best to shake it off as she placed her other foot in the stirrup and gripped onto the saddle horn as she tried to find her balance. Though the hem of her gown had risen, it wasn't too much and she thought she'd be able to ride without worrying about her gown too much.

"You look like a natural," Josh said with a chuckle. Emily shook her head, knowing that he was teasing her.

"Nice try," Emily replied as she brought up her knees a bit against the mare, feeling more secure by doing so. She then took the reins, her hips gripping the saddle as she tried not to think too much about falling off.

"Alright, just hold on one second and then we'll head out," Josh said as he quickly mounted the other horse and then guided it towards Emily. "Now, it's just like driving the wagon. More slack will tell the horse to go faster while a tight grip will keep the horse going slow." Emily just nodded as she watched Josh lead his horse out of the barn. She took one more deep breath before she rubbed her heels against the mare's sides, urging the horse forward. She tried not to pull on the reins too tightly as the mare followed after Josh's horse, seeming to know what to do.

Once they were in the pasture, Josh set his horse to a canter. Emily did her best to mimic the action, letting the reins loosen in her hands. As the mare began to canter, Emily found that she had to focus more on her balance. She did her best to move her body with the movements of the horse, which were quite jarring experiencing them for the first time. But eventually Emily got used to the quickened speed of the horse.

As soon as Emily seemed to be getting comfortable, Josh would increase their pace. He wanted to push Emily to show her that she was full of potential and really could do more than she ever thought possible. He could see the fire and determination in her eyes, close to the same fierceness he witnessed in the photo she'd sent him and also in the words she used when she'd written her letter. Josh was eager to show Emily that she had a strength deep inside her that she could avail herself to at any given time. She'd already proven herself brave by traveling all the way to Spruce Valley on her own, and now he wanted her to see that same strength for herself.

Before too long, their horses were galloping through the empty pasture. Emily smiled brightly as the wind whipped by her, the feeling of the strong horse beneath her as the hooves thundered across the grass in quick rhythm. Emily could hardly believe that she was riding a horse as they raced around the pasture. Dust flew up behind them, and Emily had never felt so free in her life. She was in complete control and she wanted this feeling to be never-ending.

After a time, Josh slowed his horse, indicating for Emily to do so as well. She figured that the horses could use a break after they'd put them through their paces. The two horses then trotted side by side as Emily did her best to catch her breath.

"So, what do you think of riding a horse now?" Josh asked, his lopsided grin having returned to his face. He looked at her with a satisfied expression and Emily couldn't help but chuckle.

"I think it's the most wonderful thing in the world," Emily said as she reached down and patted the mare's neck once more. The mare nickered in return, seeming to enjoy all the special attention.

"I knew you would enjoy it. If you enjoy poker, then I knew you'd enjoy something as thrilling as riding a horse," Josh said. Emily shook her head, wondering if it had been wrong of her to tell Josh that little detail.

"I do find riding a horse thrilling, but it's more of a sense of freedom and control that I enjoyed the most," Emily explained. "It's something I never really felt before."

"Well, you're in Spruce Valley now with all sorts of opportunities and possibilities ahead of you," Josh said, trying to be encouraging.

"I guess I need to experience these opportunities before I can appreciate any of it," Emily admitted. "Much like being shown how to ride a horse and learning that it's quite enjoyable."

"As long as you're willing, I'm sure you could accomplish anything you put your mind to," Josh said, his voice growing soft. They shared a particular look and a part of

Emily wanted to say something in relation to marriage. But she figured that now wasn't the best time for that. It seemed that Emily first had to learn to get her feet under her before she could really start thinking about marriage with a guy like Josh. He had some pretty high expectations that she wasn't sure she could fulfill at this time.

The sound of whooping voices brought Emily's attention back to the front of the ranch house. Her eyes grew large as she saw a small group of Indians approaching. Her first instinct was to gallop away on the horse in fear of an attack, but when she saw Martha and Fiona come onto the porch with scowling faces, Emily only grew more confused.

"That is Bright Star and his sons," Josh explained. "I bet Martha is giving them a good tongue lashing for being so loud when the children are sleeping." Emily still watched the scene with wide eyes while Josh simply chuckled. "Come on. I'll introduce you."

"But aren't Indians dangerous?" Emily quickly asked, uncertain about getting close to them.

"Yes, Emily, Indians can be dangerous. Just like a wild bear can be dangerous when provoked," Josh explained. "The local Crow Tribe is very friendly to everyone in Spruce Valley. Dr. Slater even employs a few to watch over his sheep further down the road." Emily was finding this all rather bazaar but was willing to meet them if Josh assured her that she would be safe. Slowly but surely, they led the horses out of the pasture and back into the barn. And once the horses had been released of their saddles and brushed down, something Emily really enjoyed doing, Josh then took her hand once more and led her towards the house to meet Indians for the first time.

# CHAPTER 11

Emily tightened her grip on Josh's hand as he led her from the barn towards the front of the house where the women were visiting with the Indians as though they were old friends. She watched as the older Indian laughed loudly, finding something rather funny. They seemed so normal that Emily almost forgot that the three men were Indians. They were dressed in deerskin trousers, but their chests were bare, save from the long necklaces they wore. Emily had never seen a man so exposed before and did her best not to look at their bodies.

"Oh good, the Sheriff is here," Martha spoke up as they came near. "Now he'll have to order you to wear some clothing when you come to the ranch."

"I think the next time I come to visit, me and my sons shall only wear our breechcloths and have your husbands wear them, too. Then you won't complain so much," Bright Star replied, causing them all to laugh at the idea while Emily only watched with much curiosity. Eventually, she made eye contact with the older Indian and had a hard time looking away.

"Bright Star, may I introduce you to Miss Emily Middleton," Josh spoke up as he watched the exchange between the two. "She has just come in from the East."

"Ah, it is nice to meet you, Emily Middleton," Bright Star said. "I am pleased that you are here for the Sheriff. If he is married soon, then perhaps he won't be so grumpy all the time." Emily couldn't contain her smile then and Bright Star felt pleased to have caused the newcomer to smile. He could tell by the way she looked at him that she'd never seen an Indian before.

"Come now, Bright Star. I am not a grumpy person," Josh said in his defense.

"You forget, Josh Ryder. I did travel with you for many days. I know how you are in the morning," Bright Star retorted, causing Emily to chuckle this time. She was enjoying watching this banter between the two. Josh scowled at the Indian then, even though there was a smile on his face.

"And if Josh doesn't prove himself worthy of such a beautiful creature," Bright Star continued as he focused his gaze on Emily, "I have two sons that are eligible." Running Bear and Sky Bird, Bright Star's sons, both rolled their eyes while remaining silent. Emily had a feeling that Bright Star liked to tease everyone, including his sons.

"Then I shall have to remind Josh often that I have other suitors to consider," Emily teased back, another round of laughter rising into the air.

"I think I will very much enjoy your company, Emily Middleton. I am glad you are here now," Bright Star said, a twinkle in his eye.

"The feeling is mutual, I assure you," Emily said with a smile. But that smile was quickly wiped off her face as she witnessed a small furry thing race across the grass to climb up onto Bright Star's shoulder. She stared at the animal as it screeched at Bright Star, completely in shock. It took her a second to realize that the animal was in fact a monkey.

"Why hell, Jack," Bright Star said in a fond voice as he took the monkey from his shoulder and cradled it in his arms. "How are you doing today?" The monkey seemed to chatter back at him and continued to do so until Bright Star gave the monkey a date. Satisfied, he relaxed into the Indian's arms like a baby.

"I'm guessing you've never seen a monkey before," Fiona spoke up as she watched Emily's surprised expression, finding it rather humorous.

"Not this close before, no," Emily said. "There was a circus I once went to, but all the animals were in cages." Bright Star scowled at hearing Emily's words.

"That is very unfortunate," Bright Star said as he petted the monkey.

"I won Jack in a poker game," came the voice of a man. Emily turned to see several men having rode in from the pasture and were now making their way to the ranch house. The one that had spoken was a bit taller than Emily with very broad shoulders. He had light brown hair and dark colored eyes.

"Emily, may I introduce you to my husband, Eddie Sawyer," Fiona said as she went to her husband and wrapped her arms around him. Such signs of affection were new to Emily, and realizing she still held Josh's hand, she quickly let it go and folded her hands together in front of her. Josh noticed what she'd done but didn't mind at all. Emily might have come to Spruce Valley with designs to marry him, but he wasn't going to put any pressure on her.

"It's a pleasure to meet you, Eddie," Emily replied. "I didn't think people kept monkeys for pets."

"And I never knew a woman who played poker," Eddie

said with a wink. Emily pretended to be surprised as she glared at Josh. He simply raised his hands and took a step back, much to the amusement of everyone.

"Well, I'd be glad to show you just how well I play poker anytime you wish," Emily said to Eddie. "But you may keep your monkey when you lose." This really tickled everyone's funny bone and eventually, Martha called everyone inside for a light snack before dinner was done. Josh couldn't help but be proud of the way Emily had stood up for herself. He could tell that she was finally coming out of her shell and showing everyone her true character.

Emily ended up meeting all sorts of people. Gray, the foreman, and Martha's husband, was introduced to her. She found him to be a very intimidating man, but when the children woke from their nap, she saw that he had a soft side to him as he played with the children in the sitting room. Emily also met the other two ranch hands. Sawyer, who was Eddie's brother, and Tom Barker, one of Sam's original ranch hands. Eventually the good doctor joined all those that had gathered when he returned to the ranch later in the afternoon after closing the clinic a bit early in town.

Emily enjoyed putting in a helping hand with finishing up the rest of dinner. She was surprised to learn that most meals happened in this way as Lucy had been cooking for everyone on the ranch since she came to Spruce Valley. She couldn't imagine cooking for so many people every day and had to give the women a lot of credit. They not only cooked and cleaned while raising children, but also managed a small business in town. Lucy eventually joined the group and sat at the head of the table after showing off the beautiful gown she'd finished while she had been resting in bed. Emily could tell that the woman was very determined, but also mindful of how her body was reacting to this pregnancy. Josh eventually told Emily the deal the two had made that

Lucy would listen to her husband's instructions if Josh was willing to share gossip with her when he came out to the ranch from town.

"I never thought a Sheriff would ever admit to being a gossip," Emily said in the hopes of teasing him.

"And I never thought a beautiful debutante would ever ride a horse as well as you have," Josh quickly replied with a wink. Emily couldn't contain her mirth, thinking that Josh would be a good contender for her witty remarks.

As the sun set, candles were lit all around the ranch house. Everyone settled down at the table for dinner, including the Indians. Emily never thought that she'd be sharing a meal with Indians present, but was finding their company rather amusing. Bright Star's sons seemed to relax after a while and proved to be as witty as his father. Another thing that surprised Emily was how delicious all the food was. The shepherd's pie with homemade apple sauce and bread were absolutely delicious and she could imagine herself trying her hand at the dishes once again.

When dinner was through, Martha and Gray took their son home while Lucy went to bed with Francene. That left Fiona and Emily as the only women present when everyone settled down at the table to play poker.

"It's been a while since I've played this game," Bright Star said as Eddie started to pass out the cards for the first round. "I'm not sure if I remember how to do so."

Sawyer, who had been rather quiet during dinner, spoke up and said, "Don't believe a thing this Indian says." Emily chuckled as the two shared a particular look. Emily enjoyed playing poker because it often showed a person's true nature. People who were mostly charming and nice could turn mean and nasty when they started to lose. But tonight, they were only playing for toothpicks so hopefully there wouldn't be so much tension.

Emily quickly learned that her original idea was wrong as she saw how competitive everyone became as the game progressed. Emily and Fiona often laughed together as they watched the men quickly raise bids just to see if they could prove something. It wasn't long before one by one, the men started to lose all their toothpicks while Fiona and Emily's piles continued to grow larger and larger.

"How is it that you two have all the toothpicks," Josh said at one point, gesturing to the women.

"That is because women have more patience than men," Emily reasoned.

"And you all make it so easy," Fiona added, causing everyone to laugh.

After a while, it was only Emily, Josh, and Eddie left playing cards. Even Fiona had lost all she had when she thought she'd had a great running but lost it all in the end. Emily was determined to win and was keeping a very close eye on her competitors. The other two seemed to be sizing her up as well and Emily did her best to keep her breathing steady and not to give away any signs of what cards she held in her hands. But eventually, she started to bid them up, feeling like she'd finally gotten a spread of cards that could win her the game.

With all three of their toothpicks in the middle of the table, everyone watched and waited for the remaining players to start laying down their cards. Everyone was dying to see if Emily would be able to beat the two men, and as Josh and Eddie laid down their cards, both with straights, Emily did her best to contain her glee.

"Read 'em and weep, boys," Emily said as she laid down her cards, showing that she had a flush. It took a second for everyone to realize that Emily had won, and before they could raise a fuss, Dr. Slater was quick to shush them all.

"Remember, Lucy and Francene are sleeping," Sam said,

his serious eyes meeting everyone else's. They all covered their mouths till their mirth had subsided. Emily didn't even bother grabbing all the toothpicks from the middle of the table as she simply laughed with the others.

"My goodness. I should really be heading back to town now," Emily said as she helped clean up the toothpicks and all the cards.

"I'll take you back to town then," Josh said as he stood from the table with Emily.

"Miss Middleton. Why don't you consider coming to stay with Lucy and I till you can get on your feet?" Dr. Slater offered. "We have a spare bedroom that isn't currently being used." Emily was surprised by the offer. She glanced at Josh, wondering what he thought of the plan. She didn't really like the idea of being so far from town, and Josh, but knew that she couldn't afford to stay at the inn forever.

"I'd be happy to accept that offer, Dr. Slater. I don't have many skills, but I'd be willing to offer my help in return," Emily said.

"I'm sure Lucy will appreciate hearing that," Dr. Slater agreed.

"Then we shall come once again to play poker with you, Emily Middleton. This was very enjoyable," Bright Star said as he rose from the table with his sons. Without another word, they slipped from the house almost soundlessly, showing Emily just how skillful the Indians were.

"Well then, we shall see you all tomorrow. I'll bring Emily back out with her things then," Josh said. "Good night everyone." Emily took the time to say goodnight and to thank them for such a wonderful day. Then, she followed Josh out of the house and into the night air. It was cool and refreshing since Emily had grown quite warm during the poker game. But she was pleased with herself for having played another good game of poker and left with more friends than she felt she ever had.

Emily accompanied Josh as they got the wagon ready to head back into town. Though it was dark, the moon shed enough light on the Earth to allow them to see what they were doing. And by the time they were done and ready to head out, Emily couldn't deny that she felt a little proud of the small accomplishment. There were so many new things that she'd learned to do in one day that it was a bit overwhelming to process. She let Josh help her up into the wagon. This time, as Josh drove them into town, he kept the reins to himself, allowing Emily to simply relax and enjoy the ride back to town.

The world seemed to be cast into a soft glow of the moon, giving the scenery a mystical appearance. Thousands of stars shone from above and Emily took a minute to watch them. She was grateful for the day she'd had on the Slater's ranch, simply learning new skills and enjoying the company of others. She felt more satisfied than she had in months and thought for a moment that she could really learn to love Spruce Valley.

Even though Josh knew he needed to keep his eyes alert for danger, especially since they were traveling by night, he couldn't help but watch Emily from time to time as her eyes drifted towards the heavens. He was immensely proud of Emily and all that she'd accomplished today. He felt like she could really fit into the community of Spruce Valley and find her own way. He wasn't certain how she felt about him or whether or not they had a shot at marriage, but he was willing to be patient and continue to watch Emily bloom and prosper in her new environment. He didn't particularly like the idea of Emily staying so far away from town but was certain that Lucy could use the extra help around the house since she was bedridden. Josh knew that Lucy had become quite restless at home since Martha took the kids into town with her during the day. And having another lady in the house would surely do Lucy as much good as Emily.

By the time they reached town, Josh was almost sad that their time together had finally come to an end. He stopped the wagon in front of the inn and went to hop down to help Emily from the wagon, when she reached out and touched his shoulder, stopping him.

"I just wanted to say thank you for everything today," Emily said, her hand still resting on his shoulder. He smiled at her and nodded.

"It was nothing," Josh replied.

"Fiona told me how it was your idea," Emily admitted with a smirk on her lips. Josh chuckled, thinking he'd want to throttle Fiona right now for letting that detail slip. But he was certain the woman was only trying to be helpful.

"Well, it was really the women that made it happen. I only made sure everyone knew about it. Mayor Stavros unfortunately couldn't make it to the get together tonight, but promises to make it up to you," Josh explained.

"I'm sure I will get to meet her soon enough," Emily assured him. "It's a small town after all." Josh nodded, certain of her words. He then finally got down from the wagon and then helped Emily down before walking with her to the front door of the inn.

"I also wanted to apologize," Emily spoke up, trying to muster up all her courage. "It was wrong of me to assume so much of you in relation to my ideals of marriage." Josh had assumed that they'd visit this topic of conversation once more and figured now was as good as any time to discuss it.

"I think people often have the wrong idea of what marriage is supposed to be like," Josh said, trying to be reassuring. "It's why people who are married say that it takes hard work from both people to make a marriage successful."

Emily simply nodded, hoping that Josh accepted her apology. He surprised her then as he neared her and lowered his lips to hers. Emily had never really been kissed before because she didn't want people to be able to gossip about her in that way. She was surprised by how warm Josh's lips were and returned the kiss with eagerness. But as quickly as the kiss started, it soon ended, leaving Emily wanting more.

"I hope you don't mind me being so forward," Josh said in a husky voice, his words sending shivers all over Emily's body.

"No, I don't mind," Emily replied as her chest rose and fell with excitement. "It's good to know if we are compatible in that way."

"And do you think we are?" Josh asked, his lopsided grin showing once more.

"I feel like I do have a pretty good idea," Emily agreed. "Goodnight, Josh." Emily turned the handle of the door and pushed it open.

"Goodnight, Emily," Josh replied as he took a step away from the inn, tempted to follow Emily to bed. But he didn't want to treat Emily like other women of his past. He wanted to treat her like a real lady.

When Emily shut the door, Josh got back into the wagon and made quick work of getting over to the livery stables to put away his mare and store the wagon. He knew that tomorrow he'd return the wagon to the ranch, along with Emily and all her things. He was grateful for his friend offering to house Emily, and it was turning into a mail-order-bride tradition. He was certain that Emily would enjoy being out on the ranch even if it seemed to put distance between them.

When Emily got to her room, she locked the door behind her and began to get ready for bed. She couldn't believe how wonderful her day had been and a part of her was looking forward to returning to the ranch. It was so peaceful out there and she'd really enjoyed herself. And though she'd have to rely on Josh coming out to the ranch to visit with her, she was certain that peaceful scenery would really help her to feel relaxed in Spruce Valley. She wanted to find her place in the community and figured that she could spend this time discovering what she wanted to do with the rest of her life.

Just like riding a horse for the first time, Emily suddenly felt this huge sense of freedom she hadn't really felt before. Though her father had been very lenient of Emily in Atlanta, she'd always adhered to society's rules of how she should act and dress.. But now that she was in Spruce Valley, she seemed to be able to act however she felt. To a certain degree, of course. But here in this small Montana town she felt she could become whomever she wanted to. Or perhaps the young lady she'd always dreamed of one day becoming.

# CHAPTER 12

After about a week out at the Slater's ranch, Emily was finally starting to get a hang of things. While Lucy rested in bed or in a chair, she gave Emily instructions on how to do the simplest of things. Whether that was cooking or washing her own laundry, Lucy was there to make sure that Emily knew what she was doing. And now, after doing so for a few days, Emily thought she was finally starting to learn a few things instead of constantly burning the food or not cooking it well enough. Thankfully, everyone had been supportive of Emily as she continued to learn and never said anything that would put her down.

One particular afternoon Josh rode out to the ranch, hoping to steal Emily away from the ranch house for a bit to enjoy a ride into the countryside. He hadn't seen Emily since he'd dropped her and the wagon off at the ranch. After a whole week, Josh was eager to spend some time with Emily again and to learn for himself how she'd been doing at the ranch. As he came down the lane and saw her pinning wet clothes on the line, he smiled brightly. After the conversation they'd had about Emily never working a day in her life, he was pleasantly surprised to see her doing such housework.

"Well, hello there, pretty lady," Josh said as he rode his mare over to where she was in the yard. "I don't suppose you can tell me where I can find Miss Middleton, a debutante from the famous city of Atlanta?" Emily chuckled at Josh's teasing as she finished hanging up a gown before turning her attention to the Sheriff.

"I'm afraid the Miss Middleton of Atlanta no longer exists, and instead you'll just have to visit with Emily," she replied with a happy grin on her face.

"Well, I think I'd like that very much," Josh replied. She was so happy to see him that for a moment they simply stared into one another's eyes. But after a little while, Emily became conscious of herself once more and soon invited him for a bite to eat.

"Actually, I was hoping you wouldn't mind joining me for a ride?" Josh said. Emily was excited about the idea as she looked down at the basket of washed clothes she still needed to hang up.

"If you'll help me hang the wash, I'm sure Lucy won't mind me being away from the house for a bit," Emily suggested.

"I guess I can help out," Josh said in a mocked voice as he climbed down from his mare and began to help Emily clip up all the wet laundry to dry on the beautiful spring day. The moment they were done, Emily went inside to hang up her damp apron and let Lucy know where she was going.

"Ye two have fun," Lucy called after her as Emily left, thinking the woman would want to know all the details when she returned. Josh hadn't minced his words when he said that Lucy liked to gossip. She herself didn't mind doing so as well and spent most of their time talking while they worked.

Back outside, Emily joined Josh by his mare. "Are you going to go saddle up another horse?" Emily asked.

"I thought you wouldn't mind riding double with me," Josh said. "I'll have you ride in front." Emily thought it was rather forward, but as she remembered their kiss, she thought that she'd like to be a bit more daring with Josh. She could tell that they had a mutual attraction to one another, but marriage was much more than just that.

"Just help me up and I'm sure we'll make do," Emily replied. Josh smiled as he helped Emily up into the saddle, loving the feeling of her in his hands, and once he was in the saddle behind her, he did his best to keep his mind clear instead of muddled with different thoughts.

With the reins in his hands and Emily's on the saddle horn, Josh steered the mare for the open countryside and took off at a trot before going into a full gallop. Emily smiled brightly, loving the feeling of riding a horse and traveling quickly across the land on such a strong animal. Her joy was increased with the feeling of Josh right behind her. With all the work she'd been doing the past week, it was surely nice to take a break from it all and simply enjoy the day.

After a while, Josh pulled on the reins and brought the mare to a stop. He slid down from the saddle and then helped Emily down before leading her to a tree where they could get out of the sun for a bit. They settled under the tree and Josh made sure to give Emily plenty of space as they sat and watched the clouds pass by. His mare grazed on the grass and Josh placed his full attention on Emily, thinking she'd really progressed since she first arrived in Spruce Valley.

"You know, Josh. I really do think you'd make a good marshal," Emily spoke up at one point. Josh was surprised to hear this and was worried she was going to start pressuring him again. "You are so kind and helpful, Josh, that it makes me wonder what kind of good you'd be able to do in that sort of position." Josh breathed a sigh of relief then and certainly appreciated her kind words.

"You know, I'm sure I could do the job right," Josh said as he stared out towards the landscape. "But I can never imagine myself leaving Spruce Valley behind. I've come to love this place ever since I came here, and this community really means something to me." Emily admired his words, wondering if she'd ever feel that way about Spruce Valley. She'd come to make some great friends and really appreciate all their kindness to her, but she'd never really felt love towards anything or anyone.

"What do you want for your future then?" Emily asked as she turned her head and looked at him. Their eyes met and Josh thought he'd like to keep her in his future. But for now, he'd keep those thoughts to himself.

"I want to do everything in my power to see Spruce Valley continue to grow," Josh said. "One day, I want to build my own home in town and move out of the apartment above the Sheriff's Office. I want to hire two deputies and really start making sure this town stays safe as it continues to grow." Emily thought his dream was very admirable and was certain that Josh would be able to accomplish those goals.

"But what about you, Emily? Now that you're here, what do you want for your own future?" Josh asked, pulling Emily from her thoughts.

"That's hard for me to think about anymore," Emily said honestly. "All my life, I was groomed to be a wife and mother. I was tutored so that I'd have the knowledge and skills to land me a wealthy husband." Josh chuckled about this idea and now Emily felt like she could finally laugh about her first thoughts about marriage. "I only ever thought that I'd get married and just listen to whatever my husband said, much like I listened to my father or tutors."

"But you really don't have to listen to anyone but yourself," Josh commented. "So, what do you want to do with yourself?" As Emily looked at Josh, she wondered if he'd be a part of her future. But if she was going to remain as an independent woman, she'd have to really think and act on her own.

"I think it's going to take me some time to discover that for myself," Emily said after a while. "I'm still learning so much that I haven't really thought what I might be good at in order to get some sort of employment to support myself." Josh smiled at her, at least pleased that she was willing to give the idea of working a try.

"I'm sure after a while you'll find something that you'll end up loving in the end," Josh said, hoping to encourage her. "When I was young, I worked on my father's ranch and did the work, but it wasn't what I loved to do. Helping people and stopping bad people from hurting good people is what really got me all stirred up. And I know one day you'll discover that, too." Emily smiled kindly at Josh, glad that he saw so much potential in her. She only hoped that in time she'd come to see the same in herself.

~

LATER THAT DAY, after Josh had taken her back to the ranch house and enjoyed a cup of coffee with Lucy and Emily at the table as they talked about town gossip, the women were surprised when another visitor came to the house. Emily answered the door when someone knocked, and she opened the door to reveal an older woman with a stern posture but very friendly eyes.

"Good afternoon, my dear. Is Mrs. Slater in?" the woman asked.

"She is," Emily replied. "Might I let her know whom has come to call upon her?"

The older woman smiled as she said, "My name is Mayor Stavros." Emily's eyes went wide as she took in the appearance of the woman. She'd always imagined that mayors were wealthy and wore fancy clothing. But this woman looked like any other member of Spruce Valley.

"Please, come in Madam Mayor," Emily said as she held open the door. She chuckled as she came into the house and hung her cloak on the hook by the door.

"Oh my dear, please address me as Delphina. My husband was the real Mayor of Spruce Valley, and I'm not sure if anyone has called me madam since I was very young," Delphina chuckled. Emily felt a little embarrassed, but as soon as she showed Delphina into the sitting room, her attention soon turned to Lucy who had been sitting in a wing backed chair, working on another gown.

"Delphina, what a pleasant surprise," Lucy said as she looked up to see who had come by. Lucy's feet were up and resting on a stool and a gown sat on her lap with her sewing kit beside her on the floor.

"It's been a while since we've visited, and with you being home and resting, I thought I'd make the trip out to see you," Delphina explained as she took to the chair across from Lucy.

"That is very kind of ye. Have ye met Miss Emily Middleton yet?" Lucy asked as she glanced at Emily as she stood in the doorway, unsure if she should stay or go.

"No, I don't believe I've had the pleasure yet," Delphina replied with a kind smile.

"Well, ye see, Emily here has come to live in Spruce Valley. She's the Sheriff's mail-order-bride," Lucy explained with a smirk. Though Emily often enjoyed being the center of attention, she also didn't want to place any pressure on Josh. She only hoped that he didn't feel any pressure when other people introduced her as his mail-order-bride.

Delphina was surprised to hear this since she often heard all the news in town. She looked quizzically at Emily then, thinking that she was rather beautiful with her dark hair and sparkling blue eyes. She had perfect posture, making Delphina think that this woman was classically educated.

"Can I get you two something to eat or drink?" Emily asked, wanting to be of good use for something.

"We just made some lemonade this morning," Lucy offered as she turned her attention to the Mayor.

"I'd hate to trouble you, but a glass of lemonade does sound rather good," Delphina agreed. Without hesitation, Emily left the sitting room and walked over to the kitchen. She poured three glasses of lemonade and put together a small plate of maple cookies that had been baked the day before. Emily then returned to the sitting room and distributed the items before finding herself a seat in the rocking chair. Never had Emily thought she'd serve another person, but the task wasn't off-putting. In fact, it was almost a pleasure because Emily had helped in making the lemonade and cookies. It was as though she could show off the products of her own two hands.

"So, Emily, I'd love to know more about you," Delphina said after taking a long sip of her lemonade. "As Mayor of Spruce Valley, I take it upon myself to know everyone in order to best serve the community. Lucy smiled at Delphina as she returned to her needlework. She had guessed that the Mayor had come by after learning about Emily's arrival into town. Though Delphina was an older woman, she had many skills that made her a great mayor. And one of those skills was keeping tabs on everyone. Where Lucy just liked to gossip, Delphina was always thinking about the welfare of everyone in Spruce Valley.

"Well, I'm originally from Atlanta, Georgia," Emily started with. "My father ruined my family's reputation there, so I decided to become a mail-order-bride to hopefully start over with my life." Delphina nodded, understanding that is why most people came to Spruce Valley. They always came running to the West, carrying their hopes and dreams.

"I like that you are honest, Emily," Delphina commented. "It must be difficult for you to admit such things. Your posture alone tells me that you were highly educated." Emily smiled, knowing that old habits would be hard for her to quit. Even in a rocking chair, she still sat up straight.

"My father was a very wealthy man. He spared no expense in my education in the hopes of making me appear more attractive to possible suitors," Emily explained. "I know many modern languages, as well as mathematics, astronomy, economics, and calligraphy."

"My word, that is really impressive," Delphina exclaimed. "I can think of several men in town who could use a calligraphy lesson. I can hardly ever make out their writing." The women giggled at this, and Lucy couldn't help but think of Eddie Murtaugh. When he had first published his mail-order-bride ad, he also needed to improve on his reading and writing skills in order to exchange letters with Fiona.

"Since most of the farmers and cattle hands drop out of school around the eighth grade, most men and women in town don't have a very good education," Lucy added. "It truly is a shame." Delphina nodded her agreement as an idea started to form in her mind.

"Have you ever considered teaching, Emily?" Delphina asked. Emily was surprised by the question. Since she'd never considered any sort of employment before, she had never dreamed of teaching professionally. But as the idea started to form in her head, she reasoned that she'd always enjoyed instructing others. Back in Atlanta, she fondly taught other young ladies her age about fashion and etiquette, as well as what they could honestly get away with in public. It was Emily's way of teaching young ladies that they could have a sense of independence, too.

"I can honestly say I've never considered it before," Emily replied. "I was raised to marry a wealthy husband and never have to worry about working. But since I've come to Spruce Valley, I understand now that employment is not only necessary, but can be enjoyable as well." This caused Delphina to laugh hardily, thinking she'd never really looked at work that way.

"I would have to agree with you, my dear. If you don't love what you do for work, then you'll just regret each day," Delphina said. "But with all your education, if you have a desire to teach others, then I think you should pursue that interest. With Mrs. Crawford also expecting a little one any day now, she'll need someone to fill in for her at the church for the children's lessons."

Emily smiled as she remembered spending part of her day with Mrs. Crawford and all her students. "I do know Mrs. Crawford," Emily said. "On my first day in town, I found it so interesting to see the students gathering in one place for their daily lessons. Since I was privately tutored, I was very curious and did spend some time with her and the children."

"If we are being honest here, then I shall tell you that Mrs. Crawford did speak to me about you coming and visiting with everyone at the church. She was the one who told me that you'd make a good teacher," Delphina confessed.

Lucy chuckled as she shook her head. "Delphina, me dear, I knew there was a real reason for your visit," Lucy said.

"Well, I don't do anything without pure intent and purpose," Delphina agreed. "And when I see a need in the town, I make sure to find a solution as soon as possible." The Mayor then turned her attention back to Emily as she said, "So, what do you think, Emily? Would you like to try your hand at teaching?"

Emily didn't respond right away. Though the idea filled her with much excitement, she didn't want to be too hasty in her response. There was a lot about teaching she didn't know, even if she did have a lot of education.

"I feel excited about the idea, I do admit," Emily said. "But I'm afraid I don't know much about teaching."

"That part will come naturally as you get used to doing it," Delphina reassured her. "And Mrs. Crawford will be able to direct you. After you've taught for some time, you'll be able to be certified by the state and make things official." Emily was surprised by how easy the Mayor made this all sound. And if she had the Mayor supporting her, Emily figured that she could at least give it a shot.

"Alright then," Emily said, her southern accent coming through in her excitement. "I would be happy to try teaching."

For the remainder of Delphina's visit, the women talked all about teaching and how Emily would be able to get to and from town to accompany Mrs. Crawford for the daily lessons till Emily could take over permanently. At first, Lucy had suggested that she get a ride into town with Martha and Fiona, but after much thought, Emily decided that she'd like to ride her own horse. This had surprised the women, but soon found out that Emily was more daring and bolder than what she appeared to be on the outside.

"We'll talk to Sam and Gray tonight about which horse would be best suited for ye," Lucy said. "I think it's a grand idea that ye'd be willing to ride a horse and be truly independent."

"And I know Mrs. Crawford and the children will be delighted to see you again," Delphina added.

After they had discussed what Emily's pay would be, which she thought was reasonable, Delphina left the ranch house with the promise to come and visit again soon. It only caused them all to chuckle as the older woman left. Lucy went to go lie down after the Mayor left, leaving Emily alone. She was beside herself with how lovely the day had gone. She'd spent the morning with Josh, thinking they were finally starting to see eye-to-eye, and now she had a teaching position in town. It was hard to take it all in and believe, so to make good use of her time, Emily found a piece of writing paper and started to write out a letter to her dear friend, Cynthia.

# CHAPTER 13

Nerves ran through Emily the next morning as she rose early to help prepare breakfast and then try her hand at riding a horse into town. She wanted to reach town extra early so she could be at the church before the children started to arrive, but that also meant that she needed to get to town first. Thankfully, Dr. Slater would be accompanying her because he also needed to be at the clinic in town for his patients.

"Are ye excited, Emily?" Lucy asked from the head of the table as Emily came in carrying a plate of pancakes and fried eggs. Gray was in the kitchen fixing breakfast and Emily was doing her best to bring it all to the table so the cattle hands could eat and get out into the pasture. It would be calving season soon and they'd need to be on constant watch in case any of the cows needed help birthing. From what had been explained to her, it was the busiest time of the year.

"I sure am," Emily replied as she sat down at the table

and quickly made her plate. “I want to get into town early and maybe even surprise Josh at some point.”

“I think that’s a great idea,” Lucy agreed. She was holding Francene on her lap and convincing the toddler to eat something before she’d go into town with Martha and Fiona. Thankfully, Francene and Samuel got along and normally kept each other occupied. Lucy was really looking forward to giving birth just so she could join everyone in town again.

As soon as Emily was finished eating, she cleaned up her dishes and headed out to the barn after bidding Lucy farewell. She carried a side bag filled with writing paper she promised to pay Dr. Slater back with her first paycheck. She wasn’t sure what she’d need, but figured she’d bring at least something. If nothing else, she could use the paper to take notes.

In the barn, Sam showed her how to saddle up one of his older horses that could use the exercise. “Now, he’s not going to go real fast, but he’s very reliable,” Dr. Slater explained.

“I guess I won’t be doing any horse racing with him, then,” Emily teased as she pulled herself up into the saddle. Sam was impressed that she was able to do so all on her own. He diverted his eyes from her exposed ankles and calves as he mounted his own horse.

“No, there won’t be any horse racing for Duncan anymore,” Sam replied. “When we were both a bit younger, he was the horse I’d ride when an emergency would come up and I was needed in the dead of night. I won’t say he’s retired, but he’ll make a good riding horse.”

“Well, I have faith in Duncan that he won’t lead me astray,” Emily quipped. Sam laughed as he led them out of the barn. The cattle hands had already saddled up and had ridden out to the pasture, so the morning seemed almost quiet as they rode out of the barn. The sounds of cattle in the distance rose into the air, and though the smell of the ranch had first made Emily a little leery of being out on the ranch, she'd gotten used to the smell and almost considered it homey.

Together, Sam and Emily rode into town at a gallop. Though she wasn't about to push Duncan, she was at least pleased that the older horse could keep up with the mare that Sam was riding. She thoroughly enjoyed the feeling of riding and was sure she'd look forward to the end of the school day just so she could ride home. The morning sun was still peeking over the horizon, sending shades of blue and pink through the sky. With this being the first day of her teaching, or at least learning to, she couldn't have imagined a more perfect morning.

They slowed their horses to a trot as they entered town. Sam bid her good luck before making his way to the clinic. After thanking him, she led Duncan down the main street till she reached the church just outside of town on the north end. She had passed by the Sheriff's Office on her way and for a moment she thought about stopping and saying hello to Josh. But on her very first day, Emily did not want to be late.

When she reached the church, Emily took her time dismounting from the horse. She was grateful that Duncan was such a strong horse for his age and seemed to handle her awkward movements as she set foot on the ground once more. She then took his reins and tethered him on the hitching post before walking up the stairs to the church.

Seeing that the front door was opened, Emily stepped right inside. Though she didn't see Mrs. Crawford, she did see a couple sitting in the front pew with their heads bowed. Emily felt like she'd just stepped into a room she shouldn't have and was just about to turn around and leave when Mrs. Crawford came walking slowly up the steps.

"Ah, good morning, Emily," Mrs. Crawford said once she reached the top of the steps. She took a deep breath and let it out slowly. "This baby is going to be the death of me!" she chuckled.

"Good morning, Reverend. Mrs. Gibbons," Mrs. Crawford said as she continued into the church. The couple looked up when they saw Mrs. Crawford coming in.

"Ah, good morning, Mrs. Crawford," said the man as he stood. Emily followed close behind Mrs. Crawford, not wanting to appear rude. She figured it would be wise for her to meet the reverend and his wife since she'd be teaching in their church.

"May I introduce you to the new schoolteacher, Miss Emily Middleton," Mrs. Crawford said as she gestured to Emily. "She's been classically trained in Georgia and will make an excellent addition to the classroom."

"Ah, Miss Middleton. It's a pleasure to meet you," Mrs. Gibbons said. She was an older woman with blonde hair and a round figure. But her smile was her defining feature. She appeared very kind and welcoming. "You'll soon meet our three children. Henry, Timothy, and Jessica."

"I'm looking forward to visiting with all of the children once more," Emily said. "I had come by one day before and was eager to see so many coming together for their daily lessons. I was privately tutored and find this setting much more enjoyable."

"Well, we are just pleased to hear that Mrs. Crawford will have someone with her during the day," the reverend spoke up. "No offense, Mrs. Crawford, but it seems that you'll pop any day."

"No offense taken, Reverend," Mrs. Crawford said with a chuckle. She sat down heavily onto a chair near a desk that had been placed at the front of the church to be used for teaching. On Sunday's, the desk and chair were removed and replaced by the pulpit for the reverend to deliver his weekly sermons.

"We'll get out of your hair now and send the children over shortly," Mrs. Gibbons said as the two of them left the church. "Have a good day."

"They are such a lovely couple," Mrs. Crawford commented once they were gone. "It's so kind of them to let us use the church for these lessons."

Before the children arrived that morning, Mrs. Crawford did her best to get Emily caught up on what all the children were currently learning and working on. It was a lot for Emily to take in because even though she understood what Mrs. Crawford was teaching the children, it was hard to keep track of every student and their current progress.

"With your helping out, we'll be able to focus on the children's needs individually. There are a few I'm worried about reaching high enough marks to go on to the next grade," Mrs. Crawford explained. "And with this little one coming any day, I want to make sure the students are ready for this transition."

"Don't worry, Mrs. Crawford. Even though I am not certified by the state, I am eager to help these children succeed and to teach them all I know," Emily said with much conviction in her voice. Mrs. Crawford smiled, feeling reassured.

"And that's what makes a teacher great. Her passion and concern for her students," Mrs. Crawford declared. With Emily just starting out, she wanted to prove to everyone that she could not only teach but do a good job at it as well. She needed to prove to herself that she could really enjoy working, and perhaps even show Josh that she could be his ideal wife.

Emily had little time to think as the children started to arrive at the church. She followed Mrs. Crawford's instructions as she rang the church bell, signaling that school was starting for the day. Emily loved seeing all the happy children as they came running into the building and were quick to find their spots in the pews as they all sat together with those of similar ages. Emily was also surprised when she saw several Indian children from the local Crow Tribe also attending. It wasn't long before Emily was caught up on the daily lessons, helping each child to improve and understand the lessons for the day.

~

SAM CAME into the Sheriff's Office carrying a picnic basket of food that he'd picked up from The Eatery. He set it on Josh's desk where he was busy filling out a few papers in response to an inquiry from a nearby sheriff. Josh was always willing to help local authorities track down criminals and Josh was trying to remember all the characteristics of a burglar he'd helped bring to jail a few years back, who may be back at it again. But when Sam set the picnic basket on his desk, he was forced to look up at the doctor and try to figure out what the meaning of all of this was.

"I'm flattered, Sam, I really am. But I don't really have time to go on a picnic with you right now," Josh said with a smirk. He really did not want to lose his train of thought right now, but figured he could pay his best friend some attention for a moment.

"Josh, this isn't for me. It's for Emily," Sam said with a chuckle. "I thought you two might enjoy lunch together."

"Sam, I think that's a great idea, but I don't have time to ride out to the ranch right now with this report I need to fill out for another sheriff. We might have a repeat crime in Montana and I want to make sure I telegram this back to him today," Josh explained, starting to feel frustrated. He appreciated what Sam was trying to do for him, but he simply didn't have the time today.

"Well, then it's a good thing that Emily is now working with Mrs. Crawford on schooling the children and not all the way at the ranch," Sam said with a wicked grin, finding himself very amusing. His plan worked as Josh stilled and looked at him as though he didn't believe him.

"Emily took a job as a schoolteacher?" Josh asked, wondering if he'd heard Sam wrong.

"She sure did. I guess she made a real good impression on Mrs. Crawford and the Mayor. Seems she has the education if not the skill. But Mrs. Crawford says she has real potential," Sam explained, pleased as punch for coming up with this idea.

"Well I'll be damned," Josh said as he looked down at his report. "Sam, let me get this done real fast and I'll be sure to head over to the church to see for myself."

"Sounds like a mighty fine plan, if I do say so myself," Sam said with a chuckle as he moved towards the door.

"Yes, thank you, Sam," Josh said in a sarcastic voice as the doctor left the Sheriff's Office. Josh did his best to focus on the task at hand as he finished the report and then took it and the basket over to Frost's to send over the telegram. Once that was finished, he speedily went over to the church to see for himself what Emily was up to.

As he came over to the church with the basket in hand, he saw Emily and Mrs. Crawford standing outside the church while the children played during their break. He saw the way she smiled as she watched the kids closely. She laughed when they convinced her to play tag with them, and as he watched her picking up the hem of her gown and chase after them, he thought he'd never seen anything so beautiful before. The fact that she was willing to play with children really warmed his heart.

"Good day, Sheriff," Mrs. Crawford said as he came up to the church. He took his eyes off Emily only for a moment to say hello to the schoolteacher.

"I heard that there was a new teacher in town," Josh said as he watched Emily play with the children.

"Oh yes, there sure is," Mrs. Crawford confirmed. "And she's really good with the children, as you can see."

"Had to see it to believe it," Josh stated. A few minutes later, Emily looked up to see Josh standing there, a funny smile on his face. She stopped immediately and rubbed her hands down her gown to smooth and straighten it out. She almost felt embarrassed for what she had been doing, but as she smiled down at the children as they all ran to tag her, she figured that she couldn't help it. Though she might be their teacher, she also wanted them to know that she was also a person they could come to when they needed help with something.

After she encouraged the children to go play without her, she approached Josh. She noticed how he was carrying a basket in his hands and wondered what idea he had.

"Hello, Josh," Emily said as she walked up to him. "How is your day going?"

"It's been busy, but a little birdie told me about the new schoolteacher in town," Josh said, his lopsided grin appearing. It made Emily weak in the knees and she did her best to keep her composure in front of the children. "I figured I'd come see for myself and ask if you'd care to join me for some lunch." Emily didn't reply but looked to Mrs. Crawford, who nodded in response.

"The children and I will be fine on our own for a bit," Mrs. Crawford said before she turned and made her way up the stairs. There, she rung the church bell, signaling for the children to come back inside for the afternoon lesson.

"Well, let's have a seat over here," Emily said as she

pointed to the base of a tree. It looked shaded and comfortable enough to sit and enjoy some food.

"Ladies first," Josh gestured. Emily smiled as she led the way over to the tree. As they settled down, Josh started to pull out the food that Sam had gotten for them. He couldn't help but smirk at it all, thinking that Sam had really outdone himself this time.

"So, you said you've had a busy morning?" Emily inquired, hoping to start some sort of conversation between them while they ate.

"Yes, I had to fill out a report this morning," Josh said as he dished out plates of food for them both. It all looked delicious as he portioned out fresh rolls, baked chicken, and buttery green beans. "A nearby sheriff reached out to other officers in Montana. He's on the lookout for a bank robber matching a few descriptions I remember from a burglar I nabbed a few years back. I would have been by earlier if I hadn't needed to finish that report as soon as possible."

"I completely understand, Josh," Emily reassured. "It's simply nice to get to spend some time with you." Josh nodded, appreciating Emily's understanding of the demands of his position in town.

"But enough about me. Tell me more about you," Josh said with a smile. "I was surprised when I heard that you'd taken the teaching job." Emily sighed as she nodded, remembering some of their previous conversations.

"I really took into consideration what you said about finding something that you're passionate about. I really didn't think that employment could ever be something that someone enjoyed," Emily admitted. "When I met with Delphina, she encouraged me to consider the position because of my extensive education. And since I've always enjoyed instructing others, I figured that I could give it a shot." Emily was a little nervous about what Josh would say in response and for a moment, simply concentrated on the food. It was delicious, and since she'd eaten so quickly that morning, she was rather famished.

Josh thought that Emily had come a long way since arriving in Spruce Valley. He could see that she was starting to bloom in the community and that she was starting to put her mind towards becoming the person she probably always wanted to be. It only took some encouragement to see that she had all this hidden potential, if only she was willing to give different things a try.

"I think you'll come to enjoy teaching just as much as I enjoy being a sheriff," Josh said after a while. "I saw the way you were with the children today and the fact that you're willing to play with them means that you actually care about them." Emily was beyond pleased to hear Josh's remarks. She really wanted to impress him, along with the rest of the community.

"I would have given anything to have learned my lessons with other students," Emily admitted. "I want these children to know they are not only going to get the help they need to succeed, but also be able to rely on their teacher. I don't want to be just an instructor. I want to be someone people can come to if they need help with their education." Emily could hardly believe the words that were coming out of her mouth. It was as though as she spoke, the truth of her heart came out. She never knew that she had this desire before until she was willing to give it a try.

"Well, it sounds like you have the passion needed for the position," Josh said. "And I'm sure in time, you'll get used to all the different demands of teaching."

"Yes, I will admit that today has been quite overwhelming as I learn how Mrs. Crawford keeps everyone and everything organized," Emily said with a chuckle. "And after I've gained some new skills, I'll be able to apply to be certified."

"Won't that be something," Josh encouraged. Emily nodded, thinking that she'd enjoy having the title of certified schoolteacher. She never thought a woman could ever be a teacher, but Mrs. Crawford would surely teach her more than how to teach. Emily would also learn how to be a successful, independent woman.

"Well, I should be getting back to the students," Emily said as she helped Josh pack up the picnic basket. "But thank you for coming by and bringing lunch."

"Any time," Josh said as he helped Emily to her feet. "We'll have to do this again soon when we can find time between both our work schedules." Emily thought it was rather interesting to think about having a work schedule. It pleased her no end as she parted with Josh. She was eager to return to the students and continue learning all she could about teaching effectively.

# CHAPTER 14

Josh realized that after three weeks of watching Emily continue to progress in this new teaching position that he was more attracted to her than he'd ever been before. Though Josh had first been drawn to her beauty, he was now more impressed with her mind. Not only had Emily been attending every school day and assisting Mrs. Crawford, but she'd also been tutoring different adults in the evenings over at The Eatery. And now that Mrs. Crawford had gone into labor and delivered a beautiful baby girl, Emily had taken over as lead teacher and was conducting the daily lessons all on her own.

Though it had been harder to be alone with Emily, he'd made time to see her during the day. Sometimes he'd bring her lunch or dinner, knowing that it was a long ride back to the ranch every evening. Every once in a while they'd have dinner at The Eatery and Josh would escort her back to the ranch and come back in the evening. It might seem like a lot of running around, but Josh was really starting to enjoy spending time with the new Emily.

When she'd first come to Spruce Valley, she'd been very set in her old ways. So much so that she had unrealistic expectations of married life. But as he slowly showed her what it was like to live in the West, Emily had slowly adapted to the lifestyle. She'd not only learned the basics of riding a horse and cooking, but also housework, and now a teaching position in town as well. It had only been about two months since her arrival to Spruce Valley and already she'd accomplished so much in such a short time.

The other thing Josh noticed was the way she attracted the attention of other men. Though everyone knew that Emily had come to Spruce Valley as a mail-order-bride for him, Josh knew that there were a few bold men who wouldn't mind trying their luck with Emily as well. Josh knew that the time had come for him to make his final move with Emily. He thought they had come a long way since first meeting in person and now might be the time to make things official.

That evening, Josh had something special planned for Emily. He'd invited her over for dinner and planned to cook her a good meal. He wanted Emily to see his small apartment above the Sheriff's Office because if they did marry, they'd be living together in this space. He had all sorts of things he wanted to tell Emily and hoped that tonight would be the night he'd finally tell her all his hopes and dreams. Josh felt a little vulnerable with putting himself out there, but his gut told him that everything would work out in the end.

Josh was busy in the kitchen, stirring a pot of creamy potato chowder on the stove when he heard a knock on the door below. Moving the pot over to the part of the stove that didn't have a small fire burning below, Josh hurried down the stairs into the Sheriff's Office and quickly pulled open the door. Before him stood Emily. She'd dressed in a very fashionable gown, the purple silk shimmering in the setting sun. She'd curled her long black hair and pinned it to the top of her head, exposing her long and slender neck. She was every bit the Atlanta debutante she'd been born as, but as Josh looked into her blue eyes, he could see the real Emily before him.

"Come on in," Josh said with a smile, opening the door all the way and allowing Emily to enter.

"Thank you," Emily replied as she stepped into the office. It was the first time Emily had been in the office and she found it very plain and simple. The only thing that was in the office was Josh's desk and chair. Another desk and chair had been pushed up against the opposite wall and appeared to be waiting for a deputy one day. But there were no comforting touches, even though Emily figured that a Sheriff's Office wasn't meant to be warm and welcoming.

"Right this way," Josh said, pulling Emily's attention back to him. "The apartment is right up these stairs." Emily followed his lead and took the stairs slowly. There wasn't much light, but as soon as they came through the door at the top of the stairs, she found the apartment to be a lot more welcoming than the office downstairs. What further surprised Emily was that there was an older couple sitting at the small dining table in the middle of the space. When Josh had invited her over for dinner at his apartment, she hadn't been expecting anyone else.

"Emily, may I introduce you to my parents. This is my mother, Matilda Ryder. And my father, Joshua Ryder," Josh introduced as the older couple stood. Emily was taken back by being introduced to his parents. She certainly hadn't been expecting this and called on her years of concealing her inner emotions as she shook hands with them both.

"It's a pleasure to meet you both," Emily said as she greeted them. She watched the way they observed her, and for a moment Emily wished she'd dressed in something a little plainer. She had really wanted to look her best for tonight since this would be the first time coming to Josh's home. But now she would have liked to have known what Josh had planned for them before arriving this evening.

"It's nice to meet you as well," Matilda spoke up when her husband continued to scrutinize the woman with his eyes. "Josh has told us so many things about you already." They all settled down at the table as Josh returned to the stove. Emily had an instinct to help him with the meal but wondered if it would be better to remain at the table and entertain his parents.

"I am pleased to hear this," Emily replied, making sure to keep a steady smile on her face. "Josh has explained to me that you two live a little south of Spruce Valley on the family ranch."

"Yes. Our family has been ranching for four generations. That is, until Junior decided to play law," Joshua said, glancing at his son for a moment before returning his gaze to Emily. She was a beauty, that he could admit. But he didn't trust people from wealthy families.

"One of the first things I learned about Josh is how passionate he is about being the Sheriff of Spruce Valley," Emily said proudly. She had detected the hints of tension in Mr. Ryder's voice and wanted to show how highly she thought of Josh. "After coming to stay here, I learned how this community really thinks highly of Josh and all the good work he's done here." Matilda smiled at Emily, finding it nice to hear so many good things about her son.

"When we got a copy of the article where Josh was detailed a hero, I couldn't be prouder," Matilda said as she looked to her son. He looked over his shoulder at her, grateful to hear such a compliment from his mother.

"He really become quite famous, even in the East where

I'm from," Emily agreed. "When I saw his ad in the paper, I almost couldn't believe that a man like Josh would need help in finding a wife." They chuckled over this, but Emily saw that Mr. Ryder hardly cracked a smile.

"I bet you were eager to send Josh a letter then," Joshua spoke up, seeing if he could catch Emily in any ill will towards his son.

"I will admit that I was intrigued why a famous sheriff would be writing a mail-order-bride ad. It is only one of the things that piqued my interest about Josh. But I wouldn't say it was the leading reason," Emily said very clearly, hoping to prove her point that she wasn't after Josh just because he was famous. Though her ideas about Josh were muddled and unrealistic in the beginning, she now saw Josh for who he truly was.

"Ma, I've made your favorite," Josh said as he came to the table with several bowls.

"Ah, how thoughtful of you, Josh," Matilda said, delighted to see the potato soup.

"Whenever I got sick, Ma would always make potato soup for me. It wasn't until I was older that I learned it was her favorite," Josh said to Emily, thinking that it was nice to have his parents visiting this week, and also have them meet his intended.

"My goodness, did he eat as a child," Matilda said with a chuckle. "I remember the one time he ate a whole pot of potato soup all on his own." Josh brought over the loaf of bread he'd made earlier in the day, proud of being able to make dinner for everyone.

"If it doesn't have a good amount of cheese, it doesn't taste right," Joshua said as he started to eat with gusto. Josh was put off by this, having wanted to say grace before they began. Seeming to notice Josh's discomfort, Emily bowed her head and said a silent prayer before beginning to eat.

"I've had jambalaya before, but nothing quite as creamy as this," Emily said. "I understand why you'd eat a whole pot of it."

"Well, I'm sure my mother has lots of interesting details about my childhood that she'd be happy to share with you," Josh said with a chuckle.

"Miss Middleton, where are your parents?" Joshua asked between bites. Josh scowled at his father then. "What did I say?" he asked in mocked hurt.

"Mr. Ryder, my mother died giving birth to me," Emily said as she stiffened. "And my father disappeared after he ruined our family name when he destroyed his own business." The room fell silent as Emily poked at her food, feeling a bit embarrassed having to share these particular details with Josh's parents upon first meeting them.

"Well, I think it's lovely that you'd travel all the way out here on your own and make a name for yourself," Matilda spoke up after a while.

"Emily has started working as a schoolteacher here in town," Josh added. "Mrs. Crawford just had her baby, so Emily came into town right at the perfect time to make sure the children continue on with their lessons."

"Wouldn't have expected a woman such as yourself to be eager to find a working job," Joshua then commented, making Emily's heart drop even further. She wasn't sure why Josh's father was being so hard on her, but she wasn't about to crumble under the pressure.

"You're absolutely right, Mr. Ryder. I had no designs to ever work a day in my life," Emily said in a sing-song voice. "But your son taught me not only the importance of having a job, but also that it could bring passion and purpose to one's life as well. I've come to enjoy teaching more than I ever thought I would, and I'm glad that Josh has been such a big example in my life of what it means to work for a living."

Matilda smiled at Emily, thinking she was witty and quick on her feet. She wasn't sure why her husband was being so cross with Emily, but she planned to give him a piece of her mind later.

Joshua harrumphed as he finished eating, scraping the sides of his bowl with his bread. Josh was glaring at his father, trying to wrap his mind around why the man was giving Emily such a hard time. He was starting to think that this dinner had been a bad idea, and if his father kept this up, he was going to send his parents' home early.

After they'd finished eating and the table had been cleared, Matilda and Emily took care of the dishes as they talked quietly with one another. Emily talked about how much she was enjoying being a schoolteacher and Matilda shared details about Josh when he was little. They laughed quietly together, and from where Josh was sitting in the living room, he couldn't help but smile to see them so happy. He looked at his father then, wanting to figure out why the man had picked a bone tonight.

"What gives, Pa?" Josh asked in a soft voice, not wanting to draw attention to him.

"I don't know what you're talking about," Joshua said as he puffed on his pipe, eager to get out of the small apartment and back to the inn. He couldn't understand why his son continued to live in such a small space instead of building a house or moving home.

"You do know what I'm talking about, Pa. You're giving Emily the ninth degree," Josh said, becoming more frustrated that his father wouldn't even admit to what he'd done during dinner.

"I just think that you could do better, Josh, that's all," Joshua finally said. "It's not like she's some nice country girl who can actually deal with being a sheriff's wife."

"And what makes you think I can't handle it?" Emily

asked, coming to join them in the living room. They'd finished cleaning up the kitchen right as Mr. Ryder had spoken, and Emily couldn't stand his negative attitude any longer. Joshua didn't like how Emily was challenging him and figured he'd put her in her place once and for all.

"Because a young lady such as yourself is more fit for tea parties and balls," Joshua said as he got to his feet. "The first time Josh gets called away on a dangerous job, you're going to be so filled with fear and worry that you won't be able to handle it again." Emily didn't like the way the man had raised his voice or the dagger eyes he was giving her. And since she didn't need to tolerate any of this, she picked up the hem of her gown and promptly made her way out of the apartment and down the stairs.

"Emily, wait!" Josh called after her, but Emily only quickened her pace. And as she did so, she stumbled over her feet because it was so dark on the staircase and went tumbling down the stairs. By the time she hit the floor in the office, she'd completely passed out from being knocked unconscious.

"Oh, God. No! Emily, no!" Josh hollered, terrified that she'd fallen and twisted her neck. But as he came running down the stairs, he reached her body and felt her chest to confirm that she was still breathing.

"Josh, is she okay?" Matilda asked as she came down the stairs slowly with a lantern in her hand.

"She's hurt bad, Ma," Josh said as he looked up the stairs at his mother. Matilda could see tears in his eyes as she looked down at her terrified son.

"It's going to be okay, Josh," Matilda said as she finished coming down the stairs. She looked down at Emily and saw how pale she'd turned. "I'm going to stay here with her and you're going to go get the doc."

"But what happens when I leave and she passes away?" Josh asked. "Mama, I can't lose her. I love her."

"Josh, you listen to me real well," Matilda said. "You go get that doc and you get your butt back here. I'm not going to let Emily die." Matilda gave her son a stern look, hoping he'd jump into action. Josh looked down at Emily one last time before pushing himself to his feet and running out of the Sheriff's Office. He didn't even bother closing the door as he ran into the night, moving as fast as he could over to the livery stables so he could collect his mare and get to the Slater's ranch as fast as possible. He prayed under his breath over and over again, pleading with the Lord to not let Emily pass away.

# CHAPTER 15

At first, Emily didn't understand what was happening. Her mind had still held onto the anger that had coursed through her body after what Mr. Ryder had said to her. But now that anger seemed to be transformed into some sort of fire that was raging through her body.

"We've got to get her body cooled down," she heard a familiar voice say. "The fever is making her too hot and the swelling in her head needs to come down."

"What do you need me to do?" came another voice.

"Let's strip her and start bathing her in cold water," said the first voice.

"Seems like a woman's job," came a third voice.

"Yeah, let us do it."

Emily could tell that she was surrounded by people but couldn't make out any of their faces. She tried her best to open her eyes, but the effort felt like too much for her to handle. Instead, she drifted back off to sleep, thinking it would be better to fall back into unconsciousness instead of feeling all this pain.

When she came to again, she felt different. The fire seemed to be gone, but now the pain was stronger. Her headed pounded with pain, but as she tried to raise her hand to cradle her head, she found that she couldn't do so. Just trying to move her right arm only caused more pain to erupt in that area. Emily desperately wished she knew what was happening to her, but as the pain increased, it only brought her deeper down into slumber.

Emily wasn't sure for how long or how many days this pattern had been going on. But eventually, she found the strength to open her eyes. As her eyes adjusted to the dim lit room, she saw that she was in a small room she'd never been in before. She was resting on a bed, that much she could tell. Her left hand moved, her fingers brushing against soft fabrics. She looked down her body to see that she'd been changed into a nightgown and she didn't like the idea of someone having changed her clothes.

But modesty seemed to be the last of her concerns. As she tried to move her right arm, she found it very difficult to do so. She turned her head to look down that side of her body and saw that her forearm had been placed in a cast and was too heavy for her to do very much with. She sighed, trying to remember what had happened to have landed her in this state.

When Emily tried to sit up, a pounding erupted in her head. Her vision blurred and for a moment she thought she was going to pass out again. But she closed her eyes to the pain and willed it to go away. Sitting up, she took several deep breaths. Then, she realized she wasn't alone.

Sitting in a wooden chair in the corner she saw Josh with slouched shoulders and his head resting back against the wall. His face looked as though he hadn't shaved in days, but he appeared so peaceful as he was sleeping. Emily hated the thought of waking him, but she was dying of thirst and seriously needed to use a water closet.

"Josh," Emily whispered, her voice sounding rough from not having anything to drink in however long it had been since she'd been injured. But she was loud enough to cause Josh to stir. It took him a moment to realize that Emily was not only awake but sitting up on her own.

"Dear Lord, Emily. Don't sit up," Josh said as he sprung from the chair and came to sit next to her. "You shouldn't sit up until Dr. Slater comes to check on you."

"Josh, water," Emily said, refusing to lie down anymore. Josh was quick to pour her a small cup of water from a pitcher on a nearby table and handed it to Emily, fearful about her sitting up already. Emily took the cup carefully and drank till it was empty, the water refreshing her throat immediately.

"Now please, Emily, you really should be resting," Josh insisted as he took the cup from her and set it aside.

"I need to use the water closet and I need to know what happened. Where am I?" Emily asked, continuing to be persistent. Josh couldn't believe how stubborn she was being but couldn't really fault her after everything that had happened.

"Emily, you're in the clinic in town," Josh started with. "And you've been here for almost three days now." Emily stilled at hearing she'd been asleep for three days. Her mind raced, trying to remember all that had happened to lead her to being placed in the clinic. She moved her right arm slowly, just raising it a bit to figure out why it had been casted and how broken it could be.

"I don't remember anything," Emily stated. "I don't remember getting into an accident." Emily's words pierced Josh's heart. He felt guilty enough and hated to be the one to tell her the truth. But it was only fair that he was the one to tell her.

"You were having dinner over at my apartment with my parents. I had invited you over and surprised you with meeting my parents," Josh explained slowly. "But my father was being bull-headed and said some things he shouldn't have. You left in a hurry but stumbled and fell down the stairs."

"I guess I must have tried to break my fall," Emily said as she looked down at her right hand. "But it doesn't sound real, to be honest."

"My parents are still in town," Josh said. "And my father would like to apologize." Emily only nodded, uneasy about the idea of being seen in this condition. But as she remembered that she'd been undressed and changed into a nightgown, it seemed that she had no reason to really feel embarrassed anymore.

"Does the clinic have a water closet?" Emily asked, really feeling like she needed to heed the call of nature.

"Yes. I'll help you use it," Josh said as he stood and then slowly helped Emily to her feet. As she put weight on her feet, Emily's head spun with dizziness. She closed her eyes a moment as she gripped onto Josh with her good hand. When it passed, she opened her eyes, ungripped her hand and walked slowly. Josh helped her out of the room and down the hallway.

After she'd finished her business on her own, she allowed Josh to take some of her weight as she slowly made her way back to the bed. She couldn't believe how weak her body felt, but was at least glad she was able to get cleaned up a bit. As Josh lowered her back onto the bed, Emily sat up and took a few deep breaths before allowing Josh to guide her down to a resting position on the bed.

"I feel like I just ran for miles," Emily said as she closed her eyes briefly.

"Dr. Slater said that it will take some time to heal. But the fact that you're awake is a good sign," Josh said, looking down at her with concern.

"Did he think I wouldn't wake?" Emily asked, fearing the answer.

"You hit your head pretty hard," Josh said as he winced at her question. "Sam said your brain was swelling bad and there was a chance you'd never wake up from the coma." Emily sighed heavily, thinking that the fall down the stairs had to be a lot worse than what she'd first imagined.

"Well, I'm awake for now," Emily said. "I just feel so exhausted." Josh nodded, even though she still had her eyes closed.

"Are you hungry?" Josh asked, wondering what more he could do for her.

"I'm not, but I'm sure after three days I should eat something," Emily said. A knock on the door was heard and Josh rose from the side of the bed and quickly answered it. He was surprised when he opened the door and saw Bright Star standing on the other side.

"I've brought some things for Emily Middleton that might be of use," Bright Star explained when he saw the confusion in the Sheriff's eyes. He held up a bag to show him what he'd brought, and Josh thought it all smelled funny. But not wanting to offend the Indian, Josh opened the door and bid him enter.

"Emily, Bright Star has come to visit with you," Josh said as he returned to the edge of her bed. Bright Star kneeled beside the bed and looked at Emily with great concern. Emily opened her eyes briefly and tried to give the Indian a kind smile.

"I don't think I'll be able to play poker today," Emily

quipped. Bright Star chuckled as he started to pull various things out of his deerskin bag.

"No, not today, Emily Middleton. But very soon, I assure you," Bright Star said as he pulled a salve from his bag and handed it to Josh. "This should be rubbed into the skin to help it heal faster."

"Thank you," Josh said, wondering if Emily would allow him to apply it later. He'd feel more comfortable asking Martha or Fiona to apply it when they next came to visit the clinic. Everyone had been into the clinic every day to check on Emily's progress and they would all be relieved to learn that she'd at least woken up.

"Now, here is some medicine that is meant to be put onto the gums of the mouth. It will help with the pain and a sour stomach," Bright Star explained. He scooped what looked like mud onto his fingers and promptly opened Emily's mouth just wide enough to where he could rub it onto her gums. She furrowed her brows but didn't protest, finding the substance to at least be flavorful, if not strange feeling.

"And next, I shall sing a special prayer for you," Bright Star announced as he rubbed fresh herbs together in his hands and moved them above Emily's body as he started to say a chant that Josh didn't understand. The air was filled with the smell of mint and rosemary, which Josh thought was at least pleasant smelling. He remained silent during Bright Star's chant, trying to keep a positive attitude about what the Indian was doing when he was a Christian man. Josh figured that it was the thought that counted.

"Emily Middleton will be sure to heal faster now," Bright Star said as he finished his prayer and began to gather his things again. "This pouch contains more of the medicine for her mouth. Give it to her when she's in pain."

"Thank you, Bright Star," Josh said as the Indian got to his feet. Bright Star grunted his approval before leaving the room. It was almost like he'd never been there, but as Josh looked down at the items in his hands, he felt grateful for them.

"How are you feeling, Emily?" Josh asked, but Emily had already fallen back to sleep. Bright Star's chanting had encouraged her back to sleep and the pain in her body had seemed to fade away for a moment. Josh smiled as he brushed back a strand of her long black hair from her face, at least happy to see that she was resting well again.

Setting the items on the side table, Josh returned to his chair and decided that it would be a good idea for him to catch a few more hours of sleep himself. His constant worrying had kept him up all night and now he was completely exhausted. He only hoped that Emily waking for a short time was a good sign that she would one day make a full recovery.

~

IT WAS five days after Emily had first regained consciousness till she was fit to leave the clinic. She was still weak and slow to move, but knew that she wasn't going to feel her old self again until she got back to the things she enjoyed doing. Wanting to be closer to the church to resume lessons with the children, Emily had her things moved back to the Honeywell Inn. That way she wouldn't have to worry about riding till her arm fully healed. And though the Slaters were sad to hear the news, they completely understood.

In the mornings, it took Emily a lot of time to get ready for the day. Dressing herself with only one arm was frustrating, and every time she bumped her bad arm, it would send shocks of pain along the full length of it. By the time she was done dressing, she felt exhausted and would often need to sit for a moment before she could get up and move about again. Eventually, she returned to the church to oversee the children's lessons. Thankfully, Reverend Paul and his wife had at least been at the church when the children arrived for the day and allowed the students to review basic lessons. Emily was grateful to the couple and hoped that she would be able to make it up to them one day.

The hardest part of recovering from the fall was the memories that slowly came back to her. Eventually she regained everything and remembered the words that Mr. Ryder had said to her. After everything she'd been able to accomplish since coming to Spruce Valley, she wasn't sure how she was going to show her worth to Josh's father and therefore she started to doubt her own abilities. Even though Emily was back on her feet, she hadn't gone out of her way to spend any time with Josh in fear of running into his parents again. This had proved particularly difficult since his parents were staying at the same inn as she was. So far, they hadn't run into each other—yet. And though Emily very much liked Josh's mother, she didn't want to have to look Mr. Ryder in the eyes again.

Emily thought all had been going well for a few weeks. She went back to teaching when one day she went into The Eatery for dinner and found Josh and his parents were also patrons for the evening. She did her best to avoid them and found a table at the back of the room. She then picked up her menu and pretended to be interested in it to avoid any awkward eye contact. But when someone took the seat next to her, she knew that she wasn't going to be able to avoid them forever.

"Why, hello there, Miss. I don't think we've met before," came Josh's voice. She couldn't help but smirk as she set down her menu and looked at him. "Because I know if we had met before, you wouldn't have come and sat all alone back here."

"I just didn't want to interrupt anything," Emily said, her eyes locking with Josh's. She'd missed seeing his honey colored eyes and the lopsided grin on his face. She sighed, feeling more comfortable then she had in a while.

"You wouldn't have been interrupting at all," Josh said as he carefully took her right hand in his. "It's always worth getting to spend any amount of time with you, and I know you're still recovering and getting back into the swing of teaching again."

"Well, I appreciate your consideration," Emily said.. "Dr. Slater said that by winter my arm should be fully healed." Another wave of guilt washed over Josh and now he could no longer bear it.

"Emily, I want you to come have dinner with me and my folks. My father has something he'd like to say to you," Josh said. Emily stiffened, thinking that Mr. Ryder had already said quite enough to her.

"I don't know if I can handle anything more your father has to say to me," Emily admitted as she looked away from Josh. But when he gently squeezed her fingers, she forced herself to look Josh in the eyes once more.

"You're one of the strongest women I know, Emily. You should never back down from a challenge," Josh said with a smirk on his lips. Emily couldn't help but smile herself, thinking that what he said was very true. But ever since the accident, she'd been a lot more mindful of herself and hadn't really tried anything but what she needed to do to survive.

"Alright then," Emily eventually agreed. She allowed Josh to pull back her chair so she could stand with ease. And then Josh led her over to his table as both his parents rose to their feet. Joshua pulled off his hat as Emily came near, the knots in his stomach gathered together as he started to wring his hat between his hands.

"Miss Middleton, I'd just like to say that I'm very sorry

for everything that happened. I should have never been quick to judge you like that," Joshua said, his eyes filled with guilt. It was clear to Emily that he felt sorry about the situation and she hoped the man wouldn't give her anymore trouble in the future.

"I appreciate your apology," Emily replied calmly.

"Would you care to join us for dinner then?" Joshua asked hopefully.

"Yes, I would like that," she responded. Joshua gave her a quick smile as they all settled down at the table. They ordered the special of the day and Emily enjoyed some of Nell's splendid tea.

"It's good to see you out and about again, Miss Middleton," Nell said as she poured Emily's tea.

"Thank you, Nell," Emily replied. The woman gave her a wink before moving to another table. It was hard to believe all that had happened since coming to Spruce Valley. But even with a broken arm, she was pleased with where her life was headed. During the dinner, Emily snuck peeks at Josh, thinking he was as handsome as ever. She only hoped that she could continue to prove her worth to him.

After they'd finished dinner, Josh invited her to walk with him. Emily agreed and they said goodbye to his parents as they returned to the inn. With her left arm hanging on Josh's, he led her through town and a bit away from it as they watched the sun dip below the horizon, filling the sky with waves of orange. The weather was growing warmer with signs that soon spring would give way to summer.

"I heard today that Dr. Slater was called home for an emergency," Josh said at one point, causing fear to spread over Emily.

"My goodness, what has happened? Why didn't you tell me before?" Emily asked quickly.

"Don't worry, Emily," Josh said with a chuckle. "Lucy

gave birth to another girl is all." Emily sighed deeply, thinking she should have thought about that first before jumping to conclusions. "I would have told you sooner if something bad had happened."

"I'm so sorry, Josh. I should have known as much," Emily said. "So, Sam and Lucy now are parents of two girls?" This made Josh chuckle as he shook his head.

"Seems like the men of Slater Ranch are soon going to be outnumbered," Josh reasoned. "But it really has me thinking about something."

"Oh? And what's that?" Emily wondered as she watched the sunset, thinking it was nice to simply stand with a handsome man and enjoy something so wonderful and beautiful.

"That someday soon I'd like a little one of my own," Josh declared as he started to become nervous. With Emily's left hand still in his, he knelt before her and pulled a ring out of his pocket. As he looked up into her eyes, they grew wide with surprise.

"Emily Middleton, since the first time I saw your picture, I knew that you were the most beautiful woman I'd ever seen. But after getting to know you, and seeing you grow here in Spruce Valley, I now know that beauty runs deep inside you as well," Josh said. "I see the way you treat other people, especially those children that you teach and the adults you tutor. I know things haven't been perfect since you arrived here, but I hope you'll agree to becoming my wife so that we can spend every day together for the rest of our lives."

Emily was so taken back by his unexpected proposal that at first she was simply speechless. But as he continued to wait on her response, she seemed to become alive with excitement as she began to nod her head.

"Yes, Josh. I'll gladly be your wife," Emily said with enthusiasm. Josh smiled the biggest smile she'd ever seen as he slid the ring onto her finger and then stood to wrap his arms around her, being careful of her broken arm. He kissed the top of her head, but wanting more, Emily tilted her head up till their lips met. That kiss was filled with passion and desire but was so light that it was perfect for the moment. Josh broke the kiss, wanting to be respectful as he tilted back his head and simply smiled down at Emily.

"Well, I guess we better go tell the folks," Josh said. "I think they will be expecting the news."

"You told them that you were going to propose to me?" Emily asked as they walked hand in hand back to the inn.

"The other day I talked to them about it. And when I saw you walk into The Eatery tonight, I just knew I couldn't wait any longer," Josh explained.

"And what did your father say about it?" Emily asked, wondering if Mr. Ryder was going to lose his temper again once he saw the ring on her finger.

"He was happy to know that I was following my heart and proposing to the woman I'd fallen in love with," Josh answered with a kind smile on his lips. Emily stopped dead in her tracks, surprised to hear Josh's confession of love. She'd never really expected to fall in love before, but as she looked up into Josh's eyes, she felt like she could really love him in return.

"You love me?" she asked, searching his eyes for an honest answer.

"Yes, Emily, I do love you. That's why I asked you to marry me," Josh reassured her. "There is no other reason besides the fact that I do really love you." Emily's eyes filled with happy tears as she looked up at him. As best she could, Emily wrapped her good arm around his waist, wanting to hug him the best she could.

"Oh, Josh. I love you, too," Emily declared, thinking she'd never be happier in all her life. She couldn't believe that her heart could feel like this for anyone, but the more she thought of Josh's good character, she reasoned that there was no reason why she couldn't love this man for the rest of her life.

Josh hugged her back, tears filling his eyes. There had been a time when Josh was certain he'd never marry or have children. It had been a nagging fear at the back of his mind every time he found a decent minute to think about his future. He wanted to create a home with the woman he loved, and he felt such great relief in finally finding her.

Telling Josh's parents the good news was almost as exciting as experiencing the proposal itself. Emily was warmly hugged by Matilda and even Joshua gave her a decent smile. She felt reassured that when she married Josh that she would be joining a welcoming family that would honestly care about her. Though she knew that no family was perfect, she was at least happy that things could be mended before they were married. It was all so surreal to Emily as she simply felt pure happiness for the first time in her life.

# CHAPTER 16

*Dear Emily, stop. I'm so happy for you, stop. I will send you a wedding present, stop. Cynthia, stop.*

Emily held the telegram in her hands, a bright smile on her face. She'd stopped into Frost's to pick up a few items when he gave her the telegram. It was good to hear from her friend and she thought how kind it had been for Cynthia to take the time to send her a telegram from so far away. Emily knew that she would treasure it forever.

With it being Saturday, and the day before the wedding, Emily was making last minute preparations. She'd tried her hand at making decorations for the church and had just finished putting them up when she went to the mercantile to see if she could purchase any more white ribbon. She hoped to have the decorations done by this evening in order to enjoy a family-style dinner at the Slater's that evening. Josh told her that he'd pick her up at the inn, and therefore she had a bit of time left on her hands.

Emily went down the road to the women's seamstress shop, needing to fit into her gown one last time. Since the wedding had been rushed so that Mr. and Mrs. Ryder could return to their ranch, so had the wedding plans. Lucy had done her best to construct a wedding gown as fast as she could with also tending to a newborn, and now Emily had to try it on at the shop in case the other women needed to make any other adjustments. She was eager to finally try it on, and even more excited to be married tomorrow.

As Emily stepped into the shop, she was quickly greeted by Francene and Samuel. "Emily, you're getting married tomorrow!" Francene shouted with glee. "And I get to be your flower girl."

"That's right, my dear. I couldn't think of anyone else more perfect for the job," Emily said.

But Francene placed her little hands on her hips and said, "It's not a job. It's a duty." Emily chuckled as she watched the small child, thinking that it was very suitable and similar to the way she used to think about work.

"You're right, Francene. And how is Samuel today?" Emily asked as she turned her focus to the young boy who was often very shy.

"I'm excited for tomorrow," he replied in his soft voice.

"And so am I," Emily replied. Martha came out of the back room then and motioned for Emily to come on back. There, Emily spotted her wedding dress for the first time. Her mouth fell open as she looked at it, thinking it had much more detail than she ever thought would be possible for such short notice.

"It's gorgeous," Emily exclaimed, walking up to it on the hanger and running her fingers over it. She'd never thought her dress would be made of silk because Spruce Valley was such a small town, but as she felt the fabric between her fingers, she could tell it was the real deal.

"Let's get you changed so we can see how well it fits," Martha said as she ushered Emily into the changing room.

Once she was ready, Martha helped her into the dress while being mindful of her broken arm. It was the only thing that Emily wished was different. But she reasoned that she had to be lucky for even being able to be married to Josh. He was such a wonderful man and a well-looked-after gentleman in the community that she was simply honored to be marrying a man like him.

"My goodness, it fits like a glove!" Emily declared as she came out of the changing room and stood before the tall looking glass. "How on earth did Lucy do something like this in such a short time, and when she just gave birth?"

"That woman is a miracle worker for sure," Martha replied as she started to look over the gown. "I don't think I can spot one thing more to do to it."

"I would have to agree with you," Emily said as she turned around before the mirror to see it at all angles. "Well, I'll pay for this and get back to the church. I have some more decorations to finish up."

"Alright, let's get you settled then," Martha agreed as she helped Emily back into her day gown and then placed the wedding dress back on the hanger. "I'll wrap this up and bring it over to the inn for you."

"Just bring it with you when you come out to the dinner tonight at the ranch. I'm going to be spending the night there and coming in with the Slater's in the morning. Fiona promised to help me get ready," Emily explained.

"Sounds like we could turn it into a slumber party and have all the women sleep over," Martha suggested.

"My goodness, what a fun idea!" Emily said with a giggle as she came out of the changing room. "I think that would be excellent."

"It's settled then. We'll see you all tonight," Martha said as she began to wrap up the gown. Emily paid for the gown at the counter and bid the children goodbye before she left, feeling more excited than before. It had been a long time since she'd had a slumber party and wondered if any of them would get any sleep tonight!

"ARE you sure you ladies are going to be okay on your own?" Sam asked as he stood by the front door, looking back at his wife and newborn as they sat in the sitting room. Lucy was rocking the baby to sleep, and he didn't like the idea of being away from them, even though he would just be sleeping in the bunkhouse tonight.

"Come on, Sam. Let the women have their fun," Gray said as he grabbed Sam by the arm and led him out of the ranch house. They'd just finished up having dinner together, and now the rest of the evening was left to the women.

"I'll see you bright and early in the morning," Josh said to Emily as he placed a kiss on her forehead.

"You bet I'll be there," Emily teased him as she hugged him one last time and finally let go. She watched as he left with his parents, needing to get them back to the inn. As the men departed, Emily turned to the women as they started to giggle with excitement.

"My goodness, what shall we do first?" Fiona asked.

"Well, it seems like mama and baby needs to get some sleep," Martha said, drawing everyone's attention to Lucy and little Maribel. They'd both fallen asleep in the rocker, and the other two older children had already gone off to bed.

"Alright, let's get them into a real bed," Emily agreed. The three women then carefully helped Lucy to her feet and led her to her bedroom before placing Maribel in the basinet, and helping Lucy into a nightgown.

"We're supposed to be helping Emily get ready," Lucy said as she yawned.

"I'm sure Emily is learning all sorts of life lessons by helping you two into bed," Martha said with a chuckle.

"Nothing truer than seeing a woman's body postpartum," Lucy said with a chuckle, causing the others to laugh. After Lucy was in bed, the other women returned to the dining room.

"How about a few rounds of cards?" Emily offered, thinking it had been a while since they had had a game.

"With the men out of the house, I think that's a grand idea," Fiona agreed. Martha quickly found the cards and toothpicks, and soon they were settled down at the table. Emily found the game very relaxing because it gave her mind something else to think about instead of the wedding tomorrow.

"Are you nervous at all?" Martha asked at one point.

"I wouldn't say nervous as much as eager," Emily answered. "I don't know if I'll sleep a wink tonight because I'm so excited to get married tomorrow."

"Seems like you should start drinking if you're going to get tired enough to sleep tonight," Martha said with a wink.

"I'll go open a bottle of wine," Fiona said excitedly as she quickly got up from the table and disappeared into the kitchen. She came back carrying a bottle and a few cups. "The one thing I miss about Boston is drinking wine with dinner."

"You know, I didn't think about that until now," Emily said. "I feel there is much I've forgotten about my old life in Atlanta."

"But do you think that's a bad thing?" Fiona asked as she passed Emily a cup of wine.

"Compared to everything I've learned and gained by coming to Spruce Valley, I would say that it's a good thing that I've forgotten much about what it was like to live in Atlanta. I really had to change my way of thinking when I came here and it's all been for the better," Emily explained. Martha and Fiona were pleased to hear Emily say that. They, too, had really seen Emily transform into a better version of herself.

"I can tell that you and Josh are going to make each other very happy," Martha commented as she passed out cards for another round.

"I hope we will," Emily said with a sigh. "He's such a great person that I hope I can live up to that one day."

"Emily, you already do," Fiona was quick to assure. "In just a few months, you've moved to a new state, learned a new way of living, and even started teaching despite having never done it before. You have a lot to be proud of since you've gained such a good reputation in town." Emily smiled kindly at her friends, really appreciating their words.

"And based on the way that Josh looks at you, I'm sure you'll have a little one of your own before too long," Martha quipped, causing them all to laugh heartily. Emily was very thankful for her news friends. Though Cynthia would always hold a special place in her heart, she was grateful for having so many new friends who truly supported her.

# EPILOGUE

Emily felt like she couldn't breathe as she stood at the doors of the church. They were currently closed, but inside she could hear the eager chatter of everyone who had come to attend the wedding. And since it was a small town and Josh was well known in the area, it seemed like everyone and their family had come to see Emily be married to Josh. Emily wasn't sure why she felt so nervous because she'd been in front of a crowd before, but reasoned that it had to be her excitement to finally be marrying Josh.

When the *Wedding March* began, Emily stiffened. But Mr. Ryder patted her good arm trying to help her calm down.

"Don't worry, Emily. You have nothing to be nervous about," Mr. Ryder said softly into her ear. Emily only nodded as she pushed a smile onto her face. The double doors were opened before her and though her eyes quickly scanned the crowd, they eventually settled on Josh. The moment their eyes locked, all the nerves left Emily's body. She was able to smile genuinely at Josh as Mr. Ryder led her forward. Everything else around her seemed to fall away as she only concentrated on Josh. He'd dressed in his finest suit and his light brown hair had been combed to the side and styled. She thought he was even more handsome than usual and was so happy to be marrying a man like him.

Josh couldn't believe how radiant Emily was. Her wedding gown made of silk seemed to glimmer in the morning sunlight that came in through the doors behind her. Josh saw her as a vision of an angel as she was escorted down the aisle towards him. He locked eyes with her bright blue ones and they seemed to twinkle as she smiled brightly at him, and he couldn't help but return the gesture.

By the time she'd finished being walked down the aisle by his father, something he was proud his father had agreed to do, Josh was eager to marry Emily and take her home to his apartment. But he knew that after the wedding, there would be a small reception at the Honeywell Inn. So many people had come out today to see the marriage that it wouldn't be right to skip out on the reception just to be alone with Emily. He'd have to be patient as much as he could.

Reverend Paul gave a sweet yet simple wedding ceremony. With it being Sunday, he tied a bit of his sermon into the ceremony, which neither Emily nor Josh minded. They smiled brightly at each other and made sure to recite their vows when the time came. Holding Josh's hands in hers made Emily fill up with such warmth and joy she'd never known before. Now, she wasn't sure why she'd been nervous before since it felt so right to be with him now.

As soon as the Reverend pronounced them man and wife, Josh bent down and captured Emily's lips with his. It was an eager kiss filled with promises and want. It thrilled Emily no end, and when the crowd started to whistle, she broke the kiss and blushed deeply. She looked out over the crowd then, and took them all in for the first time.

She was happy to see all her students and their families had come out to see her be married. And she was even surprised to see Bright Star and a few of his tribe members attending as well. She recognized the Indian children that often attended school lessons and was happy beyond belief to feel their support today. Of course, Sam and Lucy were present with their two daughters, along with Martha and Fiona with their families. The women had stayed up late last night drinking and playing cards, laughing and carrying on, but by looking at all three of them, no one would have been able to tell. They were all excited for this day and all the joy it held.

Josh eventually led Emily down the aisle and out of the church. There, they thanked everyone for coming as the guests in the pews slowly made their way out. Those that were able to stay joined them at the inn for the reception where the joy of the day seemed to go on and on.

Nell had taken the time to prepare a special tea for Emily and Josh. Though Josh wasn't much into drinking tea, he could at least agree that Nell made the best he'd ever had. Emmet and Ella had been kind enough to cook a meal for the reception, which everyone thoroughly enjoyed. Even though Emily was still getting used to the local cuisine, she was finding that every new thing she tried she ended up falling in love with and was eager to learn the recipe for.

"What are you thinking about, Mrs. Ryder?" Josh asked from beside her. For a moment, Emily thought that Josh was addressing his own mother, but then she remembered that she was Mrs. Ryder now, as well. She giggled as she looked at him, thinking herself rather silly in that moment.

"I think that I haven't been this happy in all of my life," Emily admitted. "I never thought that getting married could make me this joyful."

"I know how you feel," Josh said as he leaned forward

and placed a kiss on her forehead. "I knew that I wanted to get married and start a family, but I had no idea how lucky I would be to marry a woman such as yourself. You've really proved yourself, Emily, and I couldn't be prouder." Emily's heart seemed to swell with even more love for Josh, which she didn't think was possible at that point. But it taught her that her heart was capable of growing larger than she'd ever imagined before.

At one point during the reception, someone pulled out a fiddle and began to play music. It had been ages since Emily had danced and though Josh wasn't eager to do so, he appeased his wife by joining her in the center of the room for a waltz. Emily quickly learned that dancing wasn't Josh's strong point, and together they laughed as Josh did his best not to step on Emily's toes. Her gown had been designed with such intricate lacework that he'd hate to have ruined any part of it.

"Let her dance with a real gentleman," Mr. Ryder said as he cut into the dance. Emily laughed as she watched the scowl that came across Josh's face, but it was soon replaced with a smile as he watched how elegantly his father danced with Emily.

"Never knew you could dance, Pa," Josh said as his father twirled Emily around as though he'd been born doing it.

"I'm sure I still have a few surprises up my sleeve," Joshua replied with a chuckle. Emily was pleasantly surprised herself to see that Mr. Ryder had dancing skills, and soon other couples joined them for a song or too.

Eventually the day gave way to night and everyone who'd come out to attend the wedding and reception eventually said their goodbyes. Matilda and Joshua said goodnight to the newlyweds and went up to their room while a few others stayed behind to help clean up the inn with Bill. With everyone departing, Josh knew that it was finally time to take his new bride home.

Arm in arm, Josh led Emily from the inn and over to the Sheriff's Office. There, he unlocked the door and pushed it open, revealing light within. Josh had purchased several new lanterns and planned to keep everything well-lit in case he or Emily were ever called away on important business. He figured that it would make the Sheriff's Office more welcoming and that the townspeople would be encouraged to stop in from time to time or come to him when they were in trouble.

"Looks a lot better in here," Emily commented as she looked around while Josh shut the door and locked it. "But I think it could use a woman's touch."

"Well, it's a good thing that a woman now lives here," Josh said as he then took Emily's hand and led her carefully up the stairs. "I not only added more light but also a railing."

"I can see that," Emily said as she let her right hand glide softly across the railing. She was looking forward to the day when she didn't need to wear the cast any longer and could write again. Writing notes on all her students' progress was difficult as it was. But as she stepped into the apartment with Josh, she was surprised once more by his kindness and thoughtfulness. The apartment had been decorated with new curtains, a few new furnishings, and a large rug that covered the center of the room.

"I know it's not as nice as the home you had back in Atlanta, but I wanted you to know that I do appreciate you and think you do deserve a nice place to live," Josh explained as Emily's eyes wandered all about.

"You know, Josh, I've come to learn that the best things in life are not things that I could ever buy at a store," Emily said as she turned to her husband. "And the best thing I've found so far is you." Josh and Emily embraced then, sharing a tender kiss as they both agreed that they'd finally found their true purpose in life.

The End

## AMELIA'S OTHER BOOKS

**Bear Creek Brides**

#1 The Rescued Bride's Savior
#2 A Faithful Bride For The Wounded Sheriff
#3 The Untangling of Two Hearts
#4 Indian Bride for the Trusty Miner
#5 A Sharp-Witted Bride for the Troubled Doctor
#6 A Loving Heart for the Loyal Deputy
#7 The Pastor's Doubtful Bride
#8 Warming a Cold Heart
#9 A Division of the Heart
#10 An Untamed Bride for the Rancher
#11 Healing a Big Beautiful Woman's Heart

## CONNECT WITH AMELIA

Visit my website at **www.ameliarose.info** to view my other books and to sign up to my mailing list so that you are notified about my new releases and special offers.

## ABOUT AMELIA ROSE

Amelia is a shameless romance addict with no intentions of ever kicking the habit. Growing up she dreamed of entertaining people and taking them on fantastical journeys with her acting abilities, until she came to the realization as a college sophomore that she had none to speak of. Another ten years would pass before she discovered a different means to accomplishing the same dream: writing stories of love and passion for addicts just like herself. Amelia has always loved romance stories and she tries to tie all the elements she likes about them into her writing.

Printed in Dunstable, United Kingdom

65137563R00418